IN COURAGE AND CRUELTY, IN DESPERATION AND DESIRE, THEY SOUGHT FREEDOM AND ADVENTURE IN A BOLD NEW VISION OF AN UNTAMED LAND

Clardy Tyler Young, restless, and impulsive, his flirtation with a life of crime has put his very survival at risk. But one man's remarkable act of mercy will alter the course of his future and inspire him to stop running and take a stand for what's right—no matter what the cost.

Thias Tyler He has left his Tennessee homestead to fulfill his dying grandfather's last request: to find and save his troubled brother. But it is Thias who will find himself on the wrong side of the law and on the run from a hangman's noose.

Celinda Ames A shy, naive girl, barely sixteen, she witnessed a brutal, shocking act of cruelty that left her alone in the world. Now she must find the strength and self-reliance to survive in a land of untamed passion and unscrupulous men.

Junebug Horton A wandering rogue, he would sell his soul for a few pieces of silver or a few moments of pleasure. And now he has the opportunity to do both at once as he comes face-to-face with the blossoming womanhood of Celinda Ames.

Queen Fine A hardened river harlot with a soft spot for Celinda, she is determined to save the young girl from the life of decadence and vice she herself could not escape.

Micajah Harpe From Knoxville to Natchez, he and his younger brother Wiley have cut a swath of murder and mayhem across the frontier. For them, killing is sheer pleasure and they are planning to take their time with the one man who dared cross them: Clardy Tyler.

Sally Rice Harpe Her marriage to Wiley Harpe has led her into a life of terror and misery. But it is in one unspeakable act of evil that the Harpe brothers will drive her to the very edge of sanity.

Isaac Ford Strong, confident, and fearless, he embodies the virtues of the American frontier. Although he has only one good eye, his vision of the future is as clear as it is bold. Yet he will ultimately face a tragedy to test both his faith in the world and his will to endure.

Japheth Deerfield A lawyer both fair and courageous, he seeks to bring order into a lawless land—and love to a young woman who has experienced only pain and despair. But the odds are stacked heavily against him. . . .

PASSAGE
TO
NATCHEZ

Cameron Judd

BANTAM BOOKS

New York Toronto London Sydney Auckland

PASSAGE TO NATCHEZ

A Bantam Book/May 1996

ISBN 0-553-57560-0

Published simultaneously in the United States and Canada

Bantam Books are published by Bantam Books, a division of Bantam Doubleday Dell
Publishing Group, Inc. Its trademark, consisting of the words "Bantam Books" and
the portrayal of a rooster, is Registered in U.S. Patent and Trademark Office and in
other countries. Marca Registrada. Bantam Books, 1540 Broadway, New York, New
York 10036.

PRINTED IN THE UNITED STATES OF AMERICA

RAD 10 9 8 7 6 5 4 3 2 1

This novel is dedicated to Tom Beer

"If they say, Come with us, let us lay wait for blood, let us lurk privily for the innocent without cause ... my son, walk not in the way with them; refrain thy foot from their path."

FROM THE BOOK OF PROVERBS

"It is a good thing to be shiftless in a new country."

OLD FRONTIER MOTTO

1 7 9 8

CHAPTER 1

On the Ohio River, early autumn

She could not bear to look into his face, and so kept her eyes fixed on the misty and receding line that marked the river's far shore. Even without looking at him she felt his eyes upon her, studying her intently, trying to brand her features into his mind while he was still able to do so. It made her feel exposed and oddly endangered, as if it were she who was sick and doomed rather than he.

The sorrow in his face was what made her unable to look back at him. Her mother's face had displayed that same fated, lachrymose look two months ago, when the truth of her fate had at last broken through after days of denial and the peculiar, distinctive effects of her disease had begun to eat at her mind. Death came mere days later, after fierce suffering. Beulahland Ames had died choking and struggling as her daughter watched in terror from the corner of the one-room cabin, dreading the arrival of death, yet also eager for it to come and end her mother's ordeal.

Now her father appeared destined for a similar fate. He and Celinda both knew it, as did the flatboatmen who had just

evicted them from their craft. Surviving this hellish illness was
rare. When Trenton was gone, Celinda would be alone in the
world. *Alone.* The thought overwhelmed. She sat in the prow of
the skiff, her back toward the nearing Kentucky shore, trying to
comprehend it all.

A foggy haze overhung the water and a piercing drizzle
grayed the air. Her face felt chilled and pale. Water lapped at
the sides of the skiff and whipped against her cheek in a fine,
stinging spray driven up by a stout wind. No one spoke. A single rower powered the shore-bound skiff, the task forced upon
him by the drawing of straws among the boatmen. He kept his
face as expressionless as that of a corpse, but his eagerness to
be done with this business was evidenced by his posture and
hurried motions. Behind him and facing the prow, Trenton
Ames sat straight-spined, eyes ever fixed on his daughter's
face, his hand sometimes creeping to his throat for soft, evaluative touches.

The barrel-laden flatboat from which the Ameses had been
expelled was already almost lost in the fog, carried swiftly
away on a river made high and swift by two days of autumn
rain. The skiff rower would have to work hard to catch up to
the racing flatboat once he had unloaded his two solemn passengers, their meager baggage, and the food the crew had
packed for them in a sack that Celinda now held in her lap. It
came to her that she would share little of this fare with her father. He would not feel much hunger at the beginning, and before long he would be unable to swallow even if he did want
to eat. His continual touching of his neck showed that he was
already anticipating the first hints of the muscular spasms of
the throat that were one of the most terrible symptoms of his
malady.

Beulahland Ames's infection had come after the bite of a fox
whose madness was evidenced by the congealed saliva that had
clotted its jaws, and by its tormented, aggressive behavior. The
fox had come upon her unexpectedly from a thicket of dried-
out blackberry vines along the south side of the dirt yard of the
Ames cabin. It tore her ankle badly before Trenton could fetch
his rifle and kill the beast. Even though her bleeding leg was
thoroughly infused with the contaminated spittle of the fox,
Beulahland had initially denied with fervor that she would become sick. She was still denying it when the first symptoms
came. Only when she lost the ability to abide even the thought

of a drink of water because of the pain and muscular spasms swallowing brought on, did she finally accept the truth. Three days after that, she was dead.

Trenton had cared for his wife with saintly conscientiousness throughout her mortal suffering. It had not been easy. At times she had convulsed violently, and eventually her mind failed her, leaving her bereft of rationality and feral in manner. Once she even lunged at Trenton, declaring insanely that he was responsible for her having the illness, actually cursing him to die in the same manner.

Celinda wondered if a curse could account for her father's infection. She had her doubts, being less superstitious than most of the folk of her native Kentucky backwoods. Her father was literate and self-educated, and had shared his learning with his only child. Celinda suspected that her father had somehow picked up his hydrophobia from the diseased fox itself when he carried it off for burning. Or perhaps he had absorbed some sort of sickly miasma during the care of his wife. Maybe in one of her more violent and hateful moments, Beulahland had actually bitten him, and he hadn't told. Celinda could not know.

For fear of the disease, Trenton had not allowed Celinda to come near her mother during the last two days of her life. Celinda had judiciously obeyed, silently grateful for the prohibition. It wasn't without reason that those unfortunate enough to contract this disease were usually cut off from others and abandoned to their fate, just as the flatboat crew was even now abandoning Trenton Ames.

Forgetting how she herself had feared her own dying mother, Celinda thought the flatboatmen devilishly cruel for what they were doing. She despised the cold, frightened stares they had aimed at her father, their whispered, conspiratorial conversations, their unwillingness to touch or even come near him, and most of all their readiness to condemn a good man to die alone for the sake of their own precious well-being. They had told her she could remain with them if she wanted and go on to Natchez—as long as no sign of the disease exhibited itself in her. Trenton had encouraged her to go along, but she refused bitterly. Where her father was, she would be. As you wish, the boatmen had replied, and ejected them both.

The skiff reached the bank. The rower drew in his oars and waded into the water to the shore. He tied off the boat, hesitated, then put out his hand to help Celinda out. She shook her head, and he withdrew his hand with an expression of relief. She realized that he feared her, too, and she hated him all the more. If only her father hadn't been so honest about his ailment! He might have lied about the nature of the illness and been allowed to remain on the flatboat. But Trenton would have nothing of lies. At the first sign of sickness, he had confessed the truth. Perhaps it was for the best, Celinda thought wearily. A riverborne flatboat would be no place in which to suffer through an illness that would eventually make even the sound of rushing water intolerable.

She made it clumsily out of the boat with her packs and her father's, soaking and chilling her feet in the lapping shallows at the river's edge. Turning, she watched her father rise slowly, a gaunt, sallow scarecrow of a man. Using his Pennsylvania rifle like a walking stick to steady himself, he stumbled up to the prow, almost falling as the skiff rocked beneath him, then stepped into the water and up onto the shore. Watching, the boatman stood with his sweat-stained, woven cap of wool in his hand in a display of odd-seeming obeisance and awe at the presence of a man who in his mind was already as good as dead.

"I can pitch a shelter for you back in the trees yonder, if you want," the boatman said, putting his cap back on his head. The mumbled words were spoken as if out of obligation, the speaker having turned a longing gaze downriver after the flatboat.

"I'll find our own shelter," Celinda replied tautly. She paused, anger rising. "If you had cared whether we have shelter, you would have at least thrown us off where there is an inn or cabin. You're as good as murdering us as it is, scoundrel!"

Celinda was a shy girl, and never before in sixteen years of life had she dared insult another person to his face. She found doing so surprisingly cathartic. The boatman's solemn demeanor did not change. Without looking at either her or her father again, he swiftly freed the skiff, climbed back in, and rowed out into the river, oars creaking.

Only after the fog had begun to close around him did he speak. "God's mercy be with you!" he called feebly.

"Who are you to speak of mercy or God? Off with you!" Celinda shouted the words into the murk. No reply returned. The skiff receded and vanished into gray.

Trenton Ames sank onto his haunches, then sat down on the muddy bank. "You shouldn't speak so to that man," he weakly remonstrated. "He and the others on that boat, they're doomed souls, needing our prayers far more than our curses."

"Why do you say that?"

"Did you not see, Celinda? On the flatboat, when he was first rowing us away? There was a death angel there, right amongst them. I saw the same standing by your mother's bed before she choked her last. Perceived him both times as clear as I do you now. Those men are bound to die. Doomed souls, bound to die on that boat."

Celinda was sure now her father's mind was already being touched by his disease. She had seldom heard him say anything even vaguely superstitious. And even if death angels were real and her father had seen one, surely it had come not for the boatmen, but for him. It was as obvious as it was dreadful, but there was no reason to speak it, and she held her peace.

For a while they remained together on the shore, listening sorrowfully to the fading creak of the skiff rower's oars, until finally it was lost in the distance and there was no sound but the dull roar of the swift river and the caw of a jay somewhere back in the leafless forest.

"We'd best go, Celinda," Trenton said. "We need to find shelter. I don't want to die under the open sky."

"You'll not die, Pap," she said. "You'll get better."

She had felt obliged to say it, but she and Trenton knew it wasn't true, and it brought no comfort.

They took shelter an hour later in one of the caves in a bluff nearly a mile back from the river. Settling in, they ate some of the food, Trenton forcing down his meager portion. Then they built a fire near the mouth of the cave and simply sat, awaiting the onset of the symptoms that would mark the man's last days. While they waited, Trenton talked, telling Celinda that she was the greatest treasure he had ever possessed, but that now she would have to make her way in the world alone. He gave her instruction on what to do when he was gone, and urged her again and again to be strong. What little money he had he gave to her, and told her that she should find an inn along the river and lodge there until she could find new passage to Natchez. There, he said, she should seek out her aunt, Ida Post, just as they had planned to do together. Ida would help her find a new life, and better. Ida had her gruff side, as her father had warned Celinda before, but at heart she was a good woman and would see that Celinda was housed and fed until she could find a way to make it on her own.

"And it's on your own you'll be in a way that you never have been before," he told her. "You've sometimes been a weak girl, Celinda, but you can no longer be weak. Learn to be strong, and never let another be stronger than you. Your aunt Ida, she's a weak woman, too, and you won't be able to rely on her for long. In the end you'll have only yourself and God above to rely on. Trust in your feelings, and count on God to guide them. Do you understand me, Celinda? Will you do that?"

"Yes, I understand. And I will."

"And will you be strong, dear girl? No matter what comes, will you be strong?"

"I'll be strong." But she didn't feel strong at all.

Before long, sorrow and an imprecise, nervous fear began to afflict Trenton, true to the usual progression of hydrophobia. He struggled to maintain a brave mien, but it did not last. He paced in the cave and just outside it, looking around with wild eyes, wringing his hands, staying in constant motion. He began talking again, but not calmly and coherently as before. He chattered on about every subject that came to mind, his speech gradually taking on an oddly clipped quality very different than his usual drawl. Celinda remembered that the same thing had happened to her mother when the disease began to worsen.

He ate a little and even drank some water at first, but soon fever came and he lost his appetite. He complained of headache and pain in the eyes, and soon Celinda noticed a marked change in how he breathed. His breaths became long sighs, each one exhaled in a burst like a gasp or sob. It troubled her to hear it, but when she tried to approach him to offer comfort, he violently waved her away.

"I ain't going to let you get ill, too!" he said, each word a sharp, gaspy eruction. "You stay away from me, you hear? You stay away! And when I'm dead, don't you bury me! Just leave me here, and don't touch my corpse."

By the third day it was even more terrible for Trenton. The melancholy and vague fearfulness that had characterized him up until now yielded to authentic terror. Wrenching spasms of the throat set in. He raged with thirst, but every attempt to drink brought intense pain and choking, so that soon water grew intolerable. They were far enough from the river that its sound didn't reach them, but a dripping little rivulet in the rear of the cave brought torment. Only by laying her shawl beneath the drip to muffle its noise was Celinda able to lessen her father's suffering.

Other tortures, however, rose in hideous compensation. The sky had remained overcast, but even the murky light of cloud-filtered sun became hard for Trenton's eyes to bear without pain. The hydrophobia had seemingly heightened his hearing as well, or at least his sensitivity to what he heard, so that every sound or unexpected motion caused him to react. Occasionally he would start so badly that it set off tormenting muscle spasms that made his entire body rigid. Celinda learned to avoid sudden movements and to tread lightly. She didn't let it show when his company became disgusting because of the thick, phleghmy mouth secretions that began to afflict him, causing him to spit frequently, out of fear of swallowing.

About sunset on the fourth day, as a heavy storm built in the west, Trenton sat up suddenly and laughed. "I'll dance it out!" he declared. "Why didn't I remember it before, girl? I don't have to die at all! I'll dance the poison out of me, dance till the sweat purges me clean! I'll not die!"

Celinda was stung. Of course he was going to die. Any hope he felt at this point could only be generated by the cruel effects of the disease itself on his mind.

"Pap, sit down and rest yourself," she said. "You can't dance out this sickness."

"Yes I can, girl, yes I can—my own pappy told me about it years and years ago, for he knew a man who done it and lived. I'd plumb forgot it until now. Oh, Celinda, I wish I'd have remembered it while your mother was yet living. It would have saved her."

Celinda said nothing. Seated on the floor of the cave, the light fading outside as clouds thickened in the sky, she felt numb horror. The idea of a dying, babbling man dancing in the impossible hope of saving himself was tragic and ludicrous at the same time. She drew up her knees before her and buried her face in her skirt.

The storm hit just as he began to dance. Lightning seared through the sky, silhouetting his absurd form against the open mouth of the cave as he flailed weakly, his motions obviously causing him pain. "Stop it, Pap!" she called, fighting tears. "It's too late for that!"

"I'll live, girl! I'll live! You watch and see if I don't live!"

She refused to watch. Turning her back, she sat out the storm as he continued his convulsive, painful thrashing. A time or two she heard him fall and cry out, but each time he rose and danced again. The sound of the rain was surely bringing him misery, yet his will was amazingly strong. He was still dancing when she fell asleep.

She awakened in pitch-blackness. Sitting up, she shivered. Her clothing was soaked with cave moisture and smeared with greasy clay.

"Pap?"

She heard nothing. Rising, she moved toward the mouth of the cave, feeling her way along the wall. "Pap, where are you?"

Her foot nudged against his form, lying still on the cave floor. "Oh, Pap . . ." She knelt and touched his chest—and found he was still breathing. Breathing! And this time without the sighing, sobbing noises that had accompanied respiration after the advent of his most severe symptoms.

He was merely asleep, his breath coming slowly and evenly. Astounded, incredulous, she knelt in the dark beside him as his chest made her hand rise and fall. She smiled as tears flowed down her face, and despite the dank cold of the moist cave, she felt warm and well.

He had done it! He had actually danced out a disease that should have killed him! Celinda felt the awe of having witnessed a miracle. She bit her lip as hot tears coursed down her grimy face.

Trenton had doffed his coat at some point in his cavorting. Celinda found it and laid it across him. Moving to the mouth of the cave, she sat down and waited out the night. The storm was long over and all was peaceful. The world was beautiful and good. Her father had survived, and she would not have to be alone after all.

When the first light of dawn brightened the wet landscape and lifted the shadows in the cave, Celinda rose and went back to her father. He was lying as he had before, seemingly having not moved at all. His coat still lay across his chest just as she had placed it.

Kneeling, she touched him. He was cold and unmoving, his

face nearly the color of the gray rock beneath him. He had died sometime in the night.

All the happiness and hope that had revived in her earlier drained away, and the closest thing she could find to comfort her was the thought that at least he hadn't died as his wife had, choking and struggling in pain. At least he had been given the mercy of dying in his sleep.

CHAPTER 2

For a long time thereafter she sat staring at the corpse and experiencing the oddest of sensations. She found it difficult to associate the graying, unmoving form before her with the living man who had been her father. This could not be Trenton Ames, but merely a likeness of him. She felt the impulse to find the real Trenton so he could marvel with her at this remarkable, lifeless image of himself on the cave floor.

As the daylight grew and spilled into the cave mouth, painting Celinda's surroundings in ocher and amber, she sank back against the wall, knees drawn up against her bosom, arms wrapped around her knees. She was worried not only over what she would do and where she would go, but also because she didn't feel the sadness expected at moments of bereavement. In fact she felt little at all. Time had abruptly stopped and life had become mere existence. Like her unfortunate father, Celinda Ames was nothing more than the dead stone around her. Her mind had lost its capacity to think and feel. Not even sadness could quicken in her.

But an hour passed, then two, and bit by bit a thawing began. In the ice of her emotions something fluttered; a shiver of sadness stirred and she gasped out loud. Her hand moved to her mouth and she whispered secret words. A tear rose and slipped down her cheek, carving a pale rivulet through the grime on her face. "Oh, Pap," she whispered. "Oh, Pap, you've gone and left me alone."

Her emotions broke like overstrained wineskins, and she sobbed for several minutes until she felt emptied. For most of the next hour Celinda held a numb silence broken only by occasional new bursts of sobbing. She rose once to retrieve her father's rifle, powder horn, and shot pouch, but returned to the same spot. There she sat, the rifle across her lap, and stared at her father's body. As it cooled and settled in the dimly lighted cave, it made occasional sighing, moaning noises that initially gave her a wild hope that he was not dead after all. But he *was* dead, and she realized she would be best off to accept that as quickly as possible.

He had told her she would have to be strong. Strong . . . but how? And to what effort should she apply any strength she might muster? Go on to Natchez, he had instructed. Again, how? She laughed at the dark irony. Was she to walk to Natchez, or float herself downriver on a log, or convey herself magically in a flying washtub, like the shipwrecking witches a seafaring great-uncle fervently claimed he had once seen riding the sky seaward?

As fear rose, she forced it back and made as cool an assessment as possible of her situation. She had a rifle, some ammunition, and a small supply of food. She was miles from her old home, and even if she returned there by foot, no one remained to befriend or help her. The Ames cabin had been isolated, and what few neighbors the family had were gone, having moved elsewhere over the past three years.

The sad fact was that Trenton Ames hadn't been a popular man in his community. He had been bookish in a region where many were illiterate, and a difficult boyhood and introverted personality had retarded his ability to make and sustain friendships. Dark, inexplicable rumors about him had circulated, accusations that his shaded eyes could bring harm to others with no more than a glance. Some had even whispered that the mad fox that had fatally infected Beulahland Ames had been conjured up by Trenton himself. Right alongside those rumors stood others declaring that Trenton's skepticism about various popular superstitions hinted that he was a heretic, disbeliever, downright infidel. No one but Celinda and Trenton himself had ever seemed to notice the near contradiction of labeling the same man as skeptic and spellcaster, false labels in any case. False or not, the rumors about her father had stuck like pitch and cast their stain onto his family. Celinda herself was mistrusted and disliked by many in her home region. She had once seen a child cry and run away when she walked past. Celinda realized she could not return home. She would be rejected there, little better off than here.

All her hope lay with her aunt in distant Natchez. She had never been to Natchez and knew nothing of that town except that it stood by the big river and was one of the market towns to which Kentucky farmers shipped their goods. As for her aunt Ida, Celinda hadn't seen her since she was three, and would not know her if she saw her now. She could not even know certainly whether Aunt Ida would take her in when she finally reached Natchez.

Her father had told her to find an inn on the river. Then what? She could not book passage to Natchez with no money and no grounds for credit. People tended to believe a man could find some way to repay his debts ... but a woman, a mere *girl*, that was a different tale. She could offer nothing in return for passage except ... She shuddered, violently rejecting an unexpected and atrocious thought. Whatever happened, she would not lower herself to *that*. It would ruin her, body and soul. Nothing was worth that price.

She rose and walked to her father's body. Leaning on the rifle, she looked down at him. Though it was autumn and cool, decay was already setting in. His dead face was lean and hollow, his eyes beginning to sink. She wished she could bury him, but would not touch him. She had no way to dig a grave, anyway. He would have to lie where he was.

She turned away and went to the mouth of the cave. Since the morning, clouds had blown in from the west. A soft rain pattered down, but she ignored it and strode out into the forest. A walk was what she needed, a chance to escape the constricting, dark cave, and to think. Maybe she would find something to shoot for food in the meantime. By tomorrow night, at best, she would be out of the meager supply the flatboat crew had left her.

Weary, growing cold and sodden in the drizzle, she trudged off into the woodlands, the rifle heavy in her right hand.

*   *   *

A good saddle, this one. Best he had ever used, much less owned. Oblivious to the light rain, he shifted his rump in the curved leather seat and gave a grunt of satisfaction. Comfortable as a well-stuffed chair, this saddle. Clearing his throat, he sat up straighter and raised his right hand to the sky, brows lowering, chin thrusting out.

"Dear beloved folk, we gather this evening to sing heavenly praises. . . ." He stopped, shook his head, and started over in a much deeper timbre. "Beloved of heaven, we gather here beneath heaven to sing heavenly praises and to hear the heavenly word of the heavenly Father." He stopped again, unsatisfied. Something sounded wrong with that last sentence, out of balance, inauthentic. He couldn't have that. He had to sound convincing if he was to succeed at exploiting this wonderful opportunity that lay spread before him, so wonderful he would believe it a gift of heaven itself, if heaven gave gifts to such men as he.

Heaven . . . there was the problem! Too many heavens and heavenlies in that last sentence. Louder now, and even deeper, he intoned: "Dearly beloved, we gather here this evening to sing heavenly . . . holy praises and hear the glorious word of our heavenly . . . of our divine Father above." He grinned. "Nailed her down tight, by jingo!" He had liked the sound of that much better. He could imagine such words echoing sonorously across a crowded meeting ground, stirring the faithful to service and generosity. Yes indeed. Marvelous, blessed, *heavenly* generosity.

He plunged anew into his practice sermon. "Let us now turn to the Book of Revelations, wrote by Saint John the Baptist upon the banks of the Jordan River, where Noah built the ark of the covenant." He smiled again. He suspected that the content of his words was so much jabber, riddled with errors and misstatements, but he doubted it mattered. The kind of folk who responded to sermons seemed to him to be rather unthinking anyway, swayed more by sound and spirit than by content. He had watched such people a time or two at camp meetings, singing and hand-swaying and cracking their bodies like whips in the bizarre religious affliction called the jerks. Folks like that would be easy to fool. A few vague religious words spoken in a deep, conviction-filled voice, a few well-placed pious expressions and judiciously shed tears, and the Reverend John Deerfield would have the gullible righteous shouting and donating freely to his holy cause.

The happy thought brought a burst of exuberance. "Hallelujah, brethren!" he shouted to his imaginary listeners. "Hallelujah! Come with your tithes and your offerings! Come give to the Lord by giving to His servant! Glory hallelujah, glory be, and hop for heaven! Roll for righteousness! Sling salvation far and wide! Glory! Glory, glory, glory be upon us!"

A rumble of thunder suddenly rolled across the sky, and for a moment he actually wondered if . . . no, no. He chuckled softly. It had been cloudy all day, building up for a storm. He doubted the Lord would go to all the trouble of scrounging up a special thunderbolt just for the likes of one false backcountry preacher.

He turned his attention toward his immediate situation. Night would fall soon, and rain, too. He would need a dry place to sleep. He knew this part of the river country a little and realized he would find no inn within reach tonight. He would have to camp, but there was no time to build a dry shelter, and he didn't want to have to fool with it in any case. Halting his horse, he rubbed his lightly bearded chin thoughtfully, then said, "The caves. That's where we'll go, horse."

He had been following the river, but now reined his mount to the left, back inland. Soon he saw a dark line of bluffs that rose like massive crenellations against the sky, pockmarked with holes and caverns. He had spent many a night in those caves; tonight they would host him again.

He was within five or six minutes of his destination when he heard a rifle crack back in the forest. Maybe a half mile away, he estimated. Halting, he frowned in concern. Maybe somebody was already lodging in one of the caves, and considering that this was river country, the odds were good that any such person would possess a character more odorous than fragrant. Those who haunted the river were generally of the lowest ilk.

He considered moving on to caves farther down the river. Those would be less likely to be occupied, if only for the fact they were shallow and wet on the floor, while the closer ones were deep and only mildly damp. He grew stubbornly determined not to go farther. Why pass up a dry cave for a wet one?

Perhaps whoever fired that shot wasn't staying in the caves, anyway.

He went on, but more slowly, listening and watching. When he reached the closest and largest of the caves, he had grown reasonably sure no one else was about, and was glad he hadn't gone farther downriver.

The thick clouds had brought on night more quickly than he'd anticipated, so he had to fumble about in darkness. He stripped his horse of its tack gear, bags, and blanket, and carried it all into the cave, tossing the load back into the blackness. Heading back, he fetched his rifle and brought it inside, too, leaning it against the wall.

After hobbling the horse, he sent it out into a clearing where some grass remaining from the summer still grew. After the horse had grazed, he would stable it in the next cavern over and give it a few oats from the feed sack that had been slung from the rear of the saddle.

He walked back toward the cave, gathering sticks, barks, scraps of dead wood as he went.

The thunder was louder and more frequent by the time he reached the cave, but so far no lightning was striking nearby and the rain was still only a drizzle. He felt along the dark cave interior, nudging with his toe, and found the saddlebags he had dropped. With the firewood under one arm and the saddlebags occupying the other, he left his rifle where it was, near the mouth of the cave. He spoke aloud: "Now, let's see what kind of fire we can get burning, eh, Preacher Deerfield?"

He reached into one of the saddlebags and drew out flint, steel, and a little tin of charred cotton cloth. Feeling about on the cave floor, he found a few scraps of charcoal and dried wood from some previous occupant's fire. He gathered all this together at the back of the cave, put some of the cotton in the midst of the pile, and struck fire to it with the flint and steel. The charred cloth caught flame quickly. He bent over, cupping his hand behind the spark and gently blowing it to flame. He heaped scraps of the charred wood on the little flame until it caught and grew, then added larger pieces he had gathered. In some cases he had to peel back damp bark to expose dry wood beneath.

Within minutes he had a nice, hearty fire burning. He smiled, content and growing warmer, feeling both calmed and invigorated by the pleasures of fire and shelter. Delving back into his saddlebags, he brought out a couple of squirrels he had shot and skinned earlier in the day. He had wrapped them in their own skins and stowed them away for supper. Packed beside them in a piece of oiled cloth was half a loaf of bread he had filched from the last inn he stayed in. What an inn! He would long relish the memory of it. He had come away from there with far more than a mere half loaf of bread. Fate had smiled on him at that inn, and given him a gift he could exploit to no end of profit for God only knew how many months, even years, to come.

He stoked the fire further. It cast a cherry light against the cave walls and provided a delicious heat. He began to whistle, and rose to go outside and fetch a green stick upon which to spit the squirrels for cooking, and to stable the hobbled horse before the storm grew bad. He looked toward the mouth of the cave for the first time since he had gotten the fire blazing, and immediately let out a yell and stumbled back, almost into the fire.

He stared in horror at the last image he would have expected: a man, stretched out on the floor and looking very dead indeed, and beyond him, a dimly visible human figure, clad in a rain-dripping, bulky coat, standing in the mouth of the cave and looking back at him down the long barrel of a rifle.

Celinda raised the rifle another couple of inches as the man at the back of the cave gaped at her. "I don't know who you are, sir, but I'll kill you right here if you cause trouble."

He looked back at her silently, as if trying to comprehend what was going on.

"Who are you?" she asked. "Why are you in here?"

He said, "You're a woman—maybe not even a woman. Just a girl!"

"That's right—but I'll shoot you if I have to!"

"Did you shoot that man there on the ground?"

"No. That's my father. He died and left me—" She started to say the word "alone," but faltered.

The man's voice became the faintest bit smoother, taking on a slightly cunning quality. His trapped-rat expression metamorphosed to one of openhearted placidity. "You'd shoot a preacher, would you, young lady?"

Celinda lowered the rifle a bit. "A preacher?"

"That's right. My name is Deerfield. The Reverend John

Deerfield. A man of the clergy, bound for Natchez to be pastor of a new church there. I stopped in this cave for shelter . . . I didn't know you had already occupied it. I'm sorry. I meant no harm."

Celinda's mind was spinning. She felt so weary it was difficult to hold the heavy rifle level. Her afternoon's walk had yielded no inspirations about how to deal with her situation, and the forests provided no better game than a crow. She had shot it, figuring to eat it if she could stomach it. Finding a man already building a fire inside the cave had taken her aback and scared her. She still felt scared even though she noticed that his rifle was leaning against the wall near her and well away from him. He might be one of the thieves or killers known to haunt the river. But if he really was a preacher, perhaps all was well. *Bound for Natchez,* he had said. Down in her weary soul, hope flickered despite her fear.

"You're truly a preacher?"

"I am."

"Truly going to Natchez?"

"Indeed. I'm on my way now to take passage on a boat I'll meet farther down the river. Please, would you lower that rifle? I'll do you no injury, I swear to heaven. I'm not a harmful kind of man. It's my place in life to do good for folks."

She assessed him. He looked like he could be a preacher, though he was somewhat poorly groomed. His smooth voice made her tend to trust him. He *sounded* like a preacher, at least. But the fact he had calmly made himself at home in a cave containing a dead man troubled her. It didn't seem normal. The possibility he hadn't been aware of the corpse's presence until he turned and saw her had not occurred to her.

"I'll lower the rifle if you'll tell me why you came into a cave with a dead man in it."

"I didn't know he was there. I passed him in the dark and didn't see him until the same moment I saw you."

It was plausible. Celinda lowered the rifle but did not move nor lay it aside. She was trembling badly, longing to sit down but too wary to do so.

"How did your father die?" the man asked.

"My mother was bit by a mad beast. She died. He caught the same ailment."

Though he was several feet away from the corpse, the man

backed off a couple of steps. "Great God a'mighty! He died of *that*?"

Celinda raised the rifle again. "You ain't no preacher."

"Indeed I am!"

"You said 'Great God a'mighty.' Real preachers don't use God's name for an oath."

There was a pause, then he said, "You are right, young woman. That was a bit of my old and evil self coming through again. I was so surprised by what you said that I didn't mind my language. Even a man of God can backslide, you know. I was once a wicked man, swearing all the time, and sometimes the old ways show theirselves."

Celinda didn't know what to believe. She was so tired, weak, and empty that she was beginning to feel ill. She wanted to slump to the floor right there, but held up. Her thoughts, though disoriented, were clear enough to make her realize that if she showed this man any sign she felt poorly, he would suspect she had the same illness that had killed her father. He would shun her and leave her here alone—and even though he was a stranger, he was at least another living human and a possible source of aid, and represented hope. He was bound for Natchez, the very place she needed to go! In her present state it was easy to believe that it was no coincidence he had happened to come to this very cave. Maybe he was a literal godsend, a good and holy man, come to protect and aid her.

She lowered the rifle. "I won't shoot you. I'll trust you."

He looked very relieved. "Good, good. Now let's move to the next cave. It's unhealthy to stay where a corpse lies, breathing that dead air and such. I'll build a new fire, and cook this meat I've got. You're welcome to share it, Miss . . ."

"Ames. Celinda Ames. The man on the floor was Trenton Ames."

"I'm sorry for your loss, Miss Ames. I truly am."

"Thank you, Reverend Deerfield."

"Plain Reverend John will do, Miss Ames. God has throwed us together, so we may as well be friendly from here on out."

"Yes." She might have cried for joy. This man was friendly and generous. He would help her. *From here on out,* he had said. That implied togetherness, companionship for the long term. There was light in the darkness for her now. There was hope.

C H A P T E R   3

The next evening

Celinda settled her aching bones near the fire that the Reverend John Deerfield had built, pulled her legs up under her Indian-style as she smoothed her dirty dress around her knees, and extended her hands toward the blaze. Meanwhile she studied Deerfield from the corner of her eye as he unsaddled the horse, humming to himself as he worked.

During the day's travel she had developed new doubts about this man. So far he had been as kind to her as any real preacher would, insisting that she ride while he walked, calling her "Miss Ames" until she finally invited him to call her by name, and giving her all the comfort he could concerning her father's death. All these behaviors were consistent with what he claimed to be.

It was the odd, ignorant-sounding things he said while giving her comfort that roused her suspicions. Trenton Ames was beyond suffering, he told her, "up yonder with the holy angels and Balaam and Saint Moses and all them other Bible people." The fact that Trenton had been left unburied would not affect his situation on the resurrection day, he assured her, though she had asked nothing about that. "He'll light up out of that cave and sail up to glory like a cannon shot." That is, he added in somber afterthought, "unless some critter eats up his corpse, in which case his portions would be too scattered for the Lord to regather. So you pray he'll not be eat, so he can rise up again a whole man, missing no parts."

Celinda was no scholar of religion, but she knew babble when she heard it. No real preacher would talk that way. But if he wasn't a preacher, what was he? And who? Was his name really John Deerfield? And why was he pretending to be a preacher at all?

He had shot a rabbit and two squirrels along the trail earlier, and set about to skin and cook them now. He was still humming—a hymn? Celinda listened. No hymn, but a drinking song. And when his skinning knife slipped and knicked his thumb, the Reverend Deerfield let out a most unclerical oath beneath his breath, then glanced to see if she had heard him. She pretended she hadn't. Now she was sure he was a fraud. It was very distressing.

Rising, she walked in seeming nonchalance about the camp until she reached the saddle and saddlebags he had removed and set aside. With her foot she flipped back the flap of one of them, making sure he didn't see her do it.

She saw a Bible tucked just inside, and knelt and got it when he wasn't looking. She opened the cover and read the name inscribed inside: JOHN W. DEERFIELD, MINISTER. She closed the book and felt puzzled. Might he be who and what he claimed after all?

As she knelt to replace the Bible in the saddlebag, she glimpsed a small flintlock pistol tucked farther inside. On the lockplate three initials were roughly scratched in: J.B.H. Now what was this? Why did the initials on his pistol not match the name in the Bible?

"What are you doing over yonder, girl?"

She jumped and gasped. He had caught her! "I . . . uh, I was looking for your Bible. I wanted to read it for comfort. I didn't think you'd mind."

He smiled, just a flicker, but the narrowing of his eyes spoke a different message. "Of course not. But you ought always to ask a man before you get into his baggage."

"I'm sorry."

"I see you got the Bible in hand. Go on away from there and read it."

"Yes." She paused, then said, "Tell me, Reverend John, what is the best scripture for me to read for comfort?"

His best efforts couldn't mask a sudden look of entrapment that shaped his features—rather handsome features, Celinda noticed for the first time, yet not really all that handsome the closer she looked. His nose was well-shaped but a little too big, his lips even and nicely set, but too narrow, his brow smooth and healthily colored, but infringed upon by a hairline that seemed about an inch too low. And his eyes—there was another thing. Her father had always said that eyes were windows into the heart and soul of a man, but if so, John Deerfield had closed and shuttered those windows tight. There was nothing to be learned of him in those brown, narrowed orbs.

"Oh, well, uh . . . any part is good. Any old thing will do. All them thees and thous read pretty much the same, you know." He chuckled nervously.

Fraud! Liar! She managed to hide the contempt she felt. "There must be something that would best suit me in my grief. What do you read at funerals, Reverend John? What do you read when you're comfortless yourself?"

"Well . . . I'm partial to . . . uh, the first chapter of Matthew." She could tell he had pulled the reference right out of the air.

She opened the Bible to that chapter, randomly picked a verse, and to herself read: "And Salmon began Bo-oz of Rachab, and Bo-oz began Obed of Ruth . . ." And so on through most of the chapter. Nothing but odd names and "begats." Not only was he a fraudulent preacher, but not a particularly good one at that.

He was eyeing her with worry, as though sensing something wrong. "You find the chapter?"

"Yes."

"Well, I hope it's what you're needing."

You must learn to be strong, Celinda. "I believe I have found the very thing I need," she said. Stooping, she dropped the Bible and thrust her hand into the saddlebag. When she came up, she had the little pistol aimed at the Reverend Deerfield.

He threw up his hands in exasperation. "Again? What are you aiming to shoot me over now, girl?"

"Who are you? You ain't no preacher."

"The hell I ain't!" He winced as soon as he said it.

"That proves it! That's not the way a preacher talks!"

She cocked the pistol with a trembling thumb. He glared at her, then slowly retwisted his features into a cold smile. "Well, ain't you the brave girl, aiming a pistol at a man! And I thought you was naught but a timid little rabbit!"

Celinda declined to respond. In fact she, too, usually thought of herself in a similar light. She mentally replayed Trenton Ames's advice to her: *Learn to be strong, and never let another be stronger than you.* She shook the pistol, partly to look defiant, more to hide her trembling. "I'm *not* timid, and I swear to God I'll shoot you unless you tell me who you really are and what you intend to do with me!"

He studied her like a wolf evaluating a lamb, then chuckled. "Reckon you might as well know the truth. My name is Jim Buck Horton, though some call me Junebug. And as for what I intend to do with you . . ." Suddenly, he strode right toward her, fearlessly and fast. Her eyes went wide and she felt herself freeze. Her finger could not even feel much less squeeze the trigger. In a moment he was upon her and yanked the pistol from her hand. To her surprise, he turned it, lifted it to his forehead, and pulled the trigger. The flint snapped, but there was no shot. He laughed. The world swam before Celinda's eyes and she knew she was going to faint. Her senses failed her and she collapsed.

He was still laughing as she faded out. She heard him say, "Next time you aim to kill a man, girl, you'd best make sure you've got a loaded pistol!" Then she fell into darkness, and his arms.

You must be strong, Celinda . . . you be strong, no matter what. . . .

Her father's face loomed before her, urgent in expression, speaking with intensity. She struggled to awaken, forcing her eyes open. Darkness gave way grudgingly to light—and her father's face became that of Jim Horton, far too close, leering, whispering terrible things, and now not even slightly handsome.

She realized with a shudder that he was pulling at her dress, and that his hands were on her in ways that should not be. She struggled to stop him, but he had pinned her arms and she could not pull them free. She screamed. He laughed contemptuously and tried to kiss her. She gagged and almost vomited. That angered him. His smile went away, he called her a foul name, and pulled back long enough to slap her across the face, very hard. Then he leaned close and tried again to kiss her lips.

I must be strong. . . .

"No! No! Get away from me!" She screamed it into his face, so loud it must have rung his ears. He pulled away from her again, only for a moment. Swearing at her, insulting her with names that in her previously sheltered world she had never heard a man direct at a woman, he pushed against her and tried again to tear her dress. But in that brief moment he had pulled away, her arms had come free and she was able to reach his face. Curving her fingers like claws, she put her nails into his eyes and the heel of her hand just under his nose. She pushed up and in. He bellowed like a buffalo, roared in fury, drew back his fist and struck her in the jaw. The jolt was horrific and stunning. She grew limp. He was too strong for her. There was no hope of successfully resisting.

But to her amazement, he left her. Cursing, wiping at his face, he meandered off and stumbled around the fire, muttering inaudibly most of the time, sometimes cursing loudly and kicking up dirt, then returning to mumbling.

Celinda's senses slowly returned. She sat up, straightening her dress, and found that he had not torn it. That small blessing alone seemed so great that she almost cried. Sitting there, struggling against tears, wondering if he would return to hurt her again, she exhausted her meager reserve of fortitude. Her father had told her to be strong, and she had tried—but look what it had brought to her! She had been attacked and nearly raped. She wondered if Horton would have tried such a thing had she not so boldly exposed his pretensions and dared to hold a pistol on him.

I must not think that way, she told herself. *I was right to expose him, right to try to aim that pistol at him, right to fight him and not let him hurt me. The only wrong I've done was not being clever enough in how I dealt with him. Part of being strong is being clever. That's what Pap would say.*

She ached for her father. Facing the world without him seemed unbearable. She wondered how she could survive a life so dangerous that the first person she met after being left alone was so wicked a man as Jim Horton.

A sound she hadn't expected made her jerk her head upright.

Horton was laughing! She couldn't believe it. He was rubbing his face, wrinkling the nose she had nearly mashed flat, laughing—*laughing!*—as if it all were the funniest thing imaginable.

"Hoo, boy, look at us, girl!" he said, turning a pleasant expression upon her and making her wonder if she was imagining all this. "Fighting and scrapping—and all because I lost my temper at you for seeing through me! I ought to have thanked you instead. Better I should learn now that I need to do a better pretending job than to learn it later, when it could really cost me! Reckon I'll have to learn to do a better job of passing myself off as a preacher, huh?"

She had nothing to say. Her astonishment at the man grew. What kind of person could change from fury to good humor in so brief a span?

"I'm sorry I hit you. And about the . . . the other part, too. There was a fire in me that had me stirred, and I'm sorry." His words gave Celinda hope, but it was dashed when he added: "I won't be so rough about it next time."

Next time. So there would be a next time. She had warded him off for now, but not for good.

"Why won't you say nothing, Celinda? I didn't hurt you none. Why, I don't know what got into me, anyway. You ain't even really all that pretty. Skinny and puny-looking . . . a man would be hard put to tell you was a girl at all if not for that dress." He paused, brows lowering, and rubbed his chin. "Jingoes! You *would* pass for a boy, if you was dressed like one! We could cut your hair short, put you in my extra pair of britches and a shirt . . . why, I'll be shot square in the nates if you wouldn't pass for a boy in anybody's eyes! When we get to the cave, by jingo, we'll make good use of that!"

She deplored even having to speak to him, but his talk raised a question. "What cave? You said you . . . we, I mean, were bound for Natchez."

"So we are. And when we get there, I'll be the Reverend John Deerfield, and you'll be . . . let's see, you'll be a nephew of mine—no, an orphan boy I've took in. Saving you from a life of misery and such. And at the cave, with you dressed like a boy and your hair short, we won't have to worry that no scoundrel will take advantage of you in a bad way, if you know what I mean."

Indeed she did, and considering what he had tried to do to

her only minutes before, she thought that was the most ironic comment he could have made.

But what was more significant than irony was his obvious assumption that she would be with him for a long time to come. It was the most offensive presumption, considering what he had just tried to do. Why should she stay with a man capable of violence and even rape, a man who could shift spastically between warmth and fury?

She would *not* stay with him! She would escape him ... if she could. But she realized, sinkingly, that he held the advantage. If he didn't want her to get away, it would be hard to do so, and potentially terrible if she tried and failed. An angered Jim Horton would be dangerous.

And there would be other dangers if she succeeded. As much as she feared Horton, she also feared the river wilderness and the lonely trial of self-reliance. To be isolated in this dangerous river country, to not know where to go or what to do, to have to find her own sustenance—these were awful prospects. If she remained with Horton awhile longer, at least she would have food and protection—protection from dangers other than Jim Horton himself, at least.

Sadly and reluctantly, she decided she could not escape him, not just yet. Sometime later, when the alternatives weren't so fearsome, she would find her chance. In the meantime she would just have to be clever and somehow come up with some way to keep him from attacking her again.

"You didn't tell me about this cave we're going to," she said, trying to sound pleasant enough not to provoke him, and cool enough not to invite him.

"Yes. A cave on the river, where Sam Mason keeps his inn. The Rock Cave. The House of Nature. All kinds of names been laid on that place. It's a lot bigger cave than the one where your pappy lays a-putrifying." He chortled like an old man recalling some fond youthful memory. "Oh, what a grand place! And what grand times and folk we'll find there! You'll have never seen nothing like it, girl. You'll see men there who have rubbed their souls in the grit of the world and found it sweet as the touch of a woman."

"I don't know if I want to go among men like that."

"Well, you want to get to your dear aunt in Natchez, don't you? Mason's cave is the best place to go if we're to find us a boat."

"Who is Mason?"

"Quite a man, that's what he is. A man who knows it ain't the meek who are going to inherit *this* world, no ma'am! But I don't know we'll find him there. I run into a man here a few days back who says Sam left the cave sometime back and headed on down the river."

Good, Celinda thought. She had no ambition to meet Mason or any other human being of the sort Jim Horton would think highly of. Weary of talk, she returned to the fire and settled down beside it as before, feeling frightened and alone, and anything but strong.

CHAPTER 4

After they had eaten, Jim Horton dug a flask from the bottom of one of the saddlebags and settled in to drinking. Celinda could tell he was actually relieved to have his ruse exposed, for now he could openly pursue his vices. The whiskey he was drinking was so strong that Celinda could smell it from the far side of the campfire, where she had nestled to keep the greatest possible distance between herself and her companion. Or was he her captor now? Celinda was not certain of her status.

Horton remained quiet for nearly an hour. Celinda sat staring into the fire, wishing she could magically will her father and mother back to existence and herself back into her former life and situation. The extent life had changed for her in a matter of mere weeks was staggering.

"Stop doing that."

She looked up sharply. After so long a silence, it had startled her to hear him speak. He looked angry.

"Stop what?"

"Sitting there and judging me. Stop it. I don't like it."

"I wasn't judging you."

"Oh, you weren't? Reckon you expect me to believe that.

Reckon you think I'm so great a fool as to believe anything you say!" His face surged red.

Celinda's heart began racing. He seemed to be deliberately working up anger toward her. A preface to another rape attempt? She had to restrain herself from leaping up and running.

"I'm sorry if I've made you mad. I'll not judge you. I promise."

He took that in, then nodded curtly. The angry ruddiness of his face lessened. Celinda felt a sweep of relief.

Eyes fixed on her, he took another swig of whiskey, put away the flask, then turned his gaze to the flames again. "Folks have always judged me. Everybody I'm around, setting in judgment like they was kings or magistrates or something! Damn 'em, every one of 'em!" The liquor had given his voice an unpleasant grating quality.

It struck Celinda that agreeing with him might warm his attitude toward her. "Yes," she said. "People are bad to judge other folks."

"They are, yes indeed." He scratched his beard. "Ain't nobody suited to judge me unless they know the terrible thing that was done to me by my own mammy. Terrible thing. Worst thing a body could do to another. They'd know why I'm the kind of man I am if they knew what she done."

Celinda was unsure if he wanted her to ask what the terrible deed had been, and hung fire. After a few silent moments he glanced up at her. "Don't you want to hear about it?"

"Well . . . yes. If you want to tell me."

"I'll tell you. I'll tell you all about Junebug Horton, from the start! Then you'll see why I ain't a good man. It ain't my fault at all. It's my mammy's."

"I want to hear," she said, not only because she wanted to win his good graces, but also because knowing who he was and how he thought might help her protect herself from him.

"I was hard on you this evening, knocking you about and all," he said. "I'm sorry I was so rough. But I'll tell you, you don't know what a beating is! But I know. As a boy I come to know right well what a beating was."

"Your father?"

"Oh no, girl, no. He was a good man, my father. Never lifted a hand to hurt me. But he died when I was six, seven year old, and my mammy took up to living with his brother. Uncle

Jimbo, we'd always called him. I was named after the sorry old goat."

"It was him who beat you?"

"Yep. Black and blue, he'd make me, and for no more reason than that I'd belched at the table, or looked at him sideways, or touched something that was his."

"It must have been hard, living like that."

"Hard, I reckon! That man taught me how to hate. I ain't ever forgot how, neither. Hate was the one and only gift he ever give me apart from them beatings." He paused, suddenly looking sorrowful. "No, that ain't true. There was one more thing he left me, thanks to my mammy. I still carry it today. Right down in here." He slapped his chest. "I can feel it like a knot inside me." He fell into silent brooding.

Celinda didn't think she should ask him directly what he was referring to, but she wanted to keep him talking somehow. "Where were you raised?" she asked.

"Huh? Oh . . . South Carolina, right near the ocean. Big old thing, the ocean—you ever seen it? No? Well, it's a big old ugly thing, and stinks. Some folks like the smell. I hate it. To me it smells like whuppings and big ugly faces spitting and cussing at you, and drunk-man's knuckles busting your jaw. Don't care if I never smell that smell again."

"Did you have brothers and sisters?"

"Two. One a brother, about ten year older than me. He left home when our pap died, and I never laid eyes on him since and likely never will. And I had an older sister, Beth. But she got killed. Uncle Jimbo shot her dead, right before the hearth of our house while she was stringing beans into a bowl."

"Shot her!"

"That's right. But he didn't mean to, or so he said. He was cleaning on his rifle, and blam! There she lay, blood just a-pooling around her. He looks at her and says, 'I be squashed if I ain't kilt the gal.' Then he looks around the room and said, 'Now, warn't that a death throe! Look how far she flung them beans!' That's all he had to say on the matter. Never even said he was sorry. I believe he thought it was right funny he had killed her."

"That's awful. It's sad."

"Yes indeed. And it was after that he took to beating me so bad, too. Sometimes it was such a hellacious way to live that I wished it had been me instead of Beth who'd died on that hearth. That's the gospel truth. That's the life I knew, girl. It was hell on earth, pure and simple. He gave me hell in this world, and thanks to Mammy, he'll give me hell in the next world, too."

There—another cryptic and curious comment. Celinda eagerly awaited the rest of the tale, but to her regret, Horton opened his flask again and drank some more in silence. She thought he was through talking.

Then he rose, came over and sat down beside her. She wanted to move but knew that would offend him. Huddling into the smallest bundle possible, she endured his presence silently. He held silent, too, for a time, swigging on his flask and looking ever more maudlin. Eventually he sniffed and a tear rolled down his face. Celinda felt even more uncomfortable.

"I'll tell you now 'bout the wicked thing my mammy did to me. It happened when my uncle Jimbo was sick to dying—and I was glad he was dying, I'll tell you. I longed to be free of him. But then Mammy called me in to where he lay, just as gray and sunk in as a corpse already, and there sat an old hag woman who lived in a swampy little woods along the river, and I knowed her for a witch and it scared me half to death. All the young ones thereabouts knew this witch and was afraid of her. She had some kind of mix of bloods in her so that she wasn't a full darky, nor an Injun, nor a white woman neither, but all of them together, and she talked mighty strange. I stood staring at her, and trying not to look at my uncle on the bed because he was so ugly to see, and because I hated him so and hoped he'd die while I was there, so I could watch. My mammy, she says, 'Junebug, you're going to do something good for your uncle here today.' I says, 'What?' And she says, 'This here witch woman is going to take some of his blood and put it in a potion, and you're going to drink it.' My eyes bugged out big and I backed off, and she grabbed me by the shirt and said, 'Don't you go running—you're going to do it and that's that.' I says, 'But why?' and she says, 'I'll tell you after.'

"The old witch woman leaned over Uncle Jimbo and pricked at the fleshy part of his arm with a knife, and dripped three or four drops of blood into a little bottle, mumbling and saying strange things the whole time. She took that bottle and held it up and mumbled some more, then let out with a scream that made me jump like I don't know what, and then she took that blood and mixed it up in a cup with some foul mess that was already in it, and raised it above her head. 'The blood is the life!' she bellowed out, and then, 'Without the shedding of blood there is no remission of sins!' And then she handed me the cup and said to drink it, and not to retch back a bit of it, no matter what.

"It was the hardest thing I'd ever done to choke that foulness down my throat without spewing it all right back up again. Knowing there was blood in there was bad enough, and wondering what was in there that I *didn't* know about was worse. But I drained it on down and held it. They gave me a big drink of water after that to help settle my belly. I asked again, 'Why'd I have to do that?' and Mammy looked sorrowful and said, 'I'll tell you after Jimbo is dead and buried.'

"He had his traveling time early the next morning, and we buried him that same day in a plot out near the house. I asked my mammy again about what I'd done, and she commenced to crying all of a sudden and didn't want to tell me. I kept on asking, and after a time she said, 'That witch woman put all your uncle's sins in that blood she drained, and when you drunk it you took them in yourself to spare him from having to go to hell for all his wickedness. So when you die, you'll go to hell in his place, and there ain't nary you can do about it, because you've took his blood into yourself of your own free will. I'm sorry, Junebug,' she said. 'I did it because I'd come to love Jimbo so much that I couldn't bear to think of him going to hell. Junebug, I've damned you in his place.' " Jim Horton broke off his talk for a moment and visibly shuddered. He turned up the flask and took a long swallow.

"I tell you, girl, no boy has ever cried the way I cried that evening and for two or three days after. There I was, no more than ten year old, and bound for hell for the sins of a man I hated. Carrying his burden of sin, and no way to shrug it off. My own mother had made a sin-eater out of me, and I knew that knot I begun to feel in my chest was Uncle Jimbo's burden of sins, all down inside me like a nest of snakes. All I could do was sit and feel them sins in there, and cry and dread the day of my judgment."

"It must have been hard for you," Celinda said. The rationalistic streak she had inherited from her father had her mentally deriding Horton for actually believing in such wild notions, but she dared not let that show.

"I cried a mighty lot, then after I had wept myself dry, I

commenced to thinking. I thought, well, if I'm bound for hell and there ain't no escaping it, why not just make the best of it? Might as well take what life I've got and get all the pleasure I can from it, without worrying about the wrongs and rights. I could spend a whole life being righteous and it wouldn't do me no good. And so I upped from there, determined to do whatever came my way that would give me pleasure. If it was to hell with me, then as far as I was concerned it was to hell with the rest. And so it's been ever since. Me taking care of me. It'll be that way to the day I die. No need to worry over what can't be changed, and I reckon there's worse things a man could live with than a knot inside his chest."

He took another swallow, twisted his head and looked at her with bleary eyes. "Well, what do you think of me? Devil of a man, ain't I, bound for damnation no matter what I do, so I may as well do whatever I want. What do you think about that?" He edged closer, making her tense. "You know, there's some women I've met, they like that kind of wildness and freedom in a man. Like it a lot. You like it, too, I believe. I can see it in your face." He winked and took another drink, and Celinda filled with dread.

I wish I was away from here—I wish my father hadn't died, and I had never met this terrible man. I'm afraid he'll kill me before I can away from him. She dared not give voice to such thoughts. "I don't know what I think."

"You know, girl, you're a right appealing little thing even if you are scrawny. Sure wish you'd let yourself take a shine to me."

"I liked you better when you were a preacher."

"A preacher! Hah!" He laughed wheezingly, shaking his head. "Can you believe a man like me, a preacher? That's a sweet jest, yes indeed."

She seized on the chance to shift the subject matter away from herself. "How'd you come to pretend to be a preacher?"

He laughed again. Now that he had divested himself of his woeful tale, his spirits seemed brighter. "Let me tell you about that, girl! Back upriver, maybe fifteen, twenty miles, there's a rough old inn that sets back from the river alongside a little creek. I happened to be spending a night there when in comes this man who said he was the Reverend John Deerfield. We was setting at the supper table when he come in. He asked if there was room for him, and the innkeeper says, 'There is if you'll share a bed with this gentleman here,' and pointed at me. That preacher looked me over like I was Satan's stepson, let out a big sigh, and said he'd do it if he had to. Right then and there I took a dislike to that psalm-singing jackass. But the way things worked out, I'm glad he come alone.

"He was one of these full-of-talk souls, and he told us all about how he was bound for Natchez, where some folks had gathered up money to build a big church that he was to be the preacher at. Any talk of big money pricks my ears, and I wished it was me instead of him who was going to Natchez. But I never thought serious about it until that night, when all at once he quit his snoring and took to moaning. I sat up and asked him if he was well, and he just moaned some more. I went down and fetched the innkeeper.

"This preacher was bad sick. The innkeeper looked him over, yanked his tongue out and studied it, lifted up his eyelids and said, 'This man will die in the next ten and one-quarter hours.' And right then I seen my chance. While they was all busy with the dying preacher, I fetched his packs and took his horse and his coat and hat and lit out. From then on I was the Reverend John Deerfield, bound for Natchez and a potful of money. And that's where I'm still going, and you with me."

"But won't the people in Natchez know you ain't the real preacher?"

"I had that same fear myself, until I found a letter in the preacher's packs, writ by a Mr. Moses Mulhaney of Natchez, telling the good preacher that they was ready for him and looked forward to seeing his face for the first time. I knew then that they didn't know the man by his features. And the fact is, he wasn't much older than me nor made all that different anyways, so I could pass even if they've heard a description. So I'm setting real pretty. All I got to do is voyage to Natchez, fool the good saints long enough to get that money, and then I'm off, rich and ready to live like a man should. And now you'll be with me, girl. I like you, Celinda. You're a sweet thing, you are, and I'm glad I found you."

He reached over and stroked her hair gently, smiling blearily. She refrained from shuddering only with great effort.

"I'm sleepy," she said. "And I don't feel good."

"Don't feel good? What ails you?"

In truth she was well, but she said, "My belly hurts."

He pursed his lips. "It is getting late, and we do need our

rest, I reckon. I'll make us up a sleeping place. I'll make a roll near the fire. Going to be cool tonight."

"Where will I sleep?"

"Where do you think? Right beside me. You know I ain't a holy man, so there's no use to keep up acting like I am."

"I can't sleep the same place as you. That's for married folk." She felt dangerously bold for denying him, but the thought of spending a night with him was unabidable.

He studied her darkly. The firelight gleaming over his rough features also glinted in his liquor-reddened eyes and made him look devilish.

"I could snap you between my very hands, girl. Look at you, all frail and thin—and you think you can deny me what I want?"

A seemingly miraculous inspiration came. Perhaps because of Horton's earlier reference to feeling his uncles sins like a "nest of snakes" inside him, a story stirred up from Celinda's memory, an incredible tale told of a girl who had lived and died a few miles from the Ames cabin. Astounding as it was, the story was accepted as true throughout the community. "Very well, then," she said rising. He stood as well, grinning in anticipation. She glanced at him sidewise and, as offhandedly as possible, said, "I only hope you don't wind up with my snake getting in your belly."

"Snake? What are you talking about?"

"The one in my belly. It's been there for years, and nothing has been able to get rid of it. It's what keeps me scrawny. That's why my belly's hurting now. It's stirring around in there." She hoped she sounded convincing. She herself strenuously doubted the story about the snake in the girl's belly—but if Junebug Horton could believe that an old witch woman could put a man's sins inside a little boy, he could probably believe this, too.

He wasn't convinced yet, though. "How could there be a snake in your belly? That sounds like some kind of fool Indian notion, or something."

"It's the truth. It slid down my throat once when I was drinking from a creek. I was just a little child. I recall feeling it going down, just a tiny little thing, like a string. It's been there ever since, living inside me. It's a full-grown snake now."

"No! I never heard of such a thing! Snakes don't live in folks' bellies."

"I swear it's true." She pulled more of the story from memory, and adapted it even in the telling. "My father and mother even saw it sometimes, while I was sleeping. It would come up out of my throat and stick out of my mouth, waggling its head all around. Pap tried to grab it and yank it out, but it was slick and he couldn't get a hold on it. It would turn and slide right through his hand and back down inside me. You can believe it or not. I know it's true. You'll know it, too, if you see it . . . or if it goes from me into you."

Horton looked bewildered and thoroughly disgusted. "I can't figure how a snake could live inside somebody's belly!"

"It's a water snake. I reckon that's how it can survive. It swims around in there, all the time."

He looked at her with brows knitted. She wondered if she should have picked a more readily believeable tale. Then abruptly he turned away from her and shuddered. "A snake, coming up out of your mouth!" he said. "Sweet Moses on the mountain! Does that happen much?"

He believed her! Her relief, though unrevealed, was tremendous. "Not much, but whenever it did, my father said that he figured the snake was looking for a man's body to go into. A man has a bigger belly than a girl has. If I was you, I'd . . . well, no point in saying more. If you're bound to have me sleep beside you, I don't know how I can stop you." She paused, gave him a quizzical look and asked, "Do you sleep with your mouth open?"

He turned away. "I'll sleep by myself tonight."

He tied Celinda to a tree before he retired. He did provide her a blanket to keep her warm, his only kindness. Any lingering thoughts of escape were rendered moot, and the question of her status settled. She was most assuredly a captive.

But a clever captive, she reminded herself. By benefit of wits far superior to those of her captor, she would sleep unmolested. There were strengths other than physical ones, and she had used hers well, and felt proud.

The next morning, he freed her, handed her his knife, and told her to cut off her hair. She complied, fighting tears; her hair was the only part of her person she had ever thought was truly pretty, and now it was gone. He took back the blade, hacked on her tresses some more, smoothing out the ragged job she had done. He picked up her shorn hair from the ground and tossed it into the fire, where it blackened and sizzled and curled into ashes.

"Your name is George, now. George Ames. When we reach Natchez you'll be an orphan from Kentucky that the Reverend Deerfield has took under wing. Before then, at the cave, you'll be a cousin of mine. And you're a mute—can't have your voice betraying you. Here, smear some dirt on your face to cover that smooth skin . . . that's right. Yes, that's better. You look more a true boy now."

"Why do I have to do this?"

"You'll thank me when we get to the cave. If they knowed you for a girl, things would happen to you. Know what I mean?"

She nodded.

"All right. Now here. These are some of my extra clothes. Change into them."

"Where is the cave?"

"On up ahead a few miles, on the far side of the river. It's there we'll take our passage on a boat and be off for Natchez."

"How long will you keep me with you?"

"Why, where else would you want to be? You stay with me, girl, and you'll be better off than your daddy ever could have made you. We'll get that snake out of you, flesh you out some, and you might make a decent-looking she-male yet. Mark my words, Celinda, you'll bless the day you met Junebug Horton. Someday you will, when I make you rich." He paused and looked at her deeply. "I know we don't much know each other yet, but time will take care of that. You and me, we was meant to be together. I felt that almost right off after I met you. I care for you right much, girl, and you'll soon enough come to care for me. Ain't that right?"

She would not answer.

"I said, ain't that right?"

"If you say so. I reckon you're a lot smarter than me, you being a man."

That answer obviously pleased him. He raised his brows and nodded. "You and me, we'll do well. We will. Now let's be off. I want to make Mason's Cave soon as we can."

CHAPTER 5

Beaver Creek Valley, near Knoxville, Tennessee

Two young men walked in the waning afternoon light toward a burial ground that filled the clearing between an ancient maple copse and the dark, forested hills. The burial ground was appropriately somber, filled with crudely engraved stones and overshadowed by a unusually large, gnarled dogwood tree that grew in its center. Beautiful in the springtime when white blossoms covered it, the tree looked twisted and tormented now that its leaves were nothing but dead autumn husks that blew about among the gravestones.

The two men were brothers, surnamed Tyler, and so close in size, form, and facial appearance that many assumed they were twins. In fact a year separated them. As they reached the edge of the burial ground, the younger of the two, Clardy, shifted his eyes without turning his head and peeked from beneath the brim of his broad flop hat.

"He's watching us, sure enough," he said. "Hunkering down, but he's easy to see. Reckon I ought to just wave at him so he knows that we know he's there?"

"No," answered the older brother, Thias. "I'm inclined to see what he does. I'll wager he thinks us mighty brash, walking right in with a shovel and not even trying to hide it."

"He won't be able to see from where he is what grave it is we're digging," Clardy said. "He'll have to come clear down here to make certain we ain't disturbing dear old Grandmam Van Zandt." He paused, a reflective and slightly hungry look overtaking him. "Thias, you reckon all that talk might be true?"

"'Course not. Not even the Van Zandts are fools enough to bury a jewel with a corpse. Deathbed promises don't carry more weight than common sense, you know."

"True enough, but the Van Zandts ain't got no common sense. And answer me this: if there ain't a jewel in that grave, why has Abel kept watch on the burying ground ever since the day the old woman was laid away? Why would he bother guarding a grave if there ain't nothing in it worth stealing?"

"Would you want anybody digging up your grandmam's grave, jewel or not?"

"Never having known our dear old grandmam, I don't think I'd care much either way."

"That ain't my point, Clardy. Take Grandpap. If he was dead, would you want somebody digging up his grave for any reason, even a wrongheaded one?"

"If Grandpap was dead, there wouldn't nobody be able to get to his grave. I'd be in their way, dancing on it and singing to glory in the joy of being free of the old jackass at last."

Thias fell silent, shifting the shovel to the other shoulder. He looked displeased. After a few moments he said, "Clardy, no-body should speak so about kin. It ain't proper to talk that way about the man who raised you."

"Raised me—and raised welts aplenty on my rump and yours besides, most of the time for no good reason. He's a sorry old devil and I'll not cringe from saying so. As far as I'm concerned, what we're doing for him right now is better than the old boar deserves."

"He's been in a lot of pain. It's our duty to stop it if we can."

"Fine. But it's the last kindly thing I'll do for that man. It won't be long before I bid Hiram Tyler and this sorry place fare-thee-well forevermore. And if you've got any sense about you, you'll do the same and come with me. There's a bigger and better world than either of us have lived in just waiting out yonder, and two stout men like us could do mighty well by it."

"I don't believe you'll ever leave here, Clardy. You've talked that way more than a year now, but here you still are."

"You wait and see if I don't leave."

They had entered the graveyard and now wound among the stones until they reached a grave so small it appeared to be that of an infant child. But no child was buried here. On the stone were the roughly carved words:

Here LieS the Left LEg of
HirAm TyLer, cut oFF and
Berried the Month of MArch
year 1798 Rest in PEace a
good Limb muCh missED

"Well," Thias said, "reckon we'd best get to digging."

"*You'd* best get to digging," Clardy corrected. "I'm going to have task enough just doing what you don't have stomach for."

"I've never denied being weak of stomach. It's a failing I ain't proud of. But I'll do my share to make up for it—just as long as I don't have to see, smell, nor touch that leg."

Thias Tyler began digging with vigor, his broad shoulders growing taut each time he hefted the loaded shovel up to dump it. A heap of dirt quickly began growing beside the little grave.

Clardy crouched on the opposite side and filled his pipe with tobacco. Tucking the reed stem into his teeth, he brought out the fire-making supplies he always carried, struck flame to a bit of tinder with flint and steel, lit a twig, then with the twig, lit his pipe. Puffing until the tobacco burned evenly, he watched his brother work and envied the obvious strength of Thias's muscles. Thias had always been strong, worked hard, and in his rare leisure pursued activities that only strengthened him further—poling a heavy raft on the French Broad and Holston rivers, wrestling rough-and-tumble with anyone who wanted to bet they could whip him, making long hunting treks deep into the mountains. Thias was a fine physical specimen. Clardy often wondered why his brother hadn't yet married. Thias seemed the marrying type, unlike himself. Lack of opportunity, Clardy figured. There wasn't a wealth of young women worth taking for a wife close by in this valley, even by Clardy's standards. And Thias was even more selective by nature.

As Clardy smoked he began looking about for Abel Van

Zandt, who had now had ample time to sneak down off his hill. He was sure to show himself before long. Abel Van Zandt was noted for his poor skills as a woodsman and hunter. No one liked to hunt with him because he usually ran off any game long before anyone could get off a shot. Hiram Tyler, the Tyler brothers' sour old grandfather, had once declared that Abel Van Zandt was so poor at being inconspicuous that he had to "strain just to keep his own hind end hid in his britches." It was ironic that it was so unlikely a candidate as Abel upon whom fate had forced the duty of guarding the grave of eccentric old Selma Van Zandt, rumored to have been buried with an old family heirloom jewel of European origin and high value, just because she had demanded it on her deathbed.

A telltale sound tickled Clardy's ear. With a subtle glance he caught sight of Abel creeping through the maple copse, watching them in the gathering dusk. He had his rifle with him.

"There he is, Thias," Clardy whispered around the stem of the pipe.

"I hear him. I'll wager he wonders what the devil we're up to, digging up a grave that ain't his grandmam's."

"Reckon I ought to let him know we see him?"

"Don't see why not."

Clardy stood, forced a yawn, and stretched. In so doing he turned toward the maple copse. Abruptly he called, "Howdy do, Abel! How you this evening?"

There was a brief silence, then Abel emerged from the maples, rifle dangling, a disappointed look on his face. He was fleshy, balding, maybe four years older than the eighteen-year-old Clardy. Despite the wealth, by local standards, of the Van Zandt family, Abel was dressed no finer than the roughly clad Tylers, though his clothing was a little newer and much cleaner. "Howdy, Clardy. Thias."

"Faring well, Abel?" Thias asked, not stopping his shoveling.

"Well enough." He paused. "Tell you the truth, boys, I come down here to see what you were a-doing. I thunk maybe——"

"That we were going to dig up your grandmother's grave and take the jewel?" Clardy finished for him.

"Well . . . yes. Except there ain't no jewel. That's just a story. But I don't like my family graves being disturbed on any count."

"I don't blame you," Clardy said. "But you can see we ain't

digging in your grandmam's spot, so you can rest easy about us."

"You care if I ask what you *are* doing?"

"Digging up Grandpap's leg." Clardy puffed on the pipe as if that were sufficient answer, enjoying the look of puzzlement that Abel gave back to him.

"I can see that. But why?"

"Well, I'll tell you, Abel, though you may have trouble believing it. Ever since Grandpap lost that leg, he's had pains in the knee joint. Bad pains. Enough to keep him awake at night and make him harder to get along with than he is anyways."

Thias fired Clardy a harsh glance. There was a thin sheen of sweat on his brow from the exertion of digging, and he was thigh-deep in the hole. The pile of dirt beside the grave was piled quite high. "You watch how you talk about Grandpap, Clardy."

Clardy winked at Abel. "Thias, he's Grandpap's defender. He loves the old fool. Thias just relishes being cussed at from morning to night, worked like a plow horse, and forced to live on victuals all burned to ashes."

"The old man burns up your food?"

"Yep. Grandpap declares he's the only one of us that knows how to cook meat right, and won't let Thias or me help with it. He burns meat up before he thinks it's ready for the table. My mouth tastes like cinders most all the time 'cause of it."

"What was you saying about Hiram's knee hurting him?"

"Well, just that. His knee has ached on him ever since his leg was cut off."

"The knee he's got left, you mean?"

"No, no, his cut-off knee. It's pained him fierce."

"But how can a man's knee hurt when it ain't there no more?"

"Why, it happens all the time to all kinds of folk. Ain't you ever heard of that? But me and Thias have found out why. A man in Knoxville told us. We buried Grandpap's leg crooked, you see. The knee was bent. That's why it was hurting him."

Abel shook his head. "I never heard of such a thing. A knee hurting when it ain't there!"

"It's the gospel fact. That knee has ached him like a bad tooth. I've watched him grasping around in the air there beyond his leg stump many a time, moaning and cussing and declaring he could get rid of that pain if only he could rub that knee good and hard, and there being no knee there to rub. He says the torment of that is a lot worse than what he suffered when his leg got crushed up to begin with." Clardy chuckled. "When the hurt's at its worst, he wriggles around like a no-legged toad in a skillet. As foul an old shad as he is to Thias and me, I'd nigh enjoy watching him suffer if it didn't just make him all that much harder to live with."

Thias said sharply, "Clardy, you've crossed the line now. Don't talk that way about Grandpap no more, you hear?"

Abel's face had brightened with understanding at last. "Now I see! So you're digging up the leg—"

Clardy finished for him. "To lay it out straight and take the pain away. That's right."

Able laughed. "I be! Reckon it'll work?"

"We'll see. By the way, Abel, Grandpap don't know we're doing this. He don't know about what the man in Knoxville told us, neither. If he did, he'd just cuss us for not having buried the leg straight to begin with. Thias and me came down here on the sneak, and we aim to keep watch and see if he quits hurting."

"I won't say a word. You let me know how it works out, hear? You've roused my interest."

Thias paused from his digging and wiped his brow with his sleeve. "I'd forgot how deep we buried that box," he said. "Going to spell myself a second."

"Don't waste time," Clardy said. "It'll be full dark before long."

"Why don't you dig, Clardy?" Abel asked.

"Because I've got to do the ugly work. Thias's weak of stomach and can't bear the thought of touching that leg. So he's doing the digging, and I'm doing the straightening."

"Oh."

"How long you going to guard this burying ground, Abel?" Thias asked. "You can't spend the rest of your days watching a grave."

"I know. I'm being a fool, I reckon. But ever since that story about the jewel got spread, I've worried sick that somebody's going to dig the grave up, and I can't bear the thought of it."

"So it's all just a tale? Your grandmam never asked to be buried with her jewel?"

"Oh, she asked, and we told her she would be, just to make her happy. But we didn't really do it. Why, that would've been foolish, burying a valuable piece of jewelry till Judgment Day, when it can't do her a bit of good and can do her living kin a lot of good."

"Makes good sense," Clardy said. "Ain't you afraid she'll come back and haint you for lying to her, though?"

"I don't believe in haints. And if she does come back, I'll say, 'Grandma, ain't no way I'm going to as good as throw away a valuable jewel. Get on back to heaven where you belong and quit fretting over it.' That'll send her off, I'd say."

"Probably would. I'd be too scared to talk that way to a haint, though. I ain't too proud to admit it."

Thias had resumed digging, and a few thrusts later the shovel struck wood. "I've reached it," he said. From then on it was a matter of clearing out dirt from above and around the little coffinlike box that held Hiram Tyler's leg.

"Can you smell it, Thias?" Abel asked.

"No," Thias replied. "Maybe it's down to the bone now. Not that I'm going to be the one to see." He came up out of the grave so lithely that he might have been a "haint" himself. Clardy again grudgingly admired his brother's physical strength and grace, so much superior to his own. Clardy had always been lazy, slow to work and quick to rest, or play. Play in particular—the kind of play that involved taverns and tankards and dice and companions who were good in everything but the moral sense, and whenever possible, a woman of the same ilk. Such stirred the soul, mind, and body of Clardy Tyler more than anything else, and had given him a poor reputation in his community. He pretended not to care, but secretly he did.

Mostly because of Thias. Thias was different. "The good one," people had called him as long as Clardy could remember. *The good one.* Clardy couldn't help but resent it, and even from his youngest days the awareness that Thias's perceived goodness set him apart from his ornery younger brother had caused Clardy to think along a line that shaped his life like a molding hand: *If Thias is the good one, then I'm the bad, and if that's so, then bad I'll be indeed.* Out of that had arisen a dark ambition as of yet unfulfilled: Clardy Tyler would pursue a life of crime and daring. His name would be spoken in the same hushed tones of awe that always accompanied the mention of famed bandits and highwaymen. If he could not gain respect from virtue, he would gain it from vice. Someday people would look at Thias, "the good one," and say: "There goes the brother of Clardy Tyler, the famous highwayman!"

Thias brushed the clay from his trousers. "It's your work now, Clardy," he said. "But don't you open it until I'm out of range."

Abel Van Zandt asked, "Just how bad mashed up was that leg, anyways?"

"Mighty bad," Clardy replied.

"I believe I'll head on back to the house, then," he said. "My stomach ain't the strongest, either. Evening to you, boys, and I'm sorry I mistook what you was doing here. You can understand how I did, can't you, seeing two men walking into the burying yard with a shovel? And twice already there's been somebody tried to dig in the grave. Two men, judging from the tracks. Something scared them off both times, though. Probably somebody coming down the road."

Clardy said, "I didn't have any idea somebody has actually bothered the grave. Two, you say?"

"Yes. I've got my suspicions about who they might have been, too." He grinned. "The thought of you two even crossed my mind at the beginning. If it wasn't for knowing what a good and upright soul Thias is ... that is, what good and honest souls both of you are, I might have come asking to your place."

"You know it wasn't us," Clardy said curtly, his feelings hurt. There it was again, that eternal perception of Thias as good and trusty, himself as anything but.

"Who do you think it was?" Thias asked.

"I'd best not say. Good night, men. I'm going to stand guard a mite longer. I hope unbending that leg will do the job for Hiram."

"Good night, Abel."

Abel hefted up his rifle and walked away. It was very nearly dark now. "Off with you, Thias, I'm hefting her out," Clardy said.

Thias turned and strode away, off into the maples, and Clardy laid out flat on his belly and reached down into the hole with both hands.

When the task was done, Clardy stood, cleaned off his hands, and hollered for Thias to return, which he promptly did.

"How bad was it?"

"How bad do you think? I ain't never done a harder thing.

That leg smelled and crawled with maggots. You'd have thunk it was buried last month, the way it was. Your stomach couldn't have abided it." It was a lie spoken with the utter ease that comes with much practice. Lies were among Clardy's most constant companions. A man could rely upon a lie, he believed, far more than much anything else in life, whereas the truth brought trouble as often as not. "I hope Grandpap's pain will be gone now," he added in a righteous tone. "I've done the best I could for him."

"Best *you* could? I had a mite to do with this, too, you recollect." Quickly they worked together and refilled the grave. Then Thias exhaled loudly and arched his back. "Well, now we'll keep watch on Grandpap and see if he does better. And if he asks where we've been this evening, we'll say we come down here to visit our folks' graves." Indeed, the parents of the brothers did lie buried nearby, Jacob Tyler having fallen victim to ague a month before Clardy was born, Mary Virginia Tyler having died of a combination of Clardy's difficult childbirth and grief over her lost husband. "We'll look sharp to make sure we don't let him see the shovels. Now let's get on."

They strode off together. A few paces on Clardy stopped suddenly. "What's that yonder?"

Thias was already looking. "Don't know," he said in a whisper. "Looks like a man . . . no, two men. Clardy, they're over about Selma Van Zandt's grave!"

"You reckon—"

"I do. The very ones Abel was talking about, bound to be! Wonder if we can get close enough to see who they are?"

"And get ourselves shot doing it? No sir! Abel's still watching, anyhow. This is his worry, not ours."

"We ain't going to get shot. We'll just get close in and get a look at their faces. I want to help Abel. I like him."

"Blast it, Thias, you like everybody."

Clardy knew he'd never be able to change Thias's mind. He thought about coughing loudly to tell the intruders that there were others about. But he didn't, for he was growing curious himself about who they were.

"Come," Thias said. "Let's go. If we're quiet, they won't hear us."

They moved very slowly through the graves, keeping low and testing every step before putting their weight down. In the meantime they heard movement and whispers where the intrud-

ers were—and then ducked, frightened, when a beam of light
suddenly shone out. Someone had opened the shutter of a lantern.

"This is it," a whispered voice said. A paused followed, then
a burst of profane swearing, followed by: "They've filled in
what we dug out before, and put rocks on it besides!"

"That won't stop us," a second voice said. "Give me a little
more light so I can see what I'm doing."

The shutter moved some more, the beam grew, and some of
it reflected up onto the faces of the grave robbers. Clardy drew
in a gasp.

"You hear that?" one of the intruders whispered sharply.

"I did."

A voice sounded from the road on the far side of the graveyard, just at the edge of the woods. "You in there! Stop where
you are!" It was Abel Van Zandt.

The lantern shutter fell; all light vanished. In a mad burst of
running and swearing, the intruders scrambled away. Abel
shouted at them and fired his rifle. The ball ripped through the
leafless treetops.

Clardy and Thias, crouched very low now, stayed where they
were. Abel came running in, looking all around, then paused
and examined his grandmother's grave with his hands, it now
being too dark to see well. He muttered exclamations of anger.
The grave robbers were nowhere to be seen, though they
couldn't have gone far in so short a time.

Clardy hoped that Thias wouldn't hail Abel. It seemed just
the kind of thing he would do. If he did, Abel might think it
was they who had tried to rob the grave after all; or worse, the
two real grave robbers, if hidden nearby, would realize they
had been seen. That would be the worst thing that could happen, considering who they were—for Clardy had recognized
the faces illuminated in the lantern light.

To Clardy's relief, Thias did not call out. In cramped and increasingly miserable postures the Tylers waited for Abel to
leave. It took the longest time for him to do it, and then only
after he had reloaded his rifle and poked about among the
nearer gravestones. At one point he almost came to the place
where the Tylers hid, but turned away just in time.

When at last he was gone, the brothers turned and crept out
of the burial ground. Keeping in the darkest places and saying
nothing, they headed toward their cabin, about a mile away.

Halfway there, Thias asked, "Clardy, I saw their faces in the lantern light."

"So did I."

"I didn't know them. Did you?"

Clardy was about to tell the truth, but then reconsidered. If Thias realized that he knew the robbers' identities, he might insist that the information be given to the Van Zandts. And Clardy wasn't about to do that. Word might get back to the robbers about who named them. He wasn't about to turn *those* two against him.

"No," he said. "I didn't know them, either."

"You made a sound that made me think you did."

"I had a cramp in my side, that's all."

They said nothing more the rest of the way home. There they were greeted by Hiram Tyler, who leaned on his crutch and cursed them both thoroughly for having missed their supper. The young men would have been surprised by any other greeting. Murmuring insincere apologies, they pushed past the old man and into the cabin, which reeked of scorched potatoes and pork meat burned to coal.

CHAPTER 6

Two days later, at the Tyler Farm

Thias Tyler grunted in exertion as he lifted his heavy hammer and brought it down again. It rang loudly upon the flat head of a mortise axe he held in place atop a freshly hewn beam. The beam was Clardy's product, created in a travail of suffering, complaining, sweating, and swearing. Now Clardy was taking a much desired rest, leaning on the sweat-sheened handle of his hewing axe, puffing a pipe while the muscles of his arms throbbed and his fingers felt like they could never be straightened again.

Thias's mortise axe bit deeper into the wood, creating a square hole. Thias cast the eye of a careful master on his work, then frowned as he scanned the rough and uneven hewing job Clardy had done. He restrained himself from voicing criticism. It would do no good. Clardy simply didn't care about the quality of any work he did, even such important work as building a bigger house for them all.

"I don't see the need for all this work," Clardy said around the stem of his pipe. "Our cabin's small, but it's stout, and all this labor is mighty wearying. I don't see no call for it."

Thias gave the mortise axe a final strike, worked out the chisellike blade, and examined the four-sided hole. "I recollect you as being the one who's fussed the most about being cramped up," he replied.

"Me? Why, I don't mind being a mite cramped. Only time we're in the cabin anyway is when we're sleeping or eating. Other times we're outside."

"Except in the dead of winter, or when the weather's bad," Thias reminded him.

Clardy puffed a white smoke cloud and shifted postures. "What it comes down to is that for me this is a lot of work for nothing. I don't aim to be around this winter. You and Grandpap will have this place all to yourselves—unless you change your mind and come with me, Thias. Then the old man could have the run of the place, nobody but himself to cuss at, and you and me could be free as wild crows."

"We've chewed that cud enough times already. I can't leave here."

Clardy shrugged. "Suit yourself. Stay here forever and rot. Me, I'm going. Sooner than you know."

"Fine. Go. Just go ahead and leave, but whatever you do, shut up about it. Why do you keep trying to convince me you're leaving, anyway? I think it's your own self you're really trying to persuade."

"Got me all ciphered out, have you?"

"I'll never cipher you, Clardy. God knows."

Clardy swore abruptly, beneath his breath. Thias saw the reason. Coming up the slope from the old cabin, swinging along on his hand-whittled crutches, the leg stump beneath him hanging like a loose sack of grain in its tied-up trouser leg, was their grandfather. Thias grimaced. The old man was so hard to abide that there was seldom a time his approach didn't tie a hot knot in the center of Thias's belly. It was worse for Clardy, who got on even more poorly with the old man.

Thias glanced at Hiram's face. At least Grandpap looks to be in a decent humor, he thought. Bound to be because that leg feels better. Looks like he's worked up and eager over something, too.

Even though he and Clardy had refrained from asking their grandfather outright about his phantom pains, they had detected that the pain was much lessened, maybe gone. They considered the odd medical advice they had been given in Knoxville to be fully vindicated.

"Howdy, Grandpap," Thias called out. "You're moving good today."

"My ghost knee ain't hurting me," the old man said, and actually smiled—a rare sight indeed. His teeth, set in faded-out gums, were a worn-down line of yellow and brown. "I noted a couple of nights back that it was commencing to hurt less, and ever since it's felt better and better. Since this morning I ain't had even the first pang."

Thias glanced at Clardy and shared a secret, very small smile. "That's good. Maybe it won't hurt you no more at all."

"I surely hope it won't. Hey, boys, you heard the news?"

That phrase was Hiram Tyler's standard introduction to whatever bit of gossip he had picked up from someone or another—in today's case, the someone being Elijah March, a hog farmer who lived a couple of miles up the creek and who had come by earlier, asking if the Tylers had noticed any of their hogs or cattle going missing over the last month or so, as he had. They hadn't, but March's loss of swine was nothing unique. Several farmers for miles around had been complaining that they were losing stock. Speculation was there were thieves afoot.

"We ain't heard no news," Clardy said. "Who the devil would we have heard news from? We've been out here working while you sat a-jabbering with Elijah March."

Thias sighed. It crossed his mind that maybe it would be best if Clardy really did go. Whenever he and Grandpap were together, it was evermore like this—fussing and cussing and general harshness. Often it made Thias want to head out with a hound and a rifle and stay gone for a month in the hills, where there was nothing but quietness and peace.

Today Hiram didn't pick back at Clardy. He was primed to share his news. "I'll tell you, boys," he said. "Seems somebody we know has gone missing all at once."

"Who?" Thias asked.

"A gentleman we all know well, that's who. And it all has a right queer and deathish smell to it, too." He cocked back his head and looked down his nose. Thias sighed. As usual, the old man was going to let his information out slowly, so as to enjoy playing the role of tantalizer.

Thias asked, "Who, Grandpap?"

Clardy was poking at his pipe, pretending not to be interested so as not to add to the old man's pleasure. But he jerked to full attention when Hiram said, "It was none other than old Abel Van Zandt himself."

Thias frowned. "Abel has gone missing?"

"He has. Since a night or two back, Elijah said. He'd been guarding that burying ground, you know. You've heard about what they say was buried with Selma Van Zandt, I reckon?"

"Everybody's heard that jewel story, Grandpap," Clardy replied irritably. "Tell us about Abel." He fired a glance at Thias that was dark with worry. Thias knew just what he was thinking. Abel . . . *missing*. And from two nights back—the same night the intruders had tried to dig up Selma's grave and Abel had run them off.

Hiram continued: "Well, it seems old Abel was out there guarding, like always, and somebody dug into that grave. Abel run 'em off, then went back up to the house and told the other Van Zandts. Then he went back down to guard some more, even though the others, they told him not to. Anyway, he never come back that night, and when they went looking in the morning, he warn't to be found."

"Oh, God," Clardy whispered, turning pallid.

"And there was something else, too," Hiram said, then clamped his mouth shut. Up went the chin, the eyes narrowing as he held another piece of news hostage for the ransom of a begging. Thias, already fighting a gnawing, growing feeling of dread, could have knocked the old man down in frustration.

"Grandpap, confound you, tell us!"

"Calm down, Thias. I'll tell you. When the Van Zandts got down there, that grave was full dug up. The old woman's burying box was busted open. If there ever *was* a jewel in that grave, it warn't there after that."

"There never was a jewel," Thias said. Clardy fired him a warning glance: *Don't say anything that would let him know we talked to Abel.* "Least, that's what I hear that Abel was telling folks. He just didn't want the old woman's corpse bothered, that was why he was guarding it. Or so I've heard folks say."

"Maybe there really was a jewel, after all," Clardy said hopefully. "Maybe Abel just dug it up himself and lit out with it."

"Don't believe so," Hiram said haughtily. "That don't fit the balance of the facts."

"What facts?"

"Just that there was tracks about the grave, Abel's and a couple of other men besides." He looked from Clardy to Thias and back again. His slow, toying manner made the hot place in Thias's belly surge like someone was taking a bellows to it. "And there was blood on the ground, too. Fresh. Most likely Abel's."

Clardy swore beneath his breath.

"If there was tracks, couldn't they have been followed?" Thias asked.

"They was wiped out on the road. Whoever it was had covered their trail. And there was only tracks of two men leading out of the burying ground, 'cording to Elijah. Deep tracks, like them that made them was carrying something heavy." He narrowed one eye knowingly. "Or *somebody* heavy."

"Carrying Abel," Thias said. "Carrying Abel because he was hurt, or . . ."

"Dead. That's just what Elijah's thinking is. Mine, too. Most likely it was Abel they was carrying, and if it was, mercy on him. I 'spect we'll not lay eyes on Abel Van Zandt again," Hiram said. "He's been murdered, I'll wager you."

"Wait, wait," Clardy said, stepping forward, waving his hand dismissively, a forced smile on his face. "What's all this murder talk? Maybe all this is a mistake, or a jest or such. Or maybe Abel was in with the other two, and pretended to guard the grave, and pretended to fight them, and let them carry him off, just so he could make it seem he wasn't helping with the grave robbing himself. Maybe he . . ." And then he simply trailed off, his smile fading, the obvious absurdity of the scenario making it seem foolish to continue.

"No, boy, I don't think any such as that happened," Hiram said, growing haughty again. "There's yet one more fact I ain't mentioned that would make me doubt Abel had aught to do with helping rob that grave. No sir, he loved that old woman too much to let her corpse be done the wickedness it was."

"What 'wickedness'?" Thias asked.

Faded blue eyes flashed. The chin went up, and Hiram Tyler dropped his final piece of information in a tone of delicious self-satisfaction. He had been building up to this part all along. "Her head was cut off, boys. Cut clean off her corpsey shoulders."

"Cut off!"

"That's right. Cut off and laid back in its place upside downward. Purely ghastly. Purely ghastly."

A pause. Clardy turned his back, his shoulders taking on the odd hunch that tension always gave them, and began puffing his pipe very hard, as if reviving the dying coal of tobacco was the most important task in the world.

"Why would anybody cut on a poor old woman's corpse, Grandpap?" Thias asked.

"Why, to spite her! To spite her for not having fetched up the jewel they wanted off her. Yes sir, what happened in that burying ground was an ugly business, no lying. Somebody or other dug up that grave, killed poor old Abel for trying to stop 'em, and then put the knife to the corpse just 'cause they was mad at her for not rendering up no treasure. That's what happened. I'd wager my last coin on it."

He turned on his crutch, his leg stump moving in tandem, as if in remembrance of the muscular executions it would have performed had it been whole. "There's wickedness come to this valley, boys. Pure wickedness. Something to think on. Well, boys, I'm going to go down to the spring for a little while. You keep working, you hear? And next log you hew, Clardy, it'd better come out a cussed sight more true than that one there."

Thias pulled Clardy aside as soon as Hiram was gone. "Clardy, Abel's dead. Sure as the world, them two who we saw at the grave killed him. We've let a man be killed, me and you. We should have come out that night and helped Abel run down them two, whoever they was."

"We don't know Abel's dead," Clardy shot back. "And don't you go saying it's our fault. It ain't. If Abel got himself killed, it was his own doing for guarding that grave."

"Clardy, you answer me something straight out. When that lantern light hit the face of them grave robbers, you let out a gasp. Don't deny it. I heard it, and it wasn't because you had a cramp in your side, neither. You *knew* them men."

"I didn't!"

"I believe you did—and that means you know the likely murderers of Abel Van Zandt."

"I tell you, I didn't know them!"

Thias glared at his brother. "Look me in the eye, Clardy—if you can. That's right—look at me." He paused, deeply studying his brother's oddly ashen face. "You *are* lying. I can see it in your look."

Some of Clardy's color returned; anger was rising. "You can't see nothing, Thias. Not one bloody thing. And I don't like you calling me a liar."

"This ain't no game, Clardy. There's a man dead."

"You don't know that. Abel may come stepping 'round yonder bend in the next minute. And why are you spitting all this in my face? If Abel is dead, it wasn't me who killed him."

"No, but it's you who know whose faces it was we saw in the lantern light."

Clardy swore and shoved his older brother back so hard that Thias nearly stumbled and fell. Clardy strode on past him, muttering beneath his breath.

"Where you going?" Thias called after him. "We ain't finished here—and you can't run away from what's happened."

"I can run anyplace I please. To the devil with all this. I'm going to Hughes's tavern and get myself something to drink. Then I believe I'll just light up on my horse and ride out of this country once and for all. If I don't see you again for a good spell, Thias, you take care of yourself. Kick Grandpap right swuft in the fundament and tell him that's from me." Clardy grabbed his rifle, which had been leaned up against a nearby rail fence, and began walking toward the cabin.

"Clardy, come back here!"

"Good-bye, brother. I hope you'll enjoy your life here alone with Grandpap. Me, I'll be off on the old Boone road getting rich and famous as a highway robber."

"You're scared, that's what it is! You know who it was there at that grave, and you're scared to say!"

"Anybody but you said that, Thias, and I'd free him of his teeth," Clardy yelled back.

Clardy reached the cabin and went inside. Thias stood watching. Within two minutes Clardy was back out, carrying his rifle, pouch, horn, and a well-stuffed saddlebag. Without looking at Thias, he headed over to the stock pen, saddled his horse, and rode out. He lifted his right hand and waved across his shoulder without looking back.

Thias almost charged after him, but held back. There was no point. He could run Clardy down, drag him off that horse and back to the cabin, even beat him half senseless, and none of it would make Clardy name the men whose faces they both saw in the lantern light if he didn't want to. Nor would it keep him from leaving if he was set on it.

Thias wondered what kind of men they could be, to have done such foul things as desecrating the corpse of an old woman and murdering a man who tried to stop it all. . . .

Suddenly, Thias was overwhelmed with the realization that he and Clardy, now riding out of sight around the bend, could be endangered by all this, should it ever get out that they had seen the faces of the men at the Van Zandt grave. Probably Clardy had realized that, too. Maybe that's what was prompting him to make his long-promised exodus so abruptly.

Thias was torn. Maybe he should go try to persuade his brother to come back to the cabin. Maybe he should go on with him, to protect him.

Or maybe . . .

Or maybe he should even do the very thing Clardy had been advocating for so long. Maybe he, too, should simply leave. At his brother's side he could ride out of the very region and find a new life somewhere else. Run off . . . just declare his freedom and go.

The thought generated an unexpectedly strong pang of longing. To ride away, to simply leave behind not only this dilemma, but this whole mundane life—the notion had an overwhelming appeal all at once. For a few moments Thias understood his younger brother a little better. This, he thought, must be the feeling that stirred him to talk so much about getting away from this place.

Thias didn't go after Clardy. It was as if he couldn't, and that worried him.

He stood there for a long time at the unfinished cabin, looking down the road. He still felt fearful, not only for Clardy now, but in another way, for himself, too. Was Clardy the wiser brother for once? Sure, he was reckless, clung to the romanticized idea that becoming a thief would be a grand thing—a notion he should have outgrown several years before—and seemed to lack any drive to become a settled, decent citizen. Yet in the end it was Clardy who would probably escape this farm, become free and happy . . . while Thias himself would remain bound to the land, to his sense of duty, to a life that held no color or promise. He would grow old and tired and sour, just like his grandfather. Standing there at that moment, the whole scenario loomed vividly in his mind: sad, fated, inescapable.

He looked down the empty road and wondered if Clardy really was leaving for good. Surely not. Surely he would come back tonight, drunk and primed for a fight with Grandpap, and affairs at the Tyler house would take on their usual miserable turn.

But what if he doesn't come back? What if he doesn't?

Thias felt a hot, wet surging in his eyes. The feeling of distress over the probable murder of Abel Van Zandt, horror at the gruesome thing done to the corpse of an old woman, the guilty feeling that maybe he and Clardy could have stopped it all from happening . . . all these together felt like a mountain's weight on his shoulders.

Don't leave, Clardy. Whatever I've said to you, please don't leave me alone here.

He longed to go after his brother, but instead he merely turned and went back to work, while from down at the creek Hiram Tyler's thin voice came riding in the wind, singing some old tune that for some reason only made Thias feel all the worse.

CHAPTER 7

Clardy Tyler rode slowly along the road, eyes staring straight ahead. Now that he was away from Thias, he gave full vent to the horror aroused by his grandfather's story. He was sure that Abel was dead, and that *they* had killed him. And the mutilation of the buried woman's body . . . that fit in perfectly with what he knew of the character of the brothers named Harpe. He had seen the Harpe brothers a total of three times, once on the street in Knoxville, another time in the Hughes tavern he frequented—and a third time at the grave of Selma Van Zandt, by lantern light.

He knew little about the Harpes. What he did know, picked up mostly from his frequent drinking partner, Cale Johnson, was enough to make him very fearful of ever getting on the wrong side of the pair. Johnson knew a lot about the Harpes, enough that Clardy suspected he was an occasional partner-in-crime of the two.

The Harpes lived as brothers, though no one could say for sure that they were. Johnson had said he suspected they shared a common mother or common father, not necessarily both. They generally claimed to be from Georgia, but Johnson declared firmly that they had come from North Carolina. They

were free-roaming souls and had moved about frequently.
Johnson didn't know all the places they had lived, but one of
the few he did know about was chilling: the country of the
Chickamaugas. The Chickamaugas were a conglomerate tribe
of Indians, mostly Cherokee and Creek by birth, who had taken
the hardest and most violent line against the relentless encroachment of white settlers onto their lands over the past
twenty or so years. They had become legends of fear across the
frontier, with good reason—and any white man who dared live
among them had to be more Indian than white in his thinking
and devotions, and probably have a bent toward violence.

Based on what Clardy had heard from Johnson, this was certainly true of both Harpes. Johnson had become friendly with
the brothers on terms Clardy didn't fully know and which
Johnson declined to talk about much, even though he seemed
proud to know so rough a pair, and told with relish grim stories
of terrible deeds the Harpes had purportedly done in their past.
Clardy struggled to remember the details of those stories, but
couldn't recall most of them. He had heard them all filtered
through hazes of drunkenness, and few specifics managed to
pass through. He dimly recalled disturbing mentions of terrible
fights, mutilations, killings, rapes. All this gave Clardy an ingrained, almost instinctive fear of the Harpes. That was why he
had gasped when the lantern light struck their faces by Selma
Van Zandt's grave.

What should I do?

The question rang in his mind, unwelcome but persistent. He
knew that everything Thias had said was right, and that he did
hold in his hands the key to the apparent murder of Abel Van
Zandt. Murder . . . the very word gave him a bad taste in his
throat. Though he almost never prayed—to Clardy Tyler, God
was a being far too terrifying to be thought about, much less
talked to—he prayed now. *Lord, let Abel still be alive, please,
even though I feel right sure that he ain't. Let him show up and
be well, and then I won't have to feel guilty for not telling what
I know. Much obliged to you, and amen.*

It was a feeble prayer at best. The odds of Abel being alive
were slim. The thing to do if he were a *good* person, like
Thias, would be to reveal what he had seen and help bring the
Harpes to justice. But, God help him, what if the Harpes
couldn't be found, discovered he had revealed them, and decided to avenge that offense? All those vaguely remembered

tales of cruelty told by Cale Johnson made for a powerful deterrent.

He stopped his horse and dismounted, carrying his rifle in his right hand and leading the horse with his left. Reaching a familiar shaded spot under some thick willows, he filled his pipe, lit it with flint, steel, and tinder, then settled down to rest both body and nerves. He was tired from his early morning labors on the cabin, and his muscles ached. He had once heard it said that work was a curse upon mankind for its evil ways, and he believed it. He had no use for farmwork, for sweat and aching muscles and bone-weariness that even a good night's rest couldn't fully take away. There had to be a better life than being a slave to labor and Hiram Tyler.

Even now, his grandfather was probably raging around on his crutches, furious because his wayward grandson had vanished when there was so much work remaining. Picturing the old man's face, Clardy tried to remember when he had last felt affection for the man. A long time. Any love he had known for Hiram Tyler had been cussed and beaten out of him well before he reached adult stature. It seemed a bad thing to not care for the man who had been the closest thing to a father he had known. But a man couldn't help how he felt.

Clardy puffed his pipe lazily, beginning to relax. Here beneath the willows he would not be noticeable from the road because of a gentle swell of the land, but he retained a decent view of the road himself. Right now it was empty, but he found himself hoping he would see Thias come riding along, looking for him to tell him he had changed his mind and they could ride away together. If that happened, Clardy knew he would really be able to leave. If not, he wasn't so sure, despite all the big claims he had made to Thias. It would take courage to make the final break between himself and his family, himself and the only place in the world he had known; and courage, like most virtues, didn't come easily to Clardy Tyler.

Through a fog of pipe smoke, Clardy examined the land about him. His dislike of the region had nothing to do with the countryside, which he had always thought beautiful. A land of valleys and ridges, it was well-drained by countless creeks that, like Beaver Creek, spilled into the French Broad or otherwise into the Holston. It was a country molded by and in the stone that lay below the surface of the soil. Where limestone and shales had eroded away, great valleys had developed, lying between ridges generally bearing from northeast to south-west.

The countryside was so forested that in earlier days a man could walk for hours without leaving the shade. In those days, only from the mountain balds, or in the great expanses cleared by forest fires set by lightning or early Indian farmers, could a man see the sky without branches and trunks intervening. The forest remained vast even now, but clearings were more fre-quent, created by settlers who girdled the trees, waited for them to die, then felled and burned them, thus opening the land for agriculture.

Even such a halfhearted farmer as Clardy Tyler had learned much from the land. He knew how to judge the soil by the trees that grew upon it. The great hardwoods stood where the land was richest and deepest. On the poorer soils grew smaller, softer-wooded trees, such as pines, and scrubbier hardwoods, like post oaks. The forests were rich with maples of several va-rieties, hickory trees that provided one of Clardy's favorite meaty nuts, and with beeches, dogwoods, poplars, elms, wil-lows, chestnuts. Clardy could sweep a ridge with a glance and immediately name off most of the varieties of trees growing there, determine whether the ground was rocky, poor, or rich, and what kind of creatures were most likely lurking there. None of that mattered much to him, though; he disliked hunt-ing as much as he disliked farming. There was little in life that he liked, in fact, other than drinking and gambling and women.

He finished his pipe and emerged from the shaded little en-clave. The time for a decision had come. He had talked a long time about leaving home, but had never found the courage to do so. There was security in familiarity, even a despised famil-iarity.

Could he go? He thought about Abel Van Zandt, the Harpes, and the eternal pressure that Thias would bring upon him to tell what he knew. He couldn't do that. He did not dare risk in-forming on the Harpes.

So it really was time to go, at last.

That decision made, he drew in a deep breath and said, "I *will* do it. I'll leave."

Something rattled in the trees behind him. Frowning, he turned. Silence. Confused, he turned toward the road again, and something flew close by his head and struck a tree trunk nearby. A rock . . . someone had thrown a rock at him!

"So you're going to leave, are you? Where you going?"

Clardy grinned and yelled, "Cale Johnson, you old dog, what kind of scoundrel heaves rocks at his friends?"

"Just trying to break you from talking to yourself, boy." Cale Johnson came walking down from the road. He was grinning, broad-faced, with thinning black hair and an unusually pointed nose. Clardy couldn't have said how old Johnson was, but he surely wasn't as old as he looked. Johnson lived hard, and had drunk enough grog in his time to drown lesser men. Such a life left tracks on a man's face.

"Where you heading, Cale?" Clardy asked.

"Hughes's tavern. You want to come along?"

"Aye. I was aiming to go there anyways."

"What was that you said about leaving?"

"I've made a decision, Cale. I ain't going back home again. I've broke away for good."

"I've heard you talk so before. You mean it this time?"

"I do."

Johnson's eyes gleamed. "And do you mean the things you've said before, 'bout all them things you aim to do?"

Clardy had told Cale Johnson many times about his belief that a livelihood must surely be all the better when it is taken by brass and stealth rather than earned by labor and sweat. Big talk . . . now it was time to make it more than talk, as Johnson had often urged. He nodded. "I do mean it."

Johnson grinned and nodded. "It's surely fate that's brung us together today, Clardy. Surely it is. I been waiting for the day when you'd come to your senses and break off from that farm. Come on. Let's get on to the groggery. If it's a sweet life outside the law that you want, then we've got much to talk about, me and you."

Clardy Tyler took a careful sip of whiskey from a cracked crockery cup held in a hand just beginning to tremble. The sip of powerful liquor passed across his lips, and he savored the taste, swirling the liquor over his tongue and swallowing slowly, aware his throat and belly would begin to rebel if he drank too heavily, too fast, of the strong whiskey sold at Hughes's tavern. He was not nearly good enough at holding his liquor to balance his inordinate love for the stuff. He was eating as he drank—greasy pork and stale bread in a trencher—in hopes of avoiding the sickness that Hughes's powerful liquor sometimes brought on.

The Hughes tavern was of lowest reputation, as was old Hughes himself, who at the moment held his usual position behind a sturdy wicker screen covering an entire corner of the log-walled room. The screen's lower portion was woven so tightly as to make a veritable wall, and the top portion, of a much looser weave, was nevertheless sufficient to deflect any flying bottle or thrown cup that might come his way. It was broken only by a small window at waist level, through which Hughes could collect money and hand out drinks in return. Hughes put much stock in his screen, which had saved him injury many a time. During business hours he seldom ventured out from behind its protection.

Cale Johnson sat across from Clardy, talking in a steady stream. He had started as soon as they had seated themselves and hadn't stopped since. And all he had to say had told Clardy much about the increase in stock theft that had been taking place for miles around Knoxville of late.

Johnson's eyes were red from drinking, his lips glistening with drool. Those lips curled into a very hungry smile as he leaned forward to speak to Clardy in private tones. "You can be a part of it, too, Clardy. Me and my partners, we're making ourselves a decent living, and so far ain't a soul caught us. We don't aim to be caught, neither."

"They do catch you, you'll hang," Clardy said. His words were growing slurred.

"There's risks in everything a man does," Johnson replied. "This is worth the risk."

"Cale, tell me: Are you a partner of the Harpes?"

Johnson glanced from side to side and leaned forward. "Yep. I am."

Clardy drew back, silent, somber, his mind's eye seeing two lantern-lit faces in a graveyard, and he recalled his grandfather's talk about beheaded corpses, blood on the soil. . . .

Johnson frowned. "What's wrong with you?"

"Nothing. Just don't know what to think of the Harpes."

"What? You afraid of them?"

"To be right honest, I am . . . considering all the stories you've told."

Johnson laughed. "No reason to fear them, long as you don't do nothing to hurt them or make them mad." He chuckled.

"There's some good things that come from being close in with the Harpe brothers. And I ain't just talking money, neither." He winked.

"What are you talking about?"

"Women, boy, women."

"What women?"

"*Their* women. One of them in particular. Sally. Oh, my, what a woman she is!"

"You're messing with one of the Harpe women?"

"Not yet . . . but I will be soon enough. She's got an eye for me. I can tell it."

Clardy was too drunk to think clearly, but he knew Johnson was talking dangerous talk right now. Cale had always been unsensible about women, often taking absurd risks to pursue his passion for them.

"Tell me more . . . about the Harpes," Clardy said.

"They're men who know their place in this world—men you want to be on the good side of," Johnson said. "I help them, they help me."

"They surely ain't going to like you sniffing about their women."

"I don't know about that. The Harpes, they like me 'cause I help them. Those that help them, they won't hurt."

Clardy took a mental note of that.

Johnson went on: "Besides, they got a . . . *different* way of thinking about women." He looked sly. "Did you know they got three women in that cabin, and share them all? Every deuced one of them women has a belly full of baby right now, too, and God only knows who fathered which. And only one of them women is married by law to either one of them boys. That's Sally, the pretty one, and the youngest. She's Little Harpe's wife. Preacher's daughter, she is! You heard of Parson Rice? That's her pap. Ain't that a caution, eh? Why the good parson ever let his little gal marry a man like Little Harpe, I'll never figure."

"Which one's Little Harpe?"

"Wiley. He's the small-boned one. Micajah, he's Big Harpe. And he's a man to respect, let me tell you, if you want to keep your heart a-beating."

Clardy took another swallow of whiskey. His head was spinning now, and felt full of cotton besides. Rapidly he was losing the ability to make sense of anything. But one thing Johnson had said kept coming through the mental murk: *Those that help them they don't hurt.* Maybe the answer for his dilemma wasn't to flee the Harpes, but to work his way into their good graces. He could embark on his criminal career by way of an established and apparently successful gang. Rather than betray the Harpes to the law, he could become their ally. Let Thias worry about the rights and wrongs; he would worry only about himself.

Johnson talked on about the Harpes, speaking in one breath as if he admired them greatly and in the next as if he intended to use them for his own ends and wind up with Sally before it was done. By now Hughes's whiskey had let Clardy forget the beheaded corpse of Selma Van Zandt, the apparent murder of Abel Van Zandt, and the mortal fear of the Harpes he had held. The more Johnson talked, the better the opportunity being laid out sounded. Johnson said that the Harpes were busily involved in stealing hogs, cattle, and horses from their neighbors. They stole more hogs than anything else, slaughtering them and delivering the meat for sale in Knoxville. They always sold the meat fully dressed so the source couldn't be identified.

At length Clardy put aside the whiskey, realizing that if he continued drinking he would pass out. He also was dimly aware that Thias might show up, looking for him as he had sometimes before. If Thias found him passed out and took him home, he would wake up back in the cabin again, with Grandpap cussing him while his head rang with the miseries that accompany the morning after drinking. It would not do to pass out.

Johnson's ruddy face was close to his all at once. "Well, Clardy, are you with us?"

"With . . . us . . ."

"You come with me, and they'll let you join." He winked. "Maybe they'll even wind up sharing their women with you, too."

Clardy nodded. "I'll . . . go with you. . . ."

Johnson reached across and gently slapped Clardy's shoulder. "That's good, Clardy. You made the right choice. You'll be a better-off man for making it."

The next thing Clardy knew, he was struggling up into his saddle. Johnson was ahead, already mounted, urging him to move more quickly. "We'll go talk to them, let them meet you," Johnson said. "They'll like you, Clardy. They'll let you in."

Then he rode, and how he managed to remain in the saddle was a mystery to him. The night air was cold and slightly sobering. It came to him that they were riding out to meet the Harpes themselves, men frightening enough that he had been ready to flee the region because of them. But Clardy was impulsive at all times, and even more so when he was drunk. He rode on behind Johnson with no sense of fear, no thought that what he was doing was anything but sensible. Opportunity had reached out to him tonight, and he was ready to accept it enthusiastically.

CHAPTER 8

C lardy devoted full concentration to remaining in the saddle. The farther he rode, the more difficult that was, partly because Johnson had led him off the main road and onto a rugged, narrow path that sliced through a particularly dismal-looking finger of forest. Clardy was woozy and having much trouble thinking, but with what part of his mind wasn't fully beclouded, he wondered eagerly about the Harpes. Hughes's liquor had stripped him of his former worries, and he thought nothing at all about the fact he was heading into the lair of the very men he had been ready to flee earlier in the day.

After long riding, Johnson paused and sniffed the air. "Smell that? Smells like the flesh of a fine woman to me! We're near their place now—near my own dear Sally!"

Clardy slurred out, "I don't smell no woman. Just pigs."

Johnson frowned at him. "That's their swine pen you're smelling. Come on. We're nearly there."

Five minutes later they rode out of the woods into a clearing where stood one of the crudest, squatly built cabins Clardy had ever seen. No one had bothered to hew out or even debark these logs, and the notching had no style or neatness. Poorly rounded, ragged saddle notches had been hacked in the logs, some of which still had branches protruding from them, being used as hangers for 'possum, fox, and deer hides hung out to dry. The chinking looked like pure mud, with no sticks or straw to help make it firm.

The roof had no shingles, just big roof boards held down by logs pinned in place. The chimney was of sticks and mud and leaned perilously out from the cabin, ready to fall in the next good rain, yet no one had bothered to put a prop against it to hold it in place. Smoke and sparks poured out of the chimney top, which barely cleared the peak of the roof. Clardy caught a whiff of cooking meat. Fatty pork, he guessed. It was hard to be sure, considering the various competing stenches that hung about the place. The strongest of these was the fetor of the swine penned inside a crude rectangular fence standing about fifty feet east of the cabin. The swine had rooted and trampled the pen floor into muck, and were so deeply sunk in it that they appeared to have no legs. They put out such a stench, it cut through the alcoholic haze and actually made Clardy feel a little sobered.

There were no real outbuildings about the cabin, just some crude lean-to shelters built haphazardly in the clearing, which was filled with dead, girdled trees that would fall one by one over the next few years if the occupants didn't get around to cutting them down first. Considering their obvious lack of concern with their surroundings, Clardy doubted they would ever bother.

"Sorry looking sort of place, Cale," he said.

"Aw, they're not ones to pretty up their dwelling," Johnson said. "But it don't matter. They've got a good situation here. Two men, three women . . . that's the life, ain't it? Can you just imagine?"

A plain, ungroomed woman in a ragged frock appeared in the open cabin door. Even from where he was, Clardy could see that she was as filthy as the hogs that wallowed in the pen. Probably smelled no better.

"Surely *that* ain't the woman you're so hot to steal for yourself, is it, Cale?" Clardy whispered.

"Lord, no! That's Susanna. She come with them from North Carolina. Calls herself the wife of Micajah, yet generally goes by the last name of Roberts. I'd sooner take up with a she-bear than with her. Sally's the one I like—she's Wiley's wife." Johnson raised his hand and waved. "Howdy do, Susanna! It's Cale Johnson here! Is your men at home?"

The woman's voice was flat and lifeless. "No."

"Will they be coming back directly?"

"Yes."

"Where'd they go?"

She pointed west. Johnson side-spoke to Clardy: "Ain't much for talking, these Harpe women. Wears you out to get anything out of them." He called out, "Well, you reckon we could come down and wait for them?"

"Who's with you?"

"A friend of mine. A man your men will be wanting to meet."

Another figure appeared behind Susanna Roberts, and Johnson almost danced in his saddle. "That's Sally!" he whispered excitedly. He waved again, vigorously, and called, "Howdy, Sally! I see you yonder!" Then again to Clardy: "Ain't she pretty? Ain't she?"

To the extent that he was thinking at all, Clardy contemplated that the woman, hardly more than a girl, really, might indeed be pretty if you could see beneath the dirt and get past the deadness of her expression. Both her and Susanna had the most listless, blank looks that he had ever seen on any of the faces of womankind.

"They look right fat," Clardy commented, noting to himself that Sally was not waving back at Johnson.

"I told you, the Harpe boys got them all three full of babies."

"Oh. Aye." Clardy had forgotten.

Susanna yelled, "Reckon you can come on down."

"Let's go," Johnson said. "Clardy, I'm going to introduce you to the finest piece of womanflesh what ever walked the earth. And she's going to be mine one of these days."

"So you keep telling me," Clardy replied.

There was something sobering about entering the house of the Harpes. By the time Clardy's eyes had adjusted to the interior shadows, he felt the first glimmerings of doubt that he had been wise to come here. It was only a flicker of a thought, however, quickly forgotten in the midst of the distractions around him.

Cale Johnson was in the best of moods. He perched on a three-legged stool, with Sally at his side, seated on the floor and paying him no heed at all. In fact she was staring at Clardy, as were all the women. Not with evident suspicion, welcome, or desire. They simply stared. Clardy figured he was a curiosity in their eyes, like some blind fox that had wandered through the door by accident.

He mentally corrected that analogy. A fox would at least fetch a reaction out of these blank women, who would probably kill and skin it, as they had many other animals whose hides now covered almost the entire interior wall surface. The fat hadn't been scraped away very well from the underside of most of the skins, so the stagnant air reeked of dead flesh. And of other things: the stench of swine outside, of humans and dogs—there were six of the latter on the dirt floor—the foulness of the various piles of bodily wastes that lay ignored all around the place. Most looked to be the product of the dogs. Some, Clardy couldn't help noticing, looked like they might be . . . he tried not to think about it.

"Sally, you're one of them women who looks all the prettier when she's with child," Johnson was saying. "If it's a girl, I'll wager she'll be pretty as her maw."

No answer. Still the same dead stare at Clardy Tyler.

"I believe I'll step outside and smoke my pipe," Clardy said.

"Don't go out there," said the third woman, whose name Clardy would later learn was Betsy.

"Why?"

"If Micajah comes back and sees you there, he'll shoot you."

"*Shoot* me?"

"Now, don't get all fearful," Johnson cut in. "He won't shoot you if you stay put in here and I introduce you to him."

Time passed. Johnson kept talking, everything directed at Sally, his adoration for her obvious yet seemingly unnoticed, or perhaps simply ignored, by the women. The staring continued. Meanwhile, Clardy began to grow more sober and more uncertain that he should have come here. As darkness fell outside the cabin and a chill spread through the room—Why didn't they close the door? Did no one else feel as cold as he?—he thought about Abel Van Zandt and pondered the fact that the Harpes were probably his killers. He wondered how the brothers would react when they discovered him here, and found out that Cale Johnson had already revealed the facts about their criminal operations to a man they hadn't approved.

Clardy's thoughts were broken by the appearance of a figure

at the door. And what a figure it was! Clardy felt his heart jump and his extremities go cold.

It was Micajah Harpe, tall, broad, and ugly. He had come into the doorway with the silence of a ghost. Just behind him was Wiley, whose eyes were wild and bright and fixed on Clardy. On his face was a look that was anything but welcoming, anything but pleasant.

Micajah strode straight to Clardy and stared down at him. Clardy wondered if he should stand, but remained where he was. The big man's gaze upon him was chilling, aimed out from shadowed eye pits beneath thick, dark brows.

"What I want to know, Cale," Micajah Harpe said in a voice so soft it belied his fearsome appearance, "is who is this here sod, and why in hell did you bring him into my house?"

For the next two hours Clardy Tyler's life became a descent into the most bizarre world he had ever stumbled into, one that left him completely sober when he emerged from it. His impulsive desire to join the Harpes had died, along with most of his intoxication, the moment Micajah had looked into his face. An intensely disturbing moment had followed soon after when Johnson told the Harpes that he had informed Clardy about their stock theft operations. Wiley had leaped up, drawing a knife, cursing Johnson as a betrayer, and would have slashed it across Johnson's throat had not Micajah stopped him.

"Leave him be," he said. "Maybe this gent here can be a help to us. I like the look of him." He turned to Clardy. "Are you a young man of grit?"

"I am." Clardy did his best to look strong and hardened. There was no backing out of this now. He was here, the facts were out, and he had no choice but to play along.

Micajah Harpe rose and advanced closer to him. Clardy found himself compelled to stare him in the eye. "Are you a man who is loyal to them who are his friends, and the devil to them who ain't?" Micajah asked.

"I am."

Micajah came closer another step. His eyes glittered. "Are you a man who's not afraid to kiss death right on the mouth and find it the sweetest kind of woman, whether it be his own death or the deaths of them he kills?"

"I ain't afraid of nothing," Clardy declared. But he was afraid, afraid of Micajah himself.

Micajah suddenly drew his belt axe and heaved it straight at Clardy's head. Clardy yelped and ducked. The hatchet stuck fast in the log wall behind him. Had he remained unmoving, it would have missed him by less than an inch. Wiley Harpe hooted and cackled. The women remained as expressionless as ever and made not a sound.

Clardy looked up at Micajah Harpe, temper surging . . . but anger could not long survive the harsh stare from that broad and ugly face. His temper withered to a husk and was replaced by outright fear. Micajah stepped near and bent over, pushing his face right into Clardy's. He spoke so low that no one else in the room could hear him. Those glittering eyes burned more brightly than ever. "You work with us, boy, and you become one of us. You stay loyal to us no matter what, and you do what we tell you, no matter what it is. You understand me?"

"Yes."

"We're hard men, me and my brother. Hard as the hell-baked hide of Old Scratch hisself, and thrice as mean. If the devil rose in this room this very night, he'd bow to me and say, 'Micajah Harpe, I'm at your service, for in your time you've outdid the worst I've ever thunk of.' And it would be the truth. I'm a wicked man, boy. So's my brother. You ain't knowed wickedness—pure, poison-blooded, pit-of-hell, spit-on-the-Bible wickedness—until you've knowed the Harpe brothers."

Clardy was having trouble drawing his breath. The stench of Micajah Harpe's body and filthy clothing, the fetor of his breath, and the fear that had Clardy's insides in turmoil, all played their part in that. He was scared to the marrow, to the core of his soul.

And yet, curiously, when he looked into Micajah's piercing eyes, he felt a troubling, unexplainable desire to want to gain this man's favor. And he could not tear his own eyes away from Micajah's.

Micajah Harpe fell silent but kept on staring, his broad face scarcely five inches from Clardy's. There was no reading this man, no fathoming what thoughts were bubbling in the caldron of his mind. Clardy was so terrified he began to grow weak.

Slowly Micajah smiled, showing yellowed, brown-streaked teeth. "I *do* like you, boy. You could be one of us. But there's a thing you must do for me," he said, still whispering. "Your friend yonder—Johnson. Me and my brother don't like him no more. He's got an eye for Wiley's wife, and thinks we're too foolish to know it. I want you to kill him for me."

Clardy's mouth instantly went dry. "You want me to—"

"Keep your voice low, boy! That's right. I want you to kill him."

"But . . . when do you want me to do it?"

"Now. Pull that hatchet from the wall and go sink it in his noggin. Right now. Sink it right in, all the way."

Clardy felt wild desperation rising. Micajah Harpe was deadly serious. He had to get out of this somehow.

"I'll . . . I'll kill him . . . but I can't do it here and now. I'll not kill a man in front of witnesses. I'll do it later, outside, after we've left. That way you can say truthful that you never saw it happen."

"What? You don't trust us, boy? You believe we'd tell on you?"

"No . . . I . . . it's . . . it's the women I don't trust. I don't know them, you see. Women, even such fine women as yours, they can be persuaded to tell what she's seen, if somebody scares her bad enough."

Micajah smiled again, very slowly, and nodded. His breath smelled like something dead, and there were tiny bits of old meat stuck between his teeth, remnants of his last meal. He wiggled one of the longer pieces with the end of his tongue, then said, "Very well, boy. We'll do it your way. We'll see if you've got the grit to run with the Harpes. You kill him, and then you come back and tell me where me and Wiley might want to take a little walk together come morning. I expect we might find us a corpse lying about while we stretch our legs. You be back before morning. You hear me?"

"Yes."

"Don't fail me. You prove yourself to me, and you'll be glad for it later. I want Cale Johnson dead. Dead! Take his life, you take his place among us. Spare him, and you die in his place. Wiley and me will see to it."

God help me, why did I come here? "I'll kill him. I will."

Micajah stood and turned. "Wiley, I like this young man," he said loudly. Then to Johnson: "You did a wise thing, Cale, bringing this gent to us. He's going to be a true help to us. He's going to help us quite a lot."

"I knew you'd like him, Micajah." Johnson said. He looked

troubled, though, and Clardy knew he was wondering what he and Micajah had been whispering about.

"Off with you now, both of you," Micajah said. "Me and Wiley got talking to do."

Clardy and Johnson rode out together into the night. For the first half minute in the saddle, Clardy didn't breathe at all, and then his breath began coming in hard, stinging gasps and he felt hot and tight in his belly. As soon as they were well out of view of the Harpe cabin and out in the woods, Clardy halted his horse, dismounted, and became sick.

"What's wrong with you, Clardy?"

He turned to Johnson, who was still mounted. It was dark here. He could scarcely make out the outline of his form and face. "He wants me to kill you, Cale."

"Wants you to *what*?"

"Big Harpe, he wants me to kill you, and go back by morning to tell him where he can find your corpse. Wiley knows that you want his wife, and he don't like it. I'm supposed to prove my worth to them by killing you."

"Clardy . . . you ain't going to do it, are you?"

"No, Cale, no. But me and you, we've both got to leave here, now. Leave these parts completely, or else they'll be after both of us."

"Leave? Hell, I'm doing well for myself here. Me and the Harpes, we're doing fine! I don't want to go nowhere else."

"Ain't you hearing what I say, Cale? Have you lost your ears? They want you *dead*! And when I don't do what I said I would, they'll want me dead, too. Harpe said as much. We've got to leave here, both of us. You understand?"

Johnson was silent. He seemed confused. "I ain't going nowhere. I ain't afraid of them."

"I am. I'm more afraid of them than I've been of any men I've ever run across. I was a fool to even go with you tonight, and if I hadn't been drunk, I wouldn't have done it. Now I am leaving, going as far away as I can, and if you care about your life, you'll do the same."

"I figure I can take care of myself."

"I reckon you'll get the chance to prove that, right soon. They'll kill you, Cale. They will." Clardy mounted again. "I'm leaving. If you're a wise man, you'll leave with me."

But when he rode away, Cale Johnson remained where he was. Clardy called for him once, not too loudly, but Johnson didn't respond or move. After that Clardy didn't look back or call anymore. There was no place tonight for the toleration of fools, and such Johnson was proving himself to be. Clardy rode harder than he should, branches slapping at him, scratching his face, until he was out on the road again. After that he rode even harder, and felt like devils were nipping at the flanks of his horse and prickling the back of his neck and shoulders with long and clawed fingers.

CHAPTER 9

Thias yawned and combed his fingers through his hair. The dim light of a cold new dawn was intruding into the cabin through every crack in the chinking and around the edges of the closed shutters. Thias paused by Clardy's empty bed, frowning thoughtfully, then walked to the door and threw it open, looking out across the slowly illuminating land.

I wonder if he really has gone this time. The thought brought sadness. Clardy . . . gone. What would life here be without him?

"Close that door, Thias," Hiram's voice said behind him. "The cold air is making my knee hurt more."

Thias closed the door and turned to his grandfather. "Your real knee?"

"No. The ghost knee. Hurting again this morning. Hurting fierce."

So straightening the leg hadn't worked after all. Thias felt his already somber mood lower one more notch. He decided to tell Hiram what he and Clardy had done. "You know, Grandpap, a few nights back, Clardy and me dug up your cut-off leg and laid it out straight again. A man in Knoxville had told us that would take away the pain."

Hiram blinked in surprise. "Dug up my leg . . ."

"That's right. And for a time it appeared it had done the job. You said the pains had gone away."

"So they had, for a spell." Hiram hopped over to a stool and sat down clumsily, almost tipping himself over. "You boys dug up my leg . . . just so you could try to stop me from hurting?"

Thias wondered why his grandfather seemed to find it so astonishing that they would have tried to do something kind for him. But then that was Hiram Tyler. He had never been able to fit much human kindness into his own life, and it apparently seemed novel to him to consider that someone else would bother to do so. "That's right. I did the digging. Clardy did the straightening."

Hiram scratched his beard and looked uncomfortable. "Well, Thias, I reckon I owe you boys some thanks for trying." The words were mumbled, obviously hard for the old man to get out.

"I'm just sorry it didn't work," Thias replied.

Only then did Hiram notice that Clardy's bed hadn't been slept in. "Thias, did your brother not come in at all last night?"

"No, he didn't."

Hiram swore loudly, with enthusiasm. Thias grinned sadly to himself. The old man was ill at ease dealing with soft feelings such as gratitude, obviously eager to get back into more harsh but familiar emotional territory. "I'll kick that boy's arse! Staying gone all night, drinking and gambling and God only knows what . . . I'll teach him a thing or two!"

"I don't think you'll get the chance. I don't believe Clardy is coming back."

A frown. "What? Why not?"

"He's been wanting to leave here a long time. He's talked to me about it maybe a year or more. I believe this time he's really gone."

Hiram took a few moments to absorb the idea. "Gone," he said. "Clardy's gone?"

"That's right."

The old man was lost in thought for a while. His eyes lost their typical flintiness and grew soft. During that interlude Thias noticed how elderly Hiram was getting to be. Bathed in the white morning light, he looked downright decrepit. Then, abruptly, his cheeks burned red and his eyes became flint again. He stood up, hopped over to the near wall, and got one of his crutches, which he stuck under his arm.

"Run off, has he? Well, let him run, if that's what he wants. God knows I've never been able to do a thing with that boy anyhow. Let him go! I don't need him around here! Never could get a day's worth of work out of him!"

Hiram moved around the cabin, mumbling beneath his breath about Clardy, about his empty belly and the lack of anything worth eating for breakfast, about the unfairness of a world that would take a man's knee but leave him the pains, then about Clardy some more. Thias listened, hollow and lonely, wishing Clardy would come back home where he belonged. As aggravating as Clardy could be, Thias missed him badly right now—and he had been gone since only yesterday.

Abruptly Hiram turned, his crutch making a screaking noise on the puncheon floor. "When did you say you and Clardy was at the burying ground?"

"Two nights ago . . . no, three."

"That was the same night that Abel Van Zandt went missing!"

Thias cringed inwardly. He hadn't meant to let Hiram know he and Clardy had been at the graveyard that particular night. Distraction had made him careless. "Is that right? Well, I suppose it is, now that I think on it."

"Did you see Abel that night? The story I hear was that he was there, guarding that grave."

Thias was about to lie, but changed his mind. Was there any reason not to tell the truth now? "Matter of fact, Grandpap, we did see him."

"Why didn't you say so when I was telling you about him going missing?"

"Truth is, Clardy and me didn't want you to know that we had straightened your leg out. We figured you'd just cuss us for having buried it crooked to begin with."

"Pshaw! Sometimes I think you boys are 'fraid of me. Sometimes I believe you think of me as Old Scratch hisself."

"That's because sometimes you *act* like Old Scratch hisself. You ain't easy to live with, Grandpap."

Hiram seemed taken aback by such a forthright statement. "Well . . . maybe I ain't, but shut up about that. I want to hear about Abel at the burying ground. You know, you boys was probably the last to see him alive, except for whoever it was that killed him. Did you see anybody else—" Hiram cut off. His voice changed. "Thias, I hate even to say what I'm about to say, but with Clardy running off like he did, I got no choice. I want you to answer me straight out. Did you or Clardy have any kind of trouble or such with Abel, and maybe by accident sort of—"

"I know what you're trying to say, Grandpap. No, we didn't have trouble with Abel, and it wasn't us who killed him. You can rest your mind on that."

"I'm mighty glad to hear it. Did you talk to Abel at all that night?"

"Aye. And it was all friendly. He wanted to know what we was doing, and we told him, and he went off. We finished our task and came on home." He hesitated. "And that was all."

Hiram squinted and glared piercingly at his grandson. "That ain't all. I can tell when you're lying to me, boy."

Thias, his mind filled with the memories of lantern light on the faces of strangers, of Abel's rifle firing and voice calling, faltered only a moment before going on. "There *is* more. Grandpap, Clardy and me saw somebody at Selma Van Zandt's grave. They had a lantern and shovels and were talking about digging up the hole. Abel showed up again and ran them off, and then me and Clardy sneaked out and came on home."

"Did you see who they was?"

"We saw the faces of them when one of them opened a lantern shutter. I didn't know them. But I believe that maybe Clardy did."

"He said so?"

"He denied it. But I heard him give a gasp when the lantern light lit their faces. He knew them. I know he did."

Hiram put it together. "And as soon as Clardy found out that Abel was gone and most likely dead, he lit out. Left home."

"Aye. And that troubles me, Grandpap. Clardy's running scared."

Hiram shook his head and cussed at Clardy beneath his breath. He moved about the cabin, crutch clunking, stump swinging, white brows lowered. Thias could tell he was thinking, and that this was not a good time to disturb him. Oddly, Thias actually felt a little less depressed now that he had been honest with his grandfather. He had been burdened about Clardy, and it felt good to be sharing the load.

Finally Hiram swung around and faced him. "Any notion where he might have gone?"

"He said he was going to stop at the Hughes tavern, then leave. He didn't say where . . . no, wait. He talked about the Boone road." Thias weighed one more decision, and again opted to be open even though he was betraying one of Clardy's confidences in so doing. "Grandpap, Clardy wants to be a thief. He wants to make his living robbing folks on roads out in the wilderness."

Hiram's eyes flashed cold lightning. "Christmas! I hate to think I've raised such a fool!"

"I know, Grandpap, I know. But you can't talk sense into Clardy."

"Oh, I know that! How many a night have I laid awake, just thinking and fretting and . . ." The anger drained away from Hiram's face, replaced by a look of sorrow, and Thias found himself marveling over a revelation: Hiram Tyler was *worried* about Clardy. He cared what happened to him. Even with all the cursings and shouts and, in boyhood days, the physical blows, the old man cared about his grandsons.

"Thias, I want you to go after Clardy. Get yourself some food in your belly and go to Knoxville. If he's still about, find him. Tell him to come home. Tell him we'll fix whatever is wrong, whatever it is he's afraid of."

Thias felt a meager but authentic quiver of affection, the first he had known for the old fellow in many a year. He didn't let it show, though; Hiram Tyler wouldn't like that. "Yes, Grandpap," he said. "If he's to be found, I'll find him."

It felt good to be riding, to be searching for Clardy, even though he wasn't sure he could talk Clardy into coming home if he did manage to find him. He hoped Clardy hadn't already headed off toward Kentucky or some other distant place.

Knoxville was a remarkably ugly town, viewed objectively, but in Thias's view it had a lot of appeal for the mere fact of being a town. Built with little pattern as an outgrowth of older White's Fort, it was filled with crude log buildings. Being a river town, usually haunted by a strong contingent of even cruder human beings, Knoxville represented fun, music, and spirits of both the high and liquid varieties. Thias never set foot in the dirt streets without feeling a heightening of the pulse and a desire to lay aside any serious view of life and duty at least long enough to rest his bones and dampen his throat in one of the tippling houses. And if he had a coin or two to spare—which was seldom—to try his hand at one of the generally ongoing games of chance underway here. It crossed his mind today that if Knoxville held such an appeal to a man not given much to vice, it could surely represent virtually irresistible temptation to Clardy, who had never met a vice he didn't embrace like an old friend.

Thias hitched his horse to a dead tree in front of a log tavern before which sat two men, one an ancient, bearded fellow bearing the interesting name of Peabody Swett, the other an even more ancient fellow, a black man known to all only as Toad. He was a former slave, freed by a master on his deathbed years before, who was since seldom seen outside the company of Swett. Toad was famous throughout the region as an outstanding flailer of the banjo, an instrument of African roots that produced a droning sound Thias loved to hear. This time, however, the banjo was in Swett's hands, and he was managing to knock only noise, not music, out of the fretless, hand-carved instrument. The look of pain on Toad's face spoke more than words ever could. Swett mercifully laid aside the instrument as Thias stepped up.

"Howdy do, Mr. Swett. Howdy do, Toad."

The pair nodded greetings. "How you faring, Clardy?" Swett asked.

"That ain't Clardy. That's Thias," Toad corrected.

"Oh? I never could keep you boys straight, which one is which. You look so much the same."

"There's a lot of folks get us confused," Thias said. "Matter of fact, it's Clardy I've come looking for. I believe he might be in town here, or maybe was here yesterday. Have you chanced to see him?"

Swett squinted, shook his head. "No. I ain't."

"I seen him," Toad said. "Sometime yesterday. But it wasn't right here in town. Him and—what's that freckle-faced man's name, Peabody? The one with the wide ears?"

"That's Cale Johnson."

"Yes sir, Cale Johnson. Him and Cale Johnson was going into Hughes's tavern together. Seen them myself while I was passing by and waved howdy at them, but they didn't see me."

Thias had hoped to hear that Clardy was right here in town. Hughes's tavern stood a few miles north of town. A long ride loomed, with little promise of results at the end, since Clardy might have gone anywhere after the place closed last night . . . except that he probably would have been drunk. And if he was drinking with Cale Johnson—a varmit of a man whom Thias barely knew but greatly distrusted—he might have gone home with him to sleep it off. Thias decided to press his quest in that direction.

"You ain't heard mention of Clardy here in town since, have you?"

"I ain't, sir," Toad replied.

"What about Cale Johnson?"

Swett said, "Him we have seen, not more than an hour ago. He was eating squirrel meat and 'taters, setting right on that doorstep yonder. Don't know where he is now."

Thias had just opened his mouth to speak again when the door of the tavern behind the seated men burst open and a man staggered out backward, flailing his arms wildly to keep his balance. In his left hand was a knife, waving dangerously because of his motions. It sliced the air so close to Thias that he jumped away with a yell of alarm. Swett stood, exclaiming loudly. The banjo clattered to the ground. Toad pushed up as quickly as his age would let him and stepped out of the way, pausing only to pick up the banjo.

Thias recognized the man who had almost sliced him as one John Bowman. Thias knew nothing about him except his name and the fact that Clardy had mentioned him as one more of his collection of drinking companions. "Take care with that knife!" Thias yelled, growing angry.

Bowman glanced at him but said nothing. He didn't have time. Out of the door emerged a howling figure of a man, moving so fast that Thias couldn't make out his features clearly. Even so, he believed he knew the man, or had seen him before somewhere.

Whoever he was, he was armed with a hatchet that he swung with abandon at the head of Bowman, who ducked with great dexterity. Thias was still backing out of the way, and fearing his horse might be struck by the swinging hatchet, when Bowman lunged forward like a duelist with a sword and thrust the tip of the blade into the hatchet swinger's chest. The man let out a howl and ran to the side, away from Thias.

Just then Thias realized where he had seen the man before. He expected to see the injured man strike back with the hatchet and maybe take Bowman's head off his shoulders, but an odd thing occurred. The puncture, which was bleeding at a good rate but obviously wasn't deep or life-threatening, seemed to deflate the man, as if his spirit to fight was draining with his blood. He lowered the hatchet and dabbed at his chest with his free hand. "I'm bleeding," he said. He lifted his hand and showed the blood on his fingers to all around. "Look at that. I'm bleeding." Then his eyes came to rest on Thias, widened in surprise, then quickly narrowed. "You, by hell! *You!*"

"You know me?" Thias asked. "I don't know you."

"The hell you don't, you damned betraying Judas! You was at my house yesterday evening, and—" He stopped and looked more closely. "But it *ain't* you! You ain't Clardy! Who are you, boy?"

"My name's Tyler. Thias Tyler."

"Thias . . . not Clardy."

Thias stepped forward. "Wait a minute. You know my brother?"

"Brother! I see it now. That's why you have his look!" He dabbed at his bleeding chest again, then wiped his fingers on his trousers. Bowman, meanwhile, had taken advantage of the moment to prudently slip away.

Thias pressed his question. "I asked you if you knew my brother. I'm looking for him."

"I'm right keen to find him myself. He was in my house last night."

"Where is he now?"

"I don't know. Why don't you tell me? I'd surely like to get my hands on him. He's a liar and a Judas, your brother is. He don't do what he promises he'll do."

"What are you talking about?"

"Never you mind. You see him, though, you tell him to watch himself. You tell him the Harpes had best not see him if he knows what's good for him. Tell him the Harpes don't stand for folks betraying their word to them. You tell him. He'll know what I'm talking of and what will come of what he done. He'll know."

Thias was losing his temper. "You tell *me* what you're talking of! If you know something about my brother, if you're threatening him—"

A hand gripped Thias's shoulder firmly. He turned, startled. "Leave it be, Thias. Leave it be." It was Peabody Swett, his expression very somber, his gray eyes intense. "Don't anger that man. He's one you don't want to anger."

The seriousness of Swett's warning couldn't be ignored. Thias nodded, turned again to the man with the hatchet. The weaselly fellow now wore a cold smile.

Wiley Harpe said, "You find your brother, you tell him the Harpes will have their eyes peeled. He'd best not show himself."

Thias felt a wild urge to attack the man. Hearing threats against his own brother infuriated him—especially considering that this man's face was the same one Thias had seen by lantern light in the burial ground.

The comprehension hit him like a blow: *This man probably killed Abel Van Zandt.*

And now he was threatening Clardy, for reasons Thias didn't know. Did he say that Clardy had been in his *house*? Why in the name of heaven would Clardy have gone there? Had he been forced?

"Come away from here," Peabody urged quietly. "Come away with me, and let's you and me talk."

Thias, eyes fixed on Wiley Harpe's face, nodded. "Very well." Then to Harpe he said, "If any harm comes to my brother, I'll find you. Whoever you are, wherever you may be, I'll find you."

Wiley Harpe laughed, smeared his hand through the blood on his chest, then flipped his hand and flung red drops toward Thias. They struck his face, warm and repellent. Wiley Harpe cackled, turned, and loped away, disappearing around a cabin.

"God! Who *is* he?" Thias asked.

"He's Wiley Harpe," Peabody Swett replied, "and Wiley Harpe is a devil in the flesh. Him and his brother both, devils in the flesh. Come with me to my house, Thias. I'll tell you all I know about them."

"He talked like Clardy has betrayed him some way, called him a Judas. . . ."

"If Clardy's betrayed the Harpes, then God help him. That's all I can say. God help him."

CHAPTER 10

Swett's home, such as it was, stood nearby. It looked like a station camp shelter a hunter might build in the woods, a cross between a lean-to and a hut, rough and crude even by the standards of a rough and crude town. Entering, Thias had to duck. He wondered if Swett shared this slope-roofed hovel with Toad, but saw no evidence that more than one person lived here.

He sat down in the corner on a pile of rags while Swett perched himself on a log-section stool and Toad took a place in the opposite corner. The ceiling on Swett's end was low, but Swett was a short and stooped man and required little vertical space.

"Let me tell you what I know of the Harpes," he said. "And all I tell you is fact, straight from the mouth of Micajah Harpe himself. I took up cups with the man one time, and when he was good and drunk he talked free. Then when he was good and drunker, he took to fighting, and I made my leave of him."

"They appear to be dangerous men," Thias said.

"The 'dangerous' I'll grant you, the 'men' I have my doubts about. Them two are demons who've took on fleshly form, in my opinion. If all Big Harpe told me is the truth, them two have earned theirselves a place of honor in the deepest hole of hell."

Thias thought about Abel Van Zandt. "You know them to have ever murdered anybody?"

"Murdered several, most likely. Big Harpe told me for a fact only of one killing, but hinted at others. They are cruel men, hard men, men who've done things to turn a redskin pale. It was among the redskins, matter of fact, that they honed their cruel ways, though I doubt there's an Indian so cruel as them. And back in the rebellion, they was Tories. They lived and fought and killed their own kind, right alongside the Chicka-maugas. Lived right at Nickajack Town itself!"

Nickajack! Thias knew some about that town, one of the Five Lower Towns of the Chickamaugas on the Tennessee River. A kind of conglomerate tribe composed largely of Cher-okees and Creeks, the Chickamaugas had taken the hardest line against white encroachment onto what had been Indian lands only a score or so of years back. Led by such noted warriors as the dreaded Dragging Canoe, they had killed many settlers and river travelers in incursions. Their raiding parties had struck again and again, as far away as Nashville in the Cum-berland country. Dragging Canoe, though, had finally died a natural death—no white warrior had ever been able to kill him—and Nickajack had since been destroyed by an army.

"Micajah Harpe murdered a white man right near Nickajack, not long before the town was burned. A man name of Doss, I believe, who had been a friend of theirs but had took to dally-ing with one of the Harpe women. The Harpes shared two women betwixt theirselves at the time, though now they're sharing three. It's the God's truth I'm telling you. Savages, they are, and heathens of the worst sort.

"It seems this Doss fellow had come to think that since the Harpe brothers share their women betwixt theirselves, they'd share them with him, too. Ain't so. All that kind of sharing stays in the family. When Micajah caught Doss with one of the women, he killed him. And oh, how he killed him! Told me all about it with a big grin on his face. He knifed poor Doss till he couldn't run, then knifed him some more, in ways there ain't no decency in speaking of here. They took care not to let him die very quick, and when the man finally did die, there wasn't much of him left to do the dying. It was a good day, Micajah said. A good day—making a man die so bad! Micajah

Harpe loves suffering like it was honey on bread. His brother Wiley, the one you met out there, is no better."

"They are devils in the flesh, just like Peabody says," Toad contributed. "Know how you can tell it? There's a mark on Little Harpe. Two of his toes is growed together like one. Mark of Satan, that is."

"Have nary to do with them, Mr. Tyler," Swett said.

Thias felt sick at heart. "It appears my brother already has something to do with them, Mr. Swett. You heard what Harpe was saying out yonder. He said Clardy was in his house last night. He threatened him."

"I heard. And all I can tell you is that you'd best pray that your brother has taken on to other parts, for if the Harpes are after his blood, he'll not be long for this world if he remains here."

Thias spent several more hours searching for Clardy, but did not find him, nor anyone who knew anything of him beyond what Thias had already learned: that Clardy had been seen at the Hughes tavern with Cale Johnson. Thias rode on to the Hughes place and questioned Hughes himself, who gave him only a cold stare in response. Hughes didn't inform on his patrons, and Thias soon gave up talking to him and rode toward home in frustration and with a mounting concern about his brother.

He found his grandfather waiting for him in the yard, leaning on his crutches. The sun was setting, stretching the old man's shadow far across the packed dirt.

"Clardy came after you were gone," Hiram announced, sounding very weary and sad.

"He's here?" Thias leaped off his horse eagerly.

"No more. He went on. I couldn't stop him. He said it hadn't been his first notion to come here at all, but he figured he might not be seeing us again for a long time, and he was in need of food and such besides, so he did come."

"Grandpap, Clardy's in bad trouble. There's some bad men, name of Harpe, who are after him."

"Aye, the Harpes," Hiram said. "Clardy told me all about them. The whole tale, beginning to end. You were right about him recognizing them in the graveyard. He knew them to be the Harpes, and was afraid to speak up 'bout it because he feared them. Then, when I told you boys about Abel going missing, he was even more scared, and that's why he left. Aimed to run off from home without coming back, but he made him a mistake along the way. Met Cale Johnson and drank with him at the Hughes groggery. It winds up that Johnson has been in league with the Harpes, stealing hogs and such with them, and talked Clardy into going with him to meet them so he could join in the stealing. Clardy was drunk, didn't have his good sense about him, and went along. Went right to the cabin of the very ones he was so fearful of! He knows now it was foolish, says he wouldn't have done it if he hadn't been drunk."

Hiram went on, relating secondhand to Thias the details of Clardy's bizarre experience in the Harpe cabin, about Micajah Harpe's command to kill Cale Johnson, and Clardy's evasive escape. Now Clardy was in fear of his life, running for Kentucky in terror that the Harpes would murder him for not having killed Johnson, as he had promised.

"They *would* murder him," Thias said. "I chanced to run into one of the Harpes in Knoxville today, and he took me to be Clardy at first. He said that Clardy had best get himself gone or he would be a dead man. From what I've seen and heard of the Harpes, I can tell you that's a threat not to be ignored."

"Clardy ain't ignoring it. He's a mighty scared young fellow," Hiram said. His voice lowered slightly. "You know what Clardy did, Thias? He put his arm 'round my shoulder and gave me a squeeze. Told me that for years he's nigh hated me, wanted to get away from me, but now that he has to go, he wishes he didn't. Said he wishes everything was like it was before." Hiram turned away. "Said he loved me, Thias. Clardy said he loved me."

Thias could hardly hold back tears when he heard that. "Come on, Grandpap," he said. "Let's go into the house. I'll put away my horse, and then me and you are going to talk about what we need to do next."

They did talk, but found no answers. Thias wanted to go after Clardy and bring him home, but Hiram discouraged the idea, and Thias had to concur in the end because of the danger of the Harpes.

He then broached the idea of informing on the Harpes himself, revealing them as the ones who had desecrated the grave and corpse of Selma Van Zandt, but Hiram opposed that idea

even more strongly than the prior one. Thias would bring the
wrath of the Harpes down on him if he spoke out. Having just
lost one grandson, Hiram did not wish to lose another. He argued further that Thias really had little to tell against the
Harpes in any case. Abel Van Zandt's body had never been
found, so there was no proof he was dead. And Thias and
Clardy hadn't actually seen them desecrate the grave or corpse;
all they had seen was an attempt to dig it up, and even that had
been foiled when Abel intervened. What had happened after
that, the Tyler brothers had no eyewitness knowledge of. It was
even possible that someone besides the Harpes had come along
later, dug up and decapitated the body, and done away with
Abel Van Zandt. Thias couldn't prove the Harpes guilty of anything by the standards of a court of law.

Thias was in a mood to be persuaded. He had no real desire
to take on the Harpes and risk bringing down their vengeance
upon himself or his grandfather. So he relented. By the time he
and his grandfather retired to their beds that night, no course
of action had been decided. For now, all would simply stand as
it was.

Thias rolled over, voiced a quiet, inner prayer for his fleeing
brother out there on the trail somewhere, and fell asleep. He
dreamed only once that night, a terrible nightmare of Clardy
lying dead and mutilated like that Doss fellow who Swett had
told about, and woke up in a sweat. He lay awake another hour,
very disturbed, then went to sleep again and dreamed no more.

The next morning he found Hiram moaning in his bed, very
sick. The old man declared his head ached terribly, "like a
bad tooth, but right up beneath the peak of my noggin," as he
put it.

Hiram stayed in bed for three days thereafter, Thias tending
to him, forgetting all else. Hiram's headache declined but did
not go away. Thias considered riding into Knoxville to see if he
could find some sort of medical help, but he was afraid to
leave Hiram alone, and Hiram staunchly refused to go to Knoxville himself. Thias was pretty well confined to the farm as
long as his grandfather was down.

He was chopping wood in the yard the day that Edward Tiel
rode by. Tiel was a well-known, respected farmer of the Knoxville area, but he had never visited the Tylers before. Thias put
aside his axe and walked up to greet Tiel with a sense of concern, feeling instinctively that something was wrong.

Tiel's mission proved to be similar to the one that had brought Elijah McKee to the cabin days before. "I'm wondering if you've suffered the loss of stock," Tiel said. "The problem has grown fearsome bad in this area."

"We've been spared, glad to say," Thias replied. The subject was uncomfortable, reminding him of the Harpes.

"Count yourself blessed, then," Tiel replied. "Many of us haven't been so fortunate."

"I've heard that."

"I believe, though, that we know the rascals behind this," Ticl said.

"Aye? Who?"

"Have you heard of the Harpes?"

"Yes." Thias would have denied it had not his encounter with Wiley Harpe in Knoxville been seen by several people. Tiel might already have heard about the encounter and be deliberately plying Thias to see if he would deny it.

"John Miller has been of the view for a spell now that the Harpes are scoundrels and thieves." Thias knew Miller, a merchant in Knoxville who sold, among other things, butchered meats. "He's been speaking free about the Harpes lately, saying he believes that some of the very meat he's bought from them has been took from stolen hogs. The Harpes have lately heard that he's been saying such things—and two nights back some of Miller's stables were burned down. A couple of houses standing near were burned, too. He suspects the Harpes did it to punish him for speaking ill about them. I suspect the same."

"They sound like mighty vengeful men."

"I would say they are. The stories spreading about that pair are enough to turn any man's ear. Did you know, by the way, that Abel Van Zandt has been missing for days now, and that it appears he was spirited off by someone who dug into old Selma Van Zandt's grave? Her body was cut upon. Terrible thing."

"I've heard about that." Thias hoped he didn't sound or look as tense as he felt.

"The suspicion is that Abel was killed. And the Harpes were known to have talked in the groggeries about that tale of the jewel in the old woman's grave. I believe it was them who dug up the grave and killed Abel. There is no proof, sorry to say. We can't even find Abel's body."

Thias wondered if Tiel was playing ignorant, maybe knowing more already than his questions implied. Did he know or suspect that the Tylers knew something about what had happened in the burial ground the night Abel vanished? Thias felt the start of panic, but managed to squelch it. How could Tiel know any such thing? No one knew that he and Clardy had even been in the burial ground that night, except for Hiram . . . and Abel, of course. Abel had not had a chance to tell anyone he had seen the Tyler brothers—but no, Thias realized, that wasn't true. Supposedly, Abel had gone back briefly to the Van Zandt house after running off the Harpes the first time. He might have mentioned to his kin that he had met the Tylers there. . . .

Take hold of yourself. You've done nothing wrong. Don't be feeling and acting guilty when you ain't. Thias straightened and looked Tiel squarely in the eye. "Do the Van Zandts have any notion of who might have gotten Abel?"

"A notion, but no more. They suspect the Harpes."

Thias was relieved. Suspicions were turning in the right direction on their own, without involving the Tyler brothers.

Tiel went on. "Abel was guarding the grave that night—you know how he would do that—and came back to the house only once, according to his brother Michael. He said he had run a pair of men off from the grave and was going back again to guard some more as soon as he fetched more powder. One of the men was big, the other little."

"That's all the men he mentioned meeting? Just them two at the grave?"

"Yes. Why? Do you think there might have been others?"

"No, no. Just wondering if there might be witnesses or some such, you know."

"As best we can tell, it was only the two at the grave who he had seen. At any rate, he fetched his powder and went back out in case the pair returned. About two hours later Michael felt worried about Abel being there alone, and went down to join him. He found the grave dug up and Abel gone. The poor fellow blames himself for not having gone down with Abel right off."

"Hard for him. Bound to be."

"Aye. Well, good day to you, Thias. Where's your brother and grandpap?"

"Clardy's away for now," Thias said as casually as possible.

"And Grandpap is sick. I've been tending to him for a few days now."

"Sick? I hope he's well soon."

"I believe he'll be up and about in a week or so."

"That's good. Thias—should ever the need arise to gather men to bring in the Harpes, would you join us?"

Thias disliked that idea. He didn't want the Harpes seeing his face among any gang of captors. They might talk when they saw him, say things about Clardy, bring trouble on the Tylers. But he couldn't decline. "If I can, I'll do it. If it goes that far."

"It will, one of these days. Good day to you, Thias."

"Good day, Mr. Tiel."

CHAPTER 11

Within twenty-four hours of his conversation with Thias Tyler, Edward Tiel found himself in the center of a series of events that soon became the talk of Knoxville and the region round about it.

The first event was the theft of several of Tiel's best horses. He immediately suspected the Harpes. The theft was so blatant and daring that he figured it was done to spite him for his open investigation of the brothers.

Tiel responded promptly. Mounting his fastest horse, he quickly gathered a sizable body of armed men from among his neighbors and set out to find his stolen horses and the men who had taken them. Thias Tyler was not among the group; Tiel had thought about asking him, but remembering that Hiram Tyler was sick and needed help, let it go.

Tiel and his men rode to the Harpe cabin and found it had been vacated. An examination of the land around it showed evidence that a large number of horses had been penned here very recently. Tiel was sure they were his.

The tracks of the horses through the winter-browned pea vine and grass that filled the countryside around Beaver Creek created a fine trail for the men to follow. It led them away from the Harpe cabin and onto a path through the forested wilderness, leading toward the Clinch River. There they found further evidence that the horses had been swum across. Ahead, beyond several miles of rolling hills and valleys, loomed the high wall of the Cumberlands. The Harpes appeared to be leading their stolen horses toward Kentucky.

It was soon evident they were overtaking the thieves, and before long Tiel himself caught the first actual sight of them. Off in the distance, where the land began to rise at the base of the mountains, he saw a small cave that was a frequent resting place for travelers on this road. In a small clearing at the cave's mouth, several horses were grazing, and just in front of the cave itself two men sat eating. They had built no fire. They were too far away for their features to be seen, but their sizes in comparison with one another were enough to tell Tiel he had found the Harpes.

"I'd nigh let them go and say a fond farewell if not for the fact them's my horses they've got," he said to his companions. "Be ready, men. They may resist hard, for they'll know there's only the lash and jail for them back in Knoxville. And I don't see their women about, so keep watch on your backs. If they're about somewhere, unseen, they might shoot from hiding."

In fact the Harpes didn't resist. Though armed, they didn't raise their weapons when the posse showed itself, and turned their firearms over almost cordially, as if this were no more than a good-natured game they had the misfortune to lose. Neither spoke a word at first, but Wiley finally asked, "What do you aim to do with us? Will you kill us here?"

"We're not savages," Tiel replied. "We are civilized men, and we'll see you punished by the law, not outside it. We'll take you back to Knoxville. There you will be tried, and no doubt convicted. You'll receive thirty-nine lashes each on your backs with a leather whip, and probably spend time jailed besides."

"What about our wives?" Wiley asked.

"Where are they?"

"They have gone on ahead. We were to meet them at a certain place on the way."

"Tell us where they are and we'll send some men to fetch them and bring them back to Knoxville in safety. We hold this crime against you, not your women."

That obviously wasn't the response Wiley had been hoping

for. "Ain't no need for them to go back to Knoxville. The devil with that. Just leave the women where they are."

"You'd abandon these women in this wilderness alone?"

"They'll be well enough. We don't join them, they'll come back looking for us on their own."

Tiel went along, feeling a rising loathing for men who would not only steal and cheat their own neighbors, but leave pregnant women alone in wild country, unknowing of the fate of their men. Tiel could only suppose, though, that the women had suffered much worse than that at the hands of these devils. Maybe abandonment was the best thing that could happen to them.

With the Harpes parading on foot before their captors, hands tied behind them, they began the homeward journey. The Harpes showed no evident desire to escape. They seemed placid, almost happy, resigned to their fate.

They made their break near a huge field of briars and scrub brush. The pair of them simply bolted into the field and sprinted into the growth, seemingly ignoring the thorns and branches that ripped at their clothing and skin. A couple of the posse members managed to lift rifles, and one fired into the tangle, but Tiel waved down any further shots.

"Let them go," he said. "I've got my stolen horses back, and that's what matters most. And now that we know the Harpes are guilty men, we'll see no more of them in our parts. They'll dare not return."

Leading the horses, they continued on to Knoxville. Though Tiel did not say it to anyone, he was secretly almost glad the Harpes had escaped. It was no bad thing to have put a hard and nasty business behind, and certainly no bad thing to be free of the devilish Harpe brothers.

Cale Johnson was much relieved. He had learned that morning of the events regarding Tiel, the posse, and the Harpes, and no soul for miles around Knoxville was as pleased as he to know the Harpe brothers had fled. Ever since Clardy Tyler's startling revelation to him of the Harpes' desire to see him killed, he had hidden out, afraid to show himself. But he hadn't run away. Even if he lacked morals, he did have pride, too much to let him run from any man. Or so he told himself. On a deeper level he knew the real reason was that he had no better place to go—and there was always the possibility that if he laid low

and waited long enough, the Harpes' evil ways would catch up
with them, they would be removed from the picture, and the
much-adored Sally Rice Harpe could be claimed for his own.

It had worked out almost that very way, except for the part
about Sally. Apparently the Harpes had their women with
them, and Johnson was having to accustom himself to the fact
that he would probably never see his beloved again. The
Harpes, and therefore Sally, certainly would not return here,
where they were wanted as horse thieves. Ah well, he thought,
wrapping his hand around his cup, so goes life. There will be
other women, though none so fine as dear Sally.

He was seated in Hughes's tavern, sharing whiskey and a table with the Metcalfe brothers, siblings of Hughes's wife. The
whiskey had mellowed Johnson considerably. He felt good
about life, glad to be free of hiding and fear, and was even beginning to think that life without Sally might not be so hard to
endure after all. And as for the profitable dealing in stolen
beasts he had enjoyed with the Harpes, that was over anyway,
erased as an option for him the moment he learned that the
Harpes wanted him dead.

He was listening to one of the Metcalfes tell a coarse story
about an Indian woman he had once known, when the tavern
door opened. It was dusk and the tavern was growing dark, the
only light inside being the dim glow of sunset piercing the
west-facing window and the gleam of firelight on the hearth.
For a moment Cale Johnson was unable to believe that the two
men who came firmly striding into the tavern, belt axes in
hand, were Wiley and Micajah Harpe.

It was impossible. They wouldn't come back *here*. Not *them*.
Yet there they were.

Johnson stood, tipping over the stool upon which he had
been seated. He stared almost stupidly at the intruders. Wiley
Harpe's eye caught his, and Wiley smiled.

"Look there, Micajah," he said. "We've found him."

The Harpes approached him. "You're coming with us, Cale,"
Micajah said.

"No . . . I don't want to do that." Johnson licked his lips as
fear rose. He forced a feeble chuckle. "What are you fellers
doing back here? I didn't figure you'd return."

"Why, Cale, that's the very reason we come back!" Wiley
said. "We'd been looking for you, but you'd taken to laying low
on us. After old Tiel took our horses from us, we commenced

to thinking that maybe good old Cale would come out from under his rock, now that he'll be sure we're gone for good, scared to come back. 'Pears we were right. And you were wrong, Cale. We *ain't* scared to come back. Me and Micajah, we ain't scared of nothing. Now, Cale, you and me are going to settle a little business over my Sally."

Johnson looked imploringly at the Metcalfe brothers, who were still seated, gaping at the Harpes. "Men, I need some help here," he said.

"Ain't no affair of ours," one of them replied, waving his hands in a gesture of noninvolvement. They rose and quickly moved elsewhere in the tavern.

"Come on with us, Cale. Let's get this done without a fight," Wiley said.

Johnson eyed his rifle, which stood leaning against the wall near the door, far away from him. He could not hope to reach it. "Wiley, I don't want to go with you."

"Don't matter. You're going anyhow."

Johnson lunged suddenly, trying to break past the pair. In his wicker cage, Hughes watched, but made no move to intervene. He knew the Harpes and would not oppose them.

Micajah reached out a hand like a bear paw and grabbed Johnson by the neck. He threw him back across the table, scattering cups and making the table rock on its legs. Johnson yelled in fright. Wiley leaned over him, smiling, belt axe upraised. "You want me to do it right here, Cale?" He chortled. "You want these gents here to see you begging and crying? Do you?"

"Please, Wiley, please . . . don't hurt me."

"You've cast your eye on my woman too many a time, Cale. That's one thing I won't abide."

"I never touched her! I swear it, Wiley! You let me go, you'll never have to see me again . . . I'll ride away from here, far as I can go." Tears came to his eyes. "I promise you, Wiley. Swear it on the grave of my own pap!"

Without another word Wiley grabbed Johnson's arm and pulled him roughly to his feet. Johnson began to weep and beg mercy. Micajah gripped his other arm and the Harpes pulled the struggling, pleading man toward the door. The Metcalfes stood aside, letting them pass. Hughes remained behind his wicker screen, silent, expressionless. Johnson looked at him, begged for help, but Hughes's stare was without compassion. He would not involve himself.

The Harpes pulled their victim out of the tavern. For a long time silence held inside the darkening log building, while Johnson's pleas and cries faded away in the distance. Hughes stepped out from his protective cage. "I reckon I'll close up now," he said.

"That's probably the best thing," one of the Metcalfes said.

"Oh . . . one more thing," Hughes said. He went back to the wicker cage, stooped, and dug around in a box of papers. He produced one with Cale Johnson's name at the top and a string of figures below: Johnson's list of drinks bought on credit. Hughes sighed, shook his head, and tore up the paper. This was one debt that would never be paid.

He joined the Metcalfes and left, closing the door, shutting out the world, closing in the darkness.

Thias knelt beside his grandfather's bed, tears in his eyes. Hiram Tyler was dying. There was no question of it now. He had worsened terribly about sunset. Now it was pitch-black outside, the heart of night. Thias doubted the old man would linger until morning.

He had fallen into unconsciousness an hour before, after giving his grandson the last demand he would ever make upon him. The words were weakly spoken but clear. "Thias . . . go find Clardy. Find him . . . see that he is well. Sell the farm . . . Branford in Knoxville will buy it . . . divide the money with Clardy. You boys . . . make yourselves good lives someplace new, someplace better."

"Yes, Grandpap," Thias had replied, astounded that the same old man who had made him feel tied to this farm for so many years now was telling him to free himself of it. Maybe there had been more perception and wisdom in Hiram Tyler than he and Clardy had ever given him credit for. "I'll do all that. And I'll find Clardy. I promise."

The old man's face was drawn and twisted. Always a thin man, he had grown gaunt over his days of sickness. Thias wondered if he had done the right thing, just staying with the old man all that time. Maybe he should have gone to Knoxville and found help. But what help was there for such an illness? Clearly Hiram had fallen victim to the apoplexy that had killed several of the Tylers for generations back. No one could have done anything to stop this.

Gripping his grandfather's hand, Thias looked around the cabin. As strained and unhappy as his life had been here, it had been the only home he knew. Now it didn't seem like home at all. Clardy was gone, and soon Hiram would be gone as well. It would not be hard to sell this place and leave it. Without Clardy and Grandpap, this would be a hollow, sorrowful refuge of memories. He would not want to remain.

The first hint of sunrise was lighting the horizon when Hiram Tyler exhaled his final rattling breath. Thias, still gripping the old man's sallow, limp hand, imagined he could feel the life leaving him, rising and dispersing around him like a vapor. And then he was alone.

Rising, he laid Hiram's hand over on the unmoving chest and crossed the other hand atop it. Eyes flooding, he pulled the blanket up over the body, looked sadly at the still face for a moment, then covered it.

Like Clardy, he had often dreamed of being free of the sour, difficult old man, though unlike Clardy, he had never expressed the dreams openly. But he had never imagined gaining his freedom in this way. He had always imagined himself leaving Hiram, not Hiram leaving him. Odd as it seemed, he had never even considered the fact that one day Hiram Tyler would die. He had believed that somehow the old man would always be there.

Wiping away tears, Thias put on his coat and hat and left the cabin. He strode off down the road, walking like a man rushing to someplace of importance, though in fact he had nowhere to go at all. He was walking for walking's sake, trying to outpace the sorrow that loomed all around him. But it remained with him, heavy as a stone, and at last he turned, his reddened eyes stinging in the cold wind, and went back to the cabin to prepare his grandfather for burial.

He laid away Hiram Tyler with his own hands. There was no funeral; the old man had always despised ceremony and emotional display, and since he had avoided such in life, it seemed fitting to not inflict it upon him in death. Thias laid his grandfather away beside his late wife and near the small grave where his severed leg lay, then went back to the cabin, packed up his own rifle and his grandfather's, ammunition, and a few personal possessions, and rode into Knoxville. There he called on Joseph Branford, a frontier lawyer who kept office in that town, and announced that the Tyler farm and livestock were available for sale. The lawyer bought the land, cabin, and livestock himself, just as Hiram had said he would. Thias had no spirit for much haggling, and left knowing he probably had not obtained what the property was worth. It didn't matter to him at the moment. He was eager to break all ties and get away, more eager still to begin looking for his brother, a circumstance he mentioned to Branford.

"Would you want that money held in trust for you until you've found Clardy?" Branford asked. "There is danger in carrying money on the road."

"No. I'll keep the money with me, so I can divide it with Clardy as soon as I find him. Clardy may not be able . . . may not want to come back here, for reasons of his own." Thias said this in ignorance of all that had happened involving Tiel and the Harpes' escape.

"I see," Branford replied. "But you should be careful, carrying that much coin on you. There is always the danger of robbery, and if you lose that money, you've lost your inheritance."

Thias felt annoyed. He had just lost his brother to the wide world, his grandfather to death, and the only life and home he had ever known. What place was it of Branford's to worry about his money? Branford had the farm he had wanted, and the rest was none of his business.

Thias left the lawyer, then went to a nearby tavern and bought himself a meal. While there, he finally learned what had happened concerning the Harpes and Tiel's stolen horses. The irony made him shake his head. Clardy had fled the Knoxville area because of the Harpes, and now they themselves were gone. Clardy was running from a threat that had already been nullified, and if only he knew it, could now return to Knoxville without fear. Briefly, Thias thought about going to Branford and telling him that, yes, he would allow him to hold the bulk of the money in safekeeping for him and Clardy after all, and that they would return together later to reobtain it. But he didn't. He wasn't sure he could trust Branford, and was even less sure he would want to come back to Knoxville once he found Clardy.

Grandpap had told him to find a new life elsewhere. That was one Hiram Tyler demand that Thias would fulfill gladly.

The .challenge would be to find Clardy. He had told Grandpap he was bound for Kentucky, but beyond that had said nothing specific about where he would go. Probably, Clardy hadn't known himself. Thias wished he had something more to go on. The prospect of a long search over a vast territory was daunting.

Thias was on the verge of leaving town when a hoot and yell at the end of the street heralded the arrival of a flatbedded wagon bearing what looked like an irregularly shaped heap of blankets. One man drove the wagon; another rode slightly ahead of it, waving his hand above his head. Puzzled, Thias looked more closely at the approaching wagon and its odd burden, and realized with a chill that the apparent heap of blankets was in fact a single blanket, spread across what looked like . . .

Oh, no, Thias thought. Oh, no . . .

The horseman rode up ahead of the wagon and shouted, "Dead man! We've found a dead man—murdered, by grabs!"

Thias was seized with a brief but thorough paralysis. *That might be Clardy under that blanket. The Harpes are running free, and Clardy's out there.* . . . *They might have found him, and* . . .

He shoved off his paralysis and pushed his way through the gathering crowd toward the wagon. The driver halted, the horse's breath steaming. The horseman leaped down, circled around to the back of the wagon and grasped the blanket.

"He ain't a pretty thing to see," he warned, then yanked the blanket away.

Thias went pale, filled with a combination of horror and relief. It wasn't Clardy under the blanket, but it was Abel Van Zandt. His body, naked and much decayed, was well-marked by knife slashes and stab marks, and his throat was deeply sliced.

"Found him in a sinkhole," the man with the blanket said, almost proudly. "Stinks right bad, don't he? I do believe that this here is that Van Zandt man what's been missing for a spell."

Thias turned away, his stomach reminding him that it was weak and couldn't abide gruesomeness. He silently cursed the Harpes. Abel Van Zandt hadn't deserved such a terrible fate at the hands of men such as they.

He pondered briefly the fact that he was duty-bound here to speak up and tell that he and Clardy had see the Harpes at the Van Zandt grave the night Abel disappeared. But what was the use? The Harpes were gone. And Thias wasn't much in the mood for doing his duty at the moment. He wanted merely to go on his way, find his brother, and begin that better life Hiram had talked of.

Thias went to his horse, mounted, and rode out of town, saying not a word to anyone.

Thias was many miles away when the people of Knoxville received a second shock with the discovery of another corpse, also murdered. Cale Johnson had died hard, having been hacked on brutally and then shot through the head. Physical evidence indicated the crime had taken place on a road two miles south of Knoxville. His body had then been laid open, filled with stones, and thrown into the Holston River in an apparent attempt to hide the crime, but the current had turned the dead man, dumped out the stones, and he had floated to the surface.

Johnson was widely known to have been among the Hughes's tavern's most frequent customers, and the investigation of the crime soon led to that establishment. The Metcalfe brothers and Hughes himself were suspected of the crime. No one believed their wild claim that the Harpes were the culprits. Why would the Harpes return to a place where they were already wanted and would face the prospect of jail and flogging? No sensible men would do such a thing.

The Metcalfes and Hughes could only reply that anyone who had known the Harpes would realize that they were anything but sensible men.

Ultimately, nothing would happen to the Metcalfes, who fled the region at their first chance. But the law-abiding people of the Knoxville region had endured enough of Hughes and his establishment, known to be a "rowdy" place frequented by undesirable types. A band of regulators quickly formed and paid a call on Hughes. He took a severe beating, watched his house and groggery pulled down and burned, and was advised to leave the region. Unlike the Harpes, Hughes was sensible. He obeyed.

Meanwhile, the Van Zandt family buried the remains of Abel beside Selma Van Zandt's grave, which he had so vigorously but vainly striven to protect. It seemed the most appropriate thing to do.

CHAPTER 12

Cave-in-Rock, on the Ohio River

Celinda rolled over; a sharp stone beneath her blankets probed into a rib, and she groaned. A hand grasped her shoulder and shook her; she opened her eyes with a gasp.

The face of Jim Horton, half shadowed, half illuminated by firelight, descended before her. "Hush!" he whispered sharply. "You're a mute, remember? You want them to hear you making noise?"

She closed her eyes to make him go away, wondering how long he had been sitting there so close to her, watching her sleep. He did that sometimes—watched her obsessively, closely, as if worried that she would try to run away, or somehow accidentally reveal the truth of her gender. Even now he was lingering—she could feel him there, and smell the alcoholic odor of his liquored breath. When at last he rose and moved away, Celinda was relieved. She opened her eyes again and thought to herself: I am in hell.

I am in hell. The thought was familiar, an inner lament that arose again and again in her mind like a dirge. She had never known so terrible a place as this, nor such canker-souled raff as the people who inhabited it. Only when she was asleep was she free of this place, but sleep was hard to maintain in a place where the occupants were loud and coarse and often drunk. *I am in hell.*

At least she was spared from having to speak to them, thanks to the ruse of her muteness. With hair hacked short, face caked in dirt, feminine physique disguised by heavy trousers and coat, Celinda had managed so far to pass for a silent male, Horton's "cousin." The others all seemed to accept the deception, for which Celinda was grateful. She hated to imagine what might be done to her by some of these men if they knew the truth about the silent "boy" they knew as George Ames.

In fact, she didn't have to imagine. She knew. In the several days she and Horton had been here at this remarkable riverside cavern, she had seen three of the men who apparently lived here—their number seemed to vary from eight to a dozen from day to day—attempt to vent their lusts upon the only other female besides Celinda herself who occupied the cave at the moment: a plump, masculine-looking, powerfully built woman named Queen Fine, who dressed far better than Celinda would have imagined possible in such a setting as this. Queen wore a different dress every day—good dresses, all of them, some of them plain but relatively new, others very fine garments—and fought a constant battle to keep the cave's clay from sullying her garments and the cave's men from sullying her virtue . . . unless, of course, they paid for the privilege.

Celinda had never to her knowledge actually seen a real, living prostitute, which made Queen all the more intriguing. As Celinda lay there, waiting for sleep to return, she thought back to the previous night, when she had quietly studied Queen for more than an hour—until she noticed that Queen had begun watching her in turn, which was unsettling and had caused her to avert her eyes and watch Queen no more. Shortly after that Queen had left the cave, and had not returned since. Celinda had no idea where she had gone or whether she would come back at all.

Celinda wondered about Queen's origins and how she had entered her grim way of life. She did not believe any kind of mental lacking had led to it; behind Queen's black, piercing eyes Celinda was sure she could detect a sharp and clever mind at work. It was this, in part, that was so intriguing. How could anyone with a keen mind live as Queen did? Had it always been this way for her? Or had she been drawn by some accident into the underbelly of life and found herself trapped there? If so, might she herself be trapped in the same way?

That was such a terrifying thought that Celinda immediately began searching for a plan of escape. If only Jim Horton wasn't always so close by! She no longer feared the wilderness like before; she would gladly risk its dangers rather than remain with Jim Horton and his ilk.

Celinda pulled her dirty blanket up beneath her chin and closed her eyes. She wriggled and found a natural depression in the rock that accommodated the bone of her hip, and comfort immediately and greatly increased. Sleep came, but this time it didn't bring her the momentary escape from her situation that it usually did. Tonight she dreamed, reliving in surrealistic, distorted detail her arrival with Jim Horton at this place some days ago. She heard again the laughter, jovial swearing, hand-pumping and shoulder-slapping that had heralded his arrival among the human vermin that crawled about this oval-mouthed cavern on the Illinois side of the Ohio. She saw anew the look of joy on Horton's face as he greeted old friends, and the disappointment he showed when he learned that the Cave-in-Rock denizen he had most wanted to see, his admired friend Sam Mason, had indeed gone on downriver sometime before, as rumored. She felt again the burning knot in her stomach when Horton had introduced her to the others as George Ames, and the utter terror that somehow these cold-eyed men would look right through her disguise and see that in fact she was a female.

They hadn't seen. It had astounded Celinda that they couldn't see through her disguise. She made it a point of keeping her face as filthy as possible, letting the grime serve as a mask, and tried her best to walk and move and spit and scratch like a man. She had also mastered the skill of feigning utter complacency at the immodesty of the men around her. She had been forced to learn immodesty herself, at least with Jim Horton, because he did not allow her to go off alone, even to perform the most private bodily functions. At such times she was required by him to let him know of her needs with a prearranged hand gesture, and he would lead her off into the woods and remain near until she was ready to return to the cave. It was humiliating beyond anything she had ever experienced, and made her feel like no more than an animal.

Sometime later Celinda moved, grew uncomfortable again, and awakened. The fire near the mouth of the cave had died away substantially and now consisted more of red coals than flaming wood. It cast a ruby shimmer across the moist glair covering and slickening the cavern floor. Outside the cave rain fell, and the wind was gusting back into the cavern, whirling about in a smoke-lifting gurge, then back out again. The weather had driven the fifteen or so Cave-in-Rock residents back as far as possible in the cave; Celinda found herself lying in the midst of a great wallow of unwashed, snoring humanity.

She thought of rising and walking out of the cave. Walking and walking some more, spiteful of storm and lightning, leaving this awful cavern of criminals behind. It was an idle thought . . . but as she played it through her mind a couple of times more it suddenly didn't seem idle anymore. She really could do it, really could be free! She could walk out, lose herself in the storm, and go on until she found a settlement, and there be safe. The thought drove sleepiness away and made her thrill with excitement. She could do it . . . by heaven, she *would* do it!

She sat up, looking all around her. In the dim red light from the fire, she picked out the sleeping form of Jim Horton. He was sprawled out from beneath his blanket, snoring loudly, his hand still wrapped around a whiskey bottle he had been pulling from earlier. All the other assorted human vermin of Cave-in-Rock lay all around the cave floor, some on makeshift beds of evergreen boughs, others curled up in blankets or beneath peltries, anyplace they could find.

You must be strong. Celinda closed her eyes a moment, said a little prayer, and called up the mental image of her father's face to strengthen her. She took her first step and began to tremble badly. Her breathing grew tight and difficult, and she felt for all the world like she was doing something wrong. This same physical and mental stress had gripped her on two prior occasions she had considered trying to escape, and she hadn't managed to overcome it any more than she could understand it. This time, however, her determination was stronger.

She held fast a few moments, waiting for the paralyzing feeling to pass. When it didn't, she decided to go ahead in spite of it, though she wasn't certain she could. Maybe there was some curse on this place, some demonic inhabitant that made those who entered unable to leave, even though they wanted to. Maybe that was how Queen had been trapped. This was an evil place, after all, and it was just possible that ...

She gave herself a shake. Celinda Ames would not fall victim to superstitious thinking! Her father would be ashamed of her. The demons in this place wore human flesh. She would not remain among them any longer.

She put a foot forward and was filled with a thrill of joy that wiped away her fear. She was really going to escape! Quietly she moved through the cave, heading toward the great arched mouth of it. The floor was slick; she walked with great care, feeling with mounting excitement like she was sneaking out of a great, swallowing crypt. *Crypt* ... an apt word to describe this place, in Celinda's opinion. Her thought upon first glimpsing the limestone cavern through veiling trees on the day that she and Horton had rafted across to the cheers of Horton's old friends in this place, was that Cave-in-Rock looked like a crypt. Or perhaps a gaping mouth, dark and hungry. Even so, she realized that her own sad situation was probably coloring her perceptions. In fact the cave and its surroundings had a remarkable natural beauty, even in this barren season. Crowning the bluff above it were oaks and cedars in abundance, and the cave itself possessed as much of the quality of a cathedral as a crypt. It was her inability to associate Cave-in-Rock with anything holy that had caused Celinda to seize upon the latter association.

Some fifty feet wide at the mouth, the generally oval-shaped cave bored its length back about 150 feet or more into the stone bluff. It was level back some half the distance from the entrance, sloping upward from there, with shelves or benches of rock protruding from both sides. There were various cracks, crevices, and chimneys in the center roof of the cave and also at the rear, leading to a smaller upper chamber, and, in the cave's back, to the base of a sinkhole that drained water from the land above and kept the cave at least slightly damp almost all the time. The sinkhole was large enough to accommodate a person, but at the moment the opening was crossed with a series of ropes upon which empty bottles had been hung in a way to make them clink together and give an alarm should anyone try to enter that way. Of course, it also prevented anyone from exiting silently, too, to Celinda's displeasure.

It was the cave's unique setting and surroundings that made it handy for the low purposes to which it was being put, namely, the piracy of river vessels. The cave and the bluff into which it pierced afforded a good view of the broad river, with the trees in front of the cave mouth simultaneously keeping the cavern itself out of view of river travelers until they were close enough to have been long before detected by any cave-based sentinels. Celinda didn't know exactly how the river pirates operated, in that since she had been here only one boat had passed, and had been left unmolested. Naturally inquisitive, she had wanted to ask about the system of piracy and about what had happened to the people on the pirated boats, but she could not, since she was purporting to be mute.

She reached the mouth of the cave. Through the line of trees outside she saw the nighttime river, fast-moving, vitric, mysterious. She remembered that there were two or three skiffs hidden down below, and wondered if she should take one of them, or make her escape on foot. The decision loomed before her, as vast as the river itself, and she struggled to think through her options. The rain hammered down; little rivulets of water passed around her feet. Her hesitation reemerged. Could she really do this? Horton would come after her, probably. If he found her, she dreaded to think how he might punish her for trying to escape.

Yes, she would take one of the skiffs. She would have a better chance of escaping undetected by water, and Horton probably would not be as willing to pursue her if it required a river chase. She would head down the river a few miles, then take to the south bank and head inland.

"George? Is that you?"

The whispering voice made her jump. She turned and almost fell. Looming behind her was a tall, broad figure that after a half moment she recognized as a young man called Lumpkin. She didn't know if that was his true name, or a nickname derived from the rounded, lumpy appearance of his head, which seemed to have been severely injured at some time past.

"Uhnnnn," she said, trying to make a sound like a mute. She was terrified now, and deeply disappointed. This event might well rob her of her chance for escape.

"You couldn't sleep neither, huh? Same for me."

Why? Why did he have to be sleepless tonight, of all nights?

Will I ever have so good a chance as this one? Distress filled her.

"I ain't never been able to sleep during a storm. I seen a man hit by lightning once when I was just a little fellow, and I been scared of storms ever since."

"Uhhnn."

"You too, huh? Wish you could talk, George. I like talking."

Celinda had suspected before that Lumpkin was simple-minded, and his way of talking now tended to confirm the suspicion. She figured his condition was probably owing to whatever head injury had misshapen his skull. She felt grateful at least that it was he who had detected her, not one of the more savvy members of the Cave-in-Rock delegation of scoundrels. Her impression from prior observation was that Lumpkin had a more gentle soul in him than the others.

"I had me a brother named George. Did you know that? He was older than me, and mighty nice. He took care of me sometimes. He's dead now. I wish he wasn't."

Celinda was afraid she might cry out of sheer disappointment. She wanted to run from the cave and find a skiff, but was afraid Lumpkin might yell after her and waken others.

"When it would storm, George would sit by me till I went to sleep. He made me feel safe. You think you could sit by me, George?"

Celinda knew she was trapped. Lumpkin was taking away her chance for escape. She cast one last, longing look out toward the river, then turned back to him and nodded.

She spent the rest of the night seated cross-legged beside Lumpkin's sleeping place, her mind filled with a dreamlike sense of unreality as she listened to him talk softly, seemingly without end. The storm continued apace, actually worsening terribly before finally settling to a steady rain, and she tried to comfort herself with the idea that maybe it was best she wasn't out on the river with lightning searing down. But there was no true comfort for her. She would have risked the lightning gladly if only she could have had a chance for freedom. As for Lumpkin, he never fully went to sleep, though he did seem calmed by her presence and referred to her several times as "brother." She couldn't help but feel sorry for him, living among such vermin without even the benefit of a clear mind. Then again, maybe a cloudy mind was a good thing to have in the midst of this company.

By the time dawn lit the sky outside and the men of Cave-in-Rock began to waken, Celinda had come to some peace with her situation. At the very least she had proven to herself that she could push past her fears and hesitations and actually try to get away. That counted for something. Almost from the time Horton had set his hook into her, she had been too frightened to really try to escape. She had been afraid that courage would evade her forevermore. Now she knew that wasn't true.

Having slept little, Celinda was exhausted, and made her way back to her sleeping place. She settled down, pulled the blanket over her, and drifted off into sleep before Horton awakened.

Celinda opened her eyes and sat up with a sense of alarm. She had always had a good instinct for time, and even with the distortion of light that came from being inside a cave, she sensed that it was about noon. She marveled at having slept so hard that she hadn't been awakened by the noise around her.

Then she realized that, for once, there was no noise. The cave was utterly quiet, unnervingly so.

She was surprised as well to discover that the rear portion of the cave was empty except for her. The men of the cave were clustered down near the mouth, holding tense postures, peering out at the river. Curious, she rose, folded her blanket, and went toward them. Jim Horton was at the rear of the cluster. He turned and saw her. A frown crossed his face and he waved her back. Confused and growing alarmed, she obeyed, seating herself on the cave floor, wondering what could have everyone's attention so, and why they were so quiet.

Only then did she notice that, to a man, the cavern dwellers were armed with pistols, rifles, and hatchets. Comprehension came in a sickening rush.

She stood in horror. Even without seeing it, she knew that there were people out on that river, perhaps a band of boatmen shipping wares downriver, or a family traveling by flatboat . . . innocent travelers, just like she and her father had been. Innocent travelers, floating into a death trap here where the Ohio grew fast and narrow and the waters were hard to navigate.

She wanted to rush out and shout a warning, but she couldn't. Helpless, she simply remained where she was, waiting for something to happen.

A minute passed, then another. The man at the cave's mouth

visibly grew more intense. Celinda watched hatchets being raised, rifles and pistols being cocked. Tension grew heavy, heavier, and then with a rush of motion that hit Celinda like a jolt, the men surged forward, out of the cave, raising fierce yells.

"No," Celinda whispered. "Please, God, no."

She turned her back toward the mouth of the cave and put her hands over her ears, but nothing could block out the sounds that came echoing back to her. Shots, yells, howls of pain, hoots of beastly triumph. She heard a woman's scream, cut off by the sound of a shot. *Now I know where Queen gets her dresses.* The thought made her feel sick. Celinda's eyes filled, and through her tears she happened to look directly at the spill of light coming through the opening that led to the sinkhole above the cave.

She looked at the bottle-strung ropes, and realized that even if those bottles clanked together right now, no one else was in the cave to hear them. The others were all outside, exulting in slaughter and robbery.

She did not hesitate a moment. She scrambled back toward the rear opening, up the rough, gravelly slope and into the opening that led up into the hole. The bottles clinked and a few even broke, but Celinda climbed without regard to that. She grunted in pain as her hands and knees became abraded in the climb, and twice she almost fell, but in only a few moments she was in the sinkhole, then out, on solid ground and above the cave.

She heard the noise of violence continuing from below. The pirates were still at it, and apparently receiving some resistance. Celinda hoped that the people on the boat would escape, and all the better, would deliver as much death as possible back to these human devils who preyed upon the innocent. Nothing would be more just, or more satisfying.

Celinda ran as hard as she could, back away from the river and then to her right, heading upriver for no particular reason. She had no plan about where to go; all she desired was to get away, to put miles between herself and the place of death behind her.

As she ran, wild exuberance overwhelmed her. She threw her arms aloft, fists clenched, head thrown back as if she were an ancient Greek runner coming in at victorious at the end of a footrace. A great sense of freedom washed over her like a waterfall. She pushed herself harder, and suddenly came out of the woods onto a foot trail that followed the course of the river. Perhaps, she thought, she should move back off the trail and remain among the trees . . . but it was hard to run in the trees, and besides that, there was no one here to detect her. They were all back at the cave's mouth.

So she kept to the trail, rounded a curve on a run, and jerked to a jolting halt.

She was standing face-to-face with the bulky person of Queen Fine and a tall, bald, albino stranger whose ruddy face grinned at her from beneath a stained cap of woven wool.

CHAPTER 13

"Well, look here, Felix," Queen said. "It's the mute boy, running for all that's in him." She smiled, eyes narrowing. "*Him*, I say. But I got my doubts. I don't believe we're seeing the truth. Haven't from the first time I saw him. I believe our mute's got a secret."

"What might that be, Sister Queen?' the albino said.

"Just that this boy ain't a boy at all. I seen it right off, when Junebug brought him in. His 'cousin,' he says. 'George Ames,' he says, 'naught but a poor mute boy.' He's lying. If this here ain't a girl, I'm a polecat."

Celinda's eyes widened, and before she could catch herself she said, "No! I'm not—" She cut off, face blanching as she realized that her voice had revealed not only that she wasn't a boy, but that she was not mute either. She wanted to kick herself. How could she be so witless?

"Ah! And no mute!" Queen exclaimed. "Tell me true, 'George'—you *are* a girl? Ain't it so? Your voice sounds like no boy to me."

There was no point in trying to perpetuate the lie further. "Yes," Celinda said, heart sinking. "I'm a girl."

"I always knew it, girl. But old Queen Fine kept her mouth

shut. I had it figured that Junebug was trying to keep the men off you. Am I right?"

"Yes." Celinda looked imploringly at the big woman. "Please, ma'am, don't betray me!"

Queen laughed and put a finger across her lips. "Don't you fret yourself, girl. Queen Fine knows how to keep a secret. And so does Felix here—ain't that right?"

"Yes indeed, Sister Queen. I am no Judas. Not at all."

Queen grinned and said, "Felix here is my brother. He and me, we look out for one another."

"Your brother . . ."

"Indeed."

Celinda was finding a certain relief in her freedom to talk. "I haven't seen him about the cave."

"He ain't been there. He stays most all the time on the Diamond Island, up the river, with our sister Jasmine. He and Jasmine and the others there keep a watch out for flatboats and such coming downstream. When they see one, out goes Jasmine to wave at them from the bank. Jasmine, she's young and pretty, just like I was once. She hollers to the boats that pass that she's stranded on the island, and begs them to carry her on down to the cave, where there's folk awaiting who will take her in. 'Good folk,' she always says. She rides on down and then the 'good folk' come out of the cave, and that's the end of that."

"I saw you leave the cave night before last," Celinda said. "You were going to the island?"

"Aye, young lady. I go down often to see Jasmine. This time a boat passed while we were there, and Jasmine went out. They picked her up and by now should have met the 'good folk' at the cave."

"They have," Celinda said. "I heard their screaming. God help them."

"Don't weep for them, young lady, but give them honor," Felix Fine said. "All of us must someday leave this world. Those who have left it today at the cave have done so in a way that betters those of us who gain their possessions. They are deserving of our praise and laud."

Celinda was repelled at such a concept, staring at Felix in astonishment. Her eyes were inexplicably drawn to the woolen cap on his head. Something familiar about it . . .

"You've met us on our return from the island," Queen said.

"Me and Felix, we're going back now to see what treasures were on that boat. It was big, full of staves and barrels and all kinds of cargo. We watched from the trees while they took on Jasmine. Don't you think Jasmine is a pretty name, girl?"

"Yes, I suppose it is."

"And what is *your* name, young lady?" Felix asked.

"Celinda Ames. I'm captive of Jim Horton. He found me in Kentucky after my father died. We had been put off a flatboat, bound for Natchez."

"Natchez!" Queen exclaimed. "You were bound for Natchez?"

"Yes. I have an aunt there."

Felix smiled, his reddish-hued eyes sparkling. "We, too, have familial links with the fine town of Natchez," he said. His speech was, like his appearance, peculiar—precise, cleanly spoken, devoid of any backwoods accent. He was either educated or skillful at pretending to be.

"We have another sister in Natchez," Queen said with a proud tone and haughty look. "Beatrice Fine Sullivan. Your aunt will surely know her. She is a woman of importance."

"A woman of importance," Felix repeated, in the same proud attitude. "She married well and became a woman of wealth. The pride of our family."

"I may never reach Natchez if you don't let me go," Celinda said. "Jim Horton says he will take me there, but all we've done is come to the cave. I fear he'll keep me there forever. Please don't make me go back."

"There are many from the great cavern who journey on to Natchez," Felix said in his crisp manner. "Many who make the grand voyage and come back again."

Queen said, "Most of the boats that are stopped at the cave are taken on down the river to the market towns. They sell them there, and their cargo, and bring back the gain to be divided among us all. If it is undamaged, the very boat that was stopped today will be making a voyage to Natchez with a crew from among our own number."

"You will no doubt find your passage on that boat," Felix said, his words making it evident that Celinda's plea to be let go was going to go unheeded.

"I don't want to be on that boat or any other boat leaving the cave," Celinda said, growing disturbed. "I want to leave this place and find my own passage down the river. I don't want to be with Jim Horton. I know in the end he's going to hurt me, or worse." Suddenly, tears gushed out, running in brown streams down her dirty face.

Queen's expression softened, humanizing her broad, homely visage. She came forward and put her hand on Celinda's shoulder. Her tone grew motherly. "Poor child! Poor child! Why are you crying?"

"I don't belong among those people back at the cave," Celinda said in a quaking voice, diplomatically choosing her words to imply that Queen and Felix, of course, were not among the undesirables she sought to escape. "They are not the kind of people I know. I miss my father. When he died, and Jim Horton came along, claiming to be a preacher, I thought God had sent me help and protection, but all I've found is that cave and all those wicked folk around me."

"Has Junebug used you wrong, Celinda? Has he forced his way on you?" Queen asked, and Celinda knew just what she meant.

"No. I told him a false tale that made him not want to touch me. I said there was a snake living inside my belly."

"A snake?" The albino threw back his head and laughed heartily.

Queen joined in. "He believed you?"

"It's a story told for true of a girl back where I used to live," Celinda said. "Yes, he did believe me."

"You are a girl with wits about you," Queen said. "You will do well."

"You will do well," Felix repeated.

"What is Junebug's plan?" Queen asked. "Hush up that crying and tell me."

With great effort Celinda got a hold on her emotions. Sniffing, she said, "He's pretending to be a preacher named John Deerfield. The real preacher died at an inn, and Jim Horton took his possessions and his name, and now he's going to go to Natchez and claim to be the true man. There's money waiting there to pay for a church being built, and he aims to take it for his own."

Queen and her brother laughed again. Celinda took it to be a sign of admiration for Horton's scheme, but Queen said, "That strutting fool! He'll never pass for no preacher!"

"He will never pass!" the albino echoed.

"Have you not tried to run away from him before now?" Queen asked.

"Once, and he almost hurt me over it. I've had no good chance since. This time I thought I was free ... but now I'm caught, unless you'll let me go." She began to cry again, this time with a touch of sham in it. Celinda sensed she had the sympathies of this bizarre pair, and intuition said a show of fear and distress could further engage those sympathies to her own benefit. Her escape effort had sparked a new awareness that her own survival depended ultimately upon herself and her wits. Her father had charged her to be strong, and at this moment the best strength she had was to appear weak. "Please don't make me go back to the cave," she pleaded, looking childishly at Queen. "I mustn't go back there."

"No, girl, you *must* go back," Queen said gently. "For you to roam free without help would be the death of you. This country is filled with wickedness. You should know that, having fell in with Junebug as fast as you did. You may think it hard to believe, but you could have fell in with much worse than him. Much worse."

"The region is dreadfully full of immoral and evil ruffians," Felix contributed. He shook his head as if saddened by the thought of such rampant wickedness.

This whole affair was beginning to seem so outlandish that Celinda half wondered if she were dreaming it all. "But if I go back, Jim Horton will hurt me. He'll be angry that I ran away."

"Don't fret about Junebug," Queen said. "I'll take care of you. Junebug won't cross me, no ma'am."

"He is a weak man at heart," the albino said.

"But how can you protect me? And how will I ever get away?"

The haughty Felix spoke with the tone and manner of a bailiff formally heralding a judge into high court. "It is the most convenient happenstance that my dear Queen will also be voyaging to Natchez, there to find and greet after many years of separation our sister Beatrice, who is a woman of importance, as we informed you earlier."

After a moment of interpretation, Celinda said, "You're going to Natchez, too?" She was vaguely encouraged. At the very least, these people didn't seem nearly as threatening as Jim Horton, and Queen was obviously confident that she could restrain Horton from doing her any harm.

"I am indeed," Queen said. "And I'll take you with me, tuck you under my wing and keep Junebug off you, girl. Don't you worry about him as long as Queen Fine is around."

The albino said, "Come with us to the cave, Celinda. We will let you meet our sister Jasmine. And you have no worries about our friend Junebug Horton. He is manifestly afraid of Queen and will not defy her."

Celinda felt a combination of disappointment and relief. She did not want to return to the cave, but comprehended that if she did so, she would at least be under different and better circumstances, if Queen was to be trusted. She would be under Queen's protection—all the way to Natchez, if she understood properly. She wondered if Queen would keep her word. But what choice did she have but to trust her? "Thank you," she said. "Thank you so much for your kindness."

"Let's move on," Queen said. "I want to get my portion of the treasures before all the others steal it all. Felix, don't you forget: Celinda's name among the others is George Ames, and she's a mute boy. Don't you let the truth slip, you hear me?"

"I do indeed, dear sister," he replied, and tipped his cap. "Come, George Ames. Let us be off."

Jim Horton was a miserably unhappy man. He sat pulling on a bottle of whiskey he had found on the doomed flatboat, looking at Celinda, who had stayed close beside Queen and her ugly, pale brother Felix ever since the three of them had come walking back to the cave along the trail that led down along the river. The sight astounded and infuriated him; in the hubbub of slaughter and plundering that followed the landing of the flatboat, he hadn't even noticed that Celinda had escaped the cave. He had stormed toward her, ready to drag her off and give her a sound beating for her defiance, but Queen stepped in front of him, a knife in hand.

"George is my friend, now," she had said, with a telling emphasis on the "George." "You'll not lay your hand on *him*"—again the pregnant emphasis—"or I'll slice out your liver and cook it for my supper."

He backed off at once, knowing Queen Fine was not a woman to be challenged. Some months back when he had lived here before, when Sam Mason, the original Cave-in-Rock river pirate, was running a so-called "Liquor Vault and House of Entertainment" here in the cavern, he had seen her knife two men to death, one of them a flatboat piracy victim who had tried to strike her with an axe handle while she helped raid his grounded boat, the other a big brute of a man who had said something to her that offended her. Ever since then he had regarded Queen as being as dangerous as any man. And her albino brother, though foppish and seemingly harmless in manner, was himself quite a dangerous person, or so Horton had been told. He was no brawler and had no ambition to put that reputation to the test.

What had him most thoroughly riled was Celinda herself. Something had changed in the girl's manner; in Horton's perception, she now seemed smug and defiant toward him, sure she had wiggled out of his clutches. Not only was that terribly aggravating, it was also hurtful to him personally. He had enjoyed fancying that he'd won at least a share of the girl's heart, a share he was sure he could greatly expand later, once he was out on the river with her, floating toward Natchez. Her manner now gave the lie to that notion. Clearly she held him in disdain, and that stung his pride. A time or two she had acted friendly toward him, clung to him as a protector, if nothing more . . . though he had dared to hope there was something more. Now he wondered if it had all been a deception.

If so, in what else had she deceived him? The snake-in-the-belly story, most likely. He now felt a fool for having believed that. It was the one thing that had kept him from giving her the great compliment of his affections—such was his warped perception of his attempted molestation of her—and now he was almost sure that she had lied about the snake in her belly. If he had the chance now, he'd show her what he thought of lying females who denied a man his pleasures!

There would be no chances, though, not now or not even on the flatboat. He had already heard the sorrowful word: Queen Fine was to be among those who took this pirated flatboat on downriver, with another of the grizzled Cave-in-Rock residents, Lex Dunworth, serving as captain. This in itself was bad news for Horton. Dunworth was another person he disliked, and who disliked him in turn. Even worse, Dunworth held Queen in high esteem and would certainly help her protect Celinda if she asked him. Horton had always trodden gingerly in Dunworth's presence, knowing the fellow would probably welcome an excuse to put a knife in him and have him out of the way. With Queen and Dunworth looking out for Celinda, he would be effectively cut off from his object of desire—and her right there on the boat with him! He wasn't sure he could bear it.

He cursed his luck. It wasn't supposed to happen like this. Sullenly he raised his bottle for another drink, only to be jolted from behind. The bottle fell from his hands, crashing onto the floor.

"Watch your clumsy self, fool!" he yelled, leaping up and turning. Before him stood a surprised-looking Lumpkin. It was he who had given the jolt, provided by the butt of a rifle taken from one of the flatboat crew members who even now was being disposed of down by the river, his corpse weighted with rocks and tossed into the water. Lumpkin wasn't accustomed to carrying a rifle and had been moving about without taking account of the fact that the long weapon was bumping everything and everyone about.

"I'm sorry, Mr. Junebug," Lumpkin said.

Horton, who had always regarded Lumpkin as no more than a worthless occupier of space in the cave, reached out and jerked the weapon away. "Give me that thing. You got no need for such a thing anyhow. Bumping folks with it, breaking good bottles of whiskey—next thing you'll have shot somebody by mistake."

Lumpkin frowned. "That's *my* rifle, Mr. Junebug! I took it off the boat myself! Hand it back!"

"You don't merit a rifle, being a fool."

Lumpkin's usual simple, open expression vanished. He loomed up tall and threatening as a storm cloud. "I want my rifle! Give it to me, Junebug! Now!"

Had Horton looked at Lumpkin's face, he would have seen that defying him at the moment was mortally dangerous. As it happened, something else distracted him: a gravelly roar from a tall, muscled man at the mouth of the cave. The man was the sole survivor of the flatboat passengers. He was bruised and bloodied from the fight and clad only in a pair of calf-length woolen trousers, his shirt and coat having been taken by some of the pirates. Horton initially thought the man was roaring because somebody was in the process of killing him—his fate had been the immediate subject of debate among the cave folk, some wanting to kill him as a menace while others advocating mercy because he had put up such a fine fight—but quickly Horton saw that nothing of the kind was going on. The man had somehow managed to rip away the cords tied around his wrists, and now he was shaking his former bonds and snarling at his startled captors like some defiant new incarnation of Samson.

"Give me my rifle, Junebug!" Lumpkin hollered into Horton's ear.

Horton frowned and jerked his head away from the offending noise, and shoved the rifle at Lumpkin. "Take it, take it! What the devil you yelling in my ear for? Go away!"

Lumpkin grabbed his weapon joyfully and did go away, stroking the long barrel lovingly, like a child with a new toy. Equally childlike was the fact that he instantly seemed to put aside any anger toward Horton. Lumpkin's mind was far too simple to deal with more than one emotion at a time.

The boatman, who was standing on a rock sill just inside the cave door, roared again and shook his fists. His wrists were ragged and bleeding, torn when he yanked free of his bonds.

"So ye think to murder me, do ye?" the man yelled. He seemed as heedless of his blood-crusted wounds as he was of the rapidly chilling weather. "Well, think ye again, ye hell-bound eaters of dung! If there be a man among ye, and I doubt there be, send him to me and let him fight me! By jingo, I'm a fierce gator from Spanish Floridee, I am, with teeth to outchew the dullest pit saw and a disposition as ugly as the very butt of Beelzebub! If there be a real fighting man here among ye, a man with ary a hair on his rump or a speck of grit in his craw, send him down here and let Ajax McKee show him where Hades gets its fire! I scrap like a mad dog, spit like a roasting cat, claw like a skinned painter, belch like the thunder! I fear no man, run from naught but a spiteful woman, respect no one but my dear mammy, and abide all things but an insult! If ye plan to kill me, then be men enough to let me fight my last with pride! Is there any here with the gravel to face me man-to-man and fist-to-fist? Ajax McKee calls for ye!"

Horton grinned admiringly. Ajax McKee's peroration was a classic example of the lyrical kind of challenge issued by boatmen and other river folk in the humor to fight. At times such orations could achieve an almost poetic level, and Horton had just enough appreciation of words to enjoy them.

Judging from the man's muscled build and evident grit, Horton had little doubt McKee could back up his claims. Certainly it wouldn't be Jim Horton answering his challenge.

Out of the farrago of humanity moving about before the cavern and on the flatboat stepped a man who was a veritable mountain of flesh and muscle. This was Lex Dunworth, the unofficial leader of the Cave-in-Rock cabal in Sam Mason's absence and the man who would be in charge of the flatboat when it was piloted to Natchez. Dunworth was a native Virginian who had come to Cave-in-Rock in the days most still called it Rock Cave, or Mason's Cave. Scarred from many fights, Dunworth was a man who had never shown fear of anything or anyone, and who held the fear-inspired respect of everyone around him. The grin on his face revealed his pleasure at hearing the challenge of this boatman named Ajax McKee.

"Do you seek a fight, you carrion-chewing rat of the river? If you do, I answer you proud. I'm the orneriest devil ever to come from old Virginee, with the meanest dog, the prettiest sister, the drunkest pap, and the fattest maw to ever wean her babes on aquafortis! I was raised eating roast Injun for breakfast and stewed Presbyterians for supper! I'm strong as the biggest bear, scarred as the oldest oak tree on the barrenmost mountain, wild as the slinkingest mink, and ugly as a squashed hell-bender! I can skin a man alive and wear his hide for a shirt! I can bruise the whitest man so black he's fit to be sold at auction! After I wash myself, they skim meanness off the river from here to New Orleans! If you seek somebody to send your black soul to say howdy to the devil, you rank piece of river flotsam, you've found the very bruiser to do it. Whaaaah!" With that, Dunworth stripped off his coat, literally ripped his filthy hunting shirt from his body, and clawed bloody scratches down his own chest with yellowed fingernails.

Already the people were gathering in a wide circle around the two antagonists. Horton moved to a better position. He was no fighter himself, but he loved a good, bloody row as much as any river denizen. This promised to be a fine one indeed—and with any luck, would mark the end of Lex Dunworth.

CHAPTER 14

Bragadocious challenges done, the fight between Ajax McKee the boatman and Lex Dunworth the river pirate started without fanfare. For several moments there was nothing but cautious, evaluative pacing and staring by both men. Then they leaped, roaring in tandem as if in answer to some silent signal, and went hard at it. Celinda was horrified, but unable to tear her eyes away.

Dunworth strongly prevailed at first, laying in a series of blows selectively and expertly placed on the already battered body of McKee, driving him back until he was up against the rock of the bluff itself, tearing and scuffing his flesh against the stone. It appeared this would be a short and one-sided fight. Again and again Dunworth's hamlike fists tortured McKee's frame. Yet the man let out not a cry or whimper, even as it appeared he was sliding toward unconsciousness.

Dunworth coiled back his right arm for the evident death blow—a horrific smash to the face—when McKee began to show mettle until then unrevealed. He jerked his head to the right just in time to avoid the impact of Dunworth's descending fist. Dunworth smacked his right fist directly into the stone with a force so great it tore the flesh from his knuckles. Dunworth roared and drew back a ruined fist as McKee brought up his right knee, catching Dunworth right in the groin, striking so hard the nearly three-hundred-pound man was lifted a handsbreath from the ground.

The crowd, who had mostly favored Dunworth, suddenly turned against him as he sank to the ground, eyes bulging, left hand groping toward his injured crotch, right hand limp and clawlike. "Beat his nose flat, McKee!" "Snap his neck, boatman!" "Gouge out his eyes! Gouge 'em out!" Shouts of such ilk went up all around, Celinda noticed that Jim Horton held silence, but had an eager look. She already had detected that he and Dunworth did not get along, and figured Horton was hoping he would be done in but refused to join the shouting in case he wasn't. She felt contempt for Horton. The man was nothing but a self-protective and amoral coward.

McKee found himself a victim of his own tactics when Dunworth rolled onto his back and lifted his knee just as McKee was throwing his full weight down upon him. The knee, obviously aimed for McKee's own groin, missed that but did catch him very hard in the belly, driving the wind out of him and making McKee give his first pained scream of the fight. He landed atop Dunworth, who used his good hand to push him up and off. McKee rolled onto his back, and Dunworth sprang to his feet with remarkable agility.

He went down again almost as quickly, dropping his full weight, with knees bent, onto McKee's stomach again. Celinda winced as she saw McKee's middle flattened so severely it looked like his backbone would break against the rocky ground beneath him. Dunworth's left hand went to McKee's throat and began to squeeze.

Despite the weather, cold enough now that a few flakes of snow were spitting down from the graying sky, Dunworth was sweating profusely, perspiration falling from his grimacing face onto the bulge-eyed, reddening visage of McKee. Celinda felt sad; clearly McKee was going to pass out, and his brave fight, and then his life, would be lost. Though this fight wasn't hers, she felt a situational kinship with McKee, who like her was here against his will, fighting for his existence against the evil that had engulfed him.

Suddenly McKee's hands came up and pounded Dunworth on both ears at the same time. Celinda let out a quiet little cry,

then remembered she was still posing as mute and hoped nobody had heard it. Dunworth grunted and squeezed his eyes
shut, but still did not let go of McKee's neck.

McKee's next move made Celinda look away. He reached up
and put a thumb in each of Dunworth's eyes and pushed in,
hard. Celinda had heard of gouge-fighting, how sometimes it
blinded men, left their eyeballs literally hanging smashed and
bloody outside their sockets. She didn't want to see anything
like that and averted her eyes, but found herself compelled to
look again.

Dunworth screamed and trembled, jerking his head about,
trying to get the pushing thumbs out of his eyes. With his injured arm he tried to knock away McKee's arms, to no avail.
Still, he would not let go of McKee's neck. McKee dug deeper,
and a great shudder passed through Dunworth's body, and at
last he let go of McKee and jerked back.

That freed him from having McKee's thumbs in his eyes,
which were now bleeding—one orb appeared to be about to
bulge right out of its socket—but McKee made an upward
move himself and got a grip on both of Dunworth's ears. He
pulled Dunworth's face down to his and bit him on the nose.
His teeth dug in and he jerked his head like a dog tearing meat.
Dunworth screamed as the tip of his bulbous nose came off.
McKee spit it out.

Celinda expected Dunworth to yield, but he didn't. Instead
he knocked McKee's hands free and brought his own face
down and clamped *his* mouth on McKee's nose. Blood from
his own wounded nose flooded McKee's face. Dunworth suddenly jerked up, and McKee became the second man at Cave-
in-Rock to lose the end of his nose that day.

Dunworth rolled off McKee and collapsed, gripping his
nose. McKee, weak and bleeding as badly as his opponent,
stood in wobbling fashion as cheers rose. "Kill him, boatman!"
someone yelled. A knife was tossed from the crowd, landing at
McKee's feet. He stooped and picked it up. He looked at it a
couple of moments, then lifted it like a trophy, waving it above
his head. More cheers sounded, and McKee moved over toward
the supine Dunworth.

Celinda closed her eyes. She would not watch one man murder another. She tensely awaited the animal yells from the
crowd that would herald the end of Lex Dunworth. But sud-

denly the sound of brawling resumed. She looked just in time to see Dunworth, on his feet again, wresting the knife from McKee's grasp.

Once again the tide of opinion turned, and the shouts were now for Dunworth to kill McKee. He didn't. Instead he tossed the knife aside and put out his hand toward his opponent.

"By Christmas, you're a worthy fighter, you are, too fine a bruiser for me to kill. Ajax McKee, if you'll put aside differences, I'd be prime pleased to name you as friend."

The crowd moaned in disappointment, deprived of the fatal ending to this fight that had been desired.

McKee grasped Dunworth's big paw in a bloody handshake. "You're the pearl of Sheba, you are, Dunworth! I'll accept your hand, and your friendship."

McKee turned to the crowd. "A worthy man, this one!" he declared. "A man worth his salt—and he'll be with me when we pilot this here flatboat to New Orleans, second only to my command."

The mood of the crowd grew accommodating now that it was obvious these two weren't going to fight to the death. "You've earned a place among us, McKee!" someone shouted. "We're a bloody lot, but we welcome you if you'll be one of us and not shy from our ways!"

"Aye, I'll join ye, and proudly!" McKee yelled. He wore a broad grin and seemed oblivious to the blood streaming from his nose. There was something potentially comical in the sight of the two rough men standing there, hands gripped and raised and the ends of their noses gone, but Celinda did not feel like laughing.

She had thought that McKee was a man to admire, a fighter unwilling to yield before this murderous band. Now she saw he was really no different than they. He was joining the very group who had slain his earlier companions and commandeered their flatboat.

It seemed there was no goodness or decency to be found at Cave-in-Rock, except perhaps in the person of Queen Fine. Celinda determined right then that she would not leave Queen's side until she was safely ensconced in Natchez, out of the reach of Jim Horton and the rest of the foul rabble inhabiting this murderers' cave.

*   *   *

At her first opportunity, Celinda called Queen aside into a nearby grove of trees where no one could hear her speak and thereby realize the truth about "mute" George Ames.

"What will happen now?" she asked. "Did I understand that this flatboat would be taken on to Natchez?"

"No, on to New Orleans, Dunworth is saying now. But you and me, we'll get off at Natchez. There'll be a crew put together from amongst the people here to take the boat on to Orleans. There they'll sell the cargo, and the boat, too, then come back here by land to do it all over again with another boat. There's been many a flatboat stole that way at this cave. Many a corpse has sunk in these waters. It's been death for many, but it's life for us. The only kind a lot here know."

"Are there many here like Ajax McKee, who've come off other boats that have been pirated?"

"Very few. Most who fight get theirselves killed right off. Only the strongest ones make enough showing for theirselves to live for long in the fight, and only them survivors willing to join us and live like we do are spared after the fight's over. We're bad folk here. Murderers, thieves. The worst kind of sinners. Only the bad can live here, girl. Only the bad." She looked deeply at Celinda. "And you ain't bad. You'd not long survive this place or these folk if you stayed. It's good that you're bound away from here."

"It is good," Celinda said. "I've never seen such a place as this before, nor such people."

"They're hell's future population. That's what Mason used to say. And it's the truth, girl. It's the truth."

Aboard the big flatboat when it set out from the cave site were Dunworth, McKee, and three other crewmen selected from among the outlaws, plus Jim Horton, Queen Fine, and Celinda Ames, still maintaining her charade as a mute male. She wondered how difficult it would be to maintain that fraud in the close quarters of a flatboat. It might not be possible at all, and if so, she would have great cause to fear these violent men. At least there was Queen to protect her—if she really could. That remained to be proven.

She wasn't sure why Queen was being so helpful and protective of her. Maybe she saw her as sort of a pet or a new and weak little sister or daughter who needed protection and mothering in a rough and dangerous world. Whatever the case, she seemed to have evoked some soft and motherly feelings buried deep in the rough exterior of the hardened river harlot.

On the morning the flatboat left Cave-in-Rock, Celinda felt tremendously relieved even though she knew she was still in a dangerous situation. How could anyone not be relieved to be leaving hell? Such was how it felt to Celinda Ames.

She looked her last on the gaping cavern mouth and the human raff gathered before it. Her eyes fell on Felix Fine, who was waving at Queen and dabbing his eyes, tearful at this parting. He removed the woolen cap he wore and wiped his tears with it, and Celinda felt a shudder.

She had just realized why her eyes had been drawn to that hat. It looked exactly like the hat worn by the boatman who had rowed her and her dying father to shore after they had been evicted from that first flatboat. The hat had been stained and shaped very distinctively and was easy to recognize. How could Felix have come by it, except as booty? It could only mean that the flatboat crew who had evicted her and her father had soon after fallen victim to the pirates of Cave-in-Rock.

Celinda remembered her father's talk of a death angel, and shuddered at the twisting irony of it all.

She moved to the center of the boat, found a place among the casks and crates and settled there, wishing only to be alone and ignored. The world was too dangerous, too lonely, too indecipherable, and all she wanted to do was withdraw from it, as far and as long as she could, until she was safe with her aunt Ida in Natchez.

CHAPTER 15

Clardy Tyler huddled in the brown, leafless brush beside the trail, hidden behind a moss-covered fallen tree. His horse was tethered well behind him, far enough from the trail to keep any of its snorts or motions from being heard by any passing traveler. Though the early morning had been so cold that puddles were lightly frozen and frost blanketed the forest, and even the midday temperature remained too low for comfort, Clardy was breathless and his face felt hot. A crucial time had come. He was about to commit his first Wilderness Road robbery.

Many times in youth he had anticipated this moment, seeing it bathed in a light of cold glory and romance. The daring young robber, stepping out onto the road with rifle brandished, ordering the surprised traveler to turn over all his valuables, all the while basking in the fearful but secretly admiring gaze of the attractive young woman who, of course, would be among the party of travelers. With a whoop and rear of his fine horse he would be off, riding into infamy and legend, his phantom person becoming the subject of lore told around inn tables and forest campfires. And evermore the young woman who was privileged to have encountered the bold thief would carry his image in her mind and heart, wishing with sighs that she had been swept away by him to share his life of daring and continual earthly pleasures. . . .

Now that the time had come, the situation didn't feel that way at all. Clardy was filthy from the trail, his horse was growing lean and slow, hardly a great steed, and the odds of some beautiful, virginal young woman coming down the road didn't seem at all likely. Clardy was mainly aware of nerves and hunger, gnawing, painful hunger that had been with him for two days. His food had run out far more quickly than he'd expected, and he had failed to bring down any game but one single, scrawny squirrel. Little sustenance in that, and no glory at all.

He shifted his posture, wondering if this first attempt at robbery would work out any better than his hunting. At least he had a definite opportunity here. Someone *was* coming down the trail. A couple of minutes earlier the wind had carried a snatch of music, somebody singing, accompanied by odd, clinking sounds. The singing he could make sense of, but the clinking had him curious. He had scrambled about quickly to set up this ambush.

He heard it again. No singing now, just the clinking, and the faint nicker of a horse. Tensing, he steeled himself, gripped his rifle stock tightly, and peeped over the top of the fallen tree.

The smallest-framed man he had ever seen rode into view on a horse that was hung with pans, pots, bundles of cutlery, sewing goods, and the like. The cookware accounted for the clinking. The bulky coat the fellow wore accentuated rather than disguised his meager build. Further accenting it was the old, oversized tricorn hat that rode low above his ears and almost overhung his eyes. Smooth-shaven and homely, the man had a pleasant face and dark eyes. A peddler! Clardy told himself he was lucky. This fellow might have all kinds of things worth stealing.

The unsuspecting peddler rode closer, closer . . . the moment had come. Clardy coiled his muscles, prepared to leap out of the brush and level his rifle—

But he couldn't. A strange paralysis caught him and kept him right where he was. The peddler rode on past.

Hang it all! This would never do. How could a man become a robber if he couldn't even make himself confront his intended victims?

The peddler was almost out of sight when Clardy finally pushed himself out of the underbrush and onto the road. "You there!" he called. "Halt where you are!"

The peddler gave a start of surprise and turned. He looked at Clardy in bewilderment, then smiled. *Smiled*. Clardy realized he had forgotten to raise his rifle, but now he couldn't seem to do it. That smile had thrown him off balance.

"Well, howdy-do, young man!" the peddler called cheerfully. He had a piping voice that sounded appropriate to his small build. "I can't imagine how I managed to pass you by!" Then he addressed his horse. "Whoa, here, girl, hold up. Master Peyton's getting down to talk to a fellow man of the road." He slid down from the horse and walked back toward Clardy, grinning, hand extended.

Feeling foolish, Clardy stuck out his own hand and shook that of the peddler.

"Call me Peyton," the man said. "Who might you be, my fine young Christian?"

"My name's Clardy Tyler." Suddenly Clardy wanted to kick himself. He had just revealed his name to a man he planned to rob . . . but now he knew he wouldn't rob him. He couldn't. That grinning face, that friendly manner, that scrawny frame—he could never wrong a man such as this.

"I'm pleased to meet you, Clardy. One is always happy to encounter a friendly person on the road. I'm a man of the trail, as you can see. A peddler of good wares to the people of Kentuck and Tennessee."

"So I see." Just then Clardy's stomach gave a terribly loud rumble.

Peyton quirked up his brows and slipped off his hat, revealing an egg-bald head. "I believe you're hungry, Clardy Tyler. It so happens I am as well, having set off without my breakfast this morning. A mistake of judgment on my part, but one we can remedy. What would you think of sharing some victuals with me?"

Clardy nodded, feeling shy about accepting kindness from a man he had originally planned to rob. "I'd think highly of it, sir. Thank you," he mumbled.

Clardy ate his meal eagerly, but with an underlying sense of disquiet. Twice now he had bumped up against the borders of crime, once with Cale Johnson and the Harpes, and now with this clumsy effort at highway robbery. Both times matters hadn't worked out at all as he planned. The Harpe incident had put him on the run, and today's bungle had made him wonder if he possessed the nerve for crime.

Peyton jabbered on cheerfully, but Clardy paid meager attention, preoccupied with worry. If he couldn't make his way as a criminal, what would he do? He would have to find work somewhere, with someone. He wasn't sure how to go about that. He had never worked anywhere except on the Tyler farm, and even then he had shrugged off as much of the labor as possible on Thias. Now he was out on the road, heading into Kentucky and a world in which he knew no one.

Maybe he should turn around and go home to the farm. Odd, how a place he had hated and longed to leave didn't look so bad viewed over the shoulder. Sure, Hiram was hard to deal with and the farm offered more than its share of drudgery. But was that so terrible? It also offered a home, a roof, a sense of security, and a way to maintain a living.

Peyton laughed. He had just told a joke of some sort, which Clardy had only halfway listened to. Clardy laughed just to keep up appearances, and thought how Peyton's laugh was similar to his grandfather's. He felt a stab of homesickness.

He *would* go home . . . but no. He couldn't. The Harpes were there. They would hurt him, probably kill him, for having crossed them. He had never encountered such fear-inspiring men as they, men whose wickedness hung about them tangibly, like a bad smell. Clardy took another bite of Peyton's bread and inwardly cursed the day he sat down to drink with Cale Johnson and let liquor and criminal ambition get the best of his common sense.

Peyton laughed again, so he, too, chimed in, but a little too late to be convincing. Peyton's laughter faded and he looked at Clardy probingly. "Clardy Tyler, you seem to be a young fellow with much on his mind."

"Well . . . I reckon I am, sir."

"If I can help you in any way . . ."

"No, sir. Thank you."

"A woman? Is that your trouble?"

"No, nothing like that. Thank you for asking, but you needn't trouble yourself over me." He took another bite and said, "You've gave me plenty already, just feeding me."

"If we were bound the same way, I'd invite you to go along

with me, young man. There's safety for two that ain't there for one, you know."

"Yes sir, I do. And if you don't mind, Mr. Peyton, I'd like to give you some counsel myself. You need to be more wary of folks you meet on the road. For all you knew, I could have been aiming to rob you."

"And if you had, Clardy, what could I have done to stop you? If you had been a thief and I'd resisted you, wouldn't I have only got myself hurt? 'Pears to me that kindness is the best a man can give to them he meets. Sometimes it can even protect him from harm. An act of kindness can be the best shield a man has."

Clardy wondered if Peyton had been more perceptive of his original intent than he had showed. "Reckon you're right, sir," he said.

Peyton's kindness seemed boundless. Before parting, he gave Clardy a sack of cornmeal, some parched corn, flour, dried biscuits, and a tasty mix of old but palatable shelled hickory nuts mixed with dried grapes. "Be careful of yourself, Clardy Tyler," the gentle peddler said. "God go with you and give you His protection."

"The same to you, sir," Clardy said.

He watched Peyton ride away, pots and pans making their pleasant clinking sound. He was sorely tempted to accept Peyton's hospitality and turn his back on Kentucky in favor of home. But the phantom images of the Harpes loomed in his mind, and he held still. Soon the peddler was out of sight.

Retrieving his horse, Clardy mounted and rode up the Wilderness Road, very heavy of heart. He rode very slowly and at dusk made a camp. He paused to drink from a little pool by the trail. The water looked murky and had an odd taste, but he was thirsty and tired and drank it anyway. It was Thias who had problems with his belly. Surely a little stagnant water couldn't hurt Clardy Tyler.

By dawn Clardy was in misery. He knelt in his camp, heaving even though his stomach had nothing left in it to disgorge. He was pale and weak and thoroughly emptied, and if this dry retching was painful, at least it wasn't as bad as the diarrhea that had tormented him in the night. He felt like a hollow shell, emptied and scoured down to the soul.

He retched awhile longer, then risked trying to stand. His

stomach went into hard, grinding cramps and he bent double, gripping his belly and moaning aloud. His horse stood by, watching the curious display in the interested but detached manner of the animal world. Clardy held his uncomfortable posture a half minute or so, then slowly straightened, his face red and hair sodden with sweat. He glanced at the horse.

"Stand there and gape, why don't you! If you felt bad as me right now, I'd shoot you in mercy."

The horse moved its ears and began cropping at some brown grass at its feet.

Clardy moved gingerly back across the road and sat down on a stump. He was very woozy, but bit by bit his stomach was hurting less. Just when he thought he was about to feel well enough to get up and ride on, another jolt of nausea sent him to his knees, and for a couple of minutes he heaved in misery.

Never again, he vowed, would he be careless about the water he drank. Never again.

The morning passed before he was able to saddle his horse, where he slumped across the great maned neck like a man half dead. He was truly worried now. Hours had gone by and he still felt terrible. He might be seriously ill. That water might have been giving off some terrible miasma that would make him sick to death.

He urged the horse forward as best he could, hoping he could find help soon. He was panicked. He wasn't at all ready to die.

The day was waning when Clardy rode into view of an inn. By now he had regained a little of his strength and was able to sit almost upright in the saddle. When he saw the small but nicely maintained public house, he felt like weeping for joy, but he was so dehydrated that he doubted he could summon up enough moisture to make a tear. He urged the horse forward and made it into the yard, where he attempted to dismount. At the same time, a man was emerging from the front door of the building. He let out a cry of alarm when Clardy slumped off his horse and landed on his side. The man rushed forward as Clardy rolled over onto his back, groaning.

"Merciful Father, man, are you shot?" the man asked.

"Bad water," Clardy heaved again, but nothing came up.

He heard the man yelling and saw looming figures surrounding him. His body rose into the air, held by many hands, and he was carried into the building. He felt himself sinking into a soft but noisy shuck mattress. He closed his eyes.

He awakened with the man seated by his bed, holding out a cup of water. "You must try to drink. And I assure you this water is pure. Good cold well water."

Clardy did drink, and managed to keep it down. "I feel like I've been tromped by a herd of swine," he whispered.

"We'll get you on your feet again," the man said. "You just drink all you can, and rest."

Clardy slept through the night. The next morning he felt much better, until he tried to sit up and found he was weak and aching. His stomach was terribly sore from all the heaving of the prior day.

The man who had helped him appeared at his side again. "You have your color back, young man."

"I'm better," Clardy replied. "Not plumb well, but better. As bad as I felt yesterday, though, I reckon I'd have had to rally some just to have the strength to die."

The man chuckled. "If you're able to joke, you are indeed on the mend. My name is Farris, John Farris. You are at my inn."

"I'm Clardy Tyler, from Tennessee."

"Oh, we get hordes of Tennessee folk through here. I'm a Virginian myself. Mecklenburg County. Now I'm well established here in Kentucky. Do you know where you are?"

"Not precisely, no."

"Hazel Patch in Rockcastle County, just a jump and hop from Crab Orchard. We live here and take in travelers off the road. Nothing too fancy, but we like to think it's a safe and warm place, and pleasant for those who come."

Clardy looked around. The room was sparsely furnished, its walls made of logs, but to him it looked like heaven itself. He said as much to Farris, who laughed.

"Heaven it ain't, but better to be sick in a bed than in the woods, I suppose."

"I have no money. I don't know how I'll pay you for the lodging and such."

"A man with naught in his pocket can still pay through work. Don't fret. We'll neither pick your pocket nor make a slave of you."

"You're a kind man," Clardy said.

"We must look out for one another in this wild country," Farris replied. "You've passed through quite a wilderness just to reach us—between the Cumberland Gap and this place is some mighty lonely road. Few feel safe traveling it, and for good reason. There are highwaymen and such, and them who travel alone are sometimes molested. That was the very thing I had suspected happened to you when I saw you pitch off that horse."

"I met no one but a peddler, and he was a kind soul," Clardy replied.

"That would be Peyton, I'll wager," Farris said. "Peyton is a fine old fellow indeed and has lodged with us several times. But I worry for him. He's too trusting a man, a friend to everyone. One of these days that's going to bring him harm. He's going to meet up with the wrong kind of folk, and they'll hurt him."

Those words reminded Clardy of his initial intent to rob Peyton. He felt ashamed. "He shared his food with me. I hope you're wrong about what you just said. I liked him."

"I like him, too. But it's a hard country here. They call Kentucky the Bloody Ground, you know, and not without reason. But that's nothing to occupy you at the moment. You rest. Tomorrow you'll feel much better."

Sally Rice Harpe trudged slowly, wishing she had something better than worn-out moccasins to clad her feet. This was hardly better than walking barefoot, the thin deer hide doing little to shield her feet from the cold ground and the stones and burrs hidden beneath the leaves on the forest floor.

Micajah and Wiley Harpe had rejoined her and the other women in the western end of Virginia, at a place where they had lived for some months after leaving the Nickajack region, and where Susanna had given birth to a child who had died soon after. Sally had not yet been with the Harpes at that time, but Susanna had told her about all the thieving raids the men had carried out while living here, usually in cooperation with little bands of renegade Indian scavengers. It troubled Sally that the Harpes associated so readily with Indians, particularly those with a violent bent. Sally feared all Indians, but it seemed to her that her husband and his brother seemed to like Indian society better than that of their own race. It was one of the many aspects of the Harpe men, like their keeping of multiple wives, that she had detected only after marrying Wiley. Often she wished she hadn't let him push her into marriage so quickly. He was not the man she had thought he was when her father scaled their union, but now it was too late. Her father raised her to oppose divorce like the unpardonable sin. Even if that were an option, she knew she was too weak-willed to ever leave Wiley. And too cowardly. If she abandoned him, he would find and kill her. He had told her as much.

The Harpes had sent the women on toward this familiar locale shortly before the theft of Tiel's horses, a crime they had planned to be their last in the Knoxville area. They had shown up with the horses no longer with them, telling them about the posse and their escape and hinting strongly that they had killed someone back at Knoxville. Sally did not know who, but wondered if it was Cale Johnson. She had detected his interest in her and knew Wiley had as well. But she did not ask. Some things she was content not to know.

Sally wondered just what would happen now. Having lost Tiel's horses, the Harpes had nothing to sell, but they didn't seem worried. She figured they planned to commit other thefts. In the view of the Harpe men, whatever crossed their path was theirs to take as they pleased. All Sally knew was that they were heading for Kentucky.

They met a man on a rainy afternoon near the Cumberland Gap. He was a smiling, pleasant sort, a small fellow with an oversized tricorn, bald head, and a horse hung all around with bright cookware and other packs. The Harpe brothers greeted the man, who cheerfully greeted them back. For the next hour he shared his food with them and laid out his goods for the women to examine—bright baubles such as buttons and shiny sewing needles and even some jewelry handmade with pretty stones. Sally was delighted by all the wares and played with them like a child with new toys while Micajah and Wiley talked to him for several minutes, enjoying his jokes and funny manner. The peddler seemed to have put the men in a good humor, and Sally was thrilled when she heard Micajah say they would gladly trade with him for all his wares, and his horse, too. The peddler beamed in happy surprise, and asked what they had to trade. A belt axe, Micajah replied, and pulled his hatchet free. He smashed it into the peddler's head once, twice, then cleaned it on the murdered man's clothing before tucking it back into his belt. Sally watched it all in silence, and felt something inside her die along with the peddler. Before, she had dared hope that her husband's occasional hints that he and his brother had murdered were nothing but wild stories. Now she knew they were not.

They took the horse, the little bit of money they found on the man, and what items the other two women wanted. Sally herself had lost her desire for any of the poor peddler's trinkets. What they didn't take they left alongside the trail with the peddler's corpse. They made only the most cursory effort to hide their victim with brush, sticks, and leaves, then went on, crossing the Cumberland River at its famous ford while Micajah and Wiley cheerfully congratulated themselves at having performed a clever crime indeed.

They headed on up the road. Before long they overtook two other travelers, well-dressed and riding excellent horses, and made themselves known to them in a pleasant manner. The two travelers, initially wary, soon warmed to the jovial conversation. They told the Harpes their names were Paca and Bates and they came from Maryland. They were on their way to Stanford, the former Logan's Station. Micajah Harpe told them that his party's destination was the same. Might they travel together? They would be proud to travel in the company of two obviously respectable, well-dressed men, and that night they could all share the same camp for the sake of safety. There were dangerous Indians in this country, folks were saying.

Paca and Bates accepted the offer, and on they went, conversation gradually wearing away any lingering caution the Marylanders might have. It began to grow dark, and Micajah said they had best find a good campsite. Paca and Bates could help, he suggested, in that he had poor vision at dusk and they might have better fortune at spotting a place.

Sally knew what would happen and wished she had the courage to warn the pair. But to do so would be to risk death herself, and she held a silence she knew was sinful, but which she dared not break.

When Paca and Bates moved out ahead of the rest, the Harpes raised their rifles and shot both men at once. Bates took the ball through the head and died instantly, while Paca was hit in the back of the neck and continued to move after he hit the ground. The terrified horses reared and nickered and ran on ahead into the dusk.

"Run get them horses, Wiley!" Micajah ordered. "I don't

want to lose them!" He turned back toward the women, who were walking some twenty feet behind. "Good shooting, eh? What do you think of your men? Fine shots we are!"

With Wiley off retrieving the spooked horses, Micajah dismounted—he had been riding Peyton's horse—and walked casually over to the victims. Bates was dead, but Paca continued to move and seemed to be trying to get up. Micajah kicked him back down, then knelt and rolled him over.

"Still kicking, are you?" He drew out his belt axe and brought it down, and Paca moved no more.

Wiley came back, leading the horses. "Dead?"

"They are now."

"Let's see what's in their pockets."

They found a little gold and silver, along with paper money, continental issue. The paper money was nearly worthless, but the silver and gold was fine booty.

"Let's strip off their clothes," Wiley said. "I believe I could wear this Paca fellow's duds, and I need 'em. Mine are near tatters."

They removed the clothes from the limp bodies, taking care to avoid getting blood on them. Paca's clothing did fit Wiley, and he pranced about in his new outfit, crowing like a rooster and kicking up his feet. Micajah put on the clothes of Bates, a bigger man than Paca had been, and seemed equally pleased. All the while the women stood by, watching silently, their pregnant bellies bulging under their own ragged dresses.

Micajah laughed. "Take a look at me, Susanna! Don't I look like the handsome gentleman! What do you think of me now?"

"You look real purty," Susanna replied. Sally hung her head, letting her hair fall down on either side of her face, hiding her momentarily from a world that was becoming too terrible to accept.

"Purty I am! And take a look at them horses—we can all ride now. Five good horses, and peddler wares for you women—we're rich folk!"

Wiley crowed again in jubilant agreement, and danced a little jig around the corpses.

The Harpes celebrated their good fortune only a few minutes, then dragged the bodies a short way into the woods and covered them with leaves. Then they returned to the road and all mounted and rode ahead into the darkness until they found a good stream. There they made camp and cooked their supper. Sally did not want to eat, but Wiley forced her.

She felt her unborn baby kick within her while she filled her stomach with food she could not even taste, and wondered what kind of person this child would be, being conceived by the seed of a Harpe.

CHAPTER 16

Clardy Tyler was past sickness by the next afternoon and set about through labor to pay Farris for his aid and lodging. Ironically, the work was one of the tasks Clardy hated most—notching logs. Farris had dragged in a huge pile of straight poplar logs to make the structure, but none were notched. Clardy counted himself lucky that Farris wasn't interested in hewing and squaring the logs, planning to leave them round and barked and joined with simple saddle notches. Had the building been for human occupancy, he probably would have set higher standards and Clardy would have faced a harder job.

Clardy grumbled to himself about the work, yet secretly took a certain pleasure in it. It gave him a place and purpose, if only for a brief time. Freedom, he discovered, wasn't all that enjoyable when it meant freedom from purpose.

Clardy spent one more night, then another half day at labor, and Farris declared himself satisfied. "You are a fine worker, Clardy, and any debt you had is paid. Where is it you are bound?"

Clardy was embarrassed to admit he had no real destination.

"I've got kin up the road a ways," he lied. "Up about Harrodsburg. They're expecting me.

"I may know them. Who are they?"

Clardy almost panicked. "Uh . . . they're more Tylers. John Tyler. Has a wife named Mary." The names were fictional.

"Don't believe I know them."

"They keep to themselves."

Farris, like Peyton before him, seemed to delight in generosity, and gave Clardy a small supply of food for the road. "Compensation for difficulties," he explained. Clardy rode off feeling grateful, reflecting that he had been twice blessed to encounter goodness along this road. Goodness . . . far different than the criminal ambitions he had harbored.

It gave him something to think about.

He wished there really were a John and Mary Tyler waiting up the road to give him a home and honest means of making a living. He would drop his criminal ambitions in a moment if that were true. But no one waited, and Farris's food would last only a little while. After that he would have to find other means of keeping himself fed. He couldn't forever count on a good-hearted Peyton or Farris showing up at just the right time.

Reluctantly, Clardy decided that he would have to try his hand at robbery again, and not lose his nerve as he had with Peyton. Goodness and honesty might work for some folks, but not for him. He was, after all, the "bad" Tyler, the Hiram Tyler grandson everyone always expected to come to a bad end. And a man always had to live up to expectations.

He passed through Crab Orchard, seeing nothing there to hold him. Ahead lay the old Logan's Station, renamed Stanford. By now Clardy's doubts about his criminal plans had been battered into submission by a stern inner lecture. He had reminded himself that a man in no situation to make a living could only *take* his living. This was no time to suddenly develop a moral code or to get soft and sentimental about goodness and kindness. Maybe taking on a life of crime was an odd dream, but it was *his* dream, hang it all, and he would not yet throw it aside.

He made up his mind that before he reached Stanford he would prove to himself once and for all that he *could* actually go through with a robbery. The earlier failure with Peyton had been a mere case of first-time nervousness. It would be different this time.

But when he found himself crouched by the roadway, hidden among the trees, hearing the approach of a rider along the road, the situation didn't *feel* any different. It had been just like this when he waited for Peyton, the same posture, the same nervous, jittery feeling, the same dryness of mouth.

All the same, he would give it his best try. Licking his lips, he readied himself. The rider was drawing closer, closer . . . *now*!

Clardy lunged out of the brush, ready to thrust his rifle into the face of the horseman and demand that he halt or die. In fast motion he saw everything in a rush—the startled rider, the rearing horse, the long barrel of his rifle probing out before him—then the ground rushed up and slammed him so hard the wind was knocked out of his lungs and refused to be drawn in again.

He lay there, trying to regain his breath, trying to comprehend the absurd, humiliating fact that he had just tripped over a root and fallen flat on the ground before the man he intended to rob.

The rider settled his frightened horse. "Boy, what the devil are you doing down there?"

Clardy rolled over and tried to gasp in air, but still it wouldn't come. He felt childish, idiotic, and now the natural panic that comes with the inability to breathe began to grip him. He pushed up to his feet and suddenly found his breath again. He inhaled in a loud, painful gasp.

"Answer me, boy: What is this all about?"

Clardy looked up at the man and found himself eye-to-eye with the dark muzzle hole of a flintlock pistol. The man, a tall, lean, sun-browned, gray-haired frontiersman with a fringed hunting coat, a dully gleaming dead left eye, and a long scar down the left side of his face, was squinting his single good eye and looking very dangerous.

"I'm . . . I'm . . ." Clardy couldn't continue until he had gasped some more. "I'm . . . sorry . . . didn't mean to . . . spook you."

"Then why the devil are you hiding in the brush and leaping out with a rifle?"

"I was . . ." Clardy took advantage of the gaps brought on by his labored breathing to try to drum up a story. "I was . . . robbed on back up the road. I . . . run ahead through the woods up to here . . . and thought you was the man who robbed me. I was just . . . trying to get back what was took from me."

The man didn't lower the pistol. "So you thought I was your thief, did you?"

"Yes."

"And you didn't pause long enough even to take a look at the man you was a-pouncing, to make sure you had the right one?"

"I'm sorry. I was worked up."

Clardy had never before seen one eye give such an intense, scrutinizing stare. He wondered what would happen next.

He was relieved when the man lowered the pistol. "What was took from you?" he asked.

"All my money. And a pistol I had."

"What about your horse?"

"It's back yonder in the trees."

"So this thief, he didn't take your horse, nor your rifle. Right peculiarish robber, seems to me."

Clardy clamped his mouth shut and hoped he didn't look too scared. His tale hadn't been so clever after all.

The man simply looked at Clardy a few moments, brows slightly knit. "Young man, the truth is I believe that the only man among us who's faced a thief today is me. Am I right?"

Clardy's heart beat faster. "No sir. If you're trying to say . . . no sir. That ain't right."

"If you was robbed by this here thief so short a spell ago that you just now run through the woods to get here, it seems peculiarish that I didn't run 'cross the very event while it was happening. Or maybe even get robbed myself."

"Well . . . I reckon odd things happen."

"World's full of them, son. Full of them. Tell you what— don't think I don't trust you or nothing, but I'm feeling a mite aversional to riding on and leaving my back turned toward you with you having that rifle in hand. Step up here closer a moment, boy."

Clardy obeyed reflexively. This man possessed the kind of dominating, confident air that put him at the top of the situation almost from the outset.

"Hold up that rifle where I can see it good."

Again Clardy obeyed, feeling very distressed. His career as a highway robber was off to the worst of starts. Two failures, the second worse than the first!

The man's hand flashed out, grasped the rifle by the barrel, and with a twist and pull yanked it from Clardy's grip. It happened so quickly that all Clardy could do was stand gaping in surprise.

"Now you'll get to stretch your legs a mite," the man said. "Get to walking, right in front of my horse here. You veer to one side or the other or try to run off, I'll shoot you dead with your own rifle—providing you had the sense to load it right, and I ain't at all sure you would."

"But my horse—it's back there in the woods. I don't want to leave it."

"We all have to do things in life we don't want to do, boy. I reckon you'd have took my horse without a blink. 'Whoso diggeth a pit shall fall therein, and he that rolleth a stone, it will return upon him.' What's your name, anyhow?"

"Clardy Tyler." He winced, feeling foolish for having given his real name and ashamed that this man had him so cowed.

"Get them feet a-stepping, Mr. Tyler. I'll be right behind."

"I don't want to lose that horse!"

" 'So shall poverty come as one that traveleth, and thy want as an armed man.' The armed man now being me. Now get them legs to churning."

Wearily Clardy trudged on, making sure his steps were precisely straight and that he looked directly in front of him. He feared that otherwise the man on the horse would shoot him. The time or two that he had made even the slightest move that might look like an attempt to run, the man had whistled through his teeth at him in dire warning.

They rounded a curve and Clardy tripped over a rock, almost falling. The man laughed. "You're the clumsiest one bumstumble I ever did see, Mr. Tyler."

Clardy blushed and was happy his back was turned so his captor couldn't see it. He grew so angry at himself for the mess he had made of all this, and at his captor for making him abandon his horse and goods, that he couldn't restrain his tongue. "It was just a rock or something. I didn't see it. Could have happened to anybody."

" 'The way of the wicked is as darkness; they know not at what they stumble.' That's you, boy—the wicked. That's why you're stumbling. Me, I'm a good man. I don't go robbing folks on the public roadways. I'm righteous. You don't see me stumbling down the road with a rifle at my back, do you? I'm upright here in the saddle. 'For the upright shall dwell in the land, and the perfect shall remain in it.' You see? It's all right there in the Proverbs."

"Don't go spewing Bible at me," Clardy said. "I want to get preached at, I'll go to meeting."

"Somebody needs to preach at you, boy. 'Pears to me the task has been neglected, or else you wouldn't be out robbing on the highways . . . or trying to, at least. 'My son, hear the instruction of thy father, and forsake not the law of thy mother.' Didn't your folks raise you right?"

"I got no folks but a meal-mouthed old grandpap who raised me at the end of a hickory stick after my folks died."

"Didn't your grandpap tell you it ain't right to steal whilst he was using that hickory stick?"

"I didn't steal nothing. It was me who was stole from! I told you: a robber took some of my things, and I thought you was him, and that's the only reason I came at you out of the woods."

"You're a liar, boy, a liar if ever I seen one! 'Lying lips are an abomination to the Lord, but they that deal truly are his delight.' "

"Who are you, anyway? You some kind of preacher or something?"

"My name, son, is Isaac Ford, and I am no preacher, no sir. Just a man with an ear inclined toward wisdom and a heart toward righteousness. And I don't take well to bum-stumbles trying to rob me of what's mine."

"You ain't said yet what you're going to do with me."

"When we reach Stanford, I might turn you over to the authorities of the law. Or I might let you go free so you can head back and fetch that horse you're so deuced worried about. Or I might shoot you."

"Shoot me? You don't mean that, do you?"

The man laughed.

"You don't mean it—you tell me you don't mean it!"

"Don't be getting your hackles up, boy! Whatever I do to you, it'll be the righteous thing."

"You shoot me, that'll make you a murderer."

"That's right. It'll be an awful thing, being a murderer. It'll be hard for me to live with. But not nearly so hard as it'd be for you, having to live with being dead." He laughed loudly. Clardy didn't think it was funny at all.

Stanford had sprung up around one of the older settlements of Kentucky, established as a frontier station by Colonel Ben Logan. In its earlier days it had seen its share of Indian troubles, deprivation, and struggles to exist, but now the place had an established, civilized look to it. There was law and order here, with a jail and courthouse, and when Clardy caught sight of the village, he had the odd hope that he would have the chance to become familiar with the jail, the apparent alternative being death at the hands of this proverb-spouting character named Isaac Ford.

They reached the boundary of the town. "Well, boy, we're here," Ford said.

Clardy turned and faced him. "What will happen now?"

"Well, seems to me the best thing you can do is saunter back the way we came. Find that horse of yours and head on."

"You're letting me go?"

"I am. I've plumb lost the mood for shooting bum-stumbles."

"You walked me all the way here just to set me free?"

"You don't like that notion?"

"I like it, I like it. I don't understand why you're doing it, that's all."

"Mercy, boy. Pure and simple mercy."

"Well . . . thank you. I'm grateful."

Ford's demeanor became more solemn. "Mr. Tyler, there was a time when I was a bit like my myself. Poor, alone . . . and one time I done the very thing you tried to do today. And that one time a man showed me the same mercy I'm showing you now. After that I didn't steal no more. Now you do the same."

"I will, sir. I'll not try to steal another thing from now till the day I die." Overwhelmed with gratitude, Clardy meant it.

"That's good." Ford dumped the powder out of Clardy's rifle pan. "Here's your rifle. Off with you now."

Clardy headed back down the road on the run, realizing how close a call he had just experienced. For the moment he forgot his poverty and lack of prospects. All he cared about was that he was free.

His horse was where he left it. Mounting, he rode back up the road toward Stanford. He felt humbled and small.

By the time he reached the town again, snow was falling. He

looked around for Ford but did not see him. He ate some of the food remaining in his saddlebags and went on through the town, wondering how much snow there would be.

The farther he went, the harder the snow fell. It had piled up to seven inches by dusk, and the heavy clouds and continuing precipitation grew worrisome. He could find shelter in the woods somewhere and make it through the storm, but he despised such trials.

Darkness came and the storm became a full-scale blizzard. Flakes struck hard against his face, smarting like a rain of flint. His coat was inadequate to keep him warm, and the driving wind made the brim of his hat flap. His ears grew cold, began to hurt, then lost all feeling.

I should have stayed in Stanford. I'll freeze out here.

He began to look for shelter, natural or otherwise. But this stretch of road was lonely. He saw nothing. He was beginning to consider such desperate measures as killing his horse and huddling for warmth against its body when through the darkness he saw a flicker of light, very faint.

He headed for it, praying it would be a cabin and that whoever was in it would be kind enough to let a poor suffering traveler in.

It *was* a cabin! Clardy headed for it, huddling in his coat. When he dismounted, he discovered that his feet were numb and he could hardly stand. He staggered to the cabin, hammered on the door, then called through it.

"Shelter! A traveler needing shelter . . ."

He heard movement inside, then the sound of the latch bar being lifted. When the door swung open, Clardy found himself looking into one of the most lovely young female faces he had ever seen. There were others in the room behind her, but this beautiful visage was so distracting, even to a nearly frozen man, that he didn't even glance at them.

"I'm nigh froze," he said through chattering teeth. "If you could spare some shelter, this traveler would be mighty grateful."

"Come in, come in before you fall down!" the young woman said, stepping aside. She turned to a boy of about twelve who stood just behind her. "John, you can see to the horse. Get it into the stable and feed it."

The boy threw on a coat and hat and obediently plunged out

into the snow. Clardy hadn't taken his eyes off the young woman. Couldn't, it seemed. He was entranced.

"She's a fine young lady, eh, Mr. Tyler?"

The man's voice caused Clardy to turn on his frozen feet so quickly that he staggered. Across the room the speaker rose from a chair near the fire, grinning. Clardy's expression did not change, but it was only because his face was too frozen to move. In fact he was quite shaken to see who the man was.

"Still the bum-stumble, I see! Come over here by the blaze, Mr. Tyler. I'm glad to know that you found my company so pleasing that you've come for more of it. I didn't figure to see you, but you're welcome in my home. That's right, young man, I'll not turn you away. No man should have to be out in such fearsome weather. That's my daughter Dulciana who let you in. The boy seeing to your beast is my boy John, and this here is my wife, Amy."

"Pleased to meet you folks," Clardy mumbled, staggered to realize that of all places fate might have led him, it had chosen the home of Isaac Ford. "I'm grateful for the shelter."

Isaac Ford came to him and put a hand on his shoulder. "Folks tend to be kind, if a man just comes asking, as you did. When he comes demanding, or trying to steal, that's when the trouble comes. But there'll be no trouble tonight. Just a warm fire and good food. From the look of you, you'll be getting both just in time. But I think you'll be fine, if your toes ain't so froze that they mortify."

CHAPTER 17

Many miles behind his brother, Thias began building his shelter at the first sign the storm was going to develop into a blizzard. He knew woods and weather, how to read the signs. By the time the worst of the snowstorm hit, his horse was secured in a protective thicket and he himself was nearby, securely lodged inside a thick cocoon of leaves heaped onto a frame made with sticks he had laid up against a long, arching branch that thrust out from the trunk of a fallen tree. He left only enough space inside to accommodate his body, his rifle, and what little baggage he carried. The shelter was accessible by a single opening just big enough for him to wriggle into backward. Once inside, he covered the entrance hole with a plug door he had made by bending a flexible branch into a circle. He bound it so it held the shape, wove in sticks, wicker-style, and stuffed the frame with leaves.

Thias performed the work sadly, thinking back on how his grandfather had taught him to build such shelters when he was just a boy and they had hunted together frequently. Hard to believe that Hiram Tyler was dead; Thias still couldn't get a grasp on the fact of it. It still seemed, and probably would seem for a long time yet, that he should be able to go back home and find the old man busily cussing Clardy for whatever his latest offense of negligence was.

Clardy. Thias wondered if he would be able to find him, wondered if it made sense to be going to all this trouble to fulfill a dying old man's last request. Kentucky was a vast place, and Clardy had a good lead on him. Perhaps it would be more sensible to let Clardy go his way in the hope that one day he would come home to the farm and . . .

But no. Once again Thias reminded himself that there was no farm left to come home to. He had sold it. Maybe that had been a mistake. It was too late to think about that now. His course was set. He had pledged to find Clardy, and could do nothing else. Clardy had to know that his grandfather was dead, that the Harpe brothers he feared were no longer about Knoxville. What was more, he had money coming to him from the sale of the farm, money nestled at the moment at Thias's feet, inside one of his saddlebags. What could he do but go on?

He nibbled on a biscuit from his packs and did his best to get comfortable inside his shelter. Here and there the wind managed to find its way through the three-foot-thick leaf covering, and he fidgeted about, rearranging leaves here and there to plug the holes until at last his shelter was as well-insulated as he could make it. Ideally, he would have built a fire outside, with a screen to throw back the heat toward the door, but the heavy snowfall would make the fire hard to keep going. His trapped body heat would have to be sufficient for tonight.

He slept, and dreamed he was a boy again, out hunting with his grandfather.

He opened his eyes abruptly, startled without knowing why. The muted little rays of light stabbing in here and there in the shelter told him that night had passed and the sun was up. He sat up as far as the low roof would let him and listened, trying to hear again whatever it was that had roused him.

"Oh, lordy, lordy, oh help me, somebody. . . ."

Thias gently pushed open the plug door; snow fell in. He peered out over a thickly blanketed white landscape. He heard the voice again—"Lordy, oh my lordy"—and felt very disturbed.

He knew that voice; at the least, he had heard it before.

He drew up his rifle and edged out a little bit so that his head poked out of the door. Looking around, he spotted a man running wildly through the snow, out on the road about a hundred feet away. The man stopped, looking about as if maybe he sensed another person nearby. "Help me!" he yelled. "Somebody help me—Jack's under the tree, he's caught bad!"

Merciful heaven, Thias thought, that's Billy French! He's full-grown now, but that's none other than old Billy himself, sure as the world!

He pushed his way out of the shelter and came to his feet, bolstering his stiff, cold form up with his rifle. "Billy!" he shouted.

The man on the road yelled in fright and turned with a jerk toward Thias.

"Is that . . . it *is*! Thias Tyler, it is you, ain't it?"

"Aye, Billy, aye. What's the matter?"

"Thias, what are you doing out . . . never mind it—come quick, Thias! It's right atop Jack, and he's caught! Come quick—I can't get him out from under it alone, and I'm afraid he'll die!"

Confused, cold, and still muddled with sleepiness, Thias plunged as fast as he could through the thick snow and joined Billy French on the road. "Billy, I'd heard you might be dead," he said.

"I ain't dead, Thias, but Jack will be if we don't pull him free. You're a godsend, yes you are! Come with me, fast!"

A godsend, French had called him. Ironic words. As he hurried along beside the thickly built, red-bearded man, Thias recalled the time when French had been no less than a godsend himself.

The horrifying incident was yet perfectly vivid in Thias's memory. Clardy and Thias had been twelve and thirteen years old, respectively. They had been swimming in a swimming hole they had created by damming part of Beaver Creek, and like typical boys, had been careless. Clardy dared Thias to dive into the hole from an overhanging limb, and Thias did it, barely missing smashing his skull on a submerged log in the process. Victorious, he had risen from the water and dared Clardy to do the same, and together he and Clardy climbed back out onto the limb, and Clardy had dived headlong. He did not miss the submerged log. His head smacked against it sharply, and his limp form floated out in the swimming hole facedown. . . .

And Thias had frozen. Upon the branch, he stared in horror at his brother's unmoving form. His mind told him to leap in and drag him out, but his body didn't respond. He perched there, gaping like a fool. . . .

Billy French, at that time a neighbor, had come along and seen Clardy in the water. He plunged in fully clothed and dragged him out. Clardy's head was broken and bleeding. As Thias watched, French turned Clardy over, drained the water from his lungs, and pounded on his chest until the breathing started. The next thing Thias knew, French was dragging *him* out of the water, too. He had fainted up there on the branch and fallen deadweight into the swimming hole, fortunately missing for a second time the log that injured Clardy.

He and Clardy had come through it alive and without permanent injury, thanks to Billy French. From that day until the time some years later when young French and his widower father moved away from Beaver Creek up to the valley of the Powell River, Thias had been Billy French's staunchest defender. Billy had always been an odd fellow who behaved in bizarre ways, and he suffered many taunts from other boys in the region. Many was the time that Thias's fists had intervened to punish those who dared torment Billy French in his presence. Billy had saved his and Clardy's lives, and Thias considered him a hero.

Billy led him to a little camp about a half mile from Thias's own shelter. The situation at once became clear.

Billy and a partner had camped in a grove of evergreens, taking refuge from the snow beneath the overhanging boughs. Their campfire still smoldered nearby. One of the older trees had become overladen with snow and fallen, and Billy's partner had been caught beneath it. All that was visible of him at the moment was his left shoulder and head. The rest of him was firmly lodged beneath the heavy fallen tree.

"I couldn't lift it alone, Thias. I had to find help. We'd seen fresh tracks all along the road, so I knew somebody was ahead somewhere. I ran calling and looking—I'm mighty glad it was you, Thias. Help me now—we've got to get this tree off before it crushes the life from him."

Thias was surprised when the man under the tree spoke in a gruff tone. "I ain't dying. Just stuck. That's all."

"Well, sir, we'll get you free," Thias replied.

It took a monumental effort, but with Thias and French pushing together, they managed to move the heavy tree far enough for the man to pull his legs free and then roll clear.

They let the tree fall back into place, then stood catching their breath.

The formerly trapped man stood, wincing, and moved his legs about carefully, then with more vigor. "Nothing busted," he announced.

"That's good," Thias said.

"You saved his life, Thias," French said. "Just like me saving you back at the swimming hole years ago. You remember that, don't you?"

"I surely do. I'm still as grateful to you today as ever."

"You two know each other?" the third man said.

Billy French told the story, giving a few details differently than Thias recalled them and emphasizing Thias's fainting and inability to help his own brother a little more than Thias would have liked, but all in all he told the story correctly. Listening to French talk was interesting to Thias—he was the same old Billy French, eager, verbose, vaguely childish, still seeing the world in very simple terms.

The other man introduced himself as Jack Waller, "man of the road." Thias took that to mean he had no fixed place of residence. Shaking Waller's hand, he said, "I'm Thias Tyler. I live . . . I *did* live in the Beaver Creek valley, near Knoxville. I reckon I'm a man of the road myself now."

"You've left Beaver Creek?" Billy French asked.

"Yes. I sold the farm. My grandpap died just a few days back, Billy."

"I'm sorry to hear it. My daddy, he died, too. But he's still with me."

Thias wasn't sure what that latter comment meant. He didn't ask.

"Sold your farm, you say?" Waller asked.

"Yes . . . sold it and put the money in the hands of an attorney to hold in trust for me and my brother." He added the latter because he realized that it wouldn't do to have a stranger knowing he was actually carrying money in his saddlebags— saddlebags even now unguarded back in his shelter, he realized.

"I've had a bit of money in my own time," Waller said. "I've never been good at keeping it, though."

"Aye, yes." Thias wasn't comfortable with this line of talk. Maybe "man of the road" meant more than he thought. He recalled Clardy's ambitions about becoming a highwayman, and wondered if Waller was of that ilk himself.

"I'm sorry to hear your father is gone," Thias said to French to shift the subject. "He was a good man, and I know you were right close to him." The latter was an understatement. Billy French had worshipped his father in his boyhood days. Brackston French had been no more than a poor dirt farmer, but the motherless Billy, in his simple devotion, had always talked about him like he was the bravest, wisest, greatest man who ever lived.

"Billy carries his father's skull around with him now," Waller said.

"What?"

"His father's skull—Billy carries it around with him. Keeps it in his saddlebag and sticks a pipeful of tobacco in its mouth after supper every night."

Thias was stunned, and wondered if Waller was joking.

"That's what I meant when I said he's still with me," French said happily. "Everywhere I go, there's Daddy in the saddle-bag."

"He's foolish in the mind," Waller explained. "No sense at all. I guess you already knew that, though."

"Aye ... well, I wouldn't want to say that. . . ." Thias realized he was staring at French. His father's skull in a saddle-bag—that went well beyond Billy's oddest boyhood behaviors. That was downright strange.

"I reckon I'll get back to my own camp," Thias said.

"Don't go off, Thias," French implored. "Stay with us. Eat some victuals."

"I've got traveling to do, Billy. I'm trying to find Clardy. He headed up this way sometime back, and I need to find him and tell him that Grandpap is dead."

"You're traveling into Kentucky?"

"Yes."

"We are, too! We're going all the way to the Ohio River."

"Are you?"

"Jack knows some people up there who he says we'll be working with."

"That right? Well, good fortune to you both. But I'd still best be getting on my way . . ."

"You can fetch your things and come on back, can't you?"

Waller said. "The fact is, Mr. Tyler, that it ain't safe for a man to travel alone in this country."

"That's right," French chimed in. "There's robbers and such."

"Well, I know there are, but—"

"No need to talk more, Mr. Tyler. You'll be riding with us. It's the only sensible way."

Thias's instincts were against this. Waller was a stranger, and something about him put Thias on warning, and Billy French, though familiar and seemingly harmless enough, wasn't the traveling companion Thias would have chosen. Anyone who carried his dead father's skull around in a saddlebag had to be firing with a loose flint. But even so, Waller was right about the dangers of traveling alone. It was common for folk to camp out around the Cumberland Gap just to await other travelers they could join up with for the journey through the dangerous, forested "desert" country between the gap and the first real settlements of Kentucky.

Thias sighed to himself and nodded. "Thank you, men. I'll go fetch my things. And Mr. Waller, since we're to be traveling partners, just call me Thias."

"And you can call me Jack. I'll be pleased to have you with us. Mighty pleased."

The snow, though deep, didn't linger. The day warmed considerably and cleared, and by afternoon most of the precipitation had melted any place the sun could reach it. By day's end the whiteness still lingered beneath the trees and under the shade of hills and bluffs, but the road had turned to mud that sucked at the hooves of Thias's horse. Waller and French had no horses, so Thias kindly let them take turns riding his throughout the day. It was a common custom of the road to share rides in such situations, but he hadn't been able to help but feel a little resentful at having to give up his mount two-thirds of the time. He reminded himself all day that at least he was safer in the company of others—yet he didn't feel safer. He didn't trust the shifty-eyed, rat-faced Waller at all.

Waller had shot a deer earlier in the day and carved away the tenderloins. About sunset they stopped and camped, roasting the meat on a big fire and enjoying it greatly. With a nicely full belly, Thias had begun feeling better about the overall situation—and then Billy French had brought out his father's skull.

Now Thias was staring at the astonishing sight of a yellow-white, fleshless skull sitting on a log with a smoking corncob pipe stuck between its bony jaws. The oddest thing of all was knowing that this skull had once been inside the fleshy head of Brackston French, a man he had known. It was difficult to connect the smoking skull with his memories of Brackston until he noted the bottom row of teeth, featuring a familiar gap at the front. Thias had seen that very gap many a time when Brackston had grinned back in the old days. It surely was his very skull.

Thias wondered how French had actually wound up with his father's skull. Had Brackston died by getting his head cut off somehow? Or had Billy French beheaded the man after he was dead? Had he boiled off the flesh and . . . ? He tried not to think about it.

"Daddy always likes his pipe after supper," French said. "Sometimes he smokes two or three of 'em."

"Waste of good tobacco," Waller said. "But what can you say to a fool?"

Thias wondered how Waller and French had come together, and why Waller kept French around if he considered him so foolish. It was hard to account for people's ways sometimes.

"How'd your grandpap die, Thias?" French asked.

"Apoplexy, best I could tell." His curiosity got the best of him. "What killed your daddy?"

"He got sick. Don't know what kind of sick. Just sick."

"Oh."

"Critters dug up the grave after 'bout a year and scattered the bones. Billy found the head and kept it." This information came from Waller.

"It seemed the right thing to do for my dear father," French said piously.

"Oh." Thias marveled anew at the strangeness of Billy French.

"Yes sir, I've put up with a lot from Billy's foolishness these past months," Waller said, digging out a pipe of his own, which he slowly filled from the same tobacco pouch that had stoked Backston French's pipe. "But he's a good boy, and he minds me. Does what I tell him."

"I work for Jack now," French said proudly.

"What kind of work?"

French started to speak, but Waller cut in quickly, "Any kind of work needs doing. Anything we can find."

Silence reigned in the camp for the next minute or so. Waller puffed his pipe. Thias warmed his hands near the fire, and smoke curled up through the skull of the late Brackston French.

"Wise of you, leaving that money of yours with a lawyer," Waller said. "Some folks, they'd just pack it in their bags and carry it with them."

"I'd never take such a risk," Thias said, casting a glance toward his saddlebags and determining to keep a close eye on them as long as he was in company with Waller.

" 'Course, I suppose you got some money on you. Traveling money."

"Almost none. I know this is a dangerous road." He was beginning to wish he really had left his money in safekeeping back in Knoxville.

"Reckon you'll be able to find that brother of yourn?" Waller asked.

"I'll do my best."

"His brother is named Clardy," French contributed. "He's a twin of Thias."

"No, Billy, we ain't twins. There's a year's difference in our ages. We just look a lot alike, that's all."

"I had a brother of my own," Waller said. "He's dead now."

"They hung him," French said.

"Shut up about that," Waller snapped, suddenly venemous in manner. "That's nothing for you to wag your fool's tongue about."

Billy French ducked his head and scooted closer to the pipe-holding skull. He reached out a hand and caressed it, like a scolded child seeking comfort.

"Pay him no heed," Waller said. "A fool is hard to tolerate and spouts nonsense."

Waller's abusive talk made Thias feel protective of French. "He'll always be a fellow I look up to," he said. "I'd probably be dead if Billy hadn't saved me that day at the swimming hole, and Clardy, too."

Billy French smiled at Thias. Thias winked and smiled back.

"A fool is useful sometimes, no question about it," Waller said. "Lord knows that Billy is often very useful to me."

"I work for Jack," French said again. "I do what he tells me."

That night, Thias slept very lightly, with his saddlebags tucked beneath his head and his rifle very close at hand.

* * *

Sally Harpe heard Wiley's approach and lifted her head to watch as he entered the camp. My husband, she thought. My husband is a murderer. He didn't seem like her husband now. He had become a stranger.

Micajah Harpe left the fireside and walked out to meet his brother.

"Was I right?"

"Yep. There's a camp back yonder. It was their fire you seen."

"How many?"

"Three of 'em, camped together, biggest portion of a mile back behind us."

"Men?"

"All of them."

"Packhorse or anything?"

"Just one horse, for riding. They didn't 'pear to have much on them from what I could see."

They are thinking of robbing again, Sally thought. Perhaps killing again. I don't want them to kill anyone else.

Micajah scratched his beard, thinking. "I'm inclined to let them be."

Sally closed her eyes, welcoming those words.

Wiley was clearly disappointed. "I believe we could deal with them easy, Micajah."

"There's three of them. That makes it a question in my mind. More danger with three."

"Hell, Micajah, we can best them!"

Micajah thought some more. "No. Too much danger. Not worth it for only one horse. We don't need another horse now no ways."

"I still believe we could take them."

"No. I've made up my mind. There'll be easier pickings on this road. We'll let them be."

Wiley frowned. "I trudged a mile in and a mile out just for a look, and no takings?"

"Let it be, brother. Like I said, there'll be easier pickings. We're doing well enough as it is. Let them be."

Wiley argued no more. He strode off to the fire and warmed himself, fuming and muttering beneath his breath. Micajah Harpe stood off by himself, thinking.

After a few minutes Wiley came to Sally's side and sat down. "How are you, sweet thing? You staying warm enough here in the cold?"

"Yes." She did not look at him and did not want to talk.

"What's the matter with you?"

"Nothing."

"You're acting frettish." He touched her arm. "Sweet thing, you're trembling!"

"It's cold."

"You said you was warm enough."

"I am. But it's still cold." *Go away. Leave me be.* She wished she dared do more than think the words.

"If you're cold, I know a good way to warm you up." He winked.

"Don't want to right now."

"I do." He touched her cheek and smiled.

"Not now, Wiley."

"Yes, now." He grabbed her and pushed her back.

She closed her eyes and as best she could shut off her mind. He was rough and harsh and had no shame; the presence of the others would not deter him from what he wanted. She turned her face away and willed herself to endure, wishing she had never met and married Wiley Harpe, wishing she were still back in her girlhood home, where people were good and kind. She wished she could run away and return to her family, but Wiley would certainly kill her if she tried.

As she lay beside him later that night, hearing him snore and feeling his gnarly form pushing up against her, she touched her belly and thought of her unborn baby. I'll make it better for you, somehow, she pledged in her mind. I'll not let them hurt you. I promise. A few moments later she fell asleep, still thinking about her child. *Her* child. She would think of it that way from now on. Her child and hers alone. Not his, not ever.

CHAPTER 18

Waller was taking his turn at riding, leaving his two fellow travelers afoot, when Thias saw the face in the forest the next morning.

Or he thought he saw a face. It was just a glimpse, a flash that was there one moment, gone the next, as if the person it belonged to had ducked out of sight when he saw he was detected. Thias stopped in his tracks, staring, wondering if he had imagined it.

"What's wrong, Thias?" French asked.

"I thought . . . nothing. Nothing. Just thought I saw something."

"Where?"

"Yonder in the woods."

"I don't see nothing."

"Neither do I, now. It was a mistake, most likely."

But he was unsettled as he went on. The face he had seen, or thought he'd seen, appeared to be that of Wiley Harpe.

The Harpes . . . here? It was possible. They had fled the Knoxville area, so they could have headed toward Kentucky. And if so, Thias thought, he would have been almost on their heels. He had traveled fast. He could have overtaken them.

But he hoped he had merely imagined seeing Wiley Harpe's face. As he and his companions traveled farther, it became easier to convince himself that such was the case. He hadn't slept well the prior night, was tired from the trail anyway, and worried about his missing brother, who happened to be on the run from the Harpes. And there was the fact he himself had gone through a row with Wiley Harpe on the street in Knoxville. If his weary and overwrought mind was going to play tricks on him by showing him phantom faces in the forest, was it any surprise the face of Wiley Harpe would be one of them? He was tired and worried, that was all. He really had just imagined the face.

Even an imagined face, however, reminded him that this was dangerous country indeed. No one could know what, or who, hid in the forests of the Dark and Bloody Ground.

He decided he was glad not to be traveling alone, even if his company was no better than a rat-raced "man of the road" and a fool who carried his father's skull around in a bag.

Wiley Harpe spoke intensely, eyes narrowed. "It was him, Micajah. It was one of them Tylers! Him and two others, passing right down the road!"

"Which one? Clardy, or the one you had that tangle with?"

"I couldn't tell. I only seen him a few moments, through the trees. And them two look so damn much alike."

"You didn't see it was a Tyler last night, spying in their camp?"

"No. I didn't have a clear look at them then."

Micajah's eyes glittered. "If it is Clardy Tyler, I'd crave to get my hands on him. He didn't keep his word to us. Left us to get shut of old Cale ourselves. I'd like to remind him 'bout that."

"Let's go after them, Micajah. We'll carve him from loin to throat."

Micajah thought about it, eyes bright and eager. Wiley Harpe licked his lips, knowing his brother's hungry expression well, and sure that this time he would approve the hunt—and a hunt was all this was to Wiley Harpe. They were hunters, no different than a man stalking a deer. The only difference was the prey, and the heightened degree of devilish satisfaction that stirred in Wiley Harpe's soul when that game was brought down. To kill beasts was a pleasure—in boyhood, Wiley had done plenty of that just for the fun of it—but taking the life of a human being was more than pleasure to him. It was a sweet taste in his mouth and a soothing murmur inside his head, a murmur that whispered deliciously to him in gentle words he could not quite make out.

But again Micajah disappointed him. There were still three of them, and only two Harpes, he said. Too great a risk. Better to wait for other prey and easier.

Wiley was silent the rest of the morning. The blood lust had been stirred but left unsated. The voices in his head no longer soothed. They sounded angry. They were thirsty for blood.

They stayed in their camp a couple of hours more, Micajah lounging about, eating, smoking, and Wiley pacing and restless. Then they mounted and rode, the brothers in the lead, the heavily pregnant women slumping heavy in their saddles, riding ten paces behind in utter silence and with faces as lifeless as death masks.

"Don't go? Why not?" Thias made no effort to mask the irritation in his voice.

"That inn's a bad place," Waller replied. "Dangerous. That man that runs it, name of Farris, kills folks who stay there."

"I ain't never heard you say that before, Jack," Billy French said. "When we stayed there, he never—"

"Shut up, you babbler!" Waller snapped at French, face burning hot with sudden anger. The expression blanked away at once when he looked again at Thias. "Billy don't know what he's talking about. We've never stayed at that inn. Too dangerous."

"We *did* stay there!" French replied, growing angry himself. "And that man Farris throwed us out after you—"

Waller wheeled and shoved French with both hands, making him stagger backward and almost fall. "You sodding fool, one of these days I'll knock that empty head of yours with the blunt end of a belt axe and give you an excuse for being so deuced foolish!"

"That's enough of that!" Thias declared. He was quickly growing fed up with Waller, an untrusty man if ever he had seen one. He deplored the way Waller was treating French, too. French was unsophisticated, but probably far more honest than Waller. "Mr. Waller, is Billy telling it true? Have you been throwed out of that inn sometime past?"

"If I had, I'd hold my head high and admit it right out,"

Waller said. "Billy's mistook. That was another inn he's thinking about, back in Tennessee."

French opened his mouth; a harsh glance from Waller made him shut it again. He glowered silently.

"And he wasn't throwed out," Waller went on. "We left of our own free will when an old woman there objected to me gambling with dice."

He's a liar. I can tell it in his eyes and his voice. "I'm not sure what to think," Thias said.

Waller chuckled. "Why, you wouldn't believe that dummy over me, would you?"

"I don't know who to believe." He cast a longing glance at the inn, still a long way off. "All I know is I'd like to spend a night on a real bed, under a real roof."

"I tell you, young man, you'll not leave that inn with your packs full," Waller said. "That innkeeper is a thief."

Thias glanced at French, whose glum expression verified anew that Waller was lying and also made Thias realize that Billy was completely under the domination of his companion. "I'm inclined to take my own chances," Thias said to Waller.

"If you stay there, me and Billy will have to part ways, then. I'll not put *my* throat at risk."

A chance to be freed of Waller! Now the inn seemed even more attractive to Thias. "I thank you for your company as far as you've shared it."

"You're making a mistake," Waller replied.

"I'll take the risk," Thias said.

Waller had been on the horse. He dismounted unhappily and watched Thias climb into the saddle. "Sorry to have to take the horse," Thias said.

Waller grunted, said nothing.

Thias rode on toward the inn. French, watching him go, had a sad look.

Thias was well away from Waller and French when he heard French's voice: "No! *No*, Jack! I don't want . . ." The words became muddled and undecipherable. Thias resisted the temptation to turn around and look back at the pair.

He heard more words, more plaintive sounds from French, and then French's voice calling. "Thias, wait!"

Thias twisted his head and looked back. French was running toward him, looking very distressed. "What's wrong, Billy?"

"Thias, you'll ... you'll have to get down from there a minute."

"Billy—you're *crying*! What's wrong?"

"Thias, I'm mighty sorry ... please, you'll have to get down."

Thias was utterly bewildered. He looked back at Waller, who had dropped to a crouch in the middle of the road, hands together, fingers steepled. He nodded and smiled slightly. Thias's bewilderment only grew. He debated whether to get down or to heel his horse into a run.

"Thias, please ... if you don't, there ain't no telling what will ..." French faded out, blubbering, tears running down his face.

Despite the alarm surging inside him, Thias dismounted. Maybe something was wrong with French. Maybe he needed help. "Billy, what's wrong with you?"

"I'm sorry, Thias, but he says I have to. I don't want to do it. You're my friend. You were always good to me."

Thias drew back. His horse shifted behind him as he backed up against its flank. Billy drew out his belt axe. Thias gaped in amazement, then turned to remount. He was too slow. The back of his head seemed to explode in a burst of pain, and light flashed before his eyes. He heard himself grunt, felt the warm, bristly bulk of his horse as his face slid down its side. He crumpled to the ground. A terrible ringing filled his ears, so loud that French's sobs sounded distant and muffled. He felt more than heard the pounding of Waller's approaching feet.

He seemed to be falling into blackness. It engulfed him, and his last half-conscious thought was that he would almost surely never emerge from it again, never again see the light, never again hear another sound.

But within moments he did hear more, and did see light, though what he heard was a flux of noise and words, and the light was muted and sporadic, spilling in between eyelids that he couldn't manage to completely open.

"... made me do it, Jack! You made me ... didn't want to hurt him .." French's voice, shaking with sobs.

"... that saddlebag, that's right ... look at it, Billy! I *knowed* he had the money with him ... all of it, take out all of it ..."

Thias vainly tried to push himself into sensibility again. He was being robbed! Even in his stunned, pain-wracked condition the thought infuriated him. Robbed—of the money from the sale of the farm, money that represented everything the Tyler family had in the world. His money, Clardy's money . . .

Thias tried to move. All he could achieve was a shudder and groan.

He heard more clearly now.

Waller: "He's still alive, Billy. You didn't hit him hard enough."

French: "I didn't want to do it, Jack. You shouldn't have told me to."

Waller: "Drag him into the woods there and kill him. Cover him over."

French: "I won't do it."

Waller: "You don't, then I will."

God, please God, help me, don't let them murder me! Thias tried again to regain full consciousness, but instead he only sank deeper into stupor. He heard more words exchanged, but could no longer make them out.

Hands grabbed him beneath the arms and pulled him up. He groaned as he felt himself being dragged along. *God, help me open my eyes! Got to see* . . . He felt something liquid and warm drop on his face. Blood?

He managed to open his eyes. Above him he saw the face of the weeping Billy French. It was French who had him, and tears, not blood, that dripped onto his face. He was being dragged into the woods, just as Waller had directed. Billy was again being obedient.

Thias's body fell back heavily. He felt an icy wet cold against his neck and the back of his head. Billy had dragged him into the brush and dropped him in snow.

"I'm sorry, Thias. I'm mighty sorry. But he's told me I got to do it."

Thias tried to speak but only groaned.

"No, Thias, don't wake up. I don't want you to see me do it."

"Billy . . ." Thias heard his own voice, a whisper. The snow he lay in was reviving him. He opened his eyes again. Billy was standing over him, belt axe in hand. "Billy . . . no."

"He told me to, Thias. I got to do it."

"You don't have to . . . no, Billy. Please . . . don't murder me."

"Don't call it murder, Thias. Don't call it that. I'm just doing what he says, that's all."

Thias tried to sit up, but the pain in his head was too much for him. He sank back down. "It is murder, Billy. Don't let that man . . . control you. Can . . . he see us here?"

"No."

"Then . . . he won't know . . . if you let me live."

"I can't let you live . . . he told me. . . . But I don't want to kill you, Thias. I don't."

"Then . . . don't. Help me, Billy. Help me, like you did . . . all those years back."

"But if I don't kill you, he'll kill me. He said he would. I always got to do what he says, or he'll kill me."

"Leave him, Billy. Run . . . away." Thias reached up and back and touched the painful place where French's axe had struck him. He pulled his hand away and found blood thick on his fingers.

"He'll kill me. He says so. And he'll do it, Thias."

Thias felt a mounting despair. He wasn't going to be able to talk French out of murder. Whatever hold Jack Waller held over French, it was too strong for him to break. He pushed up again, fully intending to rise and run. It seemed impossible, but he had no choice; to remain where he was would be to die.

"Thias, don't get up, don't make me knock you down. I don't want to do this, Thias, but if I don't go ahead with it, he'll come here, wondering why I ain't come back yet."

Thias's head throbbed and his vision became a wavering field of dull colors. He reeled sideways and collapsed. His right cheek lay in the snow that had grown bloodied from his broken head. "Don't kill me, Billy. Don't kill me." He passed out.

He opened his eyes again sometime later. He was still on the ground, lying in the snow. The blood on it had crusted and browned. He didn't know how long he had been lying unconscious, but the light was different now and he was chilled clean through. His impression was that hours had gone by.

Billy French was gone. And he had left him alive.

Thias closed his eyes and wept silently.

Maybe an hour later he managed to rise. Only by clinging to a tree could he keep upright. His legs were numb and shaking, so weak beneath him that he wondered if his bones had turned to water. He was so disoriented that he could not remember in which direction he could find the road he had been dragged away from. He didn't know how far French had dragged him. It couldn't have been terribly far; he had worried aloud about Waller coming in from the road and finding Billy balking at his assigned task.

Waller . . . the thought of the man roused an intense fury and hatred. Had Thias been offered the opportunity and ability at that moment, he would have killed the man without hesitation. Waller was evil, a man who returned betrayal for help, a strong-minded dominator who had managed to gain control of a pitiful man with a weaker mind and soul and to manipulate him as a human tool of wickedness.

But the tool had rebelled, and now Thias had a chance to live.

An inn . . . there was an inn nearby! Thias had forgotten that. He had been riding toward that inn when Billy French called him down. If he could only reach the road, he could find that inn, find help.

Thias staggered over to another tree and leaned against it. He was terribly dizzy, and weak from loss of blood. He touched his head and felt a thick, scabby crust all down his neck. He was glad he couldn't see himself right now. If he looked as bad as he felt, he would be a terrible sight indeed.

He advanced farther, rested again, then went on. *Soon I'll reach the road. I'll make it to that inn, and live. The road will be close now, has to be.*

It wasn't. He went farther and farther, and did not reach it. He began to cry in frustration and fear. He must be going entirely in the wrong direction. What if he became lost? Night would fall, cold would descend, and maybe there would be more snow. He might die.

He stopped and rested a full five minutes, then turned in a new direction and advanced, praying that this time he would find the road. If only he could move more quickly! It was all he could do just to keep on his feet. There was no way to hurry.

Long minutes later he sensed he was making better progress. He was learning to work around his disorientation and weakness. Still, he didn't know where the road was. He might even yet be going the wrong way.

He stopped, holding himself up against a tree, listening.

A voice, rather distant : . .

Thank you, God. Thank you. He moved forward again, seeking the place from where the voice came. Not only the road, but travelers! He had found help. He would live.

The voice was closer and louder now. It was a man, talking boisterously and laughing. Thias smiled, his heart racing. He knew now that everything was going to be well. He pushed forward, chuckling to himself in pure joy.

Other voices now ... of course there would be others. No one would be traveling alone, talking and laughing that way. They were very close now, just beyond the hedge of laurel he was even now trying to break through. He heard hooves against the soft, snow-sodden roadway. He opened his mouth to shout ... but he kept his silence and his smile faded.

One of those voices sounded familiar.

He sank to the ground, eyes widening, mouth clamping shut. Peering through the laurel, he saw the road just beyond, and the travelers advancing down it.

The laughing man was young, handsome, and a stranger. The two male riders on either side of him were not handsome, nor were they strangers.

It was the Harpe brothers. On the side closest to Thias was Wiley Harpe himself, and on the far side of the young stranger was a hulking, ugly man who could only be the other Harpe brother.

The three riders passed, followed by the women, also riding, their faces turned straight ahead and their pregnant bodies bulky and heavy in their saddles. Thias dared not even breathe until the entire entourage was past.

He remained where he was, amazed. He remembered that face in the forest and knew now it had not been imagined at all. The Harpes really were here.

At last Thias stood and walked out onto the road. He found a heavy branch, a bit on the crooked side, but strong enough to serve as a stabilizing walking stick. Keeping careful watch, he advanced in the fresh tracks of the Harpe horses, wondering what to do. He remembered that terrible encounter with Wiley Harpe in Knoxville. To encounter the Harpes here in the woods, unarmed, weakened, helpless, would be a bad thing.

At length he came into view of the same inn he had made for earlier in the day. He stopped, leaning on his stick. It was growing late and the sun was setting. He was beginning to grow very dizzy and weak. He needed help and shelter, and the inn ahead offered it. . . .

But at this moment the Harpes' horses were being led around toward a stable in the rear. The Harpes themselves certainly were already inside.

He didn't know whether to go on to the inn and risk being recognized by the Harpes, or to seek shelter in the forest for the night and go on to the inn the next morning, after the Harpes left—and *if* they left. He could not know how long they would remain there.

There was nothing to do but go on and take the risk. He might not survive a freezing night in the woods, as weak as he was. In the awful condition he was in, maybe Wiley Harpe wouldn't recognize him.

He went forward, but his dizzyness made him stagger to the side. He tripped over his own feet and fell at the edge of the road. Pushing back up again, he tried to go forward, but fell again, this time more heavily, and backward. His already broken head struck hard against a boulder. Groaning, he rolled down a small slope into a bank of dead leaves and passed out.

CHAPTER 19

On the Mississippi River

She sat up, tensing as Jim Horton rose and came toward her. He seemed surprised to find her awake. It was night, and except for the firelight spilling over the flatboat's hearth, dark inside the low, wide shelter that covered nearly the full deck. All the others were asleep; he had waited until they were.

"Don't talk, Celinda," he whispered when he was at her side. "Just listen. I know you think you've been right clever, think you've give the slip to old Junebug Horton. You ain't, you ain't. And you don't want to, girl, not really. You don't want to keep company with old Queen. Hear her snoring yonder? Sounds like a waterfall roar. You don't want to hang about a smelly old harlot woman who's never had a shilling to her name. I can give you more, Celinda. I don't want to hurt you. I want only your good. You understand?"

She opened her mouth to answer. He instantly covered it with the rough palm of his hand. "Shhhh! You're still a mute, remember? Still George Ames the mute. And a good thing, eh? You think you'd be left untouched an hour if the men on this boat knew the truth about you? You've hid it well so far, girl, but you won't be able to do it forever. They'll find you out, and after that you'll be as used as old Queen before you know it. You don't want that, Celinda. But that's what will happen to you if you stay on this boat with that old cyprian. She can't protect you, no matter what she says."

She lay there, hating him, wishing she could spit in his face.

"I'm going to take you off this boat," he whispered. "Me and you, we'll leave this boat. Find ourselves another way to Natchez."

She shook her head. He clamped his hand down harder on her mouth to make her stop. His next words, harshly whispered, had an edge sharper than a blade. "Don't you refuse me, Celinda! You do, and it may be that your little secret comes out quicker than you think. That's right, girl. You resist me, and I'll reveal you, right before them all. Then I'll turn you over to them to use as they want. They'd love to get their hands on a pert young wench like you! Don't think I'm lying, Celinda. I'll do it. I will. I'll . . . uuunnghh!"

Celinda was as surprised as Horton to see a blade come flashing around from behind him to settle in tight against his throat. Queen's broad face lowered to the level of Horton's. She whispered through gritted teeth right into his ear. Celinda could have laughed in joy at the expression on Horton's face.

"Touch dear Celinda again, and I'll carve your head from your shoulders, Junebug," Queen said with a deliberate feminine softness that only made the words more ominous.

"I'll not touch her . . . please, Queen. Please."

Queen held her place for another moment, just to drive in the point of her advantage, then backed off. Horton let go of Celinda and stood. He turned and faced Queen with an expression of hatred. "So you *do* know the truth about 'George' here!" he whispered. "I had guessed you would have figured it out if anybody would."

"You figured right for once, Junebug. Now get away from here, and don't you come near my girl again."

"Why are you protecting her, Queen? What is she to you?"

"She's what I was once and can't be no more. Young and pure. Not yet fouled by such filth as you."

Horton chuckled low. "So old Queen's found herself a purpose! Got her a scrawny little girl to keep pure and untouched! Well, I'll tell you, you foul old harlot, it ain't going to be. She's mine. *Mine!* And I'll have her for myself, whatever you say about it."

"I don't 'say' naught. My blade does. I cut throats. I'll cut yourn."

Horton stood there, gnawing his lip. His expression of anger slowly evolved into one of sad pleading. "Queen, it ain't right to keep me from her. I . . . I love her. I truly do."

"You don't love her, Junebug. You ain't never loved nobody but yourself."

"I *do!*"

"Hush! You wake up the others and I'll tell them I caught you stealing from their packs. Get back to your blankets, Junebug. Leave my little girl be."

Horton moved off across the shelter and lay down on his blankets. Celinda sat up and looked around. It appeared that no one else on the boat had awakened—no real surprise, considering that a supply of whiskey had been purchased from another flatboat's crew earlier in the day. The crew had fallen asleep drunk, with the boat moored against a tiny island in mid-river.

"I heard some of what he was saying to you. He's right 'bout one thing," Queen whispered to Celinda, so softly that Celinda could barely hear her. She figured Queen didn't want Jim Horton overhearing. "You'll not make it all the way to Natchez without the truth about you being found out. It's right astonishing it ain't been found out yet."

Celinda nodded. Worry about what would happen when her secret was out had been an eternal cloud over her head.

Queen scratched her double chin thoughtfully. "If Junebug is holding the truth 'bout you as a threat, the thing to be done is cut his legs from under him. Tomorrow we'll tell the truth 'bout you to everyone, and dare them to come through old Queen if they want to get at you."

Celinda dared the faintest of whispers. "But what if you *can't* stop them? Jim Horton said you couldn't really protect me."

"I can. Trust in me, girl. I'll see that you're safe. Better to reveal you right out than to have the truth come out by accident, and it's bound to do that sooner or later. I'll take care of you. And I'll see, too, if I can't get Junebug away from us once and for all."

"How?"

"Lex Dunworth. He's always hated Junebug. I believe if I ask him, he'll put him off the boat."

Celinda felt a thrill of excitement. "You truly believe he would?"

"We'll see," Queen replied. "Trust in me, girl. Whatever happens, no harm will come to you long as old Queen is at your side."

Celinda did not sleep much for the rest of the night. She lay there thinking how fine it would be if she could simply flee the boat and make it to shore while the others slept. She had thought about it nightly since the voyage began.

The problem was, Jim Horton obviously had thought about it too, and kept himself awake at night to make sure she had no chance to flee. It was frustrating, downright infuriating. Horton napped during the day to compensate for his missed sleep at night. Today he had even foregone the whiskey while all the others were drinking, and Celinda knew it was because he didn't want to grow drunk and inattentive when night came.

She had to admit, though, that even if Horton wasn't such a determined sentinel, she might not have the courage to make her escape alone. To do so would be to lose the protection of Queen and her passage to Natchez. She didn't know how far away Natchez was. All she knew was that she was somewhere on the Mississippi River. If she left the boat, she would be on her own, without means, without friends, guidance . . . protection. If only Queen would come with her! Celinda had asked her once, but she had refused. Queen was fat, slow-walking, and subject to pain in her joints. She had declared she couldn't make a land journey as far as Natchez, which would probably be the only alternative if they left the flatboat. Further, by the code of river pirates, the only code Queen and her companions held sacred, for anyone to abandon the boat meant sacrifice of his or her portion of the money that would come when the stolen wares and boat were sold down the river. Queen could not afford to leave. Further, Queen counseled, Celinda should not make any attempt at a solo flight, even if she could find the chance for one. Queen seemed to truly believe that Celinda was safer with her, even among river pirates, than she would be in the wild river country alone.

Celinda was trapped where she was. It could be worse, she reminded herself. At least she was floating closer to Natchez every day. And better to be tied to Queen than to Jim Horton.

Queen's affection was warm and real, far different than Jim Horton's declared love—*love!* The thought of him loving her was absurd and maddening. A man such as he could know nothing of real love. His kind of love was possessive, destructive, a mockery.

Celinda looked toward the shelter ceiling and thanked God for Queen Fine. All her hope of safety was centered around that big, rough-cut woman, and all the trust Celinda had was thrown upon her and would have to remain there until they reached Natchez and her aunt Ida.

How long would that take? Celinda wished they were there already.

Unable to sleep, Celinda lay silently and listened to the sounds of the river—or what she could hear of them above the snores of the sleeping crew. Contradictory to what she would expect, she had developed an appreciation of the river during her time upon it, perhaps because it was the one thing in her world that moved along on its own, free and open, oblivious to all the things that she herself would like to be oblivious to. And it had filled her mind with scenes she would never forget.

The river was like a great highway, filled with human traffic moving along on anything that could float. Since the flatboat had pulled out onto Mississippi waters, Celinda had seen watercraft of astonishing variety. She often distracted herself from her worries by looking for new and different kinds of boats as they went along. By now she had an impressive mental inventory of images.

She had seen keelboats, rafts, ferries, arks, and many great broad-horn flatboats similar to the one she was upon. She had seen every imaginable kind of cargo: tobacco, whiskey, shingles, cotton, flour, lumber, horses, cattle, slaves. The Mississippi was a far greater artery of commerce than a simple Kentucky girl could have ever imagined.

Sometimes, when the river was foggy and visibility was down, the other craft on the river could be heard rather than seen, which seemed eerie. Phantom voices, disembodied, would come floating through the mist, amplified by the water, and it would seem that surely ghosts were floating above the river only a few yards off the boat, when in fact the speakers were thoroughly human and ensconced on unseen keelboats or broad horns quite a long way off.

Most of the boats, whatever their variety, were commercial vessels. Others carried both cargo and people, mostly emigrants traveling to new country down the river. On three occasions the flatboat came up alongside great fleets of flatboats traveling together both for company and safety, and Celinda marveled at what was for all purposes an entire floating town. Some of the flatboats were simply but nicely decorated by the hands of woman who saw no reason that a temporary, floating home shouldn't be as comfortable and domestically appealing as possible.

Some of the vessels they met in the river were dedicated to vice, such as the floating whiskey shop the crew had done business with today. Once, they met three barges strung together and filled with crude structures that served as liquor parlors and gambling halls. Lex Dunworth wouldn't allow his crew to board that vessel, fearing he would not be able to persuade them back to work again.

Most of the river traffic moved downstream with the current at a fairly fast and steady pace. The few craft coming upstream did so much more slowly, poling or "warping" against the flow. Warping involved tying hundred-yard rope cables, or warps, to riverside trees and coiling them in, pulling the boat with them at a rate that covered six or eight miles a day at best. "Yonder's why most sell their boats in Natchez or New Orleans, and walk back on the old Nashville road," Queen had explained to her the first time they encountered a barge warping its way upstream. "It takes months on end to make the journey back and down again, when you warp. Best to shuck off the boat for its lumber, once you've sold your load, and come back home on the hoof."

Sometimes, when Celinda had watched boats going past bearing families, she had fantasized about throwing herself into the river and swimming over to board. She would tell the good folk upon it that she had been kidnapped by those on the original flatboat and beg for rescue. But she was a poor swimmer and had never found the courage to really try it. And what if the people on the other boat didn't believe her and sent her back?

But if they *did* believe her . . . that would be wonderful. To escape this boat, to go on to Natchez in the company of some good, protective family—oh, God, if only you would make it so, if only you would give me the chance, and the courage, and the ability to swim ... She was thinking along these lines when at last she fell asleep.

The next morning, after the boat had pulled out from the island and found its channel in the river, Celinda came out of the shelter and saw Queen talking at length with Lex Dunworth. Their volume was low, but Dunworth seemed quiet astonished, and then animated, in reacting to what he heard. Wiping sleep from her eyes, Celinda wondered if Queen had just told him the truth about her, and maybe a few lies about Jim Horton to boot.

Celinda had no opportunity to find out before Queen, with Dunworth at her side, mounted the shelter top. She declared: "Hear me! You see the mute boy George Ames, there? Well, he's neither mute nor a boy! George Ames is Celinda Ames, a girl with her hair cut short to make her pass for a lad."

Celinda thought: God help me, she's really doing it! She's doing just what she said she would! Oh, Queen, I hope you know what you're doing. . . .

Queen went on: "It was all the notion of Junebug Horton, to protect her from being bothered back at the cave. Only problem is, it's Junebug doing the bothering now, and threatening to tell the truth 'bout her to all of you, holding that over her head like an axe. Well, I've done blunted that axe. Now Junebug's got nothing to threaten with—and I'm standing here to tell you, with Lex Dunworth to back me up, that there'll be no hand laid on Celinda Ames, or I'll chew it off with my own teeth! She's a pure girl, hardly more than a child, and I'll not see wrong done by her! You hear me?"

No one answered. The entire crew was staring at Celinda in amazement, reorienting their perceptions of the "boy" that had been among them for so many days now. Celinda's face grew red. She felt probed and exposed, and wanted to hide.

She looked at Jim Horton. His face was red, too, and twisted in fury. He met her gaze and held it until she could stand it no more and turned away. Horton then looked at Queen, eyes boiling with hate. Queen looked back, and this time it was Horton who couldn't hold the gaze. He turned his back on her with an oath.

"Figured to keep her for yourself, eh, Junebug?" one of the crew asked.

"Like your gals dressed up as boys, do you, Junebug?" another asked, evoking laughter that made Horton turn and fire a barrage of obscenities at the others.

"Junebug!" Lex Dunworth called from the shelter top.

"What?"

"Off the boat. We're done with you. Queen tells me you been making some threats 'gainst me 'mongst the others."

"What? That's a lie! A damned lie!"

"I've heard him!" Ajax McKee said. "Heard him with my own ears, just yesterday, saying he aimed to carve the gizzard from ye, Lex!" McKee grinned at the increasingly flustered Horton, and Celinda knew McKee was lying, backing up Queen and Dunworth either out of loyalty to them, dislike for Horton, or maybe just for the fun of it.

"You want to come try and make that threat good here and now, Junebug?" Dunworth challenged.

"Get up there, Junebug!" someone heckled. "Show old Lex who's the true yaller flower of the wildwoods!"

Other such calls began to arise. Horton swore and stormed into the shelter, gathered his possessions, and came out again. The laughter and hooting continued. Celinda, though feeling nervous and vulnerable because the secret of her sex was out, greatly enjoyed watching Horton suffer under the onslaught. He made for the skiff that was stored upside down at the rear of the flatboat.

"You just get away from that, Junebug!" Dunworth yelled. "You ain't taking our skiff."

"Then how am I supposed to reach the shore?"

"Swim."

"Swim? All the way to the bank? I ain't a good swimmer, Lex."

"You'd best learn, and fast."

Horton didn't look angry now. He looked scared. "But I ain't a good swimmer, really. I'll drown."

"I'd figure a junebug could just fly ashore!" one of the crew joked.

"Lex, please . . ."

Celinda was surprised to find herself pitying Horton. She despised the man, but did not want to see him drown. She climbed up on the decktop and went up to Dunworth. "Please, sir, have someone row him ashore."

Dunworth looked at her with great interest. "You *can* talk, can't you! And you really *are* a girl."

Celinda pressed her plea. "Please, sir. I'm glad you're putting him off the boat, but I don't want anybody to drown because of me."

"I'd figure you'd be pleased to see him dead."

"She ain't hard and mean like we are, Lex," Queen said. "She ain't been ruint yet. That's what I like about her. She makes me think of me, back before I was ruint."

"Ah, well . . . very well, girl." He called to McKee. "Ajax! Drop the skiff in the water there and row old Junebug ashore. Old George here—What's your name? Celinda?—Celinda, she wants us to show him mercy."

The protests of this were feeble. Now that Celinda was up in better view, most of the crew was occupied with looking her over very closely, trying to see the female in the form they had perceived as male up until now.

Celinda glanced quickly at Horton. He looked relieved until he realized she was looking at him. Then he glared. She dropped her head, grateful he was soon to be gone.

"Get your pack and be gone, Junebug," Dunworth ordered.

"I'll need a rifle, for protection."

"No rifle for you. You got a knife, you'll make do with that."

Ajax McKee was rowing Horton away from the flatboat when one of the crew called out to Celinda. "Say something, girl! We want to hear better what you sound like!"

Celinda felt shy, and ducked behind Queen.

The men laughed. "Look at her! Hiding like a child behind its mammy! Hey, Queen, you going to be Mammy to that gal now?"

"I'll be the closest she'll have to it," Queen replied. "And to any man what dares touch my girl, I'll be the very devil! I'll geld the first scoundrel what even looks too long at this girl!"

No one seemed to doubt Queen's word. Celinda was glad Queen was there, and decided to remain close by her the rest of the day, while the others grew accustomed to her in what was to them a new light. When Ajax McKee returned with the skiff now empty, she felt relieved.

Jim Horton was gone. He could no longer reach her, no longer be a threat. And if Queen really could keep the other men away from her, she had a chance of reaching Natchez and her aunt Ida Post unscathed.

She was enjoying the hopefulness of those thoughts when she sensed someone was watching her. Turning, she found

Ajax McKee studying her closely. He approached her. "Come here, girly."

"Why?"

"I want to get to know ye, now that I know ye are what ye are."

"No ... I don't want to ... no."

He stepped up to her and grabbed her shoulder. "Come on, now, girly! Ye know what the good Lord put girlies in the world for, don't ye? So a man could have his sport, that's why! Ye know about sporting, don't ye? Ye ain't no fresh little unplucked flower, are ye?"

"Leave me alone!" His hands seemed to burn upon her, reviving in her all the terror of the time Jim Horton had almost succeeded in forcing himself upon her. She put out her nails like claws and raked them down the side of McKee's face, drawing blood.

"Why, ye little trollop, I'll—"

Suddenly he was no longer there, but thrashing in the water beside the boat. Queen Fine had come upon him unseen, hefted up her skirts, and kicked him over the side.

"You touch my girl again, and I'll have my knife in you thrice before you hit the water!" Queen bellowed at him. He flailed, treading water with difficulty because of his soaked clothes, intermixing curses at Queen Fine with calls for someone to throw out a rope or extend an oar. Queen put her hands on her hips, spit toward him in the water, and turned to the others. "Let that be your lesson!" she yelled at all of them. "This here girl ain't to be touched! You hear me? Any what tried something like that again will get worse than a swim! That's the word of Queen Fine, as solid as the ten commandments!"

Someone at last tossed a line out to McKee and got him back into the boat, dripping and furious. He looked at Queen. "Ye'll pay dear for that, damn ye!"

"Don't touch her no more, Ajax McKee. No more. You hear?"

"Ye'll pay," he said, and turned away.

CHAPTER 20

That night, Celinda was jolted out of a dream of her old home in Kentucky by the sudden pressure of a hand across her mouth. Instantly she panicked, sure in one sub-rational moment that Jim Horton was back and that this time he would be far more furious than ever and lethally dangerous. Her eyes flashed open and she was poised to scream when a thumb expertly pressed at just the right point on her throat cut off her voice. She looked up not into Horton's face, but that of Ajax McKee, intense, ugly, the overscarring, scabrous place where his nose tip had been so close it almost touched her.

He whispered, "Hush now, quiet. Not a sound, not a peep. Get up and come with me."

She waited for him to remove the pressure on her throat so that she could breathe again—and scream, as loudly as she could. Seemingly sensing her intentions, he pushed his face even closer and whispered, "Ye make a noise, they'll stop us, and ye'll not be seeing Queen no more. She'll be heartbroke."

Queen? Celinda turned her eyes and looked at Queen's sleeping place by the light of the low and flickering hearth fire. Empty.

"Ye'll keep quiet, girly?"

She nodded. He let go of her. Celinda gasped in much-needed air. The thought of screaming despite her promise rose but died promptly. The mention of Queen intrigued her; she would do nothing drastic for the moment.

McKee's voice was so low she could barely follow his words. "Get up, quiet. The skiff is in the water. We're going to the far shore and will have ye off this foul boat at last. Ye'd like that, aye? Queen's waiting for us. No, no time to gather possessions. Come now, and no shilly-shally!"

She had time only to grab up the sack in which she had stored her original dress, coat, and shoes since Horton had forced the "George Ames" pseudoidentity upon her. To her good fortune, she had already been wearing her coat to keep her warm while she slept. Even though all on the boat now knew she was no male, she had continued to wear her bulky, unappealing male clothing, not only because it was warmer and more practical, but because earlier that day Queen had warned her of the foolishness of prettying herself before a cabal of lusty river pirates.

McKee led her toward the door opening out onto the deck. Celinda, groggy from sleep and muddled over Queen's involvement in this unexpected event, gingerly followed him on bare feet to and onto the skiff, heeding his gestured commands for silence. She quietly laid her pack at her feet. He slipped off the tie and gently pushed away from the flatboat, which had been tied up for the night against a big sawyer covered with glair and moss. Only after the skiff had drifted back from the boat as far as it would go on its own did he dip the oars in the water and begin rowing, very gently. Celinda realized at that moment she had been holding her breath in sheer tension.

She drew in fresh air and asked in a whisper, "Where is Queen?"

"On the shore. Now hush!" McKee whispered back. "Voices are louder on the river."

Rowing the half breadth of the wide river took a seeming eternity. As Celinda's mind slowly cleared out the murk of sleep, she was reminded by the situation of her and her father's eviction from that flatboat on the Ohio, and began to feel similar apprehensions. But under their stream flowed an undercurrent of confused but authentic hope because of McKee's invocation of Queen's name. Maybe Queen had somehow contrived this scenario as a way of saving her; perhaps all along

184 *Cameron Judd*

there had been a secret collaborative companionship between Queen and McKee that she had not seen, or which had been deliberately concealed from all for prudence's sake. Perhaps there had been more theater than reality in the brawl that had left McKee flouncing about in the river while Queen harped at him like a fishwife. At this moment all understanding was in limbo and anything seemed possible. Celinda delved into her pack for her shoes. As she put them on she squinted into the dark, trying to see the bank, and was thrilled with both fear and excitement when at last it came into view through the veiling night. She looked for Queen on the shore but saw no one.

McKee lithely hopped out of the skiff and pulled it aground. Celinda rose and stepped forward. "Why are you doing this? Where is Queen?"

"I believe I hear her coming now," McKee replied. "Aye—that must be her." He extended Celinda his hand. It was so dark she could hardly see it, and his face was fully shrouded. But he sounded cheery when he said, "Let me help ye from the skiff."

She opted not to touch him. "I can get out myself." She paused, squinting through the dark down the bank as she came to her feet. There was indeed someone coming toward them. Celinda stepped out of the skiff and sank her feet into the shoreline shallows. "Queen? Is that you?"

No answer. Celinda felt puzzled, then vaguely worried, and suddenly it was as if ice had touched the back of her neck. Intuition screamed a frenzied warning. The figure in the dark approached, the outline now dimly seen, and suddenly she knew. . . .

"Oh, God!" she exclaimed, facing McKee. "What have you done? That's Jim Horton out there! He's paid you to bring me to him!"

"Don't I know it, girly!" McKee laughed and grabbed her, pinning her arms to her sides and dragging her away from the boat. She struggled and was about to scream, but he put a knife to her throat. "Hush it, girly!" he snapped. "No call for noise!"

"Let me go!" She almost whispered the plea, fearing to defy him fully with a scream. The mere speaking motions of her throat were enough to make the knife tip prick her painfully. She felt silent.

She shifted her eyes and watched Horton's dimly outlined figure approaching on the bank. Apparently seeing the situation, he loped forward eagerly.

"She's a scrapper, ain't she!" Horton said, sounding a touch uncertain as he took in a dimly discernable vision of McKee clasping Celinda to him with a knife at her neck.

"Aye, she is, the little shrew!" McKee replied. He gave a sudden *Oof!* and a curse as Celinda's heel kicked his shin. She had decided she feared Horton even more than McKee's blade. McKee didn't cut her, but pushed her away and down. She reeled and fell back into the skiff. For a second she lay stunned, then grappled for the oars. McKee was far too fast, on her in a second. He pinned her down, swung his right hand around past his left shoulder and backhanded her across the right jaw, a stunning blow. "I'll cut ye open, girly, if ye kick me again!" he threatened.

"Don't hurt her!" Horton demanded. "I didn't pay you to bring her to me only to have you knife her!"

"The strumpet kicked me!" McKee answered. "She kicks once, I hit. Twice, I cut. Ye hear that, girly? Ye going to be a good and dear girly now and keep them feet still?"

Celinda wanted to cry but refused to do so. Her mind was spinning, her jaw aching. "Where is Queen?"

"Shut up," McKee barked.

Horton said, "Queen? What's Queen got to do with this? You didn't let that hag see you, did you?"

" 'Course not. Queen's on the boat. She saw nary a thing."

Celinda said, "She's not on the boat—her bed was empty!"

Horton pressed the question: "What's all this? McKee, did you do something to Queen Fine?"

McKee paused, breathing through his teeth, swore beneath his breath and said, "Aye, I did. I killed the fat old cow and slid her corpse quiet and peaceful as you please into the river. She put me in the river once, now I've did the same for her, and there she can stay forevermore."

The news stabbed Celinda with no less pain than if McKee had used his knife. She went limp, absorbing it. Horton swore and said, "You've *murdered* her? Curse your soul, man, I didn't pay for no murder—just for the girl! That's all!"

"Well, now ye have your girly. And the killing of Queen, that warn't for your sake in no case, Horton. That was my own doing, for my own reasons. Queen shamed me, and I'll abide no shaming."

Celinda suddenly sobbed aloud, which seemed to infuriate McKee, who turned to her and spat, "Hush! I despise a crying girly worse than a pox." Then to Horton: "I've done my work. Now I want the rest of my pay."

Horton waved his arms in a gesture of wild disbelief. "You've made me a party to murder! God above, man, do you want me and you both to hang? Our bargain is off."

"Ain't nobody going to hang because there ain't nobody knows 'cept us, and ain't none of us going to tell. She was naught but an old river harlot! What is she to make a fuss over? And if ye welch our bargain, I'll kill this girly ye want so bad right here and now." He pressed the knife against Celinda's throat.

Celinda prayed: God help me, help me now. Reach down and help me, because this is too terrible to abide. I am weak and in danger and Queen is dead. God help me, please.

"My money, Horton!" McKee demanded again. "Now!"

"It's . . . it ain't here."

"What? Ain't *here*? Then—"

"Don't get your bowels in an uproar, man. It's yonder. On down the shore that way, where I left my pack. Come with me and I'll pay you there."

McKee grabbed Celinda's arm and roughly yanked her up. "Come on, girly. Let's take a walk with Mr. Junebug."

"Leave her," Horton said. "I don't want her trying to run away while we're doing our dealing."

"All the more reason to take her. We can watch her long as she's in hand."

"No! I want her left here. We'll tie her up."

"Hell, why waste the time? Pay me and be done with it! What trick are ye up to man?"

"Trying to get you paid. That's all." Horton's voice was strained and oddly high-pitched.

Celinda had already pieced together the likely facts. While being rowed ashore, Horton had arranged to pay McKee to kidnap her and bring her to him, and had given him a little money in advance with a promise to pay more when the job was done. But Horton didn't really have more money. In his frantic eagerness to repossess her, he had made a bargain he couldn't keep, and the sure result would be an infuriated McKee who would probably murder them both, as he had Queen.

She did not expect McKee would agree to tie and leave her here, nor did she really understand why Horton was urging that course so strongly. She feared McKee would perceive that

Horton had cheated him and retaliate on the spot. So she prayed even more fervently, meanwhile bracing herself for the thrust of his blade. *Oh God, save me, oh God, save me . . .*

McKee's next words stunned her. "Very well, if ye have to have it that way. But ye'd best pay me quick, and no tricks. I want to be far from here before morning, in case them on the boat find Queen afloating come daylight. I'll hold her. Ye tie."

Though relieved that McKee had acceded to Horton's direction, Celinda felt obliged to struggle against them, unwilling to acquiesce to scoundrels. Despite her flailings, she was tied hand and foot within two minutes. McKee then gleefully added an unexpected torment to her situation: he wadded his dirty kerchief, crusted with dried sweat and rheum, and bound it into her mouth. Its taste made her want to retch. "That'll keep ye good and quiet, eh? Good girly!"

The men moved off into the darkness together. Celinda strained, pulled at her ropes, and found they would not give. If they would not, then perhaps her own flesh would. Bitting down on the gagging kerchief, she then straightened her right hand and pulled as hard as possible. She felt skin abrading, the pain intense. Blood flowed warmly out onto her fingers and palms. Tears burned her eyes. She was obliged to quit pulling, but only for a moment. Painful as it was, she had to free her hands. It was her only hope, because she felt instinctively sure that if she fell into Jim Horton's clutches again, this time there would be no escape. He had said he loved her. He would never let her go. He would die himself, or see her dead, rather than let her escape him.

Closing her eyes, she steeled herself, bit down again on the foul cloth in her mouth and gave a long, mighty, twisting pull at the ropes cutting into her wrists, struggling against them for her sole hope of life and escape, wild, pleading prayers ringing in her mind as she tried not to cry out in the self-inflicted pain of her struggle.

Jim Horton's heart pounded like a drum as his mind raced. McKee walked close beside him, still carrying his knife and muttering threats about what would happen if he was cheated. Horton faced the worst dilemma of his life. He had pledged to pay McKee a substantial amount when he brought in Celinda, but he had no money at all left to pay. He cursed himself for a fool for having made an impossible promise. Yet he knew he couldn't have helped himself. All he had thought about while McKee was rowing him ashore earlier was the fact that Celinda was slipping away from him. His proposal had been made in desperation so great it had precluded him from thinking clearly about what he was saying.

He reached beneath his coat and put his hand to his own knife. It was cold and hard; his fingers trembled upon it. Could he do what might be required? Could he kill McKee? He had never killed anyone before. And unlike McKee, he was no fighter. But he would have to do his best. He had figured it would come to this; his reason for leaving Celinda back at the skiff was to keep her from having to witness the death that would surely come of this: McKee's, or his. As rough and selfish as Jim Horton's brand of love was, it still bore a tinge of protectiveness for the object of his affections. And even more for himself: he knew that Celinda would never accept him if she saw him commit a murder.

He stumbled on his own pack, having reached it sooner than anticipated. McKee held up the knife and said, "Here we are, Junebug, and there's your bag. Now out with the money."

"I . . . uh . . ."

"Ye *got* no more money, eh, Junebug? So I had figured."

"I've got it, right in here." He knelt and fumbled with the pack with one hand, the other still beneath his coat, gripping his knife.

"What ye got your hand on 'neath your coat, Junebug?"

"I . . . nothing . . ." He stood and pulled out the knife, waving it at McKee. "This is what I've got."

"Aye, I figured as much from ye! I figured as much!" He lunged forward and tried to put the knife into Horton's chest.

Horton dodged back, taking only a small nick. He yelled and turned to run. McKee grabbed his shoulder and spun him around. Horton shoved in the opposite direction, knocking McKee down. Then he ran back inland.

McKee was after him in moments. Horton entered a grove of trees. Here the darkness was heavy. Dodging behind a tree, he stopped, holding his breath. McKee ran past, felt more than seen.

"Where ye be, damn your eyes!" McKee called, stopping a few feet away. "Are ye a coward as well as a cheat?"

Horton felt like he would faint at any moment. His heart hammered so hard it hurt. He let out his breath and drew in another—and McKee must have heard it, because a moment later he roared and came right at him.

Horton screamed in mortal terror, shoved his knife out like a sword straight in front of him, gripped in both hands, and waited to die.

He was unaware of the moments immediately thereafter despite many later attempts to reconstruct them. When his senses returned, he found himself kneeling on the ground, panting like a dog, his knife gone. All was silent. Hearing a quiet groan and a rattling hiss right beside him, he gasped, jumped up and backed away until he hit a tree. Silence again.

"McKee?"

No response.

"McKee, where are you?"

Quiet lingered. He heard the whisper of the river, then his own nervous giggle as hope sprang to life.

Horton's trembling legs grew weak and he sank to his knees again. He felt about for his knife, crawling forward, until his left hand touched something warm and fleshy. McKee's arm. The arm did not move. Horton grasped the wrist and felt for the beat of a pulse. Nothing.

Another giggle boiled up. He felt further, running his hand across McKee's unmoving torso. Wet warmth touched his fingers and he lifted them to his nose. Blood. He poked about some more and found his knife, sticking out of McKee's chest, buried to the grip in his heart.

Horton collapsed, sucking in air, drinking in the most welcome realization of his life: he was alive and McKee was dead! By pure fortune he had killed a man who was ten times his better at fighting. He had killed him and survived, and Celinda awaited back at the skiff on the shore.

When his strength had returned sufficiently, he debouched and left McKee's corpse behind him in the dark grove. The dim vision of the broad river in the night made him smile; had he seen his face at that moment he would have noted how pixilated was his own smile. He paused a few moments, stumbled forward to retrieve his pack, and headed along the shore back to where Celinda awaited.

The skiff was gone when he got there. Gone! He dropped his pack again and looked wildly around. "Celinda . . ."

Weakening again, he dropped to his hands and knees and

found her ropes. He picked them up and felt blood on them. She had wriggled out of them, taken the skiff. . . .

She was gone. She had escaped him. He stood paralyzed, astonished.

He yelled, "Celinda! Celinda!" His voice carried across the river. A few moments later he heard Lex Dunworth's voice yelling back from the flatboat somewhere out there in the water. "Junebug! Is that you!"

He rose, knowing that even now the absence of Celinda, McKee, and Queen was being detected. An impulse to run struck him, simultaneous with a much less sensible urge to dive into the river and swim out in search of the skiff Celinda had taken. But he couldn't swim.

Tears erupted and streamed down his face. He blubbered and cried, whispered Celinda's name, and turned away. He heard new yells from the flatboat, distant but amplified by the water, and knew that realizations that could endanger him were occurring on that boat even then.

Blinded by night and tears, he picked up his pack, turned inland and ran away from the river and into the forest, not knowing where he was going and not thinking about it at all. His mind was fully occupied by the terrible fact that she had gotten away from him, really gotten away, and he had little hope of finding her again.

Out on the dark water, Celinda gripped the skiff's oars with hands slickened by her own blood. Her wrists, abraded very deeply, burned as if aflame, but the tears on her face were not the product of pain, as they had been initially, nor even of the grief over Queen Fine's unjust death, which had roused a second jag of sobbing once the pain-crying was done and she had gotten well away from shore and into the river's current.

She was crying now out of joy. A pure, holy, soul-filling joy that she had found, or which perhaps had found her, when she realized that at last she was truly free. Free! She believed it only with difficulty. She was away from the flatboat, away from Ajax McKee, and most of all, away from Jim Horton, whose voice she had heard crying out her name across the dark water as she rowed away. She wondered what had happened to McKee. Had Horton killed him? It seemed to her that she had heard noises of struggle even as she made her escape.

She raised her eyes heavenward and thanked her creator for

having heard her prayer. Never mind that she had nearly scraped the flesh from her wrists and hands in gaining her freedom, or that her feet were still bound and would remain so until she had put many miles between herself and the hell from which she had fled. In a skiff, she did not need the use of her feet, only her arms and an iron will to keep on rowing. Celinda was grateful to be alive. Life lay stretched before her like the river that swept her along. She had no food, no money, no companions ... but it did not matter. She had life, freedom, and hope.

She rowed recklessly at first, thinking more of gaining distance than of the sawyers, planters, and floating river debris that could damage the skiff. At length she tired, her emotions settled, and common sense took hold. She slowed her rowing and kept watch for possible impediments. She found none.

The sun was tinging the eastern horizon a red-pink, rising light rendering up a surreal chiaroscuro of banks, bluffs, and riparian woodlands, when she saw a small, wooded island ahead, high-banked all around except for one upsloping shore of gravel and sand. She rowed toward it. Her joy at freedom remained, but tempered somewhat by the realization that Horton, if he survived the fight that must have occurred between him and McKee, could have followed the shoreline on foot ... might even have found some sort of floating craft and followed her on water! There was a chilling thought indeed. Threatened now by the rising daylight, she rowed fast to the island, laboriously pulled the skiff ashore, and hid it as best she could with brush, doing all this on the hop, in that her feet were still bound.

She went into the brush, out of sight, and worked loose the bonds around her ankles. Her feet hurt and tingled as a fresh supply of blood raced into them; she removed her shoes, rubbed her toes until they felt normal, then put the shoes on again. Rising, she walked to the center of the island and found a tiny pool beside a flat stone. Tasting the water, she found it pure and cool, and drank deeply. Hunger rumbled her stomach, but there was no hope of food. She opted for rest instead, curling up on a pile of leaves beneath an overhanging low branch.

Sleep was dreamless, delicious, restful beyond any sleep Celinda had experienced since her ordeal began. When she awakened in the afternoon, she was confused only a moment, then remembered her escape and was flooded again with joy. *Thank you, God.*

She heard voices out on the river and stiffened. Rising, she crept to the top of one of the bluffs overlooking the river and hid among the brush there, peering out onto the water.

As she had thought, the voice was Dunworth's. The flatboat was passing by the island—Thank heaven it was not stopping!—and the men of the diminished crew were talking among themselves. Celinda could not understand what was said, but she heard the word "Queen" very distinctly. That made her squint to see if by some miracle Queen was on the boat and alive despite McKee's claim to have murdered her. Wildly hoping, Celinda looked over the flatboat from end to end, marveling at the fact that she was close enough to toss a stone onto it while those aboard knew nothing of it. The boat floated on past, and on the rear of it Celinda saw a sight that made her cast down her eyes and feel black sorrow.

Queen *was* aboard, but not alive. Her already bloating corpse lay on the boat, uncovered, her gray and sodden face turned up toward the sky. They must have found her floating and fished her out. Celinda could not imagine why they had done so unless Dunworth intended to bury his old friend properly somewhere alongside the river. She hoped so. Queen deserved a good burial, not to go back to the elements in a murky river. She owed Queen a great deal. Watching the flatboat go by, she vowed to herself never to forget her.

When the flatboat was past, Celinda began to think about her situation. She was free, true enough, but possessed nothing but a meager bit of clothing and a stolen skiff. Lack of food was her biggest problem. She lacked even a container to carry clean water.

Watching the passing flatboat, she realized that the river was still a dangerous place. Recapture was possible if she grew careless and let herself be seen by her remaining former companions and—she shuddered at this thought—they felt inclined to enjoy her company without the respectively determined and sullen protection of Queen Fine and Jim Horton.

As she mulled her situation, Celinda thought back to words her father had spoken as he awaited death: "In the end, you'll have only yourself and God above to rely on. Trust in your feelings, and count on God to guide them."

She nodded. *Very well. So it will be. Lord, I pray you will heed my prayer. I pray you'll guide my feelings so that I don't trust the wrong folks, like I did Jim Horton. I pray that you'll give me a sign to let me know I'm making the right choice. A clear sign, a sure one. One there'll be no mistaking. That is my prayer, Lord. Amen.*

She rose, returned to mid-island and drank heavily at the little brook, letting the water fill her belly and momentarily obtund the gripping pains of hunger. Time to leave? No. Not yet. She would remain awhile longer, wash her clothes, bathe. This island was secure and peaceful. She was reluctant to go onto the open river. She felt right now that, if not for hunger, she could stay on this island, hidden from the world, forever.

Celinda scrubbed out her feminine clothing, let it dry, then put it on in place of her male clothing, which she also washed out, except for the coat. Hanging that clothing to dry on the leafless brush around her, she settled down to rest again. It was too late to set off today; dark would be upon her before she made many miles. Though hunger was becoming a torment, she was content to remain here one more night.

She was about to fall asleep as the sun set when she heard the sound of an approaching craft. Rising, she headed toward the bank where she had hidden the skiff and looked upriver from behind a mat of bushes.

Coming toward the island with the evident purpose of tying up for the night was a boatload of people on a massive, bargelike craft powered by a team of horses that turned a mill-like propellor in the center of the craft. The craft was so large that a full-sized cabin, larger than the old Ames home place, stood on its rear.

Hot panic flashed. She would be found! Why had she lingered here? She should have gone on when she had the chance. . . .

Calm yourself, Celinda. There is no running now. All you can do is face them—and remember that most who come down this river are good folk, not the kind you've been among until now. These people may help you. Look! There are women among them!

She watched the boat land, studied the folk who came off it, particularly the women. The sight of them brought tears to her eyes; she had not realized how much she had missed the fellowship of the kind of women she had known throughout life—good women, solid women, like her mother had been.

Even Queen had not been able to fill that role. Some of the women had small children. This was surely an emigrant party! Even the cargo on the huge boat supported that inference: dismantled wagons, tied-together heaps of furniture, casks of flour and meal, tools, chests that probably contained domestic goods, cutlery, cookware, comestibles, even a big cage of chickens. . . .

It did not take long for Celinda's eyes to settle on a dark-haired, striking-looking man with a trusty look and the mien and manner of a leader. That would be the man to approach, she decided. Steeling her will, she prepared to rise and reveal her presence. What a sight she would be, emerging from the brush, her face bruised and battered because of McKee's cruelty!

She dreaded the inevitable stares, the outcries of surprise, the initial shock that would greet her, but dread was overwhelmed by her hunger for good human companionship. Lifting her eyes heavenward for a moment—*A sign, Lord . . . remember to give me a sign*—she drew in her breath, stood, and advanced toward the gathering on the beach, eyes locked on the tall, dark-haired, well-dressed man she was sure led them. A child was the first to see her—"Pap! Look coming yonder!"—and then every eye turned, and the response was just as she had expected.

The surprised people formed a rough and unplanned gauntletlike double line through which she passed. She heard murmurings, shocked whisperings about her battered appearance. Eyes fixed on the tall man, she walked up to him and said, "My name is Celinda Ames. I have been a captive of river pirates, but I've escaped them. I'd like to ask you and your people for food and protection, and if I could, to become one of you and voyage on down the river."

The man blinked, seemingly not knowing what to make of this strange, battered young woman before him. "Miss, this is not my group in any sense but that I am traveling with them, but they are good folk and I am sure will be glad to help you."

"You are not the leader?"

"No, miss. Just a traveler, bound for Natchez. My name is Deerfield, and I—"

He cut off and reached out, catching Celinda just before she would have struck the rocky ground. "Help me, someone!" he called out. "This poor girl has fainted, dead away!"

They swarmed around her, voices mixing in a clamor of concern that she heard through the murk of half-consciousness. She felt her face gently massaged; someone put cool water on her forehead. Awareness began to return.

Deerfield ... his name is Deerfield ... Her eyes opened and fixed on him fearfully. "Let me ... go. ..."

"Miss, calm yourself. There's nothing to fear. These are good folk, all of them. My name is Japheth Deerfield. Did I startle you in some way?"

"Japheth ... Japheth ... not John ..."

Astonishment showed in his face. "John Deerfield is my brother. How do you know him?"

Celinda could not answer at once, being too overwhelmed. Her eyes closed. Japheth Deerfield, his broad hand behind her head, looked around and said, "This girl needs nourishment, quickly!"

The next several hours were filled with eating, resting, and the sharing of mutually astonishing stories between Celinda and Deerfield. It was late in the night before Celinda retired to a bed made of heaps of blankets. She nestled among them, losing herself to a sleep of utter peace.

She had asked for a sign, and in the person of Japheth Deerfield had received one. She was sure of it now: All was going to be well. She had found refuge, and the next morning would embark on the final leg of her voyage to Natchez among companions who would not harm her. Her night of trouble had passed; a better morning dawned.

CHAPTER 21

The sky, oddly enough, was a deep wooden brown, and as flat as could be. Thias examined the odd phenomenon through half-shut eyes, trying to make sense of it. He couldn't, so he began trying to make sense of himself and his situation instead. Where was he? What had happened? He smelled food cooking. Bacon. Was he back at the farm, with Grandpap burning up another breakfast?

He moved his head, opened his eyes wider, and gained more perspective. The wood-brown sky was in fact not sky at all but a wooden ceiling, and he was not at the farm, but inside a building he could not recall ever having been in before. And of course it couldn't be his grandfather cooking bacon. Grandpap was dead and buried.

Thias tried to sit up and experienced an explosion of pain in his head that stirred a heartfelt groan up from deep inside, followed by a burst of overwhelming dizziness that made him sink back and feel like he was spinning in circles where he lay.

A man's face loomed up before him in the swirl. "You're back with us, are you? Thanks be! I had worried you might die."

The seeming motion of the face stilled. Thias found his voice. "Where . . . am I?"

"You are in my inn, young man. My name is Farris. And your name, I'm willing to wager, is Tyler. And you hail from Tennessee. Am I right?"

"Yes . . . but how—"

"Don't try to talk too much. It will make you feel all the worse. It was easy to guess your name, Mr. Tyler. There was another fellow in here some days ago, nearly the very image of you. Clardy Tyler, he was. Your brother, maybe?"

"Aye." Thias was hardly able to absorb this unexpected bit of news about Clardy and totally unable to display any response to it, but inwardly he was stirred. Clardy had been at this inn! He was on the right course.

"I figured you for his brother the moment I saw you," Farris went on. "Well, actually I thought you *were* him until I had a good look at you. Remarkable, how much you look alike! There's similarity in your situation, too. Your brother was sickly when he was here, and we put him up until he was better, in the very bed you now lie in." Farris chuckled. "It seems we have a tendency to play host to ailing Tennesseans named Tyler in this place."

"Clardy . . . sick?"

"He was. A malady of the belly, brought on, he said, by drinking bad water. He recovered quickly. You needn't worry about it. Ah, but you, you are in much worse shape. Someone struck you very hard on the noggin, young fellow. Robbery?"

Memories of what had happened on the trail and in the forest returned in a flood. Thias closed his eyes. "Yes," he said. "Robbery."

Farris shook his head and clicked his tongue reproachfully. "It's a dangerous country, and this road can be a bloody stretch for those who travel alone. A man needs companions to be safe."

Thias cleared his throat, which made his head throb but did enable him to speak more easily. "It was my companions who robbed me."

"No! Who were they?"

"One was Billy French . . . I knew him as a boy. The other, a man named Jack Waller. A stranger until I met him on the road."

"Waller! That scoundrel! I know him well. And French, too.

I cast both those out of this inn one night some months ago when they were caught going through the baggage of two other men who had stopped here on their way to Crab Orchard."

"Waller said that *you* are a thief. He didn't want to stop here."

"Oh, I'd say he didn't! But no, Mr. Tyler, I'm no thief, I assure you. It's Waller who is the rascal, as you can well attest yourself now. If he didn't want to come here, it was only because he knew that he wouldn't be accepted, and that his foul nature would be revealed to you before he could get his hands on your possessions. What is your Christian name, by the way?"

"Thias. Thias Tyler."

"Thias, I regret you were hurt and I'm sorry for whatever you lost—but you are fortunate at least that you have your life. My daughter-in-law Jane found you yesterday morning, lying in leaves beside the road. She had seen dogs sniffing about where you were, and investigated, for which you can be grateful. Those leaves about you may be what kept you from freezing. Since then you've been here, and we've been awaiting either your awakening . . . or your death."

"Yesterday morning . . . I've been lying senseless that long?"

"Indeed. During that time we cleaned away the blood, bandaged your head, and said many a prayer for your life. It wasn't at all certain you would ever wake up." Farris suddenly pounded his forehead with the heel of his hand. "Oh, I'm a thoughtless fool, Thias. You're surely very thirsty. Jane, Jane! A dipper of water, please—our guest has come 'round!"

The water, administered by the gentle hand of a plain but appealing young woman with a look of tender concern on her face, made for the most satisfying, quenching draught that he had ever imbibed. "Not too much, nor too fast," Farris's daughter-in-law directed. "You must take all things slowly for now."

Thias lay back, wincing as his bandaged head resettled itself in the feather-stuffed pillow. "Thank you for finding me," he said.

She smiled. "I'm glad you have made it through. You'll be up and about soon."

Farris had risen while Thias was drinking, and he now paced about with an angry expression on his face. "Called *me* a thief, did he? I'll see Jack Waller flayed if ever I lay my hand on him again! And the same for that empty-headed French!"

"It was French who hit me," Thias said. "Struck me with the blunt part of a belt axe."

"Doing Waller's dirty job for him, no doubt. Waller controls the man. Directs him like a mule. French is his tool for wickedness."

"Yes. But it was French who spared me, too." Thias briefly recounted how French had dragged him into the woods for a final dispatching at Waller's behest, but had left him alive. "I owe French my life, in a way. Not once, like before, but twice."

"Twice? I don't understand."

Thias was rapidly growing weary of talking, but he did manage to get out a shortened version of how French had saved him and Clardy from drowning when they were boys. Farris declared that the tale was remarkable. To be saved, assaulted, and then spared by the same person was an oddity indeed. "It only shows more the devilishness of Jack Waller that he would push off murder on a weaker partner," Farris said. "But it seems there's yet some heart left in French."

Thias rested the balance of the day, and that night took some welcome food, after which he felt much stronger. There were no other lodgers in the inn, so Thias was the center of Farris's attention.

Thias brought up the subject of the Harpes. "Mr. Farris, there were some travelers on the road about the time I was hurt. I saw them on the road, and their horses being taken into your stables. Two men together, and a third younger one, and three women, all with child."

"Why, yes indeed. Interesting group, that one. The young man you mention was Stephen Langford. A cheerful soul, that boy, very pleasing company. It happens that I knew some of his family in Virginia, so I was pleased to have him as a guest. He's bound for Crab Orchard. As for the others, they were folk who had run across Mr. Langford on the road. A motley bunch . . ." Here Farris lowered his voice and leaned closer. ". . . and the three women, all carrying babes—I don't know what to make of that. Two men, three women with child . . . there's scandal there, I'll wager you. They were a poor group, though they did have horses. Roberts was the name they gave."

"Roberts? No, that's not right. The name of the men is Harpe—they're brothers—and as for the women, the youngest is the wife of Wiley Harpe, the smaller brother. The other two women keep company with the brothers, but they aren't married, or so I'm told. The older brother is named Micajah."

Farris wrinkled his nose like he had smelled something bad. "I knew there was badness in that bunch. Harpe, you say?"

"Yes. They're evil men, Mr. Farris. They've stolen horses, swine, cattle. I have good reason to believe they are the ones who murdered a man named Van Zandt down at Knoxville."

"Murderers!"

"Yes." Thias's manner grew very sober. "I worry for this Langford man, if he continued on in their company."

"He did." Farris recounted what had happened. The Harpes, along with Langford, had come to the inn seeking lodging and food, which Farris had gladly offered, though he felt some instinctive worry about all but Langford. The Harpes, though obviously hungry, had declared themselves too poor to pay for a meal, and Langford had cheerfully offered to pay the bill for them, and produced a purse heavy with silver coins. He seemed proud of his money. And the next morning, just before he left, he argued briefly with one of the Harpes over one thing or another, leading Farris to scold them both for using bad language in the presence of women. Langford had repented like a gentleman, saying that he regretted his words and wouldn't have desired to offend Mrs. Farris even if it would double the five-hundred-dollar value of all the things he carried in his saddlebags.

"Careless words, those were, and as soon as he said them, I wished he hadn't," Farris said. "It's unwise to boast about carrying wealth in a region so full of scoundrels. I could see the glitter in the eyes of the Roberts brothers . . . the Harpes, I should say. But when they left, they had settled whatever their argument was and all of them seemed happy with the notion of traveling together. They ate their breakfast—Langford paid for it, and the Harpes in turn paid for refilling his little glass flask for them all to share on the road—and they went on their way. It was shortly after that when Jane found you."

Thias said, "All I can say is, if I was traveling this road with money in my bags, the Harpes are the last folk I would want to keep company with. Stephen Langford made a fool's voice in taking up with them." He paused, then chuckled sadly. "Though I made just as foolish a one when I took up with Jack Waller and Billy French. Now I've lost everything—my horse,

my rifle and packs, and every cent from the sale of my grandfather's old farm. I was planning to divide that money with
Clardy as soon as I found him. Now I have nothing."

"But you are alive, young man. You are alive. And life is the
dearest of a man's treasures. It is one of the few things that,
once taken, can't be given back or replaced. You are fortunate
to be living." Farris's brows sank low over the hollows of his
eyes. "I can only hope that young Mr. Langford comes through
as fortunate as you."

The physical strength and great endurance Thias had developed
in years of farm labor served him well as he struggled to re-
cover from his head injury. As severe as it had seemed to begin
with, the injury was already healing, and Thias began to regain
his bearings and strength. He was eager to get fully well and
set about finding Clardy. He was greatly encouraged by the
fact Clardy had come this way and stayed at this very inn. It
made him seem close.

Having lost the money from the sale of the farm had a par-
adoxical affect on Thias's desire to reunite with his brother.
There was the natural dread of having to share bad news on the
one hand—Hiram Tyler's death, the loss of their inheritance—
but on the other was a desire for brotherly company that was
heightened by the fact that now the Tyler brothers had nothing
left in the world but each other. Despite separation, Thias felt
closer to Clardy right now than he had in years.

Fast though he was healing, it was evident it would be many
days yet before Thias would be able to go on. As long as he
didn't exert himself, he felt fairly well, but every time he tried
to do anything even mildly straining, sharp pain, a feeling of
sickness, and dizziness came rushing back. Billy French's axe
had done quite a job on him, even if it hadn't taken his life.
Thias would have to wait and heal for a time, and the waiting
was more frustrating by the hour.

One thing Farris told him confused Thias and caused him to
worry that finding Clardy might grow complicated. Clardy had
told Farris he was planning to meet relatives farther north—but
no such relatives existed, Thias well knew. He could only con-
clude that Clardy was being covert and evasive about his movements, which meant he might go anywhere. He could double
back, head toward the farther eastern settlements, or even go
north to the Ohio and catch a boat for some distant riverside

city. The longer Thias had to wait to heal, the more likely it
was that Clardy was putting untrackable miles between them.

Thias grew ever more frustrated. He had always been able to
meet challenges by using his strength and taking firm action.
This challenge was different. He had no strength to speak of,
and for once in his life action was the one option not open to
him.

CHAPTER 22

The cattle drovers pushed their herd past the inn, not noticing the tall, muscled young man who watched them from the window, his head wrapped in a bandage. They were weary, having driven this lowing, milling mass of bovine flesh all the way from Virginia, and many miles remained to be covered.

A day later they noticed that the cattle were behaving oddly, acting unsettled and nervous. "There's a killed beast about," the oldest and most experienced drover said. "They act that way when they smell a dead thing."

The farther they went, the more restless grew the cattle, until at last almost half the herd bolted suddenly off the road and into the forest. The drovers pursued them, chasing them down in the brown wintry brush, until suddenly the forest rang with the kind of explosive bellow given out by cattle when blood is smelled, followed by the kind of shout peculiar to a man who has experienced a tremendous, quick shock.

The other drovers gathered around their frightened companion, who pointed with a trembling finger at the terrible thing he had stumbled across. It was a corpse, cut up and battered, the brains literally knocked out of the head. It had been placed behind a log and covered with leaves, but those cursory efforts were insufficient to fully hide the terrible corpse, or to stifle the horrendous stench that rose from it.

"There's been murder done here," the oldest drover said. "That poor man is the victim of highwaymen."

"What will we do? Bury him?"

"Yes, but not here, and not yet. We passed an inn near the Rockcastle. We'll take the corpse there. It may be that someone there can tell us who it is. Whoever this man's family is, they should know what has become of him."

Farris's eyes watered and his face was screwed up with a look of strong repulsion, but he advanced toward the Indian-style, drag-pole conveyance the drovers had lashed together and bravely looked at the gray face of the dead man strapped onto it. The face was so distorted by fast-advancing decay that Farris had to look closely to assure himself that this was, indeed, the body of Stephen Langford.

"Yes, God help us, it's him," he said, hand across his nose and mouth in a vain attempt to filter the smell. "He was a guest here some days ago." Farris turned. "Thias! The worst has happened. Stephen Langford has been killed. Come and see."

Thias was standing up in the inn yard, watching with the terrible fear that the corpse would turn out to be Clardy's instead of Langford's. Farris's confirmation that it was Langford's brought him relief he politely didn't allow to show. "I've always been weak of stomach, Mr. Farris," he called back with some embarrassment. But better that embarrassment than the loss of his last meal before all these watchers, he figured.

"Then this sight is not for you." Farris shuddered. "Nor for me, for that matter. I propose we bury this poor fellow at once.'

The drovers did the job, and gladly, everyone being eager to put the foul corpse out of sight and smell.

"Word of this must be spread," Farris declared. "Every settlement should know of this as quickly as possible. There are murderers loose in this country, and their name is Harpe."

"I'll help spread the word," Thias said. "I probably can ride, if you have a horse to loan."

Farris looked him over and shook his head. "Not yet, though I thank you for your willingness. You stay here and heal, young man. And if it gives you any comfort, consider the fact that the scoundrels who tried to take your own life might be overtaken by the devils who killed poor Langford."

"And so might my brother Clardy," Thias replied. "It's him I think of—and the Harpes have hard feelings toward him already, because of something that happened in Tennessee. Until they're caught, I consider him in danger."

"Until they're caught, every traveler on this road is in danger," Farris replied. "And they must be caught . . . and I know the man to do it, if anyone can."

"Who?" Thias asked.

"Devil Joe Ballenger," Farris replied, nodding resolutely. "If any man in Kentucky can bring in the Harpes, it's Devil Joe."

"Who is he?"

"The toughest old pine knot in the Kentucky Commonwealth," Farris said. "The Harpes will have little hope of escape with Devil Joe on their heels."

"He'd better be a devil if he finds them," Thias said. "God knows they're devils enough themselves."

Despite his diabolical nickname, Captain Joe Ballenger was a highly respected man. A former Indian fighter turned merchant in Stanford, he was as tough and dogged a frontier citizen as could be found, and just as John Farris had anticipated, he proved to be the best choice of leader for the quickly formed band of "regulators" that went out in pursuit of the Harpes.

"Devil Joe" Ballenger, it so happened, had already chanced to lay eyes on the Harpes. They had passed through Stanford shortly after the time that Langford had been killed. The motley bunch had drawn attention, but no one had known at that point of Langford's murder, and they had passed through the town unimpeded.

Now that the truth was out and the story of Stephen Langford's murder was spreading all over the region, Ballenger had no difficulty in rounding up his regulators. The men of the Kentucky frontier, scarred and hardened from years of fighting Indians in the earlier days of settlement, were accustomed to taking law and order into their own hands, and with such a stalwart leader as Joe Ballenger to guide them, they readily answered the call. Murder could not be tolerated. Already stretches of the Wilderness Road of Kentucky, particularly between Cumberland Gap and Stanford, were fearsome places.

Cameron Judd

Public safety and confidence demanded that demons such as the Harpes should be exorcized from the dark forests with the greatest of dispatch.

The regulators rode out of Stanford fully expecting to face a difficult tracking job and likely resistance from the culprits. Typical murderers were prone to leave neither clear trails nor to take a cordial attitude toward capture. But the regulators learned quickly that the Harpes were not typical murderers.

They had made no effort to hide their tracks. The regulators trailed them with ease, riding across Brush Creek, where a resident named John Blain reported seeing the pursued party earlier, and then over the Rolling Fork of the Salt River. Here the trail grew extremely fresh.

"We must be very wary from here out," Ballenger instructed his men. "They are armed, and I don't anticipate they will be taken easily."

Ballenger didn't let his men see how bewildered he was. He could see no logic in the obvious lack of caution being shown by these criminals. But he knew from hard experience that too-clear trails often led to traps. He led his regulators along the course of the ever-fresher Harpe trail with a sense of wariness that grew with every mile.

They would find the Harpes, he was sure, within a day.

Sally Rice Harpe saw it all playing out in her mind as clearly as the day it had happened. She was young, no more than ten or eleven, standing beside the outdoor oven her father had built at their old family home, attentively following her mother's directions as she prepared, at her own request, a pigeon pie for her father in celebration of his birthday.

On a stone slab beside the oven lay a pile of plucked and washed passenger pigeons, a heap of vegetables, slab of beef, molded square of butter, and containers of seasonings. Sally's immediate task was carefully spreading a puff-paste dough across the bottom of a pan and up the sides. Her fingers, greased with a dab of lard, smoothed the crust under the watchful eye of her mother, who at length gave a curt nod and said, "Good, Sally. Very good. Now we'll begin laying in the makings."

Eyes closed in memory, Sally smiled to herself as she replayed each step of the process: seasoning the pigeons with salt and pepper, knifing off pieces of butter and working them inside the birds along with seasonings, carefully piling each pigeon into the pan and then laying the beef in the middle of them, and finally, that most aesthetically important step of laying on and molding the top crust. This pie was to be Sally's gift to her father, so she desired that it be perfect. She wanted deeply to please him, to earn his praise. Her father was a beloved man; he made her happy, especially when he found something she had done or made to be praiseworthy. Those occasions didn't come as often as Sally would have liked, but when they did, they were epitomical experiences that she treasured like keepsakes in her mind.

She remembered the tension of waiting beside the oven for the pie to bake, her continual sniffing to make sure the crust wasn't burning, and at last her careful removal of the finished pie. It looked as good as she hoped, and the smell of it was superb. When it was laid before her father, he had smiled, put out his hand, tousled her hair, and told her it was the finest pigeon pie ever set before a living man, kings and emperors included. She relived the pure joy that simple fatherly praise had given her, and thought again that the gift of it was far finer than the pie itself.

"What you grinning at, Sally?"

She opened her eyes to the sight of Wiley squatting before her, grinning curiously. All the happiness of her memory was jolted aside to make way for a wave of revulsion. *Murderer.* That word arose in her mind every time she looked at her husband now. *Murderer!* How could she have ever bound herself to this man? How could her own father have been so blind to the character of the human demon he had allowed to become his own son-in-law?

"Just remembering," Sally murmured, and looked away.

Wiley shifted on his feet to enter her line of sight again. She knew better than to avert her eyes again; that would anger him. "Remembering what?"

"Just things. Things I like to think on."

"Like our marrying night, eh?" He winked, reached out, stroked her leg through her dress, grinning devilishly.

"No. Not that."

Wiley's smile faded and Sally was afraid. He had never hit her, but since witnessing his capability for violence, she had realized it could happen. She wanted to curl up within herself, become small and invisible. She wanted to be free of this man, who had first stunned her moral senses by sharing her with his brother as if she were no more than a pipe of tobacco or a piece of dried beef, then stunned her all the more by killing innocent men before her eyes. The most recent was the handsome young man Langford, who had died at Wiley's own hand without ever suspecting his own danger or seeing the coming blow that slew him.

As Sally looked fearfully into Wiley's stern face an odd thing happened. Before her eyes he seemed to visibly empty, to become blank and vacant and emotionless. Her impression was that even while looking at her he had ceased to really see her. She had seen this phenomenon before in both Wiley and Micajah. She could not explain it, but when the emptying occurred, it generally heralded a time of quiet. The brothers would grow somnolent and slow, sitting for hours and doing nothing, lost in whatever thoughts it was that stirred in minds such as theirs.

The first time Sally had seen her husband that way, she asked him what he was doing. His answer puzzled her: "Listening to the voices," he had said. "They're singing sweet today. Sweet and pretty, like angels."

Wiley rose, stiffly walked away from Sally and joined his brother, who was seated on a log in the clearing where they had made this camp. Sally looked at Micajah. *He is empty, too. Both of them, empty as spilled buckets.* She was glad. They would be like this for hours, maybe days. There would be peace for her and the other women during that time, as much peace as ever was allowed them. *I hope the voices sing for a long time.*

Sally turned back to her memories again. They were her only refuge; she had begun regularly escaping into them shortly after her marriage, that very first time Wiley turned her over to be used by his brother.

She was deeply lost in her childhood when the riders came in. There were a dozen or more of them, all armed, all with stern expressions. She looked up at the apparent leader of the group and thought, I reckon they must have found one of the dead ones, and now they've come for us. I'm so glad. I don't want to go on no more like this.

The lead rider was looking oddly at the Harpe brothers, probably wondering why they did not react to this obviously hostile intrusion. Sally thought: He doesn't know that they have been emptied.

"I am Captain Joe Ballenger," the lead rider said loudly, causing Micajah and Wiley to look directly at him for the first time. Their expressions remained as vacant as before. "We've come to place you under arrest for the murder of Stephen Langford of Virginia, and to take you to the jail in Stanford, to be held under the authority of Lincoln County, Kentucky."

Micajah stood, holding out his rifle toward Ballenger. "We'll go with you," he said calmly.

Wiley turned his rifle over, too, while Captain Joe Ballenger and his men all looked thoroughly bewildered. Sally thought: They didn't expect this to happen.

One of the riders, a very young man with a nervous manner, dismounted and came to her. "Ma'am, I must ask you to come with us."

Sally rose. "Are you taking us to jail?" She sounded very childlike as she said it, which obviously surprised the nervous young man.

"Yes, ma'am. We're obliged to do that." He was shy and deferential, clearly uncomfortable with arresting a female. He took off his hat and tensely crumpled it in his hand. "I'm sorry to have to do that, it being Christmas and all."

Sally's eyes grew bright. "It's Christmas?"

"Yes, ma'am. Christmas Day."

"I've always loved Christmas," Sally said, smiling for the first time in weeks, outside those times she smiled while lost in her memories. "Back when I was small, my folks always fed me sweetening on Christmas. I love Christmas Day. Jesus was born today, you know. Born in the stables while the angels sang. The good angels, not the bad ones, like them that sing for Wiley. My pa, he's a preacher, you know. He always told us the story about Jesus and the shepherds on Christmas Day. When my baby is borned, I'll tell him, too."

"Yes, ma'am." The young man turned away. Sally wondered why he seemed so disturbed.

1 7 9 9

CHAPTER 23

Early in January, John and Jane Farris journeyed to Stanford to give testimony in the first hearing in the case of the Harpes. Farris asked Thias to consider coming along, in case the court was interested in his knowledge of the Harpes' involvement in the Abel Van Zandt murder in Knoxville.

Thias declined on the grounds that he still felt too weak and dizzy to travel all the way to Stanford, and that he really did not know that the Harpes had committed the Knoxville murder, or even if any charges had been brought against them related to it. All he really knew was that Van Zandt's corpse had been brought in just as he was leaving Knoxville, and that the Harpes were generally suspected. He shruggingly told Farris he really had no firsthand information to give on the Knoxville matter—and here he realized with secret shame that he bordered on falsehood. He had the witness of his own eyes that the Harpes had dug in Selma Van Zandt's grave the night that Abel Van Zandt had vanished. Meager evidence that might be, but evidence worth sharing—the guilty fact was he simply didn't want to share it. He wanted nothing to do with the Harpes, did not want so much as to lay eyes on them—or have them lay eyes on him, especially as he gave evidence against them—in even the sterile and protected environment of a courtroom. The truth was, Thias Tyler was afraid of the Harpes. He didn't dwell on it because it was shameful, but it was true.

When Farris and his daughter-in-law returned from Stanford the day after the hearing in Lincoln Courthouse, Thias hungrily listened to Farris's recounting of the events.

The Harpes and their women, with the sole exception of Betsy, were claiming the name of Roberts, as they had when they stayed at his inn, and though the three judges presiding over the case knew the true name was Harpe, they allowed the aliases to stand in the record, which Farris admitted he could not understand. In any case, the case was entered against Micajah, Wiley, Susannah, and Sally Roberts, and Elizabeth, or Betsy, Walker, the charge being that they "feloniously and of their malice aforethought" murdered and robbed Langford in December of the just-passed year.

The Harpes were denying their guilt despite the strong evidence against them. Among the most damning testimony, Farris said, was information given in the official affidavit of Captain Ballenger, who recounted how he learned that the murder had occurred, and how he and a body of regulators, informal in structure and nature but gathered with the blessing of the commonwealth's attorney general, had pursued the suspects and found them beyond the Rolling Fork of the Salt River. In their possession at the time of their capture, Ballenger had stated, were items including a pocket book with Langford's name inscribed upon it, three coats, including a greatcoat, a pair of trousers, a whip, a shaving glass, Freemason's apron, and various other items appearing to have belonged to the murder victim.

Further testimony came from one David Irby, who had been a traveling companion of Langford's during most of his journey. Farris said that Irby testified to having left Pittsylvania County in Virginia in Langford's company, and had traveled five days with him, sharing expenses along the way, all of which had been recorded by Langford in his pocket book, the very pocket book found in the possession of the suspects. Irby and Langford had parted ways temporarily near Cumberland Gap, agreeing to meet in the town of Frankfort. Since then,

Irby had learned of Langford's murder and hurried to the area at once.

The testimony of the two Farrises dealt mostly with the details of the visit of Langford and the Harpe clan to the Farris inn, and with details of the clothing Langford had worn, the finding and identification of the corpse, and so on.

The facts against the "Roberts" or Harpe group were sufficiently damning to lead the court to hold them in custody for trial of the murder of Langford in the Danville District Court, the trial to be held in April, and the Harpes, though declaring innocence, had nothing at all to say in their own defense. The prosecutors and witnesses were bound and bonded to appear at the trial, and the Harpes were hustled back to the log jailhouse, shortly after to be transferred to the stronger jail at Danville, some ten miles away.

"All in all, a good day's work," Farris said. "I don't believe we will have to worry any longer about the Harpes. They will be jailed until their trial, and there is no doubt that they will be convicted."

"It's a relief to me," Thias said. "I've worried about my brother Clardy, having them roaming free. They would surely kill him if he had the misfortune to cross their path."

"Their path, I believe, has come to an end—all but the final stretch of it, leading to the gallows, at least for the men. Those women—who knows what will become of them? Two of them were harsh, hard things . . . the third and youngest, Sally, seemed more pitiable than evil. A trapped woman, if I had to take a guess. Trapped in a hellish life with hellish folk."

"Do you think they will be secure where they are?" Thias asked.

"I was wondering the same. I fear they may make an escape," interjected William Farris, son of John and husband of Jane.

"Escape? No fear of that!" John Farris replied confidently as he filled a clay pipe with fine tobacco. "Danville has the finest courthouse and the stoutest jail in all Kentucky. There'll be no getting out of there." He paused long enough to light the pipe with a flaming pine twig pulled from the fireplace. Looking at the others through great white puffs of smoke, he smiled and said, "This has been an ugly business, but it's now as good as done. The Harpes have shed their last blood, and the people of our region have no need to fear them any longer."

*   *   *

About two weeks later Thias Tyler said his farewells to the Farris family and set out on a horse John Farris "sold" to him on the vague promise that "someday, whenever it's possible," Thias would return and recompense him for it. The same bargain held true of the old but serviceable rifle that William Farris put in his hands, along with powder horn and ammunition. "No man can safely travel without gun and shot in this country," he said. Then he and his father threw in a handful of money, and Jane Farris supplied an ample stock of food for the road.

"I don't merit such kindness as I've been shown here," Thias said, deeply moved.

"Neither did you merit being robbed and nigh killed," John Farris replied. "It's only fit that a man who's been afflicted with treachery and loss should have it made up for with a bit of kindness. Kindness and goodness, they're good things to be able to look back on when everything seems dark and wicked. Like a child remembering the bright daylight when he's afraid at night, you know."

"I'll come back someday," Thias said, struggling to keep his voice from breaking. "I'll set all accounts right with you then. And I will remember your kindness, and your goodness, no matter how dark it gets."

"All is well, then, young man. Now, the thing for you to do is find that straying brother of yours, fast as you can, and know that you and he are both welcome here anytime you should come."

Thias rode out with a variety of feelings mixed together— regret at parting with such fine people as the Farris family, fear at entering the open, dangerous world again after such a mentally and physically trying experience as nearly being murdered, eagerness to get on with finding Clardy, worry that he wouldn't be able to do so.

Nothing, however, made him doubt he was doing the right thing. He was alone in the world as it was, and totally impoverished except for what the Farrises had provided.

All there was out there for him was Clardy . . . wherever he might be.

Thias went on through Crab Orchard, asking all he met if they had seen another young man, probably traveling alone, who looked much like him. Some seemed to have a vague memory of such a fellow, but no one could steer him in any particular direction. Most remembered no one like that at all.

On he rode, until he reached Stanford. There he searched all the harder, but with no better results. He began to believe that Clardy had probably passed through but not lingered, and maybe hadn't paused to meet anyone. It would be just like Clardy to do that. It made Thias angry. Even in absence, Clardy could get to him.

If Clardy wasn't here, then he must have continued on north—assuming he had meant it when he told Farris he planned to go on toward Harrodsburg. There was no way to be sure.

A secret worry plagued Thias and wouldn't let him go no matter how hard he resisted it. What if the corpse of Stephen Langford wasn't the only one hidden in these vast Kentucky forests? What if the Harpes had encountered Clardy either before or after they killed Langford? For that matter, what if Jack Waller and Billy French had met up with him? It was possible Clardy was dead and no one knew.

No one might *ever* know. Thias might search for weeks, months, years, and never find what became of Clardy. A more dismal prospect couldn't be imagined.

He wished Clardy had never left home. It was all the fault of the Harpes, really. If Clardy had never become entangled with them, he wouldn't have had to flee home. He would have been there to say his final good-bye to his grandfather. He would have been there to claim his half of the inheritance, an inheritance now lost, probably forevermore. Together the Tyler brothers could have sold the farm and went out into the world, side by side, protecting each other and finding that new and better place Hiram Tyler had talked about in his final words.

It had all come so close to working out as it should. A mere difference of a few days and Clardy wouldn't have become lost out in the world, separated from his own flesh and blood. A few days difference, and circumstances would have been so very different for Thias right now.

He was lost in such thoughts, riding on some miles past Stanford, when he heard the distant crack of a rifle in the woods, high up on a ridge. He looked up and made out the tiny form of a hunter a long way off, visible only because he was limned against the gray-white sky at the very peak of the ridge, a lone human silhouette among the dark outlines of the leafless winter trees. It seemed to Thias that the man waved, though distance made it impossible to be sure. He waved back nonetheless, then returned his attention to the empty road ahead.

High on the ridgetop, Clardy Tyler watched the rider moving slowly down the narrow road. What was it about the man that caught his eye so? He was too far away for Clardy to tell anything about him, but there was something about him . . .

The man went out of sight. Clardy shrugged to himself, paused to reload his rifle, then went to retrieve the squirrel he had just barked right out of the top of an oak. When it was added to the string of squirrels already tied to the sash of his hunting shirt, he set off down the slope on a woodsman's lope, heading for the cabin of Isaac Ford and a supper table where he was feeling more at home and welcome every passing day.

An hour later Clardy watched Amy Ford stirring the kettle of stew she had cooked using the squirrel meat he had provided. *Right there is the kind of woman I hope I'm married to when I'm Isaac Ford's age.*

He blinked in surprise at that unbidden thought. Clardy Tyler thinking about marriage, even if only abstractly? *It ain't like me to think in a family way. But come to think of it, I ain't never been amongst a happy family until now.*

Happy indeed the Ford family clearly was. The bonds of affection between each member were so solid and evident that Clardy felt he could reach out and pluck at them like harp strings. It all gave Clardy a bittersweet awareness of how much he and Thias had missed, being raised without benefit of a father or mother. Old Hiram had done the best he could, maybe, but that hadn't been much. Clardy looked sidewise at Amy Ford and wondered if his own mother would have been like her. He would like to think so, and wished he could know. Hiram had always talked poorly about her, saying she hadn't been hardworking enough to have been a fit wife for his son— but that was Hiram. He had never said much nice about anyone in his life.

Clardy thought it remarkable how much coming to the Ford household had changed him. His perceptions and attitudes were going through all kinds of novel mutations. These people had a way of bringing out new things in him and making him think in uncommon ways. It was really very unnerving.

But Clardy had to admit he enjoyed being here, enjoyed the family's company and mix of personalities, even if he wasn't fully comfortable with them. That was his fault, he well knew, having to do with the mode of his first encounter with Isaac Ford. Ford hadn't told his family about that incident, as far as Clardy knew. Clardy wondered if Amy Ford and her two children would be so kind to him if they knew he had met their father in a robbery attempt.

Most unnerving of all to Clardy was the mystery of why Isaac Ford himself was being so hospitable, considering what he had tried to do to him. Clardy had done his best to rob the man, but Ford had returned only kindness, even opening his home, and not only for the brief duration of the snowstorm that had brought Clardy here in the first place. The snow was long melted, but still Clardy remained, encouraged to stay as long as he wished, on the sole conditions that he not make himself a nuisance and that he contribute something in return for the hospitality.

Lacking money, all Clardy could contribute was work with Isaac and his son, and meat he brought in from the forests. He had provided plenty of both. The aversion to labor that had characterized him through all his life so far was inexplicably lessened here, and the bad luck at hunting that had plagued him since he left Beaver Creek was entirely gone. In his brief residency here, Clardy had brought in deer, squirrel, and rabbit meat in abundance, bringing praise from the sober-faced Amy Ford, who declared him "the mightiest hunter before the Lord since Nimrod of old." Like her proverb-spouting husband, Amy Ford was a habitual quoter of the Bible.

Clardy was learning more about his hosts every day. The Fords were unusually open people, talking freely about their lives. He had learned from young John, who seemed to idolize him, that the family was small because his mother had lost no less than five babies within days of their births. "Me and Dulciana are the only two to make it through," John had said. "Pa says that must mean we're truly special folks, me and Dulciana."

Dulciana. Clardy had never heard a girl's name he liked more. It was like music on the tongue. *Dulciana.* A beautiful name, a name to linger in the mind . . . just like Dulciana herself lingered in his.

Of all the good things he had discovered here in the cabin of

Isaac Ford, Dulciana was the best. She was only fifteen years old, but already she had the face and frame of a lovely grown woman, and Clardy had to struggle to keep from staring at her all the time. It distressed him that she displayed no evident interest in staring back. Her manner was graceful, her voice delicate and as musical as her name, her hair a rich brown, like her eyes, and her hands tapered and supple, strong without being fleshy or masculine, like the hands of so many hardworking frontier girls he had seen.

"The stew is done," Amy Ford declared loudly. "John, go call in your father."

John ran to the door, threw it open and yelled to his father, who was out in the stable. Isaac Ford made his living by farming, hunting, and horse trading, and already he had taught Clardy more about horses than he had ever known before. The Tylers had never done much trade in horses, keeping only what horse stock they needed to work the farm and provide transportation, and Clardy had always been pretty much indifferent to anything equine. Now he was developing a true interest in the animals—just one more of the fast-coming changes sweeping over him.

Isaac Ford never allowed a meal to be eaten at his table without a long, expansive prayer being said first. Clardy's stomach rumbled with hunger as he sat with head bowed and listened to Ford give his supplication, full of references to the "Almighty Father of all who walk and breathe" and thanks for "the glorious bounty of the world, which you have lavished upon us for our nourishment, due to the kind labors of our guest, Clardy Tyler." Clardy sneaked a secret glance or two at Dulciana while Ford finished his prayer, then at the final "Amen," raised his head and suffered through another long wait while the bowl of stew made the rounds of the table before reaching him.

They ate without words for several minutes, then Ford leaned back, belched without shame, and folded his hands across his chest.

"I seen Thomas Pitt today," he said. "He was herding some swine down the road. Told me some interesting news. Says there's been a murder on the road back in December. A Virginia fellow, name of . . . what was it? Lángford, I believe. Killed and his body hid behind a log, all mutilaterized and mayhemed. Some cattle drovers found it when the blood smell sent their herd running into the woods. Cattle will do that when they smell blood—did you know that, John?"

"No."

"Isaac, I do hate to hear talk of blood while I'm eating stew," Amy Ford said.

John Ford didn't share his mother's revulsion, showing a young boy's normal eager curiosity about crime. "Who done the murder, Pa?"

"Some folks name of Roberts. Two men and some women. Joe Ballenger and some regulators rounded them in, and they're locked up in the Danville jail. Seems this business has been the talk of the region since it happened. I'm surprised I've just now heard about it."

Clardy wasn't surprised. The Ford family, though residing fairly close to the road, lived an isolated life and seldom had visitors. In the time he had been here, he had not seen another living soul outside the Ford family, except for that distant traveler he spotted from the ridge.

"Why did they kill the man, Pa?"

"Robbery." Isaac Ford glanced subtly at Clardy, who ducked his head in shame. "Some of the dead man's possessions were found on the killers when they were caught. Strange bunch, Thomas said. They were just sitting there on a log when the captain and his men found them. Didn't try to run nor fight. Strange thing indeed."

"Will they hang them?"

"John, I do hate to hear you talking so," Amy Ford said.

"They'll have to put them on trial first, and that won't happen until April," Ford said. "In the old days they might have hung them right off, John, but these are civilized times. We have government and appointed authorities to deal with such things. Keepers of the law, you know, who contend with them who break it. 'They that foresake the law praise the wicked, but such as keep the law contend with them.' The Robertses will face their earthly judgment in the end, though it does seem a long time to wait, all the way till April."

"Can we see it when they hang them, Pa?" John asked.

"That's enough of that," Amy Ford said firmly. "Isaac, you shouldn't talk of wicked things at the table. I don't think it's fitting."

Isaac Ford winked at his son. " 'It is better to dwell in a corner of the housetop, than with a brawling woman in a wide house.' " Amy Ford frowned, but her eyes were bright with the same underlying good humor in which Ford's teasing proverb had been spoken.

The subject dropped at that point, though, and Clardy was glad. Talk of robbers on the road roused a hot shame in him, reminding him anew of his own attempted crime against a man who had turned out to be a kind benefactor. It was downright astonishing when Clardy thought about it. Twice now folks he had intended to rob had been kind to him, first Peyton the peddler, and now Isaac Ford. It appeared that not everyone followed the same eye-for-an-eye philosophy that sour old Hiram Tyler had always advocated and which Clardy had assumed ruled the world.

Clardy ate listlessly through the rest of the meal, then put on his coat and hat and left the cabin to smoke his pipe. A few minutes later the cabin door opened and Isaac Ford joined him.

"Pretty evening. Not as cold as I would have thought it would be."

Clardy looked Ford directly in the face. "I want you to tell me something, Mr. Ford. Why is it you've been kind to me when you know I tried to rob you?"

Ford grinned. "Kind to you? If you recollect, I marched you before my horse, then sent you packing back the way you'd come."

"But that's the point. You could have locked me up, but you didn't. And when I showed up at your door, you took me in. Since then you've treated me as good as your own family. I don't understand why."

"Well, I don't know how to answer." Ford rubbed his chin in silence a couple of moments. "I'll go at it this way. Do you believe that things just happen, Clardy, or that there's a cause and purpose for things?"

"Well . . . I never thought about it."

"I have. Don't know that I've got a firm answer, but I do believe that, quite often at least, there's a reason for folks crossing paths. And when a pair of strangers like me and you crosses paths not only once, but twice, maybe there's a particular important reason for it. Maybe they're *supposed* to meet, you see. When you showed up at my door, it struck a surprise in me. It seemed to me right then that maybe there was a cause for you being there. That's why I didn't throw you out. Tell you the truth, I wouldn't throw much anybody out in a snowfall like that one. Wouldn't be decent, you see. But there was more to it than just that in your case. I believed you had come for a reason."

"There was no reason. It was the snow that drove me in. That's all."

"Maybe so. Maybe not. Whatever, I did what I thought right. I judge folks by my instincts, Clardy. My instincts about you is that there's something decent in you, down under the top of what you show. Your cream may not have riz to the top yet, but I'm betting it will in time."

"I still don't know why you've been kind to me."

"I ain't for sure myself, Clardy. But I'll tell you this: you ain't yet proved me wrong to have took a chance on you. You ain't stole nothing from me, at least not that I know of. You ain't hurt nor offenserized any of my family here. I believe that cream is beginning to rise."

Clardy lowered his head. "I feel ashamed of myself for what I tried to do, Mr. Ford. I'm sorry."

Ford's one good eye glittered happily. "Well, now I *know* the cream is rising! Feeling sorry for bad steps done took is the first turn toward taking better ones."

"I don't know how to take better steps. I ain't a good man, Mr. Ford. I got a brother who's good, but folks have always said I was good for nothing. They've been right, every time."

"Why, you ain't bad. You're free, that's all, like every man. We're all free to decide what our nature is going to be. A man's nature ain't no more than the choices he makes. The main trouble with all of us is that for most folks, at least, it seems easier to make the bad choices than the good ones. I've made plenty of bad ones myself. Now I try to do better. It's all freedom, you see. Whatever you wind up to be, it's in large measure because you make yourself that."

Clardy had not thought along those lines before. He was a very unphilosophical fellow and had not been seeking complicated answers. He shook his head.

"All that is beyond me, Mr. Ford. Let me tell you, sir, I don't know whether a man makes his nature or his nature makes him, but whichever, my nature ain't never been worth half a heap of horse dung. You know what my ambition has been, since I was a boy? To be a robber. What do you think of that? I've always thought being a robber would be the finest thing a man could aspire to. That was what I thought of as good."

"Well, I can't agree with that ambition. But the point is, I don't believe you agree with it, either, not really. If you did, you wouldn't be ashamed of what you tried to do."

Clardy puffed his pipe, thinking. This talk was intriguing, but he wondered if any of it really made any sense or any difference. He was what he was, and that was that.

"What's your ambition now, Clardy?" Ford asked. "You still wanting to turn robber?"

"I don't know. I don't believe I'd make a good one."

"Not bum-stumbling around like you done with me, no sir, you wouldn't."

"I reckon I'll have to find honest work."

"Tell me, boy, why'd you leave your home to come to these parts?"

"Didn't want it to be my home anymore. It was always a hard and trying place to live. And finally, I was forced to leave because of some things that had happened. It's a long story I don't feel inclined to tell right now."

"Your business is your own." Ford held silent, finishing his pipe. He knocked the dead ashes out on his heel. "Clardy, I need to let you know that I can't keep you on here forever."

Clardy's face flushed and grew hot. "I've stayed too long, I can see. I've imposed. I'll leave tomorrow morning."

"Wait now, don't read me the wrong way here. You can stay long as you want, as far as I'm concerned. Why, the help you've give me, the food you've put on my table, all that more than makes up for your keep. You've been a boon to me. What I'm saying is that I can't give you enough recompense for your own good. I can't give much anything to you more than a roof over your head and a table to feed you. And you need more than just room and board. You're young. It's time for you to start making a place for yourself in the world, and I ain't talking about becoming a highway robber who'll wind up shot dead or hung. Like you said, you need honest work that pays real money."

"I don't know where to find it."

"I know of one job you might get. Don't pay much, but it's honest, and it would be a start."

"What is it?"

"Helping guard jail in Danville. Thomas Pitt told me today that there's a lot of worry in Danville that these Roberts folks will bust the jail. I always thought it a stout jail, but Thomas had talked to the jailer hisself, and even he is worried. He's wanting to keep the place guarded night and day, 'specially because the women they had with them are going to birtherate babies. All three of them. There needs to be somebody keeping watch on them all the time, so that there'll be someone to fetch help when the babes come."

"Two men . . . three pregnant women . . ." Clardy frowned, his mind flashing back to the Harpe cabin on Beaver Creek. The Harpe women were pregnant. "You sure these murderers are named Roberts?"

"That's what Thomas called them. Why?"

"Oh . . . nothing." He cleared his throat. "Work guarding the jail, you say?"

"That's right. I can't assure you of it, but Thomas said that Biegler—that's John Biegler, the jailer—hasn't found him enough guards yet to keep watch. He'd probably be glad to have your help, and there'd be some pay for it."

Clardy knocked out his pipe. The prospect of guarding a jail held no appeal, but he could tell that Ford wanted him to try for the work, and he wanted to please him. "I may ride over to Danville tomorrow, Mr. Ford."

"Good luck to you there. If you don't find work, just come on back. And if they can only put you to use part of the time, you can keep living here and working with me when you ain't at the jail. Just consider this your home for now, until something better comes along for you."

"Thank you, Mr. Ford. I do appreciate your kindness."

"It ain't nothing. God knows, lots of people have been kind to me. You just go and do likewise. It'll give you a lot more joy in the end than being the best highway robber ever could, and you'll never get hung for it."

Clardy had been sleeping on a pallet before the hearth, and though it made a hard bed, he slept very well every night. This night, though, it took longer to fall asleep. He was thinking about the jailed criminals Isaac Ford had talked about, and wondering. . . .

It didn't seem likely that these Roberts folks would actually be the Harpes. He had no reason to think they were anywhere but back on Beaver Creek, where he had last seen them. But the coincidence between numbers and genders, and the fact that the three jailed women were pregnant, just like the Harpe women, was remarkable.

The possibility of common identity seemed strong enough to make him uncomfortable. Wouldn't it be an unwelcome irony, taking a guard job only to find the Harpes on the other side of the jail door! He wouldn't like that at all. Neither would they. Maybe the thing to do would be to ride to Danville, loiter about for a time, then return and tell Ford the job was already filled. Not a very honorable thing to do, maybe, but when had he worried about honor before? Maybe being around the Fords was bringing out good things in him, but he saw no sense in letting that process go too far, too fast. Moderation in all things, he told himself. Even virtue.

He closed his eyes, basking in the heat of the banked fire close by him. Thoughts about himself, the Fords, Dulciana, and the Harpes mixed together in increasingly nonsensical ways until all of them faded into nothingness and he was asleep.

CHAPTER 24

Clardy was more impressed with Danville than he had expected to be. Like most frontier towns, the bulk of its houses and buildings were of log, though more finished, sawed-wood buildings were beginning to show up. The log courthouse, already about fifteen years old, was simple and typically styled, just large enough to cast an appropriate aura of sober, authoritative institutionality. The jail, also of logs, caught Clardy's eye the most: a place as unappealing and bleak as a grave.

Last night he had been ready to make this day into one great pretense, but this morning the new and improving Clardy had carried more sway than the old, sneaky one. He had ridden all the way here with the full intention of actually inquiring about the job—and now the time had come.

He gazed at the jail with his mind full of Harpe-inspired trepidation, then scoffed at himself for fearing phantoms. It was highly unlikely that the Roberts people lodged behind those nine-inch-thick log walls were the Harpes.

A bowlegged man padded around from the back of the jail to the front, and Clardy wondered if this was the fellow he needed to see to ask about work. To his aggravation, he couldn't remember the name Ford had attached to the jailer, so he went to the courthouse and asked a nicely suited man he found inside who the local jailer was and if that was him over by the jailhouse. The man looked at Clardy with undisguised suspicion. "Why do you ask?"

"I understand there might be a need for guards to help keep watch over some prisoners in the jail yonder."

"Well . . . maybe so. If the man you saw is a shortish fellow with no hair on the top, probably wearing a black sailor's coat, then that's John Biegler, the jailer."

"Thank you." Clardy turned to go.

"Young man . . ."

"Yes?"

"Are you a hardy soul?"

"Reckon I am."

"You'd best be if you want to guard that bunch. I've not seen so ugly and brutish a bunch as them in that jail in all my days."

Clardy saw an opportunity to gain advance information. "Let me ask you, sir: What is the name of the prisoners?"

"Roberts, they informed the court. Apparently, though, their true name might be Harpe."

The blood drained from Clardy's face. The man looked at him closely. "Are you well, young man?"

"Yes, aye, yes. I'm fine. Thank you. Thank you for what you told me."

He left the courthouse, went to his horse, and rode—in the opposite direction from the jail. The Harpes after all! They must have left Tennessee approximately the same time he had. That was enough to chill his backbone. He had been riding alone on a road that also hosted a cruel pair who would have killed him in half a moment had he chanced to meet them.

It made him afraid, then angry—and then to his utter surprise he felt a third emotion. He halted the horse, evaluating this new feeling, trying to identify it. He finally analyzed it as not one feeling but two: contempt for the Harpes and shame at himself.

Contempt was a familiar feeling for Clardy, but shame?— that had afflicted him only rarely. A fellow who recognized no standards had no cause to feel bad about failing to meet them. Obviously that was different now. He shook his head sadly at this newest evidence of personal improvement—again undoubtedly because of the influence of the Fords. It was a deuced shame.

He looked back toward the town. Why was he running away? Was he so cowardly that he feared men locked behind thick walls? Had he no pride?

Well, no, he admitted. At least not before, and certainly not in private. He would bluster and strut before others, but shamelessly slip out the nearest back door as soon as eyes were off him. What had always mattered was the public perception, not the private reality.

"Blast and flail you, Isaac Ford," Clardy muttered. "All that high moral swill you pour down my throat is going to ruin me, sure as the world. Probably get me killed. You've rubbed off on me like a stain, you old one-eyed cuss." He listened to the conflicting voices inside him, almost choosing to follow the one that spoke with Ford's voice and to turn his course back to the town. He stopped himself with a desperate burst of self preserving volition. "Uh-uh, no sir!" he declared. "Not me!" He heeled his horse back into motion and rode away from town.

Ten minutes later he rode back through the same spot again, in the opposite direction, his expression very sad. It was the oddest thing that any kind of serious moral battle had been waged in the no-man's-land of Clardy Tyler's soul; odder still that the righteous side had actually won. Clardy was in despair. Keep up this course, and the next thing he knew he'd turn schoolmaster, or parson, or missionary to the heathen Indians! It was begrieving to see how the intrusion of even a smattering of pride and moral standards could impede on what had always been a carefree, shiftless life.

He rode back into Danville and to the jail, which looked even more sobering up close. The thought of being locked up in a jail like that gave him a shudder, and he was glad he hadn't succeeded in becoming an outlaw. Most outlaws found their way in the end to such miserable confinements as this.

"What can I do for you, young man?"

Clardy started, not having seen the speaker approach. It was the same bowlegged man he had spotted before. He touched his hat. "Hello, sir. My name's Tyler. If you're Mr. Biegler, you're a man I want to speak with."

Caution swept across the man's eyes like the subtle shadow

of some flock passing overhead. "I'm Biegler. What do you want?"

"I'm looking for guard work, sir. I'm told you might have need of such."

"I done hired a man for guard, 'bout an hour ago."

"Oh." Clardy concealed the relief he felt behind a mask of disappointment. "Well, reckon I've come too late then. Thank you anyways." He turned and began to walk away.

Biegler said, "Hold up there. The man I hired can only work a portion of the time I need him. I could use another man for watching overnight a few nights a week. Especially them women. All three of them are ready to out with a baby here before long."

Clardy was disheartened, but he wouldn't back out after having gone this far with it. "I'd like to offer myself for the job, sir."

"I'd be glad for the help, but I don't know you. Ain't sure I can trust you. A man must be trusty to guard a prison."

"I'm trusty."

"Anyone to speak for you?"

"Do you know Isaac Ford?"

"Know of him. Lives over above Stanford, I think? One-eyed man who says a lot of ten-pound words?"

"Yes sir. I'm living there with him, helping him out at his place. It was him who told me about the guard work."

"Ford, eh?" Biegler rubbed his chin. "Well, you look decent enough, and if Ford speaks for you, I reckon that's good enough. He's a good man, I hear. This ain't a pleasant job, though. Them folks in there, they're murderers of the foulest kind. They been calling theirselves Roberts, but their real name is Harpe."

Clardy felt a twinge of uncertainty, but he masked it. "I reckon I can deal with them, long as they're locked up safe."

"They are, or they will be. I've put in an order for a couple of new chains and horse locks to keep the men pinned to the ground, and there'll be a new lock coming for that door there, too. I don't trust them. Little one looks like a weasel. Big one's more like a bear, but uglier."

"Where does the overnight guard keep post?"

"There's a little guard room in yonder." He pointed. "Has a stool, cot, and table. Young man, you sure you want this kind of work? Ain't much money in it."

Clardy didn't want it, but to say so now would embarrass him. "I believe I would, Mr. Biegler, if you'll have me."

"I will . . . and you can begin this evening."

Clardy nodded and smiled. "Thank you, sir," he said. "I'll do a good job for you."

The thought that accompanied those confident words, however, was of a far different stripe. Clardy Tyler, he thought to himself, what the devil have you got yourself into here? That's the Harpes in there! The very men who tried to make you a killer yourself, the very men who probably killed Abel Van Zandt—and here you are, putting yourself up to guard them, all to put a handful of coin in your pocket and a grin on the face of Isaac Ford! Has ever a bigger fool than yourself walked this earth?

He hoped those horse locks Biegler had mentioned would arrive very soon.

Clardy Tyler quickly became a young man who lived in two worlds. When he wasn't on duty at the jail, he continued to live at the Ford cabin with its warmth and domestic cheer. When he was on duty, his home was the tiny guardroom at the jail, a dank, cold place bereft of color or comfort and any company a sane man would desire. Life at the jail had a definitely surreal quality and kept Clardy continually plagued with the same kind of vague unsettlement that trails in the wake of a nightmare whose content has been quickly forgotten but whose terror lingers.

For their part, the Harpe brothers were initially furious to discover that none other than Clardy Tyler was one of their guards. They spit a continual string of verbal venom at him, snarling at him like beasts from a cage, but that didn't last long. Their attitude toward him became mocking and scornful, until Clardy began to perceive the Harpes less like dangerous beasts and more like nagging, whining, persistent gnats in the ear. This was particularly so concerning Wiley Harpe, who sometimes remained awake the night through, mocking at Clardy through the closed door of his dark cell, whose only access to light and air was a single narrow window crossed with iron bars.

Sometimes the mockery was meaningless, almost childish, designed merely to annoy. Other times it took on a far darker and more threatening quality, and Clardy was glad for the thick walls and the heavy chains that kept the brothers' ankles shackled to the floor, even though the sound of those chains clinking and dragging as the Harpes moved about lent a sinister, almost ghostly aura to their unseen persons.

It grew the most sinister yet on the evening in early February when Clardy arrived at the jail to begin his nighttime duty and found Biegler the jailer in a foul humor. "The little one is worked up today," he said. "He's cussed and cried and sung and laughed all day, moving from one right to the other. And he's talked of you."

The skin on the back of Clardy's neck grew taut. Since beginning this work, it had been his secret fear that the Harpes might reveal they knew him in the past and say he was an associate of theirs. The worst part of that would be that it would be partly the truth. "What did he say?"

"Nothing much. Just that he was looking forward to you getting here. And then he'd say, 'Johnson! Johnson!' and make a funny sound. Sort of a *scriiiiiick!* kind of noise, like fingernails on a board of slate. Can you make sense of that?"

"No," Clardy said. *Johnson.* He didn't like that. He figured Wiley had Cale Johnson on his mind, a subject that cut too close to Clardy's heart for comfort.

Biegler left hurriedly, obviously glad to be away from what had become a miserable, nerve-grinding toil. Hardly had he gone before Clardy heard movement just on the other side of the Harpe cell door, and Wiley Harpe's voice came through. "That you, Tyler?"

Clardy lay down on the cot in the little guardroom, hands behind his head, and said nothing.

"I said, is that you, Tyler?" A pause. "Hell yes, that's you. I can *smell* it's you! Old Clardy Tyler, back on the good side of the law! Making sure the devils don't get out of the box!"

"Just hush!" Clardy called back. "I got nothing to say to you."

"Oh, but I got plenty to say to you, Clardy Tyler! I'm in the humor to talk about old Cale Johnson." Then he made the odd noise that Biegler had tried to imitate.

Clardy made no reply, though he was curious about what Wiley had to say. He suspected that the issue of Cale Johnson was about to be raised in some threatening manner. Wiley Harpe was a conniving soul and had enjoyed plenty of time in that cell to realize that he might be able to make trouble for his guard. Clardy wished he had thought things through a little more completely before asking for this job.

"There's naught to say about Cale Johnson," Clardy replied. "You told me to kill him, and I didn't. I ain't like you. I ain't a murderer."

"Maybe you ain't, maybe you are." This came from Micajah, surprising Clardy. Micajah had kept silence most of the time, leaving the harassment to his weasel-faced brother.

"You know I ain't. I didn't kill Cale. I warned him!" Clardy was irritated enough to be a little incautious. "What do you think of that, you pair of devils? You thought you had me tied around your finger, thought I'd go out and kill for you just because you wanted it. Reckon I proved you wrong."

"That's right—then you run like a chickenheart!"

"I left Tennessee because I had a chance for some good Kentucky land," Clardy responded. It was not the first time he had used this falsehood with the Harpes. He wasn't about to let them know he had left Beaver Creek mostly for fear of them.

Wiley said, "Your warning didn't do old Cale much good. He's dead anyways."

Clardy sat up. "Cale ain't dead."

"I hear otherwise," Micajah replied. "I hear old Cale might have gone and gotten himself knifed. Maybe even cut open like a butchered hog and stuffed full of rocks and throwed into the Holston River."

"Cut wide open," Wiley added. "Sharp knife right through flesh. *Scriiiiiick!*"

"Merciful God!" Clardy said. "You've murdered him?"

"We ain't said that," Micajah said. "Just telling stories we've heard, that's all."

A long silence followed, during which Clardy felt sick at heart. He wondered if Cale really was dead, or if the Harpes were lying outright, trying to get to him.

"Sad thing for old Cale, huh?" Wiley said through the door. He laughed.

Clardy grew angry. "Shut up. Both of you. You got worry enough without wasting your time blabbering through jail doors. And you won't have that much time. They'll hang you."

"We won't hang," Micajah said. "You know why we won't?"

"Why don't you tell me."

" 'Cause we're going to be set free of this place, and you're going to be the one to do it."

"Never!"

"And when you do set us free, you'll have a fatter pocket for it," Wiley contributed.

Clardy laughed coldly. "You are bigger fools than I had thought. You think I'd turn two murderous whoresons loose in the world for any amount of money?"

"Might as well be you who gains the good from it. Otherwise you might gain only the bad."

Micajah chuckled. "It'd be a shame for old Clardy Tyler to wind up like Cale Johnson. Shame for his belly to be laid open and stuffed with rocks. Shame for him to be eat up by fish in some river."

"Don't threaten me, Harp."

"Just talking. Just talking. Just being friendly."

"Say whatever you want to say, and still I'll not let you out of there for bribes nor threats."

"If you don't, somebody else will."

"Nobody's going to help you."

"We'll be seeing about that," Wiley said. "And after we're out, Clardy Tyler, we'll find you one dark evening, old Micajah will pull out his blade, and *scriiiiiiik*!"

They laughed together, behind their door. Clardy hated them. A moment later their foot chains rattled as they moved back farther into the room. The momentary reprieve was welcome. He pulled out his pipe, filled it, and lit it at the little fireplace on the side of the guardroom. He sat smoking, more unsettled than he wanted to admit.

Betsy Harpe, jailed under her alias of Betsy Walker, gave out her travailing cries a day or two later. Clardy sent out for a local midwife who had been on call for the inevitable birthings since the women had been jailed. The birth was lengthy and trying, and in the end gave forth a healthy young boy.

Born in a jail, and of such a brood as this! Clardy thought it a sad birthing, full of foreboding for the child. Innocent now—but how long could innocence linger, considering the foul kind of folk into whose world he had mischanced to be born? Clardy dreaded the future this child would face unless he could somehow be rescued from his own mother and father . . . whichever Harpe brother his father was. The Harpes themselves couldn't say.

Clardy had sugared tea brought in at Betsy's request the next day. Biegler frowned at giving such niceties to prisoners, but grumpily added the cost of the beverage to the list of costs brought on by the birth: a pound, eight shillings, and ten pence.

The next baby, a girl born to Susanna, came exactly a month later, rousing even greater pity in Clardy. A boy, after all, could grow up and break free from his situation far more easily than a girl. This child would probably grow up to be a common whore.

The public, fascinated with the Harpes, evidently was thinking along similar lines. In the tavern where he ate and drank at the beginning and end of his long spells of duty, Clardy heard more and more sympathetic talk toward the Harpe women and their babies. Poor waifs, they were, trapped in the web cast by the evil men who dominated them. What was needed, Clardy heard from all sides, was for these poor women and their innocent babes to be freed from the demonic men who threatened to ruin them.

Clardy hoped that was just what would happen, and was sure the women felt the same way. How could they actually want to keep company with the Harpe brothers? It went against reason.

When he thought about the women, Clardy saw a deeper significance to his guard duty than mere jail-tending. He was overseeing the beginning of a process that would finally result in the removal of two evil men from the world, and in particular from the lives of three women and two babies—soon to be three babies, because Sally Rice Harpe's pregnancy was rapidly nearing its end. Thinking about this work in that way made the drudgery and the haranguing from the Harpes a little easier to abide.

Clardy had to smile at himself sometimes. He was certainly growing more philosophical, looking at the world from many angles he hadn't before, and with far more seriousness. Life couldn't be predicted, he decided. He had set off for Kentucky with the idea of becoming a criminal himself, and now here he was, guarding a jail in the name of the law and thinking tender, moralistic thoughts about women and babies and the salvation of innocent lives—who would have thought it?

The world was a far bigger and more surprising place than Clardy had ever anticipated it would be.

The other guard hired by Biegler was named Beaumont Malory, and a more unpleasant and unlikable fellow Clardy had hardly ever encountered. He wasn't sure what it was about

Malory that had made him instantly distrust and dislike him. Something in the looks, the narrow face, the beadlike eyes, the set of the lip, and the eternal furrows in the forehead.

Clardy perceived that Malory didn't like him in turn. It was hard, however, to be sure, because Malory had little to say to either Clardy or Biegler. He was aloof to the point of being rude. Clardy sensed that even Biegler didn't trust Malory, and wondered why he had hired him. Desperation, perhaps. Not all that many people were willing to bear responsibility for the Harpes, even for money, and even with the Harpes locked up.

But public fascination with the criminal pair was alive and thriving, particularly since the birth of the two babies. All during daylight hours, and sometimes after dark, clumps of people would gather at the jail, talking about the "Robertses" or the Harpes, depending upon how they had heard the brothers designated. The more daring ones would go right up to the barred window and stare at the Harpes like patrons of a human zoo. The Harpes sometimes seemed offended by this, other times just as entertained as the observors. Wiley grew particularly fond of thrusting his face toward the window suddenly, snarling and snapping and drooling down his chin like a mad dog, then laughing at the startlement of his audience.

Micajah, the more practical of the pair, tried to make the best use of these frequent public viewings. He issued a standing challenge to the crowd: Let the two best fistfighters they could recruit come forward and take him on, two against one, and he would gladly submit to whatever punishment befell him should he lose. If he should win, however, he and his brother would go free.

No one took up the challenge, though some strutted about and claimed to be willing to do so "if only the dang court would allow it."

Clardy had his doubts about the sincerity of such puffy braggarts. Micajah Harpe was fearsome merely to behold. The memory of that frightening visage shoved up near his own face, talking fondly of death and murder like they were the sweet kisses of a beautiful woman, still haunted him. It was that image more than anything else that had driven him away from his home in mortal fright, and which still served to make him wonder why in the name of all that was sane he was associating himself with the Harpes now, even as a paid, official guard of the court. He thought a time or two of turning the job over to Malory completely, but his desire to please Isaac Ford, and a certain pride at having taken on such a daring task as this, and his comprehension of the public importance of his work, kept him from doing it.

Clardy initially made efforts to be friendly with Malory at the times one relieved the other. As time went by, he gave up on it. Malory was silent, brooding, unapproachable. At length he and Clardy were down to passing duty one to the other with hardly a word of mutual acknowledgment, and the glances that Clardy found Malory firing at him were dark and ugly. Clardy mistrusted him more every day.

One clear day when he wasn't on jail duty, Clardy helped Isaac Ford drive horses toward Crab Orchard, where a buyer awaited. Clardy was quiet and preoccupied all the way, causing Ford to question him, but all Clardy could say was that he felt something, somewhere, was wrong. He couldn't explain it.

The next day he rode to Danville to take on his usual duties and found a town with a transformed atmosphere. It was disturbed; the very air crackled with tension, and he fancied that many unusual and indecipherable expressions were turned his way as he approached the jail.

Biegler came out to meet him. "Down off that horse, Clardy. I must have words with you."

Clardy dismounted. "What's wrong?"

Biegler led him over to the side of the jail, out of earshot of anyone on the street. "The prisoners are gone."

"Gone . . ."

"That's what I said. They left their cell last night. Town's in an uproar. The women are still here, but the men have fled. There's a hole right through the far side of the wall of their cell." Biegler paused. "There is suspicion being cast toward you."

Clardy grew taut as a bowstring. "Cast by who?"

"Beaumont Malory declares that he saw you lingering around near the jail last night, off in the dark. He declares that later in the night he was struck by an unseen assailant and rendered senseless. The prisoners were freed during that time. He's alleging that you were the one who struck him and set them free, most likely because of a past association with them. He says that Micajah Harpe himself confided to him that once you were part of a stock-thieving organization they ran down in Tennessee."

"That's a lie."

"I hope it is, boy. Because if it ain't, you've made John Biegler look the biggest fool in Kentucky, hiring on guards without knowing enough about their past."

Clardy felt a wave of contempt. *Here I am, being accused of freeing murderers, and he's worried only about how he looks to the public.* "I wasn't in Danville last night. I was at the house of Isaac Ford, and if you don't believe me, you can ask him or any of his family."

"That will be done, I assure you. It would have been done by now except that Malory told his full story only this morning."

"You see? He's made it up late. Trying to keep his own hind end out of trouble. If anybody set them two free, it was Beaumont Malory himself."

Clardy was startled by a sudden change in Biegler's demeanor. He shifted from nervous worry to sudden anger. "Perhaps so. It does appear the horse locks on their foot chains was unlatched by someone with a key. That would be me, you, or Malory. One of us will take the brunt for this, and I assure you, it matters not a whit to me which of you two it is. But it will *not* be John Biegler, no indeed!"

"Nor will it be Clardy Tyler, sir, because I'm innocent and I can prove it."

"Can you, now?" As he spoke, Biegler gave Clardy a look he didn't like. Clardy thought: This man *hopes* I'm guilty. "Well, we'll have the chance to see about that. We will. It's you or Malory who's responsible for this, and I'm drawed, quartered, and stewed for mush if I'll let *that* mantle fall on my shoulders!"

"If I was guilty, I wouldn't have come back here today, would I?" Clardy pointed out. "Where is Malory right now, by the way?"

Biegler, red-faced and with a neck vein bulging and throbbing, looked around and said, "I don't know," and turned away.

Clardy faced the hardest and most intense questions he had ever been hammered with in his life, and in the end prevailed. Isaac Ford was called in all the way to Danville to verify that Clardy was with him at the time the Harpes escaped. The testimony of Ford, a trusted man, was sufficient to erase any official suspicion. Added to that was the fact that Malory had mysteriously vanished. Some declared that he had been paid off by the Harpes and had vanished with his bribe in hand, others that he had gone off with the Harpes themselves, still others that the only reward he had wound up getting from the Harpes was probably a sharp knife through the throat. Whatever the case, he was gone, and no trace of what had happened to him or where he had gone was found.

The entire affair humiliated Clardy. In the course of answering questions, he was forced to admit he had been acquainted with the Harpes back in Tennessee and had actually been on the edges of their criminal activities for a very brief time. But he had been no friend or ally. He had spurned the first criminal demand they made on him—he didn't mention specifically what that demand was—and been threatened as a result. Clardy also deliberately failed to mention the Selma Van Zandt grave robbery and corpse mutilation, and the disappearance of Abel Van Zandt. He wasn't proud of having evaded his duty related to those situations before, and too ashamed to lay them out for public inspection now. Clardy emerged from his interrogations cleared of suspicion but feeling his reputation had been sullied. That mattered a lot more to him now than it would have only a handful of weeks before.

The real sullying, however, was inflicted upon the reputation of Beaumont Malory. Within two days of the Harpe escape, a general wisdom rapidly settling into firm assurance was that Malory was the true villain in the prison escape. After casting suspicions at Clardy Tyler, he had abruptly vanished.

Malory's disappearance left Clardy and Biegler in sole charge of the jail. Biegler was happy to let Clardy take on most of the extra work. It was easier with the Harpes no longer around to harass him, but Clardy felt unsettled. He worried secretly about his own safety, reasoning that if, as they had implied, the Harpes had returned to Knoxville to murder Cale Johnson despite all their legal dangers there, they might just as readily return here as well. A further consideration was that their women were still here, potential Harpe magnets. Clardy couldn't quite picture the Harpes abandoning their women for good. They had probably left them behind only because they didn't want to be slowed in their flight by two newborn babies, two women still recovering from childbirth and a third on the brink of it.

But time would pass, Sally's baby would come, and both the women and the children would grow stronger. And then the

Harpes might return to claim what was theirs and to punish those who had stood against them.

Such were Clardy's secret thoughts, haunting him like his own shadow, making him hate the Harpes as much for the torment they inflicted on him in absence as for that they had inflicted when present.

Sally Rice Harpe's baby, a daughter, came into the world on the night of April 8, aided not by a midwife, but by the other two Harpe women. It seemed a very odd thing to Clardy to be guarding a jail occupied by three women and as many babies, ranging in age from newborn to about two months.

Clardy's worries about the Harpes returning after all the women had given birth had declined by now. He had the feeling that the Harpes were long gone, probably off in some remote corner of Kentucky, or maybe north of the Ohio River. They wouldn't have lingered in the wilderness this long, just waiting for babes to be born. This time they had abandoned their women for good. If so, that indeed *was* good. The best thing that could happen to the women and children would be to lose all contact with the brothers.

A few days after the birth of Sally's baby, Susanna "Roberts" went on trial for the murder of Langford. A jury of twelve found her guilty after a brief review of evidence from the initial hearing in Stanford, preserved in written affidavits. The next day a second jury heard precisely the same evidence given against Betsy "Walker," yet found her innocent. On the same day, the judge ruled that no trial of Sally "Roberts" would be held and she was declared acquitted. Clardy was glad. He had come to pity the childlike Sally.

Susanna appealed her conviction at once, and the judge granted her a new trial. The district attorney, however, decided not to prosecute her a second time, and the clerk of the court entered, to the cheer of a soft-hearted public, a nolle prosequi entry under her name in the court record.

"Isaac Ford predicted this would happen," Clardy told others in a tavern he had taken to frequenting. "Nobody wanted to see them women hurt for the crimes of their men, nor them babies left without mothers."

The perception was correct. The people of Danville now rose in a swell of sympathy for these poor, fallen women and their helpless infants. Clothes were collected, food gathered, money scraped up and given them for a gift. Even an old mare was scrounged up to help convey the little ones and the various goods charitably given for their care. The women, as somber and listless as ever, accepted these gifts with as much gratitude as they were capable of showing. They told their benefactors that they were through with the company of the men who had victimized them, and would travel together back to Tennessee and resettle in Knoxville, using the kindness shown to them in Kentucky as a foundation upon which to build a new and better life. They would seek forgiveness for their sins and live good lives from here on out.

Clardy watched as the procession of women and babies, accompanied by Biegler and various others, moved in a line toward the edge of town. All along the way men tipped their hats and women swiped away tears of sympathy and goodwill. It seemed that not a soul for miles around was displeased to see these women cleared of their crimes and sent on the way to a brighter future. They were perceived as witnesses rather than doers of evil, their wills overwhelmed by the evil of the men who had dominated them. Just weak women, that's all they were. Clardy saw it that way along with everyone else. He knew better than most how fierce and mesmeric a hold the glittering eyes of the Harpe brothers could take upon the will of those around them. He had very nearly fallen into that trap back on Beaver Creek. No longer could he be totally skeptical about the reality of the "evil eye" some people were purportedly able to cast upon others. If any man possessed a true evil eye, it was Micajah Harpe.

Emotional aspects aside, the departure of the women created an ambivalent situation for Clardy. With the Harpe men escaped and the women freed, there was no longer a need for guards at the jail. Clardy was out of a job. He returned to Isaac Ford's house, proud of the time he had spent at an honest enterprise, but with hardly a shilling more in his pocket than he had begun with.

He knew the time was nearing when he would have to move on and find a means of supporting himself that was more permanent and lucrative. He knew as well that the best future he could find probably would involve returning to the past: to the farm at Beaver Creek and the life he had lived before. He had no way of knowing that the farm was no longer Tyler property, that the grandfather he had sparred with through the years was dead in his grave, and that his brother Thias was no longer there, either, but had come to Kentucky on his very heels, only to pass him by.

To return to Beaver Creek . . . Clardy mulled the possibility very seriously. It seemed sensible—yet he didn't want to go back. He had tasted freedom and some measure of honest labor, and found he liked it. Beaver Creek seemed distant, part of a past he did not want to return to.

And there was a secret, nagging fear that also served to deter him from returning to the farm: The Harpe women had said they were going back to Knoxville. If so, the Harpes themselves might look for them there, and the Harpes were men Clardy could not afford to run across on his own.

So for days he lingered where he was, working for Isaac Ford and trying to decide what best to do.

CHAPTER 26

Sally Harpe, having given birth more recently than her two companions, was allowed to ride the already laden mare most of the time, while Susanna and Betsy walked, packs of donated goods on their backs and babies riding their broad hips.

Sometimes while she rode, Sally would hold her new baby in her arms and look into its face, feeling emotions she could not put a name to. But mostly she spent her time lost in her beloved fantasies of lost days of innocence. Riding with babe in arms or on her breast, her mind would be secretly immersed in phantom images of happy girlhood, seeing herself eating at the family table or listening to her father singing hymns as he worked the farm. She remembered the corn-shuck dolls she would hold as she held her living child now. Yet those corn-shuck dolls had seemed more real than this baby of flesh, blood, and bone. It was that way for her now: the shadow world of the past was more present and corporeal than the fleshly reality of a life that had turned too ugly to endure.

Though the three women were ostensibly traveling toward Knoxville, Sally knew they were not really bound there. It was just as well; she was sure she could never return to her old life and place. Her father was a good man, a holy man; she was far too fouled to go back to him. She was where she was and what she was. Nothing could be done for it now.

The women traveled toward Crab Orchard, then changed their route to follow the Green River. There, they encountered a man with a canoe and traded mare for craft. Piling into the canoe, babies stuck like weevils in cotton among the mounds of personal goods given to them by the kind people of Danville, they traveled down the Green River, heading for the community of Red Banks, where the Green spilled into the Ohio. From there it was only a short distance to the place they really had been bound for all along, in faithful obedience to the instruction given to them by Wiley and Micajah the night the young jailer named Malory had helped the men escape.

At their destination they expected to find their men awaiting them. If not, they would tarry there until they came. Whenever the reunion occurred, they would go together to a place the men had told them about, a big cave that overlooked the Ohio River, an awesome, infamous place called Cave-in-Rock.

After the departure of the Harpe women, a lull held in the regions of Danville, Stanford, Crab Orchard, and Hazel Patch. It did not linger.

Corpses were found, decayed and wolf-chewed but still identifiable. According to the word that reached Clardy Tyler near Stanford, two of the killed were Marylanders known to be traveling in the region approximately the same time as the unfortunate Stephen Langford. Their names had been Paca and Bates.

A third dead man, found at another area, was a well-known and much beloved Wilderness Road peddler named Peyton.

Clardy was deeply shaken to hear of Peyton's death, and told Ford of his meeting with the peddler and how kind the man had been to him—a sort of foreshadowing of the even greater kindnesses given to him by Ford himself.

"I've met Peyton myself a time or two," Ford replied. "A hard thing, a gentle man like that being murdered."

"The Harpes done it. Had to be them."

"All the signs point to it. The corpse was hid much the same way as Langford's. God! That pair is Satan doubled! Men without souls, they are. Men without souls." Ford's dead eye took on a new egg-white luster, as it always did when he was angry.

Clardy said, "I want to see them caught. I want to see them hanged. And not just for the killing they've done here. There's others, back in Tennessee, I believe they've murdered."

"Them two will have their punishment in time, Clardy. But who will deliverate it, nobody can say. I know of no indication that they're yet about this region. Most likely they're far away, doing their devil work among other folk."

But within a day other rumors reached Stanford. The Harpes had been seen by witnesses, moving through the forests in the region of the Rolling Fork, the very area where they were captured the first time.

When Joe Ballenger revived his regulators to being another search, Clardy Tyler and Isaac Ford were among their number. Had he seen his own face, Clardy would have been surprised at the iron fury it displayed and the coldness glinting in his eyes. He had never known so righteous an anger as this one. He was eager to sweep in the two murderers like a housemaid's broom sweeping rubbish, to see them convicted, most of all to see them hang.

Clardy's old dream of a criminal life was dead, murdered by the Harpes just like old Peyton had been. Clardy had seen pure, wicked criminality embodied in two human forms, and could no longer see anything of the romance, happiness, or wild pleasure he'd formerly associated with it. Ugliness, that's all it was. Nothing but grotesque ugliness.

Ballenger's regulators were a band of grim demeanor and blood anger. Ballenger, perhaps sensing a dangerous overeagerness in his men, warned them that the Harpes would not likely be captured so easily this round. He expected a difficult search, a prey hard to find and stubborn in resistance. They would have to be ready for dangerous surprises.

The regulators were deep into the search when they heard a whisper of noise in the forest near the Rolling Fork. Every man raised his rifle and readied himself, but the lean, sun-baked figure who emerged to face them was no Harpe. He was astride a horse that looked as lean and weathered as himself. With eyes the color of an old rifle barrel, the man swept a confident, experienced gaze across the cabal of manhunters.

Clardy lowered his rifle. "Who's *that?*" His tone evidenced the kind of impression the newcomer had made.

Isaac Ford replied, "A good friend of mine and one of the

finest of the old long hunters ever to tromp through Kentucky. His name is Henry Skaggs."

Clardy had heard of Henry Skaggs. Hiram Tyler had known of the man through his reputation as a fine hunter and woodsman. Skaggs was among the first to penetrate the wilderness west of the mountains. With one Elisha Walden and more than a dozen other excellent woodsmen, he hunted all along the then-wild country of the Powell, Holston, and Clinch rivers back in the early 1760s, fresh on the heels of the great Cherokee uprising that accompanied the siege and surrender of Fort Loudoun in the Overhill towns. Hiram Tyler was never a long hunter, but always wished he had been, so men such as Skaggs were near idols to him. Clardy had heard the names of Skaggs, Walden, Newman, Blevins, Cox, and Colter extolled so many times in his home that he was now duly impressed to see one of that famed number.

"I know who you're searching for," Skaggs said to Ballenger. "I've come to lend my hand."

"You're welcome, Henry," Ballenger replied. "Have you any wind or sign of them devils?"

"Nope. But I hear they've been seen. If so, we'll meet them soon enough."

The incidents that happened shortly after Skaggs joined the regulator party would be seldom discussed by the men who participated, but well remembered, and with shame. Clardy himself didn't quite understand how or why matters fell out as they did, especially with such a hardened group of capable woodsmen as these.

They met the Harpes without warning, at the edge of a wide canebrake near the Rolling Fork headwaters. It was as if the Harpes had simply materialized there in the woods, facing the big band of regulators with rifles—stolen rifles, almost certainly—cocked and lifted. Clardy gaped at the two figures and seemed to lose control of his will and muscle. He could hardly feel the rifle in his own hands.

Micajah and Wiley Harpe stared at the men before them, and Clardy remembered the "evil eye" tales that had been spreading about these men since their escape. A deep, panicked fear grasped him by the throat. All outrage and thirst for Harpe blood drained away, to be replaced by a wild need to be away from this place. Clardy broke free of the torpor that had held him, jerked the reins of his horse and heeled its flanks, riding off into the woods. He hardly noticed that the others in the party, except for Skaggs, Ballenger, and Isaac Ford, were doing the same. Clardy was well away from the Harpes, almost out of sight of them in the trees, before he realized with deep shame that he and his companions had just bolted like cowards, all because of two men! He stopped, wheeled his horse.

He saw Skaggs, Ballenger, and Ford approaching now. With the Harpes having the drop on them, even they had been forced to break away once the others abandoned them. Clardy could hardly bear Ford's furious gaze and dared not even glance at the others.

"They've got past us," Ford said in disgust. "Rode right on through while six times their number in good hardy men scatter from them like quail!"

The others were gathering around now, regaining their composure after the unexpected burst of group cowardice. "My horse bolted with me," one of them mumbled. "Couldn't get him stopped . . ."

"I was riding off for cover, aiming to shoot at them from hiding," another said.

"It was the evil eye that done it," a third contributed. "I felt the burn of it on me, and next thing I knowed, here I was out in the woods."

"That's damned nonsense," Skaggs said. That stentorian voice, exploding with authoritative finality from so respected a figure, put an immediate end to excuse-making. "What happened was fear, men, pure old weak-kneed, belly-burning fear. I've seen it strike many a man in Indian fights." He paused, looking around at the group like a stern father evaluating sons who have let him down. "But I've never seen it strike so many, faced by so few."

"I'm mighty sorry I ran," Clardy heard himself mumble.

" 'Least you admit it was running and put up no excuse," Skaggs said, and even so faint a praise as that from a man such as he was enough to make Clardy lift his head and feel the beginnings of resurging pride.

"They can't have gone far," Ford said. "We can run them down yet."

"They went into the canebrake," Skaggs replied. "Seen 'em sliding in there myself."

"The canebrake!" one of the party said. "We'll never find them amidst all them stalks! They've give us the slip, men."

"Hell's bells, we *handed* them the slip, handed it right to them like a chicken leg at Sunday dinner!" Skaggs replied disdainfully. "I stand with Isaac. We can yet run them down."

"In that cane? I got my doubts," another replied, then wilted when Skaggs gave him back a burning stare.

Ballenger, his own face a chiseled image of displeasure, looked around at the group. "Let it be, Henry," he said. "We'll never catch them if there's no heart give to the purpose. What we need is hounds."

Skaggs sighed. "Very well, then. Hounds we'll have." He pointed northeast. "My cabin stands yonder way. I've got good hounds. We'll fetch them and see what they can do."

The men seemed glad to have something to do that didn't involve direct pursuit of the Harpes. Clardy was ashamed of them all, but couldn't chide them. He had been the first to turn tail. He was fiercely glad Grandpap and Thias hadn't seen this. Grandpap would have cussed him as a coward from here to next Christmas, and Thias would have inflicted upon him that familiar look, the one that had reminded Clardy time and time again through the years who was the good brother and who was the bad.

They fetched Skaggs's hounds and renewed their pursuit, regaining their courage and puzzling to the last man over why such a mortal fear should have gripped them. No good answer could be found. Like so much concerning the Harpes, there was mystery here and questions to distress the heart and chill the blood.

The dogs caught the trail at the cane and led the pursuers in among the thick stalks, but soon the brake became too thick to allow them to go farther at more than a snail's pace. Most of the men grew discouraged, and despite the urging of Skaggs to continue, began to fall away. The Harpes had won this round, several declared. No point in continuing a chase when the fox has already found his hole.

In the end only Skaggs, Ford, Ballenger, Clardy, and a few others remained. Needing more manpower, they proceeded on to another cabin not far distant. Here a party was under way, a "log rolling" involving the gathering of wood for a new dwelling. Skaggs broke up the festive atmosphere only with difficulty, liquor having already been flowing free for a couple of hours prior, and announced that he was in need of brave men to help find the notorious Harpes, who were hidden, he believed, in the big canebrake not far from there.

"I've lost nary a Harpe today and feel no compunction to go looking for one," one of the revelers said. "Besides, Henry, if they're in that cane, you'll never roust them. A man can hide in the cane till doomsday and not be found."

"There's enough of us here to do the task," Skaggs said. "Have you not heard of the murders these men have done? You let them keep roaming free, and it will be one of your own who feels their blades next."

"I agree with Henry," said a man Clardy later learned was named James Blane. "We should pursue these men before the trail grows cold."

All the pleading Skaggs could do had no effect on any man there except Blane, though, and at last the old long hunter and his handful of companions turned their horses and rode away from the party. Skaggs, sounding weary and discouraged, suggested that perhaps the best notion was for him to ride on the next morning to the home of Daniel Trabue, south of there, and discuss with that fine gentlemen the need to mount and maintain a serious search until the Harpes were apprehended. Trabue was a worthy soul, highly respected. He would not dismiss such an important matter as a joke to be laughed over at a log rolling.

Skaggs rode on, trailed by his followers. Leadership of this pursuit had shifted to him without ceremony or even discussion. Among frontiersmen, leadership was based less on rank and title than on natural ability and experience. Clardy was determined to stay with the search as long as Skaggs and Ford did, but he was weary and discouraged, hardly able to muster up the indignation that had stirred him so deeply earlier in the day.

It had not been a good day's work. There was little done in this effort that any man would be able to look back on in pride. They rode only a short way before making camp in the woods for the night. Few words were spoken.

Clardy was surprised when he met Daniel Trabue. Ford had told him some about the man as the manhunter party rode toward his home. Trabue was about forty years of age and a

longtime resident of the region, having been around in the days
when the Shawnees attacked Boonesborough and life in the
Kentucky country was a very uncertain affair day to day. Yet
when Clardy saw Trabue, the man looked at least fifteen years
older. He was standing in his yard, pacing about, as the party
rode in.

The reason for Trabue's sudden look of age, Clardy discovered, was that at the moment he was deeply burdened with
worry. He had sent his son to a grist mill some distance away
early that morning to fetch flour and seed beans, and the boy
hadn't returned, even though there had been ample time for it
and he'd been instructed to hurry.

"I wish I could give you less reason for worry, Daniel, but
I'm afraid I can give you only more," Skaggs said. "There are
dangerous men on the run in this region, name of Harpe.
They're murderers of the worst sort, two coarse-haired sons of
whores who made their escape from the jail in Danville. We're
searching for them at the moment, and came here hoping you
could lend us some aid, and give us news if you've heard or
seen anything of this pair."

The news seemed to put yet another five years of age onto
the weathered, troubled face. Trabue said he was willing to
help, but until his son returned he felt compelled to stay where
he was. No one faulted him, but Clardy did fault himself and
his companions for their poor showing the prior day. He feared
that Trabue's son had probably become the most recent victim
of the murderers. If only they had pursued the chase more vigorously, and not given in to panic when they had the pair in
their very hands!

At that moment a small dog limped whimpering into the
yard and groveled at Trabue's feet. It was cut badly and bleeding. Trabue's face blanched. "God help me," he said. "It's
John's pup."

"Was that dog with the boy when you sent him to the mill?"
Ford asked.

"Aye. Oh, God!"

"Calm yourself, Daniel," Skaggs said. "Mount your horse
and let's be off to the mill ourselves, and see if we can find
news of your son."

They rode in morose silence, and at the mill learned that
John Trabue had arrived safely and set off home again long be-

fore. Trabue grew so distressed, he become sick at his stomach on the spot.

The search changed from that point on. Led now by Trabue himself, the men searched for the missing boy. They found some meager sign of his earlier passing along a buffalo trail, but it was trampled by subsequent travelers and they could not track him far.

The day passed slowly yet quickly, as days will that are full of worry. By the time night fell, the searchers were no better off than before, having found neither the Harpes nor any trace of John Trabue.

Efforts to find the boy and the Harpes continued for days thereafter. About fifteen miles to the southwest of Trabue's home, the first substantial evidence that the boy might have indeed become a Harpe victim was uncovered in the form of a dead calf and dead campfire. Tracks indicated that two men had been there and had hacked out moccasins from the fresh skin of the calf. Remnants lying about showed they had cooked and eaten a meal of meat and cakes made of flour. The flour John Trabue had been carrying? No one doubted it.

They searched hard for footmarks that would indicate the boy himself had been here, but there were none. There had been only the two men. Hope that John Trabue was still alive faded fast.

The worst was confirmed not long afterward. Another band of searchers found the corpse of John Trabue, disemboweled and literally hacked into pieces, and tossed into the bottom of a sinkhole. Lying amid the gore was a small sack, soaked in blood that had since dried. An examination of its contents showed it contained only seed beans.

When Clardy Tyler heard the news, he cried like a child.

The savage murder of the twelve-year-old boy became the fastest-spreading, most fury-inspiring piece of news that had come out of Kentucky for many years. Across the young state the name of the Harpes became known, and men searched for them with fierce determination.

Twelve days after the murder, the governor at Frankfort issued a proclamation offering three hundred dollars for the capture of Micajah Harpe, and the same amount for his brother. With the proclamation was given the following descriptions:

MICAJAH HARPE alias ROBERTS is about six feet high—of a robust make, and is about 30 or 32 years of age. He has an ill-looking, downcast countenance, and his hair is black and short, but comes very much down his forehead. He is built very straight and is full fleshed in the face. When he went away he had on a striped nankeen coat, dark blue woolen stockings, leggins of drab cloth, and trousers of the same as the coat.

WILEY HARPE alias ROBERTS is very meagre in his face, has short black hair but not quite so curly as his brother's; he looks older, though really younger, and has likewise a downcast countenance. He had on a coat of the same stuff as his brother's, and had a drab surtout coat over the close-bodied one. His stockings were dark blue woolen ones, and his leggins of drab cloth.

The proclamation, accurate in all physical descriptions except its presentation of red-haired Wiley Harpe as having black hair, was widely copied and circulated. All across Kentucky, men hunted for the murderers, mothers kept their young children close to home, and travelers lingered in the taverns and inns until large traveling parties could be formed for the sake of safety.

But safety for some was in short supply, as passing days showed.

Not twenty miles from the Daniel Trabue home, the Harpes murdered a man named Dooley. No one knew why; the death seemed as meaningless and unprovoked as the John Trabue slaying.

The next victim was a man named Stump, an impoverished, idle hermit of a fellow who lived in a crude riverside cabin and kept himself alive by fishing, a meager bit of gardening, and hunting. Though an isolated man, he was friendly to those who passed by and was fond of entertaining people with his fiddle playing. As best could be ascertained by the evidence left behind, he had been fishing at the river when he saw the smoke of a camp on the far side of the stream. He had rowed over in a skiff with a big string of fish, a freshly killed wild turkey, and his fiddle, aiming to share a meal, conversation, and music with whoever was camped there. The Harpes killed him and disposed of him with their usual rock-and-river method. By the time his corpse washed up against a bar down the river, the Harpes, having sated their appetites on the food Stump had brought them, were long gone.

As best could be told, they appeared to be heading for the Ohio River.

CHAPTER 26

Night, near the mouth of the Saline River

Three men sat together in the circled light of a campfire, shooting openly amused glances and occasional outright guffaws at one another at the expense of a fourth fellow who sat on the other side of the fire, facing them. He was a stranger . . . and as one of them had privately quipped to the others moments before, was proving to be the "strangest stranger" they had run across since the beginning of this extended hunting trip. The man had wandered in from the woods, drawn by the smell of their stew, introduced himself and asked for food. They had shared the victuals and settled into a conversation that had become far more bizarrely entertaining than they could have anticipated.

The stranger was a thickly built, hatless man with a tangle of dark hair and an open, simple look on his face. He was seated on a log; beside him was a yellowed skull with a smoking pipe thrust into its mouth. The skull was what prompted the greatest astonishment and was the centerpiece of most of the fun being poked at the newcomer.

"So, Mr. French, your pappy likes his pipe of an evening,

does he?" one of the three hunters was saying to the tousle-haired fellow. "Does he cuss you when you forget to give him one?" The other two snickered loudly.

"I never forget Daddy's pipe," the tousle-haired fellow said. "But even if I did, Daddy wouldn't cuss me. He never cusses."

"I doubt he does. I reckon he never says much at all." More laughter.

"Please don't laugh at my daddy. He don't like that, and I don't neither."

"Oh, I beg your pardon, Mr. French." The man looked solemnly at the smoke-wreathed skull. "And you as well, Mr. French the elder." The others could scarcely restrain their raillery at that one.

"You travel alone, Mr. French?" one of the hunters asked.

"I ain't alone. Daddy is with me."

"Oh, why, of course." They laughed some more. "What I mean is, do you and your daddy always travel alone?"

"We do now. There was another man with us, named Jack Waller. But he got him some money and next thing we knew, he was gone."

"Took off and left you and your daddy without a shilling, eh?"

"Yes." The tousle-haired man sounded very sad.

"Well, that was an unkindly thing to do."

"Yes it was. Jack was mean to do that. If I find him again, I'll kill him dead." The flat way he said it made the threat sound shocking. A brief silence followed, humor stilled for the moment.

"Now you're on your own—just you and your pa?"

"Yes. But we're going to find Jack. You wait and see."

"Don't believe I'd want to be him when you find him."

"No sir. You wouldn't want to be. He shouldn't have took my part of the money. It was wrong for him to do that. Daddy's mad over it. Me, too."

"Yes sir. It was mighty wrong to steal from you two. He should never have . . . Mr. French, why you looking at me that way?"

But Billy French was not actually looking at the man, but past him, into the woods. "Who are them two men?" he asked.

"What? Who?"

The man was twisting to look behind him when a rifle fired from the woods behind him. He grunted and pitched forward.

Billy French leaped up, screamed, and grabbed for his father's skull. He had just picked it up when a second shot rang out; a second man fell, having just begun to rise, and pitched dead into the fire. French screeched again as he saw two wild-eyed, ragged men, one large as a bear and the other small and weasely, come breaking out of the woods and into the camp. *They must have been in there, watching us for a long time.* Turning, French ran blindly and hard into the woods, away from the oncoming pair, who were now sweeping down on the third hunter. From the corner of his eye French saw a toma-hawk rise and fall with a terrible thud just as he vanished into the woods, branches and brambles tearing his clothing and skin.

Oh, Daddy, oh Daddy, one of them's chasing us!

The realization put new speed into his moccasined feet. He ran like he hadn't run since youth, pounding up and down wooded slopes until at last he was sure he'd given the slip to his pursuer.

A name he had heard spoken often recently in taverns and camps whispered through his mind in the same fearful inflec-tion in which he'd always heard it intoned: *Harpe.*

French stopped, panting, and looked for a hiding place. There! He went to a nearby, leaning, great hollow sycamore, squeezed painfully inside, and hid there the whole night. He was scared through and through. For the first time in his life he felt what it was to be on the quarry side of violent crime; be-fore, with Jack Waller, he had always been victimizer rather than victim. He had never known what it was to feel his insides wrench and twist inside him, cramping in pure terror, making him breathless and sick. Even hours after the event, the image of those men being murdered in the camp was stark before his mind's eye. He hadn't much liked those men because they laughed at him, but they were hospitable and generous with their fire and food. He wondered why they had been killed. Maybe for no reason. Folks said the Harpes killed for the same reason fish swam: it was their way.

Only when the sun was near the middle of the sky did French dare squeeze out of the tree and make his way cau-tiously back to the camp. He had realized with distress that he lost his father's skull sometime during his run, and that drove him from hiding even more than the terrible physical discom-fort of his situation. He searched the ground as he went toward

the camp but did not find the skull, whispering, "Daddy ...
Daddy ..."

When he reached the camp, he found the dead men lying in
blackened blood where they had fallen, though it appeared they
had been moved somewhat, as if to be searched. And in the
midst of them he found his father's skull. Crushed. Someone
had stomped it until the face imploded back into the hollow
where the brain had been.

Billy French knelt in the camp of death, stroking the ruined
bit of bone. Tears streamed down and he felt more utterly alone
than he had ever felt in his life.

Sally was on Diamond Island when the Harpe brothers found
her. She greeted them with as much enthusiasm as she was capable of showing—virtually none—and presented her baby to
them. In her husband's eyes she saw what an unwelcome gift
that child was, and drew it back to her own breast.

On to the cave they went together, and there found Betsy
and her child among an even larger assortment of human vermin than was usual at that criminal refuge.

The Harpes themselves were indirectly responsible for the
crowded situation, though it took them some time to realize it.
All the regulators, lynch mobs, and deputized bands stirred up
by their murders and robberies in Kentucky had, in the process
of scouring for the Harpes, managed to drive out much of the
criminal element of Kentucky. The quickest and safest refuge
for such had been Cave-in-Rock and its vicinity. Being on the
side of the Illinois territory, Kentucky militia and regulators
were reluctant to follow because of the jurisdictional issue.

Once ensconced at the cave, the Harpes sent across the river
for Susanna and her child, who awaited them in a small settlement there, posing as a widow to gain the sympathy of the lo-
cals. The splitting up of the three women had been planned in
advance. It made them less likely to be identified as the now-
famous Harpe women, and also gave them a wider field of
view, as it were, across which to watch for the arrival of their
infamous menfolk.

Reaching the imposing cave brought Sally out of her nearly
perpetual fantasy state for a brief time, and she observed the
situation with a keener eye than her mien and silence would
have indicated. She observed that word of who the Harpe
brothers were and what they had done had preceded them to

the cave. Even the most hardened of the river pirates watched them with awe and treated them with respect.

Sally knew that it was a novel experience for Wiley and Micajah Harpe to enjoy the respect of others, and wondered what effect it would have on their behavior. A good one, she prayed. God only knew she had already witnessed more evil and carnage than she could stand.

Soon it became evident her hope was vain. She felt a fool for ever hoping for an improvement in such men as Wiley and Micajah, especially in the company of such foul people as those crowded into and around this cavern. They all seemed to be evil folk, every one of them, and before long Sally ascertained that her husband and brother-in-law were determined to show themselves the most evil of the lot. The way they went about it drove her back into her mental sanctuary of fantasy more deeply than ever.

The first display of their wickedness came in the form of a flatboat that landed for repairs less than a mile above the cave, beneath a bluff about fifty feet high. The flatboat crew went to work on the boat, but a young couple who were among the passengers slipped off alone and found a trail that led up to the top of the bluff which overlooked the broad river.

The pair were sitting at the very edge of the bluff, arm in arm, the young woman's head on the young man's shoulder, when the Harpes detected them. Sally was with the brothers at the time, watching in silent dread as they crept up behind the couple on moccasined feet. Closer they drew—Sally wanted to scream a warning, but dared not for fear the Harpes would only do worse because of it—and then they yelled like Indians, ran forward and gave the couple a great shove from behind.

Two voices screamed in unison as the couple were launched out into space, kicking, flailing, still locked arm in arm. The Harpes roared with laughter. Sally came forward, expecting to see the crumpled dead bodies of the couple below, but was pleased to see both of them up and running toward their boat, obviously terrified but seemingly unhurt. Her relief was so great that she laughed and clapped. Wiley turned to her with a bright grin, mistaking her relief for glee over his joke. "Ain't that a funny one, Sally? What did you think of that, pretty lady?"

She withdrew at once, blocking out the present and his face, giving no answer.

Surprise waited when the Harpes returned to the cave and told the tale. Hardened and cruel as the Cave-in-Rock criminals were, they didn't seem to find much to laugh at in what the Harpes had done. A tall, thin, very pale man named Felix Fine, who they would have supposed would be far too weak and timid to face the dreaded Harpe brothers, rose and spoke forthrightly to them in a strange, elegant manner: "We here are a hard people, but we do not look kindly upon such a jest as yours. To do such crimes shows the most evil of spirits, and threatens to bring retribution to all of us besides. You, sirs, are scoundrels beyond measure, and we will not abide such dangerous and cruel treacheries that will ultimately threaten us all. It is, after all, your own brutalities that have caused regulators to rise and sweep the country, threatening our way of life."

Sally feared that Micajah might knife the impertinent fellow, but fortunately, he seemed so utterly surprised to hear this protest that he was momentarily unable to react. She also noted that the albino was carrying an even bigger knife than Micajah's, and thought that might account for some of Micajah's unresponsiveness as well.

A few more days passed, and the Harpe brothers enjoyed a first excursion into river piracy, culminating it with an act so wicked that it literally made Sally ill. A flatboat was lured to the bank by an apparent sister of the albino who waved and called for help while the pirates hid. When the attack was launched and the killing began, Sally sat in the midst of it all with her baby, nursing it, lost so deep in her escapist dreams that she did not even hear the cries or see the violence. In a life that offered no real escape from miseries, she had found a way to make her own meager but acceptable substitute.

A particularly hideous scream broke through her reverie during the sorting of the booty. She looked up and saw an amazing, appalling sight: a naked man was falling from the cliff above the cave mouth. He was tied onto the back of a horse which, like him, was blindfolded. The rider and his horse crashed into the earth with a hideous crunching thud, and Sally watched numbly as both died where they fell, broken and bleeding. Hearing laughter from above, she looked up and saw Wiley and Micajah looking over the edge of the bluff, enjoying the results of their cruel act. Turning, Sally staggered off with her baby crying in her arms, and was sick.

That night she prayed for the first time that her husband and his brother would die, and do so horribly. If there was justice in the heavens, no less would satisfy it, or her.

The next day the Harpes were told by the assembled group of cave residents that they were no longer welcome at Cave-in-Rock. Their cruelty was too great even for river pirates and their idea of pleasure far more twisted than anyone had yet displayed even at such a place at this. It was the fault of the Harpes that Kentucky was still being scoured free of outlaws at that moment. If they remained at the cave, they would eventually draw the regulators here, state and territorial jurisdictions notwithstanding.

Too stunned by this unexpected rejection to feel the full measure of rage that would have been expected, the Harpes gathered their women and babies and left at once. On down the river a ways they found and stole a sizable raft someone had beached and tried unsuccessfully to hide. Then they took to the river, floating out into the great waterway and on toward the Mississippi, having no real plan of exactly where to go. Kentucky was closed to them; they had committed too many crimes there to risk going back just yet.

And so they floated, drifting in the current, going wherever the water would take them, while Sally held her babe in silence and prayed that vengeance would come swiftly and painfully to two demonic men who deserved it dearly.

Isaac Ford nodded and smiled, but the gesture did not succeed in hiding the obvious sadness he felt over what Clardy Tyler had just told him.

"I understand, son," he said. "And though I despise to see you go, I support what you've chose. The best future you can find, I believe, lies in your past."

"I don't want to go back, not in my heart," Clardy said, struggling to keep his voice from choking with emotion. "I've learned much while living here, and I believe I'm far more a man than I was when I first came to you."

"There's no doubt about it. I've seen the changes in you. I regret that you've had to see the terrible times that came upon us here, the muderizing of innocent folk, and our failure to keep and punish them what done it."

"It was the very thing I needed to see, Mr. Ford," Clardy replied. "I had the notions of a fool when I left home, my mind set on becoming no more than a common thief. I can see now how foolish I was."

Ford smiled anew. "Then I was right."

"About what?"

"About there being a purpose in you and me coming together as we did. It was for your good, Clardy. It was to steer you onto better paths. You was drawed here to learn the lessons you needed."

Clardy shrugged. "I don't know whether I believe in such as that. All I know is that I have to go back where I came from. I've got a grandfather and a brother back in Tennessee I'm aching to see again. And a lot to tell them. A lot of repenting to do for the way I've been through the years. I never was no count at all back home."

"I'm glad you crossed my path, Clardy Tyler. And I want no forever farewells here. You'll come again—I'll hold you to it— and you'll be welcome when you do."

Clardy left the next day. It had been a hard decision for him, yet not so hard in another way. Since the killing sprees of the Harpes, he had grown to be a thoughtful young man, dwelling often on the tenuous nature of life and the importance of the kin he had left behind. He had fled his home to escape danger and to find wealth, even if in the worst of ways. He had left with a mind full of distorted notions of what his future should be, and those notions had been dashed to pieces by the goodness he found in the home of Isaac Ford and by the ugliness he witnessed in the murderous persons of the Harpe brothers.

Amy Ford, who Clardy had perceived as being quite indifferent to him, surprised him with tears when he mounted his horse, newly laden with abundant gifts of food, ammunition, and gunpowder from the Fords.

Young John Ford wept, too, and gave Clardy a small, crudely carved wooden figurine he had whittled himself. It was an image of a stout, tall man holding a rifle in one hand and carrying a rather shapeless lump in the other. "The rifle's too short," John said. "I cut off the top of it by mistake, and I didn't get to finish whittling in the string of squirrels in the other hand ... but that's supposed to be you, Clardy, bringing in food for our table."

Clardy did choke up then. "I'll treasure it, John," he said. "And I'll be back one of these days, and you and me will go hunting together. That sound good to you?"

"Yes," the boy said, then burst into fresh new sobs and turned away.

Clardy left the Ford cabin with emotions churning. He had never known so difficult a parting. It was not made easier by the fact that Isaac Ford stood at the edge of his cabin clearing, giving forth from his endless supply of proverbs as if in a travel blessing: " 'Thou shalt walk in thy way safely, and thy foot shall not stumble. When thou liest down, thou shalt not be afraid, yea, though shalt lie down, and thy sleep shall be sweet . . .' "

But one thing brightened the gloom of separation. Standing in the cabin door, waving at him with tears in her own eyes, was pretty young Dulciana Ford. She had hardly seemed aware of him in all the time he was a guest in her house, but now that he was leaving, her tears revealed that maybe she had noticed him a lot more than he'd thought.

He rode out of sight with the thought that at least one portion of his original vision for himself had come true: he had encountered a lovely young maid along a wilderness trail, and he gained her admiration. He would treasure the knowledge of that as dearly as the rough little figure that had been whittled by the hands of a twelve-year-old boy.

Someday, he vowed to himself, he would return here and see if he could not nurture the admiration of Dulciana Ford into something even greater and even more rewarding. Who could know? Perhaps there had been more purpose than mere lesson-learning for his life to have been plunged into that of the Ford family.

He traveled without incident and made good speed, covering many miles. When he came within view of the John Farris inn, he considered stopping, but that day the hour was early and he had abundant food already and was growing ever more eager to reach his home. He passed the inn without stopping and made his way toward the great gap in the Cumberland Mountains, beyond which lay Tennessee and the final miles of his journey back to the home and kin he loved far more than he had ever realized.

CHAPTER 27

In a tavern on the south bank of the Ohio River

Thias Tyler stared into his cup. Little in it now, but soon it would be refilled, and when it was emptied once more, refilled again. He would drink until he no longer felt regret over long weeks of searching for Clardy and not finding him, until he was so drunk that he no longer cared that he had lost everything he'd ever owned that was of value, and every bit of his family besides. He would drink until he was beyond all worry, including worry about his own empty pockets, so empty he couldn't even pay for the liquor he was consuming. So far the landlord hadn't demanded payment, happily. Whenever he did, Thias could only imagine how hot he would be to find out no payment was to be had for the liquor, or the hot meal that preceded it.

This is like something Clardy would do. The thought made Thias chuckle coldly. Indeed, he was acting more and more like Clardy. He didn't seem to be himself anymore. Ever since he left the Farris inn, his situation had spiraled downward like a falling maple pod. He had left with strong hopes of finding Clardy, but now here he was, all the way to the Ohio River, and still no Clardy. And he was more worried than ever about him. All he heard about anymore was the terrible killing spree of the Harpes. He couldn't shake the fear that Clardy had become one of their victims. Bodies of several Harpe victims had been found, but who could say there were not others as yet undiscovered, hidden in the forests or sunk in the rivers?

Thias took another swig, sloshed the liquor about in his mouth, then swallowed with a grimace. He had taken to drinking like this only over the past couple of months, as his depression and poverty grew. He had taken up stealing as well, filching small items, food, tobacco . . . once he had even stolen a horse. He wondered how the folk along Beaver Creek would react if they knew that Thias Tyler, the "good" Tyler brother, had taken such a quick turn for bad. They wouldn't understand it, most likely. For that matter, Thias didn't understand it himself.

He must have fallen asleep, because the next thing he was aware of was awakening when a cool blast of moist air breezed against the back of his neck. He sat up, feeling raindrops running down the back of his shirt.

He turned toward the open door and the man who stood in it. "Close that door!" he bellowed drunkenly. "The bloody rain's nigh to drowning me!"

The man looked directly at him, and Thias blinked in astonishment. Then he rose slowly, feeling unsure on his feet, and looked more closely to make sure this rain-soaked creature was indeed who he seemed to be.

"Billy French! Billy—that *is* you!"

Thias lunged forward, almost falling. Billy French turned on his heel and ran back out into the rainy night. The landlord called from the far side of the room—"Here now, what's this? Don't you be going off without paying!"—and Thias, ignoring him, pushed on out the door after Billy.

He left the tavern behind, running as best his wobbly legs would bear him, sloshing through mud and puddles, keeping the running form of Billy French in sight. The liquor made it hard to run well, but determination and a rising fury within compensated much. The angry voice of the landlord, shouting from his doorway, receded and was lost in the sound of the driving rain.

"I'm after you, Billy!" Thias called. "You and me, we've got much to settle!"

French did not answer. Though it was dark, Thias could still make out French's form, running ahead. He was gaining ground on French very quickly. French was doing some notably poor fleeing, and when Thias overran a torn, freshly lost moccasin lying in the muddy road, he understood why. French was having trouble with his footwear.

He heard a grunt ahead and the sound of a body falling hard into the mud. Laughing victoriously, Thias charged on. The cool rain on his head seemed to be sobering him a little. In only a couple of moments he was upon French, who was struggling to rise. With a blood-chilling cry, Thias launched himself out and landed directly atop Billy French, pushing him facedown into the mud.

"Don't . . . kill me! Oh, Thias, don't—"

Thias mashed French's face into the muck, giving him a mouthful of mud and water. "Don't what, Billy? Don't kill you? Don't smother the sorry life out of you? Tell me why I shouldn't! Tell me why I shouldn't mash you like a bug, you who took all I had in the world, everything my grandpap worked for all his days and left to his boys!"

French blubbered and snorted, trying to breathe without filling his lungs with muddy water. The rain continued to hammer down on the struggling men.

Thias felt French beginning to go limp beneath him before he got the best of his senses and pulled French's face free. French took in a great, bubbly gasp of air, then exhaled very vocally and gasped some more, over and over.

"Thias . . . please . . ." He was struggling to get his words out. "Please . . . I spared you . . . now you . . . spare me. . . ."

Thias frowned. In his anger he had nearly forgotten that French indeed had left him alive after being ordered to kill him. Even though French and Waller had robbed him of all he had and left him to a likely death on the floor of a cold wintry forest, it had to count for at least a little that French hadn't crushed his head with that axe.

"I will spare you—but only on the condition that I get back what was took from me."

"Thias, I ain't . . . got it! It was Waller! He—"

Thias mashed French's face back into the mud. He blubbered and struggled for another minute or so. By then Thias's anger was substantially expended. He pulled French's face back up, then grabbed him by the collar of his ragged coat and dragged him to his feet.

"So my money is spent, is it?"

"I don't know. I never had none of it. Jack, he took it and run me off. Said he'd kill me if he seen me again."

"Aye? Well, I can believe that. You were naught but a tool to him, Billy. He made you do the worst of his crime, then he took the benefit."

"Now Daddy is gone, too," French said. "The Harpes busted him."

"The Harpes!"

"I *believe* it was them. I was in camp with some strangers I'd met, me and Daddy together, and Daddy was having his pipe when the Harpes came in and commenced to killing. I run, and one chased me, but I hid and he went away. When I went back to the camp, all the men was dead and Daddy was busted like an egg. They'd stomped his poor face. Poor Daddy. Poor Daddy." French sounded as if he could weep.

Thias was astounded, and stabbed with fresh worry about Clardy. It was amazing that the very men who drove Clardy away from Tennessee had wound up in the same locale to which he had fled.

"Thias, you going to kill me?"

"No," Thias replied. "Me and you, we're going to be together for a spell. We're going to find Jack Waller and take back from him what he took from me. You helped him against me, and now you'll help me against him."

"I'll kill him for you, if you want," French said. "Whatever you want, I'll do, just like I used to do for Jack. You'll be my new good friend." French grinned. "You have a horse and rifle and such?"

"Yes," Thias replied. "Back at . . ." He slapped his brow with the heel of his hand. "Oh, no! I'm a fool, Billy. A great bloody fool!"

"What's wrong?"

"I left my rifle and horse back at the tavern. But I can't go back there and fetch them. I left there without paying, you see, and I've got nothing. If I go back to fetch all my truck, that landlord will be wanting his pay."

"I got nothing, too. No rifle, no money, no Daddy. He's buried away. I made him such a nice grave, so wee and pretty . . . why'd they bust him, Thias? What did Daddy ever do to them?"

"Well, I reckon that landlord is getting paid after all," Thias mused darkly, ignoring French's prattle. "*More* than paid. That was a prime horse and rifle both."

"We'll steal some horses, Thias. Rifles, too."

There was a time not so long before when such a proposition would have been out of the question for Thias Tyler. But much had changed for him. He was impoverished, put upon by a hard world, and he resented it. He voiced no protest to the idea.

"Come on, Billy," he said. "Let's find someplace to get out of this rain."

They traveled on foot together for two days, and on the third day stole two horses from a farm that reminded Thias of the old homeplace back on Beaver Creek. That made it hard to go through with the theft, but he forced himself, justifying it on the grounds he was desperate and victimized far worse than whoever owned this place. He eased his conscience by telling himself that maybe he would come back after he got his money back from Jack Waller, or whatever would remain of it, and pay for the horses, but when he rode off, he made no effort to remember how to find this farm again.

Later that same day, Billy French disappeared while Thias napped briefly beneath a tree. He awakened and thought French had simply absconded, but within half an hour French was back again, grinning, bearing two rifles, along with ammunition. Thias didn't ask where or how he had obtained them. It was better not to know. He could only hope that whoever had owned these rifles had lost no more to French than the rifles themselves. Though simple and childish in many ways, French was also a hardened and criminal man, fully capable of murder.

Right perculiar thing, Clardy. It was you who always talked of going to Kentucky to become a thief, and now it's me who's done it. Thias pondered the oddity of his situation. He would never have anticipated things turning out so. Only for now, he told himself. Just a brief turn off the straight road. When I'm on my feet again, I'll become what I was before. I'll be a good man . . . as soon as I can afford to be.

As time went by, Thias grew happy he had encountered French. Having all but given up on finding Clardy, he'd been considering trying to find Waller instead, but had no notion of where to begin. French, though, knew Waller's ways and the places he liked to go. With money in his pocket, certainly Waller would be drawn toward his favorite haunts—and among the most favored of these, according to French, was a certain string of riverside taverns up on the Ohio, places where liquor was plentiful, gambling was endless, and women were cheap.

"I'll kill him for you, if you want," French offered again on the day they rode in sight of the closest of these taverns. "I don't care to kill him at all."

"It won't come to that," Thias replied. "Waller's life isn't worth the noose for either of us. You let me deal with him. Whatever is done, it will be by my hand."

Waller wasn't at the tavern, though inquiry revealed he had been some days before. Thias was pleased anew that French was with him, because he was sure he wouldn't have been given even that information had he come alone. The keeper of the tavern knew French and that he was a frequent partner of Waller's, and so was more free with his information than he would have been otherwise.

They left the tavern, Thias expressing the wish he could have bought some liquor while they were there. Riding on, French abruptly stopped, told Thias to wait where he was, and then rode back the way they had come. When he returned, he had a full jug of whiskey. Thias was amazed and wondered how French had managed to obtain it—but once again he opted not to ask. He could not give testimony about that of which he knew nothing. French did suggest that they move on with particular haste, which they did.

The next two taverns also yielded no Waller and no word that he had been in them anytime in the last six months. The third tavern, however, gave them the encouraging news that Waller had been there only the day before, with a dark-haired woman who appeared to be traveling with him. They had left talking very openly about going to see kin of the woman on the Licking River.

"That would be Liz McDoogen with him," French told Thias as they left the inn. "She's a bad woman, and Jack, he always talked about her. She's helping him spend that money now, sure as the world."

Thias was encouraged. Waller was close, and apparently had not yet run through all the money. He felt great urgency to press this hunt very hard now, all the way to the end. He had been unable to pursue Clardy's trail while it was fresh, and as a result had lost him, maybe forever. He wouldn't make the same mistake with Waller. Waller's trail was also the trail of whatever inheritance he and Clardy had left. It was manifestly important that he not lose it.

They were riding through a thick grove of forest at dusk when French suddenly looked around in apparent fright and urged Thias off the trail. They plunged into thick brush just in time to avoid the hurried passing of a band of about a dozen armed and mounted men. When they were gone, Thias looked at French and saw him trembling.

"Billy, what's wrong with you? And who was them men?"

"Regulators," French replied. "The whole country is crawling with them, ever since the Harpes did their murders. They've been hanging men all over the place. Men who've did crimes. I hope they catch the Harpes and hang them for stepping on Daddy. But me and you, we'd best watch out for them."

Thias felt a chill. He realized what a dangerous life he was living and what dangerous company he was keeping. And Clardy . . . what if Clardy had gotten involved in criminal activity, as he had planned, and been caught by the regulators? There was more to fear in these forests than the Harpes and other scofflaws. There was the law itself to be wary of.

Thias and French traveled very quietly and cautiously for the next hour. When they reached a crossroads and saw there the dead and hanging corpse of a man with a sign around his neck—"See Here the faTe of Horse theefs and Bandits"— neither said a thing. They stared for a minute at the hanging man, then rode away, very sobered and thoughtful.

Thias lifted the jug to his lips and took another swallow. He knew he was foolish to get drunk at the moment, with Waller and the end of his immediate quest potentially so close by, but depression had descended like a veil upon him again, and he craved the release that liquor delivered.

It was dusk, and he and French were camped in the woods near a road only a few miles southwest of the Licking River. French was sad, too, talking about how he missed his father. Thias couldn't tell whether he was referring to his father as a living man or his father as a dried skull that smoked a pipe each evening after supper. In French's mind the two seemed to be blended into one.

Thias had never believed much in instinctive knowledge, second sight, intuitions, and such, but tonight he felt sure that soon he would encounter Waller. Whether Waller would have anything but a pittance left of the money he had taken was a burning question. Another question was just what to do with, or to, Waller in punishment. He could have the man arrested, maybe . . . but that option didn't seem so good anymore, now that he himself had been involved directly and indirectly with illegal activities. But if Waller couldn't be punished through legal means, then how? He might have taken a great moral plunge over the last several months, but he hadn't reached the level of murderer . . . he didn't think. Yet he couldn't deny that Waller deserved to die, and in just the way Waller had sought to make him himself die. There would be a certain satisfaction in lifting an axe above a cringing Jack Waller and—

What's wrong with you, Thias? You want to get yourself hung, like that man at the crossroads? Thias lifted the jug again.

"Jack's close," French said abruptly.

"What?"

"Jack's close. I can feel it."

Thias put down the jug. "Me, too. I've felt it all evening. But what if it ain't him? What if it's more regulators?"

French shook his head. "It's Jack. I know it is. I've, well . . . *felt* him being near like that before, and I ain't been wrong yet." French stood and peered through the darkening forest. "Look yonder." He pointed.

Thias stood, and to his surprise found himself drunker than he had thought. He could hardly keep his feet. Leaning against a tree, he looked in the indicated direction.

A light gleamed out in the woods. It was no more than a half mile away. A campfire.

"That'll be Jack," French said.

"We don't know that."

"We can go look."

Suddenly Thias wasn't so eager to encounter Jack Waller. "I'm drunk, Billy. I ought to be sober when—"

"We might never see him no more if we let him go now." French had a far more snappy and stern tone than Thias had ever heard him use before. He was accustomed to the subservient, pliable Billy French, the odd and maybe slightly half-witted one who toted a skull about and felt compelled to do what stronger personalities told him to. A new side of the man was emerging before his eyes. "I'm going over there. Are you coming?"

Thias wished he hadn't taken a drop tonight. But he nodded. "I'll come."

Rifles in hand, they moved through the woods, their eyes on the fire. They moved so cautiously and slowly that it required a full half hour for them to move from their own camp to the other. When they reached it, they found the fire burning brightly, but no one was about. Thias couldn't figure it out. A camp without a tender? A fire that had built itself?

A chill of fear overcame him. "Billy, let's get away from here."

French's face, dimly visible in the firelight, was taut with worry. He nodded curtly.

They turned and moved back toward their own camp. The forest was very dark. Thias sensed more than saw the figure that appeared suddenly beside him. He heard the voice of Jack Waller: "Think to jump a man in his camp, do you?" Then a rifle cracked, he felt a jolt of pain in the back of his head and went down.

He did not lose consciousness, only orientation and perception. He was aware of a struggle, mostly involving French but sometimes himself as well. He heard another shot, but no one fell. His own rifle was out of his hands and he couldn't find it. He felt Waller jar against him, and pushed back. There was a thud, as of a body against a tree. Waller's breath burst into his face, reeking and foul. He felt his hands grab and hold Waller's ears, felt himself jamming Waller's head back and hearing it smack hard against the tree behind him. Then he was on the ground, still fighting, tasting blood that might be his or might be Waller's.

He was still trying to fight when liquor, shock, and the exertion of struggle became too much. He swooned, feeling a fist jar against his cheekbone, then against his eye. Lingering for a moment on the edge of consciousness, still struggling, he gave up and passed out.

*   *   *

When he came to again, he was in the camp—not his own, but Waller's. French, his face cut and bleeding, was seated near the fire, staring at him.

"Billy . . ." Thias sat up. The original concussion injury he had suffered at French's hands back on the Wilderness Road throbbed almost like it was new, and he seemed to hurt at a dozen other points besides. He groaned.

"You done it, Thias," French said.

"Done . . . what?"

"Look. You killed him. Her, too."

Thias looked. Stretched out beside the fire, hardly an arm's length from him, was the body of Jack Waller. His throat was cut. Beside him lay a woman, also dead. She appeared to have been stabbed repeatedly.

"Billy . . . who is she?"

"That's Liz McDoogen. She was hid in the woods. You and Jack, you fought each other hard, all the way back into this clearing. You got hold of his knife and cut his throat. Then Liz, she come running in screaming, running at you, and you stabbed her. You killed them both, Thias. Don't you recollect it?"

Thias felt sick with horror. "No. I don't recollect anything like that."

"It's the liquor, and getting hit on your head. That's why you don't remember. But I seen it all. You killed them, Thias. It was *you*."

"No, no . . . I'd remember a thing like that."

"You done it, Thias. I seen it myself." He paused. "I could tell what I seen, too. Tell it to a judge!"

Thias's head was spinning, but he was beginning to understand. He had thought of French as half-witted, or something close to it, but now he saw that the man had a cunning all his own. "You're lying, Billy. It was you who did it, wasn't it? I passed out, and I was still in the dark woods at the time, not in the firelight. *You* killed them, not me!"

French firmly shook his head. "No, Thias. I remember. I seen it all, and I can *tell*!"

Thias held his head and groaned again. "What do you want from me, Billy?"

"Want you to leave. Just get up and go. I don't want the regulators to find me keeping company with a murderer."

"Damn you . . ."

"Talk nice to me, Thias. Don't talk mean. I never did like it

when folks talked mean to me, even when I was a boy. You remember how folks talked mean to me in them days, Thias?"

Thias had a new realization. "The money . . . *my* money . . .
did you find it on him?"

French tossed a cloth sack to Thias. Thias picked it up. It
contained a single shilling.

"That's all there was."

Thias tossed down the coin. "You're lying! What did you do
with the rest of it, Billy? Did you hide it?"

"Talk nice, Thias. Talk nice."

"I'll kill you!"

"You've done killed two, Thias. Ain't that enough killing for
you? Or are you like they say them Harpes are, just killing and
killing and killing, all for pleasure?"

Thias sank down again, his head spinning. He lay there, suffering, dizzy, hardly heeding the grim fact he was lying beside
two fresh corpses.

"You're telling me that I'm to go . . . and the money is to be
yours."

"There wasn't no money but that shilling," French replied.

"That's a lie."

"It ain't a lie. Talk nice, Thias. Talk nice." French stood.
"I'm taking these rifles and such with me. I'll find somebody,
tell them I found dead folk in this camp. By then you can be
gone, Thias, and they'll not catch you, most likely. You see?
I'm sparing your life again. Three times now, it is! Once when
we was boys, and I pulled you and Clardy out of the water, and
once when Jack told me to kill you, and I didn't, and now, here
I am, doing it again just 'cause—"

"Shut up, you rank devil!"

"Talk *nice*, Thias." And then he was gone, taking his rifle,
Thias's, and Waller's.

Thias rose and tried to follow, but he was still too dizzy. He
managed to reach the woods. Penetrating it deeply, he finally
sat down and waited until dawn. By then his head was clearer
and he felt drawn back to the camp. He resisted the draw.
There might be men there by now, looking, searching. . . .

Dogs. They might have dogs. They could track him.

Thias rose and began moving in the opposite direction from
the camp. He remembered those fearsome regulators, sweeping
down the road, and imagined they were upon him. Sometimes

he fancied he heard dogs in the distance, then realized it was only his imagination.

He hated Billy French. He realized how little he had known the man—and decided maybe French was one of those men who are truly unknowable. He was an inexplicable mix of simplemindedness, obedience, devotion, and utter, selfish treachery. Thias could not understand him, couldn't make sense of him. All he could do was hate him.

He came out at last on a road. By now he was weary, ready to drop. He staggered off and found a mossy, shaded place, and there nestled down and fell asleep.

Hoofbeats on the road awakened him. He sat up only a little and peered out through the brush. Regulators, from the look of them, and among them was Billy French. His face wore a look of blank horror. His hands were tied behind his back. At the end of the line of regulators was a horse with two bodies draped over its back. They were covered up, but Thias knew they had to be Waller and his woman.

The regulators rode on, and Thias remained where he was, resting. He felt some better already, not so much from rest as from that look on Billy French's face. French had told his tale, he supposed, and they hadn't believed him. And why should they have believed him? French was a known thief, a known cohort of the slain Waller. He had come telling conveniently self-serving tales of another man who had actually done the crime, a man who had vanished since then—and they hadn't believed him.

"Reckon you ain't as clever as you thought you were, Billy," Thias whispered aloud.

What drove him out at last was thirst. He had a little food in his pocket, just some parched corn and jerky, but nothing to drink. Finally, when there was no sign of further activity along the road, he rose and began walking. He found a spring and drank his fill, then went on. Twice lone riders came down the road, and both times Thias ducked out of sight until they were gone.

He wondered what to do next. Waller was dead, and his inheritance money was surely gone now. French had taken it, and now French was captured. If he had the money on him, who could say what would become of it? Thias wondered if he should go inquire about it. Maybe he could concoct a story about having been robbed by French and Waller. But that was very risky. Thias himself was a horse thief, two times now. A man could get hanged for that. And he had traveled with French for days now, in public. And what about those times that French had taken items—the liquor, the rifles. He might have killed in the process of those thefts, for all Thias could know.

Thias forced himself to face the fact: his inheritance and Clardy's truly was gone now, and irretrievable.

Unless . . .

He wondered if French might have hidden the money somewhere near the camp clearing, planning to come back for it later. There was no reason to think he had done so, but it was possible, it was at least a chance.

Thias was about to decide to go back and search that area again when he rounded a bend and came across the shocking sight of another hanging man. The regulators had done their work speedily, and this time the victim was Billy French. On his chest was a sign reading: "See here The fatE of Murderers." That confirmed it. The regulators had blamed him for the deaths of Waller and his woman.

Thias stood there alone, looking into French's blackening face and realizing just how serious a matter it was that he had fraternized publicly with this man. His old problem of a weak stomach soon got the best of him and he became sick. That was worse than a mere inconvenience, because now Thias's belly was empty of what little food he had, and he had no more, nor any money. He hadn't even remembered to pick up the shilling he had tossed down in the camp clearing.

Thias's plans changed at once. He would not return to the area of the killings. To be found there, probing about in the woods, would be dangerous. All he could do was get away from this area, and out of this state, as fast as possible. Maybe he would return to Tennessee . . . But what awaited him there? The farm was sold, Hiram Tyler was dead, Clardy was gone.

Thias was gone, too, in another way. He had changed from the man he was when he left home. He was no longer "good," as folks had always said. He had stolen horses, guns, liquor. He had run with thieves and rubbed up close against murder. He had started out good and turned out bad, and the idea of returning home now filled him with shame.

And so he made for the river, traveling by night, hiding by day, scrounging what food he could from the forests and stealing to supplement that. Every hour was a terror to him; he smelled regulators on every breeze, heard the pounding hooves of their horses in every distant sound, saw their faces in the countenance of every stranger he mischanced to meet.

He reached the river and found a group of men building a big flatboat upon which to ship horses and various other goods to New Orleans. Thias offered to help them if they would provide him passage and keep along the way. He was obviously strong, impressive to see, and they accepted the bargain.

And so Thias Tyler became a boatman, and left both Kentucky and Tennessee behind, sure he would never again return to either. That was a sorrowful thing to think about, but not nearly so sorrowful as the fact that he was sure he was also leaving behind any reasonable hope of ever seeing his brother again, if Clardy was even alive to be seen.

He threw himself into the task at hand and tried to keep his eye fixed on the future, because it was useless and painful to look any longer at the past.

CHAPTER 28

Knoxville, Tennessee, July

C lardy Tyler dismounted and tied his horse to the nearest hitching post, his eye on the crowd of men gathered around the front of a store a hundred yards down the dirt street. He could see from that far away that the group was agitated. Something important was going on. He walked quickly on down and joined the crowd.

A man at the center of the group was talking, and Clardy picked up his words in mid-sentence. ". . . and there he lay, right off the road on the crest of a hill, dead as could be. Seen him myself, just before they carried him off. It was murder, gentlemen. No doubt about it. He had been shot and knifed. Poor man must have died a hard death."

"What was his name?" someone asked.

"Bradbury. Just a simple farmer, far as I know. Nobody saw the killing, as best I'm aware."

Clardy touched the elbow of the closest man. "Somebody's been killed?"

"That's right, son. Farmer over in Roane County. Killed on

the road, 'cording to that man yonder. He just rode in a while ago, spreading the news."

"They know who done it?"

"Nope. It's enough to make a man wonder what's becoming of the world. All them Harpe killings last year, and now here's another man murdered! Country ain't safe to live in no more."

Clardy turned and walked away, not wanting to hear any more. Murder! He had brushed up against enough of that crime over the past few months. He wanted nothing more to do with it.

He crossed the street and sat down on the corner of a boardwalk, pulling his pipe from his pocket and filling it, watching the group of men as they talked loudly among themselves, broad hand gestures, intense expressions, and endless fidgeting movements showing their excitement. Big crimes such as murder had a way of stirring up people like nothing else. At the moment all that was stirring inside Clardy, however, was a strong sense of repulsion, and all the bad feelings that went along with his memories of the Harpe murders in Kentucky and the failed efforts to apprehend the culprits.

Puffing his pipe, he looked up and down the street and thought again about Thias. *Maybe today he'll return.* He had run that same thought through his mind ever since his return to his old home region.

That return had given Clardy quite a jolt. He had come expecting to find his brother and grandfather living on and working the old farm just as before, maybe by then having completed the new cabin and bettered their living situation. Instead he found that his grandfather was dead, the farm was sold to a Knoxville lawyer, Thias had gone off with the inheritance money, looking for him to give him his share. The irony seemed great to him: almost all the time he was in Kentucky, apparently Thias had been there as well, probably not far behind him. But they hadn't met. Clardy couldn't help but feel angry at Thias for having launched off on such an impossible chase. Had he really expected to be able to track down his brother in such a vast and wild place as Kentucky?

Yet Clardy's first impulse, once the shock of all the new discoveries was past, had been to turn back to Kentucky himself and see if he could find Thias. Common sense had stopped him. Thias hadn't found him, so how could he expect to do better? He recalled his grandfather's advice: When a man is lost in the woods, best to sit down and become an unmoving target than to roam around and be nigh impossible to find. The same principle applied here, Clardy decided with some reluctance. The best thing to do was to wait right where he was, anticipating that Thias would eventually give up his own search and come back. Now Clardy had been waiting for well over a month, but Thias hadn't shown up.

In the meantime, the now-landless, homeless Clardy had maintained a meager living in assorted ways. He had lodged in secret for a few days in the old homeplace cabin, living off game he hunted, but then had moved out and come to Knoxville, where he worked assorted small jobs—wagon driving, farm labor, carpentry for a merchant expanding his store. He hadn't made much money that way and had been forced to live in an abandoned old hut just east of town, but he did believe that through his hard and honest labor he was developing a better reputation for himself among the folks who had known him through all his prior years as a reveler and ne'er-do-well. That gave him a good feeling, but he continued to live in a state of unrest, wondering when Thias would return . . . and if he would return. What if something bad had happened to him in Kentucky? Based on Clardy's own rather skewed perceptions, it appeared a lot of people had bad things happen to them in the fabled Dark and Bloody Ground. Hearing about this new murder made him worry about Thias all the more.

He finished his pipe and stood. The day lay stretched before him, empty as a dried-up well. He had finished his last round of work and now was again unemployed. He would try today to scour up a new job, one that would last longer, if he was fortunate. If he couldn't, he didn't know what to do except leave and seek better fortune elsewhere, or maybe go on back to Kentucky and search for Thias after all, even if that was a nearly hopeless prospect.

The best thing that could happen would be if Thias returned. Life would become considerably brighter then. They would have their common inheritance to share, and together they could go off and find that better life they had always wanted. Maybe they could buy land somewhere, or go into business for themselves. Surely Thias would come back, eventually. But maybe not very soon. Thias would probably keep up a persistent hunt in Kentucky for a long time. He had always kept at his tasks with mulish stubbornness until they were done. Thias was slow to give up, tenacious at completing tasks of duty. It was part of what made him good.

Clardy stood and walked idly down the street, thinking about Thias, fighting off worry as best he could, and most remarkable of all, missing the grandfather he had always longed to be free of back in days that were not long past at all, but which seemed very distant now.

Clardy did find work of a sort—a couple of days' labor on a farm west of town—and forgot all about the Bradbury murder. A couple of days after his work was through, though, that murder was driven back to mind by still another murder, this one far more shocking.

Eight miles northwest of Knoxville, the body of a boy surnamed Coffey was found. According to the Coffey family, the boy had been out chasing stray cattle and hadn't come home with his horse. When he was found, he was lying beneath a tree, his shoes missing and his head broken. It appeared that an effort had been made to make the death appear accidental, as if the horse had run its rider hard against a tree limb, but no one was fooled. The horse he'd been riding was old and gentle, and those missing shoes hadn't vanished without help. The boy had been murdered, no question about it.

Clardy didn't like the thought that this news gave him: *It's almost as if the Harpes have come back.*

Then, only two days after that, yet another killing occurred, and this time the body—that of a man named William Ballard—was found in the Holston River. It had been opened and filled with rocks, just like the corpse of Cale Johnson had the year before, and just like the corpse of that fiddle-playing hermit up in Kentucky, as the story had it.

Disposal of bodies in such gruesome fashion was a distinctive Harpe trademark. Now, far more people than Clardy Tyler began to consider the possibility that the Harpes had returned to East Tennessee.

But surely not, surely not, others said. The Harpes already had trouble in Knoxville because of their 1798 crimes. No rational men would come back to a place where murder charges already awaited them.

Clardy Tyler knew the simple answer to that objection: the Harpes weren't rational men.

A few days later, while Clardy was finishing up another

round of low-paying labor on another farm, more news came that confirmed beyond reasonable doubt that the Harpes were back. Another man had been killed, this incident happening near the Emory River to the west of Knoxville. According to the story as Clardy heard it, what happened was this:

Two brothers, Robert and James Brassel, had been traveling along a mountain spur, one riding and unarmed, the other walking and carrying a rifle, when they encountered two rough-looking strangers, both mounted, who accosted them in a friendly way and asked them for news of local goings on. The Brassels told them about the two recent murders and how there were rumors that the "bloody Harpes" who had made their name infamous in the vicinity in the prior year might be behind these latest killings. The two strangers had nodded seriously, telling the Brassels that they knew for a fact that the Harpes were indeed guilty and they were out hunting for the villains themselves. A suggestion was made by the smaller of the two strangers that the Brassels join force with them and help them bring in the culprits. The Brassels agreed, but learned the terrible truth moments later when the bigger stranger sneaked up behind James Brassel and stole his rifle. James was immediately clubbed to the ground. Robert Brassel jumped down from his horse to try and grab James's rifle, but the smaller stranger jumped in and stopped him. Robert turned and fled for his life, with the smaller stranger—Wiley Harpe, he now realized—chasing him. Robert managed to escape, but his brother was not so lucky.

Robert traveled a full ten miles before encountering a band of travelers on their way toward Knoxville. He told them what had happened, and with only one gun in possession of the entire group, went back to see if they could rescue the captive Brassel. They reached the spot, and found James Brassel's battered body. His throat had been cut and his rifle smashed to pieces, as if in contempt.

No one doubted now that, incredible as it seemed, the Harpes had returned to Tennessee. The last anyone had heard, the brothers had broken out of jail in Danville, gone on a murderous spree over a wide territory, then vanished somewhere along the Ohio River. Apparently they had floated down the Ohio River, traveled up the Tennessee from its mouth, then headed eastward by a combination of river and land travel.

Robert Brassel and the party who had found his brother's

body followed the tracks of the Harpes for some distance, Clardy learned. Then they met the unexpected sight of the Harpes coming back toward them, this time with their women and babies in tow and terrible, harsh expressions on their faces.

Robert Brassel had pleaded with his companions to halt the Harpes, but an odd, paralyzing fear gripped them all. They allowed the Harpes to pass them by, with not a word spoken. Robert Brassel had wept afterward, declaring he couldn't comprehend such cowardice.

Clardy Tyler could comprehend it. He recalled his own throat-tightening fear the time he and the rest of the Skaggs party allowed the Harpes to pass them by in just such a fashion. He recalled also the terrible events that had happened afterward. It was a lingering, haunting awareness of his that had the Harpes been stopped that day near the Rolling Fork headwaters, several subsequent murders would have been avoided.

It made Clardy feel terribly guilty, and this time he couldn't shrug off guilt like he used to do so easily.

He also felt afraid, and he had more reason than most to fear the Harpes. Would he never be free of them? It was as if the Harpes were following him, anywhere he went. But that couldn't be literally true. The Harpes could not have known he had returned to Tennessee, and he doubted they would consider him game worthy of chasing, anyway. So it was coincidence that for a third time they were occupying a common region ... or maybe it was fate.

Fate. Something he had never thought much about, or believed in. What was it, though, that Isaac Ford had told him? Something about how there might be a purpose in it when folks are thrown together repeatedly, without design of their own making.

But what purpose could there be in his life and that of the Harpes being thrown together? He could see no sense in it, any more than he could see sense in the seemingly random movements and meanderings of the Harpes themselves. These men, if men they were and not incarnate devils, seemed to have no purpose in their own lives but the meaningless destruction of others. They seemed to go where the wind blew them, moving about without any particular goal or reason.

Clardy thought about it very hard. Maybe there *was* a pattern after all. He recalled a comment Micajah Harpe had made while jailed in Danville, a complaint that at some point or another he had been arrested and briefly detained in Knoxville for some theft he hadn't committed, and how that angered him and helped spur him to commit some thefts that truly were his own. "I done it in pure spite," he had said.

Might it be "pure spite" that brought the Harpes back here? Could it be that they were killing about the Knoxville region precisely because this region had given them trouble and difficulty before? Here, posses had been raised to find them, hard words had been said about them, and men had sought to have them punished for horse theft. Maybe they had come here to inflict some punishment of their own in recompense.

It made more sense than any other explanation Clardy could think of. The Harpes had returned to the Holston and French Broad country as punishers. Since they couldn't without insurmountable difficulty avenge themselves upon the specific people who had troubled them here, they were contenting themselves to take vengeance upon anyone and everyone.

That was a dreadful thought. It meant that no one was safe. If the Harpes' purpose was the general punishment of an entire populace, one life was as cheap in their eyes as any other.

Clardy was living in his abandoned hut and down to subsisting on scavenged wild greens and hunted game again. He was almost out of money, and what little he had left, he was reluctant to spend on food. He was more inclined to spend it on gunpowder, of which his supply was almost depleted from hunting.

He would need gunpowder if he was to hunt more. But he was thinking now not of hunting more game, but hunting Harpes.

It was a wild notion, but he couldn't shake it out of his mind. It all went back to Isaac Ford's talk about fate, purpose, and human lives that are repeatedly thrown together. Could it be that one of the purposes laid out for Clardy Tyler's life was to help rid the world of Micajah and Wiley Harpe?

He didn't like to think so, but the idea had its own kind of sense and persistence.

Sleep was slow to come with such momentous thought in his mind. For three nights he had hardly rested at all, tossing back and forth, thinking about Thias, himself, about Isaac Ford and the lovely Dulciana, and about all those who had died at the hands of the criminals he and his fellow Kentucky regulators had failed to bring in when they had the chance.

He owed it to those victims to make up for that mistake. They had lost their lives because of a failure in which he had played a part. It was only fair that he should risk losing his to set things right again.

No. No! Only a fool would take such a chance. I can't hunt the Harpes. All I would do was get myself killed, all for nothing. Let the good folk of the world take care of the Harpes. I'm Clardy Tyler, the "bad" Tyler brother. I ain't eager to sacrifice myself for the sake of righteousness.

He voiced such protests in his mind again and again, but the words rang hollow, and the feeling that pursuit of the Harpes was in some unique way *his* job would not go away.

He thought: I believe I'm turning into Thias. Getting holy and bound to the high moral law. And I ain't sure I like it.

Clardy was in Knoxville the day the latest news of the Harpes reached town. He stood in the midst of a crowd that gathered on the street and heard the grim word.

The Harpes had murdered again, this time up toward Kentucky, the victim being a man named Tully, whose body had been found hidden beneath a log. This particular murder was slightly different than most of the prior Harpe killings, which had no evident motive beyond bloodthirst. Tully was believed to have been an associate of the Harpes at one time or another. Maybe he had betrayed them, or refused to give them aid this time out. Whatever his offense, he had paid for it with his life.

Clardy, though generally shy about speaking up before crowds, stepped up and asked the man a question. "How is it you know about this murder?"

"Because I was with Robert Brassel and some others in the area at the time the dead man was found, that's why."

"Brassel? Brother of the Brassel killed at the Emory?"

"That's right. He seen it his duty to go after the Harpes and see them brought in. Me and some others are helping him out. It ain't nothing to be proud of that the Harpes were allowed to pass freely after Jim Brassel was murdered so brutal. Robert Brassel is still pursuing the Harpes, but he sent me back here to see if there was yet a man in Knoxville with enough iron in his backbone to come give us a hand." The man, a stocky, square-jawed fellow of about thirty years of age, wearing a battered old Revolutionary War–vintage tricorn hat, looked over the mostly male crowd. "Well? Is there a man here willing to ride out with me and answer Robert Brassel's call? Is there any here willing to hunt the Harpes?"

Hunt the Harpes. Those words struck close to home. Clardy fidgeted like a sinner under conviction at a camp meeting. He backed a little farther into the crowd and hid himself from the speaker.

An elderly man raised his voice. "Son, what's your name?"

"I'm Totty Kirkpatrick," the man said. "I come from the Holston country, and I back down before no one, even the devil Harpes."

"Well then, you're a fool!" another voice called, and everyone turned to see if they could determine who had spoken.

"Maybe I am, but I'm a fool who does his duty!" Kirkpatrick replied. "Show your courage, men! Is this the mettle of Knoxville folk? Half you men at least have fought Indians. Are you to hide for fear of two murdering scoundrels?"

"Better a hundred Indians than two Harpes!" a man called.

"That's right!" someone else shouted. "If the Harpes are heading into Kentucky, I say good riddance to them! I'll be shot if I'm going to risk my life chasing murderers who are leaving on their own."

A murmur of agreement passed through the crowd. Clardy's voice had no part in it. He slumped over as if to hide himself better.

"Don't believe you're going to find nobody eager to go Harpe-hunting!" someone yelled at Kirkpatrick. "If you're bound to do it, do it alone! There's no merit in foolishness! Don't you know the Harpes can't be killed? They got the evil eye, both of them, and they use it! How else you think they make armed men turn away and leave them be?"

"I hold no belief in the evil eye! The Harpes are mortal, and brave men can stop them. But if cowards you're bound to be, then off with you!" Kirkpatrick called, waving his hand. He looked to Clardy like a glowering, offended minor god there on the store porch. "If there's ary a man here with mettle, let him stay. I've no use for the rest of you."

Bit by bit the crowd broke up, most of the men not leaving too quickly so as not to appear to be doing the very thing they were doing, which was running away from what every one of them knew they should do. Kirkpatrick watched them disperse, his face looking angry at first, then increasingly sad. Within a minute the crowd was gone. All that remained was Kirkpatrick on the porch . . .

And Clardy Tyler in the street.

Kirkpatrick looked at him and slowly smiled. "One brave man in the lot, eh?"

"No sir," Clardy replied. "I ain't brave. I'm a man who has run from many a fight and many a duty. And in Kentucky, I was among a band of regulators who ran from the Harpes and let them live. There's been life after life lost since then. That's a mistake and wickedness I want to atone for, and you've offered me the only way I know to do it."

Kirkpatrick studied Clardy closely, in a way that made Clardy wonder what he was thinking. "What's your name?"

"Tyler. Clardy Tyler."

"Mr. Clardy Tyler, I welcome your help. And you are indeed a brave man, whether you know it or not."

"You say the Harpes are heading for Kentucky?" Clardy asked.

"Yes. It appears so. Though with them you can never tell. They double back on themselves, move in circles—there's no sense to their movements."

"You believe they are going to Kentucky for a reason?"

"Yes, if such as them have reasons. I believe they are going there to do harm to a Colonel Daniel Trabue, whose little boy they killed and who worked hard in their pursuit after that. I believe they intend to kill this Trabue to punish him. To spite him."

"I've met Colonel Trabue," Clardy said. "He is a good man. And you are right about the Harpes. I know that spite does move them. It's in their nature. Does Colonel Trabue know the Harpes are in his region?"

"By now, yes. Robert Brassel sent two of our party, William Wood and Nathaniel Stockton, ahead to his home to warn him. We had been told by neighbors of this murdered man Tully that Trabue might be a particular target for those two beasts."

"There are others in Kentucky who stood hard against the Harpes," Clardy said. "Good folk, all of them. The Harpes may try to harm them as well, or their kin." Before his mind's eye flashed the pretty face of Dulciana Ford, and with that image a new burst of courage. He *would* join Kirkpatrick, Brassel, and the others. He *would* see the Harpes brought to justice, or better still, brought to their graves. He had run enough, been coward enough. And even if he wasn't brave, like Kirkpatrick claimed he was, by heaven, he would *act* brave!

"Are you with me, then, Clardy Tyler? If you are, there's no time to waste. I'm eager to rejoin them I left. God knows I had hoped to do so with more than one man to add to our number."

"I'll be ready to leave within the hour," Clardy replied. "I own very little, and all I need to do is buy myself what gunpowder I can afford."

"Is your rifle in good fix?"

"Aye. And I hope it proves to be the very weapon that brings death to the Harpes."

Clardy bought his powder and gathered what few goods he had. Kirkpatrick, meanwhile, purchased food and other supplies for the trail. They rode out together, so fixed on their purpose and concentrating only on the immediate moment that Clardy barely had time to think how strange it was that he, who had once ridden from Knoxville into Kentucky to avoid the Harpes, was now making nearly the identical journey again for the very purpose of finding them.

CHAPTER 29

Red Banks, Kentucky, some weeks later

General Samuel Hopkins leaned back in his chair, eyes shifting back and forth between the two young men seated in his front room. Clardy felt like he was facing down his old piercing-eyed schoolmaster in the tiny classroom where he had obtained three years' worth of education and five years' worth of whippings many years ago, and the natural result was a bad case of the jitters. With great difficulty he supressed a schoolboyish urge to fidget before the dignified general. Totty Kirkpatrick, on the other hand, did not seem fidgety at all. He slumped listlessly in his chair and wearily sipped at his whiskey. Not feeling well again, he had told Clardy in private earlier. Clardy had been worried lately about his companion's health. The rigors of their life on the road were taking a toll.

"Gentlemen, I'm pleased you've come to me," Hopkins said. "Quite an honor, having the increasingly famous Harpe hunters in my home."

"Harpe hunters? Is that what they're calling us?" Kirkpatrick asked around the rim of his glass.

"Yes. Has a sort of ring to it, doesn't it? 'The Harpe hunters.' I tell you, young man, your fame is spreading all throughout Kentucky. People here are very frightened, and for good reason. It is a great comfort to many to know that there are two such as yourselves who have devoted their full effort to finding and ending these two murderers who are making such a menace of themselves. You two are becoming legend throughout Kentucky. Legend! I doubt you could know the number of mothers who are soothing their Harpe-fearing children at night with the reminder that the Harpe hunters are out there, on the track of the bad ones. I salute you both for the work you are doing."

"Our moral duty, sir, that's all it is," Kirkpatrick said. He sounded drained and his eyes were half shut. "Our moral duty."

Clardy shook his head self-consciously. He had known that he and Kirkpatrick were becoming known for their dogged pursuit, as evidenced by the lodging and food freely given to them by many families along their course, but had not realized the apparent extent. "Harpe hunter, growing famous, giving comfort to the people . . . who'd have ever thought it? My grandfather would have been proud to know his black sheep has turned to making himself known for chasing ruffians and giving comfort to scared children."

"Ruffian is far, far too weak a word to describe the Harpes," Hopkins said vehemently, eyes burning with the fierce enmity that had made him known as the most strident Harpe foe in Henderson County. Rumor had it that the Harpes held a particular hatred of the outspoken Hopkins and might even have ill plans for him. "Ruffians are men. Human beings. And the Harpes are not men, not fully. I'm convinced they lack the moral sense that marks humanity. No man could do the things they have over these past days and be fully a man. Animals, they are. Animals."

"Not animals, sir," Kirkpatrick countered, though respectfully. "For if they are animals, they cannot be held to account for what they do. We must refuse any idea that would not hold the Harpes accountable for their crimes."

Hopkins, obviously not accustomed to being disputed, lifted a brow and drummed the tips of his steepled fingers against one another, but after a few moments of thought pursed his lips and nodded. "Well said, young sir, and I must agree. The Harpes are indeed men, are indeed accountable to the standards

of common morality for what they do. But if they are not animals in their essence, they at least are animals in behavior,
and for that they must be captured and punished."

"Hear, hear," said Kirkpatrick, lifting his glass and then
draining off his final sip. He set the glass on the floor beside
his chair and slumped even lower.

"Are you ill, Mr. Kirkpatrick?" Hopkins asked.

"I've been feeling poorly lately, I'll be fine, though. Thank
you for asking."

Clardy thought bleakly about the bloody path the Harpes had
been threading through Kentucky, and clenched his hand
tightly around his glass, frustrated that they still remained
uncaptured. How could such wicked men get away with so
much for so long? Since he and Kirkpatrick had left Knoxville,
the Harpes had struck fatally several times. Of all their murders, these most recent ones were the most loathsome in
Clardy's view, and had filled him with a fierce determination
to see the Harpes brought to justice. From its reluctant and
half-guilty, halfhearted origin, Clardy's impulse to hunt those
brothers had grown to a fierce desire, an impetus before which
all other inner drives bowed in subservience. Indeed, he realized, he had become a Harpe hunter not only in action but at
heart.

Clardy followed his memories through the long, winding,
distressing, and often frustrating path that had led him and
Kirkpatrick from Knoxville here to the front room of General
Hopkins's Henderson County home. From Tennessee they had
entered Kentucky and gone straight to Daniel Trabue's house.
By the time they reached it, the Harpes had struck again. The
victims were named Graves, a father and thirteen-year-old son
who made the mistake of opening their new Marrowbone
Creek home for the night to two ragged strangers and a gaggle
of silent women with fussing babies. Their killers used the
Graveses' own axe to dispatch them while they slept. The
bodies were found thrown out against a fence, like so much
rubbish. The worst part of it was the seeming lack of reason
for the killings. Clardy wondered if random murder was an end
in itself for the Harpes.

News of the Marrowbone Creek murders had spread quickly
while Clardy and Kirkpatrick made a futile search for the
Harpes' trail. Settlers across Kentucky huddled in fear at the
knowledge of the murderers in their country and swiftly re-

formed bands of regulators began combing the forests for
them. No one found them.

The next to die was a young slave boy who was hauling a
bag of grain toward a mill on the back of a fine horse. The
Harpes left both the grain and the horse behind. Soon another
child died, a young girl out playing carelessly some distance
from her home. Again they left her corpse to be found and the
unanswered question to ring in every decent citizen's mind:
Why?

They struck next in Logan County, a few miles from the
Drumgool's Station settlement, killing several of a party of
about a dozen travelers who had camped for the night. Gone
was the Micajah Harpe who had once balked at attacking a
camp of three men because the risk was too great. No longer
did the Harpes exercise much caution at all, killing freely and
moving on with hardly any effort to cover their tracks. Yet they
were not captured, a fact that frustrated Clardy and Kirkpatrick
incessantly. It seemed they and every other pursuer of the
Harpes always came onto the scene too late, achieving nothing
but the hearing of one more horrible tale and the reception of
one more hot wrenching of the gut. Meanwhile, the Harpes
moved on, lost somewhere ahead of them in the Kentucky
wilds, no doubt looking for another would-be victim.

Clardy could not explain the Harpes' uncanny ability to
evade capture, but he knew that the more time passed, the
greater the difficulties that would be created by their continued
freedom. Already, fear of the Harpes was so great and wide-
spread that people saw their shadows behind every tree and at-
tributed every fresh set of tracks to the passing of the
murderers. Clardy often feared that he and Kirkpatrick might
even be mistaken for the Harpes themselves in such an environment of panic.

"We *must* find them, soon."

"Eh? What was that, young man?"

Clardy blinked and looked up at General Hopkins, blushing
as he realized that he had become lost in a sleepy, whiskey-
induced reverie and had spoken aloud without meaning to. "I
was just saying that we must find the Harpes soon. Before they
kill others, or some innocent person is mistook for them and
killed in error."

"Indeed, indeed." The General frowned as he spoke, leaving
Clardy to wonder if the expression reflected merely the gravity

of the subject under discussion or irritation at having been interrupted. Clardy had the idea the general had been in the
middle of some discourse when he made his unplanned vocal
interpolation.

The ailing Kirkpatrick weakly shot Clardy a remonstrative
look, turned to General Hopkins and said: "You were speaking,
sir, of a family that has moved into a cabin on Canoe Creek?"

Clardy, grateful for Kirkpatrick's subtle updating, turned his
attention to the general, determined not to drowse off and make
a fool of himself again.

"Yes, yes," Hopkins said. "It seems there are a couple of
families, actually—two men, three women, and two very young
children—who have moved into a rented cabin south of Red
Banks, on a stream called Canoe Creek. John Slover, an old
Indian-fighting friend of mine, was shot at by someone in that
vicinity not long after these strangers came in, but he didn't
quite see who did it. He suspects the culprits are the men who
moved into the Canoe Creek cabin."

"It certainly could be the Harpes," Kirkpatrick said.

"One thing doesn't fit," Clardy contributed. "You say there
were only two young children, General?"

"Yes. Three women, two children."

"There should be three children. All three of the women had
their birthings while I was yet their guard in the Danville
prison."

"Perhaps there was a third child that simply wasn't noticed,"
Hopkins said with the slightest trace of irritability.

"Or maybe it ain't the Harpes at all," said Kirkpatrick.

"Or maybe it is, and something bad has happened to one of
the babies." It took a moment for Clardy's implication to sink
in upon the others.

Hopkins cleared his throat. "Possibly so. Those devils have
already shown their willingness to murder even children." He
paused, lost for a moment in dark thoughts. Shuddering himself out of it, he declared, "God help us, what beasts!"

"Has anyone questioned the reasonableness of suspecting
the Harpes would return to Henderson County?" Kirkpatrick
asked. "They have had trouble here before, after all."

"The question has been raised. I doubt it holds much validity
in the minds of any of us three," the general replied.

"Indeed not," Clardy said as Kirkpatrick nodded. "The

Harpes have never feared returning to places where the law is after them."

"Precisely," said the general.

Clardy went on. "If anything, they're drawn to places they've had trouble, because generally there's scores to settle there—and the Harpes do settle scores. Wiley Harpe as much as told me himself that he went back to Knoxville to kill a man named Cale Johnson even though they were known to have stole a passel of horses there and had already run off once from capture." Clardy paused momentarily, conjuring up his memories of those fated days that had ended what he now recalled as a nearly carefree youth. "I knew Cale Johnson. He had his eye on Wiley's wife. Wiley got his revenge. And his spite. It may be those things here that have drawed them to Henderson County." He paused. "But that missing baby bothers me. It may not be the Harpes in that cabin."

"There are several reasons to believe these new folk are the Harpe gang, whatever the facts are about this baby," Hopkins said. "In addition to Slover nearly being shot, a man here has disappeared. His name is Trowbridge, and we've searched high and low for him, without result. I believe he is dead. Probably murdered. A group generally matching the Harpe description shows up, one man is accosted and another goes missing . . . it all adds up to the Harpes in my tally book."

"Then why has nothing been done?"

Hopkins bristled visibly at Clardy's blunt question. Clardy gave a sad inner sigh. Obviously he had a way of rubbing the general wrong even without trying. "Young sir, something *has* been done," Hopkins replied icily. "As soon as Trowbridge went missing, I sent scouts to examine this supposed Harpe cabin, but they saw nothing to settle the question. They are continuing to watch and are to report to me as soon as they have anything worth reporting. The fact is, the cabin seems to have been vacated for the moment. Perhaps the people in it realized trouble was upon them."

"I hope not. I'd like to get a look at them," Clardy said. "I know the Harpes firsthand. I could tell you straight out if it is them."

"Which is precisely why your coming is providential," Hopkins replied. "You will have your opportunity to see this pair, in the company of my scouts." He stood abruptly. "Well, enough talk is enough talk. The only way to find out the truth about our Canoe Creek residents is by observation, and we can't do that from armchairs. Let's get you young gentlemen fed—both of you, thin as rails! Does no one bother to feed Harpe hunters on the prowl?—and then we'll have you off."

Clardy rode away from the Hopkins house about an hour later, alone. Kirkpatrick hadn't made it halfway through the sumptuous meal Hopkins set before them before growing violently sick and collapsing out of his chair. He was far sicker than Clardy had realized. Hopkins was greatly alarmed and had Kirkpatrick put to bed at once, leaving Clardy to ponder with some disquiet that just as the Harpe trail seemed to be growing hot, he was to lose the aid of his trusted cohort.

Trailing the Harpes as a pair had been daunting enough; now Clardy was forced to adjust to the intimidating responsibility of tracking them alone. But not really alone, he reminded himself. All he was doing at the moment was riding toward Canoe Creek, there to meet the scouts Hopkins had watching the cabin where the Harpes were suspected to be.

But what if he encountered the Harpes themselves before he found the scouts? Dreadful imaginings of the miserable death the Harpes would inflict upon the man who had once betrayed them and then kept guard upon them in Danville filled his mind. He reined his horse to a stop, dismounted, and sat down by the road for a pipe of tobacco and a time of serious thought about just turning south and heading back toward Tennessee. Had he not done his share of Harpe hunting already?

It required a tremendous struggle and three pipefuls of tobacco for conscience to win the debate. Tempting as it was to cast off this fearful task, Clardy could not do it.

What settled the issue for him was in part the awareness that he had nothing worthwhile to go back to in Tennessee. The truly deciding factor, however, was the question of the seemingly missing Harpe baby. Perhaps Hopkins's scouts had merely miscounted. Perhaps not. Clardy felt no love for the Harpes or the women who had obviously gone back to them when they had a chance to leave, but he had been present at the births of those children. He had grieved for them, being born into such a terrible situation. He had to know if harm had come to one of them . . . and if it had, by heaven, he would see that the price for that harm was paid in full.

Animated by this righteous wrath, he mounted again and

rode. He reached Canoe Creek without incident, found the scouts with relative ease, and with them watched the supposed Harpe cabin without seeing any signs of life. Eventually he and the others had crept down to the cabin itself and found it was indeed empty. If the Harpes had been here, they were gone. Clardy was relieved on a superficial level, disappointed on a deeper one.

One of the scouts said, "Hang it all, we've wasted time enough already looking for them devils. If they've gone, I believe we ought to forget all this and get back home."

Clardy thought: Home . . . I have no home to get back to. I don't want to forget all this. I want to find the Harpes.

He turned to the scouts. "Well, I ain't quitting. I'm going on. But just where, I don't know. Back up to the general's, maybe?"

"If you're mad enough to keep this up, then I suggest you go see the squire instead," one suggested. "He's been watching and prowling for the Harpes, and may have news of them that General Hopkins don't."

"Who's the squire?"

"Squire Silas McBee. A big, heavy man, but good and as brave as you'll find. Lives on Deer Creek, to the south of us. Offer him your service. He'll have heard of you and be glad for the help."

Clardy obtained better directions, said his farewells to the two scouts and set off.

"There goes a brave man," one of the scouts said.

"Nope," replied another. "There goes a fool who's liable to get himself killed."

Within an hour of his arrival at Squire McBee's, Clardy was handed evidence that Isaac Ford's belief in unseen forces that prodded men along through their lives just might be accurate. He found he had come to McBee's just before the advent of a remarkable sequence of events.

He had scarcely arrived, made his identity known, and received a hearty welcome from the rotund McBee, before a man rode in behind him. McBee made the introduction to Clardy of one James Tompkins, who bore news of an encounter with men he suspected might be the Harpes.

"It so happens I've had a possible encounter of my own,"

McBee said. "Come inside and we'll sit. You tell your story first, Jim."

As Jim Hopkins spoke, he struck Clardy as a good-hearted fellow, perhaps slightly simple of mind, but clever enough to have looked below the surface of the situation he described.

"Squire, sir, I was setting at home yesterday toward the evening, when I heard my dogs commence to barking in the yard. I looked out and here come two men, wearing nice wool suits and carrying rifles and pistols, and right off I was worried, knowing the Harpes were said to be about, you see. But these two, they didn't look dangerous, being so nice-dressed and all, and I says to myself, Jim, them two are traveling preachers, I'll betcha. You know how you can generally tell a preacher, Squire. Don't know what it is, but they got a look to them, generally speaking. And these two, they had that look—"

"Yes, yes. Go on," McBee prodded.

"Well, they come up to the door and says to me, 'You won't let them dogs bite us, will you?' and I says, 'No, not if you're the kind of good folk you look to be.' And they says, 'We're Methodist preachers looking for a meal.' And I says, 'I thought you was preachers. You can generally tell a preacher by his look.' I reckon it was the clothes. They looked new. The little one of the pair was tugging and scratching at his collar, like maybe it didn't fit just right."

"Little one?" Clardy interjected. "One little, one big?"

"Yes sir. Just like the Harpes. But I wasn't thinking about that at the time. They seemed to be what they said. And I'd heard the Harpes traveled with women and babes. There was none such with these two."

"No women . . ." Clardy frowned.

"What happened then?" McBee asked.

"Well, I let them in and had the woman put some food out for them. The big one, he said he wanted to pray over the food and bless our house for us being so kind. And what a prayer it was! You never heard the like. When he was done, I was sure he was a preacher. You know how you can generally tell a preacher's prayer. Got more to it than the prayers of plain folk."

"What kind of things did they talk about?" Clardy asked.

"All the common things, you know. Weather, crops, stock and such. Then they brung up the Harpes. The big one, he did most of the talking, and he says, 'We're sorry to come to your home carrying such a bunch of weapons, but with the Harpes about we have to be careful.' And I says, 'Bad men, them Harpes,' and the big one—he give the name of Williams, by the way, and the little one Smith—he says, 'Men bound for hell, they are. Men surely put in the world by the Almighty to smite wicked mankind for his sins.' And the little one, he gave a sort of laugh, and that struck me odd, but I didn't say nothing.

"They ate some more and praised the victuals, which was truly right poor, if truth be told. I says, 'I'd have liked to have fed you better, but I'm so low of powder right now I ain't been able to shoot no meat lately.' So Preacher Williams ups and fetches his own powder horn and pecks out a teacup full of powder for me to have. 'There you go,' he says. 'Now you can shoot some meat and protect your family against the wicked Harpes.' And the little one laughs again."

"Obviously they didn't do you any harm, whoever they were," McBee said.

"No sir, they didn't, I'm glad to say. But they did take to asking about folks who lived hereabouts, names and where their homes was and all. The little one chimes in and says, 'We hear there's a man named McBee lives in this vicinity. A good man who is said to be a bane against the Harpes.' And I says, 'Yes, there is,' and then I told them where you lived. Soon as I did I thunk that maybe I'd done the wrong thing."

"Why was that?" McBee asked. His eyes had taken on an eager luster when he heard Tompkins's last statements.

"Just a feeling, you know. Once they left, I worried about it to no end. 'Fraid that maybe they really was the Harpes and had ill plans for you, Squire. You've been right loud in calling for the Harpes to be found and done away with, you know."

"I have indeed. Is there more to your story?"

"That's pretty much it."

"Then hear mine. Jim, I do believe the pair you met were the Harpes. Last night after dark, you see, I heard a stir among my bear hounds, just like you did, and looked out the window. I was able to see enough to make out two men there on the edge of the road, getting into quite a fray with my hounds. I might have called off the dogs, but it struck me odd that these two were coming in at such an hour—I thought of the Harpes, naturally—and they weren't calling for any help in getting the dogs off them, as folks with good intent would. So I let the hounds have at it, and before long this pair ran back to their horses with the dogs all but tearing off their backsides, jumped into their saddles and rode away. Odd thing—but it fits with your story like two notched logs going together."

"Indeed it does, Squire," Tompkins said.

"I wonder where the women and babies were?" Clardy asked.

"You've heard the suspicions that the Harpes are lodging on Canoe Creek?" McBee asked.

"Yes. But the cabin is empty. I came to you directly from there."

"Empty . . . well, maybe they've lodged their women and children somewhere else for the moment. They must be aware that suspicions are turned toward them."

"No doubt about it," Clardy said. "But what do we do now? Is there any chance of tracking down these 'preachers'?"

At that moment noise from outside brought all three to their feet. McBee went to his door, threw it open, and looking over his shoulder, Clardy saw riders thunder into the yard in a great state of excitement.

"What's this?" McBee asked.

"Squire McBee," one of the riders said breathlessly as he dismounted, "a bad thing has happened."

"What's that?"

"Moses Steigal's house burned to the ground last night. We found the ruins of it this morning, still smoking. Not a sign of life about the place. We fear there's been some deaths."

"Did you look for bodies?"

The man looked sheepish. "Truth was, sir, we weren't too keen on finding burnt corpses right after breakfast. We rode straight here to let you know, you being sort of a leader hereabouts, you see."

McBee, his broad face solemn, nodded. "I thank you, men." He turned to Clardy. "Mr. Tyler, this merits investigation. If our 'preachers' took lodging in the Steigal house last night . . ."

"I was thinking just the same," Clardy replied. "I'll come with you, if you like."

"You are welcome. But there may be some gruesomeness in what we find when we get there, you should know. If that family died in the fire . . ."

"I have a brother who is weak of stomach, but I've never been plagued with such," Clardy replied. "You lead, and I'll follow."

McBee faced the riders. "Will you men come as well?"

"Well, sir, we have business on down the road—"

McBee waved his hand. "Be off, then. I'll not ask anyone to come who doesn't want to. Jim, how about you?"

Tompkins didn't look eager, but he nodded. "I'm with you, Squire. Lord, I hope nothing has happened to Moses and his family. And I believe Colonel Love has been staying there some lately, too."

"What kind of family does this Steigal have?" Clardy asked.

"A wife and a baby, four or five months old," McBee replied. "God help them all. This is grim news. Very grim."

CHAPTER 30

They rode toward the Steigal house, passing by the home of another neighbor, William Grissom. Grissom was there, and when he learned what McBee was doing, joined them, bringing along some of his family, too. In short measure they reached the Steigal place, and found it burned to the ground and still smoking.

They called around the immediate area for the Steigals but did not find them. After waiting about an hour more for the ashes to further cool, they began probing around in the ruins, and before long McBee made the ugly discovery of the apparent body of Mrs. Steigal, then that of the Colonel Love whom Tompkins had mentioned. They looked for the baby's remains but did not find them, and concluded that either the child had been thoroughly consumed by the fire or perhaps had not been in the cabin at all, but was gone somewhere with his father, who also was obviously not here.

Clardy wasn't so confident about the strength of his stomach when McBee began more closely examining the dead. He stood off to the side, looking elsewhere, smoking his pipe until he noticed the smoke tasted too much like the charred-wood stench hanging heavily around this place. He knocked out the burning tobacco and put the pipe away.

McBee, who had been kneeling beside Mrs. Steigal's corpse, then Love's, stood with much effort, being a massively built man. "These two have been murdered," he announced. "This is my friend Colonel Love here, I'm sorry to say. His head has been split, probably by an axe or tomahawk. And Mrs. Steigal has been repeatedly stabbed."

Clardy strode up to McBee. "Might her husband have done this?"

"I doubt that. Moses Steigal is a man I don't fully trust, but I don't see him as a murderer."

"Then it was probably the Harpes," Clardy said.

"Aye, young sir, I feel sure it was."

"Why would the Harpes kill these folks?"

"Who can say? They seem to require no reason. But I have heard it rumored that Steigal knew the Harpes in Tennessee."

"In Tennessee?" Clardy felt a prompting of memory. "Steigal . . . I recollect the name, though I didn't make the link until now. I'm a Tennessean myself, Squire."

"So I've heard."

"What happens now, Squire?"

"First, there is some burying to be done."

Clardy dug Love's grave, the activity making him think back to that night when he and Thias had dug up and straightened their grandfather's bent leg. It seemed like a memory from a century ago, considering all that had come and gone since then.

When the graves were filled, they returned to McBee's house to prepare for the inevitable manhunt. They were greeted mere moments later with the arrival of a distraught-looking rider. Clardy recognized him from having seen him in Knoxville in times past: Moses Steigal. Steigal looked at Clardy as he swung down from his saddle, but didn't act as if he remembered him.

"Squire, is it true?"

"Moses, I'm sorry to say that it is."

Steigal shuddered as if someone had struck him in the spine with a hammer. He closed his eyes and pursed his lips. Clardy looked away, uncomfortable at the sight of a man being overwhelmed. He expected Steigal to break down and weep, but the man managed to get a hold on himself.

"The Harpes," he said, very softly. "They've done this."

"I do believe so, Moses," McBee replied.

"I intend to see them pay for this."

"You will find me beside you when you do."

"There are men I know who can help us," Steigal went on. "Three good and capable ones, all at Robertson's Lick right now."

"Then go fetch them, Moses," McBee said. "Come back here as quickly as you can, and we'll be ready to join you. It's time that all this hellishness end. The Harpes have ridden free long enough."

Clardy remained at McBee's that night, Tompkins returning to his home with the promise of joining the manhunters the next day. Clardy expected a difficult night's sleep, filled with both dread and anticipation of the next day's grim quest, but in fact he slept very soundly. He awakened in the morning refreshed, as ready as any man can be for dangerous work.

Steigal returned from Robertson's Lick shortly after sunrise. With him were three men, Matthew Christian, Neville Lindsey, and John Leiper, all of whom had been boiling down salt at the lick when Steigal found them. They seemed impressed to learn who Clardy was, no doubt having heard many tales of him as "Harpe hunter" over the past few weeks.

Grissom came riding in shortly afterward, bringing his family with him, and also James Tompkins. The family members were placed inside McBee's ample house, the women and older children being given weapons and told not to expose themselves outside the house until the posse had returned. The Harpes were a vengeful, unpredictable pair and might be close by. It would be just their kind of jest to wait until they saw the posse ride out, then come punish the people left behind.

With that grim bit of warning freshly ringing in every mind, the manhunters set out, eight in number: McBee, Grissom, Leiper, Steigal, Christian, Tompkins, Lindsey, and Clardy Tyler. With McBee in the lead both physically and authoritatively, they rode to the burned house, which Steigal looked at only a moment before turning away, his face hiding unspeakable thoughts. Nearby, they found the apparent tracks of the Harpes and began following them, grateful that the weather had been dry and no precipitation had fallen to obliterate them.

Deeper into the wild terrain they plunged, following the remarkably clear trail. Then came what struck Clardy as a potential disaster. The trail vanished, having been pounded into nothingness by the passing of a buffalo herd sometime earlier that morning.

"Have no fears about that," McBee said. "We should be able to find their spoor again by dividing, circling around over the buffalo track, and coming together some distance away on the far side."

The exercise worked, and the group regathered itself on a Harpe trail just as clear as it was before. Clardy felt encouraged. It appeared that once again the Harpes were being careless about their trail. As he had many times before, he felt astonished that such reckless men could have escaped capture so often and with such apparent ease.

Soon they encountered the first evidence that the Harpes might be worried at least a little about pursuit. The trail forked, and here the Harpes evidently had parted ways. The manhunters divided into two groups and followed each course, and soon found that the trails came together again. The Harpes' parting had been only temporary.

The clear weather of the prior night had been only temporary, too. By dusk the sky was filled with heavy, wet clouds. Clardy anticipated a rough night. They had no tents, nothing to throw over themselves but saddle blankets, which would be saturated within minutes. They made camp on the west bank of the Pond River, ate their supper, and waited for the storm.

It came with the darkness, soaking men, supplies, weapons. Only with effort did they keep their powder dry. They grumbled and swore about the rain, Clardy along with the rest, but the truth was he minded it much less than he would have only a year or so before. He wasn't nearly as occupied with his own comforts as he had been back in his reckless days on Beaver Creek.

"I hope we've drawn nigh to those murdering buggers," Steigal said beneath his sodden blanket. "There'll be no trail remaining after this kind of wash."

They rose with the sun, ate a sparse, cold breakfast, and set out. About an hour later they found two dead dogs on the road, knifed to death.

"That's Harpe work," McBee said. "Most likely these hounds were barking at them, and they feared they would give them away."

"That means they *are* worried about being chased," Clardy said.

"Aye, and that they are close," McBee replied. "These dogs are still a mite warm to the touch."

They dismounted at once and walked their horses, wanting to be able to take cover on foot in a moment's notice, if need be. Ambush was possible. But after a mile they had run across nothing new and remounted.

Almost immediately McBee let out a startlingly loud shout: "Yonder, men! See them there?" He pointed up a hill that rose ahead.

Clardy looked and saw three men standing, talking to each other. Two of them indeed were the Harpes; the sight of them made his blood chill. Micajah was holding the reins of a single horse. The third man, however, was a stranger.

The manhunters set their horses into a gallop, bearing hard up the hill toward the trio of men. The stranger with the Harpes turned and ran, taking cover behind a nearby tree. McBee, in the lead, raised his firearm, which he had loaded with buckshot, and fired a blast that caught the man in the side. He yelled in pain and fell.

Steigal yelled, "Don't shoot him no more! That's George Smith!"

"Squire McBee, don't kill me!" Smith yelled in a pain-wracked voice. "Don't you know me, Squire?"

"God help me!" McBee said in a tight whisper. Then he shouted: "Forgive me, George! I didn't see who you were!"

Clardy, who had been on the verge of shooting at the suspiciously behaving stranger, had lowered his rifle when Steigal shouted. He didn't know who George Smith was, but evidently he was not dangerous. He turned his attention to the Harpes.

They were gone. He felt a tremendous dismay. Micajah had leaped onto his horse and ridden pell-mell into the woods, and Wiley had darted off on foot, as slick and quick as the weasel he resembled.

"Don't be fretful, men—we'll track them down, track them clear to hell if need be," McBee said, and he had a way of speaking that made his words believable. "For now, let's tend to George's wounds. George, I'm mighty sorry. When I saw you run as you did—"

"It was my fault, Squire. I shouldn't have run. I brought it on myself."

"It looks like your wound isn't a bad one, thank God," McBee said. "We'll bind you up good and tight." He squatted and immediately began the bandaging himself. "How did you come across the Harpes, by the by?"

"I was looking for strayed horses early this morning, when over the hill comes the little one, carring a rifle and a kettle. Going for water, I figure. When he seen me, he commenced to threatening me and asking me why I was out and about, whether I was part of them who was chasing them. I thought he'd kill me any moment, he seemed so fierce. His voice carried so loud that the big one heard him and came riding in from their camp, which lies no more than eighty rods distant from where I sit right now. If you hadn't come on when you did, I'd be dead right now, Squire. Dead as a stone."

"It's the becursed Harpes who'll be dead," Steigal said. "Why do we stand here dawdling? His wounds are bound—and if that camp is no more than eighty rods away . . ."

"You are thinking my own thoughts after me, Moses," McBee said. "Smith, I'll leave you here for now. Hide amongst the brush and rest for a bit until the blood clots up good. And rest assured that if it is in our power, your difficulties today will be avenged very soon."

The Harpe campsite did not prove to be the open-aired bivouac Clardy had expected, but was enclosed beneath a huge, over-thrusting shelving rock poking out of a south-facing bluff, with another rock situated before it in such a way as to make a sort of room, safe from wind and precipitation. McBee dismounted and went to it, rifle ready. A moment later he said something, extended his hand inside, and brought out a woman.

Clardy drew in his breath in surprise. It was Sally Rice Harpe, yet hardly recognizable as the bedraggled but pretty young woman Clardy had guarded in Danville. She was pale, hair stringing down and matted on the top, her entire person filthy beyond description, wearing rags and clutching a tattered swaddling blanket. An empty blanket.

The sight of her brought stunned silence to the entire group. Clardy dismounted and walked up to her, awed and repelled to see her in such a state. "Sally?"

She looked at him with vacant eyes. "Mr. Tyler? Is it you?"

My God, he thought, she sounds like a child. "Yes, Sally, it's me." His voice almost caught in his throat as he asked, "Sally, where is your baby?"

Her pale eyes filled with tears and her face twisted in an expression of sorrow. "My daddy, he ruint my doll."

"Your daddy? What do you mean?"

"My daddy, he took my doll and hit its head against a tree a few nights back. Hit it real hard. Then he threw it off into the trees and wouldn't let me go get it."

Clardy tried to make sense of what she said, and when he did, his stomach lurched. "Sally, your daddy . . . do you mean your husband?"

She looked confused, eyes narrowing. Behind the puzzled mask of her begrimed face Clardy felt the workings of a mind strained almost past the point of sanity, almost bereft of the ability to discern what was imagined from what was real. After several seconds of strained thought, Sally shook her head. "No, not my husband." She sobbed abruptly. "Micajah done it! It was Micajah!"

"What does this mean?" McBee asked Clardy in a tone that said he dreaded the answer.

Clardy felt his own eyes flood. "It means that Micajah Harpe killed her baby. Broke its head against a tree and tossed it away."

McBee blanched. "Damn his soul. Damn his soul to the hottest fires of hell!"

Sally was weeping profusely. Clardy went to her and put his arms around her. The stench of her body was almost unendurable. "Why did he do it, Sally? Why did he kill your baby?"

"Crying . . . my doll, my baby was crying . . . he said someone would hear it, come and find us. . . . Wiley wouldn't stop him . . . his own little one, and he wouldn't stop Micajah from—" She sobbed; any further words were lost.

"Oh, Sally, Sally, I'm sorry." Clardy hugged her close and cried shamelessly before the silent group. McBee snorted, touched his own reddening eyes, and turned away.

"And after he . . . after he did it, he still made me stay with them. Made me go into a town, buy them clothes . . ."

Clardy forced back his tears and glanced at McBee. "The suits they were wearing when they went to Jim Tompkins's house." McBee nodded silently.

Clardy hugged Sally again and said, "Sally, we've come to punish Micajah Harpe, and Wiley, for what they did to your baby. And to so many other innocent folks. But you must help us. Will you do that?"

She looked up at him; again he was struck by her childlikeness. "You'll punish him?"

"Yes. We will."

In a mere moment her expression transmorphed from grief to hard, burning fury. "Yes," she said, her voice now that of a woman, not a child. "I'll help you."

"Then tell us where he is."

"I don't know where Wiley is. Micajah, he went yonder way." She pointed. Suddenly she sobbed again, her grief now mixed with a palpable fury. "He kilt my baby! You kill him, too!"

"That will happen unless he surrenders himself at once," McBee said. He patted Sally's shoulder and faced his men. "Gentlemen, I am a heavy-bodied man, and my horse is weary. I propose that I remain with this woman and follow on behind you at whatever pace she can make on foot. The rest of you proceed without letting me hinder your speed."

Clardy might have thought that proposition cowardly had someone other than McBee put it forth. But from what he had already observed, he knew McBee was no coward. His proposal was in fact very logical.

Clardy said, "Sally, where are the other women and babies?"

"With Micajah and Wiley. They put me off here, told me to stay."

"Abandoning her, no doubt," McBee said softly. "She had grown too . . . too lost. A burden on them."

"At least they didn't kill her," Clardy said.

Sally clung tight to Clardy. "Don't go. Don't go. You've always been good to me. Don't leave me."

"I've got to go, Sally, but just for a time. I'm going to go with these men and find Micajah and Wiley. Squire McBee here is a good man. He'll take care of you while I'm away."

She looked at McBee, sniffed back her tears, and nodded. Breaking free from Clardy, she threw herself upon McBee, wrapping her arms around his ample form and leaving him with a look of disquieted surprise that would have been comical in circumstances not so morbid.

Clardy remounted and they rode on. His heart thumped like a drum. He was scared, but grew strangely excited as they advanced, filling with a satisfying expectation that very soon

Micajah Harpe would receive the punishment he had so justly earned. Clardy believed without question that Micajah would be killed. He had escaped formal justice before. No one in this band would risk letting that happen again.

Moses Steigal most of all. Clardy had only to look in the bereaved man's determined face to know that no mercy would come to Micajah Harpe.

Clardy was the first to see him, but he had no time even to point him out before the others also caught sight.

Micajah Harpe, his two women, and their young children were riding on the crest of a low, wooded ridge just ahead, him in the lead, the women, with their children, straggling behind on doubly burdened horses that seemed to be having far more difficulty than Harpe's mare in maneuvering through the undergrowth.

Leiper, riding beside Clardy at the head of the manhunters, shouted: "Halt, Harpe! Stay where you are, or you're a dead man!"

Harpe's answer was an oath. He heeled his mare to faster speed and continued along the ridge. Leiper raised his rifle and fired, but the ball sailed high, singing off above the rider's head. Micajah veered his horse to the left and went out of sight on the far side of the ridge. The women, meanwhile, had already dismounted, and now knelt beside their panting horses, arms upraised in surrender, their children standing at their sides.

Leiper, trying to reload his rifle, engaged in a flurry of cursing. The rainstorm that had drenched them all in the night had caused the wooden ramrod of his rifle to swell in its thimbles so that he couldn't withdraw it. He shoved the useless weapon toward Tompkins. "Here—give me your rifle, and you take mine," he said. "I'm a better shot than you."

Tompkins, a gentle and compliant man, didn't argue. He handed Leiper the rifle. He turned to Clardy and said, "That rifle is loaded with powder that Micajah Harpe himself give me in a teacup when he ate supper with me, pretending to be a preacher."

Leiper said, "Tompkins, you and Lindsey stay here. Guard the women and their young. The rest of you—on! Don't let him get away!"

The rode up and over the ridge that Micajah had traveled

upon. Clardy cursed the strong mare that carried Micajah Harpe. The man might actually escape them because of it. His own horse was growing very tired, but Clardy urged it on.

"There!" one of the others shouted.

Micajah Harpe was bent low in the saddle, trying to race his mare up another ridge. But the horse was obviously growing tired. Three of the pursuers raised their rifles and fired at Harpe. One ball struck him in the leg, but he kept riding.

Clardy and Leiper had not fired their rifles. As the others paused to reload, the pair rode forward after the wounded man, who suddenly halted his mare and looked back at them.

"He thinks all the rifles have been fired off," Clardy said to Leiper.

"He thinks wrong," Leiper said. He halted his horse, lifted his rifle, and aimed at Micajah Harpe, who only too late realized that he should not have paused just yet. Harpe was about to race on again when Leiper fired the rifle—Tompkins's rifle—and gunpowder that had once belonged to Micajah Harpe himself sent the rifle ball hurtling to rip through the backbone and spinal cord of the bulky outlaw.

"You hit him!" Clardy yelled.

Astonishingly, Micajah Harpe rode on, though at the moment the ball hit him he nearly pitched out of the saddle. He was almost out of sight again when he paused once more, raised his own rifle with obviously excruciating effort, and snapped the trigger. The gun, apparently too hurriedly loaded, did not go off. Harpe swore and threw the rifle to the ground. Clardy raised his own rifle and fired. He missed. Micajah Harpe cursed at him.

"Halt and dismount, you murdering son of a whore, or I'll shoot you dead!" Steigal called.

Harpe freed and lifted his belt axe, and shouted back: "I'll halt when you do, damn you!" Clardy was awestruck by the outlaw's defiance, but noticed at the same moment that the voice that had always been strong and rich before now sounded weak and tremulous.

"He's going to fall off his horse," Clardy said.

Yet just as the words were spoken, Harpe turned his mount and headed it into the canebrake. His legs dangled limply on either side of the animal, indicating that he had no use of them. Micajah Harpe was paralyzed, holding the saddle with sheer force of devilish will.

The pursuing party quickly reloaded and followed after him. The canebrake was dense and difficult to travel through, but they were determined. By the time they reached the other side, Harpe was fully in view, only a few yards ahead. He came out of the brake, barely in the saddle now, and once in the open, leaned forward. The exhausted mare was moving slowly now, and Harpe himself appeared to be dying. Clardy was the first to catch up to him. Coming up beside the outlaw, he reached over and pulled the belt axe from his hand, then gave Harpe a shove that sent him pitching out of the saddle and heavily onto the ground.

The others rode up, halted, dismounted. They gathered silently around Micajah Harpe, who lay with eyes half closed, his breath coming hard. For a while all were silent. Then through the canebrake came the rest of the party, Tompkins and Lindsey leading Micajah Harpe's two wives and children, and a puffing, sweating McBee pulling Sally along by the hand. All joined the circle around the dying man.

Harpe opened his eyes a little wider. "Water!" His voice was a faint rasp, no more.

Leiper knelt and pulled off one of Harpe's shoes. He took it to a pool at the edge of the canebrake, filled it with water, and brought it dripping back for Harpe to drink. The man managed only a few swallows.

"You are dying," McBee said. "We shall give you mercy and hasten your death if you wish. But we will not be such hard men as to not give you time to pray and set your soul right with God while there is yet time."

"I care nothing for that," Micajah Harpe said faintly.

"Tell me," Leiper said. "What made you do the things you have?"

Clardy did not expect Harpe to have the strength to answer, but the outlaw drew in a shaky breath and said, "Wiley and me, we were put in this world to punish mankind. We had grown disgusted with men, with the way folk treated us. We decided to kill as many as we could while we yet lived."

"You are a devil, sir," McBee said. "How many have suffered because of you?"

Micajah began to tell, very briefly, of various murders he and his brother had done. The list seemed endless; Clardy quit keeping count at about twenty. Some of the murders were already known, others were unheard of by any there. Clardy listened with rising fear that he would hear something that would rouse suspicion that Thias was among those killed.

"Have you no remorse, man?" McBee said.

"Only for one death," Micajah Harpe replied. "I dashed out the brains of Sally's child against a tree. It cried and vexed me. I wish I hadn't done it."

"Tell me, sir: Did you spend last night in the home of Moses Steigal?"

"Yes."

"And did you murder the others there—Colonel Love, Mrs. Steigal, and the little one?"

"Aye, I did at that."

"Curse you, man, *why*? Why did you kill innocent folk who had given you shelter?"

"Because it is my way to kill. It is the reason I was put on this earth." He winced, a little more of himself dying before their eyes. "And that Colonel Love . . . he snored. Snored so I couldn't sleep at all."

Clardy looked into the broad face and wondered how it could be that a man could have ever become what Micajah Harpe was.

"Why did you kill Steigal's baby?"

"Life would have . . . would have been hard for the little one, with no mother. . . ."

"With no mother only because you, sir, murdered her! Have you no shame, no heart at all within you? Does the life of your fellow man not matter to you at all?"

"No sir, not at all. Never has. All them that I've killed, all but Sally's baby, none of them mattered, not a whit."

At that Steigal stepped forward, knelt, and shoved his face close to Micajah's. "None mattered, you say? Murderer ! Devil! Bastard! You killed my wife and babe without a quiver, and now you say they did not matter?" He drew a long butcher knife from his belt and held it before Micajah's face. "You see this, man? It's this blade that will take your head off your shoulders."

Micajah looked weakly at him. "I am just a young man," he said. "But already I feel the death sweat rising. I know my time to die has come. I've known it for days—I've felt the earth tremble beneath my feet time and again, telling me that soon . . ." He stopped talking, too weak to continue.

Clardy, perceiving what Steigal was about to do, said, "If

you aim to kill him, be merciful and shoot him. Don't take the knife to him."

"I'll treat him with the same mercy he treated my own," Steigal snapped back. Clardy backed away. He would say no more, nor would anyone else there.

Steigal wrapped his fingers in Micajah's coarse hair and jerked his head up off the ground. He thrust the knife in behind the neck and cut fiercely. Blood flowed out over the blade and Steigal's hand.

Micajah's eyes opened wide and he fixed them upon Steigal's face . . . and smiled. Clardy gaped, hardly able to believe what he saw.

Micajah said, "Steigal, you're a damned rough butcher, you are, but cut on and be damned!"

Steigal let out a terrible cry. He brought the blade around to the front of Harpe's neck, and Clardy turned away so he wouldn't have to see the rest. The sounds alone were almost too much to stand.

When Clardy looked again, Steigal stood with Micajah Harpe's head in his hand, held by the hair. It was a repulsive yet fascinating sight. The only thought Clardy had while looking at it was that Thias, with his weak stomach, certainly could not have abided seeing this.

He heard laughter. Turning, he gazed blankly at a sight that would haunt him for years thereafter. It was Sally, laughing and clapping her hands in childish glee, dancing about the headless corpse of Micajah Harpe.

They left Micajah Harpe's beheaded corpse where it lay. Not a man there had any interest in giving a decent burial to a man who had lived such an indecent life. As for Wiley, no one had any idea where he had gone. It appeared he had gotten cleanly away.

They took Micajah Harpe's head with them, forcing Susanna to carry it by the hair. She did so, muttering beneath her breath, over and over again, "Damn the head! Damn the head!"

Clardy was still with the group when they carried the head to a crossroads about a half mile from Robertson's Lick and impaled it on the sharpened end of a limb that extended out over the road from a large tree. On the tree itself Clardy carved the intials H.H.—for "Harpe's Head." There, the blackening trophy remained for long thereafter, gazing open-mouthed down at all who passed on that road, thereafter known as Harpe's Head Road.

The Harpe women were placed in custody and charged in connection with the deaths of Steigal's wife and child. No one expected that the charges would hold, in that it appeared the women had been nowhere around the Steigal place at any time.

Clardy waited in the region long enough to see Kirkpatrick recovered from his illness and to watch the trial of the Harpe women. Kirkpatrick, with a farm and home that sorely needed his attention, did not remain for the trials.

All three of the women were acquitted. To Clardy's pleasure, Sally's father came up from Knoxville, claimed his daughter after she was cleared and carried her back home with him. With her went Clardy's prayers. Sally Rice was a young woman who surely would never escape the haunting of a ruined past, but she was young, and Clardy hoped that what life brought her from then on would be as good as it could be.

Clardy left the vicinity financially better off than he had entered it. He possessed a thirty dollar share of a reward given by the governor of Kentucky as payment to the posse that brought down Micajah Harpe, along with twenty dollars more given as a special additional reward to Clardy for his exemplary and extraordinary earlier efforts in tracking and pursuing the Harpes. In addition, both Squire McBee and General Hopkins gave him private gifts of thirty dollars each, enough money to make Clardy feel relatively flush.

With money in hand, Clardy headed for the Ford residence, his refuge in prior months. The brilliant possibility of courting and marrying Dulciana and using his small personal treasury to start them off in housekeeping together had overwhelmed him as soon as he thought of it.

He knew something was different before he reached the cabin. Different . . . and wrong. He stopped, puzzled, concerned. His eye was drawn to a newly cleared area beside the cabin.

In it stood three gravestones, side by side.

Clardy stayed where he was another minute, gathering his courage, not wanting to see the names on the stones. But he had to, and rode over with his heart rising toward his throat. Dismounting, he knelt by the graves.

Amy Ford, John Ford . . . Dulciana. Clardy's eyes filled with tears. He stood and turned away.

A man stood looking at him. It took Clardy a moment to recognize that it was Isaac Ford. He was leaner than ever, his hair longer and grayer, his face lined and old-looking.

"How did it happen, Mr. Ford?"

"Sickness. Fever and ague . . . all of us took it. I'm the only one who lived." Ford wiped a tear with the heel of his hand. "Makes no sense. I was the eldest. I was sick the longest . . . but I lived, and they all died. Buried them myself."

Clardy said, "I'm sorry, Mr. Ford. I'm sorry."

"Me, too. Me, too. If I could give my life and bring them back . . . but that don't happen, does it? A man's got to live with what happens, good and bad." Ford looked at the graves sadly, then back at Clardy. "I hear big talk about you. I hear you been hunting the Harpes."

"Yes. Wiley Harpe got away. Micajah Harpe, he's dead. His head is posted up in a tree south of Henderson."

"I'm glad you come by, Clardy. It's lonely here now."

"I can't believe they're dead. Can't believe it."

"Nor can I, son. God knows I wake up nigh every night expecting to hear their breathing, feeling like they ought to be here with me." He shuddered. "It's an awful thing when the truth comes back to mind. Makes a man wish he was dead."

Clardy was looking at Dulciana's gravestone, but in his mind's eye he was seeing her face. It was impossible to imagine that as the face of a corpse. Impossible. He turned back to Ford. "What are you doing with yourself now?"

"Tending to my horses. Believe I'll sell them, though. Move on away from here. Can't live with the memories, you know."

"Where will you go?"

"It don't much matter. Maybe down to Tennessee. Along the Cumberland somewheres."

"Then that's where we'll go."

"We?" Something sparked in Ford's one good eye. For half a moment a glimmering of his former, lively self came through.

"Yes . . . if you'll have me. And if you're willing to go to Knoxville first. I need to go back and see if my brother has turned up there while I been away. If he has, there'll be inheritance money for me. If he ain't, then I'm shot if I can go lingering around waiting for him forevermore. Me and you, we'll go on to Nashville."

"But the horses . . ."

"We'll herd them to Nashville. I reckon they can graze Tennessee grass as good as Kentucky."

"Well ... reckon they could." Ford nodded resolutely. "Reckon I could, now you mention it." He grinned. "I'm glad you came back, Clardy. Don't know what would have happened to me if I had just been here alone for God knows how long. Don't know at all. You're a godsend, Clardy. A godsend."

"Well, I do recollect somebody telling me once that when folks cross paths time and time again, there's generally a reason for it."

"It's the truth."

"Ain't you got any proverbs to quote me, Mr. Ford?"

Ford looked at the graves again. "No. No proverbs for now. Someday ... but not now. Bring your horse around to the stable, Clardy. I'll see if I can find us something to eat."

1 8 0 3

CHAPTER 31

Nashville, Tennessee, early January

The tall man left through the open front door of the big store and stood on the shade of the porch, watching another man walk down the street, whistling, a parcel of newly bought goods beneath his right arm. That man had just left the store, where he had made his purchases without any evident awareness of the dark observation of the first man, who had skulked among the plowshares, secretly watching.

A third man sat sleeping on a bench on the sunny part of the porch, his hat over his eyes. He was enjoying a rare day of springlike warmth during a generally harsh winter month. Normally Nashvillians bundled about in heavy coats throughout January, but today was shirtsleeve weather, the kind to make a man drowsy in mid-afternoon, the kind to make a sunny porch bench look terribly inviting, particularly so since December had expired with a long stretch of bitter cold.

The tall man nudged the sleeper awake, and the man looked up, lifting his hat, blinking.

"That man walking away yonder—who is he?"

The sleepy man looked, squinted into the sunlight, and

watched as the indicated man freed a big, fine horse from a
hitch pole and swung into the saddle. "Why, that's Mr. Tyler."

"Tyler, eh? So that's the name he gives?"

"Well, aye, it is, that being his name."

"That ain't his name."

"What are you talking about? Everybody knows Clardy
Tyler. He's one of the best planters and horse traders on the
Cumberland. Him and Isaac Ford, they have them a big spread
of land. Have for about three years now."

"You're telling me this Tyler has been hereabouts for that
long?"

"That's right. Never knowed him to go nowhere else. Not
that he comes telling me his business."

"Well, I'm telling you that man *has* been elsewhere. I met
him myself a year ago, north of Natchez. And his name ain't
Tyler, neither."

"The devil!"

The tall man nodded, smiling with just the corners of his
tight, thin lips. "Well-chose words. Well chose indeed. Tell me,
friend, where would I find Mr. *Tyler's* house?" He emphasized
the name sarcastically.

The other man withdrew a little. "Don't know I ought to say.
What have you got in mind? Mr. Tyler, he's a fine citizen. Everybody knows that."

The tall man sighed and dug beneath his lightweight coat.
He brought out a coin and dropped it at the seated man's feet.
"Why don't you leave my business to me, and just tell me
where this 'fine citizen' lives?"

The seated man looked down at the coin and quietly moved
his foot over atop it. "Very well, sir. I'll tell you. I reckon it
ain't no secret, is it?"

"Reckon not."

Clardy was in a fine mood. In terms of weather, the day was
perfect, far too fine for dismal January, which vied with February for the status of being Clardy's least favorite month.
Good riding weather. Good weather for a jaunt into nearby
Nashville and back again. In fact it was more the weather than
actual necessity that had prompted Clardy to make the trip. A
touch of his old, nearly forgotten irresponsible nature coming
through again, he figured, but that was all right. Every now
and then a man needed to forget work and commerce and enjoy

the simple pleasures of life, such as a good ride in the fresh air of a clear day.

He was about to make the turn toward his own small cabin when his eye caught something that made him come to a halt. There was Isaac Ford, seated beneath that same old big oak he always took to when he was feeling low. His "thinking tree," he called it. Clardy knew that in fact it was more a place for grieving than for thinking. Grieving over the family that had been taken from him. A place for sinking into the familiar sorrow that loomed up from Ford's past.

Clardy sighed and slumped lower in the saddle. His good mood died in seconds. He had hoped that Isaac Ford's sorrowful periods would begin coming less frequently. So far they hadn't. Over the past year he had taken to his "thinking tree" more and more often. Odd, it seemed, how the death of Ford's family seemed to haunt him more now, nearly four years after, than at the beginning, when he and Clardy had left Kentucky and its bad memories and started their new life here.

They had gone to Knoxville first, and lingered for a while, waiting for Thias to show up. He didn't. At length Clardy had given up and concluded that his brother was gone, perhaps forever. Something must have happened to Thias during that time he was out searching, trying to find him and give him the inheritance money he was due. The lawyer Branford in Knoxville had said that Thias had taken the money with him, in cash. That was a dangerous thing. Probably Thias had been robbed by some Kentucky road bandit and killed. Maybe the Harpes themselves had done it, and hidden the body well enough that it was never found.

With that depressing thought in mind, Clardy turned his horse toward the place Isaac Ford sat. Beyond stood the big house Ford had built for himself at the time he was courting a woman he had met in Knoxville, a woman who had managed to turn him again into the bright, proverb-quoting fellow he had been when Clardy first met him. Ford had planned to marry her; it was that which prompted the building of the big house. Clardy had remained in the small, original cabin they had built when he and Ford first bought this Cumberland River land early in 1800. Clardy's own part of the investment had been quite small, in that he had very little money at the time, but Ford sold his horses and Kentucky land for a decent sum, and that set him and his younger partner up quite nicely in this new place. With a successful horse farm and planter operation working, and marriage looming, Ford had been a happy man. Then the woman had balked, unexpectedly. The engagement had been broken.

And Isaac Ford had promptly begun taking to his thinking tree. It was a sad thing to Clardy, seeing the change that had come over his partner. He had hoped that Ford would have rebounded by now. He hadn't.

On top of that, Clardy himself was becoming prone to brood, and to think about Thias. And dream about him. Bad dreams, nightmarish images of terrible things happening to his lost brother. Dreams that made him awaken in a sweat, startled by his own outcries.

He rode in under the spreading branches of the big oak and dismounted, leaving his horse to graze at whatever winter grass it could find. "Howdy, Mr. Ford." Despite their partnership and long acquaintance, Isaac Ford still remained "Mr. Ford" to Clardy, and probably always would. It seemed the natural thing to call him, though its formal overtones belied the depth of their friendship.

"Clardy. Pretty day, ain't it?"

"Yes. I took me a ride. Went into Nashville and picked up some flour and lard. You're welcome to share it, if you need any."

"Got plenty." Though the pair farmed together, they had begun maintaining separate kitchens in their respective dwellings, and generally shared only a midday meal.

Clardy sat down on the ground beside Ford. Though the atmosphere was pleasantly warm, the earth retained the cold of winter. "Thinking again?"

"Aye."

"About your family, I reckon?"

A pause. "Aye."

Clardy pulled his knees up to his chest, wrapped his arms around them and rested his chin atop them. He said nothing.

"You don't think I ought to be mulling them so much, do you? You think it's bad for me, grieving this long after they left me." Ford seldom made direct reference to death when talking about his family. They had "left" him, in his usual terminology.

"I didn't say nothing, did I?"

"Not this time. But you've said it before."

"Mr. Ford, if you want me to go and leave you alone, I will. I just saw you here and thought it would be good to—"

"Aw, hush, Clardy. I don't mind you being here. And the fact is, I know it *ain't* good for me to sit and grieve. I just can't help it, that's all. Seems these days I think more about them than I have for months and months past."

"I understand that." Clardy paused, then revealed something he hadn't yet mentioned to Ford. "The truth is, I've been thinking on Thias more than before, too. Can't seem to help it. I dream about him quite a lot. Bad dreams. Ugly ones."

Ford looked at him with interest. "Is that right? You never said."

"I just wonder what happened to him, that's all. Reckon he must be dead."

Ford nodded. "I believe he probably is, Clardy, though I hate to say that to you. From all you've told me of him, he don't seem the kind to stay away from his only living kin on purpose."

Clardy bristled a little. This topic had been touched upon many times before, and always brought him offense. "You mean, and keep all that inheritance money for himself? Have you been thinking Thias might do something like that? Because if you do, then—"

Ford bristled in turn, defensively, and cut him off. "Now Clardy, you keep in mind I don't know your brother. If I did, and if he's as fine a fellow as you always say, I'd probably never have one suspicion. You say he's a good young man, then I believe you. But that does force a man to conclusionize that something ill must have befell him, or otherwise you would have heard from him by now."

Indeed that was true. After coming to Nashville, Clardy had promptly sent a letter to Branford in Knoxville, informing him of where he could be found should Thias show up, looking for him. Branford had sent his own letter in response, assuring Clardy that he would certainly send Thias directly to him should he appear. That had been months upon months ago, and no Thias.

"He is dead, then," Clardy said, drawing again the conclusion that his musing always led him to. "He has to be dead."

Ford turned away. He picked up a pebble and began fingering it. "I despise death. It takes the good things from a man, the people he loves, and leaves him with nothing."

Clardy looked around at the broad, rolling river land, beautiful even when the trees were leafless and the fields were brown. "Well, you've got all this. A good farm, a good livelihood. A good name in your community."

To his surprise, Ford suddenly choked up. His eyes, both seeing and blind, grew red and wet. "It's nothing. Naught at all. None of it means a thing without my wife, my children."

"You life ain't over, Mr. Ford. You'll marry again. You'll have a new family."

"I'm getting old, Clardy. Ain't no woman that will marry me. We know that already, don't we? I'm doomed to be alone the rest of my days. Alone and lonely, setting on my backside under this tree, looking around at land lots of folks would give their left arm to own, and knowing it all really ain't worth having." He tossed the pebble away. "Sometimes I wish that I'd caught that same fever and died with my family. I believe that's what was meant to be, and somehow I messed up the plan of providence and managed to live when I should have been dead."

"Don't talk that way, Mr. Ford." Clardy hated it when Ford talked about death as if it were something desirable. It made him worry that one morning he might go to meet Ford at his home, as usual, and find that he had put a pistol ball through his head, or a rope around his neck.

"I can't help but talk that way, Clardy. Just can't help it."

Clardy remained only awhile longer. He tried to think of something comforting to say, but couldn't. He could feel Ford slipping ever deeper into his brood. Helpless and growing more depressed himself, Clardy rose. "I'm going to my cabin." Ford did not respond, didn't even grunt. Clardy went to his horse, which had strayed a good distance off by now, mounted, and rode home with Ford still beneath his tree, his eyes staring into the distance and his mind lost in a past he could not return to.

Clardy felt a strong resentment toward Ford the rest of the day. He felt bad for it, but couldn't help it. Ford's brooding was turning what had been a good situation into something sorrowful for both of them. Sure, the man had lost his loved ones, but hadn't many others?

Ford would have to change his ways, Clardy decided, or he might find himself without a partner before long.

* * *

He dreamed of Thias, drowning in a pool while he stood fixed on the bank, unable to reach him, his feet grown into the ground like roots. He tried to call Thias's name, but had no voice, tried to uproot himself, but couldn't. He was trapped where he was, and Thias was sinking, farther and farther, receding from him. . . .

Clardy awakened with a jolt and sat up. He knew from the light, and from the internal clock that seldom failed him, that it was mere minutes before dawn. Time to awaken anyway, and that was fine. He didn't want to sleep again if he was going to have such terrible dreams. This one, though not nearly so gruesome as some of his other recent nightmares about Thias, was the most mentally disturbing. The rooting of his feet—that's what was so distressing. To be stuck in one place, trapped, immobile, while someone he cared about was in trouble or danger . . . that would be horrible. Hellish. Clardy shuddered, threw back the covers and swung his feet out of bed, glad to have use of them.

The morning was much cooler than that of the previous day, and he had slept unclothed, so quickly he threw on some trousers and a shirt. Finger-combing his hair, he yawned and stretched and headed out to the outhouse in the back of the cabin. He hadn't shaved the day before, and two days' growth of whiskers made his face itch. It was rare for Clardy not to shave every day; over the last couple of years he had become almost obsessive about it, though he had no idea why. Maybe it was part of the new sense of respectability that he had about himself. As he scratched at his chin in the outhouse he grinned, thinking how funny it really was that Clardy Tyler, the "bad" Tyler brother with the criminal ambitions, had turned out to be a respected, honest planter and horse trader, and the "good" brother, Thias, had . . .

He could not complete that thought. He couldn't know what Thias had become, or what had become of him. All the factors pointed toward the conclusion Isaac Ford had stated the day before. Hang it all, why was it necessary for him to have to cipher out that grim equation every day of his life? Clardy asked himself. Why could he not simply accept the fact that Thias was gone and forget about it?

Because I don't know it for a fact. Because maybe he's alive somewhere, and in trouble, and here I am stuck like a man with feet rooted in the ground, not able to reach him or help him.

He left the outhouse and headed back to the cabin, deep in solemn thought. Thus he was excessively startled to hear the sound of a male voice coming from somewhere behind him.

"Hiram! James Hiram!"

Clardy wheeled about on his bare heels. "Who's there?"

He detected movement deep among the sassafras trees and dogwoods at the edge of the woods. "James Hiram, now we'll set things square!" A rifle blasted; a ball sang past his head and smacked into the cabin wall behind him.

And Clardy stood transfixed, just like he had in that dream, so stunned he could not move. Several moments passed before he was able to break free.

He turned and scrambled back to the cabin and literally threw himself through the open door. Rising, he slammed it shut and threw down the bar, then raced to the rear window and closed the shutters. Shutters! What good would those do him? Why hadn't he fortified this cabin against attack? Why hadn't he ever considered the possibility that he might have to defend himself here?

Because it hadn't seemed a possibility. Because the Indians had been defeated in these regions years ago.

But that was no Indian out there. That voice had belonged to a white man. James Hiram? Why had he called him *that*? Mistaken identity, that had to be it. He was being mistaken for someone else.

Clardy ran to the front of the cabin and took his rifle off its pegs. Thank God he always kept it loaded! He went back to the door and with the butt of the rifle hammered down the wooden patch he had put over a knothole in the rough wood. Peering out, he saw more motion in the woods.

"You there!" he yelled as loudly as he could. "Who are you? Why you shooting at me?"

"I'm here to even the score, Hiram!" the man called back. "I'll see you pay in blood for all you took from me on the old Chickasaw trail!"

The Chickasaw trail . . . one old name for the narrow war and trade route that ran from the Cumberland down through the Indian country to the southwest. Also called the Natchez Road, the Choctaw Road, the Boatman's Trail, or any of several other names, it was now used most often as a return route for boatmen who took wares down the river to Natchez and New Orleans, and came back by land to Nashville and from thence to their various homes. "Kaintucks," such were coming to be called, regardless of whether they came from Kentucky or elsewhere. But Clardy had never been on any part of the Chickasaw trail other than its northernmost portion, and certainly he had taken nothing from anyone there or anywhere else.

"You've mistook me for somebody else!" Clardy yelled. "My name's Tyler!"

"What name you go by means naught to me! I'll not forget the face of the man who took a year's worth of money from me!" Then the rifle fired again, a heavy charge this time, the ball ripping right through the door and barely missing Clardy. He pitched down to the floor, still holding his rifle, and yelled in pure fright.

The man outside yelled something else. This time Clardy couldn't make out the words. He rose and went to the window, preparing to thrust the rifle through and shoot back—but before he could there was another call, this one from some distance away, and the voice familiar. It was Isaac Ford! Clardy grinned. Ford must have heard the shots and come from his own place.

Clardy pushed open the shutters in time to see Ford ride in, half dressed and mounted on a bare-backed horse, his rifle gripped in his right hand. He slid down off the horse with easy grace and darted into the woods. The sound of scrambling told Clardy that his attacker had suddenly gone on the run.

He went to the door, threw off the bar, and swung it open. He ran out and joined the chase. By now Ford was through the dogwoods and into the woods. Clardy ran as hard as he could, following. He could see his attacker well ahead of Ford, a tall, lean figure racing hard through the stubbly undergrowth. By heaven, the tables were turned now! Clardy pushed himself harder, ignoring the pain of running on tender bare feet, and began to close in on Ford, who meanwhile was closing in on the first man.

The chase continued another five minutes before Ford finally reached the man and brought him down. He was firmly atop the panting, panicked fellow when Clardy reached them. Clardy thrust the muzzle of his rifle right into the struggling man's face.

"Lie still!" he commanded. "You move, and I'll shoot you!"

"I—I won't move! I'll lie still! I will!"

Ford, sweating and heaving for breath, rolled off the man,

lay panting on his back a few moments, sending up white gusts with each gasp, and then stood. He picked up his rifle, which he evidently had dropped when he dived for his quarry, then snatched up the first man's rifle as well.

"Look at me," Clardy said. "Look in my face. You see now I ain't the man you think I am, whoever the bloody devil James Hiram might be!"

The man, face blanched and mouth wet with saliva he had exuded during his hard run, gaped at Clardy and went more pale than before. "Oh, God," he said. "You got no scar! No scar on your jaw!"

"That's right. No scar. And this Hiram fellow had one, right?"

"Aye . . . oh, God, I'm sorry, mister. I'm sorry. I knowed you was him, I just knowed it! You look nigh the image of him, but for the scar!"

"I ain't him. I'm Clardy Tyler, and you came near to killing an innocent man! What's your name?"

"Uh . . . Smith. Jim Smith. I live up in Kentucky. I was robbed north of Natchez by a man name of James Hiram. I swear, you look just like him, Mr. Tyler! If you'd have seen him, you'd know how I made such a mistake!"

"Next time you want to revengerate yourself against somebody, you'd best make sure you have the right man," Ford said. He had only just then regained enough breath to speak.

"Well, Mr. Jim Smith, or whatever your name really is, I'm inclined to haul you off to Nashville and turn you over to the jailer," Clardy said.

"Oh, no sir, no—please don't! I'll go away, I swear it! I'll plague you no more. I admit it was a mistake, a bad one, and I'm grateful to you for being men of mercy. You are men of mercy, ain't you? You won't do me harm, will you?"

"You whine like a whupped schoolyard boy," Ford said.

Clardy stood considering, then waved his rifle. "Up with you. Take your rifle and get out of here. Don't let me lay eyes on you again."

"Clardy, you reckon you ought to let him go?" Ford asked.

"Why not? All I want of a troublemaker is to be shut of him. Let him go."

The man came up, fell on his knees and thanked Clardy profusely. Ford grunted with disdain and Clardy shook his head.

Then the man rose, took his rifle, and ran off into the woods, stumbling and scared, making strange, whimpering noises.

"There goes a man who's a waste of the skin God gave him to wear," Ford said. "Look at him run, and nobody even after him. 'The wicked flee when no man pursueth.' "

Clardy, though still nervous and upset by all that had happened, felt a flicker of relief just then. Ford had just quoted a proverb—a good sign. When he was depressed, the continual proverb spouting was the first of his usual traits to vanish. When they returned, it evidenced a shifting back to his old, healthy-minded self.

"Sure glad you came when you did," Clardy said.

"I heard that first shot and knew something was wrong," he said. "I ain't never scrambled so fast. It like to have killed me, though. I'm wore out. Too old to flax myself this hard."

"He almost killed me," Clardy said. "If that first shot had hit me, he'd have found out his mistake too late."

"The Lord has watched over you," Ford said. "He's protected you, and that means there's still important things for you to do."

Clardy grinned. "You always twist everything around to find some kind of purpose in it, don't you?"

"This old world's way too a mysteriosity for there *not* to be a purpose in things, Clardy. The real mysteriosity would be if there warn't."

Clardy was glad to hear Ford talking that way. He seemed a brighter and happier man than he had the day before.

"Lord have mercy, I'm shaking like a leaf," Clardy said. "Let's get back indoors. It's going to take me some time to get the scare out of me, I believe."

They walked back to Clardy's cabin side by side.

CHAPTER 32

S haking off the case of nerves roused by the morning encounter took Clardy most of the remainder of the day.
Like the realization of bereavement, the full shock of almost having been murdered didn't come until past the actual
event. He developed a case of trembling so bad that he was no
good for work and soon gave up any notion of pursuing labor
this day. He sat in his cabin, trying to calm himself, trying to
quit shaking, and that only seemed to make the shaking worse.

Ford suggested he might do better away from his own cabin,
where the shredded rifle ball hole through the rear door served
as a constant reminder of the morning's terror. So they went to
Ford's house, and Clardy did begin to calm down some, and
managed to eat. He was embarrassed by his nervousness and
hoped that Ford wasn't thinking badly of him for it. If he was,
Ford didn't let it show, and at length Clardy noticed that Ford
seemed quite visibly nervous himself, and was spewing out one
proverb after another. It had been a frightening event for both
of them. Clardy hadn't felt so scared since the time he had
stared into the ugly face of Micajah Harpe back on Beaver
Creek and listened to Harpe's command that he murder Cale
Johnson.

By afternoon Clardy felt much better and was beginning to think about what had happened in broader terms. He felt very strong affection toward Ford for what he had done. He detected that, despite his nervousness, Ford had taken on more of a fatherly bearing and attitude than he had shown since those first days after Clardy came to the Ford cabin in Kentucky. Clardy wondered if the act of saving his life had given Ford a renewed sense of his own usefulness and purpose. He saw reason to believe so.

Clardy and Ford were at their supper when the realization came. It swept over Clardy in an overwhelming rush, causing him to drop his fork. Ford, alarmed, stood and almost knocked over the table. "What's wrong?"

"Mr. Ford, it just came to me. Why didn't I see it before? And why did I let that man go before I found out more! God help me, I've been blind!"

"What are you babbling about?"

"Don't you see it? A robber, named James Hiram, who looks almost like me—James Hiram, the Christian names of my own grandfather! James Hiram Tyler, though he always went by Hiram alone. . . ."

Ford looked bewildered. "What does your grandfather have to do with this?"

"Nothing, directly. But there's only one other person I can think of who looks enough like me that folks have confused us before, that's my brother Thias. And the James Hiram name only makes that seem all the more possible."

"Thias! So you think . . . by jiminy, Clardy, could it be?"

"It could be indeed."

"But that man said he was robbed, and you always declared that your brother was an upstanding and moral fellow. He wouldn't be the kind to rob folks on the trails."

"I know. It don't match up to what I know of Thias. But maybe there was misunderstanding. Or maybe he was forced to do it. I was nigh forced into committing a murder once myself, so I know such things can happen. And if for some reason or another Thias did commit a crime, it makes sense he'd use another name to throw off any who might go after him, or to cover up his own shame. And he might just use the first names of his grandpap. They'd be quick to come to mind, and do as well as any other."

Ford stood there with a look of awe, letting it sink in. "It could be, Clardy. It really could be."

"I've dreamed lately of Thias being in trouble. I've never been one to put stock in signs and such truck, but who can say?"

"I stand and marvel. I do indeed."

"I wish I hadn't let that man go. I'd like to know more about this fellow who robbed him, and just where and when it was he saw him."

Clardy quit talking and began pacing the room. He was breathless, shaking again, but this time with excitement instead of fear. For his part, Ford merely stood there, apparently awed by the amazing but utterly plausible possibility revealing itself before them.

Clardy stopped pacing abruptly. "Mr. Ford, I've got to go to the Natchez country. I've got to see if Thias is there."

"Yes, you do. I was ponderating that very thought myself."

"And I've got to know if he's in trouble. And he's bound to be. Otherwise he would have found me, and gotten that inheritance rightly divided. He's the kind who'd never rest until everything was set right."

Ford, about to delve into a subject that had generated hard feelings before, looked solemn and said, "He *was* the kind, you should say. You ain't seen him for years now. You don't know what he might be like now."

"Thias would never change."

"I don't know about that, Clardy. *You* changed."

Clardy couldn't deny that. The point left him unresponsive for a moment or two, and then, as always in such conversations, he grew irritated. "Don't you go trying to persuade me that Thias could turn dishonest. He'd never do anything he knew was wrong."

"You yourself have been voicing the notion that he was the one who robbed that fellow near Natchez. Robbery ain't what I'd call honest."

"No . . . but anyone might be tempted into it in a time of need or trouble."

"So they might. But it wouldn't be honest. Wouldn't be no excuses for it."

"Why do you always have such a preachy way about you?"

"I ain't preachy. Just forthright."

"You are that, yes sir." Clardy was stirred by a spontaneous burst of animating excitement. "Think of it! My brother might be alive, Mr. Ford! I've longed to have hope of that for the longest time!"

"Aye, yes. It's a good hope." Ford coughed, cleared his throat, and adopted a serious tone. "Clardy, I must say more of the thing you ain't liking to hear. I'll try not to anger you, but let me tell you from the base of having lived a few years more than you have that sometimes folks can turn different on you. You need to be aware of that in case you do find Thias. You made a change toward the good. If your brother has met him a hard row to hoe or had some great trouble in his life, he might have changed toward the bad. That would account for why he would rob a man." He paused before delving into a far more personal area. "And maybe even why he never divided that inheritance with you."

Clardy had to restrain himself from anger. He knew that Ford was merely trying to give him the wisest counsel he could. "I understand why you think that way, Mr. Ford. But like I've said before, you don't know Thias like I do. I really don't believe he'd change. And maybe he did try to find me to share the inheritance, and couldn't. Maybe he thinks I'm dead."

"Maybe. Only one way to find out, and that's to go see if we can find this here 'James Hiram' and see if he might be Thias."

"*We* can find? So you'd go, too?"

"You're deuced right I will. I need a change of scene. Tired of sitting and moping under my thinking tree. I mulled it all last night. Decided that maybe what I ought to do, if I want to avoid blowing out my own brains, is to make me a journey. Maybe go down and sell some horses down the river. It 'pears providentialized that this news come along when it did."

Clardy might have laughed. A voyage to Natchez . . . there, Ford could sell their horses, and he could scout about for Thias, if Thias was there to be found.

He recalled right then what his attacker had said this morning. *No scar on your jaw* . . . So if Thias was indeed the true robber, he apparently now had a scar. That indicated injury, accidental or otherwise. Or perhaps that the robber really wasn't Thias at all, despite his apparent similarity to Clardy, and that the James Hiram name was merely coincidental.

Clardy did not share these thoughts with Ford, not wanting to say anything that might change his inclinations to make the journey. Clardy was entirely willing to go alone, but far better it would be to have good company.

"We'd best go have a word or two with Sweeney McCracken tomorrow," Ford said.

"Who?"

"You don't know Sweeney? Lives by the river, makes and sells flatboats. Fine ones. Pilots voyages down the rivers, too. He's been down the big water more times than most folks have gone to privy. I'm inclined to hire him to pilot us."

"You really are serious about all this, ain't you?"

"Of course I am. And, hey, there's more that Sweeney might be able to do for us. He knows the Natchez country up and down, and all the talk among the Kaintucks. If there's a James Hiram robbing along the road from Natchez, he'll probably know of him."

McCracken was a short and stocky man, broad in the rump and thick in the thighs. He wore a loose, very greasy hunting shirt that was made for a taller man, thick-soled boots, and a mass of tangled, salt and pepper hair that merged into the thickest tangle of whiskers Clardy had ever seen on a human face. Gray whiskers, as gray as the eyes.

Ford dealt with business first, and with much success. McCracken was just completing what he called the "best bejiggered broad-horn ark ever pieced together by the fangers of a man." Clardy took note of the fact that the art of flatboat building had taken a toll on McCracken's "fangers," in that he had only eight and a half of them, a little finger on his left hand being entirely gone, and the ring finger on his right missing to the first knuckle.

Ford made arrangements to buy the flatboat, then hired McCracken as pilot on complicated terms involving giving McCracken a percentage of the profits from the sale of the horses and the flatboat itself at Natchez. Clardy paid little attention and hardly cared if Ford simply gave everything away, including his own cut of the proceeds. All he could think or care about was the possibility of actually finding Thias.

When the business was finished, Clardy asked McCracken if he had ever heard of a criminal names James Hiram operating along the road out of Natchez.

"Indeed I have, though never have I laid eyes on him," McCracken replied. "He's young, from all I hear, and right about your age. Got him a scar across his jaw, and tries to hide it with a beard, but it shows up above his whisker line. He's robbed a whole passel of Kaintucks over the last year or more."

Clardy felt some rising anguish. So Thias—if Thias and this James Hiram were identical—hadn't just robbed once, under duress or out of desperation, as he had hoped was the case. He had done it often. Ford's warnings about the way individual behaviors could change suddenly seemed more potentially on the mark than he had wanted to believe.

It was sobering to realize that even if he found Thias, he might not be finding the Thias he had known before.

"Has he ever killed any of his victims?" Ford asked, and Clardy gave him a hard look because of the forthrightness of the query. Yet that very question was heavy in his own mind at the moment, though he had been unwilling to ask it.

"Don't know. It ain't Hiram that I've heard most about. The worst scoundrel in the Natchee country is a man name of Mason. Mason of the Woods, they call him sometimes. First name is Samuel. He commenced his robbing up at Cave-in-Rock on the Ohio River. You heard of that place? Pirate's haven. Terrible little bit of hell, right on God's green earth.

"Anyways, Sam Mason left his cave some years back and took up his crimes in the Natchee lands. Oh, he's a devil, he is, maybe as bad a man as them Harpes you're so famed for having chased, Clardy Tyler. Didn't know I knowed about that, did you? You're famous, boy, whether you know it or not."

Clardy felt self-conscious. He hadn't pursued the Harpes for fame, and never had been happy with having his name closely associated with theirs. He steered the subject back on course. "Does this Hiram work with Mason?"

"Not that I've heard. Mason has plenty with him, though, so I couldn't say for certain. Let's see . . . there's a fellow name of Setton, mean as a snake, and another name of May. Plenty more, too. Trouble is that not too many who Mason gets his hands on live to tell many stories about what they've seen."

"A murderer, is he?"

"Aye. Preys on Kaintucks like a wolf on sheep. Loves them full pockets and pouches that go up along the road toward Nashville."

Clardy was beginning to feel depressed. The prospect of finding Thias seemed less real now. He couldn't picture his upright brother being part of the dark criminal world that McCracken was describing.

"Why you asking so much about this Hiram, anyways? You afraid of him?"

"I heard he looked a lot like me," Clardy replied. "Made me curious, you see." He wasn't in a spirit to tell more than that at the moment.

"Looks like you? Well then, you'd best beware about Natchee town! Some gent who's been robbed by Hiram might make him a mistake about who you are."

"I'm right aware of that already," Clardy said.

McCracken squinted one eye. "There something going on here I don't know about? Something maybe I *should* know about?"

"Not a thing that will involve you, Sweeney," Ford replied. "We'll tell you all about it later on, once we commence."

They sold some of their horses in Nashville, rented out their grazing lands and fields for the remainder of the year, and drove the best of their herd to the waterfront to be loaded on McCracken's big flatboat. Whenever he had time to mull on it, Clardy was astonished that mere days after having first learned that Thias could be alive, he was actually on his way to Natchez. The timing of it all couldn't have worked out better had he planned it. He hardly dared hope that things would continue to go so well.

Clardy did tell McCracken his full story, and about his reason for being so inquisitive about the outlaw James Hiram. McCracken, a man who appreciated a good bit of drama, loved to tell stories even more than he loved to voyage on the rivers, declared Clardy's quest would make a "prime good rip of a tale," and that he was glad to be firsthand witness to seeing it played out. "By gawl, we'll find that bother of yourn, if we can," he said. "Won't that make for a yarn to spin, eh? I'll be mighty eager to see the ending of it. By gawl, I hope it's a good one!"

One good thing already was evident to Clardy. Isaac Ford was in better spirits than he had been since his family died. The labor and excitement of a big river voyage, the drastic change of lifestyle and locales that were inherent in it—all these were boons to his mental health. His eyes became bright again, his posture sturdy and erect, and his lips dripped proverbs until Clardy could hardly stand to hear them.

McCracken owned two slaves, Tate and Dewey, who worked expertly as his crewmen, aided by Clardy and Ford. The bulk of the work, however, fell on the first three in that they were true rivermen and knew the secrets of flatboat navigation. It seemed to Clardy that Dewey in particular could read the river almost mystically. He seemed to know in advance where the currents were dangerous, where sawyers and planters were likely to be, and even what the next day's weather would be by the look of the sky and water. Clardy soon learned that at best he was hardly more than a glorified passenger, able to contribute little more than muscle to this enterprise. As days passed, he became familiar with the river in a superficial way, but in a deeper sense it remained a stranger whose back was turned to him while it whispered its deepest secrets into the ears of McCracken, Tate, and Dewey.

It hardly mattered; Clardy had no ambition to become a riverman. Of more interest to him than what he could learn of river navigation was what he could learn of the Natchez country from the abundant talk of McCracken. Seldom did McCracken's verbosity dispense outright history. Mostly he told stories, anecdotes, experiences of his own and experiences he had heard of from others. Clardy began to develop a mental picture of the town he was soon to see, a town built from a mix of French, Spanish, Indian, and American culture. It was also a town divided into two segments. The upper portion sat high atop a bluff, overlooking the river. There, stood fine houses, churches, respectable edifices of every kind. Below, on the flats beside the river itself, was Natchez-under-the-Hill, a most unrespectable place, full of saloons and gaming houses and places where women came cheap and smelled of cheap perfumes and sweat. There, many a Kaintuck lost his year's income within a few days, spending it on drink, gambling it off, putting it in the hands of women in return for crude favors.

There was a time when such a place would have held strong appeal for Clardy. But he was different now. His sole interest was in finding Thias, if he was there to be found.

On a peaceful evening when the flatboat was moored along the left bank of the Mississippi River beneath an unusually bright moon, McCracken told a story of Natchez that happened to stick more firmly in Clardy's mind than any of his other tales, partly because it was so unusual but mostly because it gave him a hard-to-explain sense of hope about his own quest for a missing brother.

McCracken told the story with a smoking clay pipe stuck between his yellow teeth. "There's a certain young woman in Natchee town—I've seen her with my own eyes—and she's known through the whole town because of the torments she went through to get there. She's a Kentucky girl, seventeen year old or so when she first reached the town, that being back in 'ninety-nine. I heard her story from a Natchee town lawyer who is in a prime place to know this particular gal's story well, as you'll soon enough know.

"Her name was Celinda Ames. She was a frail sort of critter who back in the fall of 'ninety-eight had set out down the Ohio on a flatboat with her pappy after her mammy died a hard death. Mad dog or fox or such had bit the poor woman, you see. Her pappy decided it was best if he and his girl head on to Natchee town, where he thunk at the time that his sister was living, and they took passage on a boat full of goods. When her pappy took sick the same way his wife did, the boatmen shoved them both off on the Kentucky shore, fearful of catching the plague theirselves. Sure enough, the pappy died, dancing hisself to death trying to sweat out the poison of his illness, and soon after, the girl was come upon by a fellow who claimed to be a preacher name of Deerfield, on his way to Natchee town to start up a church. She thought at first that she was surely saved, being found by a preacher, but before long she learned different. This fellow was no preacher, but a no-account scoundrel name of Junebug Horton, fairly well-knowed up and down the Ohio and Mississippi among your lower breed of folk. I've seen him myself two, three times, up on the Ohio. The real preacher Deerfield, you see, had took sick unto dying in an inn back up the river where Junebug happened to be, and he'd just up and took that preacher's place, figuring on getting his hands into the church till in Natchee town."

McCracken went on with the story, telling it with the kind of detail that revealed both a sharp, retentive mind, a nearly first-hand source of information, and the natural storytelling skill he loved to exercise. Clardy was both appalled and entranced to learn of all the girl named Celinda had endured. A time of captivity at Cave-in-Rock, further captivity among the outlaw crew of a pirated flatboat, and finally a narrow escape from the man who had enslaved her, who, during her very flight in a riverborne skiff, was embroiled on the dark shore in a battle with a betrayed boatman he had used to bring her back into his clutches.

"It was an amazing thing, though, how that poor gal's fortunes changed after she broke free of Junebug Horton. I reckon the hand of the Lord was on her, for there was surely a miracle in it all. She asked for a sign from above, you see, and right after that found passage on a big horse-powered boat heading down the river. And who would be on that very boat but a man named Deerfield, younger brother to the very preacher whose place Junebug Horton had took."

"So she had her 'sign from above,' eh?" interjected Ford.

"Aye, so she saw it, and though I ain't the most devoted and wise where it comes to religion, I'm hard-pressed to see it different myself. In any case, this new Deerfield fellow was a lawyer, and bound for Natchee town hisself, aiming to set up a law practice there and be near his brother, who was his only remaining kin. Or he thought he was remaining until Celinda told him her tale. That was the first he had heard of his brother having died. It shook him bad, but at the same time he also seen it as providence that this here girl had turned up when she did. And if you've got a mind toward doubting my story here, I'll have you know I heard every word of it from Japheth Deerfield hisself. I've come to know the man, and think highly of him."

"Did this Junebug fellow live through his fight with the boatman?" Clardy asked.

"Well, Celinda heard them fighting, then Junebug's voice calling her name over the water whilst she rowed away, but after that no one can say what become of him. He never showed hisself in Natchee town, never went through with his false preacher scheme. Maybe he was hurt in the fight and died there by the river after hollering for her. Maybe he just went on his way somewheres else. No one knows."

"That's a deuce of a tale, McCracken," Clardy said. "What's become of Celinda now?"

"Well, she's done right well for herself, it seems. That aunt she was looking for in Natchee, she was dead and gone even before Celinda and her pappy left their homeplace. They didn't know it, of course. But the lawyer Deerfield, he seen to her care. I reckon he must have took quite a shine to her. They was married not five, six months after they reached Natchee. And by the by, the last time I seen Celinda Deerfield, she was moving right on toward giving birth to their first little one." McCracken puffed his pipe and cast a gleaming eye at Clardy. "So you can see, Clardy, that sometimes matters work out just prime good for folks who come to Natchee. It all depends on whether the hand of providence is upon them, the way I see it. Maybe it will be that way for you."

"I hope so," Clardy said.

"You'll just have to see how things work theirselves out once't we get there," McCracken said, knocking the ashes from his pipe. "One never can figure such ahead of time. Sometimes the right happens, sometimes it don't, and all you can do is take it as it's dealt."

Pointe Coupee, one hundred miles below Natchez

The guard, seated on the deck of the sailing vessel, was nearly asleep. Though the men he had been placed in charge of guarding were said to be violent folk, they had shown no inclination toward attempting escape at any point since they were hustled on board at New Orleans, and he'd grown complacent. At the moment he was also quite content, happy that he had escaped the much harder duty of cutting a tree on the bank and preparing it to replace the mast of the ship, which had broken two days earlier. The rest of the crew had been put on repair duty this morning, and he was posted as the day's sentinel by Captain Robert McCoy, the militia commander to whom had been given the duty of transporting these prisoners from New Orleans to Natchez for trial. McCoy himself was neither laboring on the shore nor helping stand guard, but lodged in his cabin on the ship. Probably taking a rest himself, the guard figured. And if the captain wasn't worried about the prisoners, well, he wouldn't worry either. They were all in chains, anyway. They couldn't escape if they wanted to, and they didn't seem to want to.

The look and manner of the prisoners themselves contributed to his lack of concern. The main prisoner, a big, fine-looking Virginian and alleged former Cave-in-Rock pirate named Samuel Mason, struck him more as some well-off, distinguished planter than the murderous robber baron folks claimed he was. He had come to actually like Mason during the journey up from New Orleans. Giving an equally calming impression were Mason's four sons, who were also prisoners. One of those sons, John, had a wife and three children with him, and seemed quite the peaceable family man. And the other sons were young, seeming more like boys than men. No one to be all that concerned about.

Only one of the prisoners seemed in any way worrisome, that being the small-framed man named John Setton. Setton, purported to be a confederate in crime with Samuel Mason, was kept away from the other prisoners by orders of Captain McCoy. Though sometimes Setton's cold glares could be unsettling, even he seemed a calm, quiet man. The story was, he had given evidence against Mason at the hearing following his recent arrest up in New Madrid, and was going to turn state's evidence against the others in the actual trial in Natchez. Thus it was only natural that he not be held where the others could get their hands on him—just in case they weren't as peaceable as they seemed.

His thoughts were just beginning to take on the random, nonrational quality of dreams when he felt a sudden jolt. Jerking awake, he tightened his hands to grip his rifle, and found no rifle in them. Alarmed, he lifted his head, stood, and found himself face-to-face with the grinning person of John Setton.

His chains were gone. It was impossible! The guard gaped, disbelieving. "How did you—" He never had time even to finish his question, much less find the answer to how Setton had slipped his chains. Setton raised the rifle, aimed it at the guard, and fired. The guard fell, struck the deck, and passed out in great pain.

Captain McCoy emerged from his cabin in time to see an unchained John Setton yanking a pistol free from the belt of his guard, who lay in a pool of spreading blood. McCoy jerked to a halt and saw that Mason himself had also just appeared from somewhere. He, too, was no longer chained. McCoy stood confused as Setton flipped the pistol to Mason, who, with a smile, raised it and fired. McCoy felt a sharp sting in his chest and staggered back, groping for his own pistol.

He was dying even as he fired it.

But he didn't die at once. He lay in darkness and heard the sounds of battle. The men on the shore must have heard the shots, and were trying to regain the ship. McCoy tried to move and couldn't. His last thought was a bitter condemnation of whoever among his crewmen had succumbed to bribery and secretly freed the prisoners of their chains. No other explanation of how they had gotten free could suffice.

McCoy was dead by the time the freed prisoners managed to dump out the guard Setton had injured, drive back the crewmen who attempted to reboard and stop them, and push the boat back out into the river. When pursuers found his corpse later in the day, Mason and his companions were gone, having vanished into the forests on the American side of the river.

CHAPTER 33

Natchez, Mississippi Territory

She had given her daughter the first name of Beulahland, in memory of her mother, and the middle name Queen, in memory of her departed friend and protector. Now she nestled the sandy-haired infant to her breast, enjoying the unique pleasure of nursing and nurturing, her mind filled with a whelming happiness that had been hers almost continually since this marvelous new life had come to her.

Celinda Ames Deerfield, alone in the house with her baby, sang in a quiet, plain voice, soothing both herself and her child. The tune was of her own making, the words taken from the song of Mary, whose feelings had become her own. " 'My soul doth magnify the Lord, and my spirit hath rejoiced in God my savior. For He hath regarded the low estate of His handmaiden . . . He that is might hath done to me great things. . . .' "

Great things. More apt words could not be found to describe the way Celinda perceived what had come her way. From the moment she had fled Jim Horton on the Mississippi shore and found refuge with Japheth Deerfield and all the others on the big, horse-powered boat, she felt safe and happy during her waking hours. At night, though, she still dreamed sometimes about her ordeal, and woke up frightened. But that was happening less often, and even when it did, there were the arms of her husband to hold her and the familiarity of her room to reassure her that all was well. And now there was little Beulahland as well, adding the happiness that only a child could bring.

Since leaving her Kentucky home with her father under the delusion that her aunt Ida was still alive, Celinda had been ready to see Natchez merely as a refuge. Her feelings for the town were much stronger now that it was her home. She loved Natchez. It was an old, well-established city, the capital of the Mississippi Territory up until the prior year, when the governmental seat had shifted to the town of Washington. The houses here ranged from fine and sometimes ornate dwellings in the upper portion—Celinda and Japheth lived in that section, though in a relatively small and modest home—down to the hovels and cabins of Natchez-under-the-Hill, the waterfront district. Celinda shunned that area, filled with saloons, brothels, gambling halls, dance establishments, and a population that reminded her of the foul rabble of Cave-in-Rock.

She had visited Natchez-under-the-Hill only once since coming to Natchez, and that reluctantly, out of duty rather than desire. She remembered Queen Fine's talk of a sister in this town, Beatrice Fine Sullivan, a "woman of substance." Oddly, Celinda's inquiries for such a person in the respectable upper portion of Natchez had yielded no results. No one seemed to have heard of her . . . until one man, scuffing his feet and looking embarrassed, mentioned that just perhaps he had heard of a "fallen woman" by that name in the lower part of the town.

Celinda went to Natchez-under-the-Hill after that, fighting away her fear, and inquired among the ragged populace after Beatrice Sullivan. At last she found someone who pointed out Beatrice to her—a slump-shouldered, sad-faced woman who looked like an emaciated, shrunken imitation of Queen herself. She was sitting at a table in the corner of a dive, drinking liquor from a square green bottle and eating some kind of thick gruel from a bowl. Celinda approached her, hesitated, then turned away, overwhelmed with a reluctance to face her. Clearly, Beatrice Sullivan's life was sad and empty enough as it was. What could be gained by telling her that her sister, whom she had so obviously deceived with stories of success and substance, had been murdered on a flatboat?

Celinda had slipped away, sorrowful and guilty because of her unwillingness to face Beatrice Sullivan. Despite good intentions, she found she couldn't bring herself to entwine her life again with coarse, crude strangers living in foul situations. She had experienced enough of that already, and now desired only to put the kind of world and people exemplified by Natchez-under-the-Hill behind her forever. So she easily persuaded herself that Beatrice Sullivan was not her concern.

Celinda's visit to Natchez-under-the-Hill had occurred within the first six months of her arrival and shortly before she married Japheth Deerfield. Japheth knew about Queen, but Celinda never told him of the existence of Queen's local sister. She had known he would never allow her to become involved with any of the potentially dangerous Under-the-Hill horde, and thus she had held the secret to avoid such a prohibition. After her trip to find Beatrice Fine, and her failure of nerve when she did so, she was even less prone to tell her husband of the matter. In fact she had tried to forget about Beatrice Fine herself—but she refused to forget Queen, whose memory she treasured like a gem. She would never let Queen slip from mind . . . even if she could not bring herself to meet the sister Queen had been coming to Natchez to see at the time she was murdered.

A strand of Celinda's hair fell across her shoulder and tickled the face of her baby, who was almost asleep at her breast. Quickly she brushed the hair away. Long hair, uncut in the approximately four years she had lived in Natchez. She intended to never cut it again, no matter how inconveniently long it grew. Jim Horton had forced her to cut her hair. No one would ever make her do that again, especially no man. Her hair, like her life, was her own. Even though she was married now, and devoted to and loving of her husband, she did not consider herself to be his possession, as so many wives seemed to do. She was devoted to him without question—but only by her own choice. No one would ever own her, nor force her to do anything that she did not freely choose to do.

Beulahland was asleep now, her mouth still attached to Celinda's breast. With her forefinger, Celinda gently broke the suction and shifted the baby's position, cradling her up onto her shoulder, where she softly massaged and patted the little back to bring forth the air Beulahland had swallowed. Then she rose, laid the baby in her crib, and slipped out into the main room.

She went to the heavily laden bookshelves—Japheth owned a good library filled with legal volumes he himself had bought and classic books mostly inherited from his late father and brought with him down the Mississippi—and selected a volume of English history. The intellectual hunger that Trenton Ames had stirred in his daughter had grown all the more intense now that she had easy access to literature. History was her latest infatuation, particularly the history of England and the British Isles.

A sudden rapping on the front door startled her so badly she almost dropped the volume. She stepped back, eyes wide and hand moving toward her throat. For a couple of moments she felt a strong, choking panic. A tendency to sudden, quick-passing panics when startled was a heritage of her cave-and-river ordeal. As quickly as it was past, she laid the book down, reached over to the nearby mantel and took down a small, loaded, flintrock pistol, which she held behind her back as she advanced to the door.

"Yes?"

"Ma'am? I'm sorry to disturb you, but I'm looking for Mr. Deerfield."

"If it's a business matter, sir, he keeps office during the hours of—".

"Please, ma'am, I'm sorry, but this here is a kind of unusual situation. I just arrived in Natchez today, you see, and my partner has been arrested and incarcerated in the jail."

Probably a boatman, Celinda thought; probably just another typical brawl and arrest down in Under-the-Hill, and this man wanted Japheth to take time out of his evening to try to get his friend out of jail. This was a pet grievance of hers; it seemed that many times Japheth could hardly get home before some troublemaker from below the bluff was in need of his help—and every case was "right special," or "an emergency" to those involved.

"Sir, I'm afraid there's no help to be given just now," Celinda said, unwilling to let the caller know that her husband wasn't home. It was late in the evening, a Tuesday, the day on which lately Japheth had a regular supper meeting with Moses Mulhaney, the same man who had written the letter to the Reverend John Deerfield that had been purloined by Jim Horton. Mulhaney had recently purchased some commercial property with Japheth, and the pair were embroiled in decisions about what use to put it to. "If you'll call at his office tomorrow morning, I'm sure he'll—"

"Well, I'll be!" the man on the other side of the door declared abruptly. "Here he comes now, I believe!"

Celinda frowned, unhappy that Japheth had picked this moment to come home and thus had unwittingly walked right into the middle of the situation. She went to the window and peered out through the curtain, making sure that it indeed was her husband approaching. It was, and already the caller, a tall, gray-haired, one-eyed fellow with the earthy look of a planter, had collared him and was filling his ear with news of his plight.

Celinda sighed, opened the door, and leaned against it with her arms crossed and a wry look on her face. Japheth cast her a quick glance across the shoulder of the rapidly talking, gesturing stranger, and smiled wanly as she gave him a wave and shrug. He returned his attention to the man, and Celinda watched his face. She felt dismayed to see a growing spark of interest altering her husband's previously weary-looking expression. Soon he looked outright eager. Celinda sighed. Sometimes she wished her husband weren't so prone to grow interested in every potential case that came his way. He took on any case that piqued his interest, sometimes forgetting even to find out if the client had any means of paying.

Celinda watched as Japheth put out a hand and laid it on the other man's shoulder in a gesture that said: *Calm down.* He spoke briefly to the man—Celinda heard the words. ". . . in just a moment," and, ". . . will be glad to see your friend," and, "Let me speak to my wife." Then Japheth walked past the man and up to her. The man, fidgeting with hat in hand, kept his back turned. He seemed very nervous.

Japheth kissed her cheek. "How's Beulahland?"

"Sleeping. Japheth, are you—"

"Yes, it appears I am. This man is distraught. Seems he just came in on a flatboat today and—"

"I know. His friend was arrested and locked up. Japheth, things like that happen every week around here. Must you go tonight, at this hour?"

"This situation has an interesting twist," Japheth answered, predictably. "It seems that this man is a friend of McCracken, my boatman friend from Nashville—you remember him, don't you? Quite the character. But beyond that, I'm intrigued by the reason this man's partner was arrested. It seems he had hardly set foot in town before somebody was wagging a finger at him and declaring he was James Hiram."

Celinda drew up straight and grew very serious. James Hiram! It was not a name she liked to hear. Japheth himself had been robbed by James Hiram on a road between Natchez and Washington. Hiram, though possessing no reputation approaching that of the devilish, famous Samuel Mason, was nevertheless a bane to travelers, particularly Kaintucks with full pockets. At least he hadn't killed Japheth, as Mason or his partner John Setton probably would have.

"Japheth, you're surely not thinking of taking the case of the very man who might have killed you!"

"No, Celinda. I said this man's friend was *declared* to be James Hiram, not that he was. Merely an accusation. In fact, Mr. Ford there says that his friend is in fact named Clardy Tyler, that he's never been in the Natchez region before now, and that he has come for the main reason of seeing if James Hiram might in true fact be a missing brother, operating under an alias that, quite intriguingly, happens to match the Christian names of Tyler's grandfather. It appears this Tyler has been mistaken for James Hiram once before, up in Nashville, with nearly fatal results. Having had my own encounter with the authentic Hiram, you can see why my curiosity is raised."

Celinda saw an empty, husbandless evening looming ahead, and knew there was nothing she could do to avoid it. Sighing, she said, "Very well, go on with you. I'll read until you're home. You did eat with Mr. Mulhaney, didn't you?"

"Yes, I did. I'll tell you all about the things we talked about—and about this new case here—as soon as I'm home. And that will be as quickly as possible, I assure you."

Clardy Tyler felt like some sort of freak animal on display in a showman's cage as the lawyer named Deerfield examined him, with rather a wide-eyed expression, through the crossed, flat iron bars of the jail cell. He hardly knew what to make of his situation. He had expected that his evident similarity to the outlaw James Hiram might cause him some problems in Natchez, but he hadn't expected them to arise so quickly and to actually land him in jail. He was grateful that he had remembered the name of the lawyer in that remarkable story McCracken told back up the river a ways. McCracken himself had been absent, down guarding the flatboat at the riverfront, at the time Clardy was arrested, but rather than send Ford back to fetch the boatman, it seemed more prudent to have him look up McCracken's often-referenced "lawyer Deerfield." And after the jailer happened to mention that Deerfield himself had been robbed by the mysterious James Hiram, Clardy was all the more eager to bring him here. Deerfield, having seen the real James Hiram face-to-face, should be able to verify that he himself was not that man. And Clardy thought he might be able to find some answers about Hiram from Deerfield.

Now Deerfield stood gaping at him, making Clardy feel self-conscious and not at all certain Deerfield wasn't going to misidentify him as Hiram himself. But a moment later the lawyer shook his head and said, "A remarkable similarity. Remarkable! If it wasn't for the absence of the facial scar, sir, I'd be nigh to swearing you really *are* James Hiram."

"I'm his brother . . . or I think I might be. Except his name isn't really James Hiram, but Thias Tyler . . . but maybe I shouldn't be saying all that, 'cause I don't know yet if it's true, and if it is, I don't want to get Thias in any kind of trouble, if it really is Thias . . . hang it all! The more I talk, the more confused it sounds!"

"I understand the situation already, Mr. Tyler. Your friend Mr. Ford explained it well enough." He stopped and looked Clardy over one more time. "Remarkable! You very well may be his brother, Mr. Tyler. Either that, or by some miracle there's a man who's nearly your twin roaming this country, robbing people."

Clardy's heart pumped more rapidly; certainly grew. It *had* to be Thias whom this man, and others, had encountered! It was thrilling . . . also disheartening. It meant Thias was alive—it also meant that he was a very changed man.

"Mr. Deerfield, can you get me out of this jail?" Clardy asked. "You can see there's no scar on my face, and I've heard that there is one on the face of James Hiram."

The lawyer scanned Clardy's features and nodded. "So there is . . . and so there isn't, on you. Indeed, sir, I believe I can have you out of here promptly. Have any charges actually been filed against you?"

"I was told I was being held on suspicion."

"One moment, then. I'll deal with this promptly." Deerfield turned and strode away, to speak to the jailer.

Within ten minutes Clardy knew that he had made a wise

decision in sending for Japheth Deerfield. The lawyer came back to the cell with the jailer at his side. The jailer, looking apologetic, thrust a big key into the lock and turned it. "I'm mighty sorry, Mr. Tyler. But the fact is, I've seen James Hiram with my own eyes, and you look a sight like him. So close that even without the scar, I was obliged to hold you, just in case. But with the good lawyer here swearing you ain't Hiram, I'm going to turn you loose and tell you I'm sorry we was a trouble to you."

Clardy slipped out of the cell as quickly as it was opened, feeling the kind of relief that comes with finally opening a overly tight collar that one has had to endure for hours. "Think nothing of it," he said. "All's well now, and having this happen has only made me more sure of what I've been suspecting about this James Hiram all along."

"Come with me to my home," Deerfield said. "Meet my wife, and tell us more of your story. Most remarkable, this is."

"It happens I've heard your wife's story," Clardy said. "Now, that's what I think of as remarkable."

"Oh, old McCracken's been at his storytelling, has he? I should have guessed it. But indeed you're right. Celinda's story is remarkable, as is she. A most remarkable woman. A fine lady, as you will see." Deerfield wrinkled his nose. "This jail . . . I've smelled the stench of it a thousand times, but it always galls. Come, Mr. Tyler. Mr. Ford is waiting outside. Let's get away from here, so I can hear more about this mysterious missing brother of yours who just might have robbed me."

CHAPTER 34

She doesn't like having us here. I can tell it by looking at her.

And it was difficult for Clardy not to look at Celinda Deerfield, not because she possessed any great physical beauty, but because her story had made such an impression on him. Seeing her in person made McCracken's tale all the more real to him, and now his eyes tended to drift toward her as he tried to imagine her with hair hacked short, face smudged with grime, and her fine dress replaced with ragged men's clothing.

He was seated in the front room of the Deerfield house in upper Natchez, Isaac Ford at his side, a cup of coffee steaming in his hand. He had just finished recounting his own story, and Thias's as well, as far as he knew it, and the reaction he received from Japheth Deerfield showed enthusiastic interest. Deerfield was an open fellow with an active and inquisitive mind. He clearly thought Clardy to be a fascinating man, particularly now that he realized he was one of the well-known "Harpe hunters" who had pursued the murderous brothers through Kentucky. Deerfield insisted upon a detailed recounting of the death of Micajah Harpe, and it was during that telling that Clardy had most strongly sensed that Celinda

Deerfield wasn't happy to be playing hostess to him. He wondered why. Maybe all the talk of criminals and violence brought her own ordeal too vividly to mind.

He shifted his eyes back to Japheth, who was just beginning to tell his own story of being robbed on what he called the "Boatman's Trail," just one of several names of the narrow trace that ran from Natchez up through the country of the Choctaws, Chickasaws, and Cherokees, to the rich Cumberland River country at Nashville. This was the land route by which most Kaintucks returned home after disposing of their goods and river vessels in the lower Mississippi market towns.

Japheth proved himself a storyteller nearly of the caliber of McCracken. He gave a vivid account of how, when returning from business farther up the trace, he had been accosted along a narrow, shaded portion of the way by a man dressed in rough woodsman's clothing, his bearded face blackened with charcoal to make his features hard to make out. The man, who had seemed almost apologetic in his manner, demanded that Japheth dismount from his horse and turn over all money and valuables he was carrying. "Throughout, the man told me repeatedly that he didn't wish to harm me, that he was robbing me only out of necessity, and that my cooperation would make the entire process short and painless. He made efforts not to look me squarely in the face, and I took that at first to be because of his shame. Soon, though, I made out the clear markings of a scar across his face, a kind of furrow that the blackening he had done failed to hide because of his sweat, which tended to wash it away. I realized it was that scar he didn't want me to see, because it was an identifying mark."

Clardy asked, "Can you be sure he looked like me, if he was blackened up?"

"Indeed. The poor fellow had done a rather poor job of it, to be honest, and his sweat was unveiling him bit by bit the entire time I was in his presence. Furthermore, I've made it a point to be skilled at memorizing faces—that's a helpful ability in my line of work—and I came away from that robbery with a clear image of that man's features. I made a sketch as soon as I was home again. . . . Celinda, where is that drawing? Have I left it in my office?"

"No," she said, rising. "It's in yonder cabinet. I'll fetch it."

Clardy watched her walk across the room and open a drawer in a well-stuffed cabinet. She dug through papers and came out with a piece of folded foolscap that she unfolded and brought to her husband. She returned to her seat, her expression solemn and her manner telling Clardy all the more strongly that this entire meeting was somehow unpleasant for her.

Japheth unfolded the paper and nodded. "Ah, yes. This is it. Even though I'm no artist, I think I caught his look quite well. Certainly there is a resemblance to yourself, Mr. Tyler." He handed the paper over, and Clardy found himself eyeing what indeed seemed to be a picture, however imperfect and rough, of Thias. It unsettled him.

"This is *him*! I know it's Thias!"

"I'm both pleased and displeased that you think so," Japheth said. "To track down a missing brother is good. To find him reduced to robbery isn't. And I regret that it has been so long since I saw him. There is nothing to say he is still in this region. I've heard no reports of any other robberies committed by James Hiram in the last year or more, though prior to that there was quite a flurry of them."

"How did he come to tell you his name?" Ford asked.

"I asked him." Japheth shrugged and smiled. "I know that sounds odd, but the man was so nervous that I believed he might answer. I've dealt with enough of the criminal ilk to know that often they will reveal the most damning truths even in the midst of trying to cover them. I asked him, and he answered promptly. 'James Hiram.' I had heard that name before—two or three prior robberies having been done by a person using that name."

"It would be like Thias to not have his wits about him while doing something like that," Clardy said. "I swear to you he isn't criminal by nature. All through our growing up, it was me who leaned more in that direction, and Thias who everyone declared as good."

"I wonder where else he might be, if he don't turn out to be hereabouts?" Ford asked.

"Who can say?" Japheth replied. "My guess would be New Orleans. Many a man has fled down that way when he feels the heat on him here. It is easy to lose oneself in the underbelly of that city."

"Perhaps you should be seeking him there, rather than here, Clardy," Ford said.

"Maybe. I'm inclined to turn over all the stones here first."

"That's what I would recommend," Japheth said. "But how do you plan to go about it, Mr. Tyler?"

Clardy had thought very little about that. Up until now his goal had simply been to reach Natchez; now that he was here, he realized the bigger challenge still lay ahead. "I'm not certain. I suppose I'll sull around the riverfront for a time, asking questions, looking for sign."

"That could be dangerous," Japheth said solemnly. "Questioners aren't generally welcome among the riverfront folk. But I suppose you must. And I'll try to find out all I can to help you. Where will you be living?"

"We're on the flatboat, for now," Clardy replied. "I suppose I'll take a room somewhere."

Japheth said. "Perhaps you would consider staying with . . ." He trailed off when Celinda turned a shocked expression upon him. ". . . er, perhaps taking a room somewhere would be just the thing," he completed.

Clardy was sure then that Celinda Deerfield really didn't think much of him. Obviously, Japheth had been about to offer him board right here in this house.

"That's what I'll do, then," Clardy said. Feeling an impulse to try to put Celinda's mind at ease, he turned to her and said, "Mrs. Deerfield, I thank you for your hospitality this evening. Here it is getting on toward deep night, and we're sitting in your parlor, keeping you from your rest. I apologize. Mr. Ford, I believe it's time for us to go."

"No need to rush away," Japheth said.

"I believe we should impositionize ourselves here no more," Ford said. "Mrs. Deerfield, you've indeed been a prime hostess. I'm sorry to have been the one to first disturb you this evening."

Mr. Ford can tell, too, that she's unhappy. Clardy felt a vague dismay. He wondered what there was about all this that was so unpleasant to her.

"I'm glad that my husband was able to help you gentlemen," she replied, sounding insincere.

"Might I keep this drawing, Mr. Deerfield?" Clardy asked.

"Indeed. It might be a good reference for you to use·in your inquiries. Come, gentlemen. I'll walk you out."

Outside the house, Japheth glanced back at the closed door and said, lowly, "I apologize if my wife seemed distant or cold. I gather there is something in all this that has disturbed her.

Sometimes some odd thing or another bring her own trial back to her mind."

"McCracken told us her story," Ford said. "I stand in awe of what your wife suffered through, and I'm glad to see her life has turned out well. I'm sure you are a fine husband for her."

"I try to be."

Clardy said, "Mr. Deerfield, I'm ready to pay you for your service this evening."

"Pay? Indeed not! I'm paid already simply by knowing your story. Furthermore, any man who helped rid the world of Micajah Harpe certainly deserves to receive a few good turns in sheer gratitude. I'll charge you no fee."

Clardy was surprised. No fee! "But sir, I—"

"I insist, Mr. Tyler. I have an interest in your quest myself, as you might suppose, having met 'James Hiram.' All I ask of you is to allow me to help you in any way I can, and that you keep me informed as to your progress."

"Well . . . thank you, sir. I'll do that."

"One other thing . . . It's fairly common for me to go to New Orleans. The odds are good that I'll be going there before long. If it happens that you've not yet found your brother by then, and if you're still in the area when I go, I'll be glad to take you with me. It may be that our friend has gone on down the river."

"I'll keep that in mind, sir."

After saying their farewells, Clardy and Isaac Ford walked slowly through the Natchez streets. It was Clardy's first chance to look closely at the town; up until now he had been distracted by the rather rude event of having been thrown in and then out of jail, and all the activity that followed. Above the bluff, Natchez had a patrician air of wealth, solidity, firm establishment. Even by darkness Clardy could see the elegance of the finer houses, many of them outright mansions. A fine courthouse stood imposingly in the midst of the town. Clardy thought it generally finer looking than Nashville, his best reference point for judging municipalities. But as he and Ford descended to the lower riverfront portion, the atmosphere of Natchez changed dramatically. There was nothing beautiful or aesthetic about Natchez-under-the-Hill. Hovels, dives, taverns . . . by night it looked like a jumble of wooden boxes thrown off the bluff above and scooted roughly into order blow.

"I wonder if Thias has ever drained a cup here?" Clardy mused.

"I want to talk to you about Thias," Ford said. "Seems to me there's a part of this you ain't give much thought to yet."

"What?"

"What's going to happen to him, once you find him, and if he really has turned robber?"

"Well ... I suppose I'll try to get him away from here, try to get him straightened out. I don't know ... that ain't something I've dwelt on."

"You'd best dwell on it. If he's robbed folk, he'll have to answer to the law. Have you thought out that Deerfield might have a different motivization than you in wanting to find him?"

Clardy paused. "No. I haven't." Another pause, then a shake of his head. "No, Mr. Ford. I don't think he's aiming to avenge himself against him."

"He wouldn't see it as that. It would be just one more case of criminal justice to him. And it'd be a feather in his cap as a lawyer to be the man to bring in a highwayman who's plagued folks hereabouts. You saw them fine houses up on the bluff. This here is a city of dignity. A pretty, lush, rich kind of place, in its upper portions. It's the reputation of Under-the-Hill, and the highwaymen and killers out on the Boatman's Trail, that smirch up the name of the town. The good and upright folk of Natchez aren't going to favor going easy on robbers. And you can tell that Deerfield is among the good and upright. And didn't you notice him talking about having a 'personal interest' in what you're doing, because James Hiram robbed him?"

"I heard it, but ..." Clardy shook his head. "I don't see him like you do. I believe he's just plain interested in what I'm doing. It didn't come across to me that he's wanting to see Thias punished."

"Thias robbed him. He can't overlook that."

"Maybe he can. He overlooked my fee tonight, didn't he? He seems a big-hearted man."

"Or maybe he overlooked that fee because he figures you for a means of getting his hands on the man who robbed him, and wants to keep you feeling in his debt."

"I never knew you to be such a cynical old soul. You're starting to sound as sour on the world as my old grandpap was."

"I'm just saying you need to think through what it will be like if you do find Thias. It's clear enough he don't want to be found, else he wouldn't be using false names and hiding out. If he's turned bad, he'll—"

"Don't say he's turned bad. Maybe it's just that things have turned bad for him. Maybe he don't have any choice but to rob."

"That's a bill of goods I won't buy, Clardy. Things turn bad for all kinds of folks, but that don't unwrite the moral law. There's always two choices, whatever your circumstances: the good or the bad. Either way, it's the responsibility of him who chooses. For every man who gets hisself into a crush and steps outside the law because of it, there's a dozen more in the same kind of crush who hold out and do right, and they rise and stand witness against the first man. No sir. Bad circumstances ain't no excuse for doing wrong."

"I ain't in the mood for your preaching, Mr. Ford."

"All I'm saying is, you need to think all this through: what's going to happen now, and when you find him."

"He's *my* brother. You let me worry about him."

"Fine. But you're my partner, and my friend, and I'm shot if I'm going to quit worrying about *you*."

They reached the flatboat and found McCracken waiting impatiently. The horses were off the boat now, penned at a stable nearby, but McCracken said he had been obliged to keep watch on the boat anyway because his slaves, like horses, could be stolen. He demanded to know where Ford and Clardy had been so long, leaving him in the lurch. Ford quickly recounted all that happened, and McCracken's anger eased.

"You've had you quite an evening, then," he said. "More interesting than mine . . . but that's due to change here in a minute. I'm off to the taverns, boys. You keep watch for a time. I'll be back later on."

"Drunk as a redskin, probably," Ford muttered.

"Durn right," McCracken said, winking. Within a minute he was gone, vanishing into the rough line of buildings that made up Natchez-under-the-Hill, a place so dismal that it managed to achieve an inverted kind of splendor.

After his visitors left, Japheth Deerfield had gone back inside his house with a dark look on his face. "Celinda, I demand to know why you were so cold to our guests."

Celinda felt stung. Rarely did Japheth speak to her in anything but a gentle tone. "I didn't know I was being cold, Japheth. And I thought they were more clients than guests."

"Come now, Celinda. You were all but icy. It poured off you! And you know that anyone who steps inside our walls here, client or not, is a guest for the time he is with us."

Celinda knew better than to continue to deny her chilly behavior. She *had* felt coldly toward the two men, though she hadn't realized her feelings were so transparent. "I'm sorry, Japheth. The truth is, I don't know why. Perhaps it was . . . I don't know."

Japheth, never a man to hold his anger long, changed his manner. He was a tender man; it was one of the characteristics that made her love him. "Dear, if they offended you in some way, I'm the one who must apologize. It was late to be bringing strangers into our home. They talked loudly; I'm sure you feared they would wake up Beulahland."

"It wasn't that, Japheth. It was . . . Japheth, I beg you, please don't become involved with those men. Let Mr. Tyler hunt for his wicked brother alone. It needn't involve you."

"Well . . . it needn't, that's true. But it intrigues me. Put yourself in Mr. Tyler's place. Imagine having lost contact with a brother for so many years, and then to learn that he apparently has become a criminal, using a false name. You would want to find the truth, wouldn't you?"

"Yes," she admitted. "But there is something here that doesn't rest well. I feel like that Mr. Tyler will bring us trouble. His brother already has. You might have been killed in that robbery."

"But I wasn't. And why do you say Clardy Tyler would bring us trouble?"

"I don't know. It's just a thing I feel."

"Dear, Mr. Tyler and his friend here were no bad men. They're planters, horse dealers. Honest men of Nashville. And besides, you know that nothing more than a 'feeling' about someone really doesn't count for much without facts to back it up."

"Don't put me on trial, Japheth. I know I can't defend my feelings. But even so, they're still my feelings. I just don't want you involved with Mr. Tyler or his sorry brother. I don't."

" 'Involved.' Not really the word, darling. All I'm doing is offering my moral support." He hesitated. "That, and a means for Mr. Tyler to reach New Orleans later, if his search should take him that way. I'll be going anyway, and there would be no harm in taking him along."

"Why not let him tend his own business? You got the man out of jail. What more do you care about him or his brother?"

"I was robbed by his brother, was I not? If James Hiram really is his brother."

"Yes, but . . ." She paused, cocking her head as she did at moments of sudden realization. "Is *that* why you want to see James Hiram found? So you can bring him to justice?"

Japheth flicked his brows. "There would have to be some sort of reckoning, I would think. I doubt that Mr. Tyler expects anything less."

"So would you see him brought before the court for his crimes?"

"I would hope he would surrender himself voluntarily, and . . . but all that is for future consideration, dear. The man isn't even found yet, and the odds are high that he won't be. This is a big region, and on top of that, I haven't heard of James Hiram having showed himself hereabouts for months and months. He may be dead. Early ends often come to those who take up the criminal life."

Celinda grew silent and sad in manner. Shoulders slumping, she looked mournfully at her husband's face. "Japheth, the whole business has something about it that fills me with dread. There's a shadow hanging over it."

Japheth laughed and put his arms around her. "Is this my usually level-headed wife speaking? She who was raised by her father to be a clear thinker? Don't worry, my dear. I'd never do anything that would bring trouble on my family. Perhaps I'm overly enthusiastic. I dearly love a puzzle, and Mr. Tyler's has me intrigued. But I'll maintain sufficient distance, and *will* keep my head, I promise. There. Is that what you wanted to hear?"

"Yes," she replied, hugging him close. It was indeed what she had wanted to hear, but she also wanted to be able to believe it. And she didn't. She knew her husband far too well. He wouldn't keep his distance, and he would lose his head.

She wished that Isaac Ford had picked some other lawyer to come jog his friend free of the jail tonight.

Clardy slept with the kind of dreamless, deep slumber that left him feeling tired when he awakened. He sat up, yawned, and finger-combed his hair. It needed a trimming, something he decided he would see to now that he was in a town. Tying it behind his head with a bit of twine, he rose and went out onto the open part of the flatboat.

Ford was standing on the dock, a bleary-eyed, hung-over McCracken at his side. They were talking to another man, whom Clardy had never seen before. Not being in the mood to converse, Clardy sat down and let the sun bathe over his face. The air was chilly today. He went back to his bed, retrieved and donned his coat, then reemerged in time to see Ford shaking the stranger's hand.

The stranger left, and Ford came back onto the boat. McCracken came, too, pushing past Clardy and heading for his own bed. The two slaves busied themselves elsewhere on the boat, keeping their distance from their master.

Ford said, " 'Morning, Clardy. You were still sleeping like the dead when I got up this morning."

"I wish you'd have wakened me. I can't get the sleep out of my head now. Who was that man?"

"His name is Carter. A buyer for our horses."

"Did he take our asking price?"

"Indeed, though with one provision. We have to ship the horses on to New Orleans, as soon as we can do it."

"New Orleans . . . but I need to stay here."

"I know. Clardy, maybe I should have talked to you first, but I went ahead and made the bargain."

"But you know that—"

"Hold up. I know you need to stay. So I propose that you do that, and that me and McCracken ship the horses on down the river. Does the notion of staying here on your own for a spell bother you?"

Clardy thought it over. "No . . . just have to shift my thinking about, that's all. I'd figured you and me both would be here."

"Clardy, let me tell you something further I been thinking on. I don't want to go back to Nashville. I like it around here. I might want to buy me some land, maybe down about New Orleans. It's going to be part of the United States by the end of the year, after all. I'd considered doing some looking thereabouts, and taking the horses there gives me a good excuse to do it."

"When did you start thinking that way?"

"During the voyage. I like this river country. I'm getting old. Wouldn't mind spending my last days here in a new place."

"You ain't old. You're way too young to be talking about last days."

"Oh, I ain't curling up to die. But now's the time to be making plans before them last days do come calling. Who knows? Maybe I'd find me a pretty Orleans belle and marry. I ain't averse to the notion. If I like New Orleans, I'd be pleased to stay there the rest of my life. I have no desire to go back to Nashville, and the only way I want to be returned to Kentucky is in a box, to be buried by my wife and children. When my time comes, and if we're still partners, you see that that's done. Will you?"

Clardy scratched his stubbly face. This was a lot of serious subject matter to be taking in so early in the morning. "Aye, of course. Whatever you want. But what about right now? What will become of our Cumberland River land if you go moving off?"

"I'd sell it out, I reckon. To you. Or if you didn't want it, to somebody else. Maybe you could sell your portion, too. Stay with me. Keep on being partners, like we have been."

"Doing what?"

"Same thing. We can raise and sell horses here as well as there, can't we? And we'd be right at the heart of trade. We could do well for ourselves."

Clardy said, "This is going to take some thinking. Right now I've got a big enough bite to chew on, just figuring how to find Thias."

"No hurry. Just something to be mulling. I'm feeling right serious about New Orleans. McCracken's told me some about it. No other city like it to be found in the world. The last thing I want is to grow old somewhere where life is just the same old thing you've always knowed. New Orleans, that would be a different kind of life. Something's always happening in New Orleans. And there's money to be made there, if we don't sit idle. 'Slothfulness casteth into a deep sleep, and an idle soul shall suffer hunger.'"

"More durn proverbs."

"Can't help it. It's in my nature."

"It's in your nature to keep the cream forever stirred in the milk, too! I figured seeing some new country might get you out of all that brooding under the thinking tree you'd been doing so much of. But I didn't figure it would make you want to shove your roots into a whole different hole."

"You and me both know what I'm doing, Clardy. I'm running from memories. They caught up with me in Tennessee and left me squatted 'neath my thinking tree, thinking about putting a gun to my head. Maybe they won't catch up with me here, where everything is so different."

Clardy nodded. "You go on to New Orleans. Sell the horses and look at land. When you settle on what you want to do, come back and tell me. I'll still be here. I hope I'll have Thias with me, too."

"I hope so. And I hope there's no trouble for him." He looked away. "Though I don't see how there couldn't be."

Clardy didn't want to enter that discussion again. "I'm hungry," he said. "Is there anyplace hereabouts a man can find a good breakfast?"

"How about you and me go look and see?"

"What about McCracken?"

"He's abed. Got himself drunk as the still house cat last night, and now all he can do is absconderate to his blankets to sleep it off. Shameful. 'The drunkard and the glutton shall come to poverty, and drowsiness shall clothe a man with rags.' "

"That's right," Clardy said. "And then that man can move to Natchez-under-the-Hill and fit right in. Come on, Mr. Ford. Let's go find that breakfast."

CHAPTER 35

The flatboat, laden with horses, pulled out the next day with McCracken's slaves manning the sweeps, and began its float toward New Orleans. Clardy stood at the waterfront, waving farewell to the beaming Isaac Ford. Ford was obviously happy to be beginning his new adventure in life, so Clardy gave him a broad grin of encouragement as long as his face could be seen. When Ford was out of sight, however, Clardy's smile faded and he slipped off alone and struggled not to cry.

He would have been ashamed to cry like some child lost in the woods. Clardy felt like such a child at the moment. He and Ford had worked side by side now for years, seldom being parted by more than a few miles' distance or a few days' time. Having never had a real father, Clardy perceived himself now as a virtual son of Isaac Ford. But he didn't fully realize until now just how much he had come to value Ford's company.

Now Ford was gone and Clardy was left alone in a strange town, ready to embark on some very chancy work.

Ford had given Clardy extra money before he left—another indicator of the father-son relationship that had evolved between them—and cautioned him about how to proceed with his quest. Don't ask too many questions too soon. If you err, err on the side of caution. If folks strike you as bad, trust your impression; if they strike you as good, mistrust it. Never flash money in a crowd. Don't be lured off alone, even if someone tells you they have Thias waiting for you in an alley; the town is full of cutthroats and scoundrels.

Clardy found himself a room in the Under-the-Hill part of town. It was a low-ceilinged, attic loft with a window too small to get out of if the place should catch fire, which worried him, but the cost was low and nothing else was immediately available. Outside his room was a tiny corridor, and on the other side of that a door leading to a slightly larger second room, occupied by a woman whose trade was evident by her flashy and revealing mode of dress and the steady stream of men who came calling at the oddest hours. Clardy wondered why his own room had been available to rent instead of being put to similar use by some other painted woman, until he learned in a saloon that such had been the case until the woman died, murdered in that very room by an unhappy drunk who had cut her throat so deeply that her head had been nearly severed. Then Clardy understood what had caused that blackened stain on the pine-board floor, and felt a little edgy in the place at night. But he put up with it. Nothing else to do.

He showed around Japheth Deerfield's drawing of the outlaw Hiram and, remembering Ford's caution about being too aggressively inquisitive, asked as subtly as he could if anyone might know where the fellow could be found. He was frustrated by receiving mostly predictable comments about how much the man in the picture looked like Clardy himself, or either misleading responses or no responses at all. Only when he had moved among the Natchez-under-the-Hill crowd long enough to become known did he begin to detect some softening of the resistance. A few people acknowledged having seen James Hiram before. Several of these told him that they never would have admitted having seen him had not Clardy so obviously been a brother. *You're the very image of the man.* He heard that phrase more times than he could keep up with. Yet no one had any idea of what had become of James Hiram. He hadn't been seen about Natchez for at least a year.

As days passed, Clardy became ever more sure that James Hiram was Thias, and less sure he was still to be found about Natchez.

Then, when Clardy was all but ready to give up and turn his sights toward New Orleans, a drunk boatman told him that just maybe he had seen a man who looked like James Hiram up about Greenville, a town some twenty miles to the northeast. Couldn't swear to it, but it surely might have been. Clardy was so encouraged he pressed a coin into the man's hand and bought him a fresh drink besides.

Ford had left him a horse and paid in advance for its stabling. His heart pounding with excitement, Clardy went straight from the tavern to the stable, roused the stableman from sleep, and obtained and saddled his horse. Then, with clouds spreading over a black sky and making it so dark that no sensible man would even think of trying to travel, Clardy set out from Natchez toward Greenville, so full of hope of finding his brother that he gave no thought at all to the danger.

Two days later Clardy was riding north of Greenville, his heart heavy with yet another failure. He had searched Greenville thoroughly, questioned everyone he could find, and no trace of Thias had appeared. Just now he was returning to Greenville from a cabin belonging to an old man who several folks had told him "knows the dealings of everybody that had ever haunted these woods," but that well had proved as dry as every other one he had dipped into. He believed now that the boatman had lied to him in hope of reward. He had fallen right into the snare.

From now on, he pledged to himself, he would be slower to believe anything he was told, especially by drunks, and much, much slower to pay for information until he knew it was valid.

Clardy was so distracted by his disappointment that he did not notice a rider slowly closing in behind him as he neared Greenville. Clardy happened to have a shining tin flask of whiskey with him, and pulled it out of his saddlebag for a drink. In the midst of turning up the bottle he noticed the rider reflected in the flask.

He tensed inwardly but did not show it. The man was a stranger, very rugged-looking and with a gritty ambience about him that put Clardy at caution. As close as the rider was, it was out of the question to ignore him or try to outdistance him. Remembering the words of a certain bald old peddler named Peyton—*An act of kindness can be the best shield a man has*—Clardy turned to face the man, grinned as he swallowed his mouthful of liquor, smacked his lips and shook his head in a show of pleasure, and cordially held out the bottle toward the newcomer.

"Howdy do, friend. Would you care to have yourself a swallow?"

"I'm beholden," the man said, accepting the bottle. Now that he was close, Clardy could tell the man had been drinking on his own already. His eyes were red and looked unfocused; his face had a ruddy flush.

"My name's Tyler, Clardy Tyler," Clardy said. He was always quick to give his identity now, for he never knew what stranger he met might have had some bad experience with the outlaw Hiram and mistake him for his former victimizer.

"My name is May," the other man said, helping himself without invitation to a second swallow of Clardy's whiskey. "James May. Pleased to know you."

"You live hereabouts, Mr. May?"

"Not too far. I travel a lot. Traveling into Greenville right now. Going to travel out again a rich man. I've kilt me an outlaw and I aim to collect the reward. Thousand dollars."

Clardy felt a jolt. *What if* . . . But then he realized he had never heard of any reward being offered for James Hiram, much less one so lavish as this one.

"I can think of only one man who would have a reward that large on his head," Clardy replied.

"If you're thinking of Sam Mason, you've hit the nail square."

"You've truly killed Mason of the Woods, no jest?" In all his time of inquiring after James Hiram, Clardy had heard endless references to Samuel Mason, "Mason of the Woods." The man seemed to be cut from cloth almost as stained as that of the Harpe brothers. He robbed without mercy and had murdered many innocent travelers. At times he had disposed of them in the same manner sometimes employed by the Harpes: laying open and disemboweling the bodies, filling the body cavity with stones, and tossing the whole bloody human package into the river.

"I've kilt him, yes indeed," May said. "Me, a good and law-abiding man who's been a victim of that scoundrel, have done him in."

"You'll be the man of the hour, then," Clardy said. "Everyone despises and fears Mason."

"They needn't no more," the man replied. "I have shot him in the head above the eye."

"Where's his corpse?"

"Ain't here."

"They'll want you to prove he's dead."

"I'll convince them."

Clardy wondered how that would happen, but didn't ask. For all he knew, May was a drunk with big, fantastic notions about himself and his achievements. To claim to have killed such a well-known outlaw as Samuel Mason, but to have no body to present in proof, was rather dubious.

Clardy would have rather continued on to Greenville alone, but with May traveling the same way, his company was inevitable. He decided to make the best of it, and asked May to share the story of how he had supposedly done in Mason.

By the time they reached Greenville, Clardy had decided that this James May was either a great liar or very self-deluded. May strained Clardy's credulity beyond breaking when he said he had been "kidnapped" by Mason and forced to take part in his criminal activities. The story grew ever wilder, culminating in a description of how he shot Mason while the bandit was counting his money. He now had with him some of the money and various other items that had belonged to Mason. With these, he said, he would be able to prove that he had actually killed the outlaw, and the reward would be his.

"And I'll tell you, Mr. Tyler, if I see you after I have that money, I'll sure buy you ten drinks for that which you shared with me today. I will do it."

A day later, when Clardy left Greenville after convincing himself once and for all that Thias would not be found there, he learned from the local gossip that May had not succeeded in making his case. May lacked sufficient evidence that Mason was dead, and though he was given a serious hearing by the various authorities, in the end he'd been sent on his way. Clardy was far from surprised, and promptly forgot about May, dismissing him as merely another of the strange characters who seemed to thrive in this portion of the world.

Back in Natchez, Clardy grew frustrated and increasingly hopeless. More than ever he feared he would not find Thias here, and wished he had gone on with Ford and McCracken to New Orleans. Remembering Japheth Deerfield's invitation to join him next time he went to New Orleans, he headed into the upper part of the town and to Deerfield's office. Deerfield was not there, so Clardy headed farther on, toward the Deerfield house. He was within a hundred feet of the place when Celinda appeared, walking out of the front door with her child in her arms. Clardy stopped; she turned and saw him. The look in her face told him he was not welcome. But he tipped his hat to her, smiled, and came on.

"Good day, Mrs. Deerfield."

"Mr. Tyler." Her tone was formal and cold.

"I've come to see if your husband is here. I'd like a word with him."

"You can see him in his office."

"I tried, ma'am. He wasn't there."

"I see." She stopped speaking and looked at him in a puzzlingly intense way. "Mr. Tyler," she said softly, "I want to make a request, and please forgive me if it is rude. I request that you find yourself another attorney. Natchez is full of them."

Her candor surprised him. He quirked his brows. "I don't understand, ma'am. If it's because I didn't pay your husband before, it's only because he refused to charge me a fee. I'll pay for any other help he gives."

"It isn't the fee. I honestly don't know why I would prefer you to stay away from my husband, Mr. Tyler." She lowered her eyes as if embarrassed by her next words. "I have a fear that harm will come to him through you. It's a conviction I can neither explain nor shake off."

Clardy was confounded. "I would never harm your husband, Mrs. Deerfield. He was a benefactor to me."

"Please, do not see my husband, Mr. Tyler. I ask you that as sincerely as I can. Please . . . go your way, and don't call on him again."

Clardy was hurt and mildly insulted. Then he remembered that Japheth had been victimized by James Hiram. That must be it, he guessed. She didn't want her husband trying to help him roust out a man who robbed him.

It grated in his craw some to do it, but he tipped his hat and nodded. "Very well, ma'am. I was coming to ask again about going with your husband to New Orleans, but if it means so much to you that I not be around him, well, I'll go along with that."

Her look showed surprise; evidently she had expected him to

argue with her. That in itself told him something about her apparent perceptions of him. "Thank you, Mr. Tyler. And I . . . apologize if I've been rude or . . . thank you, sir. Thank you."

"Good day to you, ma'am."

"Good day."

He turned back the way he had come. She called to him: "Mr. Tyler, for what it's worth to you, my husband's trip to New Orleans has been put off until early next year."

"Oh. Well, that's that. Good-bye, ma'am."

"Good-bye, Mr. Tyler."

Clardy secretly visited Deerfield's office the next day, driven by curiosity about whether Celinda had told him the truth about the New Orleans journey.

She had. "I'm sorry," Japheth said. "I would have been happy to take you with me, but if you want to get there sooner, it would be best if you found some other means of transport. It shouldn't be particularly difficult, given all the traffic from this city to that one."

"Perhaps so, Mr. Deerfield," he said. "I thank you in any case."

"Will you be going to New Orleans soon, then?"

"I don't know just yet. Maybe. Or maybe I'll sniff around here a few days more."

"Well, if you do end up still being around here and still needing passage when my trip comes up next year, my invitation still stands."

Clardy saw nothing to gain in telling him about his conversation with Celinda the day before. The point was moot, anyway; he couldn't imagine still being in Natchez all the way into the next year.

He left the office with the intent of rounding up some alternative passage to New Orleans, or perhaps just mounting his horse and riding there.

It happened that on that same day, however, he heard a rumor that a man who might be James Hiram had been seen recently on up the Boatman's Trail a few miles. Hardly daring to hope that this was true, Clardy ventured out onto the trail again, still looking, still hoping. Days of searching passed, and he became convinced that this rumor, too, was false.

He returned to Natchez and suddenly became ill. All the searching, worrying, and living in poor conditions had lowered his resistance to the surfeit of sickly miasmas that moved like zephyrs through the squallid quarters of Natchez-under-the-Hill. For two weeks he wallowed in misery in his bed, trying to throw off his sickness. When he emerged on the other side of it, he was weak and thin, very changed physically, but changed in a more important and fundamental way mentally.

His spirit for the quest was broken. He had lost the will to continue. The prospect of going to New Orleans no longer appealed to him. There, in such a large, complex city, he would face only more difficulty and frustration. Besides, wasn't Isaac Ford asking about for Thias there already? What was the use of him going as well?

Clardy began to grow more like the Clardy Tyler of youth. He began drinking too much, distracting himself with the illicit pleasures of Natchez-under-the-Hill. He ceased to think much about Thias at all, even stopped wondering why Ford was gone so long. What did any of it matter? All he would allow himself to care about at the moment was finding whatever entertainment and pleasure he could to see him through from morning till night.

Weeks went on like this, summer fading into fall. Isaac Ford still did not return, and Clardy, having grown cynical, concluded that his old partner had abandoned him. He told himself that he did not care. To the devil with Isaac Ford, Thias, all of it. He plunged deeper into his debaucheries, deeper into a lingering despair whose very existence he declined to acknowledge.

He was drinking in one of the worst riverside dives one night when a voice out on the street roused him. Staggering out, he found a crowd gathering around an odd-looking man who wore Indian clothing, moccasins, a tall pipe hat, and a cross around his neck. He was standing on a cask and waving a Bible.

"The end is coming!" he bellowed. "Years away yet, but it comes! Prepare yourself! There are visions being seen, dreams being had, prophecies being made . . . the earth will shake, the rivers will run backward, and the end will come! Prepare!"

Clardy turned away. Another river country babbler, out spinning verbal illusions. Clardy had no desire to become acquainted with any chimeras beyond those generated by the contents of a cheap bottle of whiskey. He went back to his dive and did not see the odd prophet again. But the memory of him lingered. He had made for an odd sight, and his words, though inane in Clardy's view, had been spoken with such force and conviction that they had branded themselves quite effectively into his drunken mind.

In October an event occurred that stirred up lots of talk in Natchez. One Elisha Winters had been robbed while on his way up to Natchez from New Orleans, and had narrowly escaped with his life. He had continued on to Natchez, very shaken, and while there, happened to see the two men who had robbed him. After Winters identified them to the authorities, they were arrested and jailed; their names were James May and John Setton.

Clardy greeted news of May's arrest with the old youthful cynicism that had resurrected within him. He wasn't surprised May had turned out to be criminal; he had felt strong doubts about the fellow when he'd met him. Sometimes it seemed to Clardy that there was no one in the world who was truly decent and respectable. It was all a sham, a veneer. Even Isaac Ford had turned out to be a deserter. Clardy believed that nothing could surprise him anymore.

But he was surprised when some days later he learned that May and Setton had been released by the authorities. The pair had claimed to know the whereabouts of the infamous Mason of the Woods; they bargained for their release on the pledge that, if freed, they would go find and kill Mason, and this time bring in proof of it.

Clardy laughed. What sort of fools governed the law in this territory? May and Setton had duped them, and they were too dense to see it. Had not the governor himself recently sent out federal soldiers to find Mason, all to no avail? Why anyone would believe that two common criminals would do better was beyond Clardy's sardonic comprehension.

Japheth Deerfield was in Natchez-under-the-Hill, having just seen off a client who, through some hard work on Japheth's part, had narrowly escaped conviction on a mayhem charge. He was walking along the waterfront when a gathering crowd caught his attention. The lawyer joined the throng and saw a canoe bearing two men riding into the levee. The man in the prow was grinning broadly and holding up a big ball of bluish clay, tightly packed, and shouting: "See here the head of Mason of the Woods! We've kilt Mason of the Woods!"

Japheth gaped, astonished, when he recognized the man as John Setton, whom he had chanced to see while Setton was imprisoned in Natchez back in October for the Elisha Winters robbery. The other man in the canoe was his companion, James May.

"You're a-lying!" someone challenged. "Break open that ball and show us the head!"

"Not here," Setton replied. "We'll do it before the eyes of the law, and no sooner."

"There stands a lawyer!" someone called, pointing at Japheth, who was immediately grasped by several callused hands and swept through the crowd and up to Setton.

"You're a lawyer?" Setton asked him.

"I am." Japheth sniffed; there was a muffled but pungent stench of decay lingering here. He blanched a little. Indeed there was something of flesh and bone inside that great ball of blue clay. "Did I hear you say, sir, that you have the head of Samuel Mason there?"

"Indeed I do, and we've come to claim our reward." Setton lifted the ball as if to smash it down and break it open.

"Wait!" Japheth said, putting out a hand to stop him. "Not here. Come up to the courthouse with me. Governor Claiborne is in town today."

"The governor!" the red-haired Setton exclaimed. His left eye twitched spasmodically. Japheth was coldly amused. Evidently this man wasn't comfortable with the idea of appearing before such an exalted representative of the law. No surprise there. Setton had the ratty look of a criminal if ever Japheth had seen one, and he had seen plenty.

"Why, we'll gladly see the governor," May interjected. "Come on, John. Let's go get our reward."

"I don't care for governors," Setton said.

"You ain't never even seen a governor, John," May replied. "It's a stroke of good fortune for us. The governor can put the reward right into our hands."

In a great parade led by Japheth, the crowd marched through Natchez-under-the-Hill and up to the finer part of town. Setton now carried the clay ball, May at his side, grinning and joking with all around him.

Clardy emerged from his boardinghouse just as the processional went by. Because of its size, he couldn't make out what the hubbub was about, but out of curiosity he fell in behind.

"What's happening?" he asked a man.

"There's two men come in, claiming they've got the head of Sam Mason in a ball of clay," the man replied. "They're taking it up to the governor to bust it open."

"Who are the men?"

"One's named Setton. The other is James May."

Even in his current jaded condition Clardy had to be impressed. May and Setton had actually done the task they had been freed to do. He could hardly believe it—and wouldn't, until he saw for himself that they really had brought in the head of Samuel Mason. He pushed his way up through the throng, trying to move toward the front and get a look at the pair. All he could see, however, was their backs. He noticed Japheth Deerfield beside them and wondered how he had come to be involved in this.

They reached the courthouse, May and Setton going inside with Japheth. The crowd was restrained from entering by some of the soldiers who were about the place, guarding it because of the governor's presence. Clardy was disappointed; he hadn't gotten a clear look either at the purported clay-covered head or at May and Setton, either. He wished to meet May and see if May remembered him from their earlier ride together into Greenville. Clardy was catching the spirit of the crowd, which was beginning to laud the pair as great heroes for having brought down so vile a scourge as Mason.

The crowd grew while May and Setton were inside; word of what was going on was spreading rapidly through Natchez and new curious folk were joining the throng. Clardy looked about to see if Celinda Deerfield might show up among the newcomers. He did not see her. He hadn't really expected to see her; she did not seem the type to be attracted by such lurid spectacles as this one promised to be.

A few minutes later the courthouse doors opened and May emerged, still holding the ball of clay. Several soldiers accompanied him, and after them came various courthouse officials and magistrates, followed by Japheth Deerfield. Then came a distinguished-looking man Clardy assumed was Governor William Claiborne. Clardy had the impression that someone was missing . . . Setton. Where was the man named Setton?

Clardy had just begun looking for Setton, curious about him, when the door opened a final time and Setton emerged. Clardy took one look at him and was jolted. His throat went dry and he could do nothing but stare in astonishment.

His eyes were still locked on Setton when May broke open the clay ball and revealed the hideous trophy. A loud gasp rose from the crowd, followed by shouts, cheers, babbles of rapid conversation.

"That's Mason! That's him!"

"Mason! They warn't lying, b'jiminy!"

"They've kilt him! They've kilt the scourge hisself!"

Clardy hardly heard the exclamations of recognition of the severed head. The recognition he was experiencing was even more significant and overwhelming. And then the smiling Setton, looking over the crowd, caught sight of Clardy's face, and from the expression that came over him, Clardy knew he had just been recognized in turn.

CHAPTER 36

O n down the street a lone rider entered town and rode toward the nearest inn and around to the stable. He dismounted and led the horse inside. A black stableman approached.

"Put him up for me; give him some grain and rub him down," the horseman instructed. "I'm going into the inn to get myself a room."

"Yes sir."

"What's all that going on at the courthouse?"

"They say there's two men what have brought in the head of Mason of the Woods, sir."

"Is that right? I'll be. Hope it's true." He sounded tired.

He stepped out onto the street a moment and watched the crowd before heading into the inn. He could hear its excited babble from where he was.

The innkeeper met him inside. "May I help you, sir?"

"I'd like a room."

"We do have one available, sir. How long will you be with us?"

"I don't know. Say, is it true what your stable boy said about Samuel Mason having been killed?"

"They're saying it's true. You could go up to the courthouse and find out for yourself, if you want."

"I believe I will."

"How should I list your name on my register, sir?"

"My name is McCracken. Sweeney McCracken."

"McCracken. Yes sir. You are alone?"

McCracken's eyes showed a flash of sadness. "Yes. I am alone."

"Good to have you with us, Mr. McCracken. Have you any luggage?"

"What luggage I had was stole from me north of New Orleans."

"Stole, you say? Merciful heaven! Were you hurt?"

"Not badly." He paused. "But I lost two slaves, both shot down like dogs. And a good friend. He was . . . never mind it. Ain't in the spirit to talk about it right now."

McCracken left the inn and headed down the street, his eye on the crowd. As he drew closer he was stunned to see a man on the courthouse steps holding up what looked like a withering, decaying human head, severed halfway down the neck. It was a revolting but eye-holding sight, and distracted him several moments before he took a closer look at the man who held it. When he did look, he stopped in his tracks, muttering an oath beneath his breath.

He held still as a statue for a couple of moments. Then he noticed and recognized a second man near the one who held the head aloft, and anger boiled up inside him.

"Them men there!" McCracken yelled, startling those close to him and getting the attention of most everyone else in the crowd, and that of the two men on the porch who were the obvious center of all the commotion. "Them men are the very two who robbed me near New Orleans in September! Lay hands on them—don't let them run!"

What followed was fast and, from McCracken's viewpoint, confusing. The man who had been holding up the head saw McCracken, blanched, laid the head down and trotted off the step as if to leave. The other of the pair, a red-haired, small-framed man, followed his partner after glancing first at McCracken, then over at another man on the other side of the crowd, then at McCracken again. He had eyes full of fear. McCracken noticed that the other man who had been sharing the attention of the red-haired man was none other than Clardy

Tyler and Clardy was now pushing his way up toward the front of the crowd. Meanwhile, an important-looking man—the territorial governor himself, McCracken now saw—spoke to a couple of soldiers near him; they leaped down and apprehended the fleeing men in the midst of the sudden hubbub.

McCracken pushed through the crowd but was cut off. Clardy Tyler, on the other hand, had just made it out of the rabble and jumped onto the step. He pointed at the red-haired man, who now wriggled in the grip of a big soldier. "That man there is not named Setton!" he declared loudly. "That man is Wiley Harpe!"

McCracken managed to make it through the crowd, which was now in a great roaring tumult because of what Clardy had just said. Everyone there knew of the infamous murderer Wiley Harpe and his late, vile brother. "Clardy!" McCracken called. "Clardy Tyler! It's me!"

"McCracken? Is that you?"

"Aye, it is. Clardy, I must tell you—"

Nothing could be told just now, though. May and his partner were being hustled back up to the courthouse. Governor Claiborne put out a hand and touched Clardy's shoulder. "Sir, can you prove what you say about this man's identity?"

"*I* can!" someone in the crowd shouted. He emerged and came up before the glowering, fox-haired man. "My name is Bowman. Some years ago I had a row with Wiley Harpe in Knoxville and stabbed him beneath the left breast. Examine him and see the scar for yourself!"

Wiley Harpe cursed and writhed, but it did him no good. Within moments his shirt was torn open, and just as Bowman had said, there was a clearly visible scar.

"They say Little Harpe had two toes growed together like one!" a former Kentuckian in the crowd contributed. An examination of Harpe's foot proved it so.

"I told you it was him," Clardy said.

"You could have believed him right off!" someone from Under-the-Hill bellowed. "He's the Harpe hunter hisself! He was there when Big Harpe's head was cut from his shoulders! Ain't that so, Tyler?"

Clardy looked Wiley in the eye. "It's so. I was there. And Wiley Harpe wasn't. He had run off. Seen to his own safety while leaving his brother to die, and his women to be took captive."

"Go to hell, you son of a whose!" Wiley Harpe said venomously.

"No, that's your journey, soon to commence," Clardy replied. He resisted a strong urge to spit in Harpe's face. He turned to McCracken, took his arm and pulled him aside. "McCracken, you just got back from New Orleans?"

"Aye, Clardy."

"And these men here, Harpe and May, they robbed you? Is that what I heard you say?"

"It is. But it was worse than that, my boy. I grieve to tell you of it. Isaac Ford is dead. They killed him. Shot him like a dog. It was Harpe who done the act. I got Isaac back to New Orleans, nursed him for weeks on end, but he didn't survive. I'm fearsome sorry to tell you. He was a good man."

"Yes," Clardy said. His eyes began to flood. "He was a good man. Best I've ever known. The very best." He held to his composure with great effort, walked back to Wiley Harpe and looked into the weasely face. "I've seen one Harpe die. Now I'll see the second die, too. They'll hang you, Harpe. And when they do, I'll be there to watch you swing. And may heaven have more mercy on you than you've shown to God knows how many others, every one of them better folk than you. Especially the last one—the finest man you ever killed, and the last who'll ever die by your hand. It'll be your turn now. Your turn to die. Your turn to face the judgment."

Wiley grinned slowly, his narrow mouth a mere crack between hollowed cheeks, his teeth yellowed and worn down. "The voices, they're yet a-singing. Singing for *me* this time, and oh, it's the prettiest music!"

Clardy had no idea what the man was speaking of, but it was unnerving, repellent. Suddenly disgusted even to be in the presence of such a loathsome creature, he turned his back and walked off, losing himself in an alley, where he knelt and cried, overwhelmed by the shock of all that had happened, and grieving for a friend who had been very nearly a father and whose face he would see never again.

A hand touched him. He started, turned. It was Japheth Deerfield.

"Mr. Tyler, are you all right?"

"Isaac Ford is dead, murdered by Wiley Harpe," Clardy replied. "McCracken just told me."

"I'm very sorry. I wish I had known him better."

"Please, Mr. Deerfield, just leave me be right now. I am shamed to shed tears before another man."

"I want to invite you to my home," Deerfield said. "You and McCracken, too. I want to extend a hand of friendship to you both at a time I believe you need it."

"I don't believe your wife would want me about, sir," Clardy said. "I happen to know she doesn't like me."

"Nonsense. It's only her manner."

"Thank you, sir, but I won't come. I'll be well enough. All I want right now is some whiskey. All the whiskey I can pour down my throat."

Japheth put out a hand and touched Clardy's arm. "Please, Mr. Tyler, don't do that. Getting drunk will only—"

Clardy jerked away and stumbled off, very overwrought and emotional, and headed toward Natchez-under-the-Hill. The severed head of Samuel Mason, lying on the courthouse step, stared blindly after him as flies buzzed in the hollows of its eyes. Someone kicked it over, unnoticed, and it rolled out onto the street, causing a child to scream and a curious dog to come running over to investigate.

Clardy found his whiskey and drank until he passed out. When he came around, he drank again. Nothing felt like it mattered anymore now that Isaac Ford was dead. He hardly cared even about finding Thias at the moment. And that Wiley Harpe had finally been captured seemed meaningful only to the extent that it would allow him the satisfaction of seeing justice doled out to the man who killed his finest friend.

Three days after that remarkable and jumbled morning when Samuel Mason's head came to Natchez in the prow of Wiley Harpe's canoe, Clardy put aside his whiskey and sobered himself up enough to talk more to McCracken about what had happened to Ford. McCracken's story was simple, and this time told without his usual storyteller's flourish. There was no pleasure to be taken in this tale.

After selling his horses and the flatboat in New Orleans, McCracken and Ford had journeyed in and about the town, partly for pleasure, partly for Ford to see if he liked New Orleans well enough to buy land nearby. He did, and began looking. At last he found property north of town that caught his fancy. He hesitated too long, though, and the land was bought out from under his nose just when he was on the brink of making an offer for it. Disappointed, he stayed in New Orleans even longer so he could look for other property, and also to begin inquiring around about Clardy's brother. McCracken had helped with the latter. Neither quest bore fruit, and in September he and McCracken began the ride back to Natchez, Ford eager to see Clardy again and find out if he had enjoyed any success in his quest. In the region of Bayou Pierre, the same area in which Elisha Winters had been robbed, they were beset upon by the criminals who turned out to be May and Harpe. Ford resisted, and Harpe shot him. May then drew two pistols and dispatched McCracken's slaves, solely out of meanness. McCracken would have been shot, too, had not all the robbers' weapons now been emptied, allowing him time to flee and hide.

When the robbers were gone, McCracken reemerged, found Ford still alive but badly wounded, and managed to catch Ford's horse, which had spooked and strayed after Ford was shot out of the saddle. He carried Ford back to New Orleans and obtained the best medical help he could find for him, but to no avail. Ford had died, his final word being a whisper of his late wife's name.

When Ford was laid to rest, McCracken headed back toward Natchez alone, dreading the prospect of telling Clardy the bad news about his partner. That he had arrived to see the very men who put Ford in his grave standing on the courthouse steps had astonished him—more providence at work, perhaps.

"If there's providence, then I wish it could have provided for Mr. Ford to have lived," Clardy responded bitterly. "I don't know that I believe in providence any more. I had a more sensible notion of what life is back when I was younger: do what you want to do, when you want to, and because you want to, and to hell with everything else."

"Young Clardy, that's the very thinking that moves men like Samuel Mason and Wiley Harpe," McCracken replied. "Don't let grief make you speak foolishness. Don't turn sour and sorry. Don't throw aside all the purpose in your life."

"I ain't. There's one purpose I know I have to fulfill, even if I can't find Thias. I need to see Mr. Ford buried where he wanted. He told me that he wanted to lie in Kentucky, beside his family."

"He's laid now in a sepulcher outside a little chapel on the edge of New Orleans. I saw him laid away there myself."

"Tell me how to find it, then. Write it down for me. Don't

know when I'll be able to do it, but I intend to see him buried where he wanted to be."

Clardy made no effort to follow McCracken's advice about not turning "sour and sorry." After giving a statement to the court at Natchez to verify the identity of Wiley Harpe, he went back to his drinking again, shutting himself off from McCracken and everyone else. Though he didn't consciously think it out to himself, it was his full intention to drink himself to death.

What saved him from doing that was an ironic throwback to his Kentucky days: Wiley Harpe escaped the Natchez jail, May with him. Nobody knew quite how they pulled it off, but when Clardy heard about it, he threw his whiskey bottle against the wall and smashed it, furious. Was there no confinement that the weasely Harpe couldn't find a way out of? He had escaped the Danville jail. Held under his John Setton alias on the boat at Pointe Coupee, he had escaped there, too. Now he had found some way to slip out of captivity yet again.

Clardy had thrown off the mantle of "Harpe hunter" after the death of Micajah Harpe. Now he took it up once more and joined the massive sweep for the escapees. That Wiley Harpe would again escape the justice that was so overdue to him was more than Clardy would stand for.

Clardy was disappointed not to be among those who actually found the escapees, hiding near Greenville, but he was happy they were recaptured. He vowed to McCracken, who also had joined the search, that he would not venture far away until his own eyes saw the dead and swinging form of a hanged Wiley Harpe. Not so for him, McCracken replied. He had seen a hanging once before, and did not care to witness another.

Harpe and May were locked up in the Greenville jail this time, chained and watched closely to ensure there was no chance of another escape. There was a new spirit in the air, an eagerness on the part of law-abiding folk to see an end brought to the law-scoffing devils who had haunted travelers on river and trail for so many years. The worst of them, Micajah Harpe and Samuel Mason, were already dead. Soon, heaven willing, James May and the despised Wiley Harpe would be, too.

1 8 0 4

CHAPTER 37

A grand jury indicted Wiley Harpe and James May near the beginning of January, and almost immediately trials began, leading to quick convictions despite the best wranglings of their lawyers. In February, in a courtroom packed with people, including Clardy, the sentence came down: "On Wednesday the eighth day of the present month, the prisoners will be taken to the place of execution and there hung up by the neck, between the hours of ten o'clock in the forenoon and four in the afternoon, until they are dead, dead, dead."

Clardy was there again when the prisoners were hauled out to a level field near the Boatman's Trail. True to what McCracken had said, he was absent; he had headed back to Nashville. Clardy's feelings were the opposite of McCracken's. He was eager to see this particular execution. He had seen far more of Wiley Harpe's wickedness than had McCracken. Seeing the man finally pay for his crimes would, he hoped, bring a sense of closure in his own mind to one of the ugliest portions of his own experience.

In the hanging field a strong beam had been laid between the forks of two trees, and noosed ropes strung to them. Clardy watched as ladders were leaned against the trees that supported the hanging beam. With much prodding from the authorities in charge of the hanging, both men were forced to climb the ladders. May was in tears; Harpe had a cold, scared look, but showed no strong emotion.

Both men were given the chance to make final statements. May spoke first, weeping and bemoaning his sentence, declaring he was innocent of any crimes worthy of death, admitting that he had been a Mason confederate over past years, but declaring that in killing Mason he had done an act to atone for any wrong he had done. The crowd listened, but sympathy was lacking. Clardy had overheard enough conversations to know why. The prevailing opinion was that even in the act of killing Mason, May had proved the depth of his own treachery. He had worked with Mason, after all, had been his cohort and friend, yet had murdered the man—not out of righteousness or in atonement for his own past crimes, but solely for the sake of the reward on Mason's head.

Harpe spoke next, giving a broad and rambling confession that included the names of various individuals who had secretly aided him, May, and Mason in crimes through the past several years. Clardy detected a rising discomfort in the crowd, some of whose members might have feared their own names would be among those Harpe reeled off. Clardy thought that was a little bit funny until he realized that Harpe might just happen to mention that at one time, none other than "Harpe hunter" Clardy Tyler himself had associated with the Harpe brothers, even agreeing to kill a man named Cale Johnson for them. Never mind that the agreement had been made falsely and under duress; Wiley Harpe was well-situated to create a very harmful false perception about Clardy if he chose to do it.

He didn't, to Clardy's relief. When the final statements were finished, the executions took place very unceremoniously. The ladders that held the men were simply kicked away, and both bodies swung down and out together, making the beam creak. The drop was insufficient to break their necks, so death came slowly and dreadfully, with strangling noises, horrible twitches and convulsions, the voiding of bladders and bowels.

And then they were dead. Clardy stood staring at Wiley Harpe's limp body, thinking back on the fateful ways his life had decussated that of the Harpe brothers, finding it hard to fathom that now it truly was all over. The Harpes were dead, and the world was a cleaner and safer place for it.

Clardy took no part in the ugliness that followed the removal of the bodies from the makeshift gibbet, though he observed it without any feeling of objection. The crowd vented its hatred for the executed men by cutting off their heads and thrusting them down onto poles. These trophies would be displayed along the Boatman's Trail near Greenville, ugly reminders to other such criminals of the fate that often came to those who flaunted the laws of God and man. Clardy believed that if ever any man deserved to have his remains dishonored in such a way, it was Harpe.

Wiley Harpe's corpse did receive one honor his brother's had not: he was buried in a cemetery, along with May. Then even that bit of humane treatment was nullified when the families of other deceased folk buried in that cemetery disinterred their departed relatives and reburied them elsewhere, so that they would not have to lie in the same ground as the piece of human vermin who had been Wiley Harpe.

Clardy returned to Natchez after the execution of Harpe and May, and that night wandered down to the levee to hear the music of a band of some twenty Indians, comprised of members of the Natchez, Choctaw, and Muskogee tribes, who had come into town during his absence to perform for incoming flatboats. A big broad horn from Kentucky had arrived that afternoon, laden with barrels of whiskey, beef, and pork, and the entertainment-hungry crew was putting on as much of a show as the Indians, who performed their strange music on handmade instruments of cane that had been split and cut in various ways. Some of the instruments were played like great flutes, while others were stalks filled with pebbles that were shaken in time with the music. A couple of the Indians sang in their own language—altering their voices to make an eerie but pleasant sound that Clardy thought was intriguing and soothing.

The newly arrived flatboatmen certainly didn't seem soothed, however. They danced like drunkards at a log-rolling, turning and reeling, whooping, and singing along so loudly that often the music of the Indians was all but drowned out.

Another person danced nearby, too. Clardy watched her closely. She was an elderly woman he had often seen along the riverfront. He didn't know her name. He had often noted her sad eyes and the weary expression always on her lined face. This was a woman who had lived a hard life and had been ill-used; he could read that clearly in her bearing and looks. Clardy had always felt sympathetic toward her, but never had he spoken to her.

Tonight she didn't look so unhappy. She danced fluidly, in a state that was nearly trancelike, as if she had just gone through some mystical experience, but which Clardy knew was more likely the result of drunkenness. He was in a philosophical mood that evening, and pondered how this old woman was a kind of living symbol of thousands of wasted, struggling lives lived out along the great river. Who was she? Where had she come from? What dreams had once stirred her in childhood, only to fade away? Would he himself wind up as sad and lonely as she? He certainly felt very alone tonight, missing Isaac Ford, missing Thias, even missing his long-gone old grandfather and the life he had so failed to appreciate back on Beaver Creek.

Clardy had no intention of approaching the dancing old woman, but when one of the drunken flatboatman, doing a wild, high-kicking improvised reel, happened to bump into her very hard and knock her down, he went forward impulsively to help pick her up.

"Ma'am, let me help you," he said, reaching down to take her arm.

She rose, looking at him with a surprised, pleased expression. She smiled then, revealing gums mostly toothless. "Thank you, young man," she said. "You are a gentleman."

Clardy wondered how long it had been since any man had done an act of kindness for this woman. It was a sad thought. "Are you hurt?" he asked.

"No, no. I don't think so."

He touched his hat and told her good evening, then turned away.

"Sir," she said, "are you the man who was the Harpe hunter?"

He was surprised by the question. Though during his time in Natchez he had come to be fairly well known along the riverfront, he hadn't expected that such a lost old woman would have even noticed his existence, much less learned who he was. "Some have called me that. My name is Clardy Tyler."

"You have been looking for James Hiram? You believe he is your brother?"

Clardy was surprised anew. "You seem to have heard a right smart lot about me."

"Yes. It is true?"

"About James Hiram? Yes, ma'am. I am looking for him."

Abruptly she reached out and touched his face. He was startled, and experienced a feeling of vague repulsion at the thought that she was about to try and seduce him for money. Probably she had sold herself to men many a time, maybe still did. "You are such a fine-looking young man, and so kind," she said. "I'll repay your kindness by—"

"Ma'am, please . . ."

"By helping you find your brother."

Clardy wished he hadn't encountered this old woman. Her, help him find Thias? It was absurd.

"Ma'am, I don't know how you could help."

"I can. I can take you to someone who knows where James Hiram is."

That hit Clardy like a jolt. "I beg your pardon?"

"I have a friend, a young man like yourself. He knows where James Hiram is. Since you have been a gentleman to me, I'll take you to him and he will tell you."

Clardy hardly dared hope it was true. "Ma'am, if you could do that, I would be beholden to you more than you can know."

"Come with me," she said. "I'll take you to him now."

"Who are you, ma'am?"

She threw back her chin and spoke in a voice of pride worthy of a monarch. "My name is Mrs. Sullivan. Mrs. Beatrice Fine Sullivan. Now come with me, Mr. Tyler, and meet the man who can help you."

She told him her story as they walked together through the darkness, and it made him both sad for her and less hopeful that she would really be able to give him the help she had promised. She was waiting for the return of Mr. Sullivan from New Orleans, she said. He left her in Natchez while he made a journey to New Orleans, but promised he would return, and "Mr. Sullivan is a man who can be trusted, a man of substance and importance." Clardy asked her how long she had been waiting. Ten years, she replied.

Ten years. Clardy felt a deep pity for her. Abandoned for ten years, yet she still clung to the promised return of a man who probably was either now dead or had forgotten her altogether.

This woman would die here, lost in her liquor and her absurd hope, clinging to a promise that was as worthless as a continental dollar.

She took him to a ramshackle boardinghouse and up a rickety flight of exterior stairs. At the top she rapped gently on an unpainted, warped pine door. "Timothy? Are you awake?"

Clardy heard movement inside, then the sound of a latch being opened. "Mrs. Sullivan? Is that you?"

"Yes, my boy. It's me. I've brought a friend to see you."

Silence for a moment, and no more movement of the latch. "Who is it?"

"A gentleman. He won't hurt you, Timothy. He is a kind young man, and you know his brother, we believe."

The door opened slowly and a pale, dirty face looked out. Clardy smiled and nodded, not showing his shock at the looks of the young man at the door, who even by the standards of Natchez-under-the-Hill looked bedraggled and wasted. "Thias!" the young man exclaimed. "The very image of Thias Tyler, you are!"

Clardy's heart began thumping loudly. "Thias is my brother."

"Brother . . . then you are—what was that name he said? Clardy! You are Clardy Tyler!"

"Yes! Yes I am! You know Thias?"

"Aye, I know him. Come in." Suddenly he froze; his eyes narrowed. "You ain't going to hurt me, are you? You ain't going to take me back to *them*?"

"No, no. I won't hurt you. I won't take you to anyone. All I want is to find my brother."

Timothy let them in. Clardy had to fight against the impulse to hold his nose. The room stank of sweat and filth, worse even than the Harpe cabin back on Beaver Creek.

At Timothy's gestured invitation, Clardy sat down on a barrel that served as a chair. The only real chair in the room, a battered imitation of a Hepplewhite, became Mrs. Sullivan's perch, and she sat in it in regal style, looking haughty despite her humble and ragged mode of dress. For the first time, Clardy noticed that the tatters she wore had at one time been good garments. Probably she had worn these same clothes since her husband abandoned her.

"You promise me you won't take me to them?" Timothy asked again.

"I don't even know who 'them' are," Clardy replied.

"Soldiers! Who else would you think?" Timothy said it very angrily, his face twisting suddenly in fury.

Clardy realized he was dealing with an unstable man. He would have to choose his words carefully.

"I should have known who you meant," he said softly. "No, sir, I won't take you to the soldiers. You have my vow."

Timothy nodded. His anger vanished and he sat down on a side of a sagging, stinking rope-slat bed. "Good. I'm mighty afraid of them. They do hard things to folks who don't please them."

"Timothy hides here from soldiers," Mrs. Sullivan said. "He was once beaten by soldiers when he was younger, and his father was shot as a deserter."

Clardy could not restrain himself from asking the burning question. "Sir, where is my brother?"

"In prison."

"What?"

"He is imprisoned. He and Willie Jones, both of them."

Clardy asked, "Who is Willie Jones?"

"Willie Jones is Willie Jones. What kind of fool question is that?" He seemed angry again.

"I'm sorry. I'm just eager to know all I can, so I can find my brother. Where is he imprisoned?"

"New Orleans."

"Why?"

"We stole gold. From a Spanish church. Crosses and such."

"Thias stole gold from a church?"

"Yes. We all did. Stole it together. They caught Willie and Thias. Except he don't call himself Thias now. He goes by James Hiram."

And there he had it: firsthand confirmation that James Hiram was indeed his brother. Despite the horror of learning of his brother's imprisonment, he was filled with relief to at last truly know what before had been only strong suspicion. "How long ago was James put in prison?" he asked.

"More than a year. It's hard to remember."

Mrs. Sullivan said, "Timothy came here after he escaped them. Now he never leaves our room. I care for him and bring him food. I think of him as my son. He is very kind to me."

"I see." Clardy was pulsing with excitement he dared not show out of fear it might set off some other angry reaction on Timothy's part. "Timothy—may I call you by your name?

Thank you—could you tell me exactly where I could find Thias? What prison he is in?"

"I don't know the name of it. I was gone before they were put away."

"Yes, of course. Timothy, have you known I was in Natchez, looking for my brother?"

"Known it for a little while. I seen you once out my window. I thought you was Thias. You look so much like him. But no scar. You got no scar."

"We've been took for each other many a time."

"Mrs. Sullivan, she told me you weren't him. She said you were Tyler, the Harpe hunter, and that you were asking people about James Hiram. I told her, '*I* know where James Hiram is! And I know his true name!' "

"That is how I knew I could help you, Mr. Tyler," Mrs. Sullivan contributed proudly.

"I'm grateful," Clardy said. He stood and put out his hand toward Timothy. Timothy did not take it; he looked at Clardy with fear, like he was being threatened. Clardy lowered his hand.

Timothy looked at Mrs. Sullivan. "Did you bring me food?"

"I have nothing at the moment, Timothy. But I believe that tonight Mr. Sullivan may return, and if so, he will bring many good things for us to eat."

Timothy balled up his fist and pounded the wall. "I'm hungry! Curse you, hag, I want food!"

Clardy stood quickly. "I can bring you food," he said. "I'd be pleased to."

Mrs. Sullivan's brows arched. "Mr. Tyler, we do not accept charity, Timothy and I!"

"It won't be charity. You can repay me for it later . . . when Mr. Sullivan comes back."

She smiled and nodded. "Very well, sir. I will do that."

Clardy left, bought bread and meat, vegetables, whiskey. As an afterthought he purchased flour, sugar, cornmeal. With all of it laden in a box, he carried it back up to the little room and knocked on the door. Timothy opened it and snatched the box from Clardy's hands without a word. Before he slammed the door shut, Clardy saw Mrs. Sullivan lying on the bed, still fully dressed, snoring loudly.

Clardy turned away from the closed door and descended the stairs, feeling both pity and great gratitude for the two rejected human beings he had met tonight. He hoped that Timothy's information, limited as it was, would prove true. He had chased so many false clues that he was afraid to be too hopeful.

But he did hope. Timothy had known things he couldn't have if he hadn't really been with Thias.

The door opened behind him as he began to descend. Timothy's wan face, looking belligerent, appeared again. "Give me money, too," he said. "I give you help, and you can pay me for it."

Clardy brought out a couple of old continental dollars and handed them to Timothy. He took them, inspected them closely in a way that suggested his eyes were weak, grunted, and accepted them. The door slammed again. Clardy sighed and shook his head. It was astonishing how much like an animal a man could become.

Clardy went down to the street. He knew what he had to do now: reach New Orleans as quickly as possible, find Thias's place of confinement, and do whatever was necessary to get him out.

He had no idea what that would involve or how he would go about it. It could be complicated, trying to get a man out of prison. He would need help and legal expertise—and he knew just the man to provide it. So despite the late hour and the fact he would probably receive a cold reception from a certain lady he would encounter at his destination, Clardy loped through Natchez-under-the-Hill and up toward the finer portion of town and the home of Japheth Deerfield.

Three days later

Celinda Deerfield put on her finest smile as she said the final good-bye to her New Orleans–bound husband. She had known for months that he would be making this journey, and had not looked forward to his absence. Now, thanks to Clardy Tyler, her vaguely negative feelings about the journey had progressed to the point of full dread. When Tyler had shown up at the Deerfield doorstep well after midnight, breathlessly eager to tell her husband of a new and significant clue about the whereabouts of his brother, he had chanced to arrive right on the threshold of Japheth's own long-planned New Orleans voyage. And Japheth, of course, not only invited him to come along, but offered him his legal help as well. Cclinda was highly displeased. When her husband was out of earshot, Clardy apologized to her for breaking his pledge to involve her husband no further in his affairs. "I felt I had to do it," he explained. "Your husband is the best man I know to give me the aid I'll have to have to get my brother free."

She had not argued, knowing it would be pointless. Just as it would be pointless now to show her displeasure over this situation to Japheth. He already knew of her instinctive disaffection for Tyler; nothing would be gained by voicing the same to him all over again. Japheth was a man with a mind that was as logical as it was enthusiastic, and he gave little credence to a mere feeling, which was all her negativity toward Clardy Tyler amounted to. Celinda could give no good, logical reasons for her notion that Tyler was somehow going to bring harm to Japheth, and thus Japheth considered her feeling irrational and not worthy of heed. Celinda, having a logical bent herself, knew he was right—and therein lay her greatest frustration, because irrational though it might be, she still didn't like the idea of Clardy Tyler entwining his business with her husband's. She still couldn't shake off her feeling that ill would come of it all—particularly if her husband followed a certain other trait he had, of letting his ingrained enthusiasm override his common sense. Life with Japheth Deerfield had taught Celinda that a logical mind didn't necessarily equal a sensible one.

Frustrations and doubts notwithstanding, she smiled, adjusted Japheth's cravat, and give him a firm hug and kiss. "I'll miss you," she said. "Come back as quickly as you can."

"So I will. Don't worry about me, dear. It's a simple business I have to attend to, and it shouldn't occupy me long."

Celinda said, "It's not your business that I'm concerned about."

"Ah, Mr. Tyler again, is it? Don't worry about that, either. If his brother is in prison there, it should take only a brief time to find him . . . though his use of the James Hiram alias could complicate the matter just a mite. But I'm very optimistic that we'll be able to obtain his freedom, now that the big territorial transaction is complete."

The transaction to which he referred was the recent purchase by the United States of the massive Louisiana Territory. All through the prior year, the machinations of intergovernmental diplomacy, wheedling, threats, and intrigue had been churning away full-force, culminating in the official transfer of the massive territory near the end of December, at a cost of about fifteen million dollars. In New Orleans shortly before Christmas, Mississippi territorial governor William Claiborne and Army commander in chief James Wilkinson had gone through transfer-of-control ceremonies, bringing a vast new region into the domain of the United States, almost doubling the nation's size.

Japheth went on: "I'm hopeful that we'll be able to find Thias Tyler safe and sound, at which point I'll petition the governor for his release on Clardy Tyler's behalf. Given the change of governmental authority and the fact that he will have served a year or so of imprisonment already, I'm near certain I can obtain his freedom."

And then what? Celinda felt like asking the question but did not. Like her bad intuitions about Clardy Tyler, it had all been voiced before. What would Japheth do? Would he seek to have Thias Tyler tried and punished for the crimes he had committed in the Mississippi Territory, one of those being against Japheth himself? Or would his seemingly blind fondness for Clardy Tyler and tremendous personal and professional intrigue with his quest cause him to leave Thias Tyler untouched by the forces of the law he had scorned? Would that be right, professionally, ethically, personally? Had Japheth considered that obtaining the freedom of a known highway bandit might not be in the best interest of the public? As far as Celinda was concerned, a New Orleans prison was a perfectly suitable place for the man who had robbed her husband at gunpoint. Celinda was honestly concerned that this time her husband might do something he would regret.

She helped Japheth on with his coat. "Just how did Mr. Tyler hear this rumor that his brother is in jail?" The night Clardy had shown up at their door to share the news, she was too disgusted to linger and hear the story from him.

"Some poor lost soul down under the hill told him," Japheth replied. "A nervous kind of fellow named Timothy, who hides out in his room out of some inane fear of soldiers."

"And he trusts the word of someone like that?"

"Well, this fellow seemed to know details he wouldn't had he not been associated with Thias Tyler. He was apparently involved in the same crime and was almost captured along with Thias Tyler." Japheth paused and chuckled. "Funny thing, in a way—this Timothy fellow, who seems a bit touched in the mind, according to Mr. Tyler, is living with an old woman who has delusions of her own. Some sad old hag named Sullivan, waiting in ragged old clothes for the return of a husband who abandoned her here a decade ago. Mrs. Beatrice Sullivan. Quite a pitiful story, isn't it?" No answer. "Celinda? Is something wrong?"

"No," she said. "Of course not."

But later, after Japheth had met Clardy at the levee, boarding a New Orleans–bound boat and set off, Celinda held her daughter and thought about Beatrice Sullivan. Japheth hadn't had any idea that the "sad old hag" he was talking about was the sister of Celinda's old protector Queen Fine. Having her brought up in such an unexpected and unknowing way had given Celinda an odd jolt.

It reminded her of something she had tucked out of the way deep in her mind for a long time now: a lingering sense of having failed Queen by having ignored her sister. Celinda had turned away from Beatrice Sullivan, never telling her that she had known Queen, never having offered to bolster her situation, justifying this negligence to herself with the idea that learning of Queen's death would only bring more sadness to an already sad life. Celinda knew that was an excuse, especially now that she had a settled life and enough material means to make a real difference in the woman's life. It could be done secretly, if she chose. It could be done openly, but without telling Beatrice Sullivan of Queen's tragic fate. There was nothing Celinda could do for Queen now, but she could do something for her sister.

Celinda sang to her daughter, but her mind was busy. It wasn't too late for her to make up for her failure. She decided that in memory of Queen Fine, she would find some way to improve the desolate situation of Beatrice Sullivan. It was her duty, and she would no longer shirk it.

Tomorrow, she decided. With Japheth out of town she would not have to sneak about to do it. She would go find Beatrice Sullivan, maybe take her a gift or some money. Exactly how she would go about it and how much about herself she would tell Mrs. Sullivan was something she could decide later.

The decision made her feel better. She hugged Beulahland close and sang gentle words into her ear.

CHAPTER 38

Celinda's noble intentions, born in the unstable emotional atmosphere of separation from her husband, withered in the brightness of the next morning's sunshine. The idea of going to Natchez-under-the-Hill and dropping the manna of benevolence on Queen's sister didn't seem very appealing now that the time to do it had come. It was easy for Celinda to find a dozen reasons not to follow through, chief among them that it would be irresponsible to take little Beulahland into such a slovenly and dangerous area of town. Beatrice Sullivan's welfare would simply have to wait.

But with the evening came a revival of moral impulse. It had been that way with her since girlhood: the daylight turning weighty concerns as moral duties into nearly invisible, easily overlooked phantoms; the darkness giving those phantoms weight and solidity again, and putting somber and reproving expressions on them besides. She tucked her baby into bed and idly picked up a copy of the Bible as her thoughts drifted down to the Under-the-Hill section of town and the sad old woman who surely was there even now. When her eye chanced to fall on a verse in Deuteronomy: ". . . thou shalt open thine hand wide unto thy brother, to thy poor, and to thy needy, in thy

land," she promptly put the Bible aside and wished she had
picked something to read that said nothing about charity to the
downtrodden. By now she wasn't in the mood to read at all,
and went to bed early, thinking to herself that tomorrow she
would leave Beulahland with Mrs. Mulhaney down the street
and go see if she could find Beatrice Fine Sullivan. She would
take her some of the money she had saved up out of the allow-
ance Japheth provided her, and tell her that she'd once she met
her sister, Queen, and now wanted to help her in Queen's memory . . . no, in her honor. Beatrice Sullivan need not even know
her sister was dead. That would only add more sadness to a life
surely sad already.

The next day, Celinda fought away another bout of hesitance
and went ahead with her plan. She pretended to be pleased
when Mrs. Mulhaney accepted her request to watch Beulahland. Secretly she had hoped Mrs. Mulhaney would be too
busy, relieving her of her self-imposed mission without the
price of guilt.

But with her daughter in safe keeping, there was no reason
not to go ahead. Celinda descended to Natchez-under-the-Hill
as an increasingly bad case of nerves plagued her. This was a
world she had grown accustomed to pretending did not exist.
The ramshackle structures of the section seemed ugly and foreboding, their windows like peering eyes. Celinda felt the years
fall away from her as she moved farther down, further in, and
soon she felt not like the adult she was, but the girl she had
been when she was thrown into the vile world of river pirates
and confidence men. It had felt just this way that first time she
came to Natchez-under-the-Hill. She began to struggle against
the desire to flee back the way she'd come, and wondered if
she looked as frightened as she felt.

*At least I've come by morning. The light is bright and the
street is as safe as it ever is, and the worst folk here are still
sleeping. Maybe Beatrice Sullivan is sleeping, too. Maybe I
shouldn't disturb her. Maybe I should just leave, and tell
Japheth about what I want to do when he gets back. He can
come with me, and maybe help her more than I can alone. . . .*

"Morning, missy."

The voice startled her. She turned and saw a man so dingy
in skin tone and dress that he blended almost invisibly into the
equally dingy alleyway in which he stood leaning against a
wall. He grinned at her reaction.

"I skeered you."

"Sir, well . . . yes."

"Am I skeery to look at?"

"I just didn't realize you were there."

"You're a fine-looking woman. Finer looking than most that come down under the hill." His grin disturbed her.

"I'm looking for someone . . . a relative of a friend."

"That right? Who?"

"Beatrice Sullivan."

He rolled his eyes. "That crazy old harlot? What would you want with her?"

Celinda was beginning to grow offended; it was no business of this man what she wanted with Beatrice. But she was afraid to let her feelings show, in case he grew offended in turn. She wouldn't want this kind of man angry at her.

What's wrong with you? The chiding voice was her own, speaking inside her head. *Have you become soft and weak? There was a time when you held your own very well among people far worse than this man.*

"My business with Mrs. Sullivan is my own," she said.

"Well well! There's some spirit in this filly!"

She had wasted enough moments with this fool. "Good day to you, sir." She turned away.

"Hey, you're going the wrong way."

"What?"

"Beatrice Sullivan lives up yonder direction." He pointed. "Upstairs room, last building on the end. But you'd best not go there."

"I'll go where I please, sir. I'll have you know that my husband is . . ." *My husband. Do I hide behind him now? Can I no longer speak for myself?* She cut off. No need to say more.

"Ma'am, I believe I've made you mad. Didn't mean to."

"I prefer not to talk at length to strangers."

"We could get better acquainted. I wouldn't be no stranger then." He winked.

She turned and put her chin in the air, thinking what a low specimen of humanity this man was and what a shame it was that Natchez had to take in so many like him. People with filthy persons and no class or culture. People who sometimes seemed more akin to the animal world than the human, people like . . .

Like a beaten-down, mistreated, kidnapped Kentucky moun-

tain girl with her hair chopped short, her dress exchanged for a man's garments, and her virtue left unsullied only by the sheer grace of God. Once again the chiding voice, rising within. She was shaken by it. *I've forgotten who I am, and what I am. I've become soft and settled, all painted up and decorated like the mansions of this town, so much that I've forgotten what it was to be anything else.*

In the midst of this thought she had halted, and the man who was talking to her—toying with her, it seemed to her—seemingly perceived that as evidence that he was making a successful advance. He grinned more broadly and stepped toward her. She turned and saw him give her another wink.

"Sir, if you come a step closer, I'll use the point of my shoe to put you at a great personal disadvantage," Celinda said.

He mugged an exaggerated expression of fear, but did not come closer. "I don't believe you're the kind to be played with," he said.

"Indeed not. Good day to you, sir." She walked away, keeping her chin raised.

"You'll regret it if you go call on Beatrice Sullivan!" he called after her.

"I have no fear of a sad old woman," Celinda replied.

"It ain't the woman you need be fearing," he replied.

Celinda wondered what that meant, but would not condescend to ask for an explanation and give him the satisfaction of her continued attention. She began to wish she had concealed her pistol somewhere on her person.

She went on down the street and found the indicated building. It was crumbling, roughly built, the ugliest structure in a row of ugly structures. The rickety flight of stairs leading up its side was most uninviting, and she wondered if she had the will to go through with this. She was about to turn and walk away when she reminded herself that to do so would be to suffer again the pangs of conscience when night came. To fail to do something for Queen's beloved sister would be to fail herself, and worse, to fail and dishonor Queen. Steeling herself, she breathed a quiet prayer of petition, climbed the stairs and rapped on the door.

It took a long time to get a response. At last a voice—a man's voice, to her surprise—filtered out through the door. "Who's there?"

"I'm . . . my name is Mrs. Deerfield. I'm looking for Mrs. Beatrice Sullivan."

A pause. "You're alone?"

"Yes . . ." *Should I have said that?* She felt very uncomfortable.

"You ain't come to bring trouble here, have you?"

"No. I want to see Mrs. Sullivan, maybe be a help to her, if I can. Am I at the right place?"

"Aye." The door began to open, and a wan, sickly looking young man glared out of the shadows at her. She fancied that she caught the flicker of a smile on the corners of his pale lips. "Well . . . look at this!" he said. "Fine woman from above the bluff, come down to see the low folk!"

She did not like this man. She feared him. But her encounter with the forward fellow minutes earlier had roused in her a fierce determination not to be put off by anyone. *No one of this ilk will ever have the advantage over me again. I'll never again yield my will to that of wicked men. I'll allow no man to make me feel the way Jim Horton made me feel all those years ago. I will be strong, like my father told me to be.* "May I see Mrs. Sullivan?"

He nodded, his grin now apparent. "Come on in, Mrs. Deerfield."

The stench of the place was appalling. The walls seemed to tighten around her as soon as she was inside. The window was shaded with a blanket nailed across it; the air was close and stifling. The man closed the door behind her after she was inside.

"Where is Mrs. Sullivan?"

"What do you want with her?"

"That's a private matter, sir."

"Well, maybe I need to know before I let you see her. Don't want no harm coming to that dear old thing, you know."

"Believe me, I intend only good for her."

"Well, whatever you intend, she ain't here right at the moment. But I'm Timothy, and *I'm* here, Mrs. Deerfield." He said her name with an enunciation that sounded obscurely mocking, then stepped toward her and wiped the back of his hand over his mouth.

"But you said before that she was here!"

"I said no such thing. All I said was this was the place she lives. All I said was come in. And you did come in. Yes, you did. Walked in like the prettiest angel . . ." He drew closer; she backed away. "Look at that hair," he said, more to himself than to her. "Look at all that pretty hair. . . ."

"You stay away from me! I'm leaving."

"Oh, no. No. No ma'am, you ain't. Not just yet you ain't." He reached out and grabbed the comb out of her hair. It fell out, long and lustrous, across her shoulders. His eyes flashed as if with fire. "Sweet Mary! All that pretty hair . . ."

She reacted by instinct, not by plan. With a shout she shoved him back, knocking him to the floor. He fell on his rump with a grunt. Celinda grabbed the latch of the door and yanked at it, but she was panicked. Her fingers fumbled and the door did not open. He was up and on her in a moment, grasping at her shoulders, pulling her back. She screamed. He was tearing at her dress, pressing his face against her neck, cursing at her in one breath and babbling about the beauty of her hair the next.

Suddenly she was no longer Celinda Deerfield the woman but Celinda Ames the girl, and this stranger was in her eyes Jim Horton. Every detail of that terrible moment he had attacked her came back in vivid clarity. "No! Oh, God—get off me! No!" She struggled, writhed, tried to scratch and hit, but it went on and on. It was foul, intolerable, incomprehensible. She felt weak, faint . . .

No! She would not weaken. Could not, or else . . .

She was on the floor, with him at the moment clinging to her back, trying to pin her down with his meager weight. From somewhere she found the strength to roll over despite him. Her elbow pressed against his ribs; she brought it up and down again with force. He grunted, his breath a stinking expulsion, fetid like old cheese. She yanked her left hand free and clawed awkwardly but accurately at his face. He yelled and swore. She clawed some more, hit him again with her elbow, then pushed up and to the side and broke away from him.

He was fast, though, and was up almost as quickly. Celinda tried to run toward the door, but he tripped her. She fell against a crate being utilized as a shelf for fly-covered, rotting food. Something clattered out onto the floor. A knife, coated with a crust of whatever foodstuff it had last sliced. Her hand closed over it. She came to her feet, turned to face him as he came upon her, slashed instinctively with the blade—

In the next moment he was staggering backward, bleeding from the belly, his hands groping at a fresh, deep puncture wound. The knife was still in her hand. Looking at it, she saw it was coated with blood. He had run himself right into the blade, which she had not even realized had been turned out toward him. He grew even more pale, blubbered and sank to his knees. He cursed her, reached a bloodied hand toward her, and fell onto his face.

He was still writhing and moaning and cursing when she reached the door. It opened for her this time, and she ran out onto the landing so hard she struck the railing and fell over it. For a second she was suspended in air, the knife still in her hand, and then she struck the ground. The breath was driven out of her and the world grew hazy and darkened. For several seconds she lay stunned, and then her breath came back with a painful heave.

She came around slowly, then stood. She still had the knife. Shuddering, she tossed it away, into some nearby bushes. She was filthy, her dress torn, her heart hammering. She became sick and heaved her stomach empty. Then, with her head spinning, she stumbled off around the rear of the building, and with hardly any awareness of what she was doing, began making her way through alleys and around the ugly backsides of the shanties and rough edifices of Natchez-under-the-Hill, heading along a meandering and hidden route back to her home.

By the time she was out of Natchez-under-the-Hill, Celinda's mind had cleared enough to allow her to realize that she had best avoid being seen in her current tattered state. She had just killed a man—she was sure he must be dead—and though it had been an accident, all she could think of was that she would be considered a murderer. No one must know. No one must see her.

With the greatest of difficulty she managed to reach her house without being seen, as best she could tell. She entered and stripped off her torn and dirtied clothing, which she immediately burned in the fireplace, poking it and making sure not a trace remained. Then she washed, combed out her hair, and dressed again, her fingers trembling at the clasps. Knowing she must calm herself, she went to Japheth's liquor cabinet and tried to pour herself a glass of wine, but her trembling was so bad that she dropped the bottle and shattered the glass. At that point she collapsed into tears and sank into a chair, where she wept for nearly an hour.

After that she was relatively sedate again, and her mind began to evaluatively thread its way through her situation. The option of reporting what happened was far too frightening to consider; it seemed to her the most important matter in the world to keep all of this a secret, particularly from her husband. What a fool she had been to undertake her intended mission of mercy to Beatrice Sullivan, for no reason other than that she was Queen's sister! At this moment Celinda hated Beatrice Sullivan, maybe even hated Queen herself. And Clardy Tyler. It was *his* fault more than anyone else's. Had he not come to Natchez, had he not involved her husband in the quest for a missing brother, had he never come into contact with Beatrice Sullivan, then she would not have been reminded of the "duty" she'd perceived but long neglected. She would not have gone today to Natchez-under-the-Hill and involved herself in the death of the foul creature named Timothy.

Celinda cleaned up the spilled wine, poured herself a new glass and drank it, followed by another. She evaluated her circumstances and what must be done to cover the fact that she had ventured below the hill today. She hadn't told Mrs. Mulhaney what her mission was when she took Beulahland to her. She could concoct an alibi to cover the matter on that score. She had reached Natchez-under-the-Hill at a time when the street was relatively free of traffic, and hadn't seen anyone there she had recognized. And probably no one there had recognized her.

She remembered the man in the alley, whose warning she now dearly wished she had heeded. Who was he? Would he speak to the law when he learned of the death of Timothy? She wished she hadn't told that man that she had been going to Beatrice Sullivan's residence. Before long, surely, it would be known through all Natchez that a stabbed man had been found dead in that very place. The man she had spoken with would hear the news, remember the woman who had asked him about Beatrice Sullivan, and go to the law. . . .

She began to feel panicked again, and sat down. Drawing in a deep breath, she told herself that such events might never happen. The man had obviously been no saint, and the fact that he was a Natchez-under-the-Hill denizen alone showed that he probably was not a citizen of caliber. Probably he was one of the endless stream of transients who passed through the riverfront district. He might leave before word of Timothy's death leaked out.

But if he was a transient, she thought, how would he have known where so obscure a person as Beatrice Sullivan lived, and that another person shared her quarters? Obviously he had known of Timothy. It had to have been Timothy the man had in mind when he gave her that vague warning that it wasn't Beatrice Sullivan she should be fearful of in that upstairs room.

Celinda wept again, believing she was lost. The shadows would gather around her, darker and darker, and then the truth would become known and the hand of the law would close around her. She would be labeled a murderess. Her life with her husband and her beloved child would end. . . .

I must find that man. I must give him money to keep silence. Otherwise he'll be the death of me.

She shook off that desperate idea. It would be the worst thing possible to do. To offer money for silence would seem an admission of guilt.

She could find no good options. The only hope she could muster lay in an adage she had often heard her father state: The thing you waste time worrying about most is the very thing that won't happen. She hoped that was true. Maybe if she just held silence and kept her tracks covered as best she could, all this would simply fade away. The death of Timothy would be put down as just one more unsolvable criminal mystery out of a district rife with such things.

She lay down and made herself rest another hour, then left the house and went to gather up Beulahland at the Mulhaney residence. Yes, she told Mrs. Mulhaney, this is a different dress than what I was wearing this morning. The other was accidentally soiled and I changed before coming here. Yes, my business was taken care of nicely. But don't breathe a word to anyone about my being gone today. I'm preparing a surprise for my husband—his birthday is coming up soon—and I don't want any hints to give it away. Yes, that is nice, isn't it? Thank you, Mrs. Mulhaney.

She went back home with Beulahland and promptly poured and drank two more glasses of wine, praying all the while that not all terrible things that happen in secret must ultimately find their way into the light of day.

CHAPTER 39

It was an old city already, with a wider mix of cultures even than Natchez. Clardy found New Orleans an astonishing place, full of beauty and promise everywhere he looked. Especially promise—that of finding his brother after almost six years. Yet even this remarkable city had its dark and ugly aspect. There was an underside here, as in Natchez—as in every city, Clardy had come to believe. In every conglomerate citizenry there were those certain avenues, that certain breed of people, that stratum of life lived in the shadows.

Told by Japheth to make no private inquiries about Thias without his legal guidance, Clardy had to be patient for a time after reaching New Orleans. Japheth's business dealings had to be handled promptly and therefore took priority. Clardy was left to content himself with walking about the city, looking at its fine French and Spanish structures, hearing the unusual accents, smelling the enticing, spicy aromas of the foods cooked in the streetside cafés and sold by vendors who seemed to be everywhere. Clardy was not surprised that Isaac Ford, God rest him, had found New Orleans sufficiently appealing to make him try to buy land. Certainly this was a radically different world than Kentucky and Tennessee. Such was what Ford had needed, a place where he could have forgotten, maybe, the hauntings of a much-beloved family stolen from him by disease.

Dulciana. Clardy still thought of her from time to time. What a lovely young woman she had been! Different by far than the jezebels he had cavorted with during his wild, more youthful days. He might have married the girl if her life hadn't been cut short. There had been no time for a true romance to blossom between them, but it could have happened. *Would* have. Clardy knew it.

Since Dulciana's death he had not really found anyone else who intrigued him in any serious way. There had been a couple of young women in Nashville—pleasant company, interesting persons, but with so obvious an eye toward marriage that they had scared him off. So here he was, in his mid-twenties, no longer a boy, but a man old enough to have a houseful of children . . . and he had not even a wife. He had friends who had married at sixteen, seventeen years of age. Would he never settle down? He didn't seem any closer to it than in his revelfilled days of living on Beaver Creek and boyishly looking forward to a life of glorious, romantic criminality.

Following the directions McCracken had given him, Clardy cast about until he found Isaac Ford's resting place. Ford was laid away in a tiny, plain, poorly kept cemetery, in a plain sepulcher upon which his name was crudely inscribed. Not forever will you lie here, Clardy vowed to his departed friend. You wanted to be buried beside your loved ones, and I'll see that done, as soon as I can. I'll lay you to rest in Kentucky, right beside your dear Amy.

After his respects were paid, Clardy wandered down to the levee, where all the aspects of life that made New Orleans the distinctive place it was displayed themselves most vividly. All about the levee stood market stands with tables filled with all kinds of wares and produce and overseen by a population of highly diverse and fascinating merchants numbering into the hundreds. Each competed with the others for the attention of buyers by vocal means, some yelling wildly like boisterous mountaineers, some singing, many giving a droning, wellpracticed salesman's patter in a mix of dialects that combined into a cacophanous human symphony. They hawked every kind of imaginable goods: Oysters, wild ducks—some caged live, some killed, plucked, and dressed—potatoes, corn, carrots, eggs, cutlery, tinware, carrots, fish, beef, pork, oranges, bananas, sugarcane. . . . A man could find most anything he could want without ever leaving the New Orleans levee markets.

Clardy stood amid the hubbub and mostly watched the people. They sported white faces, black faces, faces a light coffee hue that showed a mixing of races. He watched a couple of dancing black women, dressed with the brilliance of spring wildflowers in long scarlet and yellow gowns and multicolored madras turbans, as they sought to draw customers to a pecan-laden table manned by a perpetually smiling, heavily accented black man who managed to converse with his patrons while also providing the music to which the women danced. Clardy watched and listened in astonishment to the man's rich baritone voice as he mixed song and conversation without ever losing the cadence to which the turbaned women moved.

Making his performance all the more remarkable was the fact that only two tables down, another man, withered and wizened and playing an odd kind of hand drum and occasionally punctuating the beat with shouts in what sounded like some African language, was providing a completely contrary beat for a second band of dancers—quadroons, these appeared to be— and both dancing groups were somehow managing to keep perfect time with their own particular backups, never growing confused by the mixing of music. Astonishing, Clardy thought, that so many different kinds of people could mix so easily and so well. New Orleans was an amazing place the like of which he had never seen.

He bought a bunch of bananas from one vendor and a bottle of some unidentifiable sweet beverage from another, and settled down to watch the whole wonderful show, letting it distract him from the urgency of the purpose that had brought him to New Orleans in the first place. He ached to find Thias at once, but Japheth's counsel had been wise and he accepted it. To launch out alone would be to fail. If Thias was indeed jailed, they would have to proceed with guided caution and delicacy to obtain his freedom. This was a situation Clardy knew he could not handle alone. He would need the guidance of Japheth's trained legal mind all the way.

He nibbled his fruit and hoped that Japheth's business wouldn't last long so they could get on with the finding and, God willing, the freeing of Thias Tyler.

*   *   *

Clardy will be angry with me for this. But let him be angry. This is the best way to proceed.

Japheth Deerfield had been running that thought through his mind for the last hour, trying to convince himself it was correct. Indeed Clardy would be angry when he learned that Japheth had moved on his own to locate the prison where Willie Jones and "James Hiram" were held, a prison at which he now nervously stood while a burly guard turned a big iron key in an ancient and rusty lock. Clardy would consider himself deceived when he found that Japheth's "pressing business" hadn't been his own but Clardy's. But Japheth had what seemed to him good reason for wanting to initially locate and meet Thias Tyler on his own. He knew the terrible things imprisonment could do to men, how it could ruin their health, break their spirit, and turn them into beings far less human than they had been before. How sometimes it could outright kill them—and that is what he had wished to determine without the burden of Clardy's emotionally charging presence. All along the way to New Orleans he had pondered the fact that Clardy might find his brother was not imprisoned, but buried in some unmarked pauper's grave. Japheth's legal work had already made him aware of three cases of men who had died in the squalor of New Orleans imprisonment. If such had happened to Thias Tyler, he wanted to learn that fact without Clardy being present, so he could break the news in as gentle a way as possible.

Now, as the big iron gate swung open into a dank, mildew-infested row of stone cells, Japheth had new grounds to fear that Thias indeed might be dead. His inquiries for prisoners named James Hiram and Willie Jones had resulted in a troubling answer: Yes, there is a Willie Jones held here, but no James Hiram. Japheth asked what had become of Hiram, but the answer was a disinterested shrug. Don't know. Seems I heard there was a James Hiram who died. Maybe he died in prison, maybe before. Haven't been here that long. Don't know nothing about it firsthand, just what I've heard.

"I'll have to search you for weapons," the guard said.

"Yes, of course."

Japheth raised his hands and let the guard search him, hoping the man's big hands wouldn't feel the wild pounding of his heart. In no prior case had Japheth felt such a deep personal emotional involvement. He fervently wanted Thias Tyler to be alive for Clardy's sake. Now he was half sure that he wasn't. In any case, an interview with Willie Jones should resolve the question.

"You can go on in," the guard said when his search was done. "But you may not get much out of Jones. He's fearsome sick. Probably going to die."

With that bit of news troubling him further, Japheth followed the slump-shouldered guard down the long and dimly lighted hallway, passing stone cages in which resided the forgotten human residue of New Orleans society. He looked straight ahead, but even so felt their sallow eyes on him as he passed. How many like these were there in the world? How many of them might there be who deserved no such foul fate as this? Japheth was no unrealistic soft heart, but he did know that no legal system was perfect, and that sometimes innocents suffered at the hands of the law. Most, maybe all, of these prisoners had been jailed under the former regime; who could say whether their treatment had been justified? As he passed down that hallway, he felt he would gladly throw open the prison doors, free them all, and declare that all had a second chance to build a new and better life. Maybe I do have an unrealistically soft heart, he thought. Maybe it's good that I'm merely an attorney and not a judge.

"Here's your Willie," the guard announced unceremoniously as he fumbled out another key and turned it in the lock of the last cell on the right side of the row. He swung open the door and stepped aside. "Don't take too long."

Japheth steeled himself against the ugly stench of the cell as he walked in and beheld a wan, thinly clad man lying on a pallet in the corner. His legs were in irons, a chain running from them to an iron ring embedded deeply in the stone wall. Japheth was struck dumb for a few moments; the man lifted a pallid face and looked at him from behind a thick growth of beard. His eyes were sad, runny, empty. He said nothing. His hair, no doubt lice-ridden, long uncut and just as long unwashed and uncombed, was dark but with much intrusion of gray.

"Don't take too long," the guard repeated. He closed the cell door and began to shuffle back down the hall.

Japheth cleared his throat and found his voice. "Guard! Why is this man chained?"

The guard didn't look back nor stop walking. "Terms of his jailing, I reckon. He was in chains when I got here. Reckon he'll be in 'em when he dies." He went on; Japheth heard the iron gate at the hall entrance squeak open and close again with a metallic clang.

"Willie Jones?" he asked the prisoner.

No answer, but a nod.

"Sir, I'm an attorney from Natchez. I've come to ask you some questions."

Something like interest flickered in the sickly eyes. "An attorney . . . from Natchez?"

"That's right. I've come because you are connected with a case in which I have an interest."

The man looked at Japheth suspiciously. "I've done been tried and sentenced. To these." He rattled his irons. "What more is there to say? Unless you can get me free of here."

Japheth looked around the tiny, stinking, moldy cell. *No wonder men sicken and die in such places.* He pondered uncertainly a moment, then said, "Perhaps I can get you free."

The first spark of real life registered in the man's thin face. "Free . . . but how . . ."

Japheth was instantly filled with chagrin for having made such a statement. He had no grounds for petitioning for this man's freedom, nor any guarantee he could obtain it if he did have such grounds. His soft heart again— now he had put into this poor man's mind a hope he might not be able to fulfill. "Sir, I can try. I can't assure you of success."

Willie Jones's face had gained a touch of color and taken on an expression showing both hope and confusion. Now a look of suspicion asserted itself again. "I don't know you. Who are you? Why would you want to help me?"

"I'm merely an attorney, as I told you. And I admit that what drew me here was not your situation in itself, but the hope of finding a man named James Hiram. I understand he may have been jailed with you for a crime you committed together."

"No. James Hiram was never jailed here. James Hiram is dead."

"Dead." Japheth looked at his feet. "I feared as much."

"But you are right that we committed a crime together. Him, me, and Timothy Rumbolt."

"Yes. It was through Timothy Rumbolt that news of all this

came out. Though I didn't know until now that Timothy's last name was Rumbolt."

"You've talked to Timothy?"

"No. But James Hiram's brother has. James Hiram, you may know, was really named Tyler."

"Yes. Thias Tyler. He told me."

"Thias has ... *had* a brother named Clardy. Clardy chanced to meet Timothy in Natchez; Timothy told him that you and Thias were jailed in New Orleans together for stealing gold from a church."

"Timothy was wrong. Thias was—" Jones's words were suddenly cut off by a fierce fit of deep coughing. This man truly is very sick, Japheth thought as he watched the frail prisoner heave and hack. After nearly a minute of coughing, Jones regained control, turned to the side and spat out an ugly mass of sputum, then continued talking in a voice now tight and wheezy. "Timothy got away, somehow. Hid himself and they never found him. Thias, he tried to get away, too. We were on the banks of Lake Pontchartrain when they caught us. James ... Thias, he jumped into the water and swam, with them shooting at him. He drownded out there. Drownded dead. God knows there's times I wish I had jumped in that water and done the same. It would have been better than this."

"So Timothy was wrong. Thias Tyler was never jailed here at all."

"I reckon Timothy told you the best he knowed. Timothy, he's a peculiar fellow. Got a deep fear of soldiers for some cause or another. Makes him afraid of the world."

"Yes."

"So you come for Thias Tyler's brother, hoping to find Thias and get him free. That right?"

"It is."

The prisoner sank back against the dank wall. "And Willie Jones, he don't matter. He ain't got no brother to come looking for him."

"Have you any family, Mr. Jones? Anyone who could petition on your behalf? With the purchase of Louisiana there came a new government that might show you lenience if one of your kin would petition the governor on your behalf."

"I got no kin. I'm alone in the world."

Japheth rubbed his chin, paced about the cell, thinking hard. He was filled with pity for Willie Jones; it seemed unthinkable not to try to do something for him. Clearly he would die in this cell, and reprehensible as the robbery of holy items was, surely he had paid a sufficient price for his crime already. A very unorthodox and even illegal notion was coursing through Japheth's mind, countered at every step by his natural caution, by images of Celinda's reproving face—but did Celinda or anyone else ever have to know? Surely it would be justified morally, if not legally, to carry out his plan. Yes, he would do it. He stopped pacing and knelt before Willie Jones.

"Mr. Jones, you *do* have kin. A brother."

"I got no brother."

"Yes you do. Me."

Deep bewilderment clouded his pallid countenance.

"I'm going to petition on your behalf, claiming you as my brother and asking for your freedom. I once had a brother, but now he is dead. You can take his place."

"But they'll know . . . won't they?"

"I seriously doubt it. I doubt they even believe your name is really Willie Jones. Many of the men who rot in these prisons probably do so under false names. I'll claim you as my brother John, and I believe we have an excellent chance of gaining your freedom. But that's all I can do for you—you must understand that. When— *If* we obtain your freedom, you'll be on your own. I advise that you turn away from crime and get yourself the help of a physician. You are very ill."

Willie Jones, wide-eyed, took it in. Tears formed and ran down his face, tracking through months' upon months' worth of oily grime. "You'd do that for me?"

"I would. I will."

The prisoner lowered his face and cried silently for more than a minute, and Japheth was happy for the course he had chosen. At length Willie Jones looked up at him and smiled. "You are a saint of God, sir. You surely are."

"Just an attorney with too soft a heart for his calling. Now understand me, Willie: from now on you are my brother. You must answer to his name, admit that you lied about your identity. My brother was a preacher, by the way; we'll say that he . . . that you went wrong and changed your identity out of shame. If anyone asks you details of your life—and I doubt anyone will—say that you are from Kentucky, but that all your trials and sickness had bereaved you of your memories until I showed up and jolted them back into you. It's a tricky tale, but in your condition I think it will be believed. Not that it is likely, mind you, that anyone will even bother to ask. I suspect the authorities will be glad simply to be rid of you."

"Bless you, sir. God bless you. Whatever happens, sir, whether they free me or not, I'll never forget that you did good for me. I'll never forget the name of ... what is your name, sir?"

Japheth, animated with an excitement of moral purpose that had momentarily made him forget his sorrow over the disappointing news about Thias's fate, rose and turned to the cell door. "Guard!" he called. "I'm ready to leave now." Then, in answer to Jones's question, he said with back turned, "My name is Deerfield. Japheth Deerfield. My brother was named John. That's who you are until you are free and clear—Lord willing. Ah, here comes the guard."

He paused as the bulky man shuffled up and unlocked the cell. When he was out of the cell, Japheth turned and nodded at Willie Jones with a smile. Jones was staring at him with an expression of tremendous awe. And no wonder, Japheth thought. Surely I must seem quite a savior to him right now. "Good day, John," he said. "I'll see you later, hopefully with some very thrilling news."

Japheth headed down the hallway at a lope, out through the open iron gate and out of the prison before the somnolent guard had even made it halfway back up the hall from the cell.

Clardy Tyler returned to the inn where he and Japheth had rented rooms. He found the lawyer there, awaiting him with a somber expression.

Something's wrong. Something about Thias.

"Clardy, sit down," Japheth said. "There's news to give you."

Clardy took off his hat and sank slowly into a chair. Dread filled him. "My brother?"

"Yes." Japheth cleared his throat, coughed into his fist, looked ill at ease. "Clardy, I have deceived you. I didn't mind my own business this morning. I minded yours. I made inquiries about James Hiram ... about Thias. Clardy, this Timothy fellow, he didn't give you fully accurate information."

"He lied to me?"

"He told you the truth as far as he knew it. He had said that he escaped, and that Thias and this other man, Willie Jones, had been captured and put in prison. Correct?"

"That's what he told me."

"He was wrong. Only Jones was captured."

Clardy frowned, taking it in. "So Thias escaped, too?"

"Yes . . . but no. Clardy, what I found out was this." And he told the story of his day, told it all except his plan for the freeing of Willie Jones. It was the hardest thing he had ever done, and the growing look of dread comprehension that came over Clardy's face distressed him deeply.

When Japheth was finished, Clardy said flatly, "Thias is dead."

"As best can be told, yes. But Timothy didn't know. He had already made his escape before Thias took to the water."

"Thias . . . dead . . . But where is his body?"

"Never found, I presume. Quite honestly, I was so saddened by what I found that I didn't ask."

"Then maybe he's alive! Maybe this Willie Jones has it wrong!"

"I don't think so, Clardy. As hard as it is to do, you must resign yourself to the truth. Thias is dead. You did your best to find him, but he is gone and now it's over. It was the fear that we would find just such news as this that made me go out alone today. If we found out the worst, I wanted to be able to spare you having to learn it as straightforwardly as I did." He paused, drew in a deep breath and let it out with a sigh. "There. Now I've told you. I dreaded having to strike you with this."

"So I've come to New Orleans only to find that the brother I wanted to see is dead. God." Clardy put his face in his hands. "God!"

"I'm sorry. What can I say? It's a tragedy none of us wanted to find."

Clardy lifted his head sharply and in an angry heat said, " 'Tragedy,' you call it. 'A tragedy none of us wanted to find.' I wonder, Mr. Deerfield."

"What do you mean?"

"Isaac Ford asked me some questions about you that night you sprung me out of the jail in Natchez. He asked me why a man like you would be interested in finding and freeing the very outlaw who robbed him at gunpoint. He asked me if maybe your notion was to see Thias brought before the court for having done that. I told him he was wrong. Now I wonder. I wonder if the 'tragedy' you see in this is that now you won't get the chance to haul my brother before the court and get him locked up or pilloried for robbing you."

Japheth was taken aback to hear his motivations so mischaracterized. "You're speaking rather impertinently, Clardy. I've done nothing to justify that kind of insult."

"Insult? Or truth? What *would* you have done if we had found Thias alive? And why did you go sneaking off, trying to find him yourself, without me around?"

"I told you: I did it because of the very possibility that we would uncover news you didn't want to hear. I wanted to spare you having to be slapped in the face with any bad news that might turn up."

"Why do I find that hard to believe?"

Japheth's face went crimson. "Mr. Tyler, after all I've done for you, I see no need for me to stand here and endure this kind of abuse."

"I should never have trusted you," Clardy said. "All you ever wanted was to see Thias punished."

Japheth said, "That, sir, is a lie."

"*Now* who's insulted?" Clardy spat back. "I should knock your head off your shoulders!" He drew back his fist.

Everything froze for several seconds. Clardy's upraised fist began to tremble. He lowered it slowly and swallowed hard.

"I'm sorry, Japheth. I'm sorry. I had no call to say what I did."

Japheth lost his angry color. "Well, the truth is, I can't much blame you. My own wife asked me what my intention was should I find your brother alive and well, and I had no answer for her. I suppose I should have thought all that out."

"Don't matter now, does it? There's no Thias left to be freed *or* brought to trial."

"I am sorry. And not because I had some plan to avenge myself on your brother. Please believe that."

"I believe you."

"What will you do now?"

Clardy seemed overwhelmed by that question. Japheth suspected that this was the first time he had really faced the possibility of his quest coming to a truly final negative end . . . now not merely a possibility, but the grim reality. "I ain't sure. I've got land. Not only my own holdings, but now Mr. Ford's, too. With his family dead, he wrote me in his will just like a son. So I reckon I can go back to Nashville . . . but not just now. There's no task seems worth doing at the moment. Now I don't want to do nothing but . . . God! He's dead! Thias is dead!" He turned away and stormed out of the room, slamming the door behind him so hard that it rattled the pitcher and basin on the far side of the room.

Left alone in the sudden ringing silence, Japheth shook his head. "What a day!" he said aloud. "What a day!"

CHAPTER 40

Clardy roamed New Orleans in a daze of grief until late in the night. Knowing he had been rude to Japheth, who had never given evidence of having anything but the highest intentions, and who had gone to much effort on his behalf, he returned to their rooming house, where he found Japheth abed but awake. He mumbled his apologies, again, which were accepted graciously by the lawyer.

"It's been a difficult turn of events for you, Clardy," Japheth said. "I don't fault you for being consternated. Think no more about it. But have you thought now about your plans?"

"I suppose I'll stay here for a time. There's Isaac Ford's remains to be relaid where he wanted to be buried. A promise to keep, you know. I reckon I can deal with that."

"Yes. Did Isaac retain ownership of the place he wanted to be buried?"

"He did. Sold the farm, kept the burial ground."

"I see. That simplifies the legal side of reinterment. Of course, simply having the remains removed and shipped to Kentucky will be difficult practically. Maybe costly. I wish I could help you to—"

"No no. Thank you, but no. You've done enough already,

and I do appreciate it all. My harping at you yesterday was, well, unforgivable."

Japheth smiled. "If so, how is it that I've already managed to forgive it? Now, Clardy, if you'll excuse me, I want to get some sleep."

"Roll on over and go to sleep, then. I believe I'll sit yonder by the table and smoke a few pipefuls, if that won't bother you."

"It won't. Good night."

Clardy sat with pipe in hand, the bowl glowing red in the darkness, listening to Japheth snore and pondering the pivotal point his life had reached. Isaac Ford was dead, as was Thias. He had no partner left to work with, no brother left to find. It was as if he stood at a place where many roads crossed and he was free to choose any of them ... and yet he had lost his drive, his sense of motivation for choosing any road at all. He was wounded, deeply hurt. All he wanted to do at the moment was merely to be, answering to no one; to follow no ambition, make no plans. Maybe during that time he could adjust to a reality that had taken a turn he didn't want to accept.

Or maybe he would do what he had done before at such low times: turn back into the sorry, drinking, debauching Clardy Tyler he had been in youth. He clenched his fist, bit the stem of the pipe. No. He wouldn't do that this time. He'd control himself, stay away from the taverns and dance halls and gaming tables. . . .

The devil with it. He stood in the darkness. Walking to the little fireplace in the corner, he knocked ashes from the pipe bowl and tucked the pipe into a pocket. Then moving carefully, he gathered his possessions into his pack. Pausing beside Japheth's bed, he said softly, "Thank you again, lawyer. Best wishes to you and your own. And good-bye. To you, to Isaac Ford. To Thias. Good-bye to you all."

Clardy slipped out of the room with the numbing sense that a great change had come into his life. With the soft closing of the door behind him, he closed out all that had gone before and turned into a future whose pattern he could not foresee at all. Walking the streets of New Orleans, he looked for the nearest tavern.

Japheth Deerfield concluded his New Orleans business in a somber mood, mostly because of the unheralded disappearance of Clardy Tyler. Japheth had simply wakened to find him gone. That was fine—Clardy was a grown man and independent, not Japheth's charge—but he worried about what would come of the man. He realized he didn't know Clardy all that well, but he could tell that Clardy was a man of deep feeling. He took things, good and bad, to heart. How would he take such a major disappointment as this one? His unceremonious departure was evidence of the likely answer, and it wasn't cheering. Japheth had seen men ruined by loss. He hoped better for Clardy Tyler.

With Clardy gone, however, Japheth was able to get a more objective and philosophical perspective on the total scenario. He didn't fully like what he saw, particularly his own degree of involvement. Once again he had allowed his emotions to become unduly entangled in a case, even to the point of making a rash promise to a pitiful and perhaps undeserving prisoner. It was a most unlawyerly trait, but he couldn't rid himself of it. He had always been too easily touched by a moving or unusual story.

He knew he should fight against that. Change his approach to his profession. No more free professional service, no more getting involved with the personal aspects of cases. He should be more businesslike, not become too sympathetic ... but hang it, wasn't it his inborn sense of sympathy for downtrodden folk the very part of his nature that had made him what he was? His late brother John had possessed a similar spirit, which found its outlet in the ministry. For Japheth, the practice of law provided the same spiritual kind of satisfaction. He was in his profession for the pleasure of seeing problems solved and wrongs righted as much as for money and stature.

Even so, it was clear the time had come to strike a balance between his eager personal altruism and professionalism. He knew it wore on Celinda when he was out late, interviewing some client in a situation that he had labeled an emergency when in fact it might not be. And certainly his tendency to waive fees on impulse did nothing good for his balance sheet.

No more, he pledged. From here on out, I'm going to be as tough and objective an attorney as I can be. It's for my own good. I'm changing my ways.

Of course, he couldn't fully put that pledge into effect just yet, having promised Willie Jones a petition for release. What a foolish, unprofessional promise that was! Too late to do anything now but go through with it, however.

The rest of the day was occupied with the legal affairs that had originally motivated this journey to begin with. The next day, however, Japheth wrote out his petition, addressing it to the governor, asking for the release of "John Deerfield," jailed under the name of Willie Jones. Japheth poured his best effort into the petition, which when complete read like a moving masterpiece of supplication. The fact that he intended this to be one of his last acts of legal altruism only bolstered his incentive to make it as effective a document as he could. He closed the petition with the request that his brother be released on his own authority, claiming that they had already devised plans for reuniting elsewhere. The latter was a bogus claim added for the sake of realism and to make it unnecessary for Japheth to be physically present for Jones's release, should it be granted. As far as he was concerned, he would probably never see Willie Jones again.

He had only a moment of uncertainty before delivering the petition. What if Jones were a truly bad man? What if he was released only to commit further and worse crimes? Japheth didn't know the man, after all.

The doubts almost won the day, but were overcome by the fact that he had made a promise to Jones, and the memory of Jones's sickness. To remain in prison would be fatal to him. He might die of whatever disease held him even if he went free, but outside he would at least have a chance to fight for his health. And the man wasn't a murderer, hang it. All he had done was steal some gold relics.

Thus persuaded again by his own arguments, Japheth filed the petition and promptly put Willie Jones out of his mind. His business kept him in New Orleans only a day more, then he checked out of his room, paid the bill both for himself and the still absent Clardy Tyler, and turned his path toward Natchez, Celinda, Beulahland, and home.

The night after Japheth returned home, Celinda lay beside him in their bed, listening to him breathe. She was more grateful to have him back again than Japheth could know. Since the stabbing of Timothy, her time here alone had been hellish. Every waking moment had been spent in the fear of that dreaded knock on the door, that throat-tightening glimpse of a policeman crossing the yard, which would herald the end of life as she had come to know it. Every night had been spent in terrible dreams of what would happen to her when her crime was discovered.

Crime. An ironic and inaccurate word, she realized, but still the word that came to her mind when she thought about what had happened. She had come to see that the real crime done in Beatrice Sullivan's room was not her slaying of Timothy, but his attempted molestation of her. Timothy's slaying was not a murder, but an accident: she had not deliberately stabbed him; he had run onto the knife himself. But none of that mattered now, Celinda believed. She was sure she had waited too long to come forward and report what had happened. By now her story would have the look of an alibi developed late and presented later. And how could she prove the death was accidental? No one but she knew what had happened.

Celinda's immediate worry was whether Japheth had detected anything different in her manner that would rouse questions. Every glance he had turned toward her today set her heart to racing and her mind scrambling in fear. *He knows something is wrong—he's going to ask me what it is....* He hadn't asked. Maybe he didn't see after all.

But he will see. I can't keep this from him. I won't be able to bear it. Yet I won't be able to bear it if he finds out, either. Such conflicting thoughts had dominated her mind all day, keeping her distracted and tense. Even now, as her travel-exhausted husband slept easily beside her, her body was stiff and tight; her pulse pounded loudly inside her ear.

She could not go on like this. Either she would have to relent and confess it all to Japheth, or she would have to toughen her mind, somehow, and learn to endure and thoroughly hide her inner tension. Neither prospect seemed easily achievable. For the time being, however, she would try for the latter, because all her worries and nervousness to the contrary, one small element in the overall picture continued to give her hope: So far, no news of Timothy's death had emerged from Natchez-under-the-Hill.

Celinda couldn't understand it. Usually such deaths became known very quickly. Over the past three days, for example, news had arisen of a fatal shooting on the riverfront and a serious knifing that had one man lingering on the brink of death and another only scarcely better off. Yet there was nothing, not one word, about a corpse being found in an upstairs room. Celinda was encouraged, daring to hope that the whole event miraculously would never be discovered. Could it be that Beatrice Sullivan had found the corpse, feared she would be blamed for the death, and disposed of it in secret?

Then again, might the body simply not have been found yet? Maybe Beatrice Sullivan had left Natchez, or moved to new quarters. If so, then the axe still hung over her head, Celinda thought. A corpse in an upper room could not remain undiscovered forever.

Such thoughts swam in alternating rounds of hope and despair, stealing her sleep, spoiling even the happiness of having her husband with her again.

One week later

Almost from the moment he was home again, Japheth had detected something different about his wife. She had a nervous, fearful quality about her that she hadn't had before. He wondered if perhaps it was simply an odd emotional reaction to his return, but it hadn't lessened with passing days. He caught Celinda staring fearfully out the window several times, and twice came into a room to find her hurriedly wiping away tears. She provided no explanations.

She had reacted with disinterest to all the news he brought back. It didn't seem to distress her that Clardy Tyler's quest had turned out sadly; instead, she seemed pleased to have him now removed from their lives. Japheth thought it an uncharacteristically callous attitude for Celinda, but he remembered her instinctive fears about his involvement with Clardy Tyler and understood her feelings better in that light.

Now Japheth slowly walked through the dusk toward his home, thinking over a private, somber conversation he had just held with his friend Moses Mulhaney. He had gone to Mulhaney because his wife was Celinda's closest friend. Had Mrs. Mulhaney said anything to her husband about some event occurring in Japheth's absence that had upset or frightened Celinda?

Moses replied that the only mention his wife had made of contact with Celinda while Japheth was away was that one day Celinda had brought Beulahland over to be cared for while she dealt with some matter or another elsewhere. Moses did not know what that matter was; but after much prodding from Japheth, he did reveal that his wife had said Celinda spoke of preparing a supposed "surprise" for her husband and needed a few hours alone to accomplish it. Moses apologized for giving away the fact that a surprise was in the works, and asked if Japheth's birthday, or some other special occasion in his life, was coming up. No, Japheth replied. There was nothing . . . and so far Celinda had given him no surprise except her obviously distraught emotional state. Moses admitted that he, too, had noticed that Celinda didn't seem to be herself, and his wife had commented to the same effect only the day before.

Japheth was uncertain what to do. He was more worried than ever about Celinda, but reluctant to spoil her surprise, whatever it was to be. A party of some kind? A special gift? Neither seemed likely. Celinda had never been prone to take the lead in social matters, and she was exceedingly careful with the family's tight budget, having never spent much money without first consulting Japheth. Besides, why would either a party or a gift have her upset?

He reached his home and suffered through a quiet, tense supper, during which Celinda seemed distracted and maybe on the verge of tears. Afterward she began to wash the dishes, not humming to herself, as she had always done for years when performing that job. Japheth played with Beulahland, watching Celinda from the corner of his eye. Over the course of half an hour she dropped two glasses, breaking both. When she broke a favorite platter right after that, she began to cry.

"Celinda, what's wrong?"

"I've broken three dishes, and one's our best meat platter. I'm clumsy tonight and don't know why."

"Don't cry. They're only dishes. Maybe you're tired, or getting under the weather."

"No. No. I feel fine. I'm just a clumsy fool."

Japheth prudently took Beulahland to her room, rocked her, and put her to bed, giving Celinda time alone to get over her upset. When he came out again, Celinda was seated in her favorite chair, her legs curled up beneath her, her face looking drawn and pale. "Celinda, I believe you *are* under the weather. You look like you don't feel well."

"I'm fine, Japheth."

He went to her, knelt beside her chair and put his arm

around her shoulder. "Celinda, you haven't been yourself since I came home. Something is troubling you. What is it?"

"I'm fine, I told you! Nothing is troubling me."

"I'm your husband. I know you better than anyone. You can't deceive me."

He felt her tense. "I'm not deceiving you, Japheth. What would I deceive you about?"

"I was talking about deceiving me about how you're feeling. That's all." He paused, knowing he had trodden into territory she apparently didn't want him in. "Is there something else you thought I meant?"

She grew even more tense. "How can you ask that? You don't trust me?"

"Of course I do. It's just that I can tell you're not happy, not your usual self. I'm concerned about you."

"For God's sake, Japheth, nothing is wrong! *Nothing!* Can you not take your own wife at her word?" She rose and stormed off into the bedroom, closing the door behind her.

Japheth sat up late that night, brooding by the fireside. He drank three glasses of wine, which did not make him feel better. He had less doubt than ever that something bad had happened while he was in New Orleans, and was determined to find out what it was. Yet he dreaded finding out—dreaded the domestic struggle with Celinda that he would have to endure to obtain it, dreaded the knowledge itself. Whatever it was must be very bad, considering Celinda's state these days.

At last he rose and went into the bedroom. Celinda had retired much earlier, and lay beneath the covers, her back toward him. He undressed and slipped on a long nightshirt, then crawled into bed beside her. He could tell from her breathing that she was not asleep.

"Celinda, I'm sorry I upset you. I didn't mean to."

In the darkness she turned toward him and put her arm across his chest. "Japheth, do you love me?"

"You know I do."

"Do you love me so much that you could never stop loving me, no matter what?"

"Yes, Celinda, yes. No matter what."

"You'll stand by me, no matter what the situation?"

"Of course I will. I'll always stand by you. You are my wife. I love you more than the world itself."

"I love you, too, Japheth."

"Celinda, please ... tell me what has you troubled."

She paused, seemingly thinking, and he felt a combination of hope and dread. But in the end she shook her head and said, "There is nothing to tell."

"There is! There must be."

"No, Japheth."

He was tired, worried, and her mysterious manner suddenly became too exasperating to bear. "Celinda, I demand that you tell me what is wrong!"

"Japheth, don't shout at me!"

"Celinda, there is something troubling you, and you're holding it back from me! I'll shout if I must!"

In the next room Beulahland began to cry. "See now?" Celinda said. "You've woken Beulah." She rose and left the room, her white nightgown a ghostly receding image in the darkness.

When she returned, Japheth lay with his eyes closed. She crawled into her place beside him, staying well away from him, her back turned. He opened his eyes and looked out into the darkness, filled with worry and wondering what could have happened that was so bad as to change Celinda this much, and how he could ever convince her to tell him what it was.

CHAPTER 41

Japheth's work the next day went forward in a haze of distraction. He could think of nothing but Celinda, who had been distant and cool that morning at breakfast. Today he neglected to return home for his midday meal, opting to eat in a nearby café instead. The afternoon hours dragged by slowly and miserably, and he left the office filled with frustration at a day largely wasted, and with dread of having to return to a house filled with tension and mystery.

A cool breeze was blowing down Japheth's shirt collar and tugging at his tall hat. As he rounded a corner a particularly strong gust yanked the hat from his head and dropped it into a puddle. Muttering beneath his breath, Japheth bent over, retrieved the hat, and was brushing off the water when he lifted his eyes and saw an old, bent woman in ragged clothing standing across the street, looking at him. The intensity of her stare showed clearly that this was no chance meeting of eyes. The woman was watching him.

Japheth frowned, wondering what her interest in him was. He turned and walked on, carrying his hat, and glanced back once. She was still watching him. He stopped, stepped out onto the street and advanced toward her. She turned and moved back into an alley. By the time Japheth reached the end of the alley, she was gone.

It was mildly disturbing. Who was that old woman? Was she in need of legal help but too bashful to approach him? Her ragged condition had indicated poverty; probably she was some denizen of Natchez-under-the-Hill.

Japheth reached his home, and soon the old woman was forgotten as all the now-familiar tensions in his domestic scene reasserted themselves. Celinda was as distracted and nervous as ever. It took all of Japheth's will to restrain himself from asking her again what was wrong.

The next morning he returned to the office determined to enjoy a more satisfying day's work than he had yesterday. He threw himself into his work, accomplished much, and left the office in a contented state of mind. As he grew closer to home, apprehension began to be reborn, but he took a willful grip on his feelings and reminded himself that Celinda's worries might amount to very little if he knew what they were, and she herself might, like him, have just had a mood-brightening day.

He rounded the same corner where he had lost his hat the day before when he saw the old woman again. She stood in the same place and was staring at him as before. His good humor died like a flame in water, and he felt chilled.

For a couple of seconds he actually had the impulse to run. There was something frightening in the look of the old woman. But of course he could not run; the only strange old creatures an attorney was expected to fear sat on judicial benches in courtrooms.

He made as if to go on, then turned abruptly and headed across the street straight at her. This time she did not run, though he did detect what seemed to be a flicker of fear in her expression. That pleased him; she had roused fear in him, and he was glad to know he had the ability to rouse the same in her.

"You, ma'am!" he called. "Is there something I can do for you?"

The old woman licked her lips and cocked her head in a birdlike way. "She hurt him," she said. "She hurt him with a knife."

Japheth thought he understood. Some woman had hurt this woman's husband, son, or friend with a knife, and she wanted legal aid in dealing with it. He felt quite relieved.

"I see. Of whom are you speaking?"

"My boy. She cut my boy. I found him bleeding on the floor, and he like to have died."

"I see. Who cut him?"

"Your wife."

He blinked, frowned. Surely he had misheard. "What?"

"You know what I'm speaking to you of," she said. "Your wife. She come to me and the boy's very home, and cut him with a knife. She stuck him, for no reason at all."

Japheth grew red. "Ma'am, I don't know who you are, but that is a scandalous lie, and I advise you to watch your tongue."

"My boy says he's going to tell. Tell all that devil-woman did to him. That'll fix her!"

"Ma'am, you are clearly a fool. That's babble you speak."

"No, no, I'm not a fool. Neither is my boy. It's your wife who's the fool. She hurt him and thinks it won't cost her nothing. But it will. And you, too."

"Hag! Are you threatening me?"

"No threat. Just a warning. But there's something you can do to stop him from telling. You can give him money. He sent me to tell you that."

"I don't know your boy, and all you say is preposterous. I'll give no money to anyone."

"Then he'll tell. And they'll come put your wife in jail."

Japheth was trembling. A fear was arising. As absurd as this woman's words sounded, he couldn't forget Celinda's change of demeanor. *Something* had happened while he was gone . . . but a stabbing? It seemed absurd.

"Ma'am, I don't know who you are, but I'm telling you here and now that you'd best leave me and my family alone. I'll not abide anyone, for any reason, attempting extortion on me! I'm an attorney, ma'am! You think for a moment that—"

She turned and began walking away, her head lifted proudly. "You'll pay!" she called back. "You and that wife of yours, you'll pay! Nobody hurts my Timothy!"

Japheth felt panic and a simultaneous shame that such a crazy old woman was capable of rousing such a level of fear. Through his mind flickered an image of himself going after the hag, hauling her off behind a building, and beating her until she begged for release and promised not to show her face in his presence again.

Of course such was a mere fantasy he did not allow to keep residence in his mind for more than a moment. He would beat no one, particularly not a woman—but maybe he should follow her, at least, and find out where she lived and who this Timothy she had mentioned was. . . .

Timothy! It came to him at once that Timothy was the name of the man who had told Clardy Tyler that his brother was jailed in New Orleans, the very man who had evaded the captors who had jailed Willie Jones and chased Thias Tyler into Lake Pontchartrain. And had not Clardy told him that Timothy, surname unknown, lived with an elderly woman in an upstairs room in Natchez-under-the-Hill, hiding out there in some deranged fear of soldiers? What was the old woman's name? Sullivan. Now he remembered. Clardy had called her Beatrice Sullivan, and said she was a sad, dim-witted old creature still awaiting the return of a husband who had abandoned her on the riverfront years before.

It was an astonishing realization and an unexpected connection between two situations. Japheth didn't know what to make of it. He hesitated, torn between chasing after the old woman and going home to his wife. He opted for the latter. If the old woman and her Timothy fellow lived in Natchez-under-the-Hill, he could find them later. His main worry now was the safety of Celinda. What if Timothy had been watching Celinda, as the old woman had been watching him? Japheth wondered. Might that explain why Celinda kept peering out windows, as if looking for someone?

He headed toward his house on the run, dodging pedestrians and cutting between riders and wheeled traffic on the street, taking the shortest route possible back to his house.

Celinda had strengthened and shored up her will for days on end until she believed nothing could break through it to reach her sheltered secret. But when Japheth revealed to her what had happened on the street only minutes before, her will shattered like fragile glass. Celinda confessed it all, laying it out from the start, struggling to speak when she felt like sobbing.

"Japheth, I've told you about Queen, who helped me so much. But I've never told you that Queen had a sister here in Natchez, named Beatrice Sullivan. It was her she was coming to see."

"That old woman today . . . she is Queen Fine's sister?"

Celinda's voice trembled. "Yes. And Japheth, you know how I have always cherished Queen's memory, because of all the protection she gave me. When I first was safe here in Natchez, I intended to find Beatrice Sullivan and do kind things for her, because of Queen doing such kind things for me. But I never had the courage to seek her out . . . until when you mentioned her name before you left for New Orleans. It reminded me of all that I had intended to do but hadn't. I felt guilty, like I had failed Queen by not seeing to the welfare of her sister. So when you were gone, I took Beulahland to the Mulhaneys' and went down to the riverfront. I found out where Beatrice Sullivan lived, and went there, but she was not home. Timothy was. Japheth, he got me into the room. He closed the door behind me and tried to . . ." She couldn't get out the words.

"God! Oh, God!" Japheth whispered, and an expression unlike any Celinda had ever seen him display came across his face. "Celinda, he didn't succeed, did he? Tell me he didn't!"

"No, Japheth, he didn't. But he might have if I hadn't found a knife. I got it in my hand, he ran at me . . . The next thing I knew, he was stabbed. I didn't try to do it. It just happened. Then he fell down and I knew he was dead."

"Obviously he wasn't," Japheth said. "He's apparently alive and well enough to try to extort money from us through that old hag and harlot he lives with." He had been seated, but now he stood, pacing rapidly about, rubbing the back of his neck. "Damn him!" he bellowed. "To think any man would lay a hand on my wife . . . damn him! I'll kill the foul whoreson! I'll slash his throat to the backbone with my own knife!"

Celinda was unaccustomed to seeing her husband act and speak this way. Japheth was generally a calm man, an upstanding citizen, a devoted churchman. She had never heard him even swear before . . . but never before had he been faced with the realization that his wife had very nearly been violated by a very loathsome man.

Celinda said, "Japheth, don't talk that way. You know you mustn't."

"I can't help it, Celinda. My God, is it not a husband's duty to protect his wife from such abuse?"

"It frightens me, Japheth. I'm afraid you might do something you'll regret."

"It's my duty to protect you."

"Japheth, I protected myself. I'm capable of doing it, and I did."

"Protected yourself . . . but in the process, you've roused a scoundrel to blackmail us."

"My intentions were good. All I went there to do was to help a sad old woman whose sister had been good to me."

"That 'sad old woman' is an extortionist, in league with a dim-witted, would-be rapist."

"I know I was wrong to go there, Japheth. But all of us make mistakes."

"Yes, but this time you made a big one, my dear. That mistake could have cost you your honor, or your life."

"I know. That's why I didn't tell you about it. I knew your feelings would be strong."

He closed his eyes and massaged the bridge of his nose with thumb and forefinger, like a man with a severe headache. "Celinda, why did you not think you could tell me? Did you think I would overreact?"

"You have overreacted, Japheth. You've threatened to kill a man."

Japheth shook his head. "I won't kill him. It won't be necessary. By heaven, I can deal with this maggot short of becoming a murderer! He put his hand into the wrong pot when he deigned to trifle with Japheth Deerfield!"

"Japheth, what do you intend to do?"

"I'm going to go put the fear of God and the court into that scoundrel, that's what! The fool! Does some half-wit who sits locked away in his room in some morbid fear of soldiers, some piece of human refuse who dares lay his hands on a decent woman, believe he can practice extortion on an officer of the court and member of the bar?"

"Japheth, if you don't pay him, what will he do? He'll go to the court himself and claim that I stabbed him without reason."

"No, that he won't do. I'm not an attorney worthy of the name if I can't gain the advantage over such a bit of flotsam as this Timothy."

"Japheth, I don't want what happened to me known! I don't want people looking at me and saying, 'There goes poor old Celinda Deerfield, who was touched and squeezed and fondled by the foulest man you could imagine when she went wandering through Natchez-under-the-Hill.' I couldn't abide that, Japheth. I couldn't stand it."

He grasped her by the shoulders and looked into her face. "You shall not have to, my dear. I pledge that to you. No matter what it takes, I'll ensure that nothing that makes you ashamed will ever see light of day." He wrapped his arms around her and pushed his face into her hair. "Oh, Celinda, I wish you had told me all this from the beginning!"

"I believed he was dead. I believed I would be blamed, and there would be no way I could prove my innocence."

"Well, now we know he isn't dead. Now we can deal with him, and by the eternal, deal with him I will. Don't worry, Celinda. All will be well. I promise you that."

Japheth understood the risk in what he was doing. One could never predict with certainty how various individuals would act under pressure, and where there was not certainty, there was, potentially, danger. He stood before the warped, unpainted wooden door of Beatrice Sullivan and Timothy, drew in a quick breath, sent up a mental prayer, and rapped very sharply. He had been careful to climb the stairs silently, so that his knock would startle the occupants. And when he talked, he intended to talk a little more rapidly and loudly than normal. When he looked at them, his gaze would have more than the usual intensity. He had come late at night, hoping to find them tired, and he was dressed in his best, blackest, most authoritative clothing. He intended to gain a mental advantage over these two from the outset and not let go of it.

He heard movement inside the room. Someone was at the other side of the door.

"Who's there?" It was Beatrice Sullivan's voice.

"Japheth Deerfield. Open the door."

He heard whispered conversation. "You got no soldiers with you?"

"No soldiers. Not *yet.*"

He couldn't suppress a private smile as he heard even more intense whispering inside. Not *yet.* A lot of hidden significance in that last word. Timothy wouldn't have missed it.

He rapped again, more loudly. "Open this door!" he said. "I require admittance!"

More whispering, and then the door opened. Beatrice Sullivan's wide but withered face looked back at him. Beyond her, he saw Timothy standing in the back of the room, beside a small table on which lay a battered old flintlock pistol.

"Thank you," Japheth said curtly. He pushed on in before the door was fully open, making Mrs. Sullivan stumble backward. Japheth kept his eyes locked on Timothy's pale face and advanced straight toward him so quickly that before Timothy could even react, the pistol was no longer on the table but in Japheth's hand.

"I believe I'll keep this while I'm here," he said, sticking the pistol under his belt. "Just a precaution, you know."

"That's my pistol! Give it to me! And why the hell have you come here?"

"Didn't you want to see me, Timothy? Wasn't it your idea that I come bring you money so that you'll leave me and my wife in peace? Otherwise, I gather, you'll go to the law and complain that she stabbed you? By the way, how are you healing up?" He reached over and yanked up Timothy's loose shirt, exposing a pinkish, scabbed, but obviously healing puncture. Timothy pulled back, jerking down the shirt.

"You touch me again and I'll—"

Japheth slapped Timothy across the face. "Don't dictate to me, you squirming maggot. I'll touch you, I'll strike you, I'll kick you, or I'll shoot you dead, all at my own whim." He spun and aimed a finger right at Beatrice Sullivan. "And you, you old fishwife, will stay out of our business. If I see you so much as move, I'll not take responsibility for what I do."

Beatrice Sullivan's eyes seemed to grow as her body seemed to shrink. She hunched over and held her arms tightly against her body. "Be careful of him, Timothy . . . he's a madman!"

"Madman? Me? Oh no. It's this fool here"— he slapped Timothy again, not quite as hard—"who is the madman. He believes he can attempt to rape my wife, then try to force me to pay him for it! If that doesn't define 'madman,' nothing does."

Timothy quailed back against the wall, putting his hand up to deflect any more slaps and sinking down low to protect himself. Japheth looked at him in contempt, then smiled. "Look at you, Timothy! Cowering like some whipped child! And you thought you had it in you to blackmail me! There's nothing in you but a black heart and a soul full of worms of vermin."

He wheeled about, making Beatrice Sullivan yelp in surprise and begin to tremble. "You want to know why my wife came to this place, old woman? She came to help you. That's right. To do something good for you, because your sister Queen did good things for her once several years ago."

"Queen . . . she knew my Queen?"

"Yes, she did. And Queen proved to her that there was far more heart and soul in herself than there is in you, old shrew! She was a hard woman, but she knew what it was to be kind. I wonder what she would have thought to know her own sister would fall so low as to help a worm like this man here try to extort money from a young woman she herself loved very much! I expect Queen wouldn't be at all proud of you, Beatrice Sullivan."

Beatrice began to cry. "Where is my Queen? Can you tell me? I've longed to see her!"

For the first time since beginning this verbal assault, Japheth felt a twinge of regret over what he must say. He did not allow that regret to soften his expression or tone; it was imperative to maintain the advantage here, beginning to end. "Queen is dead. She was murdered on a flatboat by a man of the ilk of your Timothy, here."

"Murdered! Oh, merciful God!" The old woman suddenly began to sob.

Japheth turned to Timothy again. "Listen to me, Timothy. You believe you hold an advantage over me, but the truth is the opposite. I know who you are. I know about the robbery of gold from a Catholic church in New Orleans, and about Willie Smith and Thias Tyler. I know it all, and even things you don't. And I know that the soldiers there want you, Timothy. The *soldiers*." He leaned forward a little as he said that and let his eyes burn into Timothy's.

Timothy opened his mouth as if to speak, but only blubbered.

Japheth stepped forward. "That's right, Timothy. The soldiers want you. They want to drag you away and hang you. They want to watch you twitch at the end of a rope until you're dead. If they find you, that's what they'll do to you. And all it takes is a word from me, just a word, and they'll know where you are. And don't think you can kill me and silence me. There's a letter already written and in the hands of a person I trust—not my wife, either—and if anything happens to me, anything at all, it will be sent and the soldiers will come. Do you understand me?" He leaned closer still. His volume had grown while he spoke, so that his last question was nearly a shout.

"Yes . . . yes, I understand."

"That's good, Timothy. I'm glad you do. And understand

this, too—there'll be no money for you from me or my wife. Furthermore, you're going to leave Natchez, you are, and never come back. You're going to leave this town and go as far away as you can, and if ever I see you, hear of you, even smell you, the soldiers will come and they'll hang you. Do you understand that?"

"Yes."

"Never let me see you again, Timothy. Never again. And never again dare to lay your filthy hands on another woman."

"I won't. I won't!"

Beatrice Sullivan was still sobbing on the other side of the room. Timothy began to cry, too. "Please, Mr. Deerfield, please . . . I'm sorry about what I done. Don't make the soldiers come! Please don't make them come!"

Japheth was quite worked up from his tirade, and the thought of this wretched man before him having attempted to molest his wife was enough to make him boil in rage, but at this moment Timothy seemed so utterly pitiful that he couldn't help but feel sorry for him. Japheth wasn't used to treating people so harshly. Timothy's fear of soldiers was obviously the result of a damaged mind, and Japheth realized it was cruel to play on that fear. Yet it was also essential. This job could not be done halfway. He had to leave here tonight assured that neither Timothy nor Beatrice Sullivan would ever dare try to harm him or Celinda again.

"I won't make them come . . . *if* you'll leave this town and not come back! *And* if you never make another threat against me or my wife again!" He reached out and grabbed Timothy by the collar. "By heaven, man, you'd best be grateful that I'm in a forgiving kind of spirit. For what you did to my wife, and what you would have done had you not been oaf enough to run yourself onto a blade, I could have you locked away until you couldn't bear to see the light of day even if you had the chance."

"I'm sorry. I'm sorry. Just don't send the soldiers."

"Good-bye, Timothy. And this is a final good-bye. We'll never lay eyes on one another again. Correct?"

Timothy blubbered and nodded. "But please, sir, can't I stay in Natchez? I'm afraid to leave here. The soldiers, they're out there, and—"

"You *will* leave here. Otherwise I'll put you in their hands myself."

Timothy squeezed his eyes shut and quietly began to sob. Japheth pushed him away contemptuously. Then he removed Timothy's pistol from his own belt, turned the screw and freed the flint, which he pocketed, shook the powder out of the pan and laid the pistol back on the table. He wasn't about to risk a pistol ball in the back as he left this stinking room.

He could still hear both of them crying when he descended the stairs. His heart was pounding, and once he was on the street he realized how afraid he felt. What he had done had been a true gamble with his own safety, but he was confident it had worked. Timothy was scared through and through; he would not dare stir up trouble again. And without Timothy's prodding, Japheth doubted that Beatrice Sullivan would create any further problems, either. She had seemed to be no more than Timothy's mouthpiece.

"Mr. Deerfield . . ."

He turned, surprised to see Beatrice Sullivan behind him. She had descended the stairs and followed him onto the street.

"What do you want?"

"I want to know more about Queen. Who killed her? Why would anybody kill her? She was always good to other folks, Queen was."

Japheth felt pity for the old woman. Life had not been easy on her. "Ma'am, I don't know much to tell you except that your sister was stabbed by a man named McKee, who was paid to do it by a man named Horton. The reason it happened was—"

The sound of a single shot from above made him cut off. He looked up; Beatrice Sullivan did the same. The shot had come from inside the upstairs room.

Japheth felt a shudder of horror. *He must have had a spare flint.*

Beatrice put her hand to her mouth. "Timothy . . ."

She turned away and headed to the stairs, which she climbed as fast as she could, with much grunting and wheezing and repetition of Timothy's name. Japheth couldn't seem to move at all. He stood frozen, knowing but not wanting to acknowledge what that single shot meant.

Others began to gather. "Heard shooting! What happened?" "Don't know." "It came from above . . ."

A loud wail was heard from the upper room. It was the voice

of Beatrice Sullivan, heavy with grief. "He's dead! Oh, help me, Jesus, he's dead!"

I didn't mean to scare him that much. . . . God in heaven, you know I didn't mean for him to shoot himself.

Japheth stood where he was as others mounted the stairs, climbed up to the room, and general hubbub grew. Out of his growing sense of horror sprang a new and terrible realization: *I am ruined here.*

The window overlooking the street had always been kept closed and covered by Timothy, but now it was opened. A man stuck out his head. "Somebody out there!" he called out. "Go find a constable! There's a man shot the top of his own head off up here!"

I am ruined. A man is dead, and I am ruined.

There would be questions asked, investigations made. Talk. Whispers. Evil speculations, growing in the telling. Beatrice Sullivan would tell the whole story, and Japheth Deerfield would become known throughout Natchez as the man who scared another man into killing himself. The man of the law who opted to deal with a private matter outside the law, and pushed a man to suicide in so doing.

The crowd grew around Japheth. Men pushed past him and ran up the stairs. Death was common in Natchez-under-the-Hill, but seldom was it self-inflicted. Like the way he had lived his life, Timothy's final act had been unusual, and as such, would gain all the more attention.

So much the worse for Japheth Deerfield, and so much the worse for Celinda. Sinking into despair, Japheth lurched off, hid himself in an alley and cried like a child.

1 8 1 1

CHAPTER 42

In a field near Danville, Kentucky

He put on an exaggerated expression of tense excitement as the yellow-haired little girl ran across the meadow toward him, chubby arms churning as fast as her legs. He held his watch in his left hand, making a show of time-keeping. The child reached him, racing past in a blond-topped streak, then pounded to a stop. Clardy Tyler pointed at the face of the pocket watch. "Less than a minute! Jenny, you've run the whole big meadow in less than a minute! Fastest you've ever gone, sweet girl!"

The child, about four years old, came puffing back to her father. "Papa, I can run it faster."

"Maybe you can, but not today you won't. Three times is plenty for one afternoon."

Jenny Tyler looked disappointed but made no complaint. Clardy chuckled to himself as he hefted Jenny up into the saddle of his horse, then swung up behind her. He wished he still had the energy of a child. At age thirty, he remained strong and vigorous—more so, in fact, than he had been in his idle youth—but his elder daughter's vigor went beyond anything he had felt in years. She was a strong, active, healthy child, and he was proud she was his own. Just as he was proud of her younger sister, Mary, and their mother, Faith.

He had met Faith by chance in the tavern her parents operated near Nashville. The meeting occurred several months after he made his sad parting with Japheth Deerfield in New Orleans. A harder stretch of time he had never known. The effect of losing first his old friend and partner Isaac Ford, then losing all hope of ever seeing Thias in this world again, had given Clardy a thorough emotional lashing, and as he was now fond of punning, it had "taken Faith" to get him through it.

For the first six months after parting from Deerfield, he had remained in New Orleans, living a dissolute life he wasn't proud to look back on afterward. He had neglected to keep contact with the renters of his Tennessee land, had spent his money as if it were in boundless supply, and had not looked beyond the next hour, much less the next day.

Eventually that life grew tiring and sad, and he put New Orleans behind him and headed back up to Natchez. He went there solely because it happened to be the southern terminus of the Boatman's Trail, not because Natchez held any attraction in itself. Quite the opposite was true; he held that town in mental association with sorrow and disappointment, and desired nothing more to do with the place. Nevertheless, while he was there, he decided to pay a brief call on the Deerfields, mostly to let Japheth know that he was still alive and well, and to thank him again for what he'd tried to do for him in New Orleans.

The visit was never made. Clardy heard reference to some "trouble" being experienced by the Deerfields, stemming from an incident that had occurred in Natchez-under-the-Hill. Remembering Celinda Deerfield's negative attitude toward him, and not wanting to insert himself into the middle of someone else's bad situation, Clardy abandoned the notion of visiting them and went on his way. He took up with a party of Kaintucks and traveled the nearly five-hundred-mile Boatman's Trail through the Indian country, finally reaching Nashville after about a month of travel. There, at a new inn he stopped at, seeking no more than a meal to quell his hunger until he reached his own home not many miles distant, he met the woman who he would make his wife a few months later.

They were married in a small church beside the Cumberland

River, in the section of town that had initially been known as
French Lick in the earliest days of settlement It was no exag-
geration to say that the former Faith Wheeler had changed
Clardy Tyler's life drastically, and for the better.

He reclaimed his Nashville land from his renters, worked
through the legalities of claiming the inheritance left him by
Ford, and moved into Ford's old house. At that time, Clardy expected they would remain on the Cumberland River for the rest
of their days. Life was good there; since Ford's death, Clardy's
holdings of land and stock were high enough to make him one
of Nashville's best-known and successful planters and stock-
men. He began planning a larger, finer house, and listened with
some bemusement as various important people from Nashville
and its environs sought to persuade him toward politics.

Then Faith's father died. Six months after that, her mother
announced that she had been asked by a Kentucky farmer to
remarry and move with him back to Kentucky. This created a
crisis in the Tyler household. Faith was unusually close to her
mother and did not want to be separated from her. She made
a very substantial request of her husband, and it was evidence
of the strength of his love for his wife that Clardy resisted only
a little while before giving in. He sold his Nashville land,
bought acreage near Danville, and moved up to Kentucky,
where Faith could still live close to her mother.

Now, as he rode with his daughter nestled in the saddle before him, Clardy reflected on how he hadn't wanted to come to
Kentucky at the beginning. He had done it entirely for Faith's
benefit, with a lot of secret reluctance and an even more secret
touch of outright resentment. No more. All that had changed.
Clardy was happier here in Kentucky than he had been at any
other phase of his life. Much of it had to do with the birth of
his daughters, who thrived in this beautiful, rich countryside.
He was a happy man. Happy to be alive, in this place, with
these people.

"Where will the big meeting be, Papa?" Jenny asked.

"Right where we were just now, honey," Clardy answered.

"In the big meadow?"

"That's right."

"Where will the people sit?"

"On the ground, on blankets, on their wagons. Anywhere
they want."

"Where will the preachers be?"

"There'll be a platform built in the midst of the field. Folks can gather all around that way, you see."

"Why are you letting them do the camp meeting here, Papa?"

"Because the preacher Coffman asked me, and I wanted to help him. He's a good man."

"How'd he get blind, Papa?"

"He was in a big battle, years and years ago, when he was a young man. A place called King's Mountain. He was struck across the eyes with a saber."

"Why would anybody hurt the preacher Coffman?"

"It was a battle, honey. People hurt each other in battles. It's sad, but the truth. It's a lot better for people to come together peacefully, like they'll be doing here when the preacher Coffman holds his meeting."

"Are we going to be at the meetings, Papa?"

"You and your mother and sister might be. Me, I'll be out of town. Way off down the river."

"Why?"

"There's an old friend of mine who passed on a few years ago. Mr. Ford—I've told you about him. He always wanted to be buried near his kin here in Kentucky, and I promised him I'd see it done. It's been a big span of years, and I ain't fulfilled that promise yet. But I've been making ready to do it lately, and about the time the big camp meeting commences, I'll be off to New Orleans to see the job done."

"Why did Mr. Ford care where he was once he was dead?"

"It's a natural thing to want to be buried in land you loved, near folks you loved. Like me. I'll want to be buried beside your mama once my time comes."

"Papa, you won't die for a long, long time!" She said it forcefully, and he caught the glint of worry in her eyes and chided himself for having brought up a matter not easy for a child to deal with.

"That's right, honey. I aim to be around for years and years to come, and your mother, too," he said with deliberate brightness. "Why, I wouldn't want to miss out on watching you grow up and have children of your own."

She hugged him, then, with the abrupt manner of children, dropped the entire subject and began to sing at the top of her voice. Clardy smiled, shook his head, and felt he was surely the most fortunate man alive.

As he rode along, listening to his daughter's high voice, he thought about the big camp meeting, to be led within a few weeks by the Reverend Israel Coffman, on the very big field where Jenny had just been running. The blind Coffman, a beloved clergyman all through Kentucky, had personally requested use of the site from Clardy, and Clardy gave his permission. Though he himself had been raised in a largely irreligious household and was yet to be comfortable with religious matters, he held great admiration for the gentle Coffman, and for that reason alone was glad to lend his support.

Camp meetings had been a big part of Kentucky life for the past decade, and had infused a great devotion to Christianity into much of the populace. At the center of much of it had been Israel Coffman, who had migrated up from Tennessee in 1783 with an entire congregation of Presbyterians. Coffman had been involved in the ministry since his younger days, when he entered what was then the pre-Tennessee frontier to establish a church at the behest of an ambitious but ill-fated empire builder named Peter Haverly. Now Coffman was a near neighbor of the Tylers and had become a close friend of the family. Clardy still retained some of his early nervous ambivalence about religion, but Coffman was doing a good job of wearing that away a little at a time, to his own pleasure and Clardy's occasional discomfort.

When Clardy and Jenny rode into the upsloping yard of their two-story, rock-walled home, Faith came out to greet him. The sun was just now beginning to set to Clardy's right; its muted evening rays caught the amber glint in Faith's lush hair and made Clardy feel a familiar surge of love and desire for his attractive wife. She was the first women he had ever met who was able to supplant the memory of Dulciana and a romance that had never had a chance to blossom. He still found it hard to believe that such a feminine treasure had become his.

"Clardy, there's been a man here to see you," she said as he handed Jenny down to her.

He dismounted. "Is he still here?"

"No. He came from the newspaper in Frankfort. He heard you were making some big political plans. Getting ready t͏ commence a run for the legislature, or something. He had t͏ notion that the camp meeting was a political rally."

Clardy laughed. "I suppose you set him straight on tha͏

"Yes. He seemed disappointed. He had come quite a͏

tance, you know. I invited him to stay for supper, but he didn't do it. Speaking of supper, we should have eaten it long ago. Where were you two?"

"Out at the big meadow. Sorry we were late. Jenny was practicing her running—less than a minute now across the whole field!"

"Well! You're growing strong and fast, Jenny." The child beamed at her mother's praise.

"What are we eating?"

"Beef stew and fresh bread. It should be ready by the time you get the horse stabled. Come on, Jenny. Let's go slice that bread. Lord knows it's plenty cool enough to cut now."

Clardy stabled and groomed down the horse, thinking about what Faith had told him. He found it amusing that so many people seemed to think him destined for politics, in which he had only a minimal interest. It all went to show how well-known and established he was becoming in Kentucky. Who would have ever thought it? A young man bent on crime, turning into a leading citizen who folks believed destined for office. It was a peculiar world indeed.

On the way back to the house he paused to watch the sun complete its descent behind the horizon. The sky was shot with splendid colors and the breeze carried the sweet, natural aromas of summer, mixed with the delicious smells that wafted out of the kitchen shed behind the house. He heard the voices of Faith and Jenny, singing together the same old tune Jenny had been rendering so loudly most of the way home. Out in the pen near the barn, the hunting hounds bayed at some creature they had scented in the nearby woods. The only dog allowed to run free, a stray that Jenny had come to love, and that therefore had found a place in the family, came dancing and nipping at Clardy's boots. He nudged it gently away.

This is a good evening to be alive, Clardy thought. A good home, a beautiful family . . . I have been blessed.

He entered the house and closed the door behind him. The hounds were still baying, so he went to one of the windows and looked out to see what had them stirred up. He saw nothing unusual.

Out in the darkness of the woods, a lone figure who had been watching the scene and silently cursing the dogs for threatening to reveal him, turned and went back to the horse he had tethered fifty yards away. He mounted and headed for the horse trail that sliced through the woods and toward the creek.

The next evening

Israel Coffman's frame was stooped with age, and his hair and beard had gone white years ago, yet he was substantially unconscious of these effects of the years. His mind was as sharp, maybe sharper, than it had been in his long-past youth. He was famed for his ability to recite almost the entire New Testament from memory, and quite a bit of the Old as well. Unable to read the Bible's words himself after losing his sight on King's Mountain, Coffman had been forced to rely on having others read to him. The memorization had come about naturally, surprising Coffman himself almost as much as those who witnessed it. It was one of the aspects of the man that had made him quite a famous clergyman. His counsel was treasured by people over all Kentucky and beyond; it was not uncommon for folks to ride more than a hundred miles just to meet the man and gain his advice on some matter or another they were having to deal with. Coffman himself seemed almost unaware of his fame, and that lack of self-consciousness was another of his attributes that made people love him.

The old preacher was dozing at the moment inside a small cabin that his servant, Jubal—a former slave of others, now a freeman who served Coffman by choice rather than necessity—had built for him in the woods near his home. Coffman could sense the solitude of the place, and loved it. Some of his happiest hours were spent inside that cabin, or in the shade of its breezy, roofed front porch.

He was awakened by his well-developed, nearly instinctive sense that others were present. Raising his head, he listened, and said, "Jubal?"

"No, sir," came the answer, in the voice of a stranger. "You don't know me. You are the preacher Coffman?"

"I am Israel Coffman." He sat up straighter, brushed down his clothing and cleared his throat, feeling embarrassed to have been caught napping, and slightly alarmed at the fact a stranger had found him in his private place. Coffman wasn't a worrying man, usually, but he did realize that a man had to be careful. "You have me at some disadvantage, sir. . . ."

"I'm just a stranger who has heard many good things about you, Preacher. I hope you don't care that I've sought you out."

"Of course not, sir." Coffman's alarm faded. The man had a gentle manner of speaking and did not strike him as a danger. "What can I do for you?"

He heard the man shuffle his foot. *He's nervous.* "Well, Preacher, I thought I might seek some counsel from you."

Coffman was not surprised; he was often sought out by people troubled by one thing or another. "I'll be happy to give what I can, sir. May I ask your name?"

"Well . . . I'd just as soon keep this private, sir."

"Very well. How can I help you?"

A pause. Then: "Preacher, just how much wrong can be forgiven a man?"

"I know of no limit to forgiveness, my friend."

"But what about a man who began as a good man, and got himself drawn away and into bad things, sins he never thought he'd get into?"

"If that's your story, sir, then it is no different than the story of a multitude of others. We are all sinful folk, knowing what is good and then failing to do it."

"I've been a thief, Preacher. I've stole horses, money, guns . . . once I even helped steal gold from a church in New Orleans."

Coffman wondered whom he was talking to. Judging from the voice, the man was still young. And somewhat familiar, too . . . the voice, the accent, the way the man spoke his words, tugged at something in his mind.

"Sir, I have no power to excuse any sins, big or small. That is the prerogative of our creator. Repent and turn to Christ. No sin is too great to be forgiven."

The man fidgeted. "You'd know more about that kind of thing than I would. I've never known much about religion. . . . Ah, hell—pardon me, Preacher—what's the use? I've ruined my life far too much to try to correct it now." Coffman heard the man turn to walk away.

"Sir, wait! Please don't leave. Believe me, you're feeling nothing but what most feel when they become weighted with their own sins. Don't give up the fight yet."

The man stopped. "Preacher, I don't know that I'll ever become a religious man. Don't think I've got it in me. But I do feel the weight of what I've done wrong. Preacher, I'm a bad man, and I never wanted to be. Even now I make my living by counterfeiting coin. I ain't done an honest deed in years, and I wasn't raised for such as that. When I was growing up, I had me a brother who was what most folks called sorry. He seen himself the same way, even had ideas that when he was grown he'd become a robber. I always mocked him for that . . . and now he's grown and is a good man, and me, the one everyone thought would turn out so good, I'm a thief and counterfeiter. I've escaped jail by the skin of my teeth. I nearly drowned myself running from the law . . . but I reckon it didn't teach me nothing. I turned right around again and went back to the sorry ways I had took up."

"Sir, you spoke of a brother. Do you have other kin?"

"Not besides him. And I'm grateful for that, in a way. Ain't nobody who would be proud to have me for a kinsman. I'm glad there ain't nobody else for me to shame."

"What about your brother? Maybe you could turn to him. He could help you in some way. . . ."

"I doubt my brother knows I'm living. We parted years ago, and I went looking for him. I had money to give him, an inheritance we were supposed to share. But it was stole from me. I never found my brother, and I reckon that was for the best. I'm shamed that I lost him what was his due. But he's done well for himself despite that. Done well despite me." He stopped, and laughed coldly. "You know, Preacher, I came to these parts with the notion of meeting my brother again. I was right there to his house, watching him and his family . . . and I just couldn't do it. I couldn't show myself. I'm too ashamed. I don't even want him to know of me now."

"With all respect, sir, I believe you do," Coffman replied. "Why else would you have come to me? You're seeking encouragement to do the thing you're afraid to do—and I want to give it. I can tell you, from having heard it from Clardy Tyler himself, that he would be happy beyond words to see you."

Coffman stopped speaking, waiting for the man's reaction. He had figured it out—or believed he had—all in a rush when the man had spoken of his brother. Coffman had heard Clardy talk about the brother he still badly missed, the one who had supposedly died while swimming away from pursuers who would have seen him jailed for a theft. As soon as he realize~ who this stranger was, he understood why his voice sound~

familiar. It was almost the same as Clardy Tyler's voice, right down to the most minute inflections.

"How did you . . . you know who I am?" The man sounded very discomfited, just as Coffman had expected.

"You are Thias Tyler, are you not? The brother of my good friend Clardy Tyler?"

The man stammered, then said, "Yes. I am Thias Tyler."

"Mr. Tyler, your brother believes you are dead. He was told that you drowned near New Orleans."

Silence. Then he said, "Good. Good. It's best that he believes that. Because the Thias Tyler he knew *is* dead. I'm sorry I've troubled you, Preacher. I'll be on my way. And sir, I want you not to tell Clardy that I was here. Don't tell him I'm alive. Just say nothing at all."

Coffman was dismayed at that. He knew that the perceived loss of his brother had left a great vacancy in the soul of Clardy Tyler. But if this man refused to grant permission, he would be bound by ministerial honor to hold silence. "Mr. Tyler, I beg you to reconsider. Your brother has grieved over you for years. You have the chance to heal a great wound."

"No. I can't. How can seeing me for what I've turned into heal him? How can he be glad to see a brother who has turned out to be unworthy to bear the Tyler family name? No, Preacher. I was wrong to come here at all. And I don't want you to tell Clardy I was here. You understand me?"

"Yes," Coffman said sadly. "I understand . . . but you are wrong. Clardy already knows about your crimes. He would still be delighted more than you can know to see you."

"He don't need to see me. I don't know why I ever got the notion to come here. Good-bye, Preacher."

"Sir, you're leaving me in a difficult situation—Clardy is my friend. For me to know this but be unable to tell him . . . it will be a torment for me."

"Then it appears I've done a bad thing yet again. It seems to be the way life goes for me. I'm sorry, Preacher. There ain't no more to be said. I'd best leave." He paused. "It's a dark world for me, Preacher. Dark as it can be. I've come to believe there is nothing but darkness, and I'll never escape it."

"Dark . . . sir, I can tell you about darkness. I live in it. Have for many years. But the mere fact that I know it is dark shows something very important."

"What?"

"It shows that there is such a thing as light, and that I have known it. Had I been born blind, had I never known what light was, I would have never detected its absence. I would have lived in darkness without knowing it for what it was. And if the light has enabled me to know darkness for what it is, doesn't the darkness also enable me to know that there is light?"

"What has that got to do with me?"

"Don't you see, Mr. Tyler? You said your world is dark, and no doubt that is true. But does not the fact that you *know* it is dark show that there is something besides darkness? It is by the darkness that we know the light. It is by the crooked that we know the straight. Don't give up your hope, sir. There *is* a light, one no darkness can overcome. No man has lived who is beyond reach of that light. Don't go, Mr. Tyler. Stay. Come with me and see Clardy, and then let's you and I work together to help you find the light and the hope you are looking for."

Silence followed; Coffman sensed the struggle going on inside Thias Tyler. He prayed fervently, waiting for response.

"No, Preacher. No. I can't stay. There's no hope for me, no point in me wasting your time. I got to be going. Thank you for talking to me. Good-bye."

"Sir!" Coffman called, hearing Thias walk away. "Let's talk more. Don't go! Please!"

No answer.

"Sir! Mr. Tyler, please come back!"

He did not come back, though Coffman called again and again, until he knew he was alone.

CHAPTER 43

Two days later, evening

Clardy stood on the porch of his big house, puffing his pipe and watching a storm build in the west. It promised to be a big one, heavy with rain and rampant with lightning. If his guess was correct, it would reach his immediate area in less than an hour. It would be a night when a man was happy to have a stout roof above his head and sturdy walls around him.

As the sky darkened he was surprised to notice a rider coming up the road toward the house. This was not the kind of night he would expect to find anyone out traveling. Squinting, he looked closely, "I'll be!" he muttered to himself. "That looks to be Jubal."

As the rider came in close, thunder rumbling over the hills and meadows around him, Clardy saw that he was right. He stepped out into the yard. "Jubal, pleased to see you this evening. But what in the devil has brought you out with such a building?"

Jubal, devoted friend and servant of Israel Coffman, swung

lithely out of his saddle. " 'Evening, Mr. Tyler. I hope I ain't come at a bad time."

"Not a bad time for me, but it could have been for you, considering all the lightning I'm seeing in them hills there. Come up on the porch. Is everything all right?"

"Well, sir, I reckon everything's all right with me. But I'm worrying about the preacher."

"What's wrong with him?"

"He's fretful. Had something worrying him for the past two or three days."

"You know what it is?"

Jubal's expression and gestures showed uncertainty, like he wasn't sure he should be saying what he was. "Yes, sir, I do. He told me. He tells me things, you see, that he don't tell nobody else. Not even Mrs. Coffman. He tells me because he knows he can trust me to keep it quiet." Jubal ducked his head at that. "But this evening I decided that this last thing he told me, I don't figure I can keep quiet about, even though I ain't supposed to tell." Jubal pursed his lips and shook his head. "Mr. Tyler, you ever run across a time when it seemed like to do the right thing you had to do a wrong thing?"

"I reckon everybody runs upon such times as that, if they live long enough," Clardy replied, somewhat bewildered.

"Well, sir, this here is one of them times for me. The preacher, he told me something that happened here a day or two back, something he wants real bad to tell you but can't, because the person who told him said he couldn't. Preachers have to abide by that, when folks tell them things in secret, you know."

"I know."

"But I reckon I ain't bound by no such promise, am I? I mean, I ain't a preacher."

Clardy could hardly tell what Jubal was talking about and so was in no position to give good counsel. "Jubal, like an old friend of mine named Isaac Ford would have said, you've got me outright confuserated."

Jubal didn't smile. Clardy realized how heavily burdened the man was. "Mr. Tyler, it may not be right for me to tell, but it wouldn't be right for me not to, either."

"Tell what, Jubal?"

Jubal took a deep breath, paused, then said, "Mr. Tyler,

man who came to the preacher a night or two ago, he was . . . he was your brother Thias."

Faith Tyler had never seen her husband in such a state as this. Clardy had never seemed an excitable man, but certainly he was excited now. Faith did not blame him. Clardy had talked to her many times about the brother he had lost to the waters of Lake Pontchartrain. She always thought the tale a fine one, tragically romantic and exciting. Now that she knew Thias Tyler was alive, however, she saw the tale in a different light. Up until now, Clardy's criminal brother had been a figure from a dead past, irrelevant to the present and the happy life she lived here. Now he was irrelevant no longer, and that was worrisome. Clardy was fired with a wild, urgent desire to find Thias. That meant he would leave here, for heaven only knew how long, and certainly would have to delve into dangerous criminal realms if he was to locate the brother who had been lost in that underworld long ago.

She watched Clardy packing his saddlebags and struggled to find some new argument to stop him from going. All the urgings she had made so far had not had any effect and had reduced her to mere pleading. That hadn't worked, either. With great mental struggle, she finally found a new tack.

"Clardy, where will you go? Thias has gone off. You can't possibly know where to look for him. He could be anywhere in the nation, and probably using a different name."

"Jubal said that Thias told the preacher he was a counterfeiter. It ain't much of a clue, but it's the best I've got."

"So he's a counterfeiter. Counterfeiters work in secret. That's not going to help you find him."

"It might. You know as well as I and everybody else that most of the counterfeit coins seen in these parts come from somewhere along the river. The law folks have been able to trace it down that far. That means Thias is most likely living somewhere north of here. Maybe right in Kentucky, or up beyond in the territories."

"So you'll search the entire state, and the territories, too?"

"No, Faith. I know I'd never find him that way. What I'll do go up to the river and lodge myself in an inn. I'll find the ⸱t of folk who know the kind of things the law don't, and put ⸱the word that Clardy Tyler wants to find his brother. I'll ⸱d around a bit of money to help prime the motivation to help me find him. If Thias is there, word will reach him that I'm looking for him. I believe he'll come to *me*, then. He must want to find me, down inside himself. Otherwise he never would have come as nigh to me as he did. He was right here, close by us, Faith! Right here nigh to spitting distance, and I didn't have any notion!"

"Clardy, this is dangerous. I don't like to think of you up in some inn where all kinds of deviltry happens, showing money and talking to criminals. You could be killed that way."

Clardy put down his saddlebags and faced his wife squarely. "Faith, I have to do this. It's as important to me as if one of our own children was lost and I had the chance to find her. Dangerous it might be, but I've been in danger before, and I can take care of myself. I have to try my best to find Thias. Otherwise I could never live content again. Can't you see that?"

She sighed. "Yes. I can. But I'll worry about you until you're home. How long will you be gone?"

"I can't say. It may take some time."

"Can't you take someone with you?"

"This is something I need to do alone, Faith. Thias might never show himself if I had someone with me. And besides, if there is any danger, it wouldn't be right for me to put somebody else in it, would it?"

"Clardy, I don't feel good about this. I understand it—but I don't feel good about it."

"Don't you worry, Faith. I'll be fine. I'll be back safe and sound, and I'll have Thias with me."

Faith replied. "Yes, maybe you will. And that worries me as much as anything else. He's a bad man, Clardy."

He turned on her an expression so fierce it stung. "Don't say that. He's my brother. Maybe he's done bad things, but he ain't bad, not down inside. All through the years growing up, he was the 'good' Tyler. That's his nature. If he's done bad, it's because he's been forced into it."

"Clardy, what value can there be in a 'good' nature 'down inside' somebody when that somebody has spent years choosing to do wicked things? It's the choices a person makes, the things they *do*, that decides what kind of person they are, good or bad."

He seemed ready to shout at her in anger, but he clamped his mouth shut, struggled visibly with his feelings for a couple of moments, then said as quietly but firmly as he could: "I' going to look for Thias, Faith. There will be no more talk about this. Is that clear?"

After that she had nothing more to say, because she knew it would make no difference.

The inn, which stood near the Ohio River shore a few miles below the famous landmark of Cave-in-Rock, was poorly built and starting to lean. Clardy, lodged in a tiny upper room that reminded him of his dismal quarters back in the Natchez days, found himself feeling the entire world was askew when he was in his room. The floor was tilted slightly, causing coins and so on to roll down the slope whenever he dropped one, and after a few days he began to think one leg was growing longer than the other to compensate for the angle of the floor.

He had to admit that Faith was right: this was a dangerous business he had undertaken. He had deliberately chosen an inn with the lowest of reputations, run by a rough, crude bruiser of a man called Smiling Jake, whose forehead sloped even more than his floors. Smiling Jake was reputed to have been a river pirate in his younger days, and now that he was growing older and somewhat crippled with arthritis, had taken up the less strenuous work of innkeeping. Stories had it that some who came to his inn with sizable amounts of money didn't come out again, so Clardy made a point of paying Smiling Jake a substantial extra payment—"in compensation for the excellence of your inn and to make sure I'm safe while here"—and then plied him with drinks and other gifts, such as a watch and a good Siler rifle lock, to make it possible for Jake to feel he was receiving his worth from him without having to go to the trouble of doing him in. Clardy wasn't really sure such a ploy would work—maybe it would even have the opposite effect than was desired—but it seemed worth trying. But just in case, he slept with two loaded pistols at his bedside and another beside his pillow.

Within a week Clardy, using money liberally, had successfully spread word through what seemed some promising underworld channels that Clardy Tyler, the well-known stockman and planter from the Danville area, was at the inn and hoping for a visit from his brother. After that it was a matter of waiting and hoping—and keeping a pistol and dirk always within ~sy rich.

Clardy was asleep one night in his sagging, rope-slat bed

when a knock on the door of his room awakened him. He sat up and reached for his pistol. "Who's there?"

"It's Jake, Mr. Tyler."

Clardy picked up a second pistol when he heard that. Perhaps his luck was about to run out and Smiling Jake was going to see if he couldn't gain more from Clardy Tyler dead than alive. "What can I do for you, Jake?"

"There's a man here calling for you."

Thias? Clardy's throat grew tight. "Who is he?"

"He says his name is Willie Jones. Says he can tell you somewhat about your brother."

Because of his sleepiness, Clardy's mind was slightly beclouded, and he didn't realize until a couple of seconds later where he had heard the name of Willie Jones before. That realization sent him bolting up and toward the door, still retaining one of his pistols in case there was trickery involved here. He opened the door slightly and peered out. Jake was there, holding a lamp whose golden light illuminated his face from below, making him even more of a demon countenance than he normally possessed. It also revealed a second man behind him, a stranger, forty years old or more, with a low hairline and shocks of once-dark hair that had gone salt and pepper.

"You're Willie Jones?"

"Aye, I am."

"You're the man who was jailed in New Orleans with James Hiram . . . with Thias Tyler?"

"I am."

"You escaped?"

"I was freed."

"I'll leave you two be," Jake cut in. Yet he didn't move away at once, and eyed Clardy as if waiting for something.

Clardy understood. "Wait a moment." He went back into his room and returned with a coin that he placed in the innkeeper's hand. Smiling Jake bit it, nodded, and withdrew.

"Come in, Mr. Jones," Clardy said. "You're a man I very much want to talk to. You have news of my brother?"

"I do indeed."

"Then I'll say up front that I'll pay you well if you can lead me to him."

"I ain't looking for money from you. I'm doing this for the sake of doing it."

Clardy hadn't expected to hear anything like that. "Come in.

There's a stool yonder you can sit on, and I'll fill you a pipe if you want to smoke. I've got no food here, nor nothing to offer you to drink."

"I don't drink. I've put it aside. It's an evil thing, drinking. I'm a man who has put evil behind him."

Willie Jones came into the room, ducking under the too-low doorway, and pulled up the stool while Clardy cranked up the lamp he kept burning all night beside the bed, another of his precautions. Jones perched himself on the short stool, long legs crooked and knees sticking up on either side of him. In that posture he reminded Clardy of a dead, crooked-legged spider.

"If you don't drink, do you smoke?"

"Yes. I see no wickedness in tobacco. But if I did, I'd put it aside, too."

Clardy filled the clay pipe bowl from his own pouch, broke off the stem an inch or so, so Jones would have a clean end upon which to pull, peeled a splinter off the unpainted wall, lit it in the lamp, and held it out for the other to use in lighting up his pipe. Then he sat down on the side of the bed, keeping within reach of the pistols he had laid aside to deal with the pipe. He was thinking of how Willie Jones seemed to be an odd sort of man. He certainly had much to say about wickedness.

Jones eyed the pistols. "You won't need those with me. I won't hurt you. I've put hurting folks behind me."

"You seem to have put a lot of things behind you, sir. Mr. Jones, can you tell me where my brother is?"

"Not for certain. I can tell you where I feel right sure he is, though, and for total certain where he's been the last few months. Me and him, we've been working together. We stole church gold together in New Orleans, and there I believed, and the law believed, that your brother lost his life in Lake Pontchartrain. But he lived through it, and after I was freed I chanced to find him again. I had just shook off a sickness that nigh killed me when I was in irons. Ain't nobody never been more surprised than when I seen Thias was still alive. Meeting him was like a sign to me that we should work together again. We commenced to being partners once more. Most recent we was counterfeiters of gold coin, working out of a cave up north of the river. It was a sinful business. I've put it behind me."

"Did you tell Thias how Deerfield and me had come looking for him in New Orleans?"

"I told him. It moved him deep, sir. But he said it was best that you didn't find him. He believes he ain't worthy of being nobody's brother no more."

"Then he believes nonsense. Is Thias still making coin at that cave?"

"Not no more. He's gone."

Clardy felt great disappointment. "Do you know where he went?"

"If I was a gambling man—which I once was, before I put it behind me—I'd bet he was heading for New Orleans. There's a woman there he cares for. She's a good woman, divorced from a bad man, and he declares he loves her and wants to marry her. I believe he would have married her long ago if he didn't think he wasn't good enough for her and her baby."

"So the woman has a child already."

"Aye. A little girl, I believe. Fathered by the man who divorced her. I happen to know a bit about that man, too, and it's probably for the best he left her. He's a dangerous sort of fellow. He threatened his own wife's life a time or two, or so Thias told me."

"Tell me more about Thias."

"You got to know that Thias, he's been down on himself for his bad ways for years. Last I talked to him, he was saying he wants to lay aside his wrong ways and make himself worthy of that woman. And he's wise to do that. It's a time for all of us to be putting our wrong ways behind us, and getting ready. That's why I've quit my own wickedness. No more counterfeiting, no more stealing and cheating, like I've done before. Now I'm going about, seeking to do good instead of bad. I'm getting ready."

"Ready for what?"

"For the pock-lips."

"The what?"

"The pock-lips. The great day of judgment. The end of the world. It's right upon us, Mr. Tyler. It won't be long at all until this world comes to an end and we all stand in judgment."

Clardy was growing dismayed. It appeared likely that Willie Jones was not merely odd, but maybe a little deranged. The apocalypse? The end of the world? His mind flashed back to the odd preacher he had seen in Natchez-under-the-Hill years ago. That man had talked of the end of the world, too.

"How do you know the end of the world is coming?" Clardy asked.

"It has been revealed to me in a dream," Jones replied. "There'll be a great shaking of the land, an opening of the earth, and then it will all come to an end. It will be a great and dreadful day."

So that was it. A dream believer. Clardy had doubts about that kind of thing, being an instinctive skeptic where oneiromancy was concerned. "Well ... I suppose we'll see. End of the world or not, I want to find my brother. This woman in New Orleans ... you could take me to her?"

"Aye, I could. If there's time before the pock-lips comes."

"Mr. Jones, have you ever thought that maybe that dream was nothing more than a dream?"

"Oh, it's more than that. It's rev'lation. My mother—she understood mysteries and such—she had dreams of rev'lation from time to time, and they come true every time. Now I've got the same gift. When you have a dream of rev'lation, you can tell it. You wake up all in a sweat, and you *know*."

Clardy wasn't sure what to make of this man. Jones's jabber about the end of the world and dreams of "rev'lation" sounded inane, casting great doubt on his general reliability. Could he rely on the veracity of anything such a man had to say, even on a nonapocalyptic topic like the whereabouts of Thias Tyler? Clardy had little choice. No more promising sources of information had come forward.

So he would just have to take Jones at his word and hope for the best. "I want you to guide me to this woman," Clardy said. "If we can find her, maybe we'll find Thias, too."

"I think along those very same lines, sir. But this is no small journey. You're willing to go clear to New Orleans on just the chance of finding your brother? I mean, there's no assurance he'd be there."

"I know that. But yes, I'm ready to go. You don't know it, but there's actually some convenience for me in all this. It happens I would have been going to New Orleans soon, anyway. There's an old and good friend of mine who passed away and was laid to rest down there years and years ago. I've been planning a journey there to fetch back his remains and bury them in Kentucky, like he wanted. God willing, now I can come back not only with his bones in tow, but my brother at my side, too—if what you tell me is right. But I have to be full honest with you, Mr. Jones. When a full stranger comes to me, saying he wants to do something good on my behalf without any kind of pay for it, my suspicions spark up like fresh tinder. What is it to you whether I find my brother or not? Why do you care?"

"I already told you, Mr. Tyler. I'm doing it because the judgment is coming. I've spent my life doing wrong. Not much time left to do good and make up for it."

"For some reason, sir, I find it hard to believe that's your only reason. Most men I've known who've spent their lives in wrongdoing wouldn't shrug it off because of a dream."

"Mr. Tyler, there's things about me that you don't know. You're looking at a man with no hope of glory once this world ends. That door was closed to me long ago, and there ain't a blessed thing I can do about it. All I can do is try to cool down the hellfires that are waiting for me as much as I can, by doing good with what time I have left." Suddenly the man's eyes went red and he choked up in tears, rousing new and stronger doubts in Clardy about his mental stability. "And there's another reason, too. I want to do good for somebody because I know what it means to have good done for me. You might think that sounds like something to scoff at, but I mean every bit of it."

"What do you mean? What good thing was done for you?"

"I was freed from that prison because of the goodness of a man who filed a petition for my release. And for the life of me, I don't know to this day why he did it. I can't figure it out at all. . . ." Jones wiped a tear that had sneaked down his left cheek. "All I know is, I was locked up, and through the goodness of a man I was set free. A man who had no cause at all to help me, none at all." He looked at Clardy in an odd way. "You ever been haunted, Mr. Tyler? I have been. Haunted by goodness. The memory of the kindness that was done me, it's haunted me ever since it happened. Always over my shoulder, always there, like a ghost. A good kind of ghost. I tell you, sir, that lawyer changed me when he got me freed from that prison. Why would a man do that for another? Why would *that* man do such a thing for *me*?"

Clardy asked, "Might that lawyer's name have been Japheth Deerfield?"

"It was. It was indeed."

"I was with Japheth Deerfield in New Orleans, probably right at that same time. We had learned from another of your partners, a fellow named Timothy—"

Jones nodded. "Yes. He told me. You was looking for Thias even then."

"I was. Timothy gave me the strongest clue I had received until then about what had become of Thias. He was hiding out in Natchez-under-the-Hill when I met him. Living with an old harlot and fearing that soldiers were going to get him. He told me Thias was in jail, along with you, in New Orleans."

"Yes . . . and then the lawyer Deerfield came to me and I told him Thias had drownded. I didn't know he had come out of that lake alive. It was a miracle he did, sure as the world is ending."

Clardy was struck at that moment with a guilty but intriguing realization: even though he had not had anything to do with the freeing of Willie Jones, he was in a position to shift the truth around a bit and thereby claim some of the credit for himself. That would play on Jones's sense of gratitude, and maybe make him even more desirous of being helpful. It was a manipulative thing to do, certainly wrong . . . but Clardy decided this was a temptation he would not resist. His desperation to find Thias was stronger than his sense of morality. He was glad the Preacher Coffman wasn't privy to what he was about to do. It would shame him clear to the soul.

"Mr. Jones, I ought to tell you: I had a bit of a part in helping you get free myself. I had told Japheth Deerfield that whether or not we found Thias in the prison, I thought we ought to help any of his companions there get free, if we could. It was something we could do sort of in honor of Thias. Helping his friends, you see." Clardy smiled, hiding a huge surge of guilt. *There. I've told the lie, Lord forgive me. Now that it's told, I hope it helps.*

Jones gave him an odd, surprised look, then his eyes filled with tears again. "Then I owe you just as much as Japheth Deerfield. Mr. Tyler, sir, I thank you. More than you can know. I would have died in that prison if not for you and Japheth Deerfield having mercy on me."

Clardy thought: I'm the lowest kind of scoundrel, lying to a man about something so near to his heart as who rescued him from prison. But what was done was done—and it had worked.

"All I ask of you is to help me find Thias," Clardy said. "I'm taking a chance, even trusting you. If it's gratefulness you want to show me, then do it by proving yourself worthy of that trust."

"I give you my pledge, sir. I'll take you to Thias's woman, and if we're fortunate, we'll find him with her. But I must tell you, Mr. Tyler, I can't promise you he'll be there. He didn't tell me where he was bound, and it's only my best guessing that he's gone to her. He was surely talking of her a lot before he went."

"I'll take my chances." Clardy stuck out his hand. "Mr. Jones, you and me are partners. I'll stick by you—and I *will* pay you for your help, even if you are willing to do it for free. All I ask of you is that you be straight and true with me, and give the best search we can give. If we find Thias at the end, then we'll have succeeded. If we don't, well, we'll have done the best we could."

"I'll be straight and true, sir. You can trust me. There was a time when you couldn't have, I'll admit, but that's changed. The Judgment Day is coming. The earth's going to open up and hell will swallow the unrighteous. When it swallows me, I want there to be more than just wickedness on my ledger of deeds. I'm a trusty man now. I've done wrong, but all that--"

"Has been put behind you," Clardy finished. "That's good, Mr. Jones. That's good. Now let me refill that pipe for you, and let's talk more about what you know of my brother."

CHAPTER 44

Clardy Tyler and Willie Jones rode away from the inn the next morning and headed to the Tyler house. There, Clardy explained to Faith what was going on, and watched her trying to hide her worry when she discovered that the stranger he would be traveling with was a man with a long criminal history. Clardy hoped she would not try to dissuade him, desiring not to part from her on bad terms—because he would not be dissuaded, no matter what she said. She voiced no argument, to his relief.

After outfitting himself and the obviously impoverished Jones for travel, Clardy brought out and strengthened his stoutest wagon, and put together a team of his strongest horses to pull it. Upon the wagon he loaded a tightly built sealed coffin, created specifically to hold the bones of Isaac Ford during the long voyage back from New Orleans to Kentucky. The coffin had been in storage now for four years; the dust and cobwebs covering it were tangible evidence of how long Clardy had neglected his promise to Isaac Ford, and made him feel ashamed.

Clardy's plan was a reverse of the pattern followed by the Kaintucks who traded in the lower Mississippi market towns. He would travel by land to Nashville, and there take to the route that Nashvillians generally called the Natchez Road or Chickasaw Trail, and Natchezians called the Boatman's Trail or the Nashville Road.

Clardy embarked on his journey ready to merely endure Willie Jones, but the farther they went, the more he began to actually like the fellow. Jones was clearly no saint, but neither did he seem to be trying to present himself as anything more than he was. He talked openly about his criminal past, seldom making excuses for it, but talked just as much about wanting to better himself "before the end-time comes." Clardy initially scorned Jones's obsessed notion that the world was about to end, but the more talk he heard about it over the miles, the more it began to actually unnerve him some. *What if* . . . But no. There was no sense in believing that Jones's dreams actually held any meaning. Clardy figured that if the Lord intended to bring the world to its closure, he would surely find some better way of announcing it than through the nightmares of a small-time backwoods criminal.

Wrongheaded though Jones's apocalyptic notions might be, Clardy suspected they had done the man's character some good. It appeared that Jones was authentically trying to be a better person. It was difficult for Clardy to ascertain whether that was because of Jones's belief that judgment was coming soon, or how moved he'd been by Japheth Deerfield's petition on his behalf while he was a New Orleans prisoner.

In spite of Jones's obvious desire to become honest and good, Clardy was not about to fully trust the man. Jones was, after all, a stranger with nothing in his record to speak good of him, and in addition, several times Clardy caught the man seemingly on the verge of calling himself a different name than Willie Jones. That was no surprise; it was common for frontier criminal folk to use any number of different names throughout their life—but it did let Clardy know that Jones was still keeping some aspects of himself a secret, and a man who held secrets was not a man Clardy intended to fully trust.

Jones's tendency was to talk about himself, but finally he began questioning Clardy about his relatively famous experience as a pursuer of the notorious Harpes.

"Are you really the Tyler they call the Harpe hunter?" Jones asked.

"Some have called me that."

"And you were there when Big Harpe lost his head?"

"I was."

"I hear that head sfill hangs in the tree where it was stuck."

"Not no more," Clardy replied. "It hung there for years, but it was finally took down by an old woman, or so they tell me."

"Why'd an old woman want a skullbone?"

"They tell me she had her a son suffering from the fits. And you know that old remedy for the fits—imbibe the powder of a ground-up skull and you'll be cured. Or so they say. I don't believe it."

"Oh, you ought not doubt what a potion can do," Jones replied. "I know from my own experience what power there is in mixtures put together in just such a way by somebody who knows what they're doing."

"You believe in witching and such, do you?"

"Yes, sir," Jones replied solemnly. "I've been witched in the worst kind of way my very self, as a boy. What my life has been ever since, you can lay at the feet of that witching. It's because of that I'm hell-bound today, with no way to save myself."

Clardy was amazed at how superstitious Jones was. He saw the world through the eyes of a crude kind of mysticism. Witching, potions, dreams of revelation, signs of the apocalypse—these things were substantially alien to Clardy, who usually viewed the world on its surface without probing much deeper. But for Jones they shaped every aspect of his fatalistic worldview.

They drove the wagon for many days, passing down through Kentucky, into Tennessee, and on to Nashville, where an accident slightly damaged the rear axle of the wagon. There remained a few days to have the wagon repaired, and inevitably word leaked out that Clardy Tyler was back in town again, heading down to New Orleans to fetch the bones of Isaac Ford for reburial in Kentucky. He received quite a stream of visitors at the Nashville Inn, a hostelry located north of the Cumberland River with Lick Branch on its east and Cedar Knob to its north. Jones seemed quite impressed to see Clardy receiving so much attention, and thereafter acted quite proud to be in his company. Clardy noticed it and thought it was flattering and a little touching, and his liking for Jones grew.

When the wagon was fixed, they continued. Leaving Nashville, they passed through the various stations and stands along the road toward Natchez: Franklin, Colbert's, Pigeon Roost, and so on. One stand that they avoided was Grinder's, where the well-known Meriwhether Lewis had come to a bad and mysterious end two years before. They plunged deep onto the trace, still a rugged route despite increased use and various efforts through the years to improve its best portions and reroute around its worst ones. Here both men were nervous and more watchful than they had been on the first portion of their journey. Despite the passing of the worst of the outlaw years, there was still danger on this often shaded and mysterious route. Every approaching party of travelers they regarded with suspicion and caution until they were past, and at night they took turns sleeping so as not to be left unguarded.

On they traveled, past Norton's, McRaven's, Gibson's, Huntstown, Union Town . . . and the closer they came to Natchez, the better Clardy felt. It appeared they were going to make it safely the full length of the trace, and that was something to rejoice about.

Jones didn't rejoice, however. As they neared Washington, the final stop before coming to Natchez, Jones was solemn and tense. Clardy was compelled to take note of it with him and ask what was wrong.

"I can't go to Natchez," Jones replied.

"Why not?"

"I got my reasons."

"I can think of one good reason to go. You've been talking about how much it meant to you that Japheth Deerfield petitioned you free in New Orleans. Now's your opportunity to go and thank him in person."

"No!" Jones replied sharply. "That's the one thing I can't do."

"Why the devil not?"

"I have my reasons. That answer suit you well enough, Mr. Tyler?"

Clardy knew better than to ask again after that, though he was curious. Was having to look Japheth Deerfield in the eye, a man to whom he owed his very freedom, simply too much for Jones to bear? An answer to that was unlikely to come.

Jones's unwillingness to go to Natchez changed Clardy's plans. He had intended to go into town and maybe even pay call on Japheth, who surely would be interested both in the fac that he was going after the remains of Isaac Ford and th Thias was alive after all. Clardy was also curious about h the Deerfields were doing; the last time he was in Natchez, years ago, he had heard that vague mention of some sort of trouble having beset the family.

That mystery would have to go unresolved. If Jones was determined not to enter Natchez, Clardy wasn't going to go in alone. He had come to substantially trust Jones, but not enough to leave him alone for any lengthy period and risk having him change his mind and vanish. Without Jones, it might be impossible to find the woman who would, he hoped, ultimately lead to Thias.

They were between Washington and Natchez when the robber appeared. He was alone, very young, very nervous. When Clardy saw him step out from among the moss-covered trees along a lonely stretch of the road, he immediately saw himself many years ago, stepping out of hiding along Kentucky's Wilderness road to try and hold up a peddler named Peyton.

"You two stop where you are," the rifle-bearing young man said. The gun's barrel was shaking so badly that sometimes it aimed at the men, other times at the ground or the treetops. "Drop your weapons on the ground. Do it easy!"

"Young man, put that rifle down and go away," Clardy said. "You don't need the kind of trouble that comes with thieving."

"Put wickedness behind you, boy," Jones contributed. "You'd best be getting ready for the day of judgment."

The young man apparently took that as a veiled threat. He also appeared to have just noticed, to his agitation, that the wagon being driven by his victims carried a coffin. "I said for you to drop them weapons!" he said, still nervous but now growing angry, too. "I'll shoot you dead if you don't!"

"If you shot one of us, you'd be left with an empty rifle. Whichever of us you hadn't shot would then be able to kill you at his ease," Clardy pointed out.

The robber gritted his teeth and did his best to level the wavering rifle at Clardy's chest. "I'll kill you right now," he said. "Then we'll see how much wise-arse talk comes from a dead man's throat."

Jones, seated beside Clardy, stood and lifted a hand. "You put that rifle down," he said. Turning, he climbed down out of the wagon. "Give it to me. You don't want to hurt nobody."

"Willie, I don't think you should be doing that," Clardy said.

"Come on, boy, hand me the rifle. I'll take it on up the road ad and leave it for you, and you can fetch it safe and sound, and without having to worry about the jail or stocks for having robbed travelers. Come on, now, hand it to—"

The robber fired the rifle into Jones's midsection. Clardy let out a yell as Jones collapsed like a puppet with the strings cut. He raised his rifle and fired it at the robber, but he missed and was instantly glad he had. He didn't want to kill anyone. The robber turned and fled into the woods. Clardy leaped down from the wagon, stilled the disturbed horses that threatened to trample right across Jones's crumpled body. Then he knelt beside his fallen companion.

"Willie, Willie—are you alive?"

Willie Jones moaned but said nothing. Clardy rolled him over and saw his eyes roll up into his head just before the lids fluttered closed. He put his head to Jones's chest. He was still breathing. But the wound was bad. It was in the general area of his stomach, and bleeding badly.

"Willie, it seems we'll be going to Natchez after all," Clardy said. "We'll get you care. We'll get that rifle ball out of you and get you better."

He managed to get Jones into the wagon, but it was very difficult and he feared that in the process of it all he had done the wound even more damage. He leaped into the seat, took up the leads, and sent the wagon rolling toward Natchez as fast as he dared drive it with a badly wounded man in the back, lying up against the tied-down future coffin of Isaac Ford.

The three-storied, brick Natchez Hospital, built in 1805, was one of the finest of the Natchez improvements since Clardy had last been in the town. He hauled the gray-faced, badly drained Willie Jones directly to the hospital and did his best to stay out of the way as a doctor began working on him.

Clardy felt terribly upset, and did not like to admit to himself that much of the reason was purely selfish. It seemed likely that Jones was going to die, leaving him without a guide. Why had he been so foolish as not to demand that Jones give him a written description of the woman Thias loved, directions as to how to find her, and so on? All he knew about her was that her name was Elizabeth Ridge, she was a widow with two children, and lived near the levee in New Orleans the last time Jones had seen her. With that information Clardy knew he might be able to find her alone, but he'd counted on having Jones with him. He swore at his luck, then at himself for goo measure for caring more about how this was going to affect him than the fact that a man was dying.

The surgical work on Jones went on for a long time, and finally Clardy left the building for some fresh air. He sat outside, seated on the ground with his back against the brick wall, and ducked his head low, hiding from the world behind the brim of his hat. He had the terrible feeling that this new quest for a lost brother was going to turn out as badly as his earlier tries. He felt like cursing the very world.

"Sir?"

The voice made Clardy look up. It was growing on toward evening, but enough light remained in the sky to cast the man standing before him into silhouette. At first Clardy thought this was someone from the hospital, come to tell him the outcome of the surgery. "Yes?"

"My Lord, it *is* you . . . or I believe it is. Clardy Tyler?"

Clardy stood, quickly brushing himself off and then sticking out his hand. "Japheth Deerfield, it's good to see you. I didn't expect to encounter you." He moved a little to alter the angle of the light and get a better view of Japheth. When he did, he was shocked. Japheth was thin and pale, with dark rings beneath his eyes and a generally sickly complexion. As he shook Japheth's hand, he noticed that the grip seemed weak.

"What brings you to Natchez, Mr. Tyler?" Japheth asked.

"I'm passing through. On my way to New Orleans. I'm fetching back the body of Isaac Ford. I plan to sail it up to Kentucky and bury him where he wanted to be laid. I should have done it years ago."

Japheth said, "Well, I'm fascinated. But why are you here at the hospital? Is something—ah, Celinda! Come here, Celinda! Look who I've run into!"

Clardy turned and slipped off his hat. He nodded at the woman who approached. This was Celinda as he remembered her, but with a few lines of the years on her face. But no. It would take more than the years that had passed since he last saw her to account for those lines. Celinda's face was that of a woman who had suffered, either mentally or physically, maybe both.

"Celinda, it's Clardy Tyler. You recall him, I suppose?"

Clardy remembered how Celinda Deerfield had disliked im, and wondered if such feelings lingered after all this time. om the look of her, he could not tell. But she gave a polite nod of the head and extended her slender hand in a friendly enough manner. He shook it, nodded back. "Mrs. Deerfield. Good to see you."

"Mr. Tyler was telling me he is on his way to New Orleans to bring back the body of Isaac Ford. We met Mr. Ford about the same time we met Mr. Tyler."

"I remember him," Celinda replied, and as she spoke it was as if a cloud passed over her features for a moment.

Yes, Clardy thought. She has suffered. I can tell it so easily. And her husband, too.

"Mr. Tyler, we were on our way home. Would you come and join us . . . if it's all right with you, dear." The last phrase was spoken to Celinda.

Clardy looked at her face. Again that dark cloud passing. "Of course. He is welcome," she said, in a way that made it impossible to know whether it was sincere or forced.

It didn't matter; Clardy could not leave without knowing what would become of his partner. "Thank you for the invitation," he said. "But I have a traveling companion here who has been hurt. Whether he will live or die is something I don't yet know, and until I do, I have to stay where I am."

"I'm sorry to hear about your companion," Japheth said. "A relative or a friend?"

"Neither, really," Clardy said. "Just a man who knows my brother."

"*Knows?* But I thought your brother was—"

"I thought the same. But he is alive."

"But I was told—"

"Yes, I know. But he didn't drown in that lake, Mr. Deerfield. Somehow he came out alive, and I know it's true because Thias came looking for me himself, though we failed to come together. And the man who's traveling with me, and who's inside this hospital, he knows Thias very well, and has worked with him over the past few years. You know him, too. It's Willie Jones."

"Jones!" Japheth's face filled with such astonishment and interest that for a moment he lost his pallor and seemed as he had been the first time Clardy met him. "Mr. Tyler, do you realize that I petitioned for Jones's release after we found out your brother was dead . . . though I suppose from what you're telling me that we hadn't really 'found out' the true facts of the case. I never even lingered to see what the outcome of my petition was for him."

"He was freed, and sir, it helped spark a change in him—from a man who never thought of right and wrong to one who began to care about such things. He's told me all this himself. He did some bad after he was freed—counterfeiting gold coin with my own brother, for one thing—but he was different, because you took the time to do something good for him. To this day he don't know why you did it."

"Pity, pure and simple. I did it out of pity," Japheth answered. "I saw that the man was bound to die in that cell, and I petitioned for his release as an act of mercy. I'm glad it had a good effect on him."

"Yes." Clardy's face grew somber. "But now I fear he's going to die. He was badly wounded."

"I'd like to meet him," Japheth said.

"I'd like for you to meet him, too," Clardy said. "I suggested the same to him, but he rejected the idea. Maybe the idea of meeting you shames him. I reckon he must see you as a saintly figure, too good for him to speak with. That's the only reason I can figure out."

"Japheth, we should be getting home."

Remembering now that the Deerfields had a daughter, and assuming that it was the need to return to her that motivated Celinda's hurry, Clardy asked, "Mrs. Deerfield, how is .... Beulahland, I believe her name is?" Clardy asked politely.

"She is fine, thank you. A strong and healthy young girl now, not the baby she was when you were here before. She has sustained herself quite well under it all."

"I'm glad she's well." Sustained herself quite well . . . What was this woman talking about?

Japheth, who had cast a sharp glance at his wife while she made her final comment, said, "Where will you be staying tonight, Mr. Tyler?"

"I ain't give it a thought. Right here, I suppose."

"No need for that. If the situation allows you to leave here, you will stay with us."

Clardy glanced at Celinda. He saw neither welcome nor rejection in her look. He thought: This is a woman who has learned to hide her feelings very well indeed.

"Thank you. I might take you up on that. You live in the same place as before?"

"No, no. We've moved farther down the street." He gave quick instructions. "A more modest place than we had."

Clardy didn't recall the original Deerfield house as anything more than modest. What they lived in now, then, must be quite small. A move down to a lesser house, the look of trials endured on Celinda's face, her talk of their child having "sustained herself quite well," the tracks of suffering on her features and Japheth's—all these things evidenced clearly that difficult times of some sort had been the lot of the Deerfields. Those earlier whispers of unspecified trouble having beset this family must have been true.

He watched them walk away. Odd, running into them like that. He wouldn't have expected to encounter them at a hospital. Maybe Japheth had been here because he was sick.

Clardy smoked three pipefuls of tobacco, then sat down where he had been before. An hour later a woman in a long nurse's dress came out and fetched him in.

The surgeon was blood-splattered and looked very tired. "He is still alive, but only barely. I don't believe he will live."

Clardy felt wrenched. "May I see him?"

"Not now. He's unconscious, anyway. In the morning, if he's come around again, you can see him. For now he must rest . . . and you must talk to the law and tell what happened to him. This young bandit you mentioned sounds like a man who shot another person in the same area about a week ago."

"I'll go report it," Clardy replied.

He left the hospital, praying that Jones would make it through, and if not, that he would at least grow strong enough to tell Clardy more about where and how to find the woman they were seeking, the woman who would be his best hope for finding Thias.

Clardy, driving the coffin-bearing wagon, went to the proper authorities and made his report, then walked out onto the street. Should he take up Japheth's offer for lodging? Part of him felt the impulse to simply take boarding in an inn and not intrude himself further into the life of a family in which ambivalent feelings, at best, were held toward him. Another part, overwhelmed with curiosity about the Deerfields' obviously difficult recent history, and his own eagerness to tell of his own family and experiences, told him to go ahead and find the Deerfield house.

The latter part won the argument. Clardy drove the wagon

slowly along through the dusk, following Japheth's earlier directions, until he found a house that seemed to be at the place he'd been directed to go. Yet this house was terribly small, certainly too small to be the residence of even a moderately successful attorney in Natchez, a town famous for being a place where one in every ten residents was embroiled in some kind of lawsuit at any given time and where lawyers therefore thrived. Clardy was about to turn away when the door opened and Japheth thrust his head out. "Mr. Tyler, you've found us. I'm glad. Drive your wagon around back and we'll deal with your horses. You've come in time for supper."

Celinda and her daughter went to their beds early, but Clardy and Japheth sat up late that night, talking. There was much to tell on both sides. Japheth was very interested in Clardy's life since they parted ways in New Orleans. He was clearly pleased that Clardy's situation had improved, that he now had a fine wife and family, a good home, and success in his business. Looking around at the condition of Japheth's own house, shabby in comparison to Clardy's big stone dwelling, Clardy thought how remarkably fine it was of the man to be capable of feeling happiness for some other person's success when his own was obviously so lacking. No wonder he had always tended to think well of Japheth Deerfield, despite those few doubts he felt early on, when he wasn't sure what Japheth's motives were for wanting to help him find Thias.

Clardy's story told, Japheth told his own. Clardy was intrigued, often shocked, sometimes repelled, and by the time Japheth was through speaking, full of tremendous sympathy for the entire family.

Japheth told about the incident involving Timothy Rumbolt and his own tragically fated attempt to deal with his attempted blackmail without going through the open venues of the law. The suicide of Timothy, who had been frightened far more thoroughly than Japheth could imagine by all the threatening talk about soldiers, had led to an investigation. Japheth had cooperated fully and told the entire story just as it had happened, and as would be expected, the news filled all of Natchez. Every detail managed to reach the public, from the attempted rape Celinda had been forced to endure to Japheth's fated visit. Of course, half the population, eager for scandal, refused to believe it. There had been talk about Celinda having carried on a love affair with a Natchez-under-the-Hill man, about Japheth having threatened the old woman who lived with Celinda's lover, about Japheth murdering the man and managing to make it appear to be suicide. Never mind that even the facts as given by Beatrice Sullivan failed to support that wild and slanderous tale; never mind that the official investigation found Japheth innocent of any wrongdoing. What mattered in the public mind, particularly that branch of the public mind embodied in the motley rabble of Natchez-under-the-Hill, was scandal. The story spread, growing ever more distorted, bringing more and more unjustified shame onto the entire Deerfield family. Japheth's legal practice had suffered, and for the sake of his partners, he resigned the firm and opened an independent, smaller office elsewhere in town. He managed to find enough business to keep food on the table, but not enough to allow them to live even in the modest home they had occupied before. They sold the place and moved to a smaller home, then sold that one, too, and moved to the tiny house they occupied now.

"I was ready many times to give up and leave Natchez," Japheth told Clardy. "But Celinda would hear none of it. She kept repeating a thing her own father had told her right at the end of his life: 'You must learn to be strong.'" He chuckled. "'Learn to be strong.' God knows that she *is* strong. She carried me through it all, kept me fighting for my own good name when I was ready to give up. She declared we had done nothing wrong, that maybe I was guilty of bad judgment in trying to deal with Timothy's extortion directly, instead of going through the proper legal channels, but that if my judgment was bad, it had been motivated out of love for her and the desire to avoid exposing my family to scandal." He paused and shuddered. "God knows I failed in that. Failed miserably. When I frightened that poor man into putting that pistol into his mouth—and I swear to you, Mr. Tyler, I had no intention of that happening—I brought more scandal on my family than most people ever endure. I almost ruined our happiness here. And the strain of it cost us much. Especially Celinda."

"What do you mean?"

"We lost a child. Another girl. She lived not even a day past her birth, which came too early. The strain of all that had happened to us—I don't doubt that is what did it. And though we still have our Beulahland, Celinda has felt the loss of that baby like a great wound that won't heal. You can see in her face how it has aged her." His eyes misted. "She dreams of that baby. Almost every night. Dreams and wakes up in tears."

"I'm truly sorry."

"Yes. Thank you. It's been difficult for Celinda, and watching her suffer so hasn't been good for my health. My spirit is growing a bit weak, you see. Occasionally I have spells of pain and weakness from it and have to seek a physician's help."

"Was that why you were at the hospital tonight?"

"Yes. Fortunately, the Lord's good grace was with me tonight and the pain went away, so here I am at home again." He forced a bright face. "And with a welcome guest I hadn't expected to see! So everything isn't dark and grim in the life of Japheth Deerfield, eh?"

"No," Clardy replied, smiling around the stem of his pipe. "Though I am regretful you are suffering poor health." He frowned in silent contemplation a few moments. "You know what you should do, Japheth?"

"Tell me."

"You should leave this town. Get away from this river air, and all the memories. Move elsewhere and start again. I'll wager your heart would be the stronger for it and your wife all the happier."

Japheth looked into the fire. "It sounds wonderfully good, Clardy. Odd that you should say it, too. Celinda said as much to me two days ago, and then again tonight, when my chest was hurting. 'Japheth,' she said, 'we've fought it out as best we could. Now we can leave with our pride still in place.' And you know, she's right. I honestly believe I've managed over the past year to regain most of my reputation. Even my business is improving. Before long we'd be able to move into a better house . . . but neither one of us feel happy about that idea. Celinda says she wants to go home."

"Meaning where?"

"Kentucky."

"That would be a fine move for you. A fine one. Kentucky is growing. There's plenty of places a good lawyer could make his living. There, you'd have no memories of scandals and struggles. You could start fresh. And that fine Kentucky air, that's as pure and healing an air as a man could breathe. It would be good for you, Japheth." And then Clardy made Japheth an offer that the lawyer took with him to his bed, to think about in the night and discuss with his wife in the morning.

At breakfast the next day, his answer was ready. "We will accept your offer, Clardy," Japheth said. "And we thank you for it."

"I'm glad to hear it," Clardy said. "And like Sweeney McCracken would have said, don't it seem providential that I'll be coming up past Natchez on a sailing vessel anyway! I'll be hanged before I'd wheel that coffin all the way back to Kentucky by land. It'll be no trouble at all to make room for three more and a bit of luggage."

"There's one thing that troubles me," Celinda said. It had not been common for her to inject herself into conversations between Clardy and her husband either now or in Clardy's prior time in Natchez, so her intrusion now startled both men.

"What's that, dear?" Japheth asked.

"There may be a man on that boat who once held you at the point of a gun and robbed you," she said.

It was true, though Clardy hadn't thought about it from that angle. If he succeeded in finding Thias, he hoped to talk him into coming back with him to Kentucky. For him to be on the same vessel as Japheth and Celinda could make for some clumsy personal frictions.

"Don't let that worry you, Celinda," Japheth said. "I'm an attorney. I'm accustomed to tense situations. Heaven knows, with what this family has endured, we're all accustomed to that by now. If Thias Tyler is on that boat when Clardy sails it in, then so be it. There comes a time when the past must be forgotten." He lifted his coffee cup. "To Kentucky, and a new world for the Deerfield family, thanks to the generous offer of Clardy Tyler."

Clardy thought: Willie Jones sees a world ending, Japheth sees one beginning. Who will be right? I can't yet know.

They raised their assorted cups—Beulahland hefting up a glass of milk—and drank. Clardy glanced at Celinda and tried to find her feelings in her face. He could not. She was as impossible for him to read as a new river to a novice boatman. An intriguing woman she was, and very full of mystery.

CHAPTER 45

Celinda walked beside Japheth, arm in arm with him, her left hand holding her daughter's. To her husband's right was Clardy Tyler, tense and solemn. They were going toward the Natchez Hospital, there to find out the fate of Clardy's injured partner. Clardy had already said that he was braced to be informed that the man had died in the night.

Celinda hoped the man hadn't died, mostly for Japheth's sake. He was interested in meeting this man, and she was glad. It wasn't that she cared so much about the meeting itself, but that her husband's enthusiastic curiosity and interest in life was a characteristic that had slowly declined under the onslaught of the difficult times they had known, and it was good to see it returning. For that she had to credit Clardy Tyler, and she did not miss the irony of it. Clardy Tyler was a man she once had felt was going to bring bad fortune to her family, and for a time she had, with rather convoluted logic, faulted him for the scandal that had descended upon her husband and herself. The passing years had matured and changed that viewpoint, however. Now she knew that it wasn't Clardy Tyler at fault. In one sense there was no one to blame; the whole sorry affair had only been borne to them on the unpredictable currents of circumstances. Her own actions had been the stimulus that set off the chain of events, and Japheth's well-motivated but misguided attempt to cut off the problem before it grew had set the stage for all the rest. Clardy Tyler's involvement had been all but nil, and quite indirect. She could not justly blame him.

Celinda had not known until the day before the story of how her husband had petitioned for the release of the former New Orleans prisoner they were now going to see. He simply hadn't mentioned it to her. That was typical of him, and endearing. Japheth had always been a kind and caring man, particularly toward those in bad situations. It was just like him to take the time to do something good for a stranger who was in no position to benefit him in turn.

Celinda was as curious as her husband was about Willie Jones, though she really didn't know why. She hoped they would find the man improved enough that maybe he would voice his gratitude to Japheth. Such a gesture would mean a lot to her husband, who had suffered so many unjustified slams against his reputation after the scandal descended upon them. It seemed a long time since anyone had thanked Japheth for anything.

They reached the hospital. Clardy turned to them. "I should tell you that if Jones is alive, bringing you in to see him will be a violation of his wishes. He was firm about not wanting to see you, Japheth. I believe maybe it was shame making him say that; he just could not bear the thought of having to face a man who had done such a kind thing for him."

"Perhaps I shouldn't go . . ."

Clardy said, "No, I want you to. I believe it's proper that you see him, and that you thank him. But if you like, I'll ask him first if he's willing to see you."

"Yes," Japheth said. "That would be best."

Clardy paused. "Besides, I have a feeling all this is just talk in the air, anyhow. I doubt he survived the night."

But to the surprise of them all, Jones had survived, and was moving in and out of consciousness. "He has a strong will, and is fighting to live," a nurse told them. "But his prospects are still poor. His wound was bad, and there are signs it is beginning to fester. You must be prepared for him to die."

Clardy turned to his companions. "I'll go speak with him now. I'll come back to tell you what he says."

Celinda and Japheth seated themselves on a bench near the

front door of the hospital. Japheth smoked a cigar and seemed nervous. Celinda sat smelling the stenches peculiar to a hospital and thinking of how she hated this place and the illness and death it represented, and how she hoped she and her husband could leave Natchez and find a better, healthier life in Kentucky, where the grief of her lost baby would not haunt her so readily, and where Japheth could again become the man he had been before.

Clardy returned a few minutes later, looking somber. "He is conscious, but weakening," he said. "I told him you had come to see him, and at first it seemed to anger him . . . but then he changed his mind, all at once. I don't know why. He wants you to come."

Celinda trembled as she moved through the oppressive milieu of the Natchez Hospital. Going to see a man soon to die . . . not the kind of thing she was normally inclined to do. Celinda hated death. She had learned to hate it while seated in the corner of her childhood home, watching her mother die of rabies. She had learned to hate it more in a cavern beside the Ohio River, where Trenton Ames had left her, with nothing to bequeath to her but loneliness, fear, and admonitions to be strong. And now she hated death more than ever when she sensed it lingering like a shadow above her husband, waiting to engulf him whenever his weak heart finally tremored its last. Death was like a stench in this building; Celinda prayed that if her husband did die, it would not be here.

Willie Jones lay in a small bed near a back corner of a big room lined with beds. His bed was segmented off from the others by a dark curtain only partly drawn back. Celinda cocked her head to one side and caught her first look at him. He was on his back, his head turned away.

Clardy went to him first, his form coming between her and Jones so that her view was cut off. He said, "Willie, they've come. Can you hear me, Willie?"

No answer. Celinda felt a chill. Had the man died already?

Clardy turned. "He's not conscious. I believe he's—" He turned again, back to the bed. "Wait . . . he's coming around. Willie? Do you hear me now?"

"Yes." The voice was raspy and soft. The voice of a rapidly weakening man. Celinda caught a weak but odious smell, like decay. She remembered the nurse's talk of how Willie Jones's wound was beginning to fester.

"Here they are, then, Willie. Here's Japheth Deerfield. And his wife, Celinda, is here, too."

Clardy stepped aside. The man on the bed turned his face toward Celinda. She took one long, astonished look, then leaned weakly against Japheth, fearing she would faint. Japheth looked at her with an expression that said he was as surprised and shocked as she.

The man on the bed was Jim "Junebug" Horton.

Celinda felt a dull, mounting pain in her stomach, as if she had been kicked. Then a burst of quick anger—Clardy Tyler had set this meeting up maliciously!—followed by a realization that of course that wasn't the case. Clardy's own bewildered look at the moment was enough to let her know that he didn't yet realize who Willie Jones really was, nor understand why both she and her husband looked so pale.

Horton's weak-looking eyes looked at Celinda's face a few moments, then shifted to Japheth. He spoke weakly. "I can see by your looks you didn't know it was me," he said. "I had wondered, Mr. Deerfield, if you had knowed the man whose freedom you put in for in New Orleans really was."

"No," Japheth said. "No, I did not . . . and if I had . . ." He said no more, but his meaning was clear. Horton looked toward the ceiling, his red eyes looking sad.

"If you had, you would never have spoke for me going free," Horton said. "I'd wondered about that. All these years, I've wondered. Didn't want to go to my grave not knowing the answer."

"Is that why you decided to give your audience to us after all, Horton? You put my wife—and me, too—through the shock and displeasure of having to see you, just to satisfy your curiosity about whether I had realized who you really were? Well, you devil, now you have your answer!" Japheth took Celinda's arm and looked at Clardy. "Clardy, we're leaving. If I had known who this man was, I would have never come here. And to think I, of all people, petitioned for *this* man's freedom!"

Clardy said, "Wait . . . Japheth, what's all this here? I don' understand what's happening."

"That men there, his name isn't Willie Jones. That's Jo Horton."

"Horton . . ." Clardy blanched. "That's the name of the man who—"

"The man who ill-used my wife so badly, the man who tried to pass himself off as my own late brother to defraud a church. God help me! And to think I petitioned for his freedom using the very name of the good man he once impersonated! I'm damned if I would have put my wife through such a trial as having to face him, without so much as a warning, if I had known who this was."

Clardy said, "Japheth, I didn't know. I swear to you, I didn't know. If I had, I would never have let this happen."

"I don't blame you, Clardy," Japheth said. "It's *this* bastard who has my contempt. Even while he lies dying, he has the rancor, the effrontery, to weasel my wife into a situation designed to slap her in the face with his miserable presence." He tugged Celinda's arm again. "Come on, Celinda. Let's leave this place."

"Wait, Japheth," Celinda replied, pulling her arm free.

"What . . . but there is no reason for—" He grasped at her arm again.

"For God's sake, Japheth, I can decide for myself when to leave! And do you not think that after all I've been through in my life, I can't abide the mere sight of a dying man, no matter who he is?"

Japheth sputtered in astonishment. "You *want* to see this— this piece of human refuse?"

"No," she replied. "I want to see this *man*." She removed her arm again from her husband's hand, took his arm in its place, turned him to face Horton and said gently: "Look at him."

Horton had closed his eyes, tears streaming out from beneath the tightly shut lids.

"Look, Japheth. The man is dying. He can't harm me anymore, or you, or anyone else."

Japheth had been tight and stiff, but slowly he wilted. His demeanor changed. "You are a wise and perceptive woman, Celinda Ames Deerfield. And a tender one."

She went to Horton's bedside, knelt there and put her hand on his. "You are dying," she said.

Horton opened his moist eyes and looked at her. "Yes. And ¬fore I do, I want to tell you, to ask you . . ." New tears came. ¬ want to tell you that I've been an evil man, and I was ¬ked to you."

"Yes, you were." Celinda was following her instinct now, feeling that nothing worthwhile would be achieved here without forthrightness. But she spoke softly, not wanting to upset a man who clearly had not even a full day's life remaining in him.

"I want to tell you that I know how wicked I was, and that I shouldn't have treated you so. Shouldn't have tried to force myself on you like I did. Shouldn't have treated you like something I could own, like a treasure I'd found in that cave where your pappy died." He paused, then said, "But you *were* a treasure. Best and finest treasure I ever run across then or since. But I didn't know how to handle a treasure. You were something beyond me, girl. All I knew how to do was treat you ill."

"I was afraid of you," Celinda said. "I feared you would harm me. Maybe kill me, in the end."

"You was wise to get away from me," he said. "Because I *would* have hurt you. I've hurt every person I've run across in my life, and you would have been no different. But I'm different now. I am. I've been trying my best to do good things, instead of bad."

"That's good, then." Questions filled Celinda's mind. Perhaps Horton would be too weak to answer them, but she felt compelled to ask. "Junebug, what happened with Ajax McKee the night I fled from you? Is he dead?"

"Yes. Yes. I killed him that night. More by accident than purpose. He ran onto my knife in the dark."

Celinda remembered the horrible moment when Timothy Rumbolt had done a nearly identical thing up in Beatrice Fine's room, and shuddered. "And what did you do then?"

"I went on to Natchez. Walked, hitched rides on wagons, finally stole a horse and rode in the rest of the way. I asked about you, found out folks knew of you, were saying that you had been saved from terrible things by a miracle. They said a lawyer named Deerfield had took you under wing and was likely to marry you. Deerfield, they said . . . they told me he was brother to a preacher who had been bound for Natchez but had died. I knowed then that the hand of God was on you, Celinda. I knowed he had sent you safe into the arms of the brother of the man I was pretending to be. I knowed then could never have you, that you was protected. I left Natch headed down to Orleans, took up the name of Willie Jo I finally wound up in prison for helping steal gold fr church . . . and then your husband came, right as I thought I was going to die. The very husband of the girl I had treated so wrong, he came and got me my freedom, and I couldn't understand why. Why would *he*, of all people, be the one man who wound up doing good for me? I had never knowed goodness like that, Celinda. In all my days, I'd never knowed such a goodness. It's haunted me ever since then, that goodness has. And now I lie here dying, and all I can say is God bless you, Celinda Deerfield. God bless you and your good husband, even if he does hate me now that he knows the full truth. I don't blame him for hating me." He touched her hand. "I'm glad now he got you instead of me. Truly glad. I'll die knowing that things turned out for you like they should have."

Celinda wiped a tear from her eye. "Maybe you won't die. Maybe you'll live."

"No," he said. "I'm dying. And even if I lived, it wouldn't be for long. This world will end soon. I know that for a fact. I believed I'd be alive to see it, but I won't. I'll be dead before the end comes. I'll be in hell before this day is out, suffering for the sins of my uncle, and my own sins besides. The end has come for me, and I can't escape it. That same weight in my chest, that weight of sin—God, it's so heavy now that I can hardly bear the press of it. I'd hoped I could make it light by doing good things 'stead of bad, but it's still just as heavy as before. My uncle's sins and my own, all mixing up together in me, choking the breath from me."

"You will not suffer for your uncle's sins," Celinda said. She remembered very well the remarkable "sin-eating" story Jim Horton had told her long ago. "You've been wrong to go through life believing that foolishness you were told by your mother and some foolish old witch woman. They had no right to put your uncle's wrongs on your account. I know of only one time in the history of this world in which one person has carried the sin and wickedness of others. If you want to die in peace, it's in his hands you ought to put yourself."

Horton said, "That door is closed to me. It's far too late for religion. There's nothing for me now but punishment. My mammy told me forgiveness was shut off to me, and so it is. God will not forgive Junebug Horton." He sank back, wincing, apparently stabbed with pain. His voice was weaker when he spoke again. "But *you* can forgive me, Celinda. If I can't die with God's pardon, I'd at least like to die with yours."

Celinda looked at the pitiful man before her and thought of how deeply she had despised him. Though since her marriage she had managed to substantially shut out the memory of Jim Horton, being near him now revived it all with terrible clarity. She remembered his body pressing against her as he attempted to violate her in the most intimate way possible. She remembered the rough feeling of his hands holding her hair as he hacked off her locks and forced her to take on the guise of a boy. She remembered his threats, the way he had looked so hatefully at her when Queen had stepped in as her protector. Now he was asking for pardon. No man deserved it less. How could she forgive him? The words would surely catch in her throat and refuse to come out.

She looked up at Japheth. He didn't look angry now, or inclined to play the protective husband. He had stepped back, leaving this matter in her hands. It was up to her alone to decide whether Jim Horton would die with or without her forgiveness. He didn't deserve it . . . but wasn't the very heart of pardon to give not what was deserved, but mercy that was undeserved? What else was pardon, if not that?

She was trembling, and almost in tears herself. Maybe she could forgive him . . . but the words wouldn't come. Instead she asked, "If my forgiveness was important to you, why is it that you told Clardy Tyler that you didn't wish to come to Natchez, or see me and my husband?"

"Because I was too ashamed. And because I wasn't dying then. Now I am. Everything is different to a man when he's dying. Everything."

She thought then that maybe, as her old abuser was dying, it made sense to let a part of herself die, too, the part that had carried the scars of her ordeal and the lingering hatred of the man who more than any other was responsible for it. To let that part live on and on did no good to her, to her family, to anyone. Let it go, she thought. Let all the hate and hurt die with Jim Horton.

He was very weak now, struggling to maintain consciousness. He looked at her, waiting, saying no more. Celinda lifted his hand and squeezed it softly. "I forgive you," she said. "I forgive you for everything."

An hour later, as they emerged from the Natchez Hospital into the light of a clear, slightly chilly day of a world that had been home to Jim Horton but was no longer, Japheth too

Celinda in his arms. "You are a most remarkable and strong woman," he said. "Most remarkable and strong indeed."

After the burial of Jim Horton and the payment of all expenses related to his medical care, death, and interment, Clardy made final arrangements with the Deerfields, solidifying the plan they had agreed upon: Clardy would go on to New Orleans, continue his search for Thias—a search that seemed much less likely to succeed now that his guide had died—disinter the bones of Isaac Jones and place them in the sealed coffin on a northbound sailing vessel. When that vessel reached Natchez, the Deerfield family would join him, and in the end wind up in Kentucky.

Clardy said his farewell and set off. As the coffin-bearing wagon rumbled away from Natchez, Clardy found that he actually missed Willie Jones . . . having come to know him by that name, it was hard to think of him as Jim Horton. What a life the man had led! Celinda had told him about Horton's belief that he was doomed to be punished for the sins of his wicked uncle, and how that conviction helped steer his course into all the worst channels. Jim "Junebug" "Willie Jones" Horton had been a most superstitious man, obviously. It made sense of certain cryptic comments Clardy had heard the man say along the way from Kentucky. It was no wonder a superstitious-gullible man had been so quick to believe that a dream could forecast the end of the world.

Clardy was secretly happy to have a justification now for discounting all the apocalyptic talk he had been exposed to for hundreds upon hundreds of miles. He was embarrassed to admit it, but it had begun to eat at him. In those mentally vulnerable moments before sleep came, he sometimes wondered if somehow the "dream of rev'lation" that his old partner had talked about really *could* have been prophetic. What if the ground really was going to open up and swallow the wicked, and the great curtain was going to fall on the final act of the world? Now he was free to put aside such fearful bogeyman notions. If Jim Horton's dreams had been revelatory of anything, it was merely his own impending death, not the death of the entire world.

Clardy traveled without incident until he neared New Orleans on a day when clouds were growing thick. Lightning was striking in the distance and drawing nearer with great heralds of steadily louder thunder peals, and the possibility of the world's end seemed a little more believable than it would on a sunny day. When a lightning bolt splintered a tree not a hundred feet from where Clardy was driving the wagon, he let out a yell that was itself of apocalyptic proportions, and realized that the bolt would certainly have been sufficient to bring an end to Clardy Tyler's world if none other. Immediately he began searching for shelter.

He was ill-fixed to find it. The area he was in was remote and wooded with twisted, tortured-looking trees, a macabre kind of place where no one seemed to live. As the storm grew closer, the wind colder, the horses more skittish, Clardy began to believe he would not find shelter at all. He was about to give up hope, free and hobble the horses, and crawl under the wagon, when he saw a distant light in the dusk and heard the sound of a large group of people singing.

"I'll be!" he said. "Must be a meeting house yonder, or some such."

Happily, he made his way off onto a narrow side road and toward the lighted place. He saw not a church meeting house, as he had anticipated, but a large barn standing beside a burnt-out house whose blackened walls and vacant windows seemed appropriately ghostly in this wasted region. The interior of the barn was lighted by lamps and torches and held about two dozen people gathered to face a very tall, wide man in odd clothing. As Clardy drew closer, he saw that the man was barefoot, wearing some sort of Indian clothing, had long, white hair and a beard trimmed down to the skin everywhere except at his chin, where the whiskers grew in thick twists all the way to his chest. He was pacing back and forth on a makeshift platform made of boards laid side by side across a square of barrels.

I know that man, Clardy thought. That's the same man I once saw preaching in the street at Natchez. Older now, but the same man.

Someone had spread a large, heavy tent cloth over pole supports along one side of a horse pen filled with the mounts of the people inside the barn. Clardy parked the wagon under a tree, turned his own horses into the pen, and entered the barn as inconspicuously as possible, hoping to find an unnoticed seat on the ground against the rear wall. It was not to be. The man at the front, who was waving a Bible in one hand and some sort of twisted vine scepter in the other, paused in his

488

Cameron Judd

oration and pointed the scepter at Clardy as he came through
the door.

"Ah! Another comes to hear the news! Welcome sir! You
have come to the place of wisdom, where you'll hear the great
and terrible things that are soon to befall our doomed world
here at the time of the end! You may have come to escape the
storm, but there is a storm coming that no one will escape,
though they beg the rocks and mountains to fall on them!"

My lands, Clardy thought, I've found some sort of outlandish preacher, and danged if he ain't talking about the end of the
world, just like poor old Willie did.

He sat down and tried not to evoke any further notice. As he
listened, the preacher, if such he was, resumed his talk from the
point when Clardy entered. Clardy soon ascertained that this
indeed was no commonplace preacher, a suspicion he'd had
when he saw the man's bizarre mode of dress. This man
spouted a mixture of biblical imagery, Indian lore, Creole and
African legendry, and backwoods philosophy, all centering on
the idea that the world was indeed on the verge of coming to
its end. When the man began talking about a fork-tailed comet
that had been seen in the sky earlier in the year—a clear por-
tent of the end, he said—Clardy halfway hoped he was going
to say that the end would come as a heavenly fireball or something similar, and not as an opening and shaking of the earth,
as in Jim Horton's version of the apocalypse.

He was disappointed and chilled by a highly unwanted foreboding when the man said, "When the end comes, and it *will*
come, before this year closes, it will be through a terrible,
great shaking of the land. The mountains will tremble as if
they are sinners before a holy God, and the rivers will run
backward, grow red with mud so that they seem to be rivers of
blood, and the earth will spew out its swallowing sands and
open in great cracks, like hungry mouths, to devour the
wicked. I tell you, my friends, it is all here in the Bible, and in
the prophecies of the greatest and wise seers of the Indian and
Negro races, and in the very sky itself. Doom! Destruction! It
will come, and there will be no way to flee it!

"Many will die, but some will live. They will go on to a new
life and a better one. Out of the old world dying a new world
arises! Out of the old world dying a new world arises!" He repeated the statement again and again until it became a kind of

odd chant, picked up by some of the truer believers in the crowd.

Clardy glanced back out the open door. The storm was raging hard now, lightning erupting every few seconds as if in authoritative seconding of the words of the supposed prophet. He was feeling so uncomfortable here that he was beginning to think it would be just as well to go out there and brave the storm. He looked around at the others and wondered if anyone else looked as ill at ease as he felt, but all he could see were a few profiles and backs of heads, and therefore could not read the faces. He grew more restless, and irritable for letting these words get to him. Normally he would have dismissed such a man as this speaker as an obvious buffoon, or maybe a money-hungry swindler with an offering plate that needed filling, but since he'd just traveled many long days and miles with a man advocating similar ideas, it was harder to discount it all, no matter how foolish it seemed. The storm continued apace, and Clardy remained where he was, wishing he weren't.

After another half hour, the prophet had gone on to more talk of coming doom and showed no sign of slacking, but the storm did. The lightning diminished, the rain slowed to a sprinkle, and Clardy Tyler rose to slip out.

"You there!" the speaker bellowed.

Clardy winced, looking back over his shoulder at the man. "You're speaking to me, are you?"

"Yes, sir. Do you seek to flee the truth?"

"I seek to flee this barn." He had hoped for a titter of laughter, but did not receive it. Apparently this barn was full of devoted believers of what had been said here.

"The end is coming, my friend! Don't scoff or mock those who come to give the warning. Seat yourself again and listen to the rest of my words!"

"Best be going. Come see me, y'hear, if the world don't open and swallow you before you can." Again no laughter, and this time there were a few angry murmurs. Obviously this crowd didn't appreciate the mocking of what it saw as a prophet. Clardy felt his face turning red.

He got out of the barn as quickly as he could, the speaker railing after him. Clardy hitched up the horses and rolled out on the wagon. By now the man had gone back to his main line of talk and was ignoring the sheep that had fled the fold. Clardy was glad to have been forgotten. He rode away, listening to the fading drone of the prophet. Then he noticed that the volume rose and took on a scolding quality, as it had when he left. He grinned. Apparently somebody else had followed his lead and was getting out of the place. That made Clardy feel better. It was good to know there were others who hadn't yet reached the point of true believing, either.

It was all nonsense, of course. All this jabber about endtimes and trembling mountains. And rivers running backward? It would never happen. Clardy spat off the side of the wagon, a show of the contempt he felt . . . or more truthfully, the contempt he wished he could feel.

"I'm as big a fearful fool as some old granny with a pocket full of charms," he said to the sky. "It seems that if you say something to a man long enough, he takes to halfway believing it, no matter what it is."

He rode on through the night, eager to put at least two miles behind him before making camp. Finally he stopped, found as dry and sheltered a spot as he could, and pitched his camp. He cooked a meal and ate, then lay down to sleep, his rifle at his side, within reach.

He awakened sometime later without knowing why. His fire had died, but enough light lingered to reveal the form of the big man who stood beside his bedroll, so close that his booted toes almost touched Clardy. Clardy sat up with a hiss of fright and grabbed for his rifle, only to find it gone.

"Here you are, Clardy," the man said, handing the rifle to him. "Take it if you want. Though I'm sorry to see you seem to be so ready to shoot your own brother."

CHAPTER 46

Clardy sat by the newly built-up fire, listening to his brother speak, feeling overwhelmed with awe and gratitude that the meeting he feared would never happen had come about as if of its own accord. He was manifestly glad he had been forced into the barn by the storm, glad the self-proclaimed prophet of the end had made such a show of calling attention to him. It was at that point, Thias said, that he'd turned from his own place among the crowd and seen the brother he had last laid eyes on the day he fled Tennessee and the Harpes back in 1798.

"I had come into that barn to escape the storm," Thias said, scratching at the scar marking his bearded face. "I was on my way up from New Orleans when the weather drove me in. I tell you, when I turned and seen you coming in, I like to have fell over dead then and there. I couldn't believe it."

"I still can't," Clardy replied. "Thias, I came down this way looking for you."

"With a coffin in the back of your wagon? You thinking of taking me off dead?"

"Of course not. The coffin is for the bones of a man named Isaac Ford. A fine man and old friend and business partner of mine, laid to rest in a New Orleans sepulchre for a lot of years now. But he always wanted to lay beside his wife and children in Kentucky, and I'm fulfilling an old promise to him. That's the second reason I've come this way. You were the main one."

"Now you've found me, with the help of luck or the good Lord. But what you've found is a man not worth the finding, Clardy."

"I'll make that judgment, not you," Clardy replied. "Thias, it's been a lot of years, and I've missed you every one of them. For a long spell now I've thought you were dead. It wasn't until you came to Preacher Coffman that I found out the truth."

"A man can't trust anybody to hold his tongue anymore," Thias grumbled. "Not even a blind preacher."

"It wasn't the preacher who told me. It was his manservant."

"But the preacher had to have told the servant, all the same."

"What does it matter now? We're together. I only wish you'd have gone ahead and come to me when you were in Kentucky."

"I was close, Clardy, so close I could have hit you with a stone. I watched you from the trees beside your house. And that's a fine house, and finer family. You've done well for yourself, Clardy. I'm proud of you. You've held up the Tyler name real proud—a lot better than your older brother. You've become a well-known citizen, you know it? Well-known enough that I heard talk of you among the Kaintucks all the way down here. Clardy Tyler, the big planter. Clardy Tyler the Harpe hunter. It wasn't hard to find out how to reach your farm, well-known as you are."

"You should have just showed yourself when you were there. I'd have been happier to see you than you could have guessed."

"I wanted to, Clardy, and intended to, but when the time came, I couldn't. I was too ashamed of what I've turned into. I'm a criminal. A lawbreaker. I've stole and hurt folks. I've cut men with knives when I was so drunk I didn't know what I was doing. There's charges held against me almost every place I've been. Every time I see a constable or a jail or a courthouse, I break into a sweat. I've lived the kind of life I never would have thought I'd come to, and it all seemed to happen *to* me, you know, more than me choosing it. After you left home, and Grandpap died, I turned the farm into cash money and went off to find you, to give you your part of the inheritance. I lost that money, Clardy. It was stole from me. I reckon I wasn't careful enough with it. And that's haunted me ever since, and shamed me so bad, me losing that money that should have been yours."

"I don't care about that money. I've made my own money. I'm a well-off man now, Thias." He paused. "Not outright rich, but well-off enough to afford the best attorneys, men who could do a right smart to ease you out of whatever trouble you've gotten into."

"Attorneys? A man needs attorneys only when he's facing a court of law. And that won't happen to me. I'd die before I'd face down a judge in a courtroom."

Clardy began to see the relevance of the issue raised by Isaac Ford years ago when he was making that first downriver search for Thias. That issue was simply: What does a man do with a criminal brother once he finds him? How does one escape the shadow of the stigma, or evade the moral requirement of punishment that comes of having broken the law? Even though Clardy and Thias were together again, they were still cut off from one another. The life that both of them had lived had created a chasm that would not go away just because they wished it would.

"Let's talk of that another time," Clardy said. "Thias, I was traveling with your old companion Willie Jones. He was taking me to find a woman he believed you had gone off after."

"Willie? Where is he now?"

"He's dead, sorry to tell you. Wounded by a robber. He died in the Natchez Hospital this very week."

"Willie's dead? God! I liked old Willie, before he went crazy and started worrying about his life of sin and declaring his dreams had told him the world was coming to an end—same kind of nonsense that white Indian or whatever he is was babbling back yonder in the big barn."

"Do you know his name wasn't really Willie Jones?"

"I figured it wasn't, though I never knew his true one. Most of the men I've known the last few years ain't used their real names, me included."

"James Hiram—right?"

"That's right. From Grandpap's name. But tell me, who was Willie, really?"

"A man named Jim Horton. Nickname of Junebug."

"Junebug Horton? I'd heard that name. Never had a notion it was Willie." He paused thoughtfully. "So old Willie's dead Hard to believe. But maybe there's worse things than beir dead. It's harder being alive, when everything that's good in your life has gone to squat and the only hope you got is that the woman you love will let you be hers."

"So Willie was right. You *did* come down this way looking for that woman he told me of. Have you asked for her hand yet?"

"Not yet. Takes a bit of nerve, you know. I'm afraid she'll tell me no. And there's a problem with the man she was married to. They're divorced now—some folks declare her a scandalous woman for that, but that divorce had to happen. He's a bad man, treated her and her little one rough. He may get it into his head to treat me rough if I marry his woman. He still sees her as his, even though he left her."

"You be careful of him, Thias."

"I will be. I ain't worried. I can handle myself. If there's one thing the life I've lived has made me, it's stout. And I've always been good with my fists. You remember that from when we was boys."

"You get that scar on your face from fighting?"

"Yep. Good big old slash across the face with a butcher knife. The fellow who give it to me went away with worse."

"Sounds like life *has* been hard for you."

"Indeed. Indeed. But maybe it'll be good for me, if Elizabeth will give me her hand. I want to be a husband to her. Want to care for her, and let her give me the kind of life a man needs. I even want to be father to that young'un of hers."

"What if she turns you down?"

Thias lowered his head. "Don't know. Maybe I'll just put a pistol to my head and put an end to a life that wouldn't be worth living without her."

Clardy stiffened, eyes flashing. "Don't talk that way, Thias. I ain't going to hear you talk about dying, not after you and me are finally back together again, like we ought to have been years ago. No death talk, no babble about things being too far gone to change—none of that! I heard such from your old partner 'Willie' as he lay dying, and I'll not stand hearing it from you!"

Thias's face was cast in gold by the firelight. It smoothed his weathered features, softened the outline of the scar and the ragged texture of his untrimmed beard. For a few moments the face looking back at Clardy was, except for the whiskers, the face of the youthful Thias he had played beside and—when he couldn't escape it—labored with in days of boyhood and young manhood. Seeing him that way fanned up a sudden wild hope in Clardy that things really could be as they had been, that the chasm he had sensed earlier wasn't unbridgeable.

"Thias, things are going to be right again. I can feel it in my bones. Your Elizabeth will say yes to you, and when she does, you bring her and the child back up to Kentucky. You can live right on my place until you get your own roots sunk. We'll make up for all them years apart. We'll—"

"Hush that talk, Clardy. Ain't you heard what I said? Nothing can be like it was before. I'm a lawbreaker. There's trouble waiting for me anyplace I go. I can't go to Kentucky. I can't go anywhere."

"Then how the devil do you plan to live with a wife and child?"

Thias reacted as if Clardy had jammed a needle into him, making Clardy realize that he had just struck a point that Thias did not want to think about. Clardy studied his tense brother, comprehending. Thias was a man without hope, a man who believed there was nothing good left in life for him—with one exception, that being the woman he loved. It must be a great and deep love, too, Clardy thought, because he's not being sensible about it. If his life is so destroyed that he can't live on his own, how can he expect that taking on the burden of a wife and child is going to change anything?

Right then Clardy did something he would never have imagined doing: he burst into tears. Thias looked at him, astonished, but could have felt no more surprise than Clardy himself. The odd thing was that his tears were not tears of frustration or anger. They were tears of pure grief, the same grief felt when one loses a close loved one to death. The grief had come as quickly and unaccountably as that burst of hope only moments before, and now Clardy sat weeping, crying as if Thias were dead.

Thias stared at him, rose, and walked away. Clardy feared his brother would leave, so he stood and went after him. "Thias, wait! Don't go."

Thias was standing just outside the ring of light coming from the fire, his back toward Clardy. When Clardy grabbed his shoulder and made him turn, he was astonished to see by the dim reflected firelight that Thias, too, was crying, his rugged face streaked with tears.

"Clardy, I've throwed my life away, and I don't know how to

get it back again," Thias said, his voice shaking. He ducked his head and dabbed at his face with the heel of his fist. "Lord have mercy, I'm shaming myself here right before you! Crying like a bed-baby."

"I done it first. But what does that matter? We ain't boys no more, Thias. It's boys who are ashamed to shed tears."

Thias sucked in a great breath and forced himself to cease weeping. "I wish I *was* a boy again. I'd surely live my life different. But there's no turning back. I can't go the other way again any more than a river can turn and run backward, like that fool in the Indian clothes was prophesying about this evening. Maybe my whole idea of marrying Elizabeth is a fool's notion. Maybe it really is all over for me. I don't know if the whole world is coming to an end, but maybe mine is. Maybe mine is."

World coming to an end . . . Clardy thought back to the mystic in the barn. " 'Out of the old world dying a new world arises.' "

"What?"

"It's what the man in the barn said, Thias: 'Out of the old world dying a new world arises.' Maybe it can really be that way, for you. Maybe there is a way out. A new world."

"I wish it could be. God, how I wish it!"

"Then let's don't give up hope, Thias. We're back together again, and it's all come about in such a curious kind of way that I can't help but think maybe there's good things going to happen for us. Why don't you come with me to New Orleans? Help me fetch up the bones of Isaac Ford. Then we'll go back to Kentucky together and do whatever we have to do to make things right. We'll be brothers again, just like nothing that has happened ever happened at all."

"That can't be, Clardy. God knows I wish it could. Things *have* happened. More than you know. I can't wipe out my past."

"Yes you can. Come to New Orleans with me," Clardy urged again. "That's where Elizabeth is anyhow, ain't it? Ain't you aiming on asking for her hand?"

"She ain't there no more. I went there, looking, and found she had gone, left to get away from her troublesome old husband. She's up about Greenville town now, I hear. And I hear the old satan she was married to has headed up after her."

"Then go to Greenville. Find your Elizabeth and marry her.

I'll go on, fetch Isaac Ford's bones, and meet you again, you and your new family. We'll find a way then to make things right for you. We *will*, and don't let yourself doubt it a minute. We *are* going to be together again, like brothers ought to be, and everything *will* be the same. I don't know how just yet, but it will. You are going to come back with me to Kentucky, and we'll begin to work it out from there. I know a good lawyer, a man named Deerfield, who can get us started toward finding some answers."

"Deerfield . . . seems I recall having robbed a man by that name one time. The name was writ on a leather wallet he carried."

"The same man. But don't worry—he'll still help; he's just that kind of man. It was him who petitioned for Willie Jones to get free, purely out of having a kind heart. He and his wife and daughter are already set to move up to Kentucky from Natchez. I'll be taking them aboard there. They're good folk. You'll like them."

Thias scratched the back of his neck, a common gesture of his that Clardy had long forgotten but which now leaped back to his mind with utter familiarity, generating a new burst of love for a long-lost brother now found again. He knew Thias was thinking, weighing his proposition. . . .

"Well . . . I reckon I could try."

"Yes sir, you can. You surely can. Now tell me where we can meet. Somewhere along the river, someplace safe for you to be, someplace you and your new family can make a warm camp and nobody, not the law, not jealous old husbands, not nobody, can find you. I'll be coming back up in a sailing vessel once I've fetched up Isaac Ford's bones."

Thias thought some more for a few moments. "Have you heard of Cutbank Island?"

"No. Would a boatman know it?"

"Yes. Any of them would."

"Well, I'll be taking on a good boatman in New Orleans, so we'll find this island, no fear."

"Then that's where you'll find me, and God willing, Elizabeth and her little Deb. Nobody lives on Cutbank most of the time, but sometimes I've made a home there for myself, when I was in need of hiding away. I'll go straight there from Greenville. I'll wait for you . . . *we'll* wait for you, and keep watch."

"And then you'll go to Kentucky with me?"

"Aye, brother, I will. Though I still don't see how I can get out from under all the trouble I've—"

"Thias, shut up. Close your mouth. No more talk about trouble. We're ending your old world and making you a new one, and I'll not have you already messing it up with all your worrying."

Thias smiled. "You've turned into quite a man, Clardy. Quite a man. I swear, you give me hope when there's no grounds for it at all."

"I reckon that makes me useful, then. Now let's get back to the fire and cook up some of the victuals I've got. We'll both feel better for having hot food under our belts, and there's still a mighty lot of catching up we've got to do."

"Sounds good, Clardy. Sounds good."

They headed back to the fire, each feeling for the first time in a long time what it really was to have a brother.

Clardy found it terribly hard to part ways with Thias when the morning came. He recalled their last parting that long-ago day he and Thias had been working on expanding the Beaver Creek cabin. There had been no ceremony, no adequate good-byes, and certainly no anticipation that the two of them would not see each other after that day for more than a decade. What if it happened that way again? Clardy wondered. What if he reached Cutbank Island and Thias, for whatever reason, was not there?

He was ready to consider postponing his plans to disinter Isaac Ford, but he didn't. He was close to New Orleans and the journey had been long and difficult. To turn back now with that long overdue job still undone would be foolish. All the legal clearances for the disinterment had been done in advance by mail, and would have to be reworked if he threw aside the task now. And besides, Isaac Ford had simply laid in rest too long apart from his family. So with a push of his will Clardy separated from Thias and headed on to New Orleans on his wagon, the covered coffin bouncing along in the bed and Thias vanishing into the dead winter landscape behind him, heading north to Greenville and Elizabeth and hope.

The rest of the travel and the carrying out of the disinterment went on with Clardy's mind only half on what was happening. He thought constantly about Thias, wondering how far he had traveled now and whether he would be able to safely find refuge on his little island. He prayed frequently that nothing would go wrong and that he would find Thias waiting for him as he had promised. Mostly he prayed that Thias wouldn't yield to the despair that obviously hung like a dark cloud around his shoulders, trying to overwhelm him.

When Isaac Ford's remains were safely sealed inside the heavy, virtually airtight coffin, Clardy drove his wagon to the New Orleans docking area, this time hardly noticing the colorful activity of the eternally operating levee marketplace that had intrigued him on his first New Orleans visit. The scents and sounds of this remarkable Creole region hardly made an impact on his preoccupied mind. He was eager to get under way back up the river.

He made arrangements toward chartering a small but sturdy boat, equipped with a sail, to carry him and Isaac Ford's coffin back up the river. For three frustrating days he struggled against some minor difficulties that came up, but at last the journey began.

When they reached Natchez, Clardy half wished he hadn't offered to give passage to the Deerfields, simply because having to stop for them created delay, not to mention the possibility of losing some of the boatmen to the siren attractions of Natchez-under-the-Hill. But Clardy had made a promise, and furthermore needed Japheth's counsel on dealing with Thias's legal problems, and so the boat stopped as planned.

Clardy was relieved to find the Deerfields virtually ready to leave at once. He had sent a letter up from New Orleans before the boat's departure, and the Deerfields had used the time well. They had sold most of their possessions, and what little remained occupied only meager space in the cargo hold of the boat. Within a day of arriving at Natchez the boat was off again, all the crew still in place, Clardy explaining in secret to Japheth how he had found Thias so unexpectedly and the difficult situation his brother was in. Japheth pledged to give what help he could.

"Do the boatmen know who Thias is and what his situation is?" Japheth asked.

"No," said Clardy. "They know I have a brother waiting on Cutbank Island, but that's all they know."

On the journey continued, far too slowly and laboriously to suit Clardy, until finally, in mid-December, a small island came into view farther up the river, and one of the boatmen pointed it out to him.

"There's Cutbank Island," he said. "That's where your brother be, you say?"

"It is," Clardy replied. "Or so he should be. We arranged to meet here."

The boat moved up toward the island, slower than ever, it seemed, until at last it tied up beneath the high, rocky bank that gave the island its name. Celinda looked at the island with an unusual expression, then tightened her hand on her husband's wrist.

"Japheth! Do you know what island this is?"

"No. Should I?"

"Look at it, Japheth! Don't you see?"

He examined it; his eyes widened in recognition. "Celinda! It's the island where I first met you! The very island!"

"An island where a new world began for me, and for you, too," she said.

Clardy overheard, and prayed: Let the same be true for Thias, Lord. And for me. Let Thias's old world end, and let a new and better world arise for him.

Japheth turned to Clardy. "I'd like to go onto the island with you. You shouldn't go there alone, certainly. There might be others besides Thias here, you know."

"I'm wondering why he ain't showed himself yet," Clardy said with a tone of worry. "I hope he's there. I surely hope it."

"He will be. I'm sure of it."

Clardy and Japheth took a small skiff around to the farther and lower side. Mindful that Japheth suffered some with his heart, Clardy handled the rowing. They pulled the skiff up onto the bank.

"Thias!" Clardy called. "Thias! It's Clardy—where are you?"

No answer came. Clardy called some more.

"We'd best go look for him," Japheth said. "It's not too large an island, and he may be hiding out to make sure of his safety. Maybe we could get help from some of the crew."

"No," Clardy said. "Too many strangers crawling this island might be spookish to Thias. It's early. We'll look alone. If he's here, we'll find him. We'll meet back here in an hour."

"Very well."

They separated, Japheth bearing left, Clardy bearing right.

It was the afternoon of December 15, a Monday, and from somewhere high in the sky or deep in the earth, Japheth Deerfield sensed an odd, almost inaudible rumbling, and felt the most curious mental and physical sensations, impossible to put a finger on. Was it merely the rush of blood through his veins that he felt? He couldn't tell.

He searched, beating his way through the barren brush and trees of the island, calling out for Thias Tyler and hearing Clardy's steadily receding voice do the same.

CHAPTER 47

Fifteen minutes later Japheth Deerfield stopped and cocked his head. He had detected another unusual noise, different than before. This one continued longer and sounded very different. He listened, identified. It was unmistakably the cry of a child.

He was bewildered until he realized what it must mean. Clardy had told him his brother intended to seek the hand in marriage of a certain divorced woman with a baby daughter. Surely that crying child must be the daughter, hinting that Thias's proposal had been accepted. Japheth smiled and continued on, following the sound.

At length he reached a clearing in the center of the island, and there found them. Clardy was already present, seated on the ground, facing a similarly seated man, the sight of whom initially sent a shiver through Japheth. He remembered that face well enough—the face of the outlaw who had once robbed him on the Boatman's Trail. Thias Tyler turned to look at Japheth as he stepped into the clearing; their eyes locked. Then Japheth's gaze lowered, taking in the child who sat on Thias Tyler's lap, eating some sort of gruel from a cup. He glanced around, looking for the child's mother, but saw no one else.

Clardy stood. "Japheth, come on over. Meet my brother Thias."

Japheth approached, slapped on a grin, stuck out his hand. Thias didn't rise because of the child in his lap, but put up his right hand and shook Japheth's. "Pleased to see you, Mr. Deerfield. And let me say straight out that I'm sorry for the wrong I done you those years ago."

"Forgiven and forgotten," Japheth replied. "Mr. Tyler, you are indeed much the image of your brother."

"So I've always been told. Call me Thias."

"And you call me Japheth. Now tell me, who is this wee and pretty lady?"

Thias gave a tight, weary smile. "This is little Mary."

"The daughter of . . . what is her name? Elizabeth?"

Thias lowered his head quickly. "Yes. Elizabeth."

Before Japheth could say anything more, Clardy interrupted. "Japheth, Thias has given me some sorrowful news concerning Elizabeth."

Growing solemn, Japheth squatted on the ground, weary from his hike. "I'm sorry to hear that. What's wrong?"

"Elizabeth is dead," Thias said, stroking the hair of the now-content child.

"Oh, no. Oh, my. Sickness?"

"She was killed," Clardy said. "Thias has been telling me about it. She was killed by the man she used to be married to. Murdered out of jealousy when she married Thias."

"No. Lord help us." Japheth eyed Thias, who subtly wiped a tear from his downturned face. "The man . . . he was caught?"

"*I* caught him, yes sir," Thias said, looking up with his face gone florid and fierce. "I caught him, and he paid the price."

Japheth pondered, understood. "You killed him."

"Yes, I killed him. And if ever I've done a righteous act, that was it."

No one said anything more for several moments. Japheth stood and paced about. "I assume that you are wanted for the killing," he said at length to Thias.

"Yes. I had to flee. But I brought Mary with me. I'll not have Elizabeth's child raised as some pauper orphan. No sir."

Japheth glanced at Clardy, saw the despair in him, felt a pity almost as deep as that he had felt for Willie Jones in that stone cell in New Orleans. He knew how Clardy had awaited this moment of reunion. Now, as it had in almost every other dealing having to do with his brother, deep, disruptive trouble had intruded itself.

"Mr. Tyler . . . Thias . . . what will you do?"

"I don't know."

Japheth minded his words carefully. "To try to flee the law with such a young child . . . have you considered whether this is in her interest?"

"I have. And it ain't. That's why I brought her here. I'm giving Mary to Clardy."

Clardy gaped. "Give her to me? But how . . . why . . ."

Japheth went to Thias and knelt before him, looking at the child. He smiled at her; she smiled back. Fortunate, he thought, that small children cannot comprehend the sorrowful situations into which adults stumble. Fortunate and merciful. If only they could retain such gentle ignorance forever.

"How old is she?" he asked.

" 'Bout a year."

"She is beautiful. Beautiful like my own little daughter would have been had she lived."

"You lost a child?"

"Yes. Our youngest. We still have our older daughter, thank God."

Thias looked deeply at Japheth, frowning in thought. He spoke to his brother. "Clardy . . . step aside with me a minute. I want to speak to you of something."

He rose, leaving Mary with Japheth. He and Clardy stepped off to the edge of the clearing and into a rough tent pitched there. It blended so naturally into the surroundings that Japheth hadn't even noticed it initially.

The brothers talked a long time. Japheth held the little girl, feeling a deep natural affection for the child and simultaneous sorrow at the thought of his own lost infant. He wondered what it would be like for Celinda when Clardy brought this child back to the boat. Would she grieve more deeply in the presence of such a living reminder of what she had lost?

It was almost completely dark when Clardy and Thias came out of the tent and approached him. Clardy spoke. "Japheth, Thias and I have been talking, and there's a thing we must discuss with you."

They sat down together as night fell, and it was an hour before they rose again, young Mary in Japheth's arms and tears streaming down his smiling face.

* * *

"She is happy," Clardy observed, standing on the deck of the boat and watching Celinda hold and caress Mary.

"Yes, she is," Japheth said. He had finished with his crying on the island, but his voice still trembled with joy. "There is no greater gift that could have been given to her ... and to me. It's as if what we lost has been restored—thanks to your brother." He waved his hand toward the island. "God bless this place! It has given me my most precious gifts—first Celinda, now Mary. It's an island of gifts. A place of new beginnings."

Clardy nodded, said nothing, looking broodingly past Celinda and toward the dark island where Thias still was. "I dearly hope that's true."

Japheth, grasping his meaning, nodded. "I hope so, too. But I wish Thias had come to the boat with us. Why would he want to stay behind, alone, on that island with all of us here on the boat?"

"He said he needed to be alone. To think about what he can do next. Maybe he'll come on and join us later. He's got a skiff hid in there, he says."

"You know, Clardy, that it can't be as you hoped now with Thias. Not with a murder charge hovering over him."

"Japheth, might you be able to defend him? It seems clear to me that the killing he did was deserved."

"What is deserved morally isn't always acceptable in the eyes of the law," Japheth answered. "I could defend him, but the odds of exoneration would be poor. Thias committed what could only be seen, through legalistic eyes, as a vengeance murder. He can't expect not to have to face consequences ... unless he follows the course you suggested."

"There is another course open to him ... and that's the course I fear he is taking right now on that island."

Japheth was puzzled a moment, but when understanding unfolded, he drew in his breath sharply. "You believe he may end his own life? Then why are we standing here, God help us! Let's go find him, bring him back here kicking and screaming if we must!"

"No," Clardy replied firmly. "Leave him be. We've got to leave Thias's situation in his own hands now. It's up to him to choose his options. He can die, or he can do the only other sensible thing. I'm standing here praying with all that's in me that he'll choose the latter."

"Yes," Japheth said. "But what a hard thing it is to have to wait. What a hard thing." Then he meandered off to join his wife and the child that so suddenly and unexpectedly was theirs.

Clardy went to the prow of the boat, filled his pipe, and stood smoking in silence, eyes ever on the island. It seemed to him at the moment that his entire life, and Thias's, had been following an inevitable course leading up to this night at this place. He knew now that he and Thias would never have the brotherly companionship they had in boyhood days. The years had driven them down divergent courses, put distance between them, made them unchangeably different men in unchangeably different life situations. Clardy was sorry it had to be that way, but he would accept it and go on. He had no other choice. He hoped Thias would accept it, too, and choose life over death, even if it was life that might seem momentarily poor in meaning and rich in pain. But it was life, and as long as a man lived, he could hope and try and make the best of what he was handed. Too often what came a man's way was bad, but sometimes it was good. Like Mary coming into the bereaved lives of Japheth and Celinda. Like Isaac Ford coming into the life of a young and misguided Clardy Tyler, setting him right again and putting him on a course that had led to success, a happy home, a beautiful and loving family. Maybe something like that could yet come Thias's way, if only he would give life another chance. Maybe sometimes a new world could rise from the ashes of an old and ruined one.

Clardy cleaned the ashes from his pipe and put it away, then headed for his blankets. He was weary in body and even wearier in mind. Yet initially he could not sleep. His mind was heavy with worry for Thias. Further, from where he lay he could see Isaac Ford's tightly sealed coffin, and that made him think of and dearly miss his elder friend and partner. He wished that Ford could have met Thias. He would have had good and sensible advice for him, no doubt.

Clardy was just about to fall asleep when a loud, booming crack echoed up as if from the heart of the earth. A jolt unlike anything he had ever experienced threw him bodily upward, and his groggy mind filled with images of Jim Horton and that crazed barn preacher, and the notion that just maybe they had

been right, for it surely felt like the earth had given its death
shudder, and was indeed coming to an end.

It was an experience of the sort never to be forgotten by those
who lived through it.

The earth shrugged in the night, setting off jolts that almost
instantly wiped out a river country town called New Madrid,
set the tranquil Mississippi to flowing in rapids that sometimes
turned backward upon themselves, making the river flow opposite its normal direction. Along the collapsing Mississippi
banks and for miles inland great cracks opened in the earth,
swallowing trees, hills, cattle, barns, houses. At other spots the
soil kneaded itself into softness, then opened wetly as great
fountains of sodden sand spewed up from below. Buildings
fell, ancient trees crashed to the earth, and massive boulders
that had lay still as sleeping giants since centuries before Christ
went suddenly tumbling into motion, rolling and bounding
down bucking hillsides, breaking trees like twigs while fowl
screeched in alarm overhead and animals died of fright. Land
rose here, sank there, causing enormous shifts of waterways,
creating fast-filling lakes where minutes before there had been
only dry land.

As far away as Charleston mortar and brick cracked and
church bells rang of their own accord. In Washington City,
men of government paused, swearing they felt the earth shifting beneath them and secretly wondered if this were a sign.
Hundreds upon hundreds of miles away, as far as Canada, grazing cattle lifted their heads and cats crawled beneath porches,
struck with fear at the vibrations that rippled through the earth.
Where the quake could be felt the strongest, fearful husbands
and wives clung to one another in their beds, some of them, in
fear of imminent divine judgment, confessing past infidelities
to one another and then realizing that if the end didn't come
after all, nothing could be the same between them from then
on.

Of all these things Clardy Tyler knew nothing. He was aware
only of chaos, violent shaking, then chilling cold water that engulfed him and shut out light and air. He was swirled about,
moved, bumped, tortured, sucked down and spat back up again,
completely at the mercy of the river and the apocalypse that
had come upon him.

His last thought was of Thias.

*   *   *

Celinda clung to a piece of broken, floating mast with one arm and held the squalling Mary above the cold water as best she could. Beulahland was beside her, clinging hard to the same mast and crying in terror. Celinda longed to comfort her and tell her what was happening, but she couldn't. She didn't know herself. The moment the quake had struck had come so quickly it had not even ingrained itself in memory. One moment she was on the boat, babe in arms and elder daughter beside her, and the next she was in the river, clinging to this mast and fearing more for the lives of her children than for her own.

As minutes passed, a few memories returned. She recalled seeing the high, blufflike bank of Cutbank Island come heaving down from above. She remembered how she and the little ones narrowly escaped being crushed by the tons of heavy earth and rock that splintered the boat like a fist crushing a toy. The boatmen hadn't been so fortunate. Every last man of them took the full impact of the falling bank and were driven deep into the suddenly churning river. What had happened to Clardy Tyler, she did not know. Nor Japheth. *God above, let nothing have happened to Japheth!*

"Mama!" The cry was Beulahland's as her grip on the soaked and slick mast gave way. She sank out of view, making Celinda scream. Yet there was nothing she could do with one arm holding the baby and her other clinging to the mast. If she let go, all of them would drown.

A small hand grasped her skirt below the water, then another. A moment later Beulahland's face broke through the surface; she gasped for air. "Grab the mast again!" Celinda shouted in her face. Beulahland flailed, got a grip with one hand, then both. Wrapping her arms around the mast, she cried and sputtered, water streaming out of her mouth.

They clung to the mast as hard as they could, keeping hold of life in a world that had become chaos.

"I'm scared, Mama." Beulahland's voice was quivering and high, birdlike. "I'm scared."

"You must be strong," Celinda heard herself say. "Keep holding on. You must learn to be strong. If we are strong, we will live."

"Where is the boat, Mama?"

"The boat is gone. But we are here. We will be strong. We will live."

"Where is Daddy?"

"Wherever he is, he is in God's hands. So are we, as we always are through everything bad and good. Be strong, little girl. Be strong."

They clung, hands going numb, fingers turning white. Beulahland whimpered. Celinda encouraged her with words, then began to sing, because her singing had always comforted Beulahland when she was distressed. She sang old songs, minor tunes from the mountains that had come from Europe with the first immigrants. She sang one song after another, and looked for some place they could come to land. But they were in the midst of the river and no land was to be seen. So she sang some more, and together they held on to the broken mast.

Japheth wasn't sure how he was managing to stay afloat, never having been all that strong a swimmer. Yet somehow he was doing it, treading water in the turbulent river, occasionally going under but always managing to come up again.

But he couldn't keep it up forever, and his heart was beginning to feel strained. A kind of numbing pain throbbed in his arms—was it the cold, or a herald that his heart was about to fail him? He looked wildly about, hoping something substantial would float by that he could use for bouyancy.

Something brushed against him; he twisted his head and saw it was the corpse of one of the boatmen. Wincing away from it, he felt it slide past, facedown in the water, then turn in the current and twist out of sight into the darkness.

He sensed more than saw that another thing was floating toward him. Dark, shapeless until it was right upon him—a skiff! Miraculously, it was even floating right side up. Japheth supposed it must have been tossed into the water when the initial jolt struck.

He grabbed for it but failed to get a grip. The skiff was about to float on out of reach when a second desperate try succeeded. He held on tightly, his fingers so cold they had grown nerveless. Pulling up, he tried to heave himself into the skiff, but the river sucked hard at his clothing. His heart was hammering far too hard. Had to quit or—

No! He could not give up. He gave another heave, the effort almost superhuman, and suddenly he was rolling into the skiff, which was about a quarter full of water. He sat up, breathing hard. The oars were locked into place in their holders inside the skiff, to his good fortune. He freed them, put them in place, and began to row.

He began calling Celinda's name as loudly as he could.

A voice called back. Celinda's voice! And along with it, a crying baby. Mary was alive as well.

"Celinda! Where are you?"

She called again, and when he heard Beulahland's voice join in, he began to weep in relief. Following the sound, he rowed, working his way around the floating matter in the river.

He found them still clinging to the mast and pulled them into the skiff. There they hugged each other, crying and laughing at the same time. Celinda took up the oars and began rowing, heading toward the eastern shore.

They reached the bank and moved inland, getting as far away from the river as they could. Progress was difficult because there were huge yawning gaps in the land, created by the earthquake. Somehow they made it past all such obstructions and finally came into a large, level meadow, free of trees. There they sat down, huddled together, to wait out the night.

Japheth had lost his watch and thus was unable to check the time when the next tremor hit. This was a particularly terrible one that literally tossed them about. They heard more trees falling in the forests all around, but there were no trees where they were and thus no danger of being struck by falling timber. And the earth did not open in the meadow. They passed the remainder of the long night in terror, but no harm came to them. Beulahland finally fell asleep in her mother's arms, but she awakened each time the earth trembled. Japheth tried to keep count of the tremors, but lost count after about twenty of them. All through the night they heard the strange, almost moaning sound of earth giving way to water, and tremendous splashes as entire banks caved in and collapsed into the river.

The morning light revealed a land much changed. The river was high and filled with floating timber, pieces of wreckage and flotsam from their boat and other watercraft that had been destroyed farther up the foam-covered river. They went down to the riverside and observed all the devastation, filled with astonishment.

"There's something missing, Japheth," Celinda said.

"Yes," Japheth replied. "The island is gone."

It was true. Nothing remained of Cutbank Island at all. The entire mass of land had crumbled away and sunk into the river.

"Look," Beulahland said, and pointed.

Isaac Ford's coffin was floating in the river, lodged up against a jam of logs. Atop the coffin was a man. Japheth looked closely. "It's Clardy!" he said. "Great heaven! He's saved himself on that coffin!"

"He may be dead," Celinda said. "He's not moving at all."

"I'll row the skiff out to him," Japheth said.

"No. Remember your heart. You've had strain enough. I'll go."

The skiff was still where they had tied it. Leaving Beulahland, Japheth, and Mary on the shore, Celinda rowed out into the river, chasing the floating coffin.

"Clardy! Can you hear me?"

He groaned. He was alive.

Celinda reached the oar out toward him. "Clardy, can you take hold of the oar? Take it—I'll get you to shore."

Fifteen minutes later, after great difficulty, Celinda rowed the skiff back to the shore. Clardy Tyler was stunned but alive, seemingly with no bones broken except perhaps a rib that was paining him terribly. With Celinda's help, he rose and came onto the shore. Celinda helped him up toward the meadow, as behind them Isaac Ford's coffin drifted free of the log jam and floated on down the river and out of sight.

Clardy sat down painfully beside Japheth, gripping his side. "The world didn't come to an end," he said.

"No," Japheth replied. "Not for us, it didn't." He looked out across the altered landscape. "But it has changed. God in heaven, how it has changed!"

"Cutbank Island . . . it's gone."

"Yes. Celinda and I saw that at first light. The whole island, pulled down into the river." He drew in his breath. "Oh, no. Thias."

Clardy nodded. "Yes. Thias. He is gone. He must be."

"I'm sorry."

"Who can say, Japheth? Perhaps he was dead even before the quake. He may have put his neck in a noose last night." He was fighting emotion. "I hoped he would have made it through and done what I told him. He could have crossed the river and gone west. There's a new world beyond the river. It could have been Thias's new world."

"Clardy." It was Celinda who spoke. She pointed.

Clardy looked, and despite his pain, stood, eyes brightening, a thankful awe filling him.

Out in the midst of the river was a skiff, and in it, a man. Clardy strained his eyes, peering through the mist rising off the water. The man in the skiff stood slowly, balancing himself in the little craft. He raised his hand slowly, and then Clardy knew. How many times had he seen Thias give that same wave out on the Holston or the French Broad back in Tennessee, in the long-ago days he passed his time rafting on the rivers?

Japheth smiled. "He lived, Clardy. He lived."

"Yes. He lived—thank God. Japheth—the little one. May I hold her a moment, so he can see?"

"Of course. Celinda?"

Celinda put the child into Clardy's arms. He smiled at her. "Can you reach the sky, Mary? Up we go!" He carefully lifted her above his head so that Thias could see her from out on the river and know she was well. Thias waved again. Clardy lowered Mary and put her back in her new mother's arms.

As they watched, Thias sat down again and took up his oars. One final wave, and then he began to row—toward the western shore.

"He's doing it, Clardy. He's doing what you said. Heading west."

Clardy nodded, eyes gleaming and moist with tears. "Out of an old world dying, a new world arises."

"That's right. He's going to make it through in that world, Clardy. He's going to survive. Maybe even do well."

"Yes. I believe he will." Clardy swiped his hand across his cheek. "I only wish he could have come back with me. I had hoped he could make a new beginning in Kentucky. That we could have been together, like when we were boys."

"Who can say, Clardy? Maybe this way will be the best."

Clardy watched Thias's skiff go out of view, lost in the west-lying mists. "Yes. Maybe it will. He's a good man, you know. Even when we were boys, everybody knew that. Thias was the good brother. Me, I was the bad one . . . but yet I was the blessed one, too. Blessed with friends, with family . . . with mercy time and again when I didn't merit it. I'm thankful. I truly am. If Thias has even half the happiness and good friends I've been given through the years, he'll be doing well indeed."

They remained in the meadow by the river for two full days,

not daring to leave the safety of the open space until the earth had quit its fitful motion. Celinda bound up Clardy's ribs, which greatly reduced his pain, but he would have to move stiffly and with caution for some time to come.

Tremors large and small occurred sporadically throughout the entire two days, frightening but not hurting them. They had nothing to eat until Celinda managed to fish a floating barrel of flour out of the water and with the flour make simple, bland cakes. It wasn't good fare, but no one complained except the baby.

At last they left the meadow, walking east and north, taking the first steps homeward in a world that, though destroyed and devastated, also seemed fresher, more virgin, more full of promise than the world they had known before. A new world would rise from the old. It would be up to them to make it a better one.

AFTERWORD

T hough *Passage to Natchez* is a novel and most of its main characters are fictional, the story includes many historical figures, and several incidents of the narrative either depict or are closely based upon events that actually occurred.

Among the historical figures in the story are the Harpe brothers, Micajah and Wiley. The "Terrible Harpes," as they came to be known, were among America's first recorded serial killers. Unlike most of their latter-day ilk who terrorize our society, however, their crimes had a random, patternless quality that only makes the pair seem all the more wicked. In *Passage to Natchez* I have occasionally taken novelist's license with fine details and chronology in the Harpe story, and have added some fictional characters to the mix, but all in all their bloody tale is presented as it happened.

Some readers may be curious about what became of the three Harpe "wives." After her Harpe days were through and her legal waters settled, Betsy Roberts reportedly went on to marry a man named John Hufstetter, who settled as a tenant farmer near Russellville, Kentucky, where Betsy raised chickens. Later the family moved on to the Red River in Tennessee, then possibly on to the Duck River. Betsy's son, called Joe

Roberts, grew up and eventually became a soldier. Susanna (often called Susan) Harpe remained in Kentucky, near Russellville, weaving cloth for a living and raising her daughter, named Lovey. Susanna apparently remained a woman of gruff, hardened character throughout her life and was disliked by her neighbors; her daughter, though reportedly a pretty girl, had a similar personality and stigma. Eventually the two of them moved to Christian County, where Susanna died. Lovey thereafter headed down the Mississippi River and eventually ended up in Texas.

As for Sally Rice Harpe, perhaps the most pitiable of the Harpe women, she returned to Knoxville with her preacher father, a man reportedly of high character and public respect despite his daughter's waywardness. Remarrying, she had another daughter, who grew up to be "a fine-looking young lady," as one eyewitness recorded.

"Parson Rice," as Sally's father was known, later moved his family, including Sally and her second husband, to Illinois. While on the way, William Stewart, the former Logan County sheriff who had known the Harpe women in their darkest days, happened to see Sally and her companions. Historian Lyman Draper, who interviewed Stewart about the Harpes, described the encounter as follows: Stewart "did not recognize them, but thought he knew them, particularly Sally, who eyed him closely and, after a little, went to one side, sat down and, with her face in her hands, had a weeping spell, doubtlessly recounting her Harpe adventures, prompted by the presence of one of the few persons who had treated her with civility and kindness in her wayward career. After he left them, Major Stewart recollected hearing the old gentleman called Rice and the identity flashed upon his mind."

Among other historical figures who come into *Passage to Natchez* are a host of secondary characters, such as the outlaws Samuel Mason and James May, the innkeeper John Farris and his family, "Devil Joe" Ballenger, Henry Skaggs, and Daniel Trabue—a prominent figure in Kentucky's frontier history, who made an appearance as a younger man in one of my earlier historical novels, *Boone*—and various other characters.

The Ames, Tyler, Deerfield, and Ford families are all fictional, as is Jim "Junebug" Horton. The briefly appearing Reverend Israel Coffman is a fictional character whose earlier life is described in my trilogy of novels of the Tennessee frontier, *The Overmountain Men, The Border Men,* and *The Canebrake Men.*

Almost all the towns, communities, and major settings mentioned in the novel are, or were, real. The famous cavern called Cave-in-Rock still looks out over the Ohio, and in earlier times was frequently used as a base for river piracy as described in the novel. Samuel Mason and other criminals used it as a headquarters, and the Harpe brothers did lodge there briefly and perform the actions described in the novel. That they were asked to leave by the other outlaws living at the cave is evidence of just how repellent the cruel brothers were. The stench of outlawry no longer mars Cave-in-Rock; today it serves the happier purpose of being the centerpiece of an attractive recreational area and park in Illinois.

The town of Greenville, Mississippi, that comes into this novel was a real town in the early nineteenth century, but is not identical with the present-day Mississippi town of that name.

The earthquake that culminates *Passage to Natchez* is the famed New Madrid earthquake, which was actually a lengthy series of major quakes and hard aftershocks that occurred starting in 1811 and lasting into 1812. The effects of the series of quakes were so tremendous that it is difficult to get a grasp on them today. The original town of New Madrid, Missouri, was completely wiped out, and the sinking and flooding of a large area not far from that town created Reelfoot Lake, today a popular recreational spot in Tennessee with a tranquility that belies its violent origins.

The New Madrid quake forever changed the character of the land and river and struck apocalyptic fear into many hearts. Today, however, this upheaval that terrified our forebears is largely forgotten. Massive mid-American cities built mostly of unreinforced concrete, and transportation arteries stretching across regions that would turn to liquefied sand in a major earthquake, have grown up all through the New Madrid quake zone.

The terrors of 1811 and 1812 may someday return. Scientists now predict that the likelihood of a 6.3-magnitude quake occurring sometime between now and the year 2040 is from fifty to ninety percent. Odds of a quake of 7.6 magnitude are as high as twenty-five percent. Should quakes of such potency occur as predicted, this time they would shake not a wilderness but a great center of American population, and we might come

to understand ourselves why some who went through the first
New Madrid quake were prone to talk about it in terms of a
world coming to an end.

                                        Cameron Judd
                                        September 30, 1994

ABOUT THE AUTHOR

CAMERON JUDD is at the forefront of today's new generation of historical fiction writers. Marked by a love for the land and the men and women who died upon it, his writing is authentic, entertaining, and bursting with the spirit of the frontier. Hailing from Tennessee, he has just finished the first book in a new Civil War series called, *The Mountain War Trilogy*.